Inspirational Romance Reader

• Historical Collection No. 2 •

A Collection of Four Complete, Unabridged
Inspirational Romances
in One Volume

When Comes the Dawn
Brenda Bancroft

Shores of Promise
Kate Blackwell

The Sure Promise
JoAnn A. Grote

Dream Spinner
Sally Laity

A Barbour Book

© MCMXCVII by Barbour & Company, Inc.
ISBN 1-55748-952-1

When Comes the Dawn
ISBN 1-55748-407-4
© MCMXCIII by Susan Feldhake.

Shores of Promise
ISBN 1-55748-362-0
© MCMXCIII by Kate Blackwell.

The Sure Promise
ISBN 1-55748-408-2
© MCMXCIII by JoAnn A. Grote.

Dream Spinner
ISBN 1-55748-404-X
© MCMXCIII by Sally Laity.

Published by Barbour & Company, Inc.
P.O. Box 719
Uhrichsville, Ohio 44683
http://www.barbourbooks.com

ecpa Member of the
Evangelical Christian
Publishers Association

Printed in the United States of America.

When Comes the Dawn

Brenda Bancroft

Chapter One

May 1864
Atlanta, Georgia

Heat and humidity made the late afternoon air cling to the skin like wet wool. Amity Sheffield's cheeks were red from the warmth, and her wavy blond hair curled in tight wisps that accentuated her oval face with its pert dimples near her small, neat mouth.

"Hurry and change your frock, Amity! The gentlemen callers will be arriving before we know it. We must be ready," the older, severely dressed woman said in a stern voice.

The slim, pretty belle halted and glanced over her shoulder, sighing, a look of supplication on her weary features.

"Oh please, not tonight, Ophy! I can't bear it," the seventeen-year-old girl protested. "I'm tired, and besides, I have plans of my own. There are things I want to do. Laboring for the cause as we all are, there simply aren't enough hours in the day to get accomplished what we desire."

Amity looked away and so escaped seeing Ophelia's reaction. Her half-sister pursed her lips, and her brows forked over indignant eyes.

"And what plans, pray tell, are more important than graciously entertaining the troops of the glorious Confederacy? What can possibly take precedence over giving our brave young men a moment's respite so that they can return to the front lines and gallantly fight the blue-belly Yankees with honor and hope, protecting the way of life that we cherish and hold dear?"

Ophelia's tone brooked no argument and convinced Amity that it was futile to try to reason with her. The young belle swallowed her feelings.

She wasn't about to admit to a staunchly Confederate woman like Ophelia that her plans centered on a promise given to Serena, one of their household slaves. Amity had been helping Serena with her reading and writing each day after the Sheffield slave finished her many tasks.

Amity instinctively knew that Ophelia wouldn't approve of educating a servant. Her recently married half-sister often decried the plight of the South since the Yankees had begun rabble-rousing, encouraging dissent, and inspiring once loyal household servants and field hands to abandon the townspeople and plantation owners who had provided for them.

Amity couldn't risk incurring Ophy's wrath. It had been pointed out to her time and again that Ophy had been invested with sole authority when their papa had galloped off to war. Amity knew that Ophy took perverse delight in thwarting her younger sister's desires.

Ophy wouldn't cotton to the news that Amity had located a tattered primer from her own early schooling and was teaching their servant to read. But Serena had a quick mind and a love for knowledge. With an eye to being able to read the Good Book for herself, Serena had the motivation to stick with the task and seek random moments for study throughout her task-filled day.

Amity gave a resigned sigh. Ophelia had certain expectations, as well as specific ideas, of what was proper behavior. Teaching household slaves how to read and write wasn't a task with which she'd feel her younger sister should concern herself, nor a pastime that she could condone by looking the other way.

For days now, under the guise of Serena helping Amity tend to her hair and draw her bath, the two girls had closeted themselves in Amity's rooms. They kept their voices hushed, their heads close together, as they focused on the page. By the flickering light of an oil lamp, Amity helped Serena sound out the letters to form words.

Amity couldn't help grinning with delight when she saw the triumphant smiles that tugged at Serena's lips when she succeeded in haltingly reading line after line. The night before, after Serena had finished reading a section from the primer, Amity had read a chapter from the Bible.

"Time for us to get to bed," Amity had said when she had finished reading.

"Yes, Miss Amity. Ah reckons it is. We's got de washin' to do in de mornin'. Not only that for de fambly, but some for de folkses at de hospital, too."

"Then this had better be all for tonight. We can read again tomorrow night. I promise. You're doing so well, Serena. Soon you won't need help at all."

Serena's eyes had sparkled in the light of such praise, and her face had grown soft with dreamy reflections.

"I cain't hardly wait 'til I can read the Bible," the young slave had said, beaming. "Leastways, someday I hope to be able to. 'Til then Ah'l be prayin' that some kind soul will let me hold their precious Scripture between my hands, so's I can read the words of our dear Lord m'self. Mayhap you will?"

"Maybe someday," Amity had said, giving a quick smile, "you'll have your very own Bible to look at anytime you have the desire."

Amity knew that there were unread Bibles tucked away here and there in the Sheffield household, and she had made a mental note that when Serena's birthday neared, she would try to locate one to give to the servant without Ophelia's knowledge.

Generally, slaves' birthdays came and went, unnoticed by the people they served. Amity sensed that Ophelia wouldn't approve of her presenting a slave with a gift, even one of small value. Well, what Ophy didn't know wouldn't hurt her!

Amity sometimes wished that not only could she give Serena a Bible, but that she could give the girl her freedom as well. As quick a student as Serena had proven to be, and as friendly and sweet as she was to be around, a sudden bond had sprung between the girls of such differing stations in life. Serena had always been so thoughtful and helpful that it now gave Amity a pleasant feeling to consider the way Serena would treasure a book that the Sheffield family owned but apparently hadn't had any desire to read.

While Serena had made wonderful progress during their weeks of clandestine study, Amity knew that she herself was receiving the most valuable education. She had a new appreciation for the knowledge that she had always taken for granted. Seeing the miracles possible in the arrangement of letters in the alphabet through Serena's appreciative gaze had opened Amity's eyes to the injustices between owners and slaves throughout the South.

"The young gentlemen will be arriving at any time," Ophelia said, jerking Amity from her thoughts with another sharp reminder. Ophelia crooked her neck, casting a sharp glance down at her bosom where an elaborate golden brooch-watch was securely fastened. "See to it that you are present on the front veranda in time to welcome them."

Amity sighed wearily, helpless not to let her pique show. She dragged a tired hand upward to rake her heavy hair away from her face and off her shoulders.

"Ophy, I'm so tired I can hardly put one foot ahead of the other. Those wash baskets of linens were so heavy. I was worn out by the time I arrived, and then Serena and I faced the long walk home from the hospital."

Ophy gave a piffling wave of her hand.

"And isn't it a pity that Milady Sheffield had to walk to the hospital because a gallant beau couldn't come callin' in a dashing hack to ease the burden of duties that obviously you are unable to perform without complaint!"

"I'm not complaining. I'm glad to do my part. But I'm exhausted, Ophy. Tired!"

"I don't care if you are tired!" Ophelia snapped, her hazel eyes flashing as her temper flared. "Have Mammy tighten your stays to fit your best frock.

Brush your hair. Bring a smile to your lips and a sparkle to your eyes.

"Then get out on the veranda so you'll be there when our gallant Southern soldiers come to call. I shan't have them marching on down the street to dally with other belles on the block because there's no one with a ready welcome at the Sheffield residence."

Ophelia paused long enough in her litany of commands to narrow her eyes, and their hazel color turned greener as jealousy overtook the plain girl's features.

The envy that Amity believed she saw did not become Ophelia, and for a moment Amity was struck by how unappealing the bossy young woman really was. How Ophelia had managed to appeal to the man who had married her was more than Amity could imagine.

"Your poor, poor husband," Amity sighed under her breath, not caring if Ophelia heard or reacted.

But that thought was overshadowed by the uncharitable idea that her older sister was so insistent about Amity making a timely appearance on the front veranda every night because the soldiers expressed more affection and admiration toward Amity than toward herself. At least with Amity present, Ophelia was offered reflected attentions, and the gentlemen favored her with courtly, gallant conversation.

Then there was the possibility that Ophy's competitive nature motivated her to want to constantly triumph over their neighbors. While Ophy seemed to dislike Amity as a person, she did approve of her younger sister's looks, if only because they prompted the soldiers to call at the Sheffield home rather than at the Brewster girls' home farther down the street.

It was little social contraventions like that which mattered in Ophelia's eyes, and mattered more than Amity believed was necessary. Sometimes Amity felt pity when she detected such fear, insecurity, and desperation in Ophelia's myopic stare.

Recently there had been an air of utter seriousness in Ophy's earnestness about Amity being on the veranda. No evenings was she excused from the activity. A thought washed into Amity's mind and made her feel as if she'd been caught in a cold wave. Perhaps with their father off to war and Ophy invested with power, she saw it as her duty to marry off her young sister before tongues could start wagging and Amity could be labeled a pitiful spinster.

Amity could almost hear the way people would whisper behind their fans. They would start to genteelly and oh-so-worriedly wonder whatever was wrong with Miss Amity—so pretty on the outside, but perhaps so inwardly flawed that no gentleman had seen fit to claim her for his bride.

Well, she had had her chances. The truth was that she'd had no desire to wed. While the beaus she'd spent time with had been handsome and attentive, none had ever made her heart beat fast nor filled her daydreams with affectionate notions. She'd never entertained the sensations that had made some of her girlfriends become giddy, giggly, and in Amity's view, silly.

"*Let* the soldiers visit elsewhere," Amity said in a testy tone, "if that's what they prefer."

"But they *don't* prefer those simpering silly girls to ladies like us," Ophelia assured. "How could they?"

Amity gave an unladylike shrug.

"Perhaps they do," she said, yawning. "Did you ever stop to ponder the idea that they might stop here to do us a favor by passing time with us rather than have us spend a lonely evening?" Amity patently enjoyed watching her sister's complexion grow mottled and florid in reaction to her question.

"Balderdash!" Ophelia snorted in a display of worried ill-temper. "Now, whatever your prior plans, postpone them and do as you are told. Papa would be very dismayed if he knew how defiant you have become since he placed you in my care. When he returns home from the battlefield a hero, I shan't spare a word in telling him exactly how recalcitrant you've been!"

At the thought of her father off to war, his life in danger, Amity was drawn back to the present moment's needs. That grave specter drew her away from her desire to assert what independence she could muster in the face of Ophelia's bullying.

"And furthermore, young lady," Ophy said in a snippy tone, "you can make up your mind to be charming instead of wallowing in your usual mulish attitude!" Ophelia withdrew a lace-decorated linen handkerchief from the basque of her best frock and mopped at her face, suddenly dripping with perspiration.

"You should be thankful that you can do your part for the cause," she added, "by reminding our brave boys in gray of the genteel belles and courageous womenfolk they're fighting and dying to protect! It's the least you—we—can do."

Ophelia took a deep breath and archly patted her wilted, frizzing hair into place. "I fully intend to entertain the brave gents on this fine summer's eve—just as I hope some other woman is giving my dear, brave, patriotic husband a moment's respite from the war."

Amity grimaced. Perhaps that was it! Was Ophelia desperate for Amity to marry so that she could shed the responsibility of caring for her young half-sister? The way Ophy carried on, the appearance of Union General Grant or the dreaded William Tecumseh Sherman wouldn't dissuade her from insisting that Amity take up her position on the porch.

It was as if Ophelia were manning the trenches in a desperate battle to rout soldiers from their competitors' front porches and victoriously capture their presence on the sheltering Sheffield veranda shielded by towering sweet gum, sycamore, and magnolia trees.

Amity physically weakened over the thought of the evening's activities. Further arguments would only tax her reserves. She admitted defeat.

"Very well, Ophelia. But could I please postpone my appearance for a little while? After all, I spent all morning in the backyard with Mammy and Serena stirring boiling kettles full of putrid bandages.

"My afternoon was spent pinning cleaned bandages on the clothesline, taking them off when they had dried, and then folding them with Serena and loading them in baskets that we bore halfway across town to the hospital. That is, when I wasn't being forced to stand still while Mammy dabbed buttermilk on my skin to keep me from freckling in the sunlight.

"Haven't I done *enough* rushing around for one day? Can't I at least take my time freshening up and dressing?"

Ophy's back stiffened, and a flash of hatred sizzled through her eyes. Amity suddenly became aware of the depth of resentment the older girl experienced whenever her authority was challenged.

"Don't be such a selfish goose! I labor too, but do I complain?" Ophelia asked in an imperious tone. "One would think that you would be flattered that young men come to call. Those cross-eyed, weak-minded Brewster girls can't get the gentlemen to visit them, not even during these troubled, war-torn times. No doubt they'll live and die piteous old maids, the focus of everyone's scorn.

"So consider yourself fortunate that you are receiving social calls and are enjoying the attentions of prospective young men from good Southern families. Those girls would give anything to get a swain to cast so much as a glance in their direction."

Silence spiraled between the two. Ophelia was waiting for Amity to defy her, and the younger girl found it impossible not to respond.

"They're nice girls, at least," Amity muttered. "Far easier to get along with than some people I know."

Ophelia gave Amity a haughty glare.

"You're an insufferable piece of baggage, you are," she hissed, and her eyes widened with outright malice.

At that moment, Amity knew that Ophy would love nothing better than to be freed of any obligation to her sister. Marrying Amity off would remove the burden of the solemnly sworn commitment she'd given their aging father.

When Amity made no retort, Ophelia spoke on.

"Such mulish behavior! Did they teach you nothing at the Academy for Young Ladies? If you don't learn to conceal your unseemly attitudes," Ophy added in a dour tone, "you'll live and die an old maid.

"Most of your friends are already married; I work with them at the hospital. Believe me, they are talking about you. What they are saying isn't flattering, either.

"And," Ophelia hesitated in her tirade long enough for another attempt at taming her tangled, strawberry blond tresses, "I shan't be surprised if your prior reputation didn't harm my chances of making a good matrimonial match earlier than I did. The young gentlemen considered us as alike as two peas in a pod until my dear, insightful husband took a closer look. He liked what he saw and realized that I am nothing like you."

"Why, thank you," Amity purred, giving a serene, unruffled smile that caused her dimples to merrily come into play. "I do declare, Ophelia, that's the sweetest compliment I've heard all day."

Mammy walked through the hallway and gave a rotund chuckle.

"Ah 'spects that ain't been no problem fo' de young gemp'mums, Miss Ophelia. Yo' two young misses be as diff'rent as day an' night! Sho' nuff ain't no worry 'bout *dat* consideration!" She lowered her voice so that only Amity would hear her. "She best be hopin' her young gemp'mum don' take an even closer look. He might be tempted to step afore a Yankee bullet!"

Amity smiled as Mammy winked.

"I didn't catch what you said, Mammy, but it's clear that you're aiding and abetting my recalcitrant sister. Therefore, you'll hush your mouth—or risk the consequences," Ophelia said in an angry hiss. "Continue on as you have been, Mammy, and perhaps I shall dispose of you as Pa should have done decades ago."

Before Mammy could react, Amity did. She crossed the room, her eyes narrowed. Drawing up to her full height, the outraged girl faced Ophelia.

"You hush *your* mouth," Amity spoke, her tone flaring hotly as it trembled with anger. "You know the esteem in which Pa holds Mammy! He put her in full charge of the household when he rode off to join the troops and fight for the cause. He only invested you with the power of the elder white woman of the household."

Ophelia gave an unconcerned sniff.

"Mammy may think she's in charge of the household, but I am in authority over the persons in it. See how much authority she would enjoy if I didn't give it to her. Now, this is an order: freshen up and join me on the veranda, Amity. At once."

Chapter Two

Stoically resigned to the night ahead of her, Amity set about bathing and fixing her toilette. Twenty minutes later, as she arranged her hair in a becoming style, she studied her reflection and realized that the bloom of womanhood was upon her youthful features.

It was there for young gentlemen who were considering settling down with a wife and family to notice, even though Amity had tried to ignore the feminine changes herself.

She was well aware that most of her childhood friends were married, just as Ophelia had pointed out, and some of them held babes of their own. A few girls who had married young had toddlers at their knees.

An alarming number of them were aged beyond their years, and more than a few were already wearing black. Scarcely had their brave Southern soldiers made them wives, than the hated Yankees had made them widows.

While their positions as wives of the Confederacy had given the belles certain social freedoms, it had also presented exhausting burdens for them to take up in service to the glorious cause. Matrons, who were no longer viewed as innocents needing protection, were not excused from the gruesome tasks that it was deemed unseemly and indelicate for belles to perform.

The matrons were expected to do the worst tasks at the hospital, shrinking from nothing lest they be accused of shirking. Married women and widows were expected to aid in surgery, nurse the infected, delirious soldiers, and touch the dead.

Amity was a practical girl with a thirst for knowledge. She had an innate ability to apply logic to situations in what Ophelia frequently accused was a most unladylike manner. Amity knew she would earn the scorn of eligible beaus who didn't wish to be challenged by a mere woman.

After spending no small amount of time thinking it over, Amity could see no benefit to marriage. Rather, her logic led her to see many drawbacks, not the least of which was that she had not met a gentleman who stirred within her any sense that he might be the man meant for her: the one who could make her heart quicken, who could fill her with warm feelings by a mere look, a tender smile.

In times gone by, sometimes at cotillions, barbecues, and family reunions, Amity's friends had talked in giggly tones and blushed with indescribable emotions that they shared like members of a secret society of those who were loved and were in love.

But Amity was not one of them. Because she was a pretty girl, Amity had always had plenty of beaus. Not one had ever caused her to feel the emotions that she knew her girlfriends had suffered when they had met the men of their dreams. She had never felt that united with any beau—certainly not to the point of being unable to imagine life without him. She had never met a young man with whom she could imagine herself growing old, content to love only him.

Amity wasn't going to settle as easily in love as Ophy had. Once Ophelia had focused on Schuyler, the poor fellow hadn't stood a chance. Ophy had seemed desperate that he might get away before he said, "I do."

Fortunately, with her appealing looks, Amity believed that when she chose to marry, she wouldn't have to marry for anything less than true love.

Amity touched the powder puff to her nose. She ached with tiredness and felt anything but charming and vivacious. Even the application of scented talc failed to liven her spirits.

The young girl dreaded the evening ahead. Sometimes Ophy could be embarrassingly transparent in her efforts to marry off her younger sister. Amity hoped it wouldn't be another evening of humiliation featuring Ophy presenting her as a shopworn item to be disposed of to the first person willing to take possession.

Love and marriage weren't supposed to be like that. Amity couldn't imagine marrying a man for whom she felt no more than she did for the men she regularly encountered. She knew from the descriptions of her closest girlfriends that she had not once entertained the feverish passions of the heart they had enjoyed when they had become betrothed.

Amity corrected herself. She had not known what such feelings were like until that very afternoon. She closed her eyes and relived the thrilling, heartwarming experience.

Hours earlier, as the searing sun had begun to travel a western path, Amity and Serena had struggled with the willow laundry baskets brimming with freshly laundered and folded bandages.

Straining to catch their breath, the two women, a respected young belle and her house servant, had made their way into the massive brick building pressed into service as a hospital.

Surrounded by the hubbub—crowded bodies on pallets, humming conversations, and screams from the surgical quarters—the two women, one white and one black, had gazed around the cavernous room, intent on catching the eye of a staid matron so that they might release the bandages into her care.

Amity had been searching for a familiar face when she had seen him. Him! The man of her dreams.

Serena had been unaware of the transformation her mistress was undergoing. For her part, Amity had felt as if she had been suspended in time. It had seemed as if that very moment had been ordained from the world's beginning.

The handsome soldier, as if guided by a power far greater than the both of them, had looked up. Amity's heartbeat had quickened, wondering if there would be a special element of recognition. Although they were total strangers, she had felt that they had always in some special way known each other.

The soldier's expression had at first been fathomless, but a moment later he had regarded her with a touch of curiosity, if only due to the boldness of such a pretty belle's stare.

Amity's lips had curved into a hesitant, trembling smile. She had fervently wished that she were wearing her most becoming gown. To her relief, the soldier had given her an acknowledging smile. His frank gaze had never left Amity's eyes, and she had been incapable of breaking his capturing glance.

"Yo' all right, Miss Amity?" Serena had asked, concerned that her mistress had frozen in her tracks. She gave the young belle a worried, scrutinizing look.

Amity had tried to reclaim her poise.

"Yes—yes, of course. Just feeling a bit faint," she had added in a breathless tone.

"Yo' sure?" Serena's concerned frown had deepened. "Yo' seems to be takin' on a might bit strange, iffen yo' pardon my sayin' so, Miss Amity."

"Don't worry, Serena. I won't swoon," she had promised, but a moment later she had feared that she might, such was the intensity of the man's gaze. His eyes—blue eyes that she could drown in—had been riveted on her.

"See that yo' don', Miss Amity. Ah expects dey's gots 'nuff to do here 'thout yo' causin' them concern." Serena had wrinkled her nose at the malodorous scents that attracted buzzing flies and increased the suffering of the sick and dying men.

"How the matrons an' widder women stands to serve the cause myst'fies me. Ah 'spects dey's consolin' theyselves they's allowin' the Lord to use 'em as He will to give comfort to dey fellow mans."

"I expect so," Amity had echoed agreeably, her mind wandering off as her eyes had remained riveted upon the soldier who had turned back to his labors of mercy. Amity had been left feeling bereft, robbed of something precious.

"Oh, there's Miz Crispin!" Serena had cried with hearty relief.

Without waiting for her mistress, she had plowed ahead with the brimming basket, calling out to the stout, stern-faced matron, whose demeanor made it clear that she tolerated no lallygagging nor tomfoolery.

In Serena's sturdy wake, Amity had stumbled along, struggling with her own basket. She had not been concentrating on where she was going. Repeatedly she had looked over her shoulder for one more glimpse of the handsome man who had somehow touched her heart, a handsome soldier of the Confederacy who was destined to disappear from her life, never to be forgotten.

"We's got fresh bandages, Miz Crispin, ma'am," Serena had said softly to the weary woman wearing a bloodstained gown and gore-splattered apron.

Beulah Crispin had distractedly taken custody of the baskets. She had positioned her considerable bulk so that she shielded Amity from catching sight of an indecent display in the surgical rooms.

Then with brusque, dismissive movements and a quick word of thanks, she had shooed Amity out, pointedly gesturing toward the front doors and the street that was teeming with Confederate soldiers who were milling around, waiting.

The recent influx of troops had swelled the city's population beyond the customary twenty thousand inhabitants. Johnny Rebs seemed everywhere now that the Yankee devil, William Tecumseh Sherman, had forced his way into Georgia, commandeering the railroads to do so.

It was rumored that Sherman was intent on placing a stranglehold around the city and bringing Atlanta, and the South, to its knees. Southerners didn't doubt Sherman's plans, for he had forged steadily onward, destroying everything in his path as he neared his destination: Atlanta, the heart of the Confederacy.

On recent nights while seated on the veranda fanning herself, sipping lemonade or sweetened fruit juices, Amity had heard men argue and discuss battle strategy until sometimes her thoughts swirled from the onslaught.

In the darkening moments of those evenings, she had wished only that people could live in peace. But she kept her own counsel, never daring to breathe a word that she much preferred her servants' companionship and conversation to her sister's. Such sentiments falling from the lips of a genteel Southern woman would have appalled everyone present.

That afternoon, as Beulah Crispin had showed her to the door, Amity had glanced in the direction of the tall, dark-eyed, ebony-haired Rebel soldier. Desperate for the opportunity to exchange another smile with the stranger, she had sought an excuse to stay in the building, if only for a few moments.

"Perhaps Serena should run along home," Amity had suggested, her voice casual. "I could remain and help, leaving when Miss Ophelia departs for the day. Miz Crispin, y'all seem terribly busy today. I could pass out water, fan away flies, read to the men, write a letter home to a loved one, or—"

Beulah Crispin had given a tired smile and patted Amity's arm gently, as if she wasn't fooled. Even among the rigors of war, the dour matron could recall what it was like to feel one's heart stir for the first time. But duty was duty, and decency must be maintained.

"We *are* busy, child," she had acknowledged in a gentle tone. "Another train-load of wounded arrived in Atlanta an hour ago on the Western and Atlantic line. They were spillin' off the trains and bein' unloaded off litters before the surgeons had dispatched with all the sick and wounded who had come here last night.

"But you run along and leave now," the matron continued. "These are not scenes to be taken in by innocent eyes. 'Tis getting bad enough that I'll be dismissing Miss Ophelia to go home within the hour. She's got several years on your age, but even so, she's innocent compared to those of us who are mothers and grandmothers, and if 'tis in my power, she will remain thus. So be off with you, girl!"

Amity had known that there was no room for further discussion. As a brash and chattering Serena had led the way to the street, Amity had glanced back, hoping for one last look. The Johnny Reb who had so suddenly captured her heart was gone from sight. Amity had been awed by the void that his absence created within her.

But it didn't make sense, she had told herself. It was silly. Surely such feelings as she had entertained weren't returned by the handsome soldier. It was just a girlish whim. It was more likely that laboring beneath the noonday sun and standing over a wash kettle in the suffocating heat had made her feel giddy and susceptible to odd and unacceptable ideas.

On the walk back to the brick house where she had lived with Mammy, Serena, and Ophelia since her father had galloped off to the front in a rush of political fervor, Amity had hardly noticed their surroundings. Her thoughts were filled with vivid impressions of the handsome Rebel whose likeness would always remain within her heart.

When she had realized that she didn't even know his name, Amity had experienced an acute sense of loss. The sensation had refused to go away, even when she had reminded herself that there was no such thing as love at first sight. That it would be futile and foolish to daydream about a hauntingly handsome Johnny Reb she would never see again.

The girl was yanked from her musings by Mammy, who finished lacing Amity's stays by giving a solidly crisp tug. Dusk draped over Atlanta and footsteps could be heard progressing up the city sidewalks, as soldiers strolled beneath the boughs of sheltering trees.

"There, Miss Amity," Mammy said. "That's done."

"Thank you, Mammy." Amity turned away, hesitating, making careful movements as she adjusted to the added pressures exerted by the whalebone corset.

"Which gown yo' goin' to wear this evenin', Miss Amity? Dey's all clean an' pressed."

"Her best frock." From across the upstairs bedroom came Ophelia's flat-toned, irritating answer.

"I'm quite capable of speaking for myself and of deciding which dress I'll wear!" Amity flared. Then, even though she knew her best frock was the most becoming, she selected a less elaborate gown.

"This one, Mammy," she said, retrieving the gown from a hook as she cast her bossy sister an impudent look.

"No, Mammy. I specified exactly which frock Miss Amity was to wear. Re-place the one in your hand with the garment on the hook," Ophelia instructed.

"I don't give a tat what you said, Ophelia Sheffield! If Pa were here—" A furious Amity sputtered with resentment as her eyes flashed like heat lightning across a summer sky.

"It's not Sheffield anymore, my dear," Ophelia trilled in a proud tone. "It's Emerson. Mrs. Schuyler Emerson. Or did you forget?"

"How could I?" Amity retorted. "You won't let me—or anyone else—put from mind that your husband is a major in the Confederate Army. Is that why you are suddenly issuing so many commands? Did he entitle you with military power as well as give you his name?"

"Don't be petty, Amity. It's not becoming," Ophelia ordered.

"If Major Schuyler Emerson is as awful to his troops as you are to the members of this household, his men must feel like throwing in their lot with the blue-bellies or shooting him in the back and considering the glorious cause well served!"

Ophelia's cheeks became red splotches and her eyes narrowed. She whirled to face her sister, and her slashing eyebrows met over glaring, yellow-green eyes.

"Breathe another word like *that* within my hearing, Amity Sheffield, and I'll have Mammy make your mouth foam with lye soap!"

"Why, you—"

Amity's lips clamped shut against the furious words that sputtered in her mind as once more Ophelia's behavior brought out the worst in her. She feared that if the confrontation continued, she would be squalling like a scalded cat, and the soldiers in the streets would be able to overhear an unladylike debacle.

Mammy's kindly pat on her bare shoulder encouraged Amity to act like the proper lady that beloved Mammy—who had raised the girls when pneumonia had taken Amity's mother, and Ophelia's stepmother, eight years earlier—had seen to it that she was.

"There, there, Angel. Don' you pay her no mind. It don' matter what she thinks of y'all. Not when yo' know that you're doin' an' behavin' in ways to give yo' own heart content."

"Mammy, why can't she—won't she—just leave me alone?" Tears filled Amity's eyes. Her beseeching whisper rose to a miserable wail after Ophelia swept out of the bedroom and down the stairs to oversee efforts in the kitchen where Serena was preparing dainty refreshments to be offered to what troops would come calling that evening.

"I don' know, Lambie. Maybe because Miss Ophelia wants yo' to fin' a gemp'mum, marry, an' be as happy as she is."

"Happy?" Amity gave a weary laugh. "How can she be happy—unless she finds joy in making others miserable? In persecuting those unfortunate enough to be around her?"

As Mammy helped her dress, Amity poured out a deluge of words describing the horrors of the war in a low-pitched litany of hardships, denial, disappointment, and despair.

If only she could spend the evening with her head close to Serena's curls, their eyes riveted on the velvety pages of a primer worn soft from the use of many students learning how to read.

Amity knew that Serena would be disappointed, and she vowed that she would make it up to the slave girl. She would find a private moment to whisper to Serena that they would steal away to read at a later date.

"These be tryin' times, Miss Amity. You're right, darlin'. But what all you jus' said 'bout de war. Well, that makes Miss Ophelia right, too. The brave gemp'mums needs to be able to slip away from the hospital, them that's well 'nuff to walk, and go callin' on Atlanta's pretty belles. That way they can forget 'bout the misery 'til the trains take 'em back to de front lines again."

"I suppose you're right."

"And who knows?" Mammy said, tossing Amity a wink as she gave her a comforting hug. "Maybe one of these gemp'mums will touch your heart the way Mister Schuyler did Miss Ophelia's, or. . . ."

As Mammy droned on with reason and encouragement, Amity felt increasingly morose. It had been a lifetime since she had known balls, barbecues, hunts, cotillions, and grand parties.

The young men she had known then, who she had believed had been destined to become her beaus, had been dressed in foppish fashions. They had come to call astride the finest saddle horses in the South.

With swaggering good health, dashing looks, and doting, wealthy families to indulge their whims and back their bravado, they had joined the Confederate Army, looking stunning in exquisitely styled gray worsted uniforms of the finest quality fabric.

There were times when Amity doubted that there was a man left whole to be found in the entire Confederacy. Girls who a few years before would have turned away from impoverished, disfigured beaus were wedding them in droves. They were marrying while they had the chance—before eligible men could be returned to the front lines and the girls would find themselves forever pitied as spinsters.

The once debonair boys in gray were now clothed in ragged garments of butternut brown homespun. Their health and wealth had been stripped. Still they gallantly came courting—minus an eye, missing an arm, limping on a peg, supported by a crude crutch—possessed with the air of redolent swains who knew that they only temporarily endured hardship and viewed it as a minor inconvenience.

These boys believed that victory was as close as the next battle, but Amity couldn't take such a belief to heart when many situations within the South contradicted what, deep down, she knew was right.

"Yo' pretty as you can be," Mammy pronounced as she set the hairbrush down on the marble-topped dresser and adjusted the tortoise shell comb holding back Amity's honey blond hair that fell in swirling waves around her shoulders, accentuating the creaminess of her skin. A locket drew attention to the frilly, ornate bodice of her gown.

Mammy winked at Amity, crossed the room on quiet feet, snatched the cut glass decanter containing Miss Ophelia's lavender toilet water, and dabbed the cool, expensive scent to her favorite's skin.

"Amity!" Ophelia called up the stairwell. "There are young men arriving on our neighbors' verandas. Your presence is required!"

"She'll be right there, Miss Ophelia," Mammy assured. She gave Amity a consoling pat.

"You jus' ignore her, Miss Amity," she suggested in a kindly whisper. "I knows yo' tired, so jus' think about your dear papa out there fightin' the blue-bellies, an' yo' content yourself that yo's entertainin' each young gemp'-mum as iffen yo' were having the Good Lord come to call. Consider how grateful yo'd be for a chance to lighten our Savior's cares. Then yo' can more graciously do the same for some others. An' do it with a glad heart."

"Yes'm, Mammy," Amity agreed, sighing, although the kindly woman's faith-inspired words were lost upon her. Faith was something the slaves concerned themselves with, but Amity had never found the time for such issues. Nor the need.

Chapter Three

Just as Ophelia had announced, tattered Confederate soldiers were proceeding up the streets. Although their clothes would have been discarded by them at one time, deemed unfit to serve as rags to rub down a lathered horse, their courtly manners remained endearingly intact.

A few beaus whom Amity had been acquainted with before the war, she now viewed with pitying alarm. Once they had been well-fed, glowing with good health, immaculately groomed. Now they were aged beyond their years, their frames emaciated from hard work, lack of sleep, and poor diets.

Too many meals were made of doughy paste of flour, cornmeal, water, and a bit of salt formed into ropes and wrapped around ramrods. The dough-covered ramrods were extended over open campfires and baked until hard. The resulting hard biscuits filled the soldiers' bellies but did not nourish their spirits, and accomplished little else for their bodies.

The southern boys had been able to endure such deprivation for a short while, but as the battles had dragged on, and supplies had grown more scarce, their physical stamina had been depleted, leaving them prey to sickness and other complications.

Banter was lighthearted even during times of war, as if the soldiers recalled their upbringing and managed to find the wherewithal to assume the role of gallant swains come to call.

But instead of a band playing background music at a cotillion or ball, there was the muffled report of cannons in the distance. So accustomed were the men to the cannons' boom, the crack of rifles, and the report of black powder pistols that they seemed immune to the noise that Amity still found disconcerting.

She marveled that the nearing battles somehow seemed remote from them as they relaxed on the veranda and entertained themselves with harmless gossip and the news of the day.

After a decent interval that allowed the men time in which to feel at home, Mammy and Serena quietly circulated among them, graciously serving delectable refreshments.

Without making comment, seeming as functional and undemanding as pieces of furniture, the household servants threaded their way among the clusters of soldiers gathered at the home that Morgan Sheffield had recently departed, going north to join forces with the men attempting to block the

Union Army's progress into Georgia.

Recently talk had been of little else.

Ol' Joe Johnston and his troops were dug in up in the mountains, forming a stronghold. Johnston vowed to stand strong forever, but he needed men to do so, and he begged for troops. Begged to little avail.

The Confederate forces were outnumbered two to one, and morale was low. The soldiers were in dire shape. Their feet were bare, their bellies were empty, and they knew that their kinfolk at home were suffering just as terribly.

Desertion had become a real problem. There were those who simply walked away from the battlefield with no intention of returning. They were footsore and heart-weary, tired of fighting. Then there were those who had left, but only temporarily, and without bothering to get permission. They were taking "plough furloughs" to go home and help their folks on the plantations.

Who was going to plant the crops with the darkies running away? How were their families going to support themselves with no crops in the fields? How would their kin subsist when the Confederacy's own commissary department was as ruthless as the Yankees?

Citizens of the South felt that the commissary officers were as deplorable as the Yankees. What the hated blue-bellies didn't steal, the Confederacy's commissary officers commandeered.

And so the numbers of men fighting for the South dwindled.

Patriotism moved some of the soldiers to request transfers from their units. There were soldiers who were serving with the commissary forces, mail units, hospital staffs, and those assigned to maintain the railroads. Some of them began to request transfers that they might be sent to the side of Ol' Joe Johnston who desperately needed them.

In recent weeks the Yankee scourge, Sherman and his forces, had worked to rout Major General Joseph E. Dalton from the rugged terrain in northern Georgia, unmapped territory with underbrush so thick that the Rebs and Yanks could pass within a few feet of each other, unable to see the enemy that they could hear nearby.

There was fierce fighting. Sherman knew better than to try to dislodge Ol' Joe and his men, for it would require bloody hand-to-hand combat. So he sought to cause Ol' Joe and his men to give up their position. He began to swing out, arcing wide of the area, planning to sweep around the Rebel stronghold and reach the railroad.

Ol' Joe, realizing the Yankee officer's intent, ordered his men to fall back and then fight. It became a pattern. Fight. Fall back. Fight some more. Retreat. Battle again. Always the Rebels remained with their backs to the railroad.

The Confederates had seen what the Yankees had done in the past to destroy their transportation systems in an attempt to cripple the South. When a rail line was captured, droves of blue-bellies set upon the gleaming tracks. They ripped up the steel rails, rooted out the ties, then stacked the timbers in huge mounds. They slanted the heavy rails over the windrows of wood and then set the piles ablaze.

When the heat from the ties turned the rails red-hot, the Yankees, with sweat pouring from their skin due to the intense heat, used timber to bend the rails so that they would be unusable. In the South, where supplies were precious and replacements were difficult or impossible to acquire, such destruction left the railroad unsalvageable.

Amity had heard more than she cared to know about how the battles were being fought not many miles to the north. There were times when she let her mind drift to more pleasant thoughts in order to escape the reality of her existence. Some of the callers at the Sheffield residence, seeming to sense the young woman's boredom with details of the battle, sought to introduce more pleasant topics.

Most nights soldiers who came calling either spoke of their families back home, discussed kinfolk or friends held in common, or mentioned prominent political acquaintances so that conversations were more like those they had enjoyed before the war.

But on that evening, talk was only of war. Almost everyone still had faith in Ol' Joe Johnston, the respected Confederate officer in his midfifties. He had taught the accursed Yankees a lesson at Chickamauga, and any day now, they contented themselves, he would teach the blue-bellies another that they wouldn't soon forget. They had confidence in him. Ol' Joe wouldn't let them down. There was no way that he would allow Atlanta, the storehouse of the Confederate States of America, to be overrun by Yankees.

Atlanta, with her foundries, produced cannons, rifles, train rails, armor plating, and warehouses to store goods that provisioned the whole South. Atlanta—the city that provided huge hospitals to preserve life within the wounded—also manufactured wooden coffins to contain the remains of the dear and glorious dead who had given their lives for the Confederacy.

The pride and faith the soldiers had in Ol' Joe was matched only by the contempt and hatred they had for the Union General William Tecumseh Sherman.

Although it galled the soldiers to admit it, the dreaded Yankee commanding officer knew the northern Georgia terrain as well as Ol' Joe, and he wasn't about to be tricked into a trap that would make his men fight in close quarters.

"Don't worry," one of the soldiers assured everyone gathered on the veranda. "General Johnston can stand forever at Dalton."

Silence spiraled up.

"I don' know," another Johnny Reb murmured worriedly. "We're in trouble if they can't hold 'er. I've heard talk that maybe Jeff Davis is thinking of replacing Ol' Joe with Lieutenant General Hood."

There was some quiet dissent, then one voice rang out above the others, firm with assurance.

"Jus' rumors. Maybe a threat. He won't do it, though. Not if Ol' Joe can stand strong," the first soldier stressed. "And he will, especially if they'll send him the troops he's crying for."

There was a murmur of voices, creating a dull roar of conversation. Each man had an opinion on that score.

"Y'all know Gov'nor Brown's refusing to release his militia?"

"Well Ol' Joe wouldn't be beggin' for Governor Brown's Pets if he wasn't in dire need. Maybe he's gettin' too old to command. Mayhap we do need a feller like Hood to step in. He's a young fellow—only thirty-three—and wild as a bay mule. Full o' spit and vinegar. Perhaps that's what's called for. An officer with some spark an' fire to impassion and inspire the troops as he leads 'em into battle!"

An older man with a heavily bandaged leg thoughtfully puffed on his pipe and dolefully shook his head.

"He's impulsive, that Hood. When I was a young pup, I used to be a tad on the impulsive side, too." He drew on his pipe. "An' I learned quick enough what it got me."

"That's right," the fellow next to him agreed. "Too rash, if you asked me. He came within four demerits of bein' kicked out of West Point, y'know. That says somethin' about his character and his capacity to lead when a cool head an' calm manner may be required to sort out the various options."

There was a gabble of disagreement from across the porch.

"Regardless, you can't discount his bravery. Hood's left arm was shattered at Gettysburg. An' he lost a leg at Chickamauga a year ago. But does he sit in a rockin' chair and let action pass him by while he fills his mind with past glories? No sir! They have to strap him into the saddle so he can lead his men—but lead 'em he does!"

"Well, iffen he's goin' to lead troops, they'll have to be sendin' them to him in numbers sufficient for him to do what must be done."

"I'll be there soon as I get the word," a young man vowed.

"Me, too."

"I'm with y'all!"

"We'd be in good company among each other. When we go back to the front, who'd want to do battle alongside troops like Gov'nor Brown's Pets anyway? Too pampered to face the war and fight like other Confederate men."

"Don't y'all worry. Jus' remember Chickamauga a year ago!"

They did, and in discussing that rousing victory, faith and hope for immediate triumphs sprang anew, even though there were wary mentions of recent skirmishes at places where Rebs had strongholds, where Union forces had bivouacked too close to home: Rocky Face Ridge, Crow Valley, Ringgold, Dug Gap, Snake Creek Gap, Dalton, Reseca.

As the velvety warm night cloaked Atlanta and katydids scratched in the darkness, Amity hid one yawn and then another behind the fan she wafted to create a breeze in the stultifying heat. The soldiers continued to discuss C.S.A. strategy.

In the glow of the coal oil lantern that Mammy had hung on a newel post bracing the veranda's room, Amity made out approaching figures. She looked up, and her lips parted in surprise. *He* was there. Dazed, she stared, sure that it was an apparition created by her exhaustion and the daydreams that had crowded her fanciful thoughts.

But when she blinked, the handsome Rebel soldier who had so completely captured her thoughts had not disappeared, and Amity gasped in wonder as he strode up the steps to the veranda, a pace behind Will Conner, a young gentleman Amity had met long before at a ball held near Grandpapa Witherspoon's plantation not far from Jonesboro. As an old family friend, Will was accorded a position of respect and welcome above and beyond the formal welcome offered to the pleasant strangers who congregated on the Sheffield porch.

Amity hardly heard Will as he presented himself, saying sweet, courtly, complimentary things to her. Due to her rigid training at the Academy, she murmured instinctive greetings and managed to afford Will a quick smile before her eyes were drawn to the handsome stranger.

At close quarters she savored his perfection. Surrounded by the South's men, the tall, dark-haired stranger was the only one who wasn't relying on crutches, or dealing with cumbersome bandages, or obviously recovering from near fatal infection or disease.

Even so, a fresh pink scar created a thin line at his temple, disappearing into his hairline and signifying a grazing wound that, but for a miracle, would have been an instantly fatal injury. Around his upper arm was a bandage, soiled, but otherwise dry, offering evidence that it was a minor injury and he would soon be returned to the front. Perhaps he would not be so fortunate during a second encounter with the dreaded Yankees.

At the realization, Amity's heart skipped a beat then flew to a staccato rhythm as she fleetingly considered the unfairness: just when she had met a potential beau who stirred feelings in her from the first glance, it was clear that he was destined to depart without a chance to woo her, if that was his intent.

Amity suddenly understood what her friends had experienced. And she knew why they had agreed to almost indecently quick weddings in order to have time to spend with the men they loved.

"My new friend saw you at the hospital today, and he let me know that he would like to make your acquaintance," Will Conner drawled, gesturing toward the silent stranger who gave Amity a reserved smile and ducked his head forward in humble greeting.

"Yes. I. . .I noticed him," Amity breathed, returning his smile while trying not to appear too forward.

"His name's Jeb Dennison, Miss Amity," Will said. "And Jeb, I present the loveliest belle in all the South, Miss Amity Sheffield of Atlanta, the fair city's most charmin' female o' courtin' age."

Jeb took Amity's hand in his. The contact was as special as she had known it would be, and when she looked into Jeb's eyes, she was aware that he sensed something out of the ordinary, too.

"How you do run on, Will Conner," Amity accused, but gave him a pleased smile as she waited for Jeb to say something—anything—to which she could respond personally.

When Jeb did not say a word, the quicksilver thought flitted through Amity's mind that he was shy, although the looks they had already exchanged had certainly been bold enough.

Before Amity could plumb the significance of Jeb's silence, Will matter-of-factly offered an explanation for his friend's stoicism.

"He's a mute. Jeb can hear whatever y'all say to him, Miss Amity." Will touched his own throat. "But he cain't answer. An' paper an' a pen ain't always easy enough to come by. He wrote me a note that he was injured during a fracas with Sherman up north aways, knocked out by a blow to the head, and left for dead in the underbrush. Drifting in and out of consciousness, he finally woke up on the train bearin' him to the hospital.

"Jeb can't talk, so it's been difficult for him makin' his way an' gettin' the point across to folks about what he's doing and what he needs. He's been spendin' his days helpin' with the wounded who're worse off than he as he finishes recoverin' himself. There would probably be a few more families readin' casualty lists and grieving for their dead if not for the miracles this Johnny Reb's worked." He gave the taller man a warm look and continued his explanation.

"I expect that his pappy was a physician, for he seems t' know more than just a little about the healing arts. But if you want to communicate with him, y'all will have to phrase things so he can answer by shakin' his head yes or no. It makes it a bit easier an' less laborious than expectin' him to write out his responses."

"Very well," Amity said, managing to keep a tight rein on her emotions so that her face and tone did not give away her keen disappointment.

For long minutes Amity's smile was frozen to her features. Her heart felt as if it had shattered. She couldn't bear for those around to witness her private heartbreak, nor could she stand the thought that Jeb would know her torment in discovering him less than the perfect suitor to fulfill her every girlish dream.

As time passed, Amity felt more in control, and gallant as Jeb was, it somehow became easier to forget that he was hampered in ways that other men were not. Jeb was, by far, the most handsome man on the veranda, and Amity knew that he was also the most attentive.

His doting eyes seemed to convey more than all the other young men's bantering conversation could begin to contain. He gave her looks that spoke to her soul, and she sensed that the glances she sent his way addressed him in a similar manner.

Gradually, as streams of soldiers began to pass by en route to their army quarters or the hospital, those who had come to wile away the evening with Amity and Ophelia prepared to depart and came forward to tender courteous goodbyes and thanks for the tasty repast served by the Sheffield slaves.

When it became time for Will's leave-taking, Jeb moved forward, too. Jeb presented himself first to Ophelia, then to Amity. He took her hand, lowered his lips to it, and smiled. His eyes conveyed the intimate messages that his lips could not speak.

When their gazes met, Amity saw Jeb's desperate look and recognized the anguish of one denied something desperately desired. She realized that never before had she so much wanted to hear a man's words, and never so keenly had Jebediah Dennison desired the power to speak to a woman.

"Do come calling on us again, Mister Jeb," Amity invited. "And you, too, Will," she added, if only out of gratitude that he had brought the man of her dreams into her life once and could be counted on to arrange it again.

"Mightn't be none of us back," Will idly warned as the pair left. "We may be subjected to cannon thunder in mere days." He leaned against a brace post, and stared off into the dark distance, as if he saw a dark future.

Amity's heart squeezed in dismay as Will tendered a quick goodbye and, with a courteous nod, Jeb took his leave and followed after his friend.

With Will's last comment, the talk shifted back to the war. Those who remained seemed unable to restrain themselves from discussing the fearful future.

Ophelia Emerson began receiving quiet advice from the older soldiers who granted her a certain stature as the family decision maker. She had been put in a position they wouldn't desire for any woman, but which necessity had forced many southern women to accept.

"Y'all really should think about leavin' Atlanta while you can, Miss Ophelia," a man, the father of three, who now walked with a crutch, urged the young woman.

Another man quickly agreed. Soon it was the unanimous sentiment among the men who remained on the veranda.

"You've no doubt seen that folks have been leavin' in droves. You should go while you can. Some say there's not a need—and pray God that it won't become a necessity—but the fact is that while you may resist the idea of fleeing, you can travel now in relative safety south on the Mason and Western, and east on the Georgia Railroad.

"When the time comes that you want to leave—have to leave—that may no longer be true. Sherman took over Union railroads. Our own Confederacy may be called to do the same. Civilians will suffer in order that the C.S.A. may be served."

Ophelia's fingers flew to her throat. Her pale face grew more wan.

"But—but they have promised that Atlanta won't fall," she protested. Her mouth opened and closed, but for a moment no sound came out. "They say it can't fall. My husband, Major Emerson, has assured me that they will never allow Atlanta to come under siege."

The men nodded, but their faces were reluctantly grim.

"An' like as not it won't, Miss Ophelia. But it could be unpleasant living here, and y'all might see things unfittin' for womenfolk to witness if we're forced to drive the blue-bellies from these very streets, one man at a time."

That suggestion brought a gasp from Ophelia as she looked around, seeming to imagine Yankees swarming over every stoop and hiding behind each shrub, while cannons were booming, howitzers shrieking, and rifles cracking.

Shaken, she began to stutter frightened, disorganized pleas. Her eyes sought assurances from the soldiers that things were not as grim as these veterans of many battles had seemed to suggest.

"There's no denyin' that the battle lines are falling back, Miss Ophy. We'd be lyin' to you if we told ya different. The truth of the matter is that the Yankees are pressin' closer every day, ma'am. The Yanks can't be but much more than thirty miles t' the north. Time's running out."

"Oh my," Ophelia whimpered, looking around, her eyes darting in panic. "What'll happen to us?"

"We're hopin' that Ol' Joe will stand strong. But there ain't no guarantees in life. Atlanta is the jewel of the South. Stands to reason that the Yanks are going to work hard to capture Atlanta. The onliest way I can see for them to accomplish it is to choke off the city. To lay it under siege."

"Siege?"

"Yes'm. I'm afraid it could come to that. Prayin', mind you, that it won't. But realistically facing that it could."

"Oh my," Ophelia whimpered. "Siege. . . ."

As she said the dreaded word, the soldiers began to talk in hushed, grim tones of what this could mean. Food on short rations at first, then running out as starvation set in. There would be no newspaper, for there would be no paper supplies, nor ink with which to print.

Yankee forces would cut the telegraph wires to prevent news from getting into the city—or getting out. There would be no mail service, and no rail schedules would be maintained. In such a closed and chaotic environment, rumor could run wild, with mob action close on its heels.

"Y'all have kinfolk out in the countryside, don't ya?" A kindly, gentle-toned man inquired, seeming to take control of the situation with his question. "You should leave Atlanta before the threat of siege grows stronger. Once it arrives, there won't be no leavin'. Then it could be too late. Have you a safe place to go to wait out the war and bloodshed?"

Ophelia looked stricken. Her trembling fingers crept to her throat and nervously toyed with a locket.

"Well, yes, there's Major Emerson's kinfolk. And we've got our Grandpapa Witherspoon, too."

The man ducked his head in a gesture of respect.

"Then I'd suggest that you, your sister, Mammy, an' your cook go visit kinfolk 'til we've sent those heathen Yankees packin' and dispelled the very specter of a siege."

Ophelia wrung the linen hanky in her damp hands.

"We'll think about it," she promised.

"I ain't meanin' no disrespect, Miss Ophelia, but y'all best be doin' more than merely givin' it consideration, ma'am. Y'all had better be following through on the suggestion."

"How soon?"

The man leaned on his crutch and rubbed his bearded jaw.

"Well, if some bloke was givin' my woman and her kin this advice," he seemed to carefully choose his words, "I'd be hoping he'd give the same answer I am: Tomorrow mornin', ma'am. Jus' as soon as y'all can make arrangements to leave Atlanta. Go. An' Godspeed."

"Tomorrow," Ophelia suddenly agreed in a dazed tone. "Very well. We'll depart in the morning."

Stunned, Amity stared as if she were sightless while the soldiers took their leave until all that remained was their boots echoing against the hard sidewalk as they disappeared into the distance.

After issuing crisp words to Mammy and Serena to pack the trunks before they took to their cots for the night so that they might be able to leave as soon as Ophelia could find passage for them, Major Schuyler Emerson's wife swept into the house and up to her quarters. Amity remained alone in the darkness. Her eyes were dry, but her heart was awash with unshed tears as she realized she would never see Jeb Dennison again.

Chapter Four

The next hours passed in a nightmarish blur. There were clothes to pack, household items to store away, and furniture to cover. It was well past midnight before Amity was free to slip on a nightdress and lie down on the feather tick. She was almost swooning with exhaustion.

Alone in her bed, plagued by heady feelings each time she remembered the touch of Jeb's lips to her hand, Amity understood what had driven her friends to the altar in haste. She didn't know how she could face the dawn knowing that soon Jeb would be but a faint and fleeting memory.

Amity felt as if she'd scarcely fallen asleep when Mammy tiptoed into the girl's sweltering upstairs bedroom and shook her awake. Ophelia had already left for the railroad depot to arrange their passage and to find someone to haul their trunks to the train station.

After Amity dressed, she drifted downstairs to eat a solitary breakfast. Mammy and Serena, occupied with last minute chores, seemed relieved that Ophelia had left. From the quietly hurt remarks the servants exchanged, Amity realized that Ophelia had been inordinately sharp-tongued and short-tempered with the loyal Sheffield household help.

Mammy and Serena worked quickly and in uncustomary silence, conveying to Amity that they were as upset by the radical change as she. Amity sensed that they were as frightened by the unknown that lay ahead as she was.

It was midmorning before a heat-wilted, visibly nettled Ophelia returned home, waving her flower-bedecked straw hat since she had no fan with which to move the sultry air about her.

"That's done," she said, and wearily reiterated what extraordinary lengths she had gone to and what trials she had faced to arrange passage for the four of them on a Macon and Western railroad train departing from Atlanta later that day.

Fanning herself and passing smelling salts under her nose, Ophelia sank into a chair and sent Serena scurrying for a cup of tea with which she would revive herself for the journey ahead.

"We depart for the plantation of Schuy's family in two hours," she reported. "I've telegraphed them that we will be arriving some time late this afternoon so they will be there to meet the train. I know it's not much warning, but that can't be helped. We're family to them now. They can't—and won't—refuse us hospitality."

Ophelia's words held more conviction than the expression on her face. A chill gripped Amity's heart when she considered what lay in store for them if they were not welcomed with traditional Southern hospitality.

Mammy, Serena, and Amity exchanged concerned glances. But from the scowl on Ophelia's features, they knew that she would brook no comment nor endure any questions regarding the matter.

Although no one had spoken a word, they had assumed that they would be going to Grandpapa Witherspoon's plantation where Amity's mother had been raised. Mammy had lived there until she had come to Atlanta with her young charge who had married Mister Sheffield, a widower. They had become part of the Sheffield home which included Mister Sheffield's motherless little girl, Miss Ophelia.

The three people placed in Ophelia's care had not expected to be guests at the Emerson plantation, even though it had been an option raised by Ophelia to the soldiers the evening before. Logic had dictated that they'd go to Grandpapa Witherspoon's plantation. Amity had never given a thought to the idea that Ophy would select Schuy's family to host them. If she had, she would have registered a complaint the evening before.

Mammy and Serena exchanged unhappy glances, but said nothing. Amity, however, was unable to contain her feelings for a moment longer.

"Oh, Ophy, you didn't!" she cried, upset.

Ophelia gave her young sister a cool stare and patted her heat-dampened, frizzing hair into place as she took the cup of tea from Serena without a glance of thanks.

"Why, I most certainly did. And I will not tolerate your taking on so, my dear. I'll have you know that I am long overdue a visit with my new kinfolk at Magnolia Manor. It's my home now, too, you know.

And, it so happens that Schuy's got a cousin," Ophelia added with a knowing smile. "He's home from the front lines for good because he's wounded a bit too seriously to be expected to fight anymore, and well, he might be interested in *you*, Amity. Papa Emerson mentioned him in a recent letter as a likely and worthy prospect. You could do worse. And it's high time you found a husband, settled down, and. . . ."

Amity felt weak with horror. For a moment she stared, stunned.

"What?" Amity whispered. "What did you say?"

After the daydreams about Jeb that she'd had the day before and the sweet musings before dawn, to think of another man as a possible husband seemed an emotional infidelity. For others to have the power to strike a matrimonial bargain involving her filled Amity with horror.

"With Pa away, I have to think of such things—especially since you fail to consider your future," Ophelia blithely defended in an airy tone. She twitched her long skirts into place and nestled the teacup on her prim lap.

"Cousin Philomen would be a steady man. You could do worse. There's not much to choose from these days, I might remind you. And, my dear, you are getting older."

Only Mammy's gentle hand on Amity's forearm restrained her from uttering hot, hostile words that would have had Ophelia ordering Mammy to fetch the lye soap.

"I spoke with Hettie Adams on the way home," Ophelia announced. "Jubal and Absalom will haul our trunk and valises to the railway depot. They should be arriving at any moment."

She glanced at the timepiece brooch pinned to her dress, an heirloom that had belonged to Schuy's late mother.

"We don't have any time to waste, so I hope that you're all prepared to depart with no lallygagging nor shilly-shallying. From all I've been told, the railroads aren't terribly reliable these days. What was once a short trip now might very well take all day."

The household was a hive of activity as the four women attended to last minute tasks. When everything was ready, Ophelia locked up the residence and hurried down the street.

The two servants and Amity followed in Ophelia's wake as she rushed Jubal and Ab through Atlanta's streets. Time and again she craned around and in a testy voice bid her retinue to hurry lest they miss the overcrowded train.

All too soon, they arrived at the train station. The sun beat down, and Mammy and Serena stood in stoic silence on the weather-beaten, splintery railroad platform. They didn't dare express their fears about life at the Emerson plantation where they'd be expected to take orders from Schuyler's kin, the Emerson servants, and their own young misses.

To Ophelia's chagrin and the misery of those who were forced to be around her, the train was more than two hours late. While they waited, the travelers dared not leave their place in line for fear that they would be unable to find places on the train when it arrived.

They were hot, thirsty, and almost fainting from the searing sunlight when the belching locomotive arrived, a plume of dark smoke drifting up into the cloudless sky as it chugged toward them. With a grating clash of steel against steel, the train drew to a stop in front of the depot.

Slowly the line inched ahead as people labored up into the aged and dusty railroad cars, gingerly seating themselves on the once plush upholstery that was now threadbare, offering mute testimony to the general decline of the Confederacy.

By the time the locomotive chugged away from the depot, Ophelia's tinder-short temper had grown even flintier. She snapped at everyone she confronted, but she couldn't help offering a smug, self-satisfied smile at those who were forced to wait beneath the relentless summer sun for the next train.

"I so dread accompanying Ophelia to her new kinfolk and so detest the idea of socializing with Misses Lavinia and Maybelle Emerson and making the acquaintance of Cousin Philomen, that I would sooner remain in Atlanta and run the risk of having blue-bellies coming to call," Amity muttered to Serena. "I don't know how we will stand it."

Mammy gave an unamused chuckle.

"Maybe we be runnin' into dem Yankee gemp'mums anyways," she dared to venture an opinion. "Mist' Witherspoon's plantation is more remote. Pro'bly would've been a heap safer there than at this here Magnolia Manor."

"I doubt that safety counted for so much as a tat when Ophelia made our plans," Amity sighed.

"We're in the Lord's protection," Serena reminded. "Nothin' will happen but what He allows it."

"That's right, girl," Mammy agreed. "We cain't be a-forgettin' that. If the Lord be with us, cain't nothing win against us—leastways, not in the end."

Amity had no such solutions, herself, and she envied how calmly the slaves faced the journey to a distant area and a strange household. As the slaves quietly chatted back and forth, mentioning names Amity suspected were from the Bible, she realized that they knew stories that she did not.

She listened to Mammy and Serena remind themselves of men and women who had pleased the Lord, men and women who had faced the risk of leaving behind what they had known and wandering into a strange region because it was the Lord's will.

Let the slaves dream, Amity thought. Maybe they thought the Lord was leading them south of Atlanta and that by obeying they were doing His will, but Amity knew better. Ophelia was in full control, and she loved every moment of making decisions that could change the destiny of other people.

The locomotive roared over the countryside, seeming to chew its way through the pine forests and mowing down the hillside. But it struggled up the grade, huffing and puffing, moving more slowly as it lost momentum. Passengers seemed to strain ahead, as if shifting their body weight could help the train to crest the hill.

A groan shuddered through the passengers when the locomotive fell short of power just before the top of the hill and the train coasted back down. The engineer had no choice but to put the locomotive into reverse and chug backward, almost pushing the caboose up the hill they had just descended.

Men heaved more fuel into the fire boxes. The blaze ignited. The water roiled. A blast from the steam engine's whistle was proof of increased pressure.

The engineer let the pressure build a bit longer, then he eased out on the throttle. Faster and faster the locomotive went, chugging determinedly. It slowed, but enough of a run had been taken to provide the necessary momentum. A hearty cheer overtook the car as it conquered the hillside.

The train continued to make progress, but precious time was repeatedly lost when the engine failed to crest a hill on the first attempt.

Ophelia was simmering when, in sight of their destination, the engineer pulled onto a siding to let a train bearing weary, sickly men in blue uniforms pass.

"Yankee prisoners," someone said. "They be takin' 'em down to Andersonville."

Amity shuddered. She knew that Andersonville was the dreaded prison camp. She tried not to look into the cars that inched by, but she couldn't avoid seeing the prisoners. A few Yankees' eyes met hers, and she gave them sad half-smiles in sympathy of what lay ahead of them.

When at last the prison train had passed, the train from Atlanta pulled out from its siding and drew into the station. The Emerson girls and their pa were waiting at the depot when their weary callers from Atlanta arrived.

Raynor Emerson led his guests to a dilapidated carriage that was hitched to a mule. His horses had been commandeered by Confederate forces, a sacrifice the kindly gentleman claimed he had been glad to make. Amity wondered about this because she knew from remarks that Schuyler had made that his father's horses had been his pride and joy.

Mister Raynor was the same courtly gentleman Amity had remembered from Ophelia and Schuyler's wedding, but as the evening wore on, she realized that she liked Misses Lavinia and Maybelle even less than she had recalled. It was clear that they remained silly girls, both simpering and vain.

At Magnolia Manor, Ophelia, who considered herself a true Emerson, was in her element. Amity, Mammy, and Serena were steeped in misery, feeling like sojourners in a foreign land.

Never had Amity felt like she was such a burden, and the unpleasant emotion escalated when coy announcements were made that Lavinia and Maybelle both had intendeds and would be wed within the fortnight when their beaus came home on furlough from the front lines where they fought for the C.S.A.

Almost on the heels of that announcement came the news that Cousin Philomen would be stopping by to welcome the visiting kin from Atlanta.

"Miss Amity's looking forward to making his acquaintance," a calculating Ophelia assured, causing Amity to quail inwardly. "In fact, Miss Amity, in Cousin Philomen's honor, I think that you should go to your quarters and pretty yourself up a bit."

Ordinarily Amity would have protested, but any excuse was suitable if it removed her from the Emerson girls' presence.

"Take Serena along to help you," Ophelia ordered.

The shy-eyed slave quickly fell in step behind her mistress.

"Are you going to marry him if they want you to?" Serena whispered when they closed the doors to Amity's room.

The slim, pretty blond whirled, her eyes blazing.

"When donkeys fly!" she hissed.

"Maybe he's nice. Philomen, that's a name from the Bible," Serena said. Then she sounded it out.

"You really miss your reading and writing, don't you, Serena?" Amity asked.

The household servant gave a hesitant nod.

"Yes, Miss Amity, I do."

"We'll continue with it," Amity promised. "Even if we have to sneak to do it."

"I've seen some books that are available. Maybe if you'd ask, Miss Amity, they wouldn't mind your borrowing the Good Book. We could read it in your room."

"I was thinking more in terms of dreadful penny novels myself," Amity said. "They have some tremendously good love stories."

"The Good Book got some love stories, too," Serena said. Then she began to describe some of the stories she had been told, but had never known the joy of reading for herself. "Mayhap you'd like readin' them to me, iffen I couldn't read them to m'self right directly."

"Maybe I would," Amity said, intrigued by the idea that the Bible could have some love stories between men and women of God, written centuries before.

The two girls dawdled in Amity's room for as long as they dared before they rejoined the Emersons. Amity felt as if she had been given a reprieve when the heavily promoted Cousin Philomen failed to appear that night. She was as relieved as the matchmaking Emersons seemed disappointed.

By the time she could offer excuses and escape to the guest room assigned to her, Amity had a grinding headache. She stared out over the darkened meadows, and the sight only made her feel worse. The cotton fields were covered with weeds and brambles now that poor times were upon them all.

Silently Mammy slipped in bearing a ewer and basin containing soothingly hot water for Amity's bath. The thoughtful servant had brought linens and soap from Atlanta. Without a word, she began undoing the closures of Amity's clothes, helping her from her garments as she had when Amity had been a sleepy little girl.

"I don't think I can stand it here, Mammy," Amity murmured in a tremulous whisper. "Lavinia and Maybelle are silly and petty. It exhausts me listening to their prattle. And around them, Ophelia is even more domineering and derisive than usual. The way they are carrying on about him, Cousin Philomen is sure to be repulsive."

Mammy didn't offer a word of disagreement.

Amity clenched her hands into fists.

"I can't marry him!"

"Especially when Serena and I's knowin' you're so taken with that young soldier who came callin' last night." Mammy paused reflectively. "My, my, seems like a lifetime ago, not jus' yesterday, Lambie."

Amity met Mammy's eyes in the beveled mirror.

"You noticed?"

Mammy gave a rich laugh.

"Of course I did. And so did Serena. That mute boy couldn' take his eyes off you either. Maybe he can't utter a word—but his eyes said it all. Compared to him, you'll sho' nuff find Mist' Philomen wantin'."

"I know I'm going to hate it here. I already do," Amity whispered in a bitter tone.

"Maybe it'll be better in the morning," Mammy suggested, but the remark lacked any conviction.

"Well, if it's not, I'm. . .I'm not going to stay. That's all there is to it."

"You've—we've—got nowhere else to go, honey. Yo' heard the menfolks talkin' las' night, and again when we got off the train in Jonesboro. You've listened to what Mister Raynor said at the supper table. They's expectin' Atlanta to fall. Y'all can't go home. We ain't gots a home to go to 'ceptin' this one—and the heavenly mansion waitin' fo' all o' God's chillun when He be callin' 'em home one day."

"But I can go to Grandpapa Witherspoon's home. And I will, Mammy, I promise you that. I will even if I have to walk every step of the way."

Mammy set the basin aside. Her face took on a nostalgic cast.

"Now that's a fine man, Mister Witherspoon. Why, I remember when your mama was a lil' girl, we were all so happy there. It's still like home to me."

"You'd like to go back, wouldn't you, Mammy?"

The bulky, aging woman gave a rotund laugh.

"Heavens, yes, child, I reckon I would."

"Do you know the way?" Amity whispered.

Mammy's eyes grew large as she stared at her young mistress and plumbed the possibilities the headstrong girl might have in mind.

"Course I remembers."

"Will you go with me if I decide to leave?"

Mammy gave a solemn nod.

"I'll be beside you ev'ry step of the way, child. Where you go—there I'll go."

With that assurance Amity seemed placated.

"And Serena, too, if she wants to go along," she promised. "I'd miss Serena something dreadful."

"She'll want to," Mammy whispered with surety.

"You. . .you've heard talk, haven't you, Mammy, about servants being liberated by the Yankees? Mammies leaving the children they've raised up? Field hands runnin' off to be free. And—"

"Let them go," Mammy dismissed with a haughty sniff. She sank her bulk on the edge of Amity's feather tick and folded the slim girl into her strong embrace.

"Come what may," she said fiercely, "I'm going with my people, Miss Amity, and you're my family. Where you are is my home. An' pray God someday maybe yo' be havin' lil' ones, and they'll be Mammy's to love an' to raise up just like I done for y'all."

At the thought, Amity shuddered.

"If Cousin Philomen is determined, Mammy, we're leaving the very mornin' after he'd make such intentions clear."

"I'll be prepared, honey, anytime you give the word. Miss Ophelia, she warn't your mama's blood, not like you are. And Mist' Witherspoon, he gave me to your mother, girl. Yo' mine, an' I'm yo's an ain't no one—an' no two sides to a squabblin' nation—that's goin' to come between us. An' I promise you that, as the Lord is my witness."

Chapter Five

Amity's reprieve did not last long, for the next day Philomen Emerson arrived. He seemed delighted to make Amity's acquaintance, and it was clear to her that her reputation preceded her, for she could detect that the Emerson family had done their best to stress her attributes as a potential matrimonial possibility for their homely but pleasant relative.

When Cousin Philomen took Amity's hand in his and squeezed it in a way that she realized he hoped would express the admiring optimism he felt, she shuddered.

He was not a repulsive man, as she had feared, but there was nothing about him to set her heart afire with so much as a flicker of the heady attraction she felt for Jebediah Dennison.

Philomen, who had inherited acreage near his Uncle Raynor's plantation, was short, balding, plain, and, perhaps because of all he'd seen and endured while at war, humorless. He had a dour expression that in his better moments was merely bland.

Amity found it disconcerting to make an amusing remark and have it go unrecognized by Philomen. Even worse was when such comments drew a perplexed glance from him, as if he couldn't understand what she had meant by such a statement.

Philomen had long since concluded that ladies were a confusing lot, so when he was met with a situation or remark that was beyond his ken, he smiled agreeably and inquired no further.

Amity knew that there could be no understanding between them, and her heart rebelled against being borne along, like a leaf carried in a stream. She refused to allow herself to be married off without protest.

The Emerson kinfolk did all that they could to place the pair regularly in each other's company. Over the days and weeks that followed, Amity realized that Philomen was a cordial and pleasant man who possessed a kind nature and a well-intentioned heart.

Due to the living conditions he had endured while fighting in the War for Separation, Philomen had a poor constitution. The fact that he didn't dwell on his aches and complaints raised Amity's opinion of him.

Amity came to view Philomen as a gentleman she could never hate, but neither was he a beau she would grow to love. He hadn't the ability to stir passion within her and was bland as unsalted corn mush. For just that reason,

Amity felt alarmed whenever Philomen's looks grew more adoring. He was content with a mere crumb of attention from her.

Philomen tried to please Amity and cheer her up, an attribute she appreciated most when bad news arrived from the war. Word had been disseminated via an Atlanta newspaper that Ol' Joe had been replaced by Major General John Bell Hood, just as Confederate soldiers had predicted on the veranda of the Sheffield home weeks earlier.

Casualties had risen sharply for both North and South, as Hood, not a patient man, recklessly attacked Yankee positions, gaining only a bloodbath for his men. Ophelia and Amity discovered their pa's name on the list of the wounded, and Ophelia's husband, Major Emerson, was among the missing and unaccounted for.

Because Amity had lived with Ophelia's difficult temper and trying nature, she desperately wanted to protect Philomen's feelings. It was evident that he had already suffered much in life. She wanted to keep him as a friend while refusing him as a suitor, but she was not sure how realistic a goal that was.

"What yo' think o' Mist' Phil?" Mammy presumed to ask one night as she helped Amity get ready for bed in early July.

Mammy's question made Amity grow thoughtful. It was an issue she had already discussed with Serena, who, as an uninvolved third party, confirmed Amity's reactions to the Emerson relative who was spending more and more time with his kin that he might also be close to Amity.

The girl stared into the looking glass and carefully laid down the brush with which she'd been working her honey-colored tresses.

"Philomen's pleasant, kind, gentle, intelligent, industrious, upright. But he's. . . ."

Amity gestured with hands palm up in a display of inarticulate confusion. Words to describe her swirling, confusing feelings failed to make the journey from mind to tongue.

"But not for you, child?" Mammy finished softly as she took up the hairbrush that Amity had abandoned.

Amity gave a sigh of relief at being so understood.

"No. He's not the man for me," Amity murmured.

She lifted her eyes and met Mammy's dark gaze in the vanity mirror.

"I didn't reckon yo' be thinkin' 'bout marryin' Mist' Philomen," Mammy admitted, sighing. "Miss Ophelia, she be marrying for whatever de reason she had for snagging Mist' Schuyler, but I knows my lil' Miss Amity, an' when she be marryin' it'll be for love alone, no matter what de gemp'mum's sentiments."

Amity frowned, studying the husky black woman's fathomless face.

"Have you heard something, Mammy? Something that you believe I should know about? And don't deny that you usually know more about what's going on in a household than the folks who own it. I know you hear plenty as you move around the mansion on catfeet, with family members unaware of your passing presence. Something's on the tip of your tongue. Tell me what it is, Mammy."

Mammy paused with the boar brush midstroke. She gave a huffing sigh.

"Mayhap I jus' have heard somethin'," Mammy admitted. "Business concernin' a right private matter."

Amity was aware that the study was the usual scene for confidential conversations.

"Were you listening at a closed door?" Amity asked, her voice stern, but her eyes laughingly conspiratorial as she realized how Mammy had probably come by her knowledge.

Mammy gave an unchastened chuckle.

"Seems like as if just perhaps I was dustin' the fancy work on Mistah Raynor's study while he had a visitor there makin' a request o' him. So then I moved on to clean the portrait o' Mist' Raynor's great-grandpapa hangin' nearby in de hallway."

Such details began to drive Amity to distraction.

"Mammy, please! Don't do this to me. Be out with whatever it is you have to say. Don't keep me in suspense, Mammy. What did you learn?"

Mammy began dragging the brush through Amity's heavy hair, as if the familiar motion made the uncomfortable news a bit easier to share.

"Now that we's got Misses Lavinia and Maybelle's nuptials behind us, Miss Ophelia be gettin' mighty antsy to get yo' betrothed to Mist' Philomen, married up, and entrusted into another's care. An' if I know Miss Ophy, it be afore winter be comin' on—as I think she's considerin' how many mouths they be to feed an' how much money can be saved."

Amity stiffened at the reminder that the Emersons might view her as a burden.

"That's Mister Raynor's concern, not hers."

Mammy gave a vigorous nod.

"'Deed it is, Missy, but yo' know how Miss Ophelia can be. And now Mister Raynor is off to town a goodly amount, same as Mist' Philomen, an' somebody's gots to attend to the managin' o' this plantation, what with the fiel' hands runned off, an' Miss Ophy, she seems like she's considered that she be the mos' likely."

Amity's heart tightened as she considered what her domineering sister might be capable of doing in an effort to trim the costs of running Magnolia Manor.

"Exactly what did you overhear, Mammy?" Amity asked, her voice steady, although she quailed inwardly. "Word for word, now, if you please."

"Well, a few days ago I heard Mist' Philomen and Mister Raynor talkin' in the library when they gots home from military drills wit' neighborhood gemp'mums. They was discussin' lots o' things, but among them, Mist' Philomen asked Miss Ophelia's papa-in-law for yo' hand, seein' as he's the man of the house and yo' be livin' under his roof."

Although she had known what plans were afoot, Amity gasped. Her heart momentarily stopped before it escalated to a frenzied rhythm that made her limbs feel weak and her head swim.

"Mammy, no!"

"Oh, yes," the slave answered in a grim, resigned tone. "But Mist' Raynor, bless him, he tell the young gemp'mum that he thinks he'd best be a-speakin' of that to Miss Ophy, since Mist' Schuyler's wife be yo' next of kin, not him. Mist' Raynor said it not be in his place to make such a serious answer on behalf of another person, especially 'bout such a monumental prospect as matrimony."

Amity drew a deep breath.

"And has he? Has Cousin Philomen spoken to Ophelia?"

"Not to my knowin'," Mammy said. "Nor to Serena's hearing, neither," she added a bit sheepishly. "I shared the secret wit' her so's she could help me be alert an' pr'tect you."

"Good," Amity sighed with relief. "Philomen's a nice man, and I hate to think of ever hurting his feelings by having to turn down his proposal, but feeling as I do, there's no way I could marry him. I'll just have to discourage him from daring to ask.

"Why, Mammy, the idea of marrying him, going to live at his plantation, and being expected to let him. . . ." Amity's soft words dissolved into another shudder.

The idea of residing with Cousin Philomen as his bride left Amity cold and shaken, whereas the thought of sharing such unspecified closeness with Jeb Dennison had caused the most thrilling dreams to consume her.

"What are we going to do, Mammy?" Amity whispered when she realized that listening outside her door could be one of the Emerson servants, as loyal to their charges as Mammy was to her. If word got back to the Emersons about this conversation, Ophelia would not take kindly to having her intentions thwarted.

"There's always Mist' Witherspoon's plantation, Lambie," Mammy reminded in a hushed voice as she cast the door a dark look.

Amity gave a low and bitter laugh.

"Don't think that I haven't given that thought. But I'm afraid to try. You've heard the menfolks talking, Mammy, and you're aware of what Mister Raynor says when he returns from the home guard drills. Why, he's after us constantly not to go out alone and not to wander any distance from the house.

"There are bands of marauders, and to the shame of the South, the Rebs are pillaging the countryside the same as the blue-bellies, commandeering starving folks' last food, heartlessly robbing them of their treasured heirloom possessions, being rowdy toward the womenfolk other gentlemen have fought and died to protect. And—"

Mammy sighed and gave a troubled nod.

"Yes'm, Miss Amity, I've heard. I know it's dangerous. But—"

"Why, if we met up with the likes of them, I'd. . . ," Amity shook her head and fell silent, unable to voice the unspeakable horrors that would await them in the course of their desperate journey. By comparison, Cousin Philomen no longer seemed so unappealing.

"It be like yo' heard Serena say," Mammy reminded, "we's the Lord's— leastways Serena and I is—an' yo' could be, iffen yo' turn yo' life and heart over to the Lord and trust an' allow Him to guide you. Iffen yo' be doing exactly what the Lord wants yo' to do, Lambie, then He keep you safe on yo' mission, no matter how desperate it be.

"An' iffen for some reason you ain't kept safe, then it only be 'cause de Lord be lettin' it happen that His glory will be seen. He can take plumb awful situations and grow 'em into miracles when He uses folks who've got seeds of faith inside 'em and seek to live not for theyselves, but to live for Him, hidin' theyselves in Him, like the Good Book says."

"I don't know, Mammy," Amity said.

"Yes yo' do!" she retorted. "Serena, she's been a-tellin' me how sometimes late at night yo' helpin' her with her readin'. She gettin' plumb good, that girl is, 'cause she be telling me what chapters of Scripture she been readin' and what ones you read to her when the words got too diff'cult. So don't be telling me that yo' don' know, 'cause I knows yo' starting to understand the Good Book in your head, Lambie! But we's prayin' that soon yo' goin' to start understanding it wit' your heart."

"Mammy, I've got more important things to worry about right now than the Bible, interesting as it sometimes is," Amity pointed out.

"Yo' ain't got nothin' more important than yo' faith, Miss Amity, and yo' eternal future. But the Lord, He don't put no pressure on yo' to decide iffen yo' going to love an' trust Him. He lets ever'one make up their minds free an' unhampered. So'll it be with yo'.

"But I wants yo' to think about what yo' ol' mammy is a-sayin' so that yo' know that no matter what happens, de Lord is there and He be a-waitin' on yo'. Yo' don' have to face nothin' alone, honey, even if I should die and be unable to stay by yo'. With the Lord dey ain't nothin' yo' can't face and endure. Even marriage to Cousin Philomen. And he is a decent sort. I suspects he be a Christian from things he said. Though I know that when that special spark is missin', that don't seem to be enough."

"It's not," Amity said. "I want more—so much more. Whatever are we going to do? I like and respect Philomen, and I hate the thought of rejecting him and hurting his feelings, but I won't be pushed into marrying a man I don't love. The thought of leaving terrifies me. And if we decided to, how would we best go about it?"

"Carefullike, I reckon," Mammy finally spoke. "I suspects if we all was to light out all o' the sudden, Miss Ophy'd know where we were goin' to," Mammy sighed. "If she's determined to marry yo' off to Mister Philomen, then she'd be het to fetch us back. She might even order Serena an' me whupped."

The thought sickened Amity.

"I'd never allow that. She'd have to whip her way through me to ever get to you or Serena. But it seems we don't have a chance to escape," Amity said, her tone dismal. "At least not right now."

"Maybe the tide will turn."

"Perhaps," Amity murmured. "But until then all that we can do is bide our time and hope for the best. Even if Cousin Phil does talk to Ophelia and she dares to give in to his request that we marry, I can postpone the ceremony almost endlessly."

"There be ways for that awrighty!" Mammy said and gave a conspiratorial chuckle.

"He's a shy man," Amity pointed out.

"Could be that he'll be a spell before he gets up the gumption to ask Miss Ophelia if yo' can be his bride. He was plumb hesitant broachin' de matter with Mist' Raynor, and him the uncle who's been like a papa to the boy. So I 'spects that it may take him a while to get around to speaking to Miss Ophelia. Praise God for dat, 'cause it gives us time in which to lay our own plans in de matter."

"Yes," Amity agreed. Then her eyes widened as an unsettling thought occurred. "Unless Ophelia decides to take the matter in hand and raises the matter with *him*."

Mammy's eyes widened as she realized the likelihood of that outcome, for Miss Ophy was shameless when in pursuit of her desires.

"Miss Ophy a pow'rful woman," Mammy said. "But she, too, is in de Lord's control. He can restrain her if it serves His will, so that she'll be found makin' a diff'rent choice, not even sure, herself, why she is. She thinks she's in control, but she ain't, 'cause God is. Ain't nothing in this ol' world that happens without de Lord knowin' about and allowin' it, as He always has since de first moments of creation."

"Really?"

"Yes, Lambie. Ol' Mammy wouldn't lie to yo'. Why, when the world was a new place, de Lord, He knew already that one day I'd be standin' here big as life talkin' Scripture to yo' and tellin' yo' to trust Him. And the Lord, He already knows if yo' gonna choose to love an' accept Him or if it be yo' choice to reject Him. Serena an' me, we hopes yo' make the right choice when the moment of decision comes."

"I hope so, too," Amity murmured, even though she wasn't confident that she would recognize such a moment when it arrived. Although she was well-educated in comparison to her slaves, she felt totally unschooled in areas of faith where the household servants had a deep, practical knowledge.

"I meant to tell yo', too, Lambie, that yo' been a-pinin' for that Mist' Jeb y'all met in Atlanta, believin' yo' won't never see him again. Well, don't yo' trouble yo'self about that, 'cause if it's the Lord's will that yo' do, sure as can be, yo' will."

"And if I'm not meant to see him again?" Amity inquired, her voice cracked with emotion.

"Then de Lord will give yo' the strength and wisdom to accept that situation, trust Him, and know dat it's for de best."

Chapter Six

Even though the Emerson family and their house guests had been warned to be watchful for the arrival of Yankee soldiers and had scared themselves with talk of their coming, deep down they had believed they would be spared. But it was not to be.

Days later blue-bellies were everywhere. Neighbors sent runners or someone brave enough to ride out on spavined old mules to warn of the Yankees' approach.

The frightened residents of Magnolia Manor scarcely left the solidly built house except to hide possessions from Yankee raiders as well as from Rebels who would ruthlessly commandeer valuables for the cause even if it meant leaving Southern civilians to face a bleak winter of starvation and material hardship.

The Emerson kin and their house guests were thankful that the plantation was as far from the Macon and Western Railroad as it was, and even Ophelia had begun wondering if perhaps they wouldn't have had a safer haven at Grandpapa Witherspoon's, although there had been reports of random skirmishes in that vicinity, as well.

Almost daily, thick, oily smoke plumed into the sky, signifying that another elaborate antebellum structure had been razed. Chimneys stood like skeletons against the skyline as the Yankees torched dwellings, leaving their inhabitants homeless.

There were no local newspapers to spread the history of events, but the Georgians had only to look northerly to see the horizon glowing like an ember in the night sky and realize what was happening. The dreaded Yankees were surrounding Atlanta and had ventured south to Jonesboro and Lovejoy as well.

On September second, shortly after the midnight hour, Georgians from as far away as Jonesboro heard massive explosions and surmised that a Southern munitions train had been destroyed to prevent its capture by the Union Army.

Before noon of that same day, Yankees had entered Atlanta, the heart of the Confederacy. Mayor James M. Calhoun and a contingent of the city's gentlemen met the invading force. The city leaders waved a white flag in truce, begging for mercy on behalf of the residents in the captured city.

But Sherman was an officer without mercy. He and his army rolled over the land like some monstrous, inhuman entity consuming and routing every-thing and everyone in its path.

It was a full fortnight before those in the vicinity of Magnolia Manor ven-tured out, and then they did so only as necessary. The womenfolk went out only in the company of an armed man who was grim, watchful, and at the ready. By then they were hungry for news, a look at the latest casualty lists, and any facts that would help them determine their future.

Come mid-September, Ophelia, who was determined to travel to the vil-lage and try to discover the fates of their pa and her husband, made the trip with Cousin Philomen serving as her protector.

Lavinia, Maybelle, and Amity nervously awaited Ophelia's return. They hastily arose when they heard wheels crunching gravel on the lane leading toward the mansion, and they rushed to the window, sighing collectively when they saw Philomen's rickety wagon rather than hordes of raiding sol-diers.

"What did you find out?" Amity asked as Ophelia entered the house. "Is Papa—"

"Wounded. In a hospital," a weary Ophelia crisply informed. "But he'll live, barring the misfortune of putrefying infection causing him to become septic."

"And Schuyler?" Maybelle and Lavinia questioned in unison.

For an instant Ophelia faltered. She squeezed her eyes shut, struggling to maintain rigid control. Her trembling lips scarcely moved as she uttered the word, "Captured."

Faint shrieks escaped from the Major's sisters.

"But Cousin Philomen assures me that Major Emerson may be better off in a Yankee prison camp than he would have been fighting in or around Atlanta," Ophelia stated. She seemed to be trying harder to convince her-self than to give optimistic thoughts to her kinfolk.

"Do you really think so?" Lavinia murmured. "You know what it's like at Andersonville and Libby. Prisoners there don't fare well, I've heard. The way the Yankees have plundered our Confederate Nation, we've little enough for ourselves, let alone to share with the enemies in our prisons."

"Cousin Philomen says that at Point Lookout, Schuyler has more to fear from disease than from the Yankees. And," Ophelia drew herself up straight, "my husband has a strong constitution. Cousin Phil said that there's been talk of another prisoner exchange. We can't be gloomy girls; we must hope for the best. It's what Schuy would want. We must be brave for his dear sake if we can't find reason to manage it from the depths of our own piteous grief."

"You're right," his sisters agreed and fell to their sister-in-law, smothering her in comforting hugs.

"Let's speak of more pleasant things." Ophelia turned to Amity. She seemed to physically shake off her gloom as she would whisk off a cloak.

"You'll never guess who I saw while I was in town today," she trilled.

"I shouldn't hazard a guess, as I know so few people in these parts," Amity said.

Ophelia decided to make a game of imparting the information.

"One of your old beaus who used to come to call."

"There were dozens," Amity reminded and offered a careless shrug. She felt herself blush when she saw Maybelle lift an eyebrow, and Lavinia whispered a remark about Amity remaining unwed, a state of affairs that challenged her claim to having been so popular.

"Since you can't guess, then I'll tell you: Will Conner!"

"How nice!" Amity cried, even as she felt a stab of disappointment that the name had not been that of Jeb Dennison. Warm memories of Will washed over Amity, and she tendered a dozen rapid questions about Will's health, his family, his arrival in the area, news of home, messages from mutual friends, and information about how Grandpapa Witherspoon was faring.

"One at a time," Ophelia laughingly stipulated. "I knew you would be brimming with more questions than I could probably answer in one breath."

Forcing patience that she did not feel, Amity primly seated herself near the hearth where a low fire glowed to remove the damp chill from the cavernous parlor.

"Is Will on furlough?" Amity began.

"No. He's with a detachment of soldiers who are bivouacking in this area. It seems that when Atlanta's fall became imminent, troops began moving south to protect the railroads. Sherman circled around the city with the intent of capturing the Macon and Western line. There's been some terrible fighting, although Will hasn't been involved in anything except light skirmishes."

Amity felt relief.

"Then Will's well?"

"Looking marvelous, actually, considering what he—what all of them—have been through."

"Did you see any of the other soldiers who had stopped by the house to dally of an evening? Any of Will's friends with whom we became acquainted?"

"Not that I recall, although I suppose there could have been one or two I had met before. They tended to cluster around you since initially I was spoken for and later I was wed," Ophelia reminded and gave Schuyler's sisters a quelling glance, upholding family pride by confirming that Amity had been as sought after as she had claimed.

"Oh. I thought perhaps you'd have recognized others."

"Maybe under better conditions, Amity, but Will's the only one who spoke to me. In butternut brown homespun and unkempt, all Johnny Rebs tend to look the same."

Amity's heart skipped a beat when she realized that there was still a slim hope that Jeb was nearby, a member of Will's detachment. Could it be possible that he was mere miles from Magnolia Manor? Dare she hope that they would one day see each other again?

Amity considered what Mammy had said about the will of God, the purpose for each life, and how if it was in God's plan she and Jeb meet again, they would, but in God's own time.

"Until this moment, I hadn't realized how homesick I have been to see a familiar face and talk to an old friend," Amity mused, fluffing her fair hair around her wistful face.

"I'll admit that I felt the same when I saw dear Will Conner standing there."

"I wish I could have seen him."

A knowing smile appeared on Ophelia's lips.

"Perhaps your wish will come true, my dear," she said. "I gave Will permission to come calling on us. And, as an old family friend he's got the right, although I did make it discreetly clear that he would be greeted as an old family friend and neighbor of Grandpapa's, not received as a beau. Since you've been—well, you know how Cousin Philomen feels. We do have his sensitivities to consider."

"Will never was a beau. He's more like a brother," Amity said. "Will's always been a family friend, and I hope he always shall be."

"That's all he will ever be," Ophelia agreed. "It is all he can be," she warned, and a knowing smile played on her face, deepening the crow's feet that crinkled at the corners of her eyes.

"Exactly what do you mean you by that, Ophelia?"

Pausing to let suspense build, Ophelia smoothed a fold in her faded calico gown.

"Cousin Philomen was good enough to see me to town and back today. En route home, Amity dear, he addressed some business of a personal nature, as I have been anticipating he would," she explained, carefully picking at an imaginary piece of lint on her sleeve. Ophelia bought more suspense by adjusting the brooch on her dress and taking time to wind the ornate timepiece.

Amity's heart leaped within her chest, then felt as if it stopped. Heaviness pervaded her being, and her pulse sounded a death knell.

"Well?" she questioned.

"He's asked for your hand, Amity dear, and I have affirmed that his intentions are honorable, that he will provide for your welfare, and that he is a man to be relied on. I have given him my permission to ask for your hand which, of course, you will be honored to accept."

"Ophelia. . .no. . . ." Amity's dazed whisper was drowned out by Maybelle and Lavinia's excited chatter.

"In Papa's stead, I have granted Cousin Phil the opportunity to offer you his proposal of marriage. I have also intimated that your answer will be to accept with honor and great pleasure. That foreknowledge should do much to encourage Cousin Philomen not to be dilatory in making his request."

"Of course she will accept!" Lavinia chirped. "He's a real catch. She probably couldn't do better."

"Cousin Philomen's so shy and sweet, Amity. Don't you dare trifle with his heart and keep him on tenterhooks until you agree to be his bride!" Maybelle gaily warned. "And there's no need to postpone a wedding. Philomen's home to stay, you lucky girl. Why, we can have you two married just as soon as we can decently arrange the details and plan a party."

"This is just what we need to chase away the gloom from the awful fighting, the horrible blue-bellies' recent presence, and the depressing news that Atlanta's fallen."

They rushed toward Amity in a swirl of skirts, and their arms twined around her as they bestowed joyous hugs and showered impulsive kisses on her hot cheeks.

"You'll be content with a man like Cousin Phil," Lavinia assured.

"And won't we have fun when the war is over, and our men are home? We will all live nearby, and. . . ."

The rest of Maybelle's speech was lost on Amity. She felt herself being pulled down into an eddying whirlpool of unhappiness, swept along against her will.

Stunned by the news, weakened by gnawing hunger, Amity felt the room tilt and whirl about her. She struggled to keep her balance but was powerless to stop the movement, too disoriented to counter it.

"Goodness, she's swooning!" Ophelia cried. "Quick—help me! Get the smelling salts!"

Chapter Seven

There was a flurry of activity as Amity crumpled to the floor. Schuyler's sisters shrieked in alarm and stood rooted in horrified dismay, of little help. As was her nature, Ophelia took charge, her tone brusque and snappish.

"Mammy, fetch the smelling salts from my reticule!" she cried and impatiently shook her sister.

Amity groggily blinked and then turned her face aside and moaned. The world continued to spin around her like a child's top gone out of control, causing her to feel disoriented and sick to her stomach. She went hot, cold, then feverish again, before a consuming chill overtook her. The gabble of the other women's voices sounded from a distance.

Serena carried Amity to the worn horsehair settee and wafted a palmetto leaf fan over her.

"What...where...?" Amity asked as she tried to sit up, not sure how long it had been since she had collapsed.

She sank back on the velvet throw pillows and remembered with horror that she was now destined to become Philomen Emerson's bride.

"Won't Cousin Phil be proud as a strutting bantam rooster to learn how utterly he has swept Miss Amity off her feet?" Lavinia teased.

"Cousin Philomen has succeeded where many other beaus have failed," Ophelia assured. She gave a tittering giggle. "It would seem that the Sheffield belles are especially partial to the Emerson beaus."

"Before Amity swooned I believe she was inquiring about when this wonderful event is going to come to pass," Lavinia reminded them.

"Why, I can remember how eager I was when Papa told me that he had given my Gaylord permission to seek my hand in marriage. I'm sure Miss Amity is as excited as I was. She must want to know how long it will be before Philomen will arrive with his hat in hand, prepared to go down on bended knee to seek her hand in marriage."

"Well, it won't be tonight," Ophelia said in a regretful tone. "Cousin Philomen mentioned that he and Papa Emerson have patriotic business that cannot be postponed.

"But that's perhaps all for the best because earlier in the day, Will Conner—the old family friend Amity and I have been talking about—inquired if he could come calling. As eager as he seemed to see us again and to be received into the parlor of proper people after having to live off the land, I shan't be at all surprised if he doesn't favor us with a visit this very day."

"How wonderful!" Lavinia cried. "It seems ages since we have entertained company—especially a charming gentleman."

"Although staples are precious, we will have our cook prepare something especially lovely," Maybelle promised.

"You might have her ask our Serena for her recipe for tarts," Ophelia suggested. "Mammy will know exactly which little tasty tidbit it was that Mister Will was most partial to when he would come to call, and if we possess the ingredients, Mammy can prepare it for his enjoyment."

"Today started out so damp, grim, and gray, but it's become quite lovely," Lavinia declared. "Think: a wedding in the offing and tonight the first company we've had come calling in ages! Things are looking up, girls."

To Amity they had never looked more bleak. Although she kept a careful smile fixed on her features and hoped that her misery wasn't visible, she knew that Mammy understood and was reviewing possible options that would allow them to escape the fate Ophelia had planned for them.

As much as she wanted to see Will Conner and enjoy being in his company, Amity hoped even more to arrange to speak with him privately. She needed to press him for any news regarding Jeb Dennison and perhaps ask his opinion regarding which way to run, should they choose to flee Magnolia Manor. She would swear Will to secrecy and hope that out of respect to an old friend, he would honor her request and plead ignorance if later questioned.

The other members of the household prepared for the evening with special zeal, even though several times Ophelia hastened to remind them that there was a chance Will wouldn't be able to come calling.

Amity prayed that he would arrive exactly as anticipated. If he didn't come calling at Magnolia Manor that very evening, she would be unable to see him at all, for she had decided that when Mammy helped her undress for bed that night, she would give her servant notice to prepare to flee. There was no time to waste.

Soon after the next day's dawn, Amity was going to leave Magnolia Manor and escape an unwanted marriage. Granted, she liked Cousin Philomen, but in her heart, irrational as it was, Amity loved Jeb. Without his having ever told her his feelings, she also believed that Jeb loved her.

If she was destined one day to meet Jebediah Dennison again, she couldn't bear to be introduced as the wife of Philomen Emerson. Instead, she would wait for Jeb the rest of her days. Better to pine for a true love than to live in comfortable harmony, adjusted to a man not really meant for her by the God her servants had assured her had a special plan—and a special man—just for her.

Chapter Eight

That evening shortly after the supper hour, Will Conner arrived astride a mule he had borrowed from a superior in his detachment. He had promised that he would return early with the beast after a hasty visit with old family friends who resided at a plantation in the area.

As Will made his way up the winding lane sheltered by towering trees, members of the Emerson household flocked from the mansion to greet him. Ophelia ordered a servant to catch the bridle of the beast Will rode and take control of it, freeing him to immerse himself in the attentions of his eager hostesses.

Amity hung back demurely, knowing that if she appeared too forward, she would risk drawing criticism from Schuy's sisters and Ophelia. Inwardly, Amity was thrilled to see Will. His presence at the plantation momentarily took her mind off her troubles.

While Amity was still determined to leave the plantation the next day, she was disturbed by a conversation she had overheard between Raynor Emerson and Philomen. The two men had talked in low, disgusted tones of Confederate deserters from whom southern women were no more safe than if they confronted an enemy Yankee. Such southern men would callously burn out their own people and would view a woman alone, or in the company of her household servants, as a diversion to be used and then cast aside.

Amity knew that there were also bands of roving Yankees who were going ahead of the Union Army in order to pillage the land and holdings of plantation owners. Nothing was safe from these hordes. They would enter a house and hold the women and children at gunpoint while they searched for valuables.

As dire as her fate would be if she were set upon by a band of southern deserters, Amity's imagination failed her in chronicling the possible horrors that would be her fate if she were to encounter Yankees.

As Will was ushered into the once stately home that had begun to fall into ruin and disrepair because of the wartime hardships, a spark of hope warmed Amity's heart.

Will would be honest with her. He could be trusted to keep a secret. Somehow she had always known that about him. From what Will had been saying about his life since he and his detachment had moved south of Atlanta, he was familiar with the area.

Somehow she would get a chance to question Will in private. If there was a safer way to travel to Grandpapa Witherspoon's plantation, surely the kind and gentle soldier would know of it and advise her accordingly.

The grandfather clock incessantly ticked off the seconds of each passing minute as Amity patiently bided her time. Her mind searched for a plausible excuse to slip off with Will. She needed only enough time in private with him to find out about Jeb Dennison's health and whereabouts and to discuss her flight to Grandpapa Witherspoon's plantation.

Amity felt weak with anxiety. For months life had been out of her control. Her choices had been forced on her by others. Suddenly she could see a way to make her own decisions and provide a better environment for Mammy and Serena.

The end of Will's visit was drawing near, and still Amity hadn't been able to speak with him alone. She steeled herself to appear calm and casually made a suggestion with what she hoped was the right amount of indifferent politeness.

"I really should show Mister Will around Magnolia Manor while it's still daylight and before he has to leave," she said, covering a delicate yawn. "It's truly a pity that Schuyler or Mister Raynor aren't here to do the honors so that they could have the pleasure of showing him their acreage and enjoying his company."

"I would love to see the property," Will said.

Amity was grateful that Will seemed to sense her desire for a few private moments and was assisting her in her efforts. She rose gracefully. Will stood and, with a courtly bow, offered her his arm.

Mammy had slipped into the parlor.

"I'll go wit' you," she murmured, offering to serve as a chaperone. To prevent the appearance of a servant taking charge, she carefully qualified the remark. "Unless Miss Ophelia would rather go along. Or Misses Lavinia and Maybelle."

Amity didn't dare glance in Mammy's direction lest someone catch a conspiratorial look pass between them.

"My slippers are only now starting to dry out after my venturing into town this morning," Ophelia dismissed, much too ladylike to complain in front of a gentleman caller about her true reason for declining: corns and bunions.

"I'm afraid I feel a touch of grippe coming on," Maybelle excused herself, not wanting to seem too eager to spend time with a young gentleman in the absence of her husband. "This dreary weather may be the death of me yet.

Pity the poor soldiers who can't get in from the rain." She drew her shawl about her and gave a theatrical shiver.

Lavinia patted her neat coronet into place and gave a gentle, long-suffering sigh.

"Yes, I do think of our brave boys, especially at times like this when I'm too comfortable to move," she murmured from her place close to the fire. "Were that everyone in the world could know such moments as this all the time."

There were low murmurs of general agreement as Amity, Will, and Mammy made their way toward the front doors that opened onto the wide veranda of the Emerson home.

"Those tarts that Serena showed our cook how to make are wonderful. I shouldn't have taken the last one," Maybelle said to no one in particular. "It was thoughtless of me, considering the daily plight of our guest." She favored Will with a quick, regretful smile that caused him to immediately offer assurances that his needs had been more than met.

"Don' worry yo'self about it, Miss Maybelle," Mammy politely enjoined. "Serena saved a few of her tasties to send back with Mist' Will so he can enjoy 'em on his way back to de camp. An' mayhap share with a few o' his comrades if he chooses."

Will visibly brightened over the prospect, although his expression never lost the grimness brought on by his experiences in the war.

"Much as the idea pains me after enjoying your charming company and delicious dainties, I'll be havin' to take my leave," he said to the ladies.

"Get my wrap, if you would, Mammy," Amity said, smoothing her voluminous skirts after she passed through the doorway of the parlor and stood in the foyer.

Will turned back and courteously began tendering goodbyes to the matrons still congregated around the cozy room. He explained that he would like to tarry but had to be heading back to his detachment. It was foolhardy for a soldier from either side to be out alone after dark in case he chanced into roving bands of enemy soldiers.

"I'll be takin' my leave after Miss Amity shows me around y'all's lovely plantation," he said. "And I do hope that perhaps I can return to savor your company again before our regiment moves on—none of us having any idea how long we'll be in these parts. We could leave tomorrow, or we might be here for a few weeks.

"Even our officers don't seem to know. I reckon it depends on what the blue-bellies are up to. But, if I'm here, I would beg your permission to come calling again. This has been most enjoyable, seein' y'all."

"It's been our pleasure," Ophelia said, smiling.

"Oh, do hurry back!" Lavinia encouraged.

"You're welcome anytime," Maybelle agreed.

"If you have gentlemen friends who would like to spend a pleasant evening, feel free to come in their company, Will," Amity made it unanimous. Her heart skipped a beat when she considered that maybe Jeb could have—would have—come calling if he'd had an express invitation.

"Give our greetings to anyone who knows us," Ophelia reminded. "And give them news of Papa and Major Emerson, of course, for I'm sure they'll be interested."

"By all means. Consider it done," Will politely agreed.

Amity's heart was thumping as she headed for the front veranda with Will in her wake, her steps as light as her soaring heart now that she knew she was moments away from being able to discuss Jeb with a trusted friend.

For the first time since Ophelia had delivered the stunning news of Cousin Philomen's intentions, Amity's heart felt at peace. She stood still so that Mammy could slip a cloak over her slim shoulders and tie its ribbons beneath her pert chin.

As they left the main house, Mammy took her position a pace or two behind her young miss and her gentleman caller. The pair walked down the path toward the various outbuildings, a grove of trees, an overgrown meadow, and then to a bower formed by decorative bushes.

Mammy trailed behind Will and Amity, keeping a distance sufficient to allow privacy to talk, but not so far away that Ophelia could complain about impropriety.

"I'm so glad that you came calling tonight, Will, and that you agreed to accompany me for a walk around the grounds so that we could talk," Amity said in a fervent tone. "I've been almost wild with distraction, hoping—praying—for this time alone."

"My pleasure, Miss Amity," he assured in a gallant tone. Will stood at a safe distance from her, for he had heard enough about Cousin Philomen that evening to know about the expected engagement.

"I'll admit I've been wantin' to speak with you, too," he added, "an' not have everyone there to overhear it."

Amity quailed, wondering if Will was preparing to tell her that Jeb Dennison had departed this life after entrusting Will with the responsibility of sharing the details of his passing with the woman they both knew would care. But it couldn't be that! She decided to take her risks and speak honestly, hoping for the best.

"I so wanted to see you before—" Amity swallowed quickly. "Before I leave. For I don't know when I will see you again, and you have been a cherished and trusted friend to me since we were both small children and I met you at Grandpapa Witherspoon's barbecues and cotillions when our family visited him from Atlanta."

"I possess many fond memories of those days at home, Miss Amity, as well as of those evenings when you bestowed upon me your gracious hospitality and charming company in Atlanta. While I could have sought you as my belle, I wished to always keep you as a friend rather than to risk more and end up with less."

"Oh, Will!" Amity said, blushing. She was pleased to know the depth of her friend's admiration.

Will gave a hapless shrug.

"You sometimes toyed with suitors' hearts," he reminded in a teasing tone. "But it would appear those coquettish days are over. From what I've heard this evening, am I to discern that congratulations will soon be in order?

"Seems that Miss Ophelia's been hintin' that you'll be marryin' soon. An' Major Emerson's sisters seemed to be a-tossin' out a few sly remarks, too. With all of 'em mentioning a Philomen Emerson and speakin' of him in the highest of regard, it sounds like you've done well by yourself and have at last found the right man to marry."

Amity sighed.

"There's the threat of that, yes."

Will halted abruptly beneath a sweet gum tree and stared at Amity in amused shock.

"Threat?" he whispered, stunned by the choice of words made by a young woman who always tried to be the epitome of tact.

Silence spun between them and tears filled Amity's eyes.

"Threat?" Will repeated the word. "Somehow, pardon my makin' the observation Miss Amity, but that doesn't sound like the words of a happy bride-to-be who's head-over-heels in love.

"Why, for my part, if a woman I wanted to take as my bride considered me a threat, I'd be wounded to the core. And I'd probably decide to love her enough to free her to be with another than to wish to bind her to myself."

Amity squirmed with misery. She smoothed her hair away from her troubled face. Finally, she lifted her sad eyes to Will's face.

"That's because I'm not happy, nor am I in love with Cousin Philomen. Nor will I ever be."

"What's the matter?" Will was concerned, his voice gentle. "Don't you even like him a little bit? From what I've heard sometimes merely likin' someone a great deal is a wonderful foundation upon which to base enduring love that comes later."

"I don't even really like him. I'm in a position where I find myself tolerating him for others' sakes."

"Your sister and her husband's family seem to think the sun rises and sets on Cousin Philomen. But appealing as you are, it seems to me, Miss Amity, that you could have had your pick of beaus. Why him if you don't even cotton to the fellow? It'd be awful to wed a person you didn't like very well."

Amity dabbed at her eyes with a threadbare linen handkerchief. She tried to smile.

"Actually, Will, I was probably wrong. Or in my unhappiness, exaggerated. I suppose I like him well enough. In fact probably quite a lot. He's certainly not an offensive, abrasive person. He's rather easygoing and comfortable enough to be around. But it's just that—"

"Ah," Will said, and his tone took on sudden clarity of understanding. "But likin' and bein' comfortable with's not love."

"Exactly," Amity said, knowing that Will Conner would understand what she meant and how she felt. "Philomen's not the man I'd have chosen to marry. He's a kind man. I know he'd never harm me. But to wed such a boring and unimaginative person would cause me to die a little every day.

"I'd—well, to be unabashedly honest, Will, feeling as I do I'd almost sooner marry a lively, interesting, and passionate blue-belly than such a bland, plodding Southern gentleman."

Will gasped.

"Surely you jest!"

"I'm sorry, Will, I suppose I didn't mean that. At least not about preferring a Yankee. But Cousin Philomen is so predictably dull and so lacking in passion or imagination, that I already feel frustrated by him. I know it would only become worse if we were married.

"Maybe it wouldn't be so bad, but I can't resign myself to marrying him, adjusting to his personality, consigning myself to a lifetime of tending his household, and seeing to his needs. Not when I. . . ."

Amity's courage failed her.

"You can't fathom becoming Philomen's wife when you love someone else?"

Will finished for her. "Is that it? Because you've already given your heart to another?"

Amity gave Will an almost defiant stare. His lips curved into a faint, knowing smile.

"Yes," she whispered. "Yes I have. Not because I intended to, mind you, but because somehow I was helpless not to."

"That's what I thought."

"But how did you know that?" Amity asked, hoping that Will didn't misunderstand and believe that it was *he* whom she professed to love above all others.

"Because I saw you on the veranda the night before y'all fled Atlanta for Magnolia Manor, Miss Amity. Don't forget that I was in Jebediah Dennison's company that night, and for many nights after. I saw what was in your eyes, my dear, and I know what's in Jeb's heart."

At the mere mention of his name, Amity's heart quickened, and her hands trembled.

"Pardon me if I'm speakin' out of turn, Miss Amity, but could you be pinin' for Jeb? Or have you met another?"

Amity knew that for the sake of decency, she should demurely turn away from what was becoming an intimate and inappropriate conversation with a man, but she couldn't. Her heart—her love—demanded that honesty be served.

"Yes. I suppose that, well, unreasonable as it may seem after such a brief encounter, I am in love with Jeb. I do pine for him, Will. And it's been my sweetest dream to believe that he longs for me, too, that he cares as I do. If God is willing and miracles happen, perhaps someday he and I could be together."

Will nodded.

"Then I was right, for I thought so, and in the time that's passed I've witnessed Jeb longin' for you, even though he'd never had the chance to whisper sweet words of love in your ear.

"Something special occurred that night in Atlanta, Miss Amity. Something powerful passed between you. You know it. Jeb knows it. I know it. And the way he almost wears out the pages of the Good Book in his knapsack, I think he's seekin' godly answers—perhaps a miracle—so that you might see each other again."

"I want that more than I want life!" Amity passionately proclaimed.

"Is Miss Ophelia aware of your feelings? Do Major Emerson's sisters know your heart in this matter?"

"No. Only Mammy's aware of how I feel. And Serena," Amity admitted.

"Jeb would be a mighty happy man to know that his feelings are returned. I know that he's unceasingly prayed for that—and for you."

"Then you have seen him? Recently?" Amity asked, her excitement knowing no bounds.

"Up until two weeks ago we were together almost constantly," Will affirmed. "We got split up during a minor skirmish with the Yankees over toward the road leading to Mist' Witherspoon's plantation.

"I think Jeb might've been wounded, I'm sorry to say. Shelling was such that I wasn't able to return to him, nor, if he was unharmed, was he able to locate me. I hated to move on without him, but I had no choice."

"Oh, no!" Amity cried.

"If it'll make you feel better, he wasn't on the ambulance laden with injured. For my own peace of mind, I checked. And I've read casualty lists. His name's not appeared on any of them, so there's hope."

"Oh, I hope so," Amity breathed.

"Jeb might've gotten separated and linked up with some other Rebs. I sure hate to think of that; Jeb an' I got pretty good at communicatin'. I got so's I could read his gestures.

"That failin' he'd write a bit on the back of casualty sheets that we carried with us and used to tuck beneath our clothes to break the bite of the early autumn wind. He had a right neat hand. I expect that he was an educated fellow."

As Will talked on, Amity understood what Jeb's life had been like since she had last seen him in Atlanta. She felt grateful relief to know that Will had made Jeb's life easier, and that in return, Jeb had been a true friend. If only there hadn't been the skirmish that had parted them.

"I miss him," Will admitted. "Jeb was always someone to visit with, an' he never tired of listening to me. But then, perhaps that's because he usually saw fit to keep me talkin' about *you*, Miss Amity. I expect if I know somethin' about you, Jeb Dennison now treasures that knowledge as well."

"You talked about me?" Amity asked, surprised but pleased.

"About you, Miss Amity. He couldn't hear enough about you. Other Johnny Rebs would be around the fire talkin' about their wives or their intendeds or simply reminiscing about the belles they'd courted back home. Jeb, he seemed to hunger for the same. Don't reckon he's had many belles to court, him bein' a mute an' all.

"Jeb would write questions on the back of casualty sheets, and I'd answer 'em as best I knew, talkin' till I tired, or until I could no longer think of stories from our childhood at your Grandpapa's plantation. That seemed to satisfy Jeb, considering that I've known you an' your kin for as long as I can remember. I know that bein' close to me somehow made Jeb feel as if he was closer to you."

"What did he ask you?" Amity murmured, realizing that she wished she could learn the same kind of information about Jeb.

"Oh, lots of things. So long as I was talkin' about you, Jeb was happy. Why, I can pro'bly tell you *exactly* what he asked," Will exclaimed and began reaching into voluminous pockets, pulling out tightly folded casualty sheets.

"Maybe I'm still carryin' some of them that Jeb wrote on. With damp, cold days comin' on, sometimes I'm called on to help in startin' a fire, so I carry a wad of casualty sheets with me."

"Oh, I hope you haven't already burned the sheets that he wrote on," Amity said, her heart aching as she considered that an accident of selection could have robbed her of precious contact.

Will frowned as he scrutinized the wrinkled, fraying papers.

"Here's one. An' another. This's one, too, although it ain't all there, I'm sorry to say. But 'twill serve as better than nought."

Soon there was a small sheaf of papers with smeary charcoal writing still visible for Amity to hug to her heart. Upon seeing proof that her deep feelings were returned, Amity knew a pang of happiness unlike anything she had experienced since the moment on the veranda in early summer when she had lifted her eyes and seen Will approaching with the man of her dreams.

Amity stared at the papers bearing Jeb's script as if to memorize them. She was loathe to return the papers, but before she could offer them back, Will bid her keep them.

"You've told Jeb all that you know about me," Amity said, "so can you tell me all that you recall about him?"

"He's from an area north aways, far closer to the Mason-Dixon line," he began.

Will sketched in a story of a man not too different from himself, a young gentleman whose life had been on an even course until the War for Separation disrupted his plans.

"Naturally, him bein' a mute an' all, I don't know all about him that I'm sure you wish I did. But I can vouch that he's an upright soldier," Will assured. "Intelligent. Kind. Compassionate. Brave. Decent. Ethical. Amusing, though he can't crack jokes.

"He's the kind of fellow I've been glad to have beside me in the trenches, although I can tell that totin' a rifle doesn't appeal to him, while helpin' to heal mankind does. I guess that's because he's a Christian. Judgin' by my own familiarity with the Good Book nowadays, I'd say that Jeb Dennison lives his faith."

"You said at one time that you believed his papa was a physician."

"I was wrong," Will said. "It's Jeb himself, I gather, who's had some medical trainin'. He was schoolin' up North—Harvard, I think he said—when the war broke out. So obviously he came home to be with his own people, fightin' side by side, as many of our boys bein' schooled in the North did when the time came to have to plumb loyalties and make a choice."

"A doctor who can't talk?" Amity mused, then shrugged away the problems such a situation might present.

"May be that he ain't always been that way," Will said. "I never asked him. He could've lost his voice from an injury. Scars bear testimony that he's been through his share of difficulties at the hands of the blue-bellies."

"Yo' best be gettin' back, Miss Amity," Mammy approached them and ducked her head, giving Will a warm smile as she reluctantly intervened. She did not want to arouse the suspicions of Miss Ophelia and her sisters-in-law.

"Yes, Mammy," Amity agreed.

Carefully Amity refolded the precious casualty slips bearing her beloved's scrawl, and she turned toward the mansion.

"So what are you going to do?" Will asked. "If I may be so bold as to risk offendin' your sensibilities by askin'. It seems you're committed to one man while truly lovin' another. That's not an easy plight in which to find yourself. I know you Miss Amity. What're you proposin' to do about it?"

"Do?" Amity inquired.

"You'll marry one man while lovin' another?" Will's expression revealed that he couldn't believe that the belle he knew so well would ever accept such a situation.

"I don't want to," Amity admitted carefully, not yet prepared to take Will fully into her confidence. "But I don't know what I'm going to do to prevent it."

He nodded, misunderstanding her intent.

"Yes, an' you might never see Jeb again. An' from what they've been saying, Mister Philomen will provide for you. Maybe you'll even come to love him the way a wife should, given time and kind treatment and consideration."

Amity shook her head.

"No, Will. Never. And I'll never marry Philomen Emerson."

Will gave a rueful smile.

"Y'all seem plenty determined, Miss Amity," he said. "But I recall that Miss Ophy can get pretty single-mindedly het up, too, when she's settin' store to accomplish somethin'."

"I will not be marrying Philomen!" Amity said, her tone adamant. "I decided that months ago. Now's simply the time for me to see my options through to fulfillment."

"Options?" Will echoed.

The moment had come to risk complete honesty with her childhood friend and hope that the future would uphold her belief that he would never betray her.

"Mammy, Serena, and I are going to leave Magnolia Manor."

A flash of alarm crossed Will's features.

"Does Miss Ophelia know this?" he asked.

"Of course not. We're going to run away. And if you breathe so much as a syllable about it to anyone—I'll never forgive you, Will Conner, for as long as I shall live."

Will looked more amused than alarmed by Amity's bold plans.

"Your secret is safe with me, Miss Amity. You know that. If questioned, I will profess ignorance of your intentions."

"Thank you. Is there any way you can help me, Will? I'm thinking about going to Grandpapa's plantation. He would take care of us."

Will was a long time responding.

"I can't actually assist you in your escape, Miss Amity. While I feel loyalty to you, of course, my first obligation is to the C.S.A. I can't be away from my regiment to escort you, unfortunately, for I would if I could. But I can tell you what I know about troop movements. How best to travel. What to look for to keep yourself as safe as possible. I wish I could offer more."

"That's a start," Amity sighed in grateful acceptance.

"When are y'all leaving?"

"Soon. Very soon."

"Good. Then the information I can share will at least be current. It's ever-changing out there," he said, giving a gesture that swept in all directions.

Amity listened intently as Will told her what she and her household help could expect as they made their way from the Emerson property toward her grandfather's plantation.

"There are both Yankee and Rebel detachments in the area," Will warned. "At night, you may not be able to tell which you are nearing. So be careful when you travel. You may not see soldiers because you haven't trained yourself to be alert. They will know you're in the area long before they see you."

He cautioned her about making an undue amount of noise or using campfires.

"I'll remember," Amity promised, and nodded to encourage him to speak further.

"Sometimes the safest thing might be to forgo walking across the countryside. You might want to consider floating down a creek on a raft at night. It would be perilous and unpleasant, but it could be safer. If y'all lie still on a raft, you'd have a better chance at traversing the area undetected."

"We can manage that. Thanks for suggesting it."

"And iffen y'all do have to skirt close to regiments that are camped, check for Quaker guns. They're a dead giveaway it's a Rebel unit, not Yankees."

"Oh, Will, I know the difference between a pistol and a rifle, but that's about the extent of my knowledge. I'm afraid I wouldn't know one rifle from another."

"You don't have to, Miss Amity. You'll have no problem recognizing a Quaker cannon." A bitter smile came to Will's face.

"We Rebs are poorly armed, you know. So we have to do what we can to contribute an illusion of strength. When we dig in foxholes and rifle pits, we saw down trees with straight trunks, lop 'em off to appropriate lengths, and insert these logs along the rifle pit. From a distance it's hard to tell if it's a log or a cannon barrel. Yankees don't use Quaker guns, but we Rebs have no choice."

"Oh, Will," Amity murmured.

"And if you see a wheel of buzzards hoverin' in the sky, try to avoid the area. It probably marks a battlefield where some unfortunates' bodies lie molderin' in the sun. Y'all don't want to pass too close and have enemy forces discover you if they're lootin'. And y'all don't want to end up gettin' contaminated with a sickness, either."

By the time Will had finished giving Amity all the information that he felt she should know, her head was fairly swimming.

"You're determined to go?" he asked.

Amity gave a grim nod.

"I have to, Will. I can't stay here."

Will nodded understanding of her plight.

"That's what I thought. Well, good luck, Miss Amity, and Godspeed. If Mist' Witherspoon's plantation happens to be burned out, you're always welcome at the Conner estate. Mama and Papa would be delighted to see y'all and help out as they can.

"I'll rest easier knowin' your mind, and where you're goin'. That way, if Jeb and I happen t' link up again, I'll be able to share with him the sweetest knowledge he'd ever extract from me: where to find the woman he loves."

"Oh, Will, I'm so grateful I could hug you!" Amity cried.

Laughing contentedly he opened his arms to her.

"I should like nothing better, my brave and beautiful friend. Jebediah Dennison is a lucky man, possessin' the heart of a woman like you."

"Until we meet again," Amity breathed as she gave Will one last hug.

"Go in peace, Miss Amity. And God bless and protect you."

Will turned and strode toward the borrowed mule as Mammy and Amity lingered so that she could compose her emotions and hide her precious papers. Jebediah's hands had touched the pages that she now pressed close to her heart. His written words conveyed a faithful love that his mute lips could never express.

Chapter Nine

Had Amity had her way, she would have fled Magnolia Manor the next morning without giving any thought to preparation. But Mammy and Serena, who as slaves had had far less secure lives than Amity, raised questions about their journey that made their mistress aware of the danger they were walking into.

They would need food to sustain them, enough clothing to shield them from the elements, and sufficient time to get safely away before their absence was noticed.

If evening came before anyone realized that something was amiss, the women would have placed a full day's travel between themselves and Magnolia Manor. If their disappearance were discovered before noon, however, Mister Raynor or Cousin Philomen could hitch up a mule and locate them with embarrassing ease.

Once they had agreed on the most viable plan for their escape, they rehearsed the details several times until they were calmly familiar with their plan. When morning came, all three were certain that they could leave on a supposed task without raising anyone's suspicions.

The next morning, Mammy, Serena, and Amity met at a predesignated spot, giggling with relief that they had managed the first step of their plan and were about to set off on an adventurous journey of escape.

Their laughter was short-lived. Mammy and Serena were well aware of the fate they would face if they were separated from Miss Amity and caught by angry southern men who would wish to make an example of them. The two slaves dropped to their knees and prayed fervently.

Amity, after a moment's consideration, smoothed her skirt and sank to her knees beside her two servants. She felt humble and hesitant as she offered her own requests to the God that Mammy and Serena trusted so completely.

And so they began their journey. When it was safe, they traveled narrow country roads and winding trails. When they approached civilization, they shrank into the underbrush where briars, brambles, and prickly bushes snagged at their clothes and hair.

After Serena came within inches of stepping on a poisonous copperhead snake, the trio tended to step lively and squawk with alarm over the least movement near them in the woods.

By sundown they were exhausted, but they vowed to continue trudging on, thanking the Lord that there was a full moon to guide their steps. It made travel easier as they wound their way along the ribbons of roads cutting through the countryside toward Grandpapa Witherspoon's plantation.

Physical exhaustion finally forced the women to halt, even though their spirits desired to keep going. They huddled together for warmth, wondering if they had been missed yet and if Philomen and Mister Raynor had pressed the local militia members into service to come looking for them.

It was with relief that they set out again after several hours spent in fitful sleep. By nightfall of that next day they felt that success was possible. By the next morning, they believed success was in their future, although they admitted that they had been through a grim and grueling three days. Amity had only to glance at Mammy and Serena to know how grimy she, herself, must appear.

Although the journey had left the trio bone-weary, famished, thirsty, and suffering from an assortment of injuries from blisters to scratches, there was an air of adventurous frivolity. Any time their hearts were faint, they were revived when they realized the glorious truth. They were free!

Amity was freed from an unhappy future, and Mammy and Serena had escaped from the house that had never felt like home. Where Miss Amity went, they, too, were free to go unquestioned, for they were in a white woman's company.

There was a bond between the two servants and their mistress. Amity was theirs just as surely as they belonged to her, and recognized that they were the Lord's and that He was seeing them through their sojourn to a new and happier land.

"I can't believe we're almost there," Amity said.

"Well, we is—an' we ain't. We's close, sho' nuff, an' the worstest is behind us, but we won't make it to the big house by nightfall," Mammy clarified.

"Oh," Amity breathed her disappointment at not being able to retire to a comfortable bed after soaking in a bathtub brimming with hot water.

"We can't show up on Mist' Witherspoon's doorstep with yo' looking like po' white trash, an' Serena an me looking like no-account field hands instead of valuable household servants. We's goin' to make ourselves look respectable first," Mammy insisted.

"How? By bathing in a downpour?" Amity asked, as she cast a worried glance toward the slate gray clouds that looked swollen with autumn rains as they tumbled across the sky, their ominous movement accompanied by distant thunder.

"We're goin' to stop fo' the night at a lil' cabin not far from here. It's on Mist' Witherspoon's plantation, but quite a piece from the house. We can haul water from the creek and sponge off, change frocks, an' wash these filthy clothes."

"It will be heaven to don a clean, dry frock," Amity said. "If only we could have a hot meal, too."

"Not unless they's some way to make a fire in the hearth, honey, an' somethin' to cook in. Otherwise we'll jus' have to nibble down what I's been pickin' along the way an' eat it as the Good Lord saw fit to provide it for our needs."

"I wish we hadn't had to leave most of our clothes at Magnolia Manor," Amity murmured.

Mammy sighed, as did Serena. It was the younger servant who spoke.

"It seemed the only way we could travel fast, Miss Amity, an' the way to best convince Miss Ophy an' the others that mayhap we wasn't really going to visit Mist' Witherspoon for a spell."

Mammy gave a rowdy laugh.

"If they believes Miss Amity's note after the way we all left, they's gullible, though it be the hones' truth! With us a-travelin' so light an' not arrangin' for Mist' Raynor nor Mister Phil to fetch us over to Mist' Witherspoon's and leavin' strangelike as we did, I'll bet they's goin' to be lookin' in the wrong direction. They'll think Serena and me are runaway slaves.

" 'Stead of comin' to look for us at Mist' Witherspoon's plantation, bein' as we all left almost on the heels of Mister Will, they mayhap be a-thinkin' that Miss Amity done run off to be wit' Mist' Will, goin' after him like one o' them shameless camp follower wimmen!"

"Jus' so we have time to safely get to where we's goin'," Serena said. "Dat's all I'm askin'."

"Mammy, is it much farther?" Amity asked an hour later as the daylight waned and a smacking drop of icy rain landed on her cheek.

"It's right up ahead, Lambie. I believe's I can see the door from here! Be thankful it be a-standin' yet. I wasn't so sho'. It's been a long spell since this plantation was my home."

"Thank goodness!" Serena cried when she saw the rustic, dilapidated overseer's shack with its sagging roof and weather-beaten walls.

"Hurry!" Mammy gasped as she broke into a trot and urged Amity to pluck up her skirts and run, too. Lightning struck nearby, creating a thunderous boom, and Amity and Serena screamed. With frightened cries the women hurried toward the cabin.

They had scarcely stepped beneath the eave's sheltering overhang when the clouds opened and rain battered down.

"In just the nick of time," Amity said. "Thank God for shelter when we needed it."

She looked around her. Dust and cobwebs hung over most of the shack, but in the dim light it appeared that other areas had been swept smooth. The surface grime had been disturbed—and recently.

"Someone's been here," Amity said in a whisper.

"Wonder who?"

"I don't know," Amity said and shivered from the dampness of her clothes and the specter of Yankee forces nearby.

"Sho' 'nuff they be gone now," Mammy said, but with less conviction in her tone than Amity liked.

"Well, this is plumb snug after what we's been growin' accustomed to," Serena said in an obvious attempt to bolster their lagging spirits. "What's the big house like, Mammy? Has it got a large kitchen?"

"Indeedy it does," Mammy assured.

Mammy moved around the cabin, locating a dented enamel basin and a few rusting pots. She opened the sagging door enough to set the dishes under the eaves to collect rainwater so that the three of them could wash themselves. While they were waiting for the water to collect, Mammy spun tales about the splendors of Mister Witherspoon's mansion.

" 'Course dat was before the war," she reminded. "But I 'spects it's still a home to do its people proud. We'll get cleaned up tonight an' eat what roots an' berries I've collected in my bag an' what fruit we found unharvested and hangin' in trees at abandoned, burnt-out plantations. When comes the dawn we'll light out to go the rest of the way to Mist' Witherspoon's home."

"How long will it take?" Amity asked tiredly.

"An hour walkin' slow, honey. Who knows how quick if we're all to step high an' lively?"

With heavy rain moving in after the initial wave of thunder had passed through, the cabin grew so dark that they had to squint. Mammy struggled to her feet, dug through one of the bags she had carried, and produced a stumpy candle and matches.

"We's almost home," she said, "so we don't have to ration the candle so close." She struck a match, then deftly touched it to the wick. She held the match to the bottom of the candle, melting wax into the center of the table, then plopped the candle into the drippings and waited for it to cool and hold the taper upright.

"There! That be better."

"It's almost homey," Serena said.

"After three nights in the woods, this is like a castle," Amity conceded.

None of them raised the question of what they would do if Mister Witherspoon's plantation had been burned out, its inhabitants scattered to the four winds. In low voices they talked. Suddenly, they heard a creak overhead. The startled women stopped talking. Their eyes enlarged and they stared at one another, not daring to breathe.

"What was that?" Amity finally asked in a strangled whisper.

Serena and Mammy exchanged worried glances.

"It sounded big enough to be somebody," Amity whispered. "What if it's a Yankee?"

For a moment there was nothing but strained silence—and the faint groanings of pressure against boards in the attic.

Mammy hove to her feet and pulled Serena up with her.

"They's somethin' in that attic, sho' nuff, but I'm a-bettin' it's only a mama opossum an' her brood. Hopin' it ain't a skunk." She attempted a feeble laugh.

"I'm goin' to investigate," Mammy said. "De Lord didn't bring me this close to taste failure. Help me up on dis ladder, Serena." Mammy grabbed the rung, instinctively moved to slap dust and grit from her hands, then stared at them as she seemed to realize that the ladder steps had been scraped clean by something. . .or somebody.

Mammy climbed a step. The ladder groaned under her bulk. She lifted her other foot and stepped on another riser. Her head neared the attic opening.

"Serena, han' me dat candle," she ordered. "But keep the matches in yo' hand 'n case somethin' snuffs it out."

Serena eased the candle from the table up to Mammy. The older woman held it aloft and stared.

"Well, I'll be!" she gasped, amazement evident in her tone. "There's a gemp'mum up here!" Then she emitted a squawk that sent her dropping down the ladder and caused Serena and Amity to cling together in fear, desperate prayer on their trembling lips.

"Mammy, what's up there?" Amity cried.

Mammy's eyes were big as saucers.

"Dey's a gemp'mum in the attic," she said, "a-laying still as death. An' it's either dat mute man, Mist' Jebediah, or I be seein' his ghost!"

"Mammy, are you sure?"

"I never been so sure in all my born days!"

"Give me the candle," Amity said. Only the thought of seeing Jeb again gave her such courage, but as she lifted her head into the attic space, her bravery wilted.

"Oh, my," she breathed.

Mammy was right. It was Jebediah Dennison. But Mammy was wrong, too, thank God, for Jeb wasn't a dead man, though he soon would be if someone didn't do something right away.

"He's sick, Mammy. Very sick," Amity said. She wrinkled her nose as the odor of putrifying wounds wafted toward her. "We've got to do something, but I don't know how we'll get him down from the attic. It's very close quarters."

"You leave that to Serena an' me, Miss Amity. Yo' jus' clear us a space to make a pallet fo' him, an' we'll do the best we can."

The three worked with desperate haste. Amity chewed her lip as Mammy and Serena disappeared into the attic. The joists groaned beneath their weight. Amity was aware of their success only because of the thumpings and scrapings.

She wondered that even a mute didn't cry out in pain as they unceremoniously wrenched him from his resting place. In a moment Mammy came down the ladder, huffing for breath, and when Serena lost her balance and accidentally dumped Jeb into Mammy's arms, Amity saw why—Jebediah Dennison was unconscious.

"We's got to have some heat. This man's not only got an infected wound, but a fall cold a-comin' on."

Mammy ordered Serena to break up what was left of a rickety chair and build a fire in the grate.

"An' hope that the flue ain't plugged with a bird's nest."

When Serena had successfully started a fire, Mammy quickly gave her another order.

"Yo' fetch in one of them pans o' water, an' start tearing off lil' pieces of roots an' things so we can make a broth. We's got to get somethin' hot inside Mist' Jebediah to give him the will to fight, or he's not long for this world."

Amity hardly heard Mammy's orders, so intense were her prayers to God, a God she dared to trust to keep Jeb safe and well, even if theirs was not a love meant to be. Even if the fact that Jeb would live on might mean one day he would go to another woman and find love.

"Is there anything I can do, Mammy?" Amity asked, wringing her hands.

"Nothin' I ain't already doing. Jus' keep on prayin', Lambie, and know that Serena and I is, too."

Two hours later, Mammy finished spooning hot broth between Jeb's lips, stroking his throat to encourage him to swallow. She pronounced that he was better and that with luck, he would live until morning.

"We'll have to go to the big house an' fetch help to move him there," Mammy decided. "Mist' Witherspoon'll know what to do. Dawn be comin' early. So y'all had better rest up now."

"I'm too addled to think of sleep, Mammy," Amity said. "You lie down and Serena, too. I'll stay up and tend to Jeb."

"All right, Lambie. I am plumb tuckered. An' I know that Mister Jebediah couldn't be tended with any hands more lovin'."

Chapter Ten

Amity passed one of the longest nights of her life as she kept her vigil beside Jebediah, who groaned and writhed in his sickness. Several times during the night, she was terrified that he was going to breathe his last, and she prayed to God to preserve and protect the man she loved.

When the first rays of dawn crept over the horizon, Amity's eyes were gritty from lack of sleep, and her body felt leaden and dull from exhaustion. But Jeb seemed a bit stronger than he had the night before, and hope flamed anew.

Amity was loathe to leave Jebediah when Mammy and Serena sleepily awoke and quietly began discussing their immediate plans.

"I know yo' wants to stay with yo' loved one and nurse Mist' Jeb, Lambie, but dat ain't for de best. We's gots to think of all o' our needs. But don' you fret. Serena, she's took care of sick folkses. She knows more about healing than yo' do. She knows almost as much as I do."

"I know, Mammy."

Mammy looked at Jeb and then laid a kindly hand on his forehead.

"I'd like to stay wit' the boy an' tend to him myself, but yo' need me to guide yo' to the plantation, and dey'll need me to lead 'em back to help Mist' Jebediah when they fetch him to the big house."

"That's true," Amity said, bowing to Mammy's logic. "But we'll have to hurry. Maybe if you went by yourself, I could stay with Serena."

"The way things be, Lambie, neither Serena nor I dare be caught walking the lands alone. Someone might collect us as runaways. An' it be fittin' that yo' be there to greet your grandpappy when we arrive, 'stead of me arrivin' alone."

Amity reluctantly realized that Mammy's plans were the wisest course of action.

"Then let's hurry, Mammy," Amity said. "I'm ready to go. The sooner we get home the quicker we can get help for Jeb."

So eager was she to reach the plantation that Amity knew no exhaustion and only slowed occasionally when she realized how Mammy labored to breathe. The older, heavier woman was walking with quicker steps than usual so she wouldn't lag too far behind her young mistress.

"It's not far now," Amity said, pausing to look around her. "I recognize that grove of trees from one time when I went riding with Will when we were children. We'll be home soon."

"Dat's right, child," Mammy panted. "We's about to the fambly cemetery."

"Oh! I see it!" Amity said, feeling a burst of relieved enthusiasm when she suddenly realized that they were closer to the big house than she had realized. On Witherspoon land, she hoped that she could rush ahead a bit and that her trusted servant would be safe if she was left behind in Amity's eagerness to be home with her beloved grandfather.

Amity strained to catch sight of the big house between the cover of leaves that still remained in the towering trees. So intent was she on assuring herself that the house still stood that she didn't bother glancing into the small burial plot enclosed behind a rusting wrought-iron fence.

Mammy did, and she quailed when she saw the mound of fresh dirt rising above the tangled, dead grass. Mammy, who had made many sad trips to the cemetery to observe the committal of the folks she had loved, tended, and prayed for, slowed her steps. As she passed the gravestones, memories flooded over her along with the names and the dates inscribed on the headstones.

"Won't Grandpapa be surprised to see us?" Amity called. "Oh, do hurry, Mammy! I know you're tired, but if you could keep up with me, we would be there sooner. Maybe they will have a cart you can ride in for the return trip to Jeb. I can't wait to see Grandpapa. I know he's going to be thrilled to see us."

"I sho' nuff hope so, honey," Mammy said in a soft, unsure tone. "I sho' hope so."

Amity darted ahead before she could see the worried cast enter Mammy's dark eyes, and she didn't notice that the older woman's frown had intensified to reflect an added burden of concern.

Amity quickened her pace as she made her way through the meadow, climbed over a fence that kept her from the lane leading to the Witherspoon lawn, then made her way across the expanse of house yard before she rushed up the flagstone walk, the heels of her shoes clattering. The house—the entire plantation—seemed unnaturally silent.

Mammy caught up with her mistress and banged the ornate knocker down hard on the solid front door a few times. There was no answer, so she repeated the action. She had just lifted her hand to repeat the gesture when the door creakily swung open.

Mammy tiredly dropped her arm to her side as a hollow-eyed, frightened servant peered out.

"Who yo' be?" she asked when she saw Mammy. "An' what yo' be wantin'?"

"Denizia?" Mammy asked. "Is that you?"

The woman frowned, her expression hesitant.

"Yes, dat be me, but what yo' wantin' here?" Fear haunted the haggard woman's eyes.

"Nizy, it's Mammy, home with Mist' Morgan's lil' girl, Miss Amity. We's come to see Mist' Buford Witherspoon iffen he still be here, an' stay with y'all for a spell."

The woman stood as a statue.

"Don't yo' recognize me, Nizy? Yo' titched in the head, girl? Say sumpin'!"

The words jolted Denizia out of her daze. She shook herself, seeming to cast off the strange mood that had overtaken her, and stepped forward. Her tone warmed with welcome.

"Mammy! Of course I recognize you now. I jus' wasn't expecting to see you." She rubbed her eyes.

"Still cain't believe I'm seein' yo' again. In recent times we's known such unhappiness that I couldn't believe the joy. Was afeared yo' was an apparition, I was, and that if I'd be seein' yo' ghost, Lord pr'tect and preserve me from who else's would be comin' to call."

Mammy didn't have time for such considerations. Especially not in broad daylight. She decided to get right down to business.

"The Yankees been here?" Mammy asked. "We was stayin' over at the Emerson plantation, and they was awful in that area, robbin', pillagin', burnin' good and decent folkses out of they very houses."

Denizia nodded. Her sad expression seemed to indicate that she could match every horror story Mammy could relate.

"They passed nearby. We was luckier 'an others. Ol' Mist' Buford, he was all het up to stand de Yankees off all by hisself." A wistful smile washed over Denizia's sad features, and her eyes momentarily sparkled at the memory.

"He got plumb apoplectic an' Big Tom had to calm him down an' put him to bed, same as he had to do dis summer when Mist' Buford took a notion Gen'l Hood could use him up towards where they be fighting to drive de Yankees back from Atlanta. De ol' gemp'mum took off that day, after orderin' Big Tom t' take care of the place in his absence." Denizia gave a hearty chuckle.

"But a mighty tuckered out Mist' Buford come home a couple of hours later, without the strength to take himself to his bed. Big Tom hadda carry him to his quarters, tend to him like a chile, an' poor ol' Mist' Buford didn't leave his bed fo' three days afterward."

Mammy made a tsk-tsk noise with her teeth and tongue.

"That don' surprise me. That do sound like Mist' Buford, sho' nuff. He was quite a grand ol' gemp'mum."

"Where is he now? Is Grandpapa still ailing?" Amity asked, speaking up for the first time.

Denizia looked at Amity with sad eyes, seeing her owner's kinfolk for the first time.

"Oh no, honey," she explained softly, her voice heavy and velvety with sympathy. "Your grandpappy's not ailin' now, chile, he's dead. He won' never ail no more. An' he was such a dear ol' man, and so good to us darkies what was his, we's hopin' to see him again on dat great gettin' up mornin'!" Denizia patted Amity's arm.

"Don' yo' fret over your grandpapa, Miss Amity. He was a good man, salt-of-the-earth. His passin' be peaceful and he had an expression like he knew he was goin' home to be wit' his believin' loved ones who'd gone on home in faith before Mist' Buford was called there hisself."

For Amity, there was no comfort found in assurances of her grandfather's relationship with God. She felt only the knifing agony of loss and the sensation of being alone in the world.

"Mammy!" Amity cried out and began to sob. "Oh, Mammy! What are we going to do now?"

Mammy was thoughtful a moment, then seemed to center on the basic practicalities of living, for it was certain that nothing could be done for the dead.

She took a deep breath and licked her lips as she bought time in which to think through their basic needs and pray for the answers that would allow them to most directly fill them. She folded Amity into her arms, hugging the girl close as she wept her grief, confusion, and disappointment in all that she confronted in life.

"Well, first off, we's goin' to fetch Mister Jeb an' Serena to the big house," she decided, "an' then see what we can do to help Denizia and Big Tom around dis here plantation."

She paused and gave the premises and surrounding acreage a critical stare. It was more tumbledown than she had expected, and her hopes had not been high.

"Who all yo' got here workin' de fields, Nizy?" She asked, facing Mister Witherspoon's trusted servant who had stood by him when others had fled or sought to betray him.

The rawboned slave who had tended to Buford Witherspoon stared at her hands.

"Jus' my Big Tom an' me, Mammy. De rest o' 'em done runned off wit' the Yankees. An' me an' Big Tom, we ain't known what to do 'thout someone to tell us.

"We been a-scared, too, in fear dat someone, suspectin' ol' Mist' Buford passed on, would come and take us, an' we wouldn't have no pr'tection. We's aware dat we could go free. But dis is our home. We's allus been free here. Just now we's more free than we was free then."

Mammy nodded perfect understanding, for that was how she felt toward Mister Morgan and Miss Amity, although she felt no such loyalty toward Miss Ophelia.

"This yo' home as long as yo' wants to stay and tend it and be took care o', I'm sure, because my Miss Amity, she in charge now, an' she's a kind-hearted mistress," Mammy clarified. "She be yo' new young miss, too. An' she take care of yo' like she takes care o' us so good while we's a-doin' our level best a-takin' care o' her."

"Praise the Lord! We's glad to see y'all," Denizia said, her countenance shining with relief.

The sentiment was echoed by Big Tom when he arrived from the fields. He had heard the voices of strangers and had hesitantly sidled up to the house, keeping to the shadows. He had wanted to know if his wife was in danger before he made his presence known.

When he recognized Mammy, he let out a whoop, sprinted across the front lawn, and scooped her into his massive arms, swinging her around as he cried with glee.

"Yo' remember lil' Miss Amity?" Mammy asked him when he replaced her on the front veranda step.

He nodded enthusiastically.

"I sho' do. She was the purtiest baby on the plantation when her dear mama and Mist' Morgan and his lil' girl from his first marriage come to call."

"And she's the loveliest belle to ever grace this plantation right now, even purtier than her mama."

"Sho' sad that y'all didn't arrive in time for Mist' Buford to see his daughter's lil' girl one last time," Tom said, his voice solemn. "It'd have cheered his ailin' heart, sho' nuff."

"Guess that the Good Lord just didn't mean for it to be," Mammy said.

"Come in and rest," Denizia encouraged, bidding them to enter the mansion with a welcoming gesture as she turned to lead the way.

"We cain't rest but a moment, Nizy. We's got us a heap o' work to do afore we can. Dey's a feller down in that little cabin in the woods. We left Serena, one o' Miss Amity's loyal servants, with him to tend his needs. He been wounded. Gots an infection, I expects. An' a fall cold comin' on, too."

"We'll fotch him to de big house," Denizia said, nodding. "I'll ready another room—"

"We's gon' give him the best care. He's a Rebel, sho' nuff, though he cain't talk nary a word. But we wants to heal him so some day he can go home and hug de ol' mammy who raised him up as a boy and had a hand in turnin' him into a gemp'mum with qualities that Miss Amity was but helpless to love—even wit' him bein' a mute an' all."

"He be Miss Amity's beau?" Denizia said.

Mammy nodded.

"Sho' nuff is. And we ain't gonna let either Miss Amity or Mist' Jeb down. Lord willin', we's gonna save his life so dey can be together. Mayhap with us here.

"This be Miss Amity's plantation now. Left to her by her mama. Miss Ophelia, she warn't no relation to Mist' Buford. She ain't gots no claim to dis here land—nor to us. Mist' Jeb an' Miss Amity could be happy here iffen they'd choose to be."

"I'll be prayin' that," Denizia said. "We don' wants to have to open up another grave in de fambly cemetery. It was a sad task for ol' Big Tom an' me, committin' de master we loves body into de ground as ol' Mist' Buford's Master welcomed him home to the big mansion He has prepared in heaven. Ol' Mist' Buford, he'd had a long, full life. We don' wants to fail Miss Amity so dat her beau goes home and leaves her a lifetime o' loneliness 'til they can meets again."

"Denizia," Amity quietly said. "Please don't talk like that. You're upsetting me. Scaring me."

Mammy put an arm around Amity.

"It's the truth, Lambie, and the truth ain't always pretty to hear. But it be like it was when King David lost his little chile dat he loved so much. He was grievin' and carryin' on. Den it struck him that it be dat his lil' boy, he wasn't never gonna come back.

"But King David, he realized dat he could go to dat little boy in the great fo'ever an' fo'ever be wit' the Lord. So he chose to amend his life, so that he'd be fittin' to meet the Lord and his loved ones who'd gone on ahead. We's got them kinds o' choices, too."

"I know. I've read enough Scripture to be aware of that. But it's hard. Seeing Jeb has only made me more aware of how much I love him."

"As pow'rful as yo' love, Miss Amity, yo' keeps in mind dat de Lord loves Mist' Jebediah more. If de Lord calls him home, it's onliest 'cause de Lord loves him most—and while de Lord can share such a fine man as Mist' Jeb wit' all o' us, he belongs to de Lord what created him."

"Dat's right," Denizia assured. "But don' yo' think we're goin' to be slackers in carin' for yo' beau, Miss Amity. Iffen it's meant to be, de Lord will give us healin' wisdom like we ain't never known afore, so's we can nurse yo' loved one back to full health."

"Nizy's right, Miss Amity. We sho' know what's we want. But the Lord's will be done."

Amity swallowed tears at the back of her throat and gave a quick hug to the two women beside her. They were strong in body but had even more strength of spirit.

"Amen," Amity whispered her acceptance.

Chapter Eleven

It seemed to take an eternity for Denizia to put a quick breakfast on the table so that the plantation's new arrivals could replenish their strength. Mammy had suggested that Miss Amity rest, but Amity negated that idea, using Mammy's own logic.

"From what Will Conner said, there are roving bands throughout the area. They won't magically detour through these parts because they're on Witherspoon acreage. And if you, Denizia, and Big Tom are stopped, you might be taken into custody by someone, and then there'd be no help given to Jeb. He and Serena would be alone in the woods with no one coming to offer assistance. But if I went along, you'd be under the authority of a white woman."

"Dat's true. Den yo' be welcome to come along—needed to come along." Mammy gave a slow smile. "An' even if what yo' said warn't true, I knows yo' wants to see yo' beau again, to reassure yo'self that he still be among the livin'."

At the idea that Jeb should die before she could touch his hand one last time, Amity's heart galloped with fear. She calmed down only as she remembered what her servants had assured her: If it were meant to be, Jeb would live. If not, then his death somehow served the Lord's will, and when she passed through her grief, she would come to recognize and accept her loss.

Even so, Amity wanted to do what she could to shape the future.

"Really, we must hurry," she encouraged. "The sky's been overcast. We don't want to be bearing a deathly ill man home in a chilly autumn drizzle."

"Dat we don't," Mammy agreed.

"I'll be wrappin' up de leftovers in a cloth so's we can take sustenance to yo' gal Serena and Miss Amity's beau," Denizia offered.

Big Tom scraped his chair away from the table.

"We ain't gots no mules nor critters anymore," he apologized. "I wish we had a fine and fancy carriage and beast wit' which to go fotch yo' Mist' Jeb. I's been thinking. It be a pow'rful long ways to carry him laid out on a board, even iffen I quicklike construct some handles.

"I's been thinkin'—out in de shed dey's a pony cart that Misses Amity an' Ophelia used when they was lil' girls. Iffen he be a tall man, he gon' be kinda scrunched up, but we can make de trip quicker." He paused and puffed out his chest, flexing his arms.

"I 'spects I can pull about as well as a contrary ol' pony ever did! De cart's sturdy an' light."

Denizia laid a hand over her husband's strong grip that rested on the table.

"I'll help," she offered.

"Me too."

"With all of us working and the Lord giving us strength and knowledge, we'll do just fine," Amity assured. "Thank you so much. Y'all are a true comfort to me." Amity could see in their eyes that she was also a comfort to them.

"Of course," Denizia said. "Yo' our new young miss—an' we loves and wants to take care o' yo' an' your'n."

Hauling the pony cart to the woods was a comparatively easy matter. Big Tom hauled it with the zest of a young man half his age. But by the time they loaded the unconscious Jeb into the cart and tucked in the few possessions that Amity and her servants had carried, the conveyance's wheels dug into the ground.

Sweat poured off Big Tom as he breathlessly moved ahead. His eyes strained and his teeth ground as he struggled to haul the pony cart up rises that they had hardly noticed in their haste to reach the cabin.

Even with Mammy and Denizia's help, it was difficult going, and soon Serena and Amity threw their weight against the back of the cart. With a combined effort, the trip to the big house was accomplished. Everyone felt weak and lightheaded when they halted near the door.

"Beggin' yo' pardon, Miss Amity," Big Tom said and dropped to the ground between the traces of the pony cart. "I cain't walk another step. Iffen I's got yo' permission, I needs to rest a spell afore I can manage to pick up Mist' Jeb an' lug him to the sickroom."

Amity laid a gentle, grateful hand on the big slave's shoulder.

"You take all the rest you require, Big Tom. Thank you so much. We couldn't have done it without you."

He gave her a pleased smile.

"I'll only be a moment," he promised.

"There's no real hurry," Amity said. "Mister Jeb isn't going anywhere."

Mammy clucked and fluttered around Jeb, hoping to begin her sickroom duties even as they were clustered in the front yard. A blue jay swooped and darted, disgruntled at the activity beneath the tree where she had a nest.

A few minutes later Big Tom sprang up, seeming to feel rejuvenated. With Denizia's help, he gently boosted the inert man into his arms. Mammy rushed ahead to open the door, and the Witherspoon servants made their way with their charge, depositing him on the waiting bed in the sickroom off the kitchen.

"Big Tom, yo' shuck him out o' his clothes." Mammy began to snap orders, knowing that as Miss Amity's mammy she had the authority.

"Denizia, iffen yo' don' mind, yo' het up some water. The young gemp'-mum needs a bed bath." Mammy sniffed and her nostrils crinkled. "I do declare, white folkses or not, he be smellin' lack a pole cat! An' dese wounds do need cleaned."

"Right away, Mammy," Denizia said, and seemed relieved to have someone else in charge.

"Serena? Girl, yo' stay here an' give me a hand. I ain't as young as I used to be. I need yo' to help me move him. Even though he's among the livin' yet, he be like a dead weight."

Serena set about her work, having labored with sick charges before in the Atlanta house.

"Now yo', Miss Amity! Yo' hie on out o' here. Tain't fittin' for yo' to be here!"

"Mammy!" Amity protested, though she knew her mentor was right.

Mammy's stern manner relented.

"Go on, Lambie," she encouraged in a gentler tone. "Yo' can come back an' set up a vigil at Mist' Jeb's bedside jus' as soon as we tend to our duties an' make him fittin' to be seen by an innocent an' unworldly belle.

"Now go, Miss Amity. The sooner yo' leave, den it be dat much sooner yo' can come right back an' hol' his hand an' smooth his brow to yo' heart's content."

Amity left with reluctant steps. She paused at the doorway.

"You're all so busy, and being so needed. I wish that there was something I could do."

"They is!" Mammy said. "Yo' can pray fo' Mist' Jeb."

"An' iffen yo' wanting comfort fo' yo'self and the Lord's strength, then yo' can get ol' Mist' Buford's Good Book," Denizia suggested, explaining to Amity where it could be found.

"Mayhap it be a comfort to yo' in yo' loss o' yo' dear grandpappy if yo' young hands be touchin' the pages of the book he treasured fo' all o' his days."

Although Amity was the figurehead in power at the Witherspoon planta-tion, she did as she was told. Awe filled her as she realized that her grand-father had consulted the Bible so often that its cover was worn and the pages were velvety from use. The book fell open to the passages it seemed the Lord intended her to read so that she would find comfort, assurance, and accep-tance.

As Amity read, it became easier for her to give up her own will and instead seek God's direction. Burdens slipped away and cares were relieved as Amity placed herself and Jeb in the loving God's eternal care. She knew that if she had to face Jeb's death, the Lord would sustain her and help her live on in faith, believing that one day she would know unending joy with the man she loved in a heavenly home.

During the next three weeks, Amity was afraid a dozen times that Jeb was hours from death. But due to the strength God gave the three servants and Amity, death was defeated each time. The four worked as a united group of believers, willingly becoming servants to each other in their effort to save Jeb's life. Amity no longer saw herself as above performing chores that other southern women would have consigned to exhausted slaves.

Amity made several trips to her grandfather's new grave, and many times she prayed that Big Tom wouldn't be needed to dig a similar hole for Jeb Dennison's earthly remains.

"Maybe there's nothin' more we can do, Miss Amity," Mammy said. "I've used all of the herbs an' roots that I'm aware can heal folks. Mist' Jeb don't seem to be getting any worse, but he ain't gettin' any better, either, and if he lingers like this, he's goin' to suffer a decline, an' be gone before our eyes. We's got to do sumpin', and will, unless it ain't what de Good Lord plans for Mist' Jeb."

"No! Oh, don't even say that. I can't bear it. I've come to care more for Jeb with each passing day. He won't die—I won't allow it!"

"Then yo's goin' to hafta do something, Miss Amity. Or increase yo' prayers that the Lord will hear your pleas."

"We've got to do something, but what?"

Mammy shrugged.

"Send for a doctor," she suggested. "There was an elderly gemp'mum, a special friend of Mist' Buford's, an' he come here to nurse Mist' Buford's servants when dey took sick an' I know if he's still alive, he'd come to heal this gemp'mum."

"Send Big Tom to fetch him," Amity said, "and have him tell the doctor that we'll pay him soon; I'll get the money somehow."

"Mayhap sooner than you think," Mammy said. "When I was here in my younger days, Miss Rosalyn, yo' grandmama, used to have a jar of silver dollars buried away for a rainy day. It pro'bly ain't still there, but den, so few of us knew o' its whereabouts that could be dat it's a miracle and it still is.

"Either way, it's worth a look. We might find disappointment at the end of a spade—then again we might find the assistance that de Lord knew we'd one day have to discover."

"Send Big Tom for the doctor, and find us a spade, Mammy." Amity sighed. "Grandpapa no doubt dug it up long ago and donated it to the cause. I don't feel that the cause is right myself, but I know a lot of good Christian Southerners have philosophies that somehow allow them to reconcile slavery with the Good Book. That isn't my concern. Seeing to Jeb's health is. I pray that money hasn't been spent."

"Mayhap it ain't, and maybe Mist' Buford didn't donate it to the Confederacy, especially iffen he didn't know Miss Rosalyn had it set back for diff'cult times. He was generous 'nuff wit' her that she could've set back her lil' nest egg without troublin' him to mind to it, as he did the rest of the plantation. They wasn't but a few of us, Miss Rosalyn's most trusted servants, who knew about that jar of money. Might be it's still there."

"I hope so, for I'm so poor that I couldn't spare the pennies to weight a dead man's eyes." Amity drew a deep breath, then pulled away when she realized what she'd said. "Go talk to Big Tom, Mammy. And ask him to please hurry."

When Big Tom returned after going in search of a physician, the towering servant was so winded and weak that he couldn't find the strength to eat. His mission had taken several hours, and he had returned with a young, modern physician who had taken over the retired doctor's practice. He asked questions of the servants and Amity with a lazy drawl that belied his sharp eyes that missed nothing.

"I don' like the looks of him," Mammy said when the doctor left, staring down the lane after him.

"I don't care if he looks like a gargoyle if he can heal Jeb."

"That ain't what I mean," Mammy said. "He's presentable enough, but there's somethin' about him that I jus' don't trust. I cain't quite put my finger on what it is."

Amity saw nothing out of the ordinary when Dr. Brink stepped from Jeb's sickroom upon his return the next day, pronounced the continued care that they had given him excellent, and offered a professional opinion that with medication Jeb would completely recover. Dr. Brink lined up an array of bottles and tendered instructions to Mammy and Amity on how to correctly administer the potions.

"We thank you, sir," Amity said. "And what do we owe you?"

The doctor looked at her dirty hands, and seemed to consider that Amity had been pillaging the pitiful vegetable garden for something to prepare for their evening meal. He appeared to be taking in her almost threadbare frock when he named a low figure.

Inwardly, Amity sighed with relief. They would not have to part with any of the large coins left in Grandmama Rosalyn's discolored fruit jar that had been buried for so many years beneath the grape arbor. Such an expenditure would arouse suspicions among their neighbors about how they could have acquired such financial reserves.

"Mammy, run fetch a coin from my reticule," Amity said. "Thank you for coming, doctor, and good day."

Amity felt a prickle of alarm when she caught Dr. Brink's eyes resting on her in a manner much like Philomen's. As a popular belle, Amity had had enough experience to know that the doctor's interest in her was not simply professional.

Dr. Brink licked his lower lip.

"I'll stop back to see the patient in another day or two, Miss Amity. And," he added, "there'll be no charge for my consultation. I'll consider myself paid, and paid well, if perhaps your house girl could have a treat laid out for us and we could share a spot of tea and a bit of conversation."

"I'm sure you have overhead expenses," Amity said, using the word she had heard her papa use when transacting business. "I would like to pay my just debts, and I am able."

"Very well."

Although she knew that she should graciously invite the doctor to tea, as well, Amity simply couldn't make herself bow to social conventions. There was something about Dr. Brink that she did not like—but to bring Jeb back to health she would face anyone.

After Dr. Brink left, Amity scrupulously followed his instructions. Hours later, Mammy insisted that Amity leave the sickroom and allow her trusted servant to handle the sickroom duties.

"Yo' have to let me minister to Mist' Jeb, honey, before yo' gets sick, too, an' I've gots to take care of you. I don't know how much more these ol' bones can take."

"Very well, Mammy," she agreed.

Even though Big Tom and Mammy freed Amity from many sickroom tasks, she saw a lot of Jeb. As far as she was concerned, she saw too much of Dr. Brink, as well. He came calling more regularly than Amity believed was necessary once Jeb had begun to regain his strength. But there was little she could say to discourage the doctor, for he did not charge for his visits and Amity could hardly be so rude as to refuse his courtesies.

"Jeb's sleeping," Amity said a week later as she exited the sickroom and conferred with Mammy.

Mammy frowned.

"Miss Amity, has yo' noticed a difference in Mist' Jeb?"

"He's getting better. Stronger. His appetite has improved."

"No, Lambie, I mean somethin' *different*. Have you heard him try to talk?"

"Mammy, you know he's a mute!" Amity reminded, giving her servant an unbelieving look.

Mammy was stolid. Her lips folded in a grimace of determination.

"I'm tellin' you, Miss Amity, Mist' Jeb's able to talk. I's heard him!"

"Moans, of course," Amity was quick to agree. "He's been in so much pain. I'm sure even mutes groan in anguish."

"Well, I've heard somethin'," Mammy said, "An' I think that the doctor man, he thinkin' they's somethin' odd, too." Mammy licked her lip, then stared at the floor between her feet.

"An' I don't trust that doctor man, jus' like I tol' you, Miss Amity. The other day when he was checkin' in on Mist' Jeb, he shooed me out of the room an' gave Mist' Jeb some kind o' potion. It made him talk, but he talked real funnylike. He sho' don' sound like all of us when he speak."

"Oh, Mammy," a tired Amity sighed.

"Mist Jeb, he don' remember none of that miracle medicine," Mammy persisted. "An' I's sho' he don' recall it givin' him the capacity to speak, him bein' a mute an' all. But the po' man, he sho' nuff was groggy de next day from dat strange medicine Dr. Brink be givin' him, I been thinkin'."

"So that's what happened to him," Amity mused. "Well, you know how Dr. Brink prides himself on practicing the very latest medicine. I don't intend to give Dr. Brink another moment's consideration. I think with luck we'll have seen our last of him anyway, because he said that Jeb will be well enough to start getting up and around by the end of the week."

"If it ain't already too late by then," a glowering Mammy muttered as Amity departed for her quarters. Mammy went into the sickroom to keep a solitary, worried vigil.

"Now I'm thinking we's got even more tragedies to be a-prayin' don' befall none o' us."

Chapter Twelve

Jeb was better by the end of the week, and the week following Amity could see his strength returning almost by the hour. Mammy, deciding that the young soldier could use the mental stimulation and companionship, prepared a daybed for him in a corner of the kitchen near the potbellied stove so that as he felt up to it he could listen to those around him and remain comfortable and warm.

When he was awake, Jeb's expressive eyes set Amity's heart aflutter, and she never tired of asking questions that he could answer by either nodding or shaking his head. But there was more—so much more—that she wanted to know about Jeb.

One afternoon when she had a few moments, Amity explored the attic where she and Ophy had played as children. There she located an old slate and a minuscule piece of chalk.

Jeb's eyes lit up when she gave the slate to him, but he soon became frustrated. There was so much he had to say and so little space in which to write it, and the chalk held between his tightly pinched fingers was quickly disappearing.

Amity developed a system of asking Jeb a question and then going about her chores while he laboriously wrote his answers on the small slate nestled on his lap. She vowed that she would pillage the attic until she found old papers which they could press into service along with homemade ink and a quill salvaged from the henhouse. A few bantam hens that had been too wild for the Yankees to capture when Sherman and his troops had fanned through the area still made their home there.

Sometimes Amity grew concerned about Jeb when he struggled to phrase what should be detailed explanations as concisely as possible in the crowded space allowed by the slate. She sensed that his frustration was building, and she worried that, as weakened as his state had become from weeks of illness, he was setting back his physical recovery by becoming so mentally overwrought.

"Don't bother with writing out an answer right now," she said one evening and eased the slate from his hands. "You can write the answers when you've regained more strength. That's what matters the most."

You're what matters now! his eyes seemed to say, even as his hands fell obediently limp over the slate. He carefully set it aside, then his hand encircled

Amity's wrist. He drew her down onto the edge of the settee next to him and stroked her cheek with his forefinger.

Amity shivered beneath his gentle touch, and he noticed her reaction. He seemed to draw courage and he drew her face down toward his. Her hair fell forward, brushing across his face as she laid her head on his shoulder while he patted her smooth, soft arm.

Amity sighed, content at last to be in Jeb's arms. His fingers sifted through her wavy hair and explored the flare of her eyebrows, the line of her cheek, the curve of her mouth, the indentation of a dimple, and a beauty mark off to the side of her chin.

Their lips were mere inches apart, and their eyes were locked. Jeb's lips worked, as if he so desperately wanted to say something, but couldn't.

Amity was unsure if she lifted her lips to Jeb's, or if he drew her face up so that their mouths could meet, but an instant later their lips were pressed together in snug perfection.

Amity's pulse thundered, then warm, wonderful, weakening sensations overwhelmed her until she felt too satiated to move. She wanted only for the moment to last for eternity. Never had she been happier or more at peace in her life.

Jeb was short of breath when Amity freed herself from his arms. He gave her a beseeching look.

"You're not a well man, my darling Jeb," she reminded him. "I won't be the cause behind your having a relapse and suffering a terrible decline. I've been too afraid of your dying these past weeks to bear the idea of losing you now. You must have your rest; you're not a well man yet."

Jeb nodded.

"I'll stop in to see you tonight," Amity said, "before I retire for the evening. I'll bring Grandpapa Witherspoon's Bible and read to you from the Good Book, as I did last night when Mammy, Serena, Denizia, and Big Tom joined us."

Again Jebediah nodded. From his pleased smile, Amity knew how much the Bible meant to him, and how overjoyed he was that she shared his love and respect for it.

Jeb, who had been awake quite a while, got comfortable on the daybed by the stove that Amity had just fired up. Amity noticed his eyes grow heavy. She'd scarcely left the room to go about her chores than he was fast asleep. She tiptoed back, kissed her fingertip, and pressed it against his mute lips.

"Until tonight," she promised.

After a quiet meal, as substantial as their plain fare allowed, the servants brought order to the kitchen and Amity attended to some needlework. When they had all finished their labors, they clustered around the potbellied stove, and Amity sat down on the settee beside Jeb and opened up Grandpapa Witherspoon's Bible.

In a melodious voice she began to read from the Psalms, squinting by the flickering candlelight to make out the words that at times were shadowy upon the printed page.

Occasionally one of the slaves would murmur, "Amen!" or "Praise His sweet name!" or "Halleluia!" when they heard a favorite passage.

Finally Amity's voice grew a bit husky from reading. Big Tom was openly yawning, and Denizia and Serena were swallowing their yawns. As for Mammy, her heavily jowled face had dropped forward to her ample chest, and she was softly snoring, lulled by the poetic phrases of the Old Testament.

Gently Amity closed the book.

"That's all for tonight," she said, yawning herself.

"I be goin' to bed then, Miss Amity, iffen there ain't nothing mo' yo' needin' me to be doin'."

"Good night, Denizia. Sleep well."

Big Tom stood up, stretching and yawning.

"I's plumb tuckered out. I be retirin' fo' de night, too, so's I can git up an' face all de work 'round here when comes de dawn."

"Sleep well, Big Tom. We can hope for a sunny and warm day tomorrow."

"Indeedy we can!" he said, and ambled off, a cheerful smile on his face.

Mammy and Serena said their good nights as well.

"Is there anything you would like before I retire for the evening?" Amity inquired of Jeb.

He looked at her, his eyes brimming, and she felt a ripple of pleasure go through her as his adoring eyes expressed that there was one thing he wanted above all others—her!

With trembling hands she gave him the slate and a piece of rock that Big Tom had found down by the creek bed, which worked quite well in lieu of chalk.

A moment later Amity read the words on the slate, as Jeb suggested that she fix them a spot of tea before she departed for the evening.

"That sounds good," she admitted. She crossed to the water bucket, filled the pot, and set it on the potbellied stove. Then Amity replenished the fire with a few chunks of firewood that Big Tom had ricked in the corner wood box and slapped the dust and grit from her hands.

Jeb wordlessly patted the settee beside him. Feeling tense and nervous now that they were alone, Amity seated herself stiffly beside Jeb. Daring to be bold, he draped his arm around the back of the sofa.

As Amity relaxed, Jeb stroked her soft cheek with his forefinger. The movement lulled Amity, and before she realized it, her head was pillowed on his rugged shoulder. She felt total contentment.

Jeb shifted, reaching for the Bible that Amity had set aside. He moved it onto his lap, his fingers fanning through the pages. His fingers slowed, then carefully lifted individual pages.

He positioned the book solidly on his lap when it opened to The Song of Songs. With a gentle touch, he roused Amity. Her tired eyes flickered open.

Jeb reached for his slate. He wrote, "Please read this for me." Then he took the chalk-stone, scratched out *me* and wrote *us* in its place.

"The Song of Songs?" Amity inquired.

Jeb nodded.

"Very well," she agreed.

Amity had not yet read The Song of Songs, for she had concentrated on reading from the New Testament, Proverbs, and Psalms.

Serena had told her that there were great love stories in the Bible, and Amity had read the story of Ruth. The Song of Songs was an undiscovered treasure, and as she read the precious words, she felt a sense of correctness that she should discover that book while snuggled in the arms of the man she loved.

As she read the words and occasionally looked up to find Jeb's eyes on her, a lump formed in Amity's throat. She realized Jeb had requested that she read from that book because the various songs of Solomon expressed so beautifully the feelings that Jeb had for her. His tongue could not tell her how he felt, and they hadn't the paper, quills, and ink sufficient for him to write to her.

Amity's voice grew tired, although the book was short, but she continued reading until she had finished the Song of Songs. For a moment the Bible rested open in her lap. Then Jeb shifted, removed his arm from around her, and carefully set the Bible on a nearby shelf. He reached for her again.

His cheek was close to hers, and she had only to move her head a fraction of an inch for their lips to meet, at first hesitantly, then with a precious hunger. Jeb rained kisses on her face.

"Oh, Amity. I've waited so long," he whispered. "I've dreamed of you every night. It's a miracle to have you in my arms. I love you, Amity—I love you! And it's like sweet pain in my chest to realize that you love me, too."

"Oh Jeb, it may be shameless of me to admit it, but I do. I do!"

So accustomed had Amity become to the dialogue in dreadful penny romance novels and so caught up was she in the romance of the moment that she didn't realize at first that Jeb had spoken.

But Amity knew full well that Jeb *had* spoken, and in escalating horror she realized that it could not be a dream. In her dreams her Rebel had spoken in a soft, melodious drawl, the tones rippling and rich, sweet as pralines. Never had he uttered adoring words in the flat, clipped tongue of a Yankee!

"I adore you, Amity," Jeb whispered. "I've wanted you since that first night on the veranda in Atlanta when I was with Will. We'd noticed each other at the hospital, but we hadn't a chance to become introduced. I'd believed that I'd never see you again, but then Will invited me to accompany him to go calling on some belles and there you were. It was like a miracle. A gift from God. How I ached to talk to you, to court you."

Amity twisted out of his arms, shocked, dazed.

"Let go of me!" she cried, her voice shrill.

She struggled up from the settee. Startled Jeb let her go, releasing her before in her thrashing she burn herself against the potbellied stove.

Amity was flooded with confusion. Not knowing what to think, she was helpless to speak. She stared at Jeb as she gasped for breath. Her neatly ordered world was shattered, lying in jagged shards at her feet.

Their eyes met. Amity sensed that Jeb was as unsettled as she.

"I love you, Amity," he whispered in a voice that was no longer as shocking as when she'd first heard it. "And I will love you even if you vow to hate me with your dying breath because I am a Yankee."

Then Jeb began to tell her how much he had come to adore her, and why.

"We can't help it that I'm a Yankee while you're a Rebel born and bred. The War brought us together, Amity. Don't let politics drive us apart when there are so many things that so perfectly join us."

Jeb opened his arms to her, and she found herself moving into his hug like a sleepwalker. His lips—lips that could speak—sought hers. Helplessly, she responded to his tender ministrations. And she discovered herself even more thrilled by his loving attentions. Jeb—a sworn enemy—had become her beloved Yankee.

"I want you to marry me, Amity, and go North. I came South in search of my brother a year after I finished my own duty to the Union. Teddy lied about his age and enlisted to go fight Johnny Reb. I promised my mother I would find him and bring him back. But I arrived too late. I learned that he was killed at Shiloh.

"I prepared to return home with the sad news, but I was wounded near Dalton, knocked unconscious. Because I was a Yankee in civilian clothes, I was mistaken for a Rebel in homespun and put on the train of wounded bound for Atlanta. Enemies were everywhere, but they became people I liked." He cupped her face in his hands.

"And one of them I especially love. You!" He gave her lips a quick kiss and smiled.

"So you were forced to play the part of a mute?" Amity said, awed by what an act of will that had required.

"Yes. But the fact remains that I love you. I want you to be mine forever. Marry me, Amity, I beg of you."

"Jeb, this is so unexpected, so startling, that I don't know what to think. I don't know what to say. Go North? But—"

"My parents would adore you," he urged. "We have property and substantial holdings. You would never lack for anything, my beloved."

"Oh Jeb," Amity wailed, her words a tortured groan as she considered what it would mean to leave the land of her birth and rearing, maybe never to return. "You don't know what you're asking. I. . .I can't give you an answer. At least not right now. There's so much to think of—so many others to consider."

"Then say nothing for tonight, my darling. Give me your answer when comes the dawn."

"Very well," Amity agreed.

"I wish I could give you longer, my darling, but I must begin the long trek home soon. I will pray on your behalf, and if you pray for God's guidance, He will not forsake you. Come the dawn, you'll know your answer. We both will."

"Whatever happens, Jeb," Amity said, and her words squeaked as sudden tears salted her eyes and lips, "know that I love you—and I always will."

"Then pray to God that it is His will that we be together, with everything settled in your heart as it already is in mine."

"I shall fall asleep tonight with that prayer on my lips."

"Before you do, I want to seal those honeyed lips with my kiss."

With the strength of Jeb's arms around her, his tall, rugged form shielding her, and his lips gentle and possessive on hers, Amity could have stayed in his embrace forever. She didn't know how she would ever find the strength to turn away if, after she prayed for guidance, the answer God gave her was not the one of her choosing.

Jeb released her, and Amity turned to depart, but then, unable to restrain himself, he drew her back into his arms for one last kiss.

Amity was about to shamelessly seek a third kiss—and a fourth—from him, but at that moment the teakettle began to whistle, preparing to issue a full-fledged scream. Hastily, Amity extricated herself from Jeb's arms and snatched the kettle from the stove before it could send Denizia and Mammy running to the kitchen.

If she chose to follow Jeb and in her own manner live out the story of Ruth, Amity realized that her loving servants would know soon enough the matters of the heart and the loving choices made.

Chapter Thirteen

Amity awakened before dawn. For a moment she stared at the cover of her four-poster canopy bed, organizing her thoughts and making plans for the day. But then she came fully awake and remembered the thrilling interlude with Jeb the night before.

Her heart ached with happiness, and she felt a ripple of joy as she realized that Jeb wanted her as his wife as much as she desired to spend the rest of her days with him. Amity Sheffield knew she would be content to love Jeb as they walked through life together, trusting the Lord to guide them.

With a sense of eagerness, Amity arose and prepared to dress for the day. But as she smoothed her hair and heard Mammy coming up the staircase to lay out her clothing and help her into her dress, she paused to consider what the future would demand that she leave behind—perhaps forever—if the North and South never reconciled their differences.

In moving North, she might be viewed as a Southern Rebel for the rest of her days, and the South's citizenry, knowing she had chosen to link herself to a Yankee, would view her as a betrayer.

Amity thought of her papa, an older man who had galloped off to war, ready to fight and die for the Confederate nation that had spawned him. He couldn't have believed in all of the C.S.A.'s tenets, but tradition and loyalty had guided him to do his part to preserve a way of life he had always known.

Amity stared at her troubled eyes reflected in the beveled looking glass in the marble-topped vanity, and she realized that she was as fearful as she was eager, as hesitant as she was optimistic.

"Change is frightening," she whispered to herself, then tried to rub away the quick sprinkle of goose bumps that rose on her skin. It was human nature, she realized, to cling to the familiar rather than reach out for the fearful unknown, even when the future promised happiness.

There were no guarantees. Jeb loved her, of that she was sure. But was it enough? Could she leave behind her father and others she held dear to follow Jeb anywhere he might choose to go?

Mammy arrived and began the process of lacing Amity's stays. From what the servant didn't say, Amity knew that, as usual, nothing had gone unnoticed by her. Mammy had tried to tell her that Jeb could talk, but Amity had been adamant in her refusal to hear what her Mammy had been telling her.

Had Mammy been listening from her doorway as Jeb offered his proposal of marriage? Amity couldn't help smiling as she suspected that it was probably so.

She gave a heavy sigh as she considered the conflicts that faced her, and her mind swirled with possible ramifications. Either choice she made had drawbacks, just as both possibilities offered benefits.

The tender hand Mammy laid on Amity's shoulder conveyed to her that Mammy knew and understood.

"I be goin' an' wakin' up Mist' Jeb," Mammy said.

"Let him sleep," Amity murmured. "He needs his rest. I'll take a breakfast tray to him later."

"Yes, Miss Amity. Whatever yo' say." Mammy crossed to open the drapes. "My, but it's a pretty day. A bit overcast, but—"

"It's dawned the most beautiful day of my life," Amity murmured, "and would be still if it were pouring down rain."

She bit back more words, not yet wanting to tell Mammy that Jeb was a Yankee, and that he'd sought her hand.

"And it might rain. Oh my! Lord have mercy!" Mammy gasped.

"What is it?" Amity asked, shaken when she heard the fright in Mammy's voice.

She rushed to her side. From their second-story vantage point they could see a procession moving toward their mansion. Amity recognized Cousin Philomen's wagon and mule, Mister Raynor's saddle mule, and Miss Ophelia dressed in black, seated grimly at Philomen's side, surrounded by a motley assortment of sharecroppers and impoverished planters. No doubt these men were veterans of the War for Separation and carried physical scars, weaknesses, and painful imperfections that served as reminders of what the battle had cost them.

"What on earth?"

"Quick, Miss Amity, yo' run down t' meet 'em, and stall 'em as best yo' can—"

"But—"

"Do as yo' tol', Lambie. Dem folks's up to no good. Believe me, yo' ol' Mammy be knowin' a lynch mob when she sees one! Dey's after yo' Yankee man."

Amity felt faint.

"No!" she cried.

"Yo' keep yo' head an' wits about you, an' go down there, Miss Amity,"

Mammy ordered, giving her a gentle shove toward the door. "An' you act like they ain't no accursed Yankee never been nowheres near this house. An' you play the part as if Mist' Jeb's life depended on it—because it does!"

"What are you going to do, Mammy?" Amity cried, realizing that she'd always trusted in Mammy's wise counsel. The aged black woman had an ability to miraculously make bad situations acceptable through the sheer power and stoicism of her personality. Mammy had unbending ethics and a well-developed sense of what was right and what was wrong.

"Don't ask, child. Yo' be better off if yo' don't know nothin' about what yo' mammy's goin' to do."

Amity threw a wrap around her suddenly icy body and ventured from Grandpapa Witherspoon's mansion to greet her half-sister and the grim-faced lynch mob.

The welcoming words that Amity had selected flew from her mind when she saw the savage sneer on Ophelia's hate-filled face, noticed her red-rimmed eyes, and realized that the dark clothing signified that her half sister was consigned to the wearing of widow's weeds.

"You hussy! You tawdry harlot!" Ophelia cried her rage. "Where is he? Where's the vile Yankee blue-belly you've been sheltering, while his kind have allowed my husband to die in a wretched northern prison and caused our papa to succumb in a hospital after growing septic from his wounds?"

Amity felt the news about Papa and Schuyler's deaths like a hammer blow, but then her thoughts flew to the needs of the living and the man she loved.

"There's no Yankee here," Amity said. She didn't believe she lied, for in her mind people were no longer Northerner or Southerner, Union or Confeder-ate, Yankee or Rebel. They were all human beings created by God. She and Jeb were in a special family—Christians—united with other believers. In this world they would never know some of their brothers and sisters in Christ, but in the hereafter they would recognize strangers as dear siblings in faith.

The sisters stood eye to eye, toe to toe. Without any warning, Ophelia slapped Amity with such a force that a crimson stain spread across the younger woman's pale cheek.

Amity bore the insult and the pain without reaction, but Mammy charged forward, the fire of indignation in her eyes.

"How's come yo' striking my baby?" Mammy angrily demanded as she came thundering down the front veranda steps, impervious to the cold.

"What's goin' on here?" Her black face was set in a forbidding glower as her hot gaze swept to take in the ragtag group of Southerners gathered around her.

"We're looking to take custody of the Yankee y'all been harborin' here, Mammy," Mister Raynor spoke up. "Y'all best be handing him over."

There was a rope coiled on the horn of the saddle in which he shifted as he waited. Nearby stood a tall tree.

"They ain't no Yankee gemp'mum here, Mist' Raynor, sir."

"Ain't no *gentleman* to be found in the entire North," Cousin Philomen spat in a bitter tone.

"Don't try to tell us that he's not here," Ophelia cried in a strident voice. "We know better. The doctor you called has been telling the countryside about the Yankee he treated at Amity Sheffield's request."

"That gemp'mum never spoke a word to me, Miss Ophelia," Mammy said. "An' I tended dat sickly man day an' night 'til he was well enough to leave."

"I don't believe you," Ophelia murmured. "Nor do the men who are accompanying me." She swiveled to face them.

"You all have my permission to search my grandpapa's house. Leave not a nook nor a cranny unsearched."

She turned back to Mammy and Amity with a triumphant glint in her tear-ravaged, hate-filled eyes.

"Y'all go right ahead," Mammy invited graciously, while Amity quailed within. "Yo' won't find no Yankee. Yo' won't find nothing but de late Mist' Buford's household help an' the late Mist' Morgan Sheffield's servants in the care o' Miss Amity here, who inherited us from her late mama."

"Gentlemen," Miss Ophelia said, "make yourselves at home. Search as long and as thoroughly as you like."

"This isn't your home. It's mine," Amity flared. "This plantation is bequeathed to me. Grandpapa Witherspoon was no kin to you. But rather than thwart you, Ophelia, I will agree," Amity added after a special look had passed between her and Mammy, "we have nothing to hide. So, gentlemen, as the mistress of this manor, I bid you welcome and invite you to search. I'll have my servants prepare a repast so that you can refresh yourselves before you begin your long ride home."

Ophelia, realizing she was no longer in control, gave her young half sister a murderous look. Rather than enter the home that was Amity's rightful domain, the older woman stood outside, shivering beneath a tree. She wept with rage, disappointment, and frustration at what she was unable to control and manipulate.

Although the search took less than an hour, to Amity it seemed to last an eternity. At any moment she expected to hear brawl-like sounds of victory as the men located Jeb where Mammy had secreted him.

But in her heart, she believed that her sister and the lynch mob would leave without satisfaction, for she knew what the Good Book said about protection. If the posse was successful in locating Jeb, it would be only because the Lord had allowed it.

Finally the mob left after enjoying the tarts that Serena had prepared. It was apparent that everyone except Miss Ophelia was feeling more convivial as they rode away.

For long minutes Amity stared after them, stunned, tears running down her face when she looked out over the meadows. She felt such relief that the blood-lusting mob had not laid a hand on Jebediah.

He seemed gone, truly gone, and Mammy had said nary a word about it, suspecting that the posse would circle back to check again a short while later. She wished to continue to protect Amity from knowledge that the group of men might try to wrest from her.

Two hours passed. Amity's grief deepened when she realized that she would never see Jeb again. While she had stalled the mob at the front of the house, Mammy and Serena must have sent Big Tom out the back way, supporting the weakened Yankee until he was protected by the woods. Big Tom would then have rushed back to the house so that his absence would not arouse suspicions. No doubt Jeb was weakly making his way through the woods, cold and without food, not knowing where he'd find shelter for the night.

"Whyfore yo' cryin', Miss Amity? They's gone. An' while they might be back, I don't think it's going to be today, and by—"

"I'm crying because I miss him, Mammy, and because I love him. Jeb wanted me to marry him. He wanted for us to go North. He said he'd await my answer until morning. But now he's gone before I could give it to him."

"And what might you've decided to tell Mist' Jeb?"

"Yes, Mammy. My answer was going to be yes!"

"Then tell him, Lambie. He's here. I know this ol' house like the back of my hand. I 'spects I's the only one left that knows dey's a little hidden closet in the attic, there from the day's when Mist' Buford's papa planned de home. We had jus' enough time to get Mist' Jeb and all his belongings into it before the lynchers was ready to search de house."

At that moment Jeb stepped outside and laid his hand on Amity's shaking shoulder.

"It's not too late for me to accept your answer, Amity. But now I know that I must leave this home, even as I realize that I can't—won't—go alone. I want to take you with me. I want to take all of you home with me."

"Do you mean it, Jeb?" Amity asked, realizing that she could never be happy without Mammy and Serena, and that fond as she was of Denizia and Big Tom, and they of her, they wouldn't want to abandon the plantation that had been their lifelong home.

Things in the Southland were changing. Grandpapa Witherspoon's plantation was now hers, to do with as she would. Jeb had told her that his family possessed wealth, that she would never want for material things. That meant she could give Denizia and Big Tom not only their freedom, but the deed to the plantation as well.

Serena, Amity believed, would want to go North to the land of opportunity where she could earn her livelihood with her skills and intelligence. And as for Mammy, Amity needed her to go with them, wanted her to go. Mammy had been more of a mother to her than the woman who had given birth to her.

Mammy had always been there, and Mammy would want to always be there, to be the loving grandmother to Amity's own children. She would help Amity and Jeb guide their children in the ways of the Lord.

"I'm afraid we may have to walk all the way to Atlanta," Jeb apologized. "But once we encounter Yankee forces, there should be no problems for us."

Amity laughed.

"For years I've feared the Yankees. Now I long for the sight of them," she drawled.

"And I'm afraid that while I have money in the North, my sweet, I'm an impoverished man in the Confederacy."

"I have an inheritance, Jeb, to stake us on our freedom journey. It's from Rosalynn, a one-time Boston debutante who would understand and approve of us using her money in this way."

Amity smiled as an autumn shower began to drizzle on the veranda roof with the slow, lazy passion of a storm that would soon find itself spent.

Mammy sighed with satisfaction and shuffled into the house, murmuring to herself about the packing at hand, the tasks to attend to, and the heirlooms that should be collected to be passed on to Miss Amity's young.

"Take what you want," Jeb encouraged her. "But I can promise you, Miss

Amity's children and mine will have everything they need: a mother, a father—"

"And Mammy," Amity assured.

"An' de Lord!"

Shores of Promise

Kate Blackwell

Chapter One
1840

Please still be there, thought Sarah Brown as she rounded the corner of the house from the back. Her pulse quickened—the carriage was just about to pull away from the front gate! Gathering her skirts with her right hand and waving her left, she hastened her steps.

"Ma'am!" she called out, no longer caring if the occupants of the house heard her. The driver flicked his short whip over the horse's back. With a creak of wood and iron, the carriage started to roll, leaving Sarah too far away to catch up. Filling her lungs with deep gulps of air, she looked back at the house. Mrs. Gerty's face was at an upstairs window.

I'm done for now, Sarah thought, unable to tear her eyes away from the woman's frowning face. The sound of horses' hooves pierced through the fog of despair that engulfed her. The carriage was returning!

Spurred on by renewed hope, Sarah ran toward the carriage. Just as she could make out the puzzled look on Mrs. Carlton's face, disaster struck. The toe of Sarah's worn leather slipper caught in the hem of her dress. Down she went with a violent thud!

"My dear, are you all right?" Sarah was too mortified to move. Two hands gently pulled at her shoulder and arm, and she allowed the driver to help her to her feet. Her teeth were gritty with dirt, and there was blood on her fingers when she pulled them away from the burning place on her cheek.

Sarah knew she was a sight, but the woman in the carriage looked at her with such concern that it gave her courage to speak. "Ma'am," she began, taking a deep breath and walking over to the buggy. "You said you'd be needing a maid?"

Mrs. Carlton pulled out a lace-bordered handkerchief from a lavender beaded purse. She leaned forward and held it out to Sarah, pushing it into her hand when the girl appeared reluctant to touch the fine piece of linen.

"Now, what's that you're asking?" she said as Sarah held the handkerchief to her cheek.

"A maid. I heard you say that you'd like to have an English serving maid. I'm a hard worker. Do you think you could take me on?"

Mrs. Carlton turned toward the house, and Sarah looked back over her shoulder. Mrs. Gerty had moved from the window to the front doorway.

She was too far away to hear their conversation, but the glare on her red-splotched face told Sarah that the woman had an idea of what was taking place. Sarah turned back to Mrs. Carlton.

"You wouldn't even have to pay me," she said quickly. "I'll work for board, and I don't eat much."

The older woman laughed, but her voice was full of compassion. "You work for Mrs. Gerty, dear. I can't go stealing you away. Besides, I was just making conversation when I spoke of wanting a maid. We really have enough servants."

Sarah opened her mouth to speak, then closed it again. "Yes'm," she said as she took a step back from the buggy, lowering her head. "I'm sorry to have disturbed you."

Mrs. Gerty's eyes burned into her back, and Sarah knew she'd have to face those eyes as she walked back to the house. The thought filled her with such dread that her courage came back. She took a step forward.

"Please?" She looked directly into Mrs. Carlton's eyes, putting all her longing into her gaze.

Mrs. Carlton held a crochet-gloved hand up to her lined cheek. The girl that stood in front of her was a bit pale—probably from working long hours indoors—but there was a captivating freshness about her. The slightly upturned nose and wide brown eyes contrasted interestingly with the determined straight line of her lips.

"Well, I suppose it would be nice to have you serving my guests. You are quite lovely." Sarah's cry of joy was cut short when Mrs. Carlton held up a hand. "I must discuss this with my husband." Catching the slight drop of the girl's shoulders, Mrs. Carlton reached out and patted her on the arm. "Don't worry. He does everything I ask him, but it makes him feel good to have me ask. You understand?"

Sarah's smile returned. "Yes ma'am. Oh, thank you ma'am!"

Mrs. Carlton smiled back. "Now, we're leaving Bristol to go back to the States in two days. Meet us at the dock, and I'm sure we'll have your passage ready. Should I send a carriage for you?"

"Could I come with you now?" asked Sarah, fearful that Mrs. Carlton would change her mind if pressed too hard, but more afraid of facing Mrs. Gerty.

Mrs. Carlton studied Sarah's face. "How old are you, dear?"

"Sixteen, ma'am."

"Are things so bad here?"

"Yes'm," Sarah cried, embarrassed by the tears that gathered in her eyes. "I can't go back, not now!"

"Well, climb on in then!" Mrs. Carlton said. The driver, stately in his blue velvet waistcoat adorned with a row of gold buttons, had been patiently standing to the side. Upon hearing Mrs. Carlton's invitation, he helped Sarah into the seat next to her. When Sarah was settled in the carriage, Mrs. Carlton turned to her. "Don't you need to get some belongings from the house?"

Sarah shuddered. "There's naught that I care about. My other dress is quite worn. I just wear it when I wash this one."

Reaching deep into the pocket of her apron, Sarah drew out a bundle of coins bound up in a shabby piece of muslin, the savings she'd grabbed from her attic room when she realized Mrs. Carlton was leaving. "I can buy another dress—maybe two—so's you won't be ashamed of me."

Mrs. Carlton let out a hearty chuckle. "My dear, no one will ever be ashamed of you!" Instructing the driver to turn the carriage around, she turned her face toward Mrs. Gerty, who stood glowering.

"I didn't like that woman, anyway," she said to Sarah with a grin.

Sarah couldn't help but look back, not at Mrs. Gerty, but at the house. Most people thought Gothic-style Connelsworth Park—with its delicate bay windows and crocketed pinnacles—was majestic as any cathedral. Three years of her life had been spent there, and to Sarah no prison could have been uglier.

Chapter Two
1834

Sarah's earliest memories were of her mother's skirts swishing as she cooked in the lofty kitchen at Hadenwilde Manor. A wooden spoon and tin soup ladle served as Sarah's toys, and she quickly learned that they'd be taken away if she banged them on the stone-flagged floor.

The kitchen was toasty during damp winter months, a wonderful escape from the unheated servants' quarters. The summer months, however, were plain misery. Steam rose from the copper cooking pots, bathing Ruth, Sarah's mother, in sweat. Alice, the kitchen maid, was equally wretched.

Still, the heat was more tolerable near the floor where Sarah played and napped. Comfort and companionship could be had by toddling over to her mother and grabbing a handful of muslin skirt to hold next to her cheek. When Ruth needed to move to another part of the kitchen, she'd gently tug on her skirt to release it from the grip of those baby fingers.

As Sarah grew, she was given more chores to perform in the great kitchen. She was a willing helper and quick learner. By the age of five, she created almost transparent peelings from potatoes and beets, and by age six she could knead and fold a mountain of bread dough. Staying busy made the day pass more quickly, and when her legs ached from long hours of standing, she looked ahead to when the last meal would be served and the kitchen cleaned and polished.

"Little Sarah, let's have a walk!" her mother would say, wiping her hands on her apron. Then the two would slip out of the house and sit on a bench in the garden—if none of the owner's family or guests were there—before retiring to the tiny room they shared with Alice.

It didn't matter to the little girl that darkness prevented them from seeing the full glory of the delphiniums and roses. She could lean back and see stars peeking through holes in the sky. Often Sarah would rest her head on her mother's lap, her face pointed toward heaven, as she listened to her mother's lovely singing.

> "See the stars, like little candles
> In the deep, dark sky
> And the maid who comes to light them
> She'll sleep by and by."

Sarah liked to wonder, with a trace of envy, about the girl who had such an important responsibility. Was she as pretty as her mother, who had faint dimples at the corners of her mouth and eyes as dark as mulberries? The delivery men who brought meat or butter and eggs to the kitchen always gave her mother special attention. While Alice was ready to lean against the door frame and chat with them, Sarah's mother treated them with cool politeness.

As the evening passed, the little girl's thoughts would muddle into dreams about butter and mulberries and floating through night breezes from star to star with a fiery torch. The next thing she'd be aware of was waking up in the morning between Mother and Alice on the goose-feather mattress.

One night, ten-year-old Sarah wasn't interested in the stars. A thought had troubled her since the night before. She sat on the bench in silence, needing consolation for her pain but afraid of what dreadful things she might learn.

Though not permitted in the rooms of the house where the Norton family lived, Sarah had been called upon several times to help serve a meal, especially when the family entertained guests.

"Don't be a calling any attention to yourself, little Sarah," her mother had warned, so Sarah had tried to move silently. The previous evening had been particularly busy. All sixteen places had been filled by the guests and their hosts, Henry and Anne Norton. The Nortons' five children had been sent to bed hours earlier, and the adults were being served a late dinner after their return from a performance of "Venice Preserv'd" at the Grafton Street Theatre.

"I ain't never seen the likes of so much food!" Celly, the new serving girl, had said as she'd loaded her tray in the kitchen. Ignoring a sharp look from Ruth, she'd fingered a sliver of baked whitefish from one of the dishes and popped it into her mouth.

"Jobs is scarce around here, lessin' you want to lose your eyesight at the weaver's mill," Ruth had warned. "I wouldn't go upsetting the mistress if I was you."

Celly's cheeks had nearly matched her flaming red hair as, lips drawn into a pout, she'd haughtily tossed her head and joined Sarah and the other serving girl bringing trays back and forth from the kitchen. The meal had started out with soup, fish, meat and game, sauces, vegetables, and a sweet pudding.

After the first course, the girls had reset the table, working around the diners. The second course had included several main dishes of meat and fish and a variety of puddings, creams, and tarts.

For the dessert course, the white damask tablecloth had been removed and the table reset with fruits, pastries, jellies, and other sweetmeats, all enticingly displayed in crystal or silver dishes. Once the desserts were served, Sarah only had to stand near the sideboard table and watch to see if her services were needed. Though she didn't understand the gossip that was tittered over, it was fascinating to a little girl who spent most of her time in the kitchen.

That evening, Sarah had been so absorbed in the lively chatter that it had taken her a few seconds to realize a young lady was motioning to her. With a start, Sarah had gone to her side.

"I've dropped my napkin. Please bring me another." The lady had been wearing a white crepe dress trimmed with pink satin ribbon, the bodice and sleeves spotted with white beads. Her flaxen hair had been bound up with several pearl combs, and Sarah was sure she'd never seen anyone so elegant. The lady had been seated next to Thorton Hepplewhite, Mrs. Norton's younger brother. Mr. Hepplewhite was often a guest at the table, but he had never taken notice of the servants. Sarah had been surprised when, as she had retrieved a clean linen napkin, she'd overheard him speak her name to his companion.

"Her name is Sarah," he had said, obviously in answer to the lady's inquiry.

The lady had looked over her shoulder at Sarah and smiled, then had turned back to Thorton. "She's a beautiful child! Where did she come from?" she'd asked, loudly enough for the other diners to hear.

Sarah had wanted to run to the lady's side and throw herself at her feet. Beautiful! No one other than her mother had ever called her that. Turning her head, Sarah had sought her reflection in the silver tea pitcher sitting on the sideboard. Her distorted reflection had revealed thickly lashed brown eyes and fine cheekbones. Curly tendrils of chestnut hair framed her oval face. Turning back to the table, Sarah had wondered what Mr. Hepplewhite was whispering to the lady that made her cover her mouth and laugh softly.

"What did he say, deary?" Across the table from the couple, a dark-haired woman in a green-sprigged muslin dress was leaning forward. "Where did she come from?" The woman made no effort to lower her voice.

That was when it had happened. The fine lady, with another glance over her shoulder at Sarah, had leaned forward. Her voice had been low, but just as she whispered her response, other conversation ceased. Sarah, who had pretended not to listen, heard an expression that had turned her blood to ice.

Her heart hammering in her throat, Sarah had stood with her back to the wall, feigning ignorance. Some of the more ill-mannered guests had stared at her before turning to whisper to a neighbor. Others had given Sarah quick glances, pretending interest in the silver tea service at her side or the portraits on the wall above her. The lady sitting next to Mr. Hepplewhite had not looked at her again.

Sarah shuddered as the memory of that evening came back to her. All day, she'd managed to keep busy and let work occupy her thoughts. But sitting in the cool night air, nothing could keep her from reliving the experience.

"Are you cold, Sarah?" Her mother put an arm around Sarah's shoulder and pulled her closer. Sarah snuggled against her mother's side, closing her eyes tightly and trying to feel the way she had until last night—that Mother was her whole world.

She marveled that she had never wondered why she didn't have a father. Oh, she'd known about fathers. She saw how kind Mr. Norton was to his children, but she'd assumed that wealthy children had fathers just like they had fine clothes and toys and ponies. Poor children had none of those things.

When she'd heard Jake the gardener use the wretched word that the elegant lady had whispered, she'd had to ask Alice what it meant. When she'd been told, she'd shrugged her shoulders—it had nothing to do with her.

Now she knew. Her very existence was a profanity! A great sob tore her throat.

"Sarah?" Her mother's voice was filled with alarm as she turned Sarah to face her. "Whatever is wrong?"

Clinging to her mother's arms, Sarah wept on. Finally, her chest heaving and her throat raw, she sat up and wiped her nose on the hem of her apron. "Mother," she managed to whisper. "Why don't I have a father?"

Shoulders sagging, Ruth let out a long sigh, her lips trembling. Sarah wished that she hadn't spoken. She looked down at her mother's work-roughened hands—hands that caressed her when she needed comfort. Filled with shame for hurting the woman who'd only been good to her, Sarah reached up and put her hand on her mother's cheek.

Just then, Ruth spoke. "I used to have Sundays off—did you know that?" She was looking straight ahead. "And I was paid twice what I'm paid now."

She was quiet for so long that Sarah wondered if her mother had fallen asleep. Then she spoke again. "I had a friend who worked here until she got married to a shipyard worker. Her name was Kate. We was real good friends, and about once a month, Ben, the livery man, would take the vegetable wagon in to Bristol and visit his family. He'd drop me off near Kate's, and we'd have a lovely time, Kate and me and her husband, John." She smiled faintly, reliving happier days.

"Sometimes John's brother, Thomas, would come by. He seemed to like me. I was only eighteen and so shy, but I liked him, too. He was quiet, like me."

Taking a deep breath, she continued. "The little cottage Kate lived in was down a dirt lane that was too narrow for the wagon. There must have been hundreds of cottages thrown together there. When Ben let me out of the wagon, I had to walk past alleys and buildings and cottages to get to Kate's. We always went there in the daytime and there was plenty of people around, so I never thought I was in danger.

"I never heard the man when he came up behind me from the alley!" Sarah's mother said, her voice quivering. "After. . .I didn't even go to Kate's. I was so ashamed!" Her lips tightened. "I was raised to be a good girl, Sarah, but some men are evil.

"When I discovered that I was in a family way, I didn't know what to do. My grandmother had died when I was fourteen, and I never had no other family. Lonely and scared I was."

For a while mother and daughter sat holding hands. Sarah was stunned. She knew about babies and how they were made, but she'd never heard of anything so brutal.

"When Mrs. Norton found out, she told me she would have to dismiss me because I would shame her family and be a bad example to her daughters and the other servants. She said that none of the ladies she knew would want to hire me, either. I didn't have no other place to go, so I got down on my knees and begged her not to make me leave. After she talked to Master Norton about it, she offered to let me stay if I'd work for half-wages and no Sundays off."

Finding her voice, Sarah asked, "What about Thomas?"

"I never went back to Kate's, and when they sent me messages, I didn't get anyone to read them to me. I threw them away."

"You never saw him again?"

"Thomas came to see me a few months later. Alice was new, and she let him in before I could see who it was." Ruth's voice turned flat. "I stood there, big with child, and he didn't say a word. He stared at me. Then he turned and left."

Sarah's heart filled with rage at the man who'd hurt her mother and at the

Nortons for treating her so badly. Her anger turned inward when she realized that she herself was the cause of her mother's troubles. Fresh tears came to her eyes. "Are you sorry you have me?"

Ruth hugged her daughter tightly, almost squeezing her breath away. "Never! After you was born, I loved you from the start."

Sarah wasn't sure how long they sat together that evening, but her first thought the next morning was that she would never let anyone hurt her mother like that again.

Chapter Three
1837

"Mercy!" exclaimed Celly, pushing her chair back from the scarred kitchen table. "It's terrible hot in here!" She stretched out her legs and fanned them with the hem of her skirt.

Thirteen-year-old Sarah watched as her mother and Alice exchanged raised eyebrows. Celly had managed to sit by George, and the pock-marked stable boy was gawking at her white shins. Embarrassed for the older girl, Sarah cleared her throat, hoping Celly would notice the attention she was drawing.

Celly looked up. With a self-conscious giggle, she smoothed her skirt back over her legs and gave George a smile. Red-faced, George snapped his mouth shut and turned his eyes back to his plate of food.

"I don't see why you had to bake bread today, with the rain pourin' down like that," Celly whined, turning to Ruth. "We can't even take our dinner outside."

Ruth stopped cutting wedges from a fist-sized ball of hoop cheese. "The missus and family are comin' home from holiday tomorrow. I'll be needing some bread. But it's only light misting outside. You can carry your plate under the arbor if you're wantin' some air."

Fluttering her eyelashes, Celly smiled at George again. "I've a mind to do that. Would anyone be wantin' to join me?"

"That's a right fine idea!" From across the table, Jake, the gardener, flashed Celly a yellow-toothed grin as he picked up his plate and fork. "I'm sufferin' greatly in this kitchen!"

Glancing at George hunched over his plate spooning mutton stew into his mouth, Celly pulled her chair back up to the table. "It ain't so bad in here."

Sarah thought about the arbor. It would be great fun to sit on the stone bench and listen to the raindrops pelt the grapevine leaves that carpeted the trellis. She could almost smell the earthy aroma of wet leaves and damp air.

"Why don't you go, Celly?" she said, hoping that if the girl changed her mind and went with Jake, they would invite her along. "It's so pretty there."

"I said it ain't so bad in here." Celly gave Sarah a withering look.

"I'll go with ye, Sarah," said George, sitting up in his chair and wiping his mouth with the back of his sleeve. "I like the rain."

Sarah was fond of George. She was about to agree when she caught Celly's expression. The older girl was staring at her with such an outpouring of anger that Sarah was shaken. *Why, Celly hates me!* she thought. Confused, she tried to think of what she'd done to deserve such malice. Was it because George offered to go outside with her?

Wishing she hadn't said anything, Sarah was relieved when her mother spoke. "I'll be needin' Sarah to help me in a few minutes. She'd best stay here."

Sarah stole another look at Celly, expecting everything would be back to normal. Celly's expression hadn't changed.

ॐ

The next day was unusually busy as the servants hurried to get the house ready for the family.

"Master Henry and the family are here!" called out Fenton, the butler. The other house servants scurried to the great hall and, with much whispering and nervous excitement, took their places according to their importance in the household.

Fenton stood first in line. Albert, the footman and only other male house servant, had accompanied the Nortons on holiday, so the female servants took their places after the butler. At any other estate, the cook would have been second only to the housekeeper among the female staff, but at Hadenwilde Manor that had changed more than a decade earlier. Ruth stood at the end of the line behind Ester, the scullery maid. Sarah, who was allowed to work in the kitchen but received no salary, stood last, next to her mother.

The whispering ceased when the massive carved oak doors swung open. Albert was the first to enter, quickly standing to the side to hold one of the doors, while Fenton held the other one.

"Good evening, Master Henry!" chorused the line of servants as Henry Norton entered, carrying three-year-old Jenny Norton in his arms. His gray frock coat and nankeen trousers were uncustomarily wrinkled from the long carriage ride, and the familiar musty-sweet odor of pipe tobacco trailed behind him.

Henry Norton nodded, handing the sleeping child over to Frances, a stocky housemaid. "Put her to bed. Mind you take her shoes off," he ordered. Turning to his wife, who was coming through the doorway, he motioned toward his study. "I'll be looking over the books. Have supper sent to me when it's ready."

Anne Norton frowned at her husband's back, ignoring the greetings of the servants. "So, this is why you were so anxious to get back home. You think a fortnight away from business has ruined us?"

Mr. Norton froze, opened his mouth as if to speak, and then continued on to his study without looking back.

Sarah felt sorry for Mrs. Norton. The slender woman's pinched face had fallen, and the corners of her eyes were glistening with tears. Remembering the way her mother was being treated by this family brought her sympathy to a sharp end, but she was still uncomfortable in the sight of such distress.

"Emily, I've a headache," Mrs. Norton said to the governess, who had Frank, Elizabeth, and Celeste in tow. "See that the children are bathed before supper." The mistress of the house took to the stairs with her personal maid, Penelope, following.

As soon as the Norton family had left the room, the servants scattered, some heading out to the carriage to bring in chests of clothing, some to the dining room to set the table for supper. The kitchen workers, Ruth, Alice, and Sarah, returned to their preparations for the meal.

"Sarah, give me a hand." Ruth was folding towels to handle the iron door of the brick oven. A blast of scorched air stirred the wisps of dark hair around her forehead as she bent down to remove a sizzling roaster.

Sarah fetched a pewter platter from the cupboard and brought it to the kitchen table, where her mother was setting the hot pan. Using three-pronged meat forks, she helped lift a crisp goose onto the platter.

"There ain't much prettier than a roast goose!" said Ruth, spooning drippings from the pan over the bird. "I believe this is the—"

Her words were interrupted by a commotion at the kitchen door. Sarah and her mother looked up in surprise to see Anne Norton burst through the door, followed by Mrs. Owen, the housekeeper.

"I would like to see all of you in the front!" Mrs. Norton ordered, her eyes red and swollen. A lady of quality never set foot in her own kitchen, so the three servants knew something serious was about. Sarah had only seen Mrs. Norton that angry once—when the ham they'd served at a dinner party was a bit dry. Even then, she'd sent for them from the library.

Heads lowered, Ruth, Alice, and Sarah followed Mrs. Norton and Mrs. Owen down the long hall into the great room where the other house servants were somberly gathered. *What have we done?* wondered Sarah. The same question was mirrored on the other faces. Tension filled the room.

A wail sounded from upstairs. One of the children was sobbing loudly from grief. Although Sarah was concerned for the welfare of whatever child was in distress, she was also relieved. She'd never been allowed much contact with the children, so whatever trouble was happening couldn't involve her. She let out the breath she'd been unconsciously holding.

"Elizabeth's favorite doll is missing. Its glass case has been broken," said Mrs. Norton, facing the servants. "Do any of you know where it is?"

Sarah knew which doll Mistress Norton was talking about: the "Princess Victoria" doll, a delicate creation of china, satin, and fine artwork. A gift from a favorite aunt, thirteen-year-old Elizabeth had brought the doll to the table several times to show guests, immediately returning it to her room upstairs. A stab of guilt brought a flush to Sarah's cheeks. She'd coveted the doll every time she'd seen Elizabeth cradling it. Could whatever had happened be her fault in some way?

"I'm waiting for an answer." Anne Norton's voice was cold, but the veins standing out on her temples gave evidence of her immense wrath. She walked down the line of servants, searching each face.

Mrs. Norton was facing Ester, and though the maid's back was straight, her lips trembled at the intensity of her mistress's stare. Mrs. Norton moved on, seemingly convinced that Ester wasn't the guilty one.

No! Sarah's thoughts screamed as the woman came down the line toward her. *Don't let her look at me like that!* Standing next to her mother, Sarah tried to control her expression, but the more she willed her cheeks to stop burning, the hotter they felt.

"Sarah, look at me!"

Sarah brought her eyes up to face the woman in front of her, but the expression on her mistress's face terrified her. Cowered by the accusation in Mrs. Norton's eyes, Sarah lowered her own.

"Where did you put it, Sarah?" asked Mrs. Norton through clenched teeth.

"I. . .I didn't." She looked at her mother for help. "Mother, I didn't. . . ."

Ruth put her arm around her daughter, drawing her close. "Ma'am, the girl has always been truthful to me. She'd not be the type to—"

"Search her room!" snapped Mrs. Norton to Albert and Mrs. Owen.

Sarah felt her mother trembling against her. She wanted to reassure her that there was nothing to worry about, that she hadn't taken the doll, but the knowledge that the eyes of everyone in the room were upon her froze her tongue.

The next five minutes seemed like an eternity to Sarah. Hearing the footsteps of the returning servants, she looked up. Walking ahead of Albert, Mrs. Owen held the doll.

Sarah's mouth flew open, and she found her tongue. "No! I didn't take it!"

Mrs. Owen had always been kind to Sarah, and there was regret in her voice when she spoke. "It was under her bed, Madam, wrapped in her nightdress."

Closing her eyes, Sarah leaned her head against her mother's chest. "I didn't take the doll!" she sobbed, her shoulders heaving.

"Your daughter will have to leave," said Mrs. Norton, facing Ruth. "I'll have no thieves about here. You may stay, though. We've no complaints against you."

Ruth's head snapped back. "Ma'am, I ain't got a family to send her to, and I wouldn't if I had. Sarah's not a thief!" Humbling herself, she lowered her voice. "I've served you well these past fourteen years. Please don't do this to us."

Mrs. Norton frowned. "If you won't send her away, then your duties are no longer required in this household. Pack your things and have Ben drive you to town." Turning on her heel, she crossed the room, the doll in her arms.

"Oh, Missus Anne, please don't be so cruel," pleaded Ruth, taking a step forward as if to follow her employer.

Pausing at the first step of the staircase, Mrs. Norton put her hand on the banister rail and looked back, her face a mask of disdain. "Cruel? You dare to call me cruel, here in my own house and ahead of my servants? I should have known something like this would happen!" Her sharp voice dripped venom. "I've been too much of a lady to hold her breeding against her. I even gave her a home. But the ill-begotten will sooner or later seek their true level, won't they?"

Ashen-faced, Ruth put her hand over her heart, leaning on Sarah for support. Alice touched her shoulder. "I'll help you gather your things," she said quietly, her face a picture of ineffable sadness.

As they walked past the other servants, Sarah looked up at the sound of weeping. It lightened her heart a little to realize that they had some friends in the household. When she caught Celly's eyes she stopped short, confused at the message they were sending. Crossing her arms over her buxom chest, the red-haired maid grinned broadly.

Chapter Four
1836

"Remember to stand up straight, Sarah," said Ruth, holding open the wrought-iron gate leading to the great house.

When Connelsworth Park first came into their sights, Sarah had only been able to stare at the majesty of it. Now she found her tongue. "Mother, are you sure we should apply here? Mrs. Norton said that—"

"Lower your voice, child! You'll have us turned away before we get inside the door!"

Sarah wanted to obey, but she found herself faltering. "Mrs. Norton said that Mrs. Gerty—she's crazy! I heard the Mistress and her friends talking about her lots of times!"

Shifting the roll of clothing and belongings she carried to her other arm, Ruth took Sarah's elbow, pulling gently to hurry her along as they followed a cobbled path to the back of the house. "We've nowhere else to look," she whispered. "And our savings is almost gone."

"But there must be some—"

Stopping a few feet from the door, Ruth wheeled her daughter around to face her. "I don't like to talk ugly about the mistress, even if she did send us away, but her and her friends wasn't kind when they talked about people. Mrs. Gerty can't be as bad as they said."

She took the smaller bundle from under Sarah's arm and set it down in the grass growing near the path. "Now, let's brush the dirt from our dresses and wipe the sweat off your face with this handkerchief. We want to look presentable, don't we?"

Swallowing hard, Sarah nodded. "What if she won't hire us? Mrs. Norton might have told her about us, too." They'd found when they'd begun seeking other employment that Mrs. Norton had spread word among her friends that Ruth and Sarah were insolent and dishonest. Even potential employers who weren't acquainted with the Nortons wouldn't consider them without a letter of recommendation.

"We've got to try, little Sarah. That's all there is to it," Ruth said, bending to pick up their bundles again. Stepping up to the wooden door, she pulled the rope on a large brass bell affixed to the frame.

After a while the knob turned, and the door was pulled open by a ruddy-faced woman wearing a smeared white apron, obviously the cook or kitchen maid.

Eyeing the bundles they were holding, the woman shook her head. "We don't need nothin' today," she said, not unkindly. The door was starting to swing shut when Ruth put out her hand to catch it. "We're not selling, ma'am. We're seeking jobs."

The woman at the door laughed, then darted a look behind her. "Are you that desperate?"

"Yes."

"Do you have a wagon waiting in front?"

"No, ma'am. We walked here."

Her eyebrows shot up. "All the way from town in this muggy weather?"

Ruth nodded.

"Then you must be desperate indeed! Let me send for Miss Martin. She's the housekeeper. You can wait in the kitchen."

They followed her through a short hallway, then down a flight of stone steps. Sarah had heard of underground kitchens, but she'd never been in one. She was astounded at the coolness of the room, a welcome relief from the oppressive heat they'd walked in all morning.

Setting out from the far wall was a huge cooking range with ovens on either side of its coal grate. From hooks on the brick wall hung a multitude of iron and copper saucepans, skillets, skimmers, and sieves. The shelves covering another wall were stacked with fancy pudding molds, jelly and aspic dishes, preserving pans, bread tins, milk bowls, and numerous other utensils. Some she'd never seen before, even though she'd been raised in a kitchen.

Ruth, turning around to take it all in, let out a sigh. "The size of this kitchen!" she said. "It's twice as big as what I'm used to!"

"All the rooms are big, dear," said the woman. "Except the servants' rooms, of course." She turned to a girl about Sarah's age who was at a table peeling beets. "Frances, go ask Miss Martin to come."

The girl put her knife down and got up from the table. Wiping her hands on her apron, she gave Sarah a shy smile before trotting up the stairway and through the door at the top.

"My name is Agnes. I'm the cook. Would you be wantin' to put your bundles down?" Pulling out a chair, she motioned for them to put their belongings on it. "You look like you could use some water, too."

"Thank you for your kindness," said Ruth as she laid their things in the chair. "Have you worked here long?"

"Five years," answered Agnes, dipping two tin mugs in a bucket on the sideboard. "Longer than anyone else, 'cept for Miss Martin. Folks with any sense don't stay around here very long."

Ruth was opening her mouth to question this statement when the door at the head of the stairs opened again. In walked a stick of a woman.

Sarah's eyes grew wide. She'd never seen anyone that thin! The fullness of the woman's black skirt and white starched apron only made her arms and torso seem more skeletal. Her sparse, dull brown hair was pulled back tightly into a bun at the nape of her neck, drawing attention to her colorless sunken cheeks and severe lips.

"You are looking for positions, I'm told," she said, still standing at the top of the stairs. "May I see your letter of reference?"

"We got no letter, ma'am," said Ruth. "But my daughter and I—"

"I'm afraid Mrs. Gerty requires a reference," interrupted Miss Martin. "You may leave now."

"Do you mind if I give them a bite to eat first?" asked Agnes quickly. "They walked all the way from town."

"Hand them a loaf of bread and get on with your duties," Miss Martin answered as she turned back to the door.

"Please tell the mistress that we was fired by Mrs. Henry Norton," Ruth spoke out to the woman's back.

Miss Martin paused at the door, her hand on the knob. "Fired?"

"Yes, and wrongly too."

She turned to look at them, then shrugged. "That still doesn't—"

Ruth bit her lip, her face anxious. "Please tell her that we don't believe none of the horrible things Mrs. Norton said about her."

Miss Martin stared at them. Then, to Sarah's amazement, a corner of the housekeeper's mouth twitched.

As if embarrassed by this faint show of emotion, Miss Martin straightened her bony shoulders. "You may give them something to eat," she said to Agnes, without looking at Sarah and Ruth. "I shall see if the mistress would like to speak with them."

"I believe Miss Martin was about to smile!" said Agnes, shaking her head in wonder. She handed Sarah a soft roll, smeared with meat paste. "I'd have thought a corpse more likely to!"

"She does seem a sad one," said Ruth.

"Sad? That would take some feelings. The woman's got a stone for a heart —and a wee one at that!"

Sarah watched Frances peeling beets. She longed to speak to the girl, but the unfamiliar surroundings intimidated her. As if reading her thoughts, Frances looked up from the basket in her lap.

"I hope you can stay," she said. "Ginny is the nearest one to my age, and she's three years older than me."

"I hope so, too," Sarah replied. *Mother's right*, she thought. *Mrs. Norton said bad things about lots of people.* While it was true that Miss Martin was a bit cold, Sarah liked the idea of having a friend her age. Maybe she and her mother could be happy working in the house, even if Mrs. Gerty was odd.

The kitchen door swung open. "Mrs. Gerty would like to see you in the sitting room," said Miss Martin, her face expressionless.

Rising from their chairs, Ruth and Sarah silently followed her up the steps and down a short passageway, through a huge dining room, and down a second, longer hall. When they came to a door near the end of this hall, Miss Martin knocked softly.

A high voice called out. "You may come in."

Miss Martin opened the door and motioned for them to go inside.

"You stay here, too, Julia, so they aren't wandering around the house when they leave."

When they leave! In her disappointment, Sarah forgot to hold her back straight as she followed her mother and Miss Martin through the doorway. The sitting room was massive, with paintings of all sorts lining the walls. Burgundy velvet curtains hung at the windows, and brilliantly colored carpets nearly covered the polished floor.

As big as the room was, it was crammed almost to bursting with furniture. Damask and striped silk sofas, armchairs, a variety of little tables and cabinets, reading stands, embroidered footstools, and carved bookcases stood about in profusion, and in the corner stood a stately grand piano.

Remembering why they were visiting, Sarah straightened her back and walked from behind her mother to stand next to her. Seated in front of them was a short, stout woman. Her pink silk dress, with its rows of ruffles, silk bows, and tiny wreaths of rosebuds, was designed for someone much younger.

"What did Mrs. Norton say about me?" Mrs. Gerty demanded of Ruth. A row of flesh bubbled out from under her chin when she spoke. "Tell me everything!"

Closing her eyes, Ruth struggled with herself. Then she reached for her daughter's hand and squeezed it. "She said you was crazy."

"Crazy!" The mass of ringlets in Mrs. Gerty's graying black hair quivered, and her body shook with rage. "She's got some nerve calling me crazy!" Narrowing her small eyes, she asked, "Who did she say this to?"

Sarah could hear her mother gulp. "I heard her say it to Mrs. Waldsworth, Miss Farington, and Mrs. Helen Smith, among others."

"Do you think they believe her?" asked Mrs. Gerty. Her fleshy, pallid cheeks were covered with angry red splotches, and Sarah was shaken at the utter hatred in her eyes, even though it was not directed at them.

"Mrs. Norton talks bad about a lot of people," answered Ruth. "Only a simpleton would believe her gossip. Why, she accused my daughter of being a thief!"

Sarah looked up at her mother, not believing her ears! They'd had too many prospective employers throw that up at them, for most well-connected people around Bristol knew the Nortons. And now Mother was volunteering the information!

"Well, maybe she is a thief!" snorted Mrs. Gerty, sharply eyeing Sarah's terrified face.

"Another maid in the house has boasted to our friends that she stole a doll and hid it under my daughter's bed. When we found out, we tried to see Mrs. Norton, but she won't see us or change her mind, even though she fired the other maid a few days after we left."

While Mrs. Gerty considered her words, Ruth pressed on. "She's told everyone in town that she won't speak to anyone who hires us. We came here, ma'am, because we figure you ain't one to be told what to do."

"You're right about that!" said Mrs. Gerty. "I'll not be having the likes of Anne Norton telling me who I can or cannot hire!"

Ruth squeezed Sarah's hand again. "Then would you have a position for us? We was in the kitchen at the house, but we can do other work besides."

Mrs. Gerty reached for an almond-shaped chocolate from a dish on the settee and popped it into her plump mouth. After chewing with obvious relish, she licked her lips. "I have one position open, for the girl."

Sarah and her mother looked at each other.

"I don't like having lots of servants around," continued Mrs. Gerty, a flake of chocolate still at the corner of her mouth. "I have to feed and pay them all, and they get lazy when there's not enough work to keep them busy."

"Ma'am," said Ruth, stepping forward. "The child's not used to drawing a salary, so's if we could stay together, you'd only have to pay me."

"I don't think so. Sooner or later, you'd get to grumbling about it and walk around here with a sour face. I expect my servants to look pleasant."

Sarah couldn't help but glance at Miss Martin, who looked anything but pleasant!

Ruth pressed on, an edge of panic in her voice. "We didn't grumble at the Nortons', and we'd be grateful to you if we could have a place here."

"Food isn't free around here," answered Mrs. Gerty, "and I presume you'd want to eat. No, the girl is enough, or both of you take your leave and I'll hire someone else."

"Then, you'll take on my Sarah?"

"That would suit me fine. I'll pay four shillings a month, as I can't be expected to give full wages for a child. How old is she—ten?"

"She's thirteen, ma'am, and a hard worker."

"We'll see." Mrs. Gerty reached for another chocolate. "Miss Martin, show her where she'll sleep tonight and give her something to do."

Numb, Sarah walked with her mother and Miss Martin back down the long hallway and up two flights of stairs to a tiny, windowless attic room. She didn't speak until the housekeeper left them alone.

"Mother," she sobbed, throwing her arms around her waist. "I don't want to stay here without you!"

Gathering her daughter in her arms, Ruth sat on the flock mattress on the bed. "My child, it tears my heart out to leave you, but right now you need a place to stay."

"You need a place, too! Where will you stay?"

"I heard a woman in the rooming-house say they're hiring workers at the cotton mill. I can get a job and bed there until something better comes along. Then I can come get you."

Sarah's head shot up. "I can get a job there, too, and we can be together."

"No!" Ruth's voice was firm. "I'll never have you working in one of them places! No matter how hard you have to work, you'll have it better here than the little ones in the factories!"

Gently setting Sarah down from her lap onto the mattress, Ruth rose. "I'd best be going now, so's I can reach town before dark."

Dumb with anguish, Sarah could only reach out for a handful of her mother's skirt. Like in the old days, she held the fold of limp broadcloth to her cheek, her eyes closed.

Ruth stood for a while, her hand resting on her daughter's head. "Oh, child," she finally groaned, "this ain't forever. I'll come to see you when I can." After carefully untangling Sarah's fingers from her skirt, she bent down and kissed her forehead. "You hang on to your wages. Find a safe place. When we've got enough saved, you and me, we'll go to another town and look for positions where they never heard of Mrs. Norton!" Giving Sarah one last, quick hug, she was gone.

❧

A soft rap sounded at Sarah's door. Rising from where she'd thrown herself on the bed, Sarah wiped her eyes. "Come in," she said hesitantly, fearful of who might be on the other side.

A pretty, golden-haired girl of about fifteen came in, holding Sarah's belongings and some folded linens. "I brought you some sheets and your bundle. There's a blanket in the bottom of the chest." She eyed Sarah. "Well, you're a wee one, like Frances. You'd best dry up them tears before the missus sees you."

"Are you Ginny?" asked Sarah.

"A smart one, too, I see! That's me name, for certain. I'm the parlor maid. How old are you?"

"Thirteen."

"The same age I was when I came on," said Ginny. "The missus likes to hire 'em young 'cause we don't eat much, and so's she can pay half-wages. The only thing is, when you get older, she forgets to raise the pay." Handing Sarah a coarse cotton sheet, she turned and fetched a brown woolen blanket from the chest. "I'll help you make your bed if you'll stop standing there like you ain't got any sense."

Positioning herself at the foot of the bed, Sarah helped Ginny tuck the sheet in around the mattress. "Why don't you get a position somewhere else?" she finally asked.

"When's a body supposed to look for work? I've had only three days off since I came here—one to go to my aunt's funeral, and two more when I was taken ill." She frowned. "I get a half-day every month, but Mrs. Gerty won't let Alex drive me to town in the wagon. By the time I walked there, it'd be time to turn around and come back!"

"My mother used to have half-Sundays off every week," said Sarah, warming up to the talkative older girl. "She was a cook."

"Well, no wonder about that. Agnes gets half-Sundays off, too. Good cooks are hard to find, I hear, so's they get treated a mite better."

Sometimes they are, thought Sarah. *But not always.*

"Now," said Ginny, smoothing out the last wrinkle in the blanket. "Miss

Martin says you've had your lunch, and I'm to show you what to do." She motioned for Sarah to follow her. "Most important," she said as they started down the dark attic stairs, "is to stay busy. And when you see the missus, you'd best look happy. Even if you ain't."

&

Finished! thought Sarah, squeezing the rags she'd used to clean the billiard room fireplace. Ginny had taught her to scour the iron grate with vinegar and sand from a bucket in the tool shed. It seemed a waste to clean it when the morning fires would be laid in less than an hour, but Sarah knew better than to question an order.

Her right shoulder ached from scrubbing, but she didn't ache all over anymore. After six months at Mrs. Gerty's, her body was getting used to hard work. She looked down at her hands. They were red and coarse not only from the continual scrubbing and polishing, but also from the strong lye in the laundry soap.

It wouldn't be so bad if her mother were working with her. The ache in her chest was far worse than the pain in her shoulder, and the loneliness far worse than the drudgery. Frances spent all her time in the kitchen helping Agnes. Even though their rooms were next door to each other, they rarely had time to talk. At the end of each day it was all they could do to pull themselves up the attic stairs and fall into bed, sometimes without even pulling down the sheets.

Mealtimes in the kitchen—the bright spots in Sarah's day—were rushed, and if a maid wanted enough to eat, she'd best spend that time eating instead of talking.

Suddenly, Sarah's thoughts turned to panic. *What am I doing, just sitting here!* Holding her breath, she listened. The room was quiet. Slowly, she turned her head to the left, examining the shadowy spots out of the corner of her eye.

She let out a breath and reached for the crock of vinegar and wet rags. Rising, she looked one last time around the room, careful to keep a smile on her face.

Chapter Five
1838–1840

"You learn a lot by keepin' your ears open," advised Ginny, picking up the bread crumbs that were left on her plate with her fingers. " 'Stead of going around with your head in the clouds."

Sarah blushed, but Ginny's wink told her the older girl wasn't being unkind. The female servants were taking their time at breakfast. Miss Martin had left early for Bristol to purchase household goods, and Mrs. Gerty hadn't rung her bell for breakfast. They'd have to rush through chores at an even greater speed, but the relaxed companionship was worth it.

"So, what have you learned, m'lady?" asked Agnes, resting her elbows on the table.

"I found out how come the mister and missus is so rich."

Sarah remembered that she'd overheard Mrs. Norton and her friends tittering over how the Gertys had acquired their immense wealth, but she couldn't recall the details. That life had been over a year ago and seemed like a dream.

Pleased at having her audience so attentive, Ginny continued. "Alex told me that Leslie, that new gardener, told him they wasn't always rich. I mean, they wasn't as poor as the likes of us, but Mr. Gerty was a clerk in the shipping business, or somewhat like that."

Agnes sat up straight, a mock look of horror on her face. "You mean they ain't gentlefolk?"

"In a sow's eye!" Their giggles of delight caused Sarah to glance at the stairs. She couldn't believe they were talking this way!

"Anyhow, Leslie says he heard Mr. Gerty leased a ship and made buckets of money haulin' slaves 'cross the ocean—even after it was against the law."

Frances's eyes grew wide. "He sold little black babies?"

"Right out of their mommies' arms. Course he sold some grown ones, too."

"That's horrible!" exclaimed Sarah. "Is he still doing it?"

"No, that was a long time ago. But he made enough money to start his own shipping business and to buy this here house." Ginny leaned closer to the table. "I heard they bought it from some gentry that had more land than sense, and the mister and missus gave them a tenth of what it's worth!"

Bringing her dish and mug to the washbasin, Sarah felt keen disappointment in Mr. Gerty, though she barely knew him. He stayed mostly at a club in Bristol, close to his business. *Of course,* she thought grimly, *I wouldn't blame Mr. Gerty for staying away, even if he had sold slaves once.*

"My, ain't we jumpy these days!" said Agnes, who'd brushed against Sarah on her way to the basin.

Sarah looked down at her broken dish on the floor. "I'm so sorry!"

After helping Sarah throw the broken pieces away, Agnes put an arm around the girl's shoulders and gave her a squeeze. "You can't let the missus upset you so," she whispered, "or you'll end up as daffy as she!"

Sarah would have liked to have stayed enveloped in Agnes's plump arms. It had been so long since she'd seen her mother. When the cook finally turned away to give her attention to the dishes, Frances touched Sarah's arm. "Are you all right?"

She nodded, managing a little smile. *Poor Frances,* she thought. *At least I have a mother who'll come for me one day.* Frances had been recruited from an orphanage and knew nothing about her parentage.

Mrs. Gerty still wasn't up, so Sarah couldn't carry down the chamber pots. She reached into her apron pocket and brought out her list of duties for the day—cleaning the drawing room was next. Miss Martin had given her a list of duties for every day of the week, but Sarah had been too embarrassed to tell the housekeeper that the marks on the page meant nothing to her. Fortunately, Ginny was able to read them to her, and within a month's time, she knew what the words stood for.

Sarah brought a handful of clean rags and a jar of linseed oil into the drawing room and cleared the knick-knacks from the rosewood table nearest the door. First, the table had to be rubbed with a dab of linseed oil on a soft cloth, then buffed with a piece of lamb's wool. After the polishing was done, Sarah dusted the ornamental vase, candlestick, china figurines, and glass dome of wax flowers.

Well, that one's finished, she thought, looking around the room. She let out a sigh, for knick-knacks abounded on every surface. Why not close up the rooms that were never used and cover the furniture with sheets? Mrs. Gerty never entertained guests, yet she demanded that every room in the house be kept spotless.

"What's the matter? Don't you have enough to do?"

Sarah jumped at the familiar voice. To her right was Mrs. Gerty, her head showing from where she was crouched behind an overstuffed sofa.

"You thought I was still asleep, didn't you? Figured you'd dawdle without Miss Martin around to make sure you do your work!"

"No, ma'am, not at all. I was just—"

Standing and making her way around the sofa, Mrs. Gerty shook a pudgy finger at the girl. "You were just stealing from me, that's what you were doing! I pay good wages in exchange for your services, but you idle about!"

Sarah knew that there was no use arguing. "Yes, ma'am," she whispered, hanging her head.

"You think it was you that was crowned last year instead of Princess Victoria, is that it? Do you want to be Queen of England?" Mrs. Gerty stepped closer, hovering over the girl so that Sarah could feel her sour breath on her forehead. "Does your highness have better things to do than earn your keep?"

"No, ma'am."

"Look at me when I speak to you, you ugly wretch! Do you know that there's a cellar under this room with a big, heavy door?"

Paling, Sarah looked at Mrs. Gerty as commanded. "Yes, ma'am."

"How would you like to spend a few days down there with rats and spiders crawling all over you?"

"Please—"

"Please, what? You filthy little beast!" Mrs. Gerty drew back her teeth in a grin, enjoying Sarah's terror. "I could come down there with a big knife and rip your stomach open. Wouldn't the creatures down there love to gobble your innards!"

Don't faint. It'll be over soon, Sarah told herself, biting her lower lip as she kept her eyes on Mrs. Gerty's.

"No one would ever know." Mrs. Gerty's voice was lower, more sinister. "Perhaps I've done it before to other lazy girls, and do you see me in prison? I'd tell anyone who cared enough to come looking for a nothing like you that you stole money and ran off!

"And there you'd be, beneath their very feet, a pile of chewed-up bones! Do you think the constable would dispute my word? I'd tell him, 'I don't wish to press charges if you find the poor creature. She's suffered enough already.' And I'd look so worried about you—even wipe a tear from my eye!"

Mrs. Gerty brought her face inches from Sarah's. "I might have mercy on you this time—though you surely don't deserve it—and hold back this month's salary. But next time, I may choose something more effective!"

"Yes, ma'am," said Sarah, her forehead beaded with sweat.

"Is that all you can say, you ingrate?"

"I mean, thank you, ma'am."

"Say it like you mean it!"

Sarah stretched her lips into a smile. "Thank you, ma'am."

Mrs. Gerty narrowed her eyes. "Am I going to see you sulking about, or will you manage to look agreeable?"

The smile still frozen on her face, Sarah answered. "I plan to look pleasant, ma'am."

ᶽ▲

Sarah was carrying an armload of folded sheets up the back stairway when Miss Martin called from the foot of the stairs. Turning around, Sarah wondered if she'd done anything wrong.

"Sarah, after you put those in the linen closet, you may visit your guest in the kitchen."

Sarah nearly dropped the sheets she was holding. "Do you mean my mother?"

Miss Martin nodded, her face impassive. "You may take your half-day off today instead of waiting until Thursday."

"Oh, thank you, Miss Martin!" Sarah flew halfway down the steps before she remembered the bundle in her arms. "Oh, the sheets!" she said, tearing back up the staircase.

It only took a few seconds for Sarah to put the sheets away and head for the kitchen. Bursting through the door, she cried out, "Mother!"

Suddenly, those arms she'd longed for were wrapped around her. "I missed you so, my little Sarah," said Ruth.

"Oh, Mother. I thought I would die for wanting to see you!" Sarah said.

After a while, Ruth put her hands on her daughter's shoulders and took a step back. "Mercy, child, I believe you've grown!"

For the first time in almost two years, Sarah got a good look at her mother. Her face was sallow. Wrinkles creased her forehead. A deep cough racked her body with violent heaves.

"Sit here, Miss Ruth," offered Agnes, coming over from the stove and pulling out a chair. "You sound like you're coming down with croup."

"No, it's not that," Ruth said, lowering herself in the chair. "It's my lungs —the cotton mill."

Agnes nodded. "I've heard about such things. It's a shame you couldn't find another position as cook."

"Heard about what things?" asked Sarah, alarmed. "Are you dying?"

"No, of course not," reassured her mother. "I'm just—" Her words were interrupted by another fit of coughing.

When the coughing had eased, Ruth took a sip from the steaming cup of tea Frances put in front of her. "Thank you, child." She smiled tenderly at Frances, and some of her former beauty shone through.

"It's the cotton fibers. They float around us while we work. I've taken to keeping a cloth tied around my mouth and nose, and I expect that'll help a lot—as soon as this cough clears up."

Sarah caught the look that passed over Agnes's face, though the cook quickly smiled and started bustling around. "Mother, I don't want you to work there anymore!" Sarah insisted. "It's been over two years since we left the Nortons'. I know you can find a better position now!"

Ruth shook her head. "Nobody'd hire me. They'd be scared I've got somethin' contagious." She reached for her daughter's hand. "I'm afraid I've had to spend most of my savings at the doctor's. But I'll get better soon and start savin' again. Can you wait a little longer?"

Behind her mother's back, Agnes gave Sarah a meaningful look.

"Yes, Mother. I'll wait."

Beaming, Ruth reached across the table for her hand. "I feel better! I was so worried when I left you here, I could hardly sleep nights for cryin'. It's good to see you've got friends here. You're happy, ain't you?"

"Yes," Sarah lied. "Everyone is kind to me."

Before Sarah knew it, her mother had to leave. "They gave us a whole day off 'cause Mr. Johnson's getting married—he owns the mill. But it'll be dark soon, and I should've started back a while ago. I wanted to be with you as long as I could."

"Alex will drive you back in the wagon," came Miss Martin's voice from the top of the kitchen stairs. "I've decided we need some silver polish from town." Knowing that Alex couldn't possibly find a shop open, Sarah shot Miss Martin a grateful look.

The wagon was out of sight when Sarah stopped waving. She was glad she'd fetched the coins she'd saved and pressed them in her mother's hand— two years' wages.

Four months later, Agnes came up to Sarah's room where the girl was making her bed.

"She's gone, dear child. Pneumonia."

❧

Brush and dustpan in hand, Sarah paused outside the door to the library, checking her apron pocket for matches to light the oil lamps. The carpets in the library were too heavy to carry outside and had to be brushed by hand. Now that she was fifteen, she performed her tasks mechanically, looking forward to when she could retire at night for a few hours of blessed unconsciousness. *I'll never be able to leave,* she thought.

Pushing the door open, Sarah was surprised to see a low light coming from one of the lamps near the settee. She thought Mrs. Gerty had come to scream at her until she realized that the person seated was Miss Martin.

"I'm sorry," Sarah said. "Do you want me to clean the carpets later?"

"No, I'll leave," Miss Martin said, not moving. Her voice was unsteady, and Sarah wondered if the housekeeper had been crying.

"Miss Martin?" she said. "Are you all right?"

"No."

Sarah didn't know what to say. She walked tentatively across the room and stood a few feet away from the woman. "Can I help? You look ill."

Miss Martin smiled bitterly. "Ill? Yes, that's it. Only it's my heart that's ill."

"You're unhappy?" The thought was new to Sarah. She'd assumed that Miss Martin had no emotions. Even after the housekeeper had been so kind that day her mother had visited, she'd remained aloof, speaking to Sarah only when there was a duty to assign.

"Please, come sit with me," said Miss Martin. "I'll help you clean the carpets later so you won't fall behind."

Taking a seat on the settee, Sarah glanced timidly at the woman. Miss Martin's face was splotched, her eyes swollen.

"Sometimes I have a spell of feeling sorry for my state," Miss Martin finally said. "I haven't cried about it for a long time, but this morning I felt overwhelmed." She turned to Sarah. "You must find a way to leave here," she said, her voice suddenly stronger, determined, "or you'll end up like me—bound here for life!"

"I'm saving my wages so's I can go somewhere else and look for work. It's just taking a while."

"You'll never have enough if Mrs. Gerty has anything to do with it! And do you think she'd give you a reference if you told her you were leaving?"

"Is that why you've never left?"

Miss Martin pointed to a painting next to a bookcase. A boy of about seven years stood behind the chair where a girl, perhaps two or three years younger, sat. The boy had his hands on the girl's shoulders, and while their expressions were serious, they both looked healthy.

"My brother and I," said Miss Martin. "We were born in this house."

Sarah's mouth dropped open. "You?"

"As was our father before us. We had servants everywhere and visitors calling. When I was fifteen or so, my mother hired a serving maid my age, a Helen Andrews. She was a quiet girl and pretty—and quite smitten by my brother, James."

Miss Martin looked up at the portrait again. "James had an eye for the ladies, but he seemed to pay the servant girls no mind." Turning back to Sarah, she said, "We were disappointed when James failed at Oxford, but Mother was determined that he should marry well."

"And did he marry?"

"Never. Neither did I, though I was engaged. After my brother returned from college, Mother's maid told her that James had been seen on the servant's stairway late at night and early in the mornings. Mother inquired further and discharged Helen from her position."

Sarah didn't understand where all this was leading, but she nodded anyway.

"Helen didn't take it too well. She cursed my mother, saying that James had promised to marry her. I had never heard such profanity. And the terrible things she threatened to do to our family! James denied any such promise. He went away on holiday that same day with some friends.

"My mother and father had us children in their later years," Miss Martin continued. "They passed away within six months of each other when I was twenty-three. Four years later I was engaged to marry a dashing young man."

Miss Martin smiled and clasped her hands to her sunken chest, looking past Sarah with shining eyes. "I'd always been plain, but he told me I was beautiful! He made plans about what we'd do after we were married, and I was swept off my feet!

"Three months before our wedding, James died in a drunken brawl. Our solicitor went over the family finances and discovered that we were deeply in debt." Miss Martin shook her head. "James had squandered away a fortune."

New tears were forming in Miss Martin's eyes, and Sarah tentatively reached for her hand.

"When I told my husband-to-be the news, he bowed out of the engagement. One year later he married another plain, wealthy girl. Our family solicitor arranged to put our home up for sale, and the man who bought it paid off my debts. I was left penniless. I've always wondered if my attorney had been dishonest, especially after I heard that he had gone into business with the man who bought my house."

A bitter smile came to Miss Martin's lips. "The man's wife kindly suggested I stay here until I found a position at a girls' school. I would be expected to earn my keep as the housekeeper."

Sarah's eyebrows drew together. "I don't understand. Why did you stay as a servant when you could have done something else?"

"I regret it so much, Sarah, but my life had been sheltered. I was always a shy person, and the rejection by my suitor left me more timid than ever and ashamed to face people. I told myself that I would leave when the right position came along."

Suddenly, it dawned on Sarah. "The serving maid that your family fired?"

"Helen Gerty became her married name."

They were both quiet. Sarah broke the silence. "You can still leave, Miss Martin. Haven't you any money saved up after all these years?"

Miss Martin shook her head. "I'm too old. No, I'll die here one day, under that woman's thumb."

❧

Sarah was helping Frances scrub the pantry floor when Miss Martin entered. It had been almost a year since Sarah had had the talk with the housekeeper in the drawing room. She felt affection for her, though the woman was still tight-lipped.

"Madam would like you to wax the dining room floor again. She is having a guest tomorrow. An American woman, I'm told."

Frances's eyebrows shot up. "Somebody came from across the ocean to see the missus?"

"The lady's husband, a Mr. Carlton, is transacting some business with Mr. Gerty. Mrs. Gerty offered to entertain Mrs. Carlton."

A guest! Even though it meant more work, a change from the routine was welcome. Since Ginny was no longer here—she'd married Leslie, the gardener, six months earlier and they'd found positions elsewhere—Sarah would be helping Frances serve the noon meal.

The next day, Miss Martin caught Sarah's arm as she was returning to the dining room with a tray of dessert pies.

"Did you hear what the lady said about wishing for an English maid?" She squeezed Sarah's arm. "This is your chance. You must catch her out front when she leaves!"

"But what if—"

"Do you want to stay here forever?"

Sarah bit her lip. "Mrs. Gerty will be—"

"I'll try to call her attention to something upstairs when the lady leaves the front door. Take the chance, Sarah—and Godspeed!"

Chapter Six
1840

"Now, we're leaving Bristol to go back to the States in two days. Meet us at the dock, and I'm sure we'll have your passage ready. Should I send a carriage for you?"

"Could I come with you now?" asked Sarah, fearful that Mrs. Carlton would change her mind if pressed too hard, but more afraid of facing Mrs. Gerty.

Mrs. Carlton studied Sarah's face for a few seconds. "How old are you, dear?"

"Sixteen, ma'am."

"Are things so bad here?"

"Yes'm," Sarah cried, embarrassed by the tears that gathered in her eyes. "I can't go back, not now!"

"Well, climb on in then!" Mrs. Carlton said.

❧

"You mean, you were born and raised in Bristol, and you've never seen a ship?" Amos Carlton laughed at the expression on Sarah's face when Bristol Harbor came into view. "Do they look like you imagined?"

Reverently, Sarah shook her head. "I seen pictures hangin' on the walls at the house, but I didn't know they was this big!"

She sat up straight in the open carriage so she could take in as much as possible. A few yards beyond the stone quay was blue-green water, speckled with whitecaps. White sails flickered in the sunlight as coastal schooners and brigs picked their way through the channel leading to the Severn estuary.

"There's our ship," said Mr. Carlton, pointing to the *Eastern Star*.

Nearly six-hundred feet long, the ship had four smoking chimneys and a thirty-foot-high wall of black iron punched through by portholes. Six masts, tall as trees, rose from her decks, with enough canvas to bed a small town.

Most captivating to Sarah's eyes was the bow, where a carved woman with the body of a fish held both arms out as if to embrace the sea. On each side of the woman were dolphins, their bodies painted so that they looked cast in bronze.

As their carriage came closer to the dock, even Mr. Carlton let out a low whistle. "Well, she's the finest ship I've ever set eyes upon! They say we'll be back in the States in about three weeks if the weather cooperates." He shook his gray head. "Steam engines! When my present contracts expire, I want to ship all the company's merchandise this way. Just think of—"

"When your contracts expire?" Mrs. Carlton, seated next to her husband, looked puzzled. "Haven't you made an agreement with Mr. Gerty about your next shipping arrangements?"

Mr. Carlton cleared his throat. "I didn't sign with Gerty, though his pricing was quite competitive. I meant to tell you yesterday, but when you came back to the hotel with the little lady here, it slipped my mind."

"Slipped your mind! We came all the way across the Atlantic—"

"Now, Mary," he said, "I could have sent Wesley to handle this, but you said you wanted to see Europe before you got too old to travel. Seems to me we got our money's worth out of this trip."

"Yes, it's been enjoyable." Mrs. Carlton tilted her head in Sarah's direction. "Even interesting. But why did you change your plans?"

"Something told me not to trust the man. He and his lawyer seemed too pushy, and when I looked over the contracts, I found some changes—"

"You don't have to explain," said his wife, reaching over and patting his hand. "You've built a successful business by trusting your instincts, and I'm not going to question them now."

Mr. Carlton grinned, the laugh lines deep at the corners of his eyes. "I guess not after your instincts told you to kidnap that lady's maid!"

"My dear, it wasn't kidnapping, and that was no lady!"

At the pier, the three joined a dozen or so other people on board a harbor-taxi to be ferried out to the *Eastern Star*.

After the stewards carried the trunks to their stateroom, Sarah helped Mrs. Carlton unpack while Mr. Carlton went up on deck. Mrs. Carlton looked through the small doorway leading to Sarah's tiny berth. "It's rather small," she said, "but it's only for three weeks."

"Oh, ma'am," Sarah exclaimed, "it's only a little tinier than my room in the attic. I can't thank you enough for taking me on!"

"You're welcome. I'm sure you'll perform your duties diligently." The older woman closed her eyes. "It may be that your first duties will be quite unpleasant. I became horribly seasick on our trip over. Amos has assured me that the ship's great speed will lessen the pitching and tossing, but I'm afraid I'm feeling queasy even now."

Sarah hadn't noticed before, but the floor was moving, a subtle, rocking motion, even though the ship was in dock.

"Perhaps you should lie down a bit, ma'am," said Sarah. When Mrs. Carlton nodded, her eyes still closed, Sarah pulled down the covers and guided her by the elbow over to the bed.

"I ain't ever taken care of anyone with the seasickness," she said softly as she tucked the comforter around the lady. "Is there anything else I should do?"

"Yes," groaned Mrs. Carlton. "Pull that rope next to you and call for a steward. Ask for some arrowroot. And a bucket."

One week into the journey, Mrs. Carlton hadn't been able to leave her bed save for short walks on deck propped between her husband and Sarah. "The fresh air will do you good," her husband would tell her, coaxing her out of bed.

After four days, Mrs. Carlton flatly refused to try. "The effort is too great, and it doesn't make me feel better," she said weakly. "I was hoping this trip would be easier than the one over. I wish we'd stayed home!"

It's so beautiful, the ocean, thought Sarah, taking an appreciative whiff of salt breeze as she carried a bucket out on deck. She felt so sorry for Mrs. Carlton, who was unable to appreciate the deep blue of the water or the hazy, fine-spun clouds that pillowed the sky.

Pinching a piece from the soft bread roll in her pocket, Sarah put it in her mouth and chewed. Mr. Carlton had advised her to keep something in her stomach at all times. So far she'd been able to keep the bread down, though the slight nausea was constant.

She was emptying the contents of the bucket over the railing when the skin on the inside of her thumb got pinched between the bucket and the wire handle.

"Ouch!" she cried out, jerking her hand away. In an instant, the pail flew out of her reach. She leaned over the rail, trying to catch the lost bucket.

"Hey, that's not a wise thing to do!" Sarah felt a hand on her arm. A sandy-haired young man, only an inch or so taller than her, was at her right. "You don't want to drown because of a bucket!" he said in an American accent.

"I wasn't thinking," said Sarah, straightening. She gave the man an embarrassed smile. "Thank you for your concern."

"Of course," he said. When he returned her smile, his eyes lit up, making his rather plain features almost handsome. "I'd hate to have you fall overboard right in front of me—especially when I can't swim. Would you like another bucket?"

"Oh dear," said Sarah, glancing toward the water where the bucket had disappeared. "I can't take yours."

"Please." Pulling the top bucket from a stack under his arm, he handed it to her. "This ship was prepared to hold two hundred people, but only eighty or so are on board, so there're plenty of supplies." Looking up at the funnels at the stern, he shook his head. "People don't quite trust the steamers yet, but they're the wave of the future."

"Do you work on the ship?"

He flashed a boyish grin. "I just like ships. Actually, some families down in steerage are seasick, and there's no one to care for them. I'm helping out."

Bidding her good day, he turned and headed for a passageway. Before he reached the door, he turned around.

"What's your name?" he called out.

"It's Sarah."

"Sarah," he repeated as he disappeared through the doorway. Sarah hurried back to the Carltons' room.

"I'm sorry I took so long, but I lost—"

Mr. Carlton put his finger to his lips. "She hasn't needed it," he whispered. "She fell asleep soon after you left." He reached over and, with thumb and forefinger, moved a tendril of gray hair from his wife's cheek.

"I'll watch her now if you'd like to get some air," Sarah said softly, touched by his devotion.

"No, I'm a bit tired. I think I'll have a rest myself. Why don't you go explore the ship? You've spent most of your time here with Mary."

"Are you sure?"

He nodded, waving her away.

A steward in a blue coat was in the passageway, carrying an armload of towels.

"Excuse me," Sarah said. "Where might I find steerage?"

She followed the steward's directions. Several feet from the portal leading to the steerage hold, Sarah noticed a foul odor getting stronger as she drew closer. Tending to Mrs. Carlton had required some unpleasantness no matter how clean she kept the lady, but Sarah was unprepared for the human suffering she beheld as she stepped through the door.

Bolted to the walls were about thirty canvas bunks, double-stacked. More than half of these were inhabited by men, women, or children, either asleep or softly moaning. Vomit dried on blankets and pillowcases, and the contents of an overturned bucket seeped under a bunk. A middle-aged woman went from bed to bed, wiping faces and giving sips of water. Rinsing out a mop in a pail was the young man who'd spoken to Sarah on deck.

Sarah covered her mouth with her hand, afraid she would add to the filth surrounding her. She was about to flee when the young man looked up at her and spoke.

"Well, hello, Miss Sarah. Are you lost?"

She shook her head slowly, taking shallow breaths. "I wanted to see what steerage was like. Those poor folks. It's dreadful down here!" After a pause, she added, "Is there anything I can do?"

"Can you stand the smell?"

"I think so."

The woman tending the people in the bunks looked over and gave Sarah a weary smile. "You should use your apron to tie up your dress a bit and keep it off the floor," she said, her voice a thick brogue. "And roll up your sleeves as well."

Hesitant to show her ankles, Sarah looked at the young man. With a grin, he turned his back and continued mopping. Sarah reached behind her back for her apron strings and hitched her dress up a couple inches.

"My whole family's taken with seasickness," said the woman, wiping the cheeks of a small boy. "And these two families—every one of them is sick. The ones that are well took their mats to the quarterdeck to get away from the smell."

"How long has it been since you've slept?" asked Sarah.

"Oh, I get bits and pieces here and there," said the woman. "Mr. David has been a blessin'. I don't know what we'd do—" She wiped the corner of her eye. "Excuse me. It's been a hard trip."

Sarah touched the woman's arm. "I can stay a little while. Why don't you take a nap?"

"Oh, I couldn't," protested the woman.

"Please let me help while I can," insisted Sarah, taking the bowl of wet cloths from the woman's hands.

After a few minutes, the woman's deep breathing could be heard from her bunk. "That was kind of you," said David, his mopping finished.

Sarah looked at the woman's tired face. *She's these children's mother,* Sarah thought. *I wish more people had been kind to my mother.*

❧

I shouldn't be so happy to see her, David Adams thought when Sarah walked into the steerage compartment. It had been two days since the last time she'd helped out, and he'd found himself looking at the door every time someone walked in.

"I'm sorry I haven't been 'round lately," Sarah said. "Mrs. Carlton, my employer, is getting so weak that I'm afraid to leave her for long."

"Everything's in decent order now," David told her. "Why don't we sit on deck a while? I've been down here all day. Do you have time?"

"But I came to help."

The woman Sarah had helped before looked up from where she rested on her bunk. "Go on, children. Everyone's sleepin' now."

Outside the steerage compartment, David turned to Sarah. "Would you mind finding us a couple chairs while I change clothes?"

She smiled, and his weariness left him. "I'll try," she said.

Fairly racing down the passageway from his room, David came out on deck to find Sarah standing at the rail, the April trade winds moving her long hair about her shoulders. *Beautiful*, he thought, coming to an abrupt halt. He stared at her with his mouth agape until she sensed his presence and turned around.

"Oh," she said, her cheeks flushing. "I was admiring the water. I didn't expect you back so soon." She pointed to some deck chairs. "Will these be all right?"

"Of course," David said as they walked over to the chairs. "How long can you stay?"

"Not more than an hour," Sarah replied. "Mr. and Mrs. Carlton are resting, but I'll need to check on Mrs. Carlton."

"Are you her nurse?"

"Maid," she said quietly. "Where do you work?"

"My employer, Jacob Harvey, sent me to England to transact some business. I'm an accounting clerk with his investing firm in Charleston."

"What does one of those do?"

"One of—oh, you mean clerk. I keep books—ledgers of business transactions, prices and such—but I have other duties as well." *Like becoming engaged to Mr. Harvey's daughter*, he thought.

Taken by shyness, the girl studied her hands. David willed himself not to stare at her face. *She's apparently not well educated*, he thought, *but she has an intelligent face.* Her greatest charm was that she didn't seem to realize how intelligent and beautiful she was.

"May I ask you something?" he finally asked, aware that she would have to leave soon.

"Yes."

"The Carltons. Do they treat you well?"

She smiled. "Of course. Why do you ask?"

After a moment's hesitation, he went on. "There's a sadness about you."

A shadow crossed her face.

"I'm sorry," he said. "I'm prying. Please forgive me."

"Don't be sorry," she said. "You care about people, don't you?"

"I try to."

"You've spent most of your trip helpin' those people, yet you didn't have to. Why?"

"Please don't think more highly of me than you should," David said. "I've had to force myself to go through that steerage door every time."

"But you went."

"I put myself in their place. When Christ said, 'Do unto others as you would have them do unto you,' He had people like them in mind."

"You're a Christian, then?"

"Yes," he answered, confused by the disappointment in her eyes. "Why do you look as though that's a bad thing?"

Sarah looked at him, her brown eyes serious. "The Nortons—a family I worked for once—said we servants should all be Christians, so Mr. Norton lined us up every Sunday mornin' and read Scripture to us. I didn't understand most of it or why he always appeared so angry at us as he read. Yet you are a Christian, and you are kind."

David had her hand in his before he realized he'd reached for it. "Sarah," he said earnestly. "I've met people who claimed to be Christians but didn't have an ounce of love in their hearts. To really become a Christian is to—"

"Excuse me, but are you Miss Brown?" A steward, clad in a red coat and black trousers, stood in front of them.

Sarah sat up, panic on her face. "Yes. Is something wrong with Mrs. Carlton?"

"I don't know, miss," said the steward. "But Mr. Carlton has requested that I find you."

She's gotten worse, and I was away, thought Sarah as she hurried to the Carltons' stateroom. Knocking softly, she pushed the door open. "I'm sorry I wasn't here," she said. "Has she gotten worse?"

"I didn't mean to frighten you," Mr. Carlton answered. "Mary would like to take a walk, and I need you to help me dress her."

"A walk?"

"Yes, dear." Opening her eyes, Mrs. Carlton smiled weakly from her pillow. "I feel a little better and would like to see something other than this closet of a room."

Mr. Carlton laughed. "I know what it is. You can smell land, Mary. The captain says we're only two days from shore."

"Two days." Mrs. Carlton sighed. "And I'm still alive, after all!"

⁂

"There it is—the United States!" said Mr. Carlton, pointing to a faint mass on the horizon. A cheer went up from the passengers, most of whom were lined against the port deck railing to catch the first sight of land.

My new life, Sarah thought. Her heart was filled with gratitude for her new employers and for what Miss Martin had done for her.

"Are you excited, child?" asked Mrs. Carlton from the deck chair her husband had pulled up to the rail.

"Yes, ma'am! I can't hardly take it all in!" On impulse, Sarah knelt and kissed Mrs. Carlton's hand. "Thank you so much!"

"There, there girl," said the older woman. "You certainly made the return trip easier for Amos and me. We should be thanking you."

Blushing, Sarah rose to her feet. "I'll run down to our rooms and make sure we're packed up proper."

She was just outside the portal when she heard her name called. To her right was David, walking quickly in her direction. He was wearing a light gray coat and white drill trousers.

"David!" Sarah said, brightening. "I was afraid I wouldn't get to tell you goodbye."

David held out a package wrapped in brown paper. "I wanted to give you something." When Sarah held up a hand in protest, he pressed on. "It's a notebook I've been keeping for about a year. When I find a verse from the Bible that touches me, I write it down. I'd like you to have it."

Sarah was about to tell him that she couldn't read, when she realized that she would be ashamed for him to know that. Instead she said, "But you've spent a year writing in it, and now you're givin' it away?"

"I can start a new one. Please?"

"Thank you, David." Sarah turned the package over in her hand. "No one's ever given me a gift before."

"I've written the address of where I work in the inside cover. If you ever need help, you'll know where to find me."

A great lump formed in Sarah's throat. "Goodbye, David," she said, forcing a smile before going through the portal.

Chapter Seven
1840-1841

"Really, Mary. How could you think of entertaining the Grimke sisters! You've had strange ideas before, but to have traitors in your own house!" Dorothy Bowman stirred her tea with vigor, the metal spoon clicking angrily against the sides of the cup. "Anyway, they've got no business coming back to visit. Let them stay up North where they belong!"

Mrs. Carlton took a sip from her cup. "There's no harm in listening. Besides, you know how I feel about slavery."

A frown creasing her attractive face, Mrs. Bowman shook her head. "People who haven't got Negroes should mind their own business. They eat rice, I'm sure. How are we supposed to operate a rice plantation without workers? I suppose those Grimkes asked you for money to print those awful little papers!"

"No, they didn't ask."

"But you gave them some, didn't you? Does Amos know you're throwing his money away like that?"

Sarah was standing just outside the parlor door with a silver tray of spiced cakes when Hannah, the cook, came up behind her. "Sarah, why haven't you taken the tray in yet?" she whispered.

"They're having a disagreement," Sarah whispered back. "I thought I should wait 'til they're finished."

"Finished? You wait for that, and you'll have cobwebs hanging from your earlobes. They're first cousins and talk that way all the time. Now, shoo!"

"Shoe?" Sarah looked down at her feet where the toes of her brown morocco slippers peeked from under her skirt. "I've got them on."

Hannah sighed. "You Brits should learn to speak English. Take the tray in!" she said, giving Sarah a gentle push through the door.

Obediently, Sarah took the tray to a mahogany concertina table between the two women. "Fig cake, ma'am?" she asked Mrs. Carlton's visitor.

"Yes, I'll have one," said Mrs. Bowman, taking the flowered porcelain dish that Sarah handed her. "Mary, I suppose this is the maid you hired in England?"

Mrs. Carlton smiled from her Chippendale armchair. "In Bristol, right before we left." She gave Sarah a wink as she took a dish of cake from her hand. "Sarah has been a hard worker these three months."

Tapping at the front door sounded. The Carltons had no butler, so usually the servant who was closest to the front of the house answered it.

"I'll get that, ma'am," said Sarah, setting the cover to the butter dish on the tray. Mrs. Carlton's generous words sounded again in her mind as she made her way to the entrance hall. How different it was to be complimented for doing her best. Each word of praise from the Carltons made her work even harder.

Before pulling open the door, Sarah smoothed the gathers in her blue poplin dress, enjoying the crispness of the starched fabric. Mrs. Carlton didn't require her maids to wear caps, so Sarah kept her hair coiled loosely at the nape of her neck with a tortoiseshell comb she'd bought. It was nice to earn a salary decent enough to buy pretty things for herself.

"Good afternoon, sir," she said to the man on the front porch. About thirty years old, his tanned face was ruggedly handsome. Coal-black hair showed from beneath his hat. Brushing past her without a word, the man strode down the hall toward the parlor.

"Sir?" Sarah said, taking quick steps behind him.

"Ah, Mother," the man said, removing his hat as he entered the parlor. "My business in town is finished. Are you ready to leave?"

"Well, I suppose."

He bent down to put a kiss on Mrs. Carlton's cheek. "Mary, it's a pleasure to see you, as always. Is your health good?"

"It is, Jonathan. Will you stay and have some cake?"

"I'm afraid not," he said. "I've got some things to attend to before dark. Give my regards to Amos."

"He'll be disappointed that he missed you," said Mrs. Carlton.

"Yes, I can imagine." The man offered his arm to his mother and escorted her out of the house.

✿

Hannah shopped for groceries every Tuesday and Saturday at the outdoor market near the fishing wharf. When Florence and Adele, the other maids, found out how eager Sarah was to accompany her, they gladly gave that responsibility to the English girl. They didn't enjoy carrying heavily loaded baskets in the July humidity.

Sarah wished the walk could be longer, for she was charmed by the beauty of Charleston. Middle Street was her favorite, lined with stuccoed houses whose hipped roofs were covered with pink or purple tiles. Wrought-iron garden gates, stair railings, and balconies abounded.

At the market while Hannah went from vendor to vendor, squeezing peaches, tapping melons, and smelling fish, Sarah was allowed to walk onto the Cooper River wharf. The salt air was invigorating, and she enjoyed watching the men laying traps for crabs. When the nets were pulled up, there were usually at least two or three blue crabs clinging to the bait. Turned inside out, the nets were then shaken roughly until the crabs gave up and dropped into a wooden half-barrel.

Almost as fascinating as the crabs were the gulls, screeching to each other overhead and sometimes trying to steal bait fish. Mingled with their cries was the slap of the water against barnacle-studded posts.

It was near this place, soon after she'd set ashore with the Carltons, that Sarah had first seen black people. Fascinated as she was by the darkness of their skin and hair, she tried not to stare at them. Staring was rude—Mother had taught her that long ago.

Sarah had been surprised to see several black people walking the streets without any chains. When she'd asked Hannah about it, the cook had explained that Negroes were allowed to run errands for their owners and to "hire out" on their own time. They weren't allowed on the streets of Charleston, however, between the night and morning drum beats unless they carried a pass from their owners.

"I think I'll make a peach cobbler for dessert tonight," Hannah was saying as they walked along the brick sidewalk leading from the market area, their arms loaded with purchases. "Mr. Carlton has a sweet tooth for cobbler."

"A sweet tooth," Sarah echoed, smiling.

"I suppose you never heard that one, either," said Hannah. "Well, he does."

"Have you been with them very long?"

"Years and years. I'd say fifteen. They're good folks to work for." Giving her a sideways glance, Hannah added, "They sure don't deserve the way Elizabeth treats them."

"Their daughter?"

Hannah's lips tightened. "You can call her that, but she doesn't act like a daughter should. Her portrait is hanging in the living room next to the fireplace."

"Doesn't she ever visit?" asked Sarah, who didn't recall seeing anyone come to call who resembled the lady in the portrait.

"Not for five years or so. It breaks their hearts to have an only child who's that spoiled and ungrateful."

Looking over her shoulder to make sure no one was walking behind them, Hannah continued. "Elizabeth got married eight years ago to a sorry, no-count of a man, Gerald Mobley. You should have seen the wedding. I baked the cake myself! Soon after they were married, Elizabeth asked Mr. Carlton to find her husband a position in his company."

A handsomely dressed young couple strolled by, and Sarah dropped back behind Hannah to make way for them on the sidewalk. When the couple had passed and was no longer in hearing range, Sarah stepped back in place next to Hannah.

"Elizabeth intended for Gerald to have an important position helping run the company. Mr. Carlton wasn't willing to demote Matthew Wesley, his assistant, who's been with him from the beginning. He offered Gerald a much lower position, saying he'd have to prove himself before getting more responsibilities.

"Elizabeth pouted and fumed but Mr. Carlton wouldn't change his mind, so Gerald took the job. Folks at the company began telling Mr. Carlton that Gerald was coming in late and sometimes didn't come in at all. When he did come to work, he told the other employees what to do, threatening to get them fired if they didn't cooperate."

Hannah shook her head. "After warning him time and time again, Mr. Carlton had to let Gerald go."

Hannah and Sarah turned the corner onto palmetto-lined Dabney Street, where the Carltons' two-story brick house could be seen in the distance.

"Is that why they don't come to see the mister and missus?" asked Sarah.

The cook nodded. "After her husband was fired, Elizabeth came to the house in a screaming fit. Mr. Carlton wouldn't back down. He told her that he'd made Mr. Wesley a full partner, so if anything happened to him, Elizabeth and her husband couldn't get their hands on the business and ruin it. Elizabeth told her parents that she wouldn't set foot inside their house again. It broke their hearts, the dear old souls!"

Sarah's heart went out to the Carltons, who'd been so good to her. "It just ain't—I mean, isn't—right," she said to Hannah. "Here I am, still missing my mother, and she doesn't even visit hers!" The conversation ended as they entered the kitchen with their purchases.

☙

"Tippecanoe!" Mr. Carlton snorted. "Mute as a mule is what he is! Why, I'll bet he hasn't a thought in his head that wasn't put there by his cronies!"

"Now, Amos," scolded his wife as she tied his wool scarf around his neck. "You're just trying to get out of going to Washington, and it won't work! I've never seen a presidential inauguration, and you gave me your word."

"You've never ridden a buffalo, either. I suppose the next thing you'll be wanting is to go out West."

"Who knows?" Standing on tiptoe, Mrs. Carlton kissed her husband's cheek. "Besides, you said yourself how good it'd be to see the Powells again. We'll have two weeks to catch up on old times!"

Sarah smiled in the next room as she fastened the catch on Mrs. Carlton's trunk. After almost a year of living with the couple, she was used to their affectionate bantering. *If I ever get married, I hope my husband is as good-natured as Mr. Carlton.* Suddenly, David came to her mind. *Does he think about me at all?* she wondered. He probably had more important things to occupy his thoughts. After all, she was just a servant.

Catching a peek at herself in Mrs. Carlton's mirror, Sarah tucked a stray wisp of chestnut-brown hair back into her comb. *Did he think I was pretty?* She'd looked wretched during the voyage, pale and thin after her years in Mrs. Gerty's employ. A year's time had made her figure more womanly, and her cheeks now glowed with health.

"Sarah, did you pack my blue wool shawl?" Mrs. Carlton was standing in the doorway to her room, her eyes on the trunk in the middle of the floor.

"No, ma'am," Sarah replied. "Remember, you told me I should put it in your canvas bag for the coach?"

Mrs. Carlton looked pleased. "What a sharp memory you have! Amos tells me that my cape will suffice, but I don't trust these March winds. They can still bring a bite to the cheeks."

"I hope the weather will hold for you and that you both have a wonderful time," Sarah added impulsively.

Stepping closer, Mrs. Carlton gave her a quick hug. "I think we shall."

Later that day, Sarah and Florence waved to the Carltons as the hired carriage pulled away from the house. They would be catching a coach to take them to Washington, D.C., for the festivities. The day after the inauguration of William H. Harrison, they would take a train on to Baltimore. Adele would spend the next three weeks in the country with her family, and Hannah would be staying with her sister in Charleston.

"We won't know what to do with ourselves!" Florence said after the carriage returned out of sight. "As long as we keep the house clean, Mrs. Carlton said we can do what we like.

"Don't forget we promised Mrs. Carlton we'd go to church every Sunday." The Carltons insisted that their servants attend worship services on the Lord's day. Hannah, who was Episcopalian, was always picked up in a carriage by some of her friends on their way to St. Philip's Church, while Adele, Florence, and Sarah rode with the Carltons to the Cathedral of Saint John and Saint Finbar on Broad Street.

Though she couldn't understand the language that was spoken during the service, Sarah knew it was about God. She'd questioned Mrs. Carlton about it, and the kindly lady had tried to explain God's love. That was harder to understand than the Latin, for Sarah certainly didn't feel lovable.

"Keep your heart open, Sarah. God will draw you to Him if you listen for Him," Mrs. Carlton had finally said.

❧

David Adams was so intent on the papers before him that he did not hear the murmurs of greeting until Kathleen Harvey was standing in front of his desk.

"Goodness, David," said the comely young woman. "How your face scowls when you work!"

"Kathleen," said David, rising to his feet. "I apologize. I didn't know you were there."

She tugged at the wrist of one of her pale blue velvet gloves. "You haven't come by the house in almost a week, so I thought I should remind myself of what my fiancé looks like."

"I imagine I haven't changed that much." Startled by the sharpness of his voice, David smiled at her. "You look lovely. Another new dress?"

Kathleen glanced down at the ecru muslin, with its shell buttons and blue silk underbodice. "Mother says I shall need at least a half-dozen more. You and I will be entertaining quite often, and people will want us to call on them as well."

"If it isn't my beautiful little girl!" A voice boomed out behind David. "And you came to visit your father at work. How flattering!"

"Oh, Papa!" With a giggle, Kathleen flounced around the desk and kissed the portly man on his cheek. "I can see you at home every day!"

Mr. Harvey feigned disappointment, shaking his head. "How soon they grow up!"

Giggling again, Kathleen covered her mouth with her hand. "You know why I'm here. I told you I was going to have David take me to lunch today!"

"Oh, yes. Now I remember." Turning to David, he put his hand on the young man's shoulder. "Take as long as you like, and here." Reaching into his pocket, he brought out a handful of bills and began to count some out.

"Mr. Harvey, I can't accept—" began David, mortified that the other employees in the office were watching them.

"Oh, don't be silly," said Kathleen, plucking the money from her father's hand. Adjusting the bow at the front of her Dunstable bonnet, she held out her arm. "Well, David?"

&

"Do you think we'll recognize Addison and Martha?" Amos Carlton stretched his legs as far as possible without hitting the man seated opposite him. The thirty-foot rear passenger car of the District of Columbia Railroad line was filled with people returning to Baltimore from the inauguration ceremony, and Amos, tired of people-watching, was in the mood to chat. "I suspect they look rather old after all these years."

Mary Carlton looked up from the book she was reading and smiled at her husband. "They may be wondering the same thing about us."

"Us? Why we look like schoolchildren next to our new president!"

"Amos, please don't talk about him so loudly. There may be someone around who voted for him," whispered Mary.

"Well, excuse me for being a bad sport about it, but I still don't see why Clay was passed over."

"You wouldn't have voted for him, either."

"True, but he would have had the integrity to run a real—"

Mary Carlton put her hand to her husband's lips. "Listen! Do you hear yelling?"

"Probably someone else who doesn't like the way Harrison—" He stopped suddenly, his head cocked. Over the drone of the wheels, he could hear frenzied voices from the front of the car shouting, "Axle's about to break! Stop the engine!"

&

"I believe I'll buy that pink gingham nightgown after all!" Florence came to an abrupt halt at the middle of Church Street, jerking Sarah's arm. "My aunt would love it for her birthday, and I still have time to send it to her."

"Are you sure this time?" asked Sarah, who'd been inside the corner apparel shop with her friend twice before that day.

"Very."

Sarah looked at Florence with affection. They'd had so much fun the past week, racing through their chores and taking long walks in Charleston. Sarah had told Florence about the time she'd spent on the ship with David, though she hadn't said anything about the notebook. That was her secret, and one day she'd learn how to read it.

"Do you want to see the statue before we go home?" asked Florence, once she'd finished her shopping. Tucking the parcel under her right arm, she linked her left arm through Sarah's. "It's at Washington Park, just one street over from where we are now."

"Who is he, and what happened to his arm?" asked Sarah when the bronze statue of a man in a flowing robe came into view.

"A Mr. William Pitt, from your neck of the woods."

"My neck of the woods?"

"Sorry. He was from England, like you. His arm, or rather the statue's arm, was lost when Charleston was fired at from the British in the war, so Mr. Carlton says."

Sarah was about to ask what the Englishman had done to endear himself to Americans, when she caught sight of a familiar face. There, some distance from them, was David! At his side with her hand in his was a lady, a fashionably dressed, attractive lady who motioned animatedly with her free hand as she talked.

"Let's go home," Sarah said to Florence, her cheeks burning as she turned away from the couple and headed in the opposite direction.

"But it's this way," said Florence.

Sarah didn't look to see in which direction her friend was pointing. "Please come with me. We can go that way later."

Hastening her steps, Florence caught up with Sarah. "What's wrong?" she said, panting slightly from the exertion.

"David."

"David? Where?"

"Don't look!" Sarah grabbed the girl's arm to keep her from spinning around. "They'll see us!"

"They?"

"He has someone with him."

ぶ

I was foolish to think about him so often! Sarah thought, propping herself up on her pillow. She'd gone to bed hours earlier, but thoughts of David drove sleep away.

The agony she'd felt all evening was unreasonable, she told herself. He'd been kind to her—just as he'd been kind to that woman in steerage—because he was a decent person. Nothing more.

Trying to fill her thoughts with other things didn't work. When sleep finally came, it was full of disjointed, hurried bits of dreams.

Sarah was frantically trying to scrub an oil stain from the carpet in Mrs. Gerty's library. To her horror, she'd poured the fluid out while cleaning a lamp-chimney, and the puddle grew larger, even as she sopped it up with rags. Somewhere in the house she could hear Mr. and Mrs. Gerty talking, their voices low and menacing. She tried to call out to Ginny to ask for help with cleaning the rug, but her tongue was frozen and her mouth wouldn't form the words.

Sarah awakened, her eyes opening to sunlight slanting in from where the curtains met at her window. Confused, she could still hear the voices she'd heard in the dream. Then she realized that Florence was speaking with someone—a man—downstairs. Slipping out of bed, Sarah pulled her flannel robe over her nightgown and tied the sash. She was reaching for the comb on her dresser when she heard Florence cry out, "No! It can't be so!"

Sarah dashed from the room and down the stairs. In the front hall, a man was standing near the chair where Florence sat hunched over, her shoulders shaking. He looked up as Sarah descended the last steps.

"Mr. Wesley?" It had taken a moment for her to recognize Mr. Carlton's assistant, for his face was pale and drawn.

"I've brought bad news," he said. "Mr. and Mrs. Carlton were killed in a train wreck yesterday on their way to Baltimore."

Grabbing the banister rail, Sarah swallowed hard. "No!" The figure in front of her became blurred, but she could see that he was slowly nodding his head. "Oh, Mr. Wesley, how did it happen?"

"Believe me, it's best that you don't know all the details. I wish I didn't." He rubbed his forehead. "At least they didn't suffer. It was quick."

After Sarah had brewed some strong tea and persuaded Florence and Mr. Wesley to have some, they sat at the kitchen table.

"Do you have the addresses where Hannah and Adele are staying?" asked

Mr. Wesley. "I'd rather send word to them than have them read about it in the newspaper."

"Yes," said Florence. "In the cupboard drawer. I'll get them for you."

Taking the piece of paper from the maid, Mr. Wesley looked at the two maids.

"There is something else you should know," he said. "I broke the news to Elizabeth—the Mobleys—before I came here. I don't know what her plans will be where all of you are concerned."

❧

The next few days were busy. From the moment the coffins were delivered to the parlor until the funeral and burial at the Cathedral of Saint John and Saint Finbar, people came by to pay their respects. Having food prepared for the mourners was a constant duty, so Sarah, Adele, and Florence helped Hannah in the kitchen, speaking to each other in hushed tones.

After the burial, Elizabeth Mobley called the servants together in the living room. Sarah had been prepared to dislike the Carltons' ungrateful daughter, but she felt sorry for her. Elizabeth had sobbed throughout the funeral service, even trying to throw herself at the coffins as they were lowered into the ground.

"Humbug!" was what Hannah had whispered at the woman's emotional display, but it had brought fresh tears to Sarah's eyes.

"I want to thank you for serving my father and mother well," Elizabeth began, sitting on the sofa in front of them. "Unfortunately, I have no need of maintaining two houses, so I'm making arrangements to sell this one. You'll receive excellent references, but as of tomorrow morning, your services will no longer be required."

"Miss Elizabeth, I cooked for you when you were just a girl," protested Hannah. "You should have given us notice earlier so we could look for jobs. It isn't right to turn us out into the street!"

The woman sighed. "You can hardly blame me if my thoughts haven't been in order. I've barely slept these last four nights. Besides, you all have families, I'm sure, who can put you up until you find other employment."

"What about Sarah?" asked Florence. "She hasn't got any family."

"Then she's fortunate, isn't she?" sniffed Elizabeth. "She doesn't have relatives to turn their backs on her!"

"Can't you at least let her stay until she finds another job?" pressed

Hannah. "She's too young to be on her own."

"Oh, all right!" answered Elizabeth, shrugging her shoulders. "I have a couple coming to look at the house Friday. It would be better to keep it aired out and the furniture dusted. You may stay here until Thursday afternoon if you'll do those chores." She narrowed her eyes at Sarah. "You must be out by Thursday afternoon, do you understand? And if I discover anything missing, I'll alert the sheriff at once."

Chapter Eight
1841

The *Charleston Courier* contained advertisements placed by homeowners looking for servants, Hannah had told Sarah before she'd left. After a sleepless night, Sarah decided she would walk to the stone building that housed the Charleston Library Society and ask the librarian to read the newspaper advertisements to her.

Stepping to the mirror above her dresser, Sarah peered at the dark circles under her eyes. *No one will want to hire me. I look beastly from tossing and turning all night,* she thought, frowning at her reflection. At least the green linen dress she was wearing brought out the rich hues in her chestnut hair. *I'll need to trim it soon,* she thought as she reached for her comb. It was down to her waist, and when she coiled it into a bun, it pulled heavily against the back of her head.

Mrs. Carlton's gray hair had been even longer than Sarah's, though not nearly as thick. Adele and Sarah had combed Mrs. Carlton's hair every night and braided it in the mornings, for the woman's slight rheumatism prevented her from doing it herself.

The thought of Mrs. Carlton made Sarah's eyes burn. *You mustn't cry now,* she scolded herself. *It won't bring them back, and you've got to look presentable to find work.*

An abrupt silence made her realize someone had been knocking at the front door. *Oh dear, it's Mrs. Mobley. She'll kick me out for ignorin' her,* Sarah thought, dropping her comb to the floor.

Halfway down the stairs she realized she was still in her stocking feet, but it was too late to go back for shoes. Hastening through the hallway, she threw open the front door.

Elizabeth Mobley was nowhere in sight, but a man was walking toward a carriage parked in the street. At the sound of the door, the man turned around.

"Mr. Bowman," said Sarah. She'd only seen Jonathan Bowman twice before: the day that his mother had come to call and at the Carltons' funeral. Neither time had he spoken to Sarah, so she was startled when he removed his hat and took a step toward her.

"So, Elizabeth has a heart after all. I didn't expect anyone to be here.

Rumor is that she's kicked out the servants." His tanned face crinkled when he smiled, and his blue eyes shone under a fringe of dark eyelashes.

"She very kindly said I could stay till Thursday while I look for another situation."

"Oh, she's the soul of kindness. A saint." He started walking toward the door. "Anyway, I'm glad someone was here. There's something I have to get."

He was only a few feet away when Sarah gathered up the nerve to protest. "I'm sorry, sir, but you mustn't take anything from the house."

"I mustn't?" he said, his faint drawl vanishing as he clipped his words to imitate her accent. He sidestepped her and entered the house.

"Mr. Bowman, you must leave this house at once," Sarah said, trying to keep her voice steady as she trailed him through the hall and up the stairs.

Ignoring her, he stepped onto the second-floor landing and made his way to the closed door of the Carltons' bedroom. His hand was on the knob when he turned back to look at her.

Sarah froze. *What am I doing, following him into. . .* Biting her lower lip, she wondered what to do. Run outside and cry for help?

The sound of drawers being pulled open turned Sarah's fear into anger. How dare he try to take something! She ran into the Carltons' room. "Sir, you've no right to mess up this room. Have you no respect for the dead?"

Pushing in the bottom drawer of the carved fruitwood dresser, Jonathan Bowman moved to a black lacquered chest against the opposite wall.

"Perhaps you can help. Have you seen a handkerchief with some yellow birds embroidered around it?" He was rifling through the contents of the top drawer.

Surely she hadn't heard him right. "A handkerchief?"

"Yes," he said, not looking up. "My mother made it for Mary when they were little girls. Look. Here it is!" He brought out a yellowed square of linen, with childish, uneven stitching around the edges.

"You can't take that from here," Sarah said, stepping back to the doorway and blocking his passage.

"Oh?" He was coming toward her, his eyebrows raised. "And I suppose you're going to forbid me to leave this room?"

Hands trembling, Sarah nodded, hoping her face didn't betray her fear.

The corners of his mouth turned up again. "Well, if I'm stuck here, I might as well have a nap."

Before she could blink her eyes, he was sitting on the edge of the bed, pulling off a leather boot.

"What—"

"You know, I was up all hours last night. I figured I'd try to squeeze in a rest today after I ran this little errand for Mother." Dropping the boot to the floor, he began tugging at the other one.

"Anyway, this is better. I've got a lovely young maiden to watch over me and see that I sleep undisturbed."

When his fingers started unfastening the top button of his dark blue shirt, Sarah covered her eyes with her hand. "Sir, you aren't going to undress in here, are you?"

He sounded surprised. "Why, of course. You don't expect me to sleep fully clothed, do you?"

"All right. I'm leaving," she said, her shoulders falling. "Only, please wait and ask Mrs. Mobley about the handkerchief. I don't want to be arrested!"

"Arrested? That's ridiculous. It's just a handkerchief."

"But Mrs. Mobley said she'd tell the sheriff if anything turned up missing after I leave."

His laugh made her flinch. "That's what all this fuss is about? Prison? By the way, you can look now. My shirt's fastened again." He reached down for one of his boots. "We don't put girls in prison for missing hankies. I suppose the English send them to the gallows?"

Shaking her head, Sarah thought, *Why doesn't he just leave?*

His boots back on his feet, Jonathan Bowman stood up and stepped toward Sarah. "My mother made this handkerchief for Mary when they were children. Even though they grew apart, they were very close at one time. I'll leave a note downstairs for Elizabeth if you're going to have nightmares about prison cells."

"Thank you," Sarah whispered, backing out of the doorway. The ordeal had strained her raw nerves, and to her embarrassment, tears flowed.

"You're quite a crybaby, aren't you?" the unwelcome visitor asked. "You'd probably be halfway decent to look at if you weren't so weepy-eyed." After walking through the doorway, he stopped in front of her, slowly reached out a hand, and touched a curl of brown hair at her shoulder. "I'll wait in the carriage while you pack your things."

Her tears dried up and her head snapped back. "Mr. Bowman, you have misunderstood what kind of person I am!"

"Misunderstood?"

"Yes, very much!" she said, spitting out the words.

"I don't understand." He scratched his head. "Didn't you say that you're looking for a job?"

"As a domestic, Mr. Bowman—nothing more."

Shrugging his shoulders, he brushed a piece of lint from his cuff. "Of course. Whatever did you think I meant? My mother could use a maid, and I'm prepared to hire you if you want the job."

"A maid?"

"That's what you are, right?"

"I'm sorry," she said, feeling foolish for jumping to conclusions. Just then, Sarah remembered something from a conversation between Mrs. Bowman and Mrs. Carlton.

"You have slaves, don't you?" she asked.

"Yes, some," he said. "But Mother's getting difficult, and she doesn't trust the Negroes anymore. I'm at my wit's end as to how to handle her."

"Well, I had hoped to stay here in Charleston—"

"Perfect! In two months, Mother will be coming back here to live in our town house. She leaves the plantation every year from early May until first frost. There's danger of malaria during the warm months."

"Don't the slaves get malaria?"

"Not very often. The Negroes seem to have some natural immunity, perhaps from the African climate. I don't get sick either, so I won't be staying here in town with Mother, if that makes you feel better."

Crossing his arms, he impatiently drummed his fingers on his sleeve. "Of course, if you're not interested, I'm sure we'll have no trouble finding someone else."

Sarah knew she had to make up her mind quickly. *My savings can't last forever, and it might take some time to find a position from the newspaper,* she thought. *I won't have to be around Mr. Bowman very much.*

"Thank you," she finally said. "I'll pack right away."

In front of the Carltons' house, Jonathan inhaled deeply of his cigar. Squinting his eyes, he looked at the second-floor window where the girl was hurriedly gathering her things. *She's a real beauty,* he thought. He flicked the ashes from his cigar into the street. *They're so easily fooled when they want to be!*

❧

"My grandfather, Pierce Bowman, built Magnolia Bend between 1760 and 1770." Jonathan pointed toward the river. "I'm glad he picked the Ashley River to build on. It's not the best river for growing rice, but it's the closest to Charleston. Shipping's easier."

Sarah nodded from across him in the carriage. They'd been on the road for two hours, and she was beginning to have misgivings. She didn't expect Mrs. Bowman to be as kind as Mrs. Carlton, especially after what her son had said about her being "difficult."

Get hold of yourself! Sarah reproached herself. *You're not a thirteen-year-old child.* She could be satisfied, she told herself, as long as she wasn't mistreated. *It's good that I'm returning to Charleston with Mrs. Bowman in a few weeks,* she thought. *If things are intolerable, I can look for another job.*

The horses slowed as the road inclined sharply for two-hundred feet. Then, turning to the right, the carriage entered a shadowy avenue lined with towering oaks. High limbs stretched across the lane and met to form a high, sun-dappled ceiling.

The horses picked up speed again, hungry for their oats. At the end of the avenue waited an imposing two-story white house. Its many-windowed front was interrupted by huge white columns and delicate wrought iron.

"What do you think?" asked Jonathan.

"Your home is lovely, sir," said Sarah, thinking privately how little the appearance of a house had to do with how the people living within it treated each other.

Veering to the left around the house was a curved road. It ran through a garden to a side door. The carriage halted several feet away, and Mr. Bowman was greeted respectfully by eight dark-skinned servants.

"Miz Dora, she be lying down," said a stooped man with white hair.

"I suppose she still has a headache?"

The old man nodded. "Yassir."

Jonathan sighed as he helped Sarah alight from the carriage. "All right. Violet, show Miss Sarah to her room—the corner bedchamber next to my mother's. Then find her something to eat." He turned to a much younger black man. "Anson, saddle my horse and bring her here. I want to look at the trenches before it gets dark."

"Is there anything I should be doing?" Sarah asked.

"No, not today. Violet can show you around if you wish." Turning, he followed Anson toward the stables.

A girl about her own age stepped forward, and Sarah assumed she was Violet. The slave girl directed two adolescent boys to carry Sarah's small trunk, and she led Sarah up a short flight of stone steps and through the door. The first room they entered was a parlor, spacious and airy. A wide passageway was next with a mahogany-railed staircase curving toward them.

At the top of the stairs, Violet put a brown finger to her lips. "We have to be quiet, Missy. Miz Dora." She pointed to a paneled door.

Following the girl through an open door at the end of the upstairs hall, Sarah moved aside so the boys could set the trunk on the floor next to a four-poster bed.

When the boys had left, Violet closed the door softly, walked over to the trunk, and knelt down to open the latch.

Confused, Sarah watched Violet. She'd always packed and unpacked for herself, as was expected of servants. Could this girl be thinking she was a guest or relative?

"Violet?" she said as the girl swung the lid open.

The girl turned her head to look at her. "Yes, Missy?"

"Why are you unpacking my things?"

"Why?" Violet looked as confused as Sarah. "If I don't put them on pegs, they'll get wrinkled." Turning her attention back to the trunk, she scooped up Sarah's favorite dress, a dark-blue calico.

"But. . ." Following Violet to a wide chifforobe next to the fireplace, Sarah watched her fluff out the folds of the dress. "I can do that," she finally said.

Violet smiled agreeably, but didn't stop smoothing the blue fabric with her hands. After she put the dress away, she started back to the trunk.

"Wait." Sarah reached out and touched the girl's arm. "You're not supposed to unpack my clothes."

Something akin to fear came into Violet's brown eyes. "What do you mean, miss?"

"I'm a maid here. Mr. Bowman hired me this morning."

The slave girl shifted uneasily from one foot to the other.

"Do you understand?" asked Sarah.

The girl shook her head. "You're white," she whispered.

"You've never seen a white servant?"

"No, missy," she said, and reached down for another dress.

Violet was determined not to stop, so Sarah figured she'd at least help with the three remaining dresses and her other belongings. Silently they worked, side by side, while once in a while Violet darted a quick glance at the white girl.

When they'd finished unpacking, Violet led Sarah down the stairs, through the dining room and pantry, to another door. It was still daylight when they stepped outside, though an evening chill was settling in. They walked over a short path leading to a brick building.

"Missy Sarah, this is Leah. She's the cook," Violet said as they entered the kitchen. To Leah, she asked, "Do you have anything ready to eat?"

The older black woman, her head wrapped in a brightly colored square of fabric, looked up from the biscuits she was rolling. She looked at Sarah as if surprised to see a white woman in her kitchen.

"Suppah ain't ready for a while, but I got some sweet potato bread and a piece o' ham."

"That sounds good. I haven't eaten all day," said Sarah to the woman. She saw the cook's shoulders relax. "May I eat in here?"

Violet's eyebrows shot up. "In the kitchen?"

"I've spent most of my life in kitchens," Sarah said, taking the pewter dish that another woman—her hair also bound up in a scarf—handed her.

Though Violet sat at the huge planked oak table with Sarah, she would not eat. Sarah chewed slowly to keep from wolfing down the food. It was delicious, and not just because she was ravenous. The sweetness of the bread went well with the salty ham.

The kitchen, with its brick floor and whitewashed walls, was as long as the Carltons' whole house. The ceiling was smoked almost black. A wide fireplace took up most of one wall, and stirring the contents of a big iron pot hanging over the fire was another slave woman. A boy sat on a low stool, slowly turning the handle of a spit on which at least a half-dozen hens were roasting.

When Sarah finished eating, Violet asked if she'd like to see the rest of the plantation. Thanking Leah for the meal, Sarah walked with Violet outside around another path of flat rocks. It led to a dirt lane and several small wooden buildings.

"That's the smokehouse," said Violet, pointing to the first building. "Those two houses are the sundry barns, and the mill's on the other side."

Though Sarah paid close attention to what Violet said, she was more interested in the girl herself. "How long have you lived here?" she asked, hoping Violet wouldn't think her too nosy.

"Three years."

"Where did you live before here?"

"Master Lucas's house, down the river a bit. He sold some of us to Master Bowman."

"Are you treated well here?"

Violet locked eyes with Sarah, gave a quick, solemn nod, then pointed to another cabin. "Over there is the grain house."

Back upstairs in her room, Sarah was cleaning her hands at the washstand when a knock sounded at the door. Standing in the hallway was a black woman whom she hadn't seen earlier. "Miz Dora want to see you now."

Mrs. Bowman looked up as Sarah walked into the room. "Pull a chair up to the bed so we can talk."

Quickly, Sarah obeyed. Mrs. Bowman seemed to have lost weight. The flesh around her chin sagged loosely, and the complexion Sarah remembered as being lovely was now milky pale.

"Do you remember me?" asked Mrs. Bowman.

"Yes, ma'am. You came to see Mrs. Carlton last year."

"I look quite different now, don't I?" said Mrs. Bowman, her lower lip trembling slightly. "You've gotten prettier, and I've turned into an ugly old hag."

"Oh no, ma'am. That's not so!" protested Sarah.

"I despise a liar," said the woman sharply. "Are you trying to flatter me?"

Sarah took a deep breath. *You can always look for another job in just a few weeks,* she told herself. "Mrs. Bowman, you don't look like a hag. But if it's honesty you want, you look like you've been ill. Is that why you couldn't come to the funeral?"

"Yes." Mrs. Bowman's lip started trembling. "I wanted to go, but my head hurt so badly that I couldn't tolerate the drive. You think Mary and Amos would have understood?"

Mrs. Bowman had such childlike longing in her expression, that Sarah felt compassion. "They were kind," she said. "They wouldn't have wanted you to travel when you were ill."

"That's right," Mrs. Bowman said, almost eagerly. "But I made sure that Jonathan went, even though I was afraid to be here without him. I was in terrible pain."

"Is there anything I can do for you? Does your head still hurt?" asked Sarah.

"It hurts almost constantly, but I feel a little better now that my son is home. I've been asking him to hire a white girl to help me, but he said it wasn't necessary. I was so pleased when he told me about you."

"Pleased, ma'am?"

"Oh, yes! Mary had good sense when it came to picking dependable servants." She sniffed faintly. "She had good sense about other things too —more than I gave her credit for at the time."

Not fully understanding what response was expected of her, Sarah nodded. "Yes, ma'am."

Suddenly, the woman slipped a hand out from under the sheet and grabbed Sarah's. "I feel that I can trust you, especially if Mary trusted you." She lowered her voice. "I need to hear it from you, though. Can you keep a secret?"

Sarah blinked, startled. "I can."

"Have you ever kept an important secret?"

After a moment, Sarah answered. "Yes, ma'am." *Oh, Mother,* she thought. *I wanted to run into your arms and tell you how mean Mrs. Gerty was, but I pretended to be happy for your sake.* "A very important one."

"Good!" Letting go of Sarah's hand, Mrs. Bowman leaned forward. "Tiptoe over to the door and see if anyone's listening," she whispered.

"Listening?"

"Outside the door. Hurry!"

Rising, Sarah slipped to the door, turned the knob, and pulled it toward her a little, peeking out the narrow crack.

"Not like that! Throw it open quickly!" said the woman from the bed.

The door made a loud "whuff" as Sarah pulled it open. Sticking her head into the upstairs hall, she looked both ways. "No one's there, ma'am," she said, closing the door again.

"We still have to talk softly," Mrs. Bowman said, motioning for Sarah to sit. "The slaves are planning to revolt soon. I fear they want to kill Jonathan and me and take over Magnolia Bend. That's why I get so many headaches lately." She closed her eyes for a second. "They're poisoning my food a little bit at a time."

When Sarah didn't respond, the woman grew agitated. "You're looking at me like Jonathan does—as if I'd lost my mind. I tell you, it's true!"

"Ma'am, I didn't mean to look at you like that," said Sarah. "It's just the Negro servants seem nice."

"So, you've met them all?"

"Not all of them, I'm sure. But Violet and Leah and those that I've met—"

"We have over one hundred eighty Negroes," interrupted Mrs. Bowman. "Would it be ridiculous to think that some of them are unhappy enough to want to kill us?" She shook her head. "We've treated them almost like family. We've even made sure that each cabin has a full bolt of mosquito netting for the beds. Most planters wouldn't bother with that expense. But, you know, the longer I live, the more I realize that the people you do the most for are sometimes the most ungrateful!"

Sarah didn't know what to think. Mrs. Bowman surely knew more than she did about her own slaves. She remembered how badly she had felt when Mrs. Gerty had held her wages back. To work for nothing, year after year—perhaps Mrs. Bowman was right.

"Has Mr. Bowman been getting headaches?" Sarah asked.

"No, but I'm worried about him. You see, they won't try to kill us the same way. It would look too suspicious."

"Have you told Mr. Bowman?"

A look of pain washed across the woman's face. "Jonathan won't listen. He thinks I'm imagining things. I'm not imagining the looks they give each other when they think we're not watching!"

Suddenly, the older woman's face brightened. "Now that you're here, we can do something about it. I've been making plans."

Sarah swallowed hard before asking. "Plans?"

"Yes. I've sent word to Leah that I want all my meals sent up here, and yours, too—on account of my headaches, you see." Her voice took on a conspiratorial tone. "We'll switch trays as soon as Ben and Lucy leave the room. If you start getting headaches, we'll know they've been plotting against me.

"But don't worry," she added hastily. "As soon as your headaches come—if they do—we'll have the evidence, and you can stop. I wouldn't let you eat enough to kill yourself."

That didn't make Sarah feel any better. "Why wouldn't they poison my tray along with yours?"

Mrs. Bowman smiled. "I wondered that, myself, but after thinking it over, I know they wouldn't. If we both got sick, it would prove that they're poisoning the food."

Folding her arms together across her chest, Mrs. Bowman looked pleased with herself. "You have to outthink them, just like playing chess."

Chapter Nine
1841

"Sir, may I talk with you?"

Jonathan Bowman looked up, folded his newspaper, and placed it on the settee next to him. "Come in."

"I'd best shut the door, if you don't mind," said Sarah, still standing in the doorway of the library.

"By all means. I've been expecting you."

Expecting me? Sarah wondered. *Why?* Closing the door, she took a couple steps forward. "Sir, it's about—"

"Why don't you sit down."

Slipping into a gold damask chair across from Mr. Bowman's settee, Sarah took a deep breath. "It's about the job. I've reconsidered and can't accept it." She hurried on. "I know it's a long ride back to Charleston, but I can pay someone to take me in the morning."

Jonathan studied Sarah's face with his midnight-blue eyes. Clasping his hands behind his head, he leaned against the high back of the sofa. "I take it that you've talked with Mother," he said, a trace of a smile on his face.

"I have, and I can't accept the terms of my employment."

"She wants you to stand at her door with a gun, eh?"

"No, sir. Mrs. Bowman plans to have me switch meals with her to test for poison."

Jonathan sighed. "She's obsessed with this conspiracy idea. Did she tell you she kept a pistol under her pillow while I was in Charleston?"

"Perhaps there's some truth to what she fears," said Sarah.

Jonathan shook his head. "Not here. Believe me. I keep a close eye on my people." He leaned forward, his arms propping his weight on his knees. "It's that abolitionist tract we found last October! I wish she'd never found out about it!"

"Excuse me, sir?"

"There's a seditious little pamphlet printed by a freed slave in Boston called the Appeal. It tries to stir up the Negroes to overthrow their masters. I have it right here," he said, rising and walking over to a rolltop desk. From the bottom drawer he brought out a thin booklet with worn edges, about the size of his palm. "Would you like to see it?"

Sarah looked down at her hands. "I can't read."

Shrugging his shoulders, Jonathan sat back down. "I'll read some of it to you, then, and you'll understand my mother's fears." Opening the pamphlet, he began to read:

> *If you commence, make sure work—do not trifle, for they will not trifle with you—they want us for their slaves and think nothing of murdering us in order to subject us to that wretched condition—therefore, if there is an attempt made by us, kill or be killed.*

He slapped the booklet shut. "A white steward on a brig from Boston thought he would hand some of these out to our Negroes in Charleston while his ship was in dock. A loyal slave showed one to his master, and the steward was arrested and put in prison for a year. That was a few years ago, and I didn't think any of my people ever saw this piece of trash—until we found this in one of the quarters." Shaking his head, Jonathan frowned. "One of my most trusted workers. I used to send him to Charleston on errands by himself."

"What happened to him?" asked Sarah.

"He's dead."

"For having that paper?"

Fixing his eyes steadily on hers, Jonathan replied, "The penalty for trying to lead a revolt is hanging. That's the law in South Carolina. He knew better than to have something like that in his possession."

Still horrified, Sarah asked, "Do you kill them when they displease you?"

"Of course not!" Jonathan looked at Sarah as if she'd lost her mind. "What kind of businessman would I be if I mistreated my laborers!"

When she didn't answer, he went on. "The Negroes here are well fed, clothed, and taken care of. There are inequalities all over the world, Sarah. Take your England, for example. I've heard there are children as young as six years old working in the factories and mines. I don't send them out in the rice fields that young. When you've lived here longer, you'll understand the way things are. Now, let's talk about Mother."

"She wants me to switch meals with her to test for poison." Sarah shook her head. "I can't do that."

"Sarah," he said, smiling at her as if she were a child. "Do you think the servants would poison an old woman?"

Sarah pondered his question. "No, perhaps not. But she's asking me to risk my life."

"And your life is of great value to you, I assume."

It wasn't the words so much as the faint smirk at the corner of his mouth that enraged her. "Mr. Bowman, it's true that I'm just a servant, but my life is my own!"

"You're right, of course." He held both hands up in front of him, placatingly. "I didn't mean to say that." Putting his hands down again, he lowered his voice. "I just wanted to see the fire in those dark eyes again."

"Sir?" Not sure if she'd heard him right, Sarah wondered whether to leave the room.

"Nothing," he said. "Please reconsider staying with my mother. I can't leave my work to calm her fears all the time. You'd have no work to do other than keeping her company."

"But the food?"

"I know it sounds crazy, but it would reassure her if you could prove that she's wrong. Perhaps then she'll stop imagining plots." Suddenly, he sat up straight. "I've got it! You save half the food on your tray for me, and I'll have it when Mother's asleep."

Sarah gave a small sigh. "You're that sure there's no poison?"

"That sure."

"Then I'll try it myself—as long as my head doesn't hurt."

"Thank you, Sarah," he said, rising to open the door for her. "My mother can be quite pleasant when she's not worrying. You may even feel at home here, one day."

❧

"My husband, Charles, used to tell me all the time, 'Dorothy, holding your hand is like touching the cream at the top of the milk bucket!'" Mrs. Bowman held both hands out for Sarah to see. "I've always kept a little mineral oil spread on them at night, and I use the smallest amount of soap when washing my hands."

"Your hands are lovely, ma'am."

The woman's eyes drifted to the tray on Sarah's lap. "Is the food suitable?"

"It's delicious," answered Sarah, breaking a hot-buttered biscuit in half. "What do you call this?" She pointed to the chunks of seafood and vegetables in a brown, gravylike liquid served over rice.

"It's gumbo. We had it at the Jordans' house. Their cook is a Creole from New Orleans, so I asked Caroline Jordan to let Leah go over and learn how to cook it." Mrs. Bowman spooned down her own gumbo with relish. "I don't believe it's ever tasted quite so good," she said.

Later that night, Sarah lay in bed wondering if her head would start hurting. *I don't believe I've been poisoned,* she thought. *And Mrs. Bowman seems to like me.* Perhaps she had made the right decision, but what would David think of her working for people with slaves? She didn't think he'd approve.

Sarah wished she could talk with David about many things. Perhaps he could explain the ache she had for something she couldn't recognize, much less understand. *There's something out there that I need so much, but I don't know what it is,* she thought.

She had her eyes half open when the doorknob turned slowly. As the door drifted open, Sarah sat up in time to see a dark form slip inside the room.

"Oh, missy. I'm sorry to wake you up!" said a voice.

"Violet?"

"Yes, miss. It's me all right." In the dimness, Sarah could see the girl carried a bundle.

"I've got a log. I thought I'd make a little fire to break the chill in the room," Violet said, walking over to the fireplace.

Sarah didn't know what to say, so she watched the girl spread kindling in the hearth. From a bucket she carried, Violet poured a glowing ember on the kindling, picking up the poker to stir the wood. "When that burns a little, I'll put the log on top," she said.

Finding her tongue, Sarah smiled. "Thank you. The fire will be nice. If you'll tell me where to find the wood, I'll lay my own and save you the trouble."

Hesitating, Violet walked toward the bed. "Miss Sarah," she said meekly, "we been told what to do. If you do our work, then we'll be in trouble."

Watching Violet wring her hands, Sarah's heart went out to the girl. "I don't want to get you in trouble, but I'm not used to being waited on." Then, a thought dawned upon her. "Am I causing a problem?"

Violet smiled. "Not if you let us do our work."

❧

"As you can see, this home has been well cared for," said Elizabeth Mobley, walking over to touch the east wall of the sitting room. "The wallpaper came from France just last year, and the paneling was polished every week."

Kathleen Harvey nudged her fiancé beside her on the sofa. "The wallpaper has to go," she said under her breath. "Roses are so outdated!" To Elizabeth, she smiled sweetly. "Have you thought about our offer?"

Taking her chair opposite the couple, Elizabeth cleared her throat. "I understand why a young couple just starting out would want a good price. It's a lot lower than what I asked, though."

Kathleen's face fell. "Oh, dear. I had nightmares that this would happen!" Clasping her hands tightly in her lap, she gave Elizabeth a trembling smile. "We can't afford to go any higher."

"Not even to halve the difference?"

Kathleen shook her head regretfully. "It's very kind of you to offer, and I wish our circumstances would permit. I suppose it wasn't meant to be."

The man sitting beside her looked startled. "Wait a minute," he began. "We decided that—"

Raising her voice, Kathleen drowned out her fiancé. "We'll have to take that little house on Charlotte Street." Rising, she motioned for the man to follow. "Come, David. We won't take any more of Mrs. Mobley's time."

The young man was halfway to his feet when Elizabeth held up her hands in protest. "Please stay. It's possible that we can work this out."

As the couple sat back down, Kathleen's eyebrows raised expectantly. "Yes?"

Giving a heavy sigh, Elizabeth nodded her head. "I need to settle my parents' estate as soon as possible. My husband needs the capital to invest in a business venture. My parents died last week, you know."

"I'm sorry," offered David. He couldn't remember seeing a death notice in the newspaper for any Mobleys. "Were they ill?"

"Oh, no!" she said. "Didn't you hear about the train wreck near Baltimore last week? My mother and father were killed in that wreck."

He'd only read about one couple from Charleston who'd died on that train, a businessman and his wife. *Of course!* he thought. *Their last name wouldn't be Mobley*. "Your father is—was he Amos Carlton?"

"Yes." Reaching for a handkerchief, Elizabeth blew her nose loudly. "They were the finest people. Everyone loved them."

"The Carltons." David spoke as if in a daze. "What happened to their servants?"

Elizabeth looked puzzled. "Oh," she finally said. "You'll need servants. I'm sure the ones who worked here have found other employers."

"Do you know which employers?"

"No, I'm afraid I don't," said Elizabeth. Then she remembered the note that Jonathan had left her, telling that the English maid was in his employ. *Doesn't matter*, she told herself. *I'm here to sell a house, not to help this greedy couple find servants.*

"Perhaps we shouldn't buy the house after all," said Kathleen, elbowing her fiancé while lowering her eyelashes at Elizabeth. "You must have so many memories. . . ."

"Well, yes, but my husband needs the money. Only, he was hoping to get a little more than—" Suddenly, she sat up straight. "I tell you what. I'll take my carriage home now. He's there resting. I'll ask him if he can live with your offer, and come right back and let you know. You can stay here and look around some more."

"Thank you so much!" said Kathleen, jumping up from her seat. "I'm so thrilled, and look at my fiancé. He's speechless!"

Sarah lived in this house, thought David. *She never contacted me. I wonder where she is now?* He let his hand rest reverently on the carved cherry of the sofa arm. *She probably dusted this chair.* For the hundredth time, David reminded himself that he'd only known the girl briefly. *She's forgotten me,* he thought. *Why can't I get her out of my mind?*

When Elizabeth had left, Kathleen turned angrily to David. "You almost ruined everything. We're getting this beautiful house for a steal!"

David looked up. "We're not going to take advantage of the lady, Kathleen. She just lost her parents, and she might not be thinking rationally."

"Oh, nonsense! You heard her say it's been a week." Turning on her heel, Kathleen studied the wall. "I believe a fleur-de-lis pattern would make this room look more modern, don't you?"

David watched her go about the room, examining the furnishings. *Why did I let myself get pressured into this?*

He winced as Kathleen squealed. "These curtains are brand new—no fade lines!"

I don't even like her very much. Overwhelmed by thoughts of living with Kathleen for the rest of his life, David groaned.

"Oh, don't be so grumpy!" Kathleen said over her shoulder as she turned up the lining of the curtains on the next window. "We can buy new ones if you don't like these."

David put his head in his hands. "It's no use, Kathleen," he said. "I can't."

"Can't what?" she said, walking over to stand in front of him. "Are you ill?"

"No," he said bleakly. "I can't get married."

Kathleen laughed. "Of course you can, you silly thing!"

David knew that he'd never get another chance. "Please sit down," he said, looking up at her.

"David, you're serious, aren't you?" Taking her place next to him,

Kathleen put a hand on his arm. "Is it because of the way I got that woman to lower the price?"

She took his silence for agreement. "That's business, dear. I learned that from my father, and look where he is today."

"Kathleen, please listen!" David said, turning to her. "I've not been honest with you or with myself. It's killing me to have to hurt you, but I don't want to get married."

"You have last-minute jitters, that's all," she said reassuringly. "We still have two months for you to calm down." Her face brightened suddenly. "I know! You've been working so hard, Papa says. Perhaps you need a rest from your job for a few days. I'll ask Papa to let you—"

"No!" David interrupted. "That's why I can't marry you. You and 'Papa' would run our lives! I'd be a houseboy for you to order around, and you'd run to your father when I didn't obey."

"David, I can't believe you're saying such mean things!" Kathleen said. Covering her face with her hands, she burst into tears.

David almost changed his mind. Kathleen's tears were nothing new to him, but this time she was truly in pain. *It wouldn't be fair to her,* he thought. *She should marry a man who will love her.*

"Kathleen, if I could do anything to undo the hurt I've caused you—"

"You can marry me!" she sobbed. "What will everyone say? You're practically leaving me at the altar!"

Pulling a handkerchief from his waistcoat pocket, David tried to wipe her face. "Oh, give me that!" she commanded, dabbing at her eyes.

The grandfather clock marked off the seconds against the wall behind them. When Kathleen turned to David, her green eyes were filled with sadness. "You don't love me?"

He shook his head. "I'm sorry—not enough to get married."

"Well, I like that!" she said, jumping to her feet. "You can explain to Mrs. Mobley when she returns. I'm going to see what Papa has to say about this!"

Before disappearing through the door, Kathleen threw one parting shot. "And you're such a fine Christian, everybody says! What would they say if they could hear you now?"

The walls shuddered with the splintering slam of the door. Leaning his head on his hands, David sat, listening to his heart race. *Lord,* he prayed silently, *please help Kathleen. I've hurt her so deeply.* Another face came back into his mind. *And Sarah, let me see her again, and take care of her, wherever she is.*

David didn't know whether he should report for work Monday morning. Mr. Harvey had always praised his hard work, but Kathleen came first in her father's mind. The man couldn't stand to see his daughter denied anything.

I'll have to clean out my desk if I'm fired, David told himself as he pushed open the oak door leading to Harvey and Merrit Investment Services. Typically early, David wasn't surprised to see the three other desks in the main office empty. Hearing footsteps, he turned to see Mr. Harvey standing in front of his office door.

"Young man, we need to have a talk!" Kathleen's father boomed, his corpulent frame filling the width of the doorway. "Come in here now!"

Following the man who'd been his employer for six years, David felt like he was being led to the gallows. When they'd sat down—his boss in the huge armchair behind his desk and David on a small chair in front—Mr. Harvey surprised him by smiling broadly.

"So, you're having second thoughts, my baby girl tells me."

"You don't know how badly—" David began.

"Just wait," said Mr. Harvey, still smiling as he held a hand up in front of him. "I want to tell you that I understand."

"You do?"

"Of course. It's natural for a young man to get cold feet." The office resounded with his deep laugh. "Don't tell Mrs. Harvey, but there was a time when I wondered what I was doing, giving up the carefree life of a bachelor."

Here I go again, thought David. "Sir, I'm not going to change my mind. I'm sorry that so many wedding plans were made, but I cannot go through with it."

The man's smile fell as his heavy-lidded eyes became cold. "One of the things I've admired about you is your stability. I take it, then, that you're serious, and you've thought of the consequences?"

Squaring his shoulders, David nodded. "If you mean my job, sir, I don't expect to keep it after this."

Leaning back in his chair, Mr. Harvey drummed his fleshy fingers on the top of his desk as he stared at the young man. "I tell you what," he finally said. "I think you need a change of scenery."

"I beg your pardon?" said David, not quite believing his ears.

The smile came back to the man's face. "Kathleen's a high-spirited girl, and I've noticed she's a little bossy with you. It would do both of you some good to get away from each other."

"Away?"

"I need someone back in England for six months, maybe a little longer. I wanted to send you, but with the wedding—"

"You mean, I still have my job?"

Mr. Harvey laughed. "Of course, son. I'd be crazy to let someone like you go. Oh, I admit, I was all set to fire you, but that's no way to run a business. And what's more," he added with a wink, "I'm betting a certain young lady will be in your thoughts while you're away."

"Mr. Harvey, I want to be honest with you. This won't make me change my mind about the marriage."

"Never say never," said Mr. Harvey with a wink.

Chapter Ten

"My dear, you're becoming quite skillful at this game." Mrs. Bowman tapped her finger on the side of the chess board. "You may beat me one day, if you keep making moves like that."

Sarah's face broke into a grin. "Was that a good move?"

"Well, no. I'll have your rook. But you get better every day, so don't be discouraged."

Sighing, Sarah studied her chessmen. Mrs. Bowman had insisted she learn the game, and Sarah was surprised that she enjoyed the challenge of playing. Hesitating briefly, she reached out and moved an ivory pawn forward, only to have the woman capture it with her knight.

"Take your time, now," said Mrs. Bowman. "You don't want to make another wrong move." The woman's complexion had developed more color since Sarah's arrival, almost a month before. After two weeks of switching trays with the girl, Mrs. Bowman had realized that she wasn't being poisoned. As her appetite improved, so did her disposition, and her headaches were disappearing.

Mrs. Bowman's son had also noticed the change, and the week before, Sarah had found a large box on her bed containing a beautiful mauve linen dress. When Sarah had discovered that the dress was from Jonathan, she'd felt uneasy. She didn't like accepting such a gift from a man.

However, when she'd approached her employer about the dress, he'd rolled his eyes. "Of course you can accept it! I'm just thanking you for taking such good care of Mother." Looking down at Sarah with a smile, he'd added, "You've made such a difference around here."

"I can't tell you how much fun it is to have someone to play chess with again. Most of the women I know aren't interested." Mrs. Bowman's voice broke into Sarah's musings. "My late husband and I played often, and sometimes I beat him. I always wondered if he let me win."

"And you haven't played until I came here?"

"Oh, sometimes I talked Jonathan into a game, but he hasn't got the patience for it."

"What about the other servants?" asked Sarah. She noticed Violet was dusting the bookshelves that covered the west wall in the library.

"Don't refer to yourself as a 'servant,' dear," said Mrs. Bowman. "I like to think of you as my companion. But as to the Negroes, play chess, you said?" Her face turned solemn. "That would be cruel. Too much mental exertion. It taxes their brains and could give them fits."

Mrs. Bowman stood up. "I need to be excused for a minute. You should plan your next move."

Sarah wondered if Violet had heard what Mrs. Bowman said. She looked over at the girl, who seemed to have her mind on other things as she wiped each book with a cloth. *Mrs. Bowman is so good to me,* Sarah thought. *But I wish she wouldn't speak about the slaves that way, especially in front of them.*

Frowning at her chessmen, Sarah tried to anticipate Mrs. Bowman's possible countermoves.

"Move your knight over to take this pawn. It'll put her king in check," came a voice from beside her.

Sarah turned to find Violet studying the chess board, one hand on her slender hip and the other rubbing her chin.

"Violet? You know how to play chess?"

"Yes, missy. Been knowing since I was a little girl."

Sarah winced. "Violet, you said you'd stop calling me that. It embarrasses me!"

Hanging her head slightly, the slave asked, "Are you mad?"

Reaching out to squeeze Violet's hand, Sarah smiled. "Not if you tell me how you learned to play chess!"

"Back at the Riveroaks house—before I was sold here." Violet returned Sarah's smile. "One of Master Lucas's children taught me how."

"You've played it a lot?"

"Hundreds of times!" The sound of Mrs. Bowman's footsteps in the hall sent Violet back over to the bookcase. Picking up her dusting cloth from the shelf, she turned back to Sarah and whispered, "And I ain't had a fit in my life, ever."

Mrs. Bowman liked to retire soon after supper, and once she fell asleep, Sarah had a couple of hours to herself. Usually she sat on the back porch in a white wicker rocking chair, wondering at the goings-on in the slave cabins just north of the cornfield. Mrs. Bowman had told her that it wasn't proper for her to be near the quarters. Sarah could pick out individual families around the closest cabins only by their mannerisms and vague shapes, for their faces were blurred by the distance.

"Spinning wool?"

She turned at the sound of Jonathan Bowman's voice. "I'm sorry, did you speak to me?"

"I said your name, but you were apparently lost in thought."

"I was wondering about the people who live down there."

"Wondering?"

"Yes. How they live, about their families. They seem to care for each other a great deal."

"Callie—over there—she cares for her brood, too," said Jonathan, pointing to a calico cat stretched out against the woodbin, her stubby kittens scrambling over each other as they nuzzled against their mother for nourishment.

Sarah's eyes were grave as she looked into his. "Surely you don't think they're the same."

Jonathan shrugged his shoulders. He held his hand out to her. "Let's go for a walk."

"A walk? Where?"

"Wouldn't you like to see the cabins up close?"

Forty whitewashed cabins lined both sides of the lane. *Like beads on a necklace,* thought Sarah. About fifty feet apart, they had shingle roofs and brick chimneys. Behind each house was a vegetable garden. Most of the slaves were visiting in the yards or hoeing dirt clods in the gardens. "Hello, Massa Bowman" was the greeting from nearly every slave, and a small group of children followed from a bashful distance.

"Would you like to see the inside of one?" asked Jonathan, pointing to a house near the end of the row.

"Yes, but do you think they'd mind?"

"There's no one living there," he said casually. Walking to the front step, he lifted the leather cord from its wooden peg and pulled the door open. "Well, are you coming?" he asked, turning to look back at her.

The cabin smelled of emptiness and musky wood. It contained a good-sized front room with a fireplace, two tiny bedrooms, and a loft for the children. Sarah was at the bottom of the ladder leading into the loft, straining her neck to see as much of the children's area as possible, when she felt a hand on her arm. "You'd best not climb up there," said Jonathan. "The ladder looks in need of repair."

"Thank you," she said. "But I wasn't going to—"

Her sentence was cut off by Jonathan's mouth on hers. He pulled her close with his other arm. Sarah couldn't breathe. She slid her hands against his chest and pushed him away with all her might.

"Mr. Bowman!" she said, wiping his kiss from her mouth with the back of her hand. "Why did you do that!"

Hurt washed across his face. Then, angry, his eyes narrowed.

"It was just a kiss. Don't tell me you didn't expect it."

"I didn't!" she said, a cold chill racking her body. "I thought you were being kind."

He moved closer, a half-smile playing at his lips. "I thought that was very kind. Perhaps you'd change your mind in a little while."

Like a terrified deer, Sarah bolted past him through the front door. Dark-skinned children scattered as she ran blindly past the cabins. Their parents broke off conversations, gazing after her with knowing expressions. Nettie, a field hand, tightened her grip on the willow broom she'd been using to sweep her steps. *At least the white woman can run away,* she thought.

Jonathan strode toward the stables, his mouth set in a grim line. He could hear the familiar low neigh of his horse, Luther.

"Masta?" Isaac, the stableman, stuck a dark head out from a stall. "I was just checkin' on this here colt 'fore turning in."

With a short nod, Jonathan opened the door to the tack room and reached for the closest bridle.

"You going riding this late, Masta?" asked Isaac, scurrying over to get Jonathan's saddle. Heaving it up into his arms, he pulled open the door to Luther's stall and stood behind his master, who was pulling the bridle over the horse's ears. "Goin' to be real dark soon. You goin' break a leg if you ride in the woods."

"Then I'll stay on the road," said Jonathan. "Here, hand me that saddle."

He rode the animal hard and fast down the river road. He could no longer see the Ashley River by the light of the stars, but he could smell the water in the chilly night air.

Stupid of me! he berated himself. He should have been more patient. He'd planned to give Sarah a few more gifts like the dress, but the realization that his mother would be leaving for Charleston in less than two weeks had clouded his judgment.

The day he'd gone to Mary's for that handkerchief and seen Sarah standing in the door, her hair wild about her shoulders, he'd decided to enjoy getting to know her better. That his mother had been nagging him about hiring a white girl had worked into his plans perfectly. Now, beguiled by Sarah's beauty and innocence, he was becoming obsessed.

Pulling the reins sharply to bring his horse to a stop, Jonathan grinned.

This can work to my advantage, he thought, turning the horse around and heading back for home.

~~

"Miss Sarah?"

Sarah raised her head from her pillow. She didn't know what time it was or how long she'd been in her room. Recognizing the voice of Lucy, one of the house servants, Sarah said, "Come in."

Closing the door gently behind her, Lucy walked to the bed, the glow from her candle showing a face full of compassion. "You all right, missy?"

Sarah nodded, rubbing her eyes. "I'm going to be, Lucy." *As soon as I leave here and never come back,* she thought.

"Masta wants to see you in the library."

Sarah sat up in bed. "What!"

"He say to tell you that I'm supposed to come and stay in there with you."

Sarah was about to refuse when it occurred to her that this could be an opportunity to tell Jonathan Bowman that she was leaving for Charleston in the morning.

Sarah looked up at Lucy's face. "Do you think this is a trick?" She didn't know how much Lucy knew about what had happened earlier, but she knew from personal experience how much servants knew about what went on in households. Probably all one hundred eighty slaves had seen or heard about her running to the house in tears.

"No, Miss Sarah," she answered. "Don't look like one to me." Then she whispered something so low, that Sarah had to strain to hear it. "But be careful!"

"You may leave the door open, if you wish," said Jonathan, standing behind an oak armchair. He motioned to the sofa. "And please have a seat, both of you."

Silently, the women took their places. Lucy, ill at ease, folded her brown hands and stared at them, trying to blend into the room like the furniture. Sarah waited, watching Jonathan from the corner of her eye as he crossed to the front of his chair and sat down.

Leaning forward and resting his elbows on his knees, Jonathan studied his entwined fingers, choosing his words carefully. He looked up at Sarah.

"I apologize if you were sleeping, but I couldn't let the night pass without telling you how sorry I am for what I tried to do."

Though he looked sincere, Sarah had no pity for him. "I've no father, I can't read, and I've been a servant all my life," she said evenly. "Because of that, people have looked at me as lowborn since I was a little girl."

"But I don't—"

"Yes, sir, you do," she interrupted. "You think you can buy me a pretty dress and say pleasant things to me and then have your way with me because I'm too ignorant to know any better."

His face clouding, Jonathan opened his mouth as if to speak, but Sarah jumped in once more. "I don't have much, but the one thing I know is that I'm a lady. A lady, like my mother was. And you won't take that away from me, sir!"

Jonathan's blue eyes narrowed under their dark brows, and his face reddened. Then, as if willed back onto his face, his repentant look returned.

"I've been so wrong," he said.

Both Sarah and Lucy looked up with a start, though Lucy quickly lowered her head again.

Watch how you say this, Jonathan thought. *You may still have a chance.*

"You see, I've never had to chase women. Being unmarried and having this big home—well, women sometimes throw themselves at me." He lowered his eyes, as if ashamed by his admission.

"But then I saw you at the Carltons' house, and you were so beautiful and noble. I knew you'd be good for Mother, and I was right. You've brought peace back to this house.

"And, yes, perhaps the dress could be mistaken as a bribe, but I bought it only with the intentions of giving a gift to someone very special to me."

He lowered his eyes. "That's what you've become: special. I kissed you because I lost my head. And I know I said some ugly things afterward, but I was hurt because you didn't feel the same way about me. I'm in love with you, Sarah."

Sarah closed her eyes. "I'm sorry, sir, but I don't feel the same about you." She did not see the look of surprise that came over his face.

"You don't?"

"No. I'm sorry." Opening her eyes, she added, "And I want to leave in the morning."

"Please, no!" said Jonathan, sitting up in his chair. "It would kill Mother if you left!"

"I've thought of that, and I'm truly sorry, but it would be best."

"But you're going to Charleston soon, anyway. Planting season is in a month."

"I wish to go now," Sarah said firmly.

"All right, all right," he said. "Wait a minute." He settled back in his chair, deep in thought. "What if you and Mother left tomorrow?"

"You mean, stay with her in Charleston?"

"Yes," Jonathan said eagerly. "You wouldn't see me, and you'd have at least five months to decide whether to come back here or get another job."

"Will Violet be coming?" Sarah asked.

"She can, if you wish. Mother always takes one of the Negroes to keep house. Is that agreed, then?"

Sarah studied Jonathan's face. "Yes."

Jonathan held the door open for Sarah and Lucy to leave. When they'd gone, he walked over to the rolltop desk near the bookshelves. Grabbing a crystal whiskey decanter and a glass, he poured himself a drink.

Things hadn't worked out as he'd planned, but she wasn't gone for good—yet. He'd have to arrange a trip to Charleston once the crop was planted and be on his best behavior so Sarah would return in the fall. When she came back, he'd prove that he could be trusted.

Sloshing the amber liquid around in his glass, Jonathan frowned at the nerve of Sarah—a servant—thinking herself too good for him right after he'd claimed to love her. *It doesn't matter,* he thought, wondering why his hands trembled.

&

After Lucy had left her room, giving her hand a quick squeeze, Sarah felt her way to the bench at her dressing table. Lucy had offered to light the oil lamp, but Sarah wanted the darkness to cover her like a cloak.

He said he loves me, she thought, propping her elbows on the table and wondering why she felt nothing in return. *No man's ever told me that before.* Then she realized that one man had spoken of his love many times—if only in her dreams.

Chapter Eleven

It's so good to be back home, Sarah thought, wrapping her wool shawl against the morning chill. Not even the fishermen were out on the wharf so early. Low fog shrouded the water, and in the distance, the sun's first rays turned the eastern sky pale blue.

The intense quiet sent a shiver through her. *Something's out there. I can feel it. Whatever is there, it—or he—wants me to find him. Could it be David?* Lost in thought, Sarah held out an upturned palm as if pleading for whatever was out there to give her something she could touch and understand.

Cold dampness on her cheek made Sarah realize she was crying. An unexplainable longing haunted her. Could it be God? Was He trying to talk to her? Where could she find Him?

Suddenly, Sarah knew where to look.

❧

"I want you to teach me how to read."

Violet drew her head back as if slapped and set down the lamp globe she'd been cleaning. "What?"

Crossing the parlor to the eighteenth-century cherry bookcase, Sarah grabbed a book. "Words," she said, holding it out in front of her. "I need to read them."

"But missy—I mean Sarah—I can't do that."

"Are you going to tell me that you can't read?"

Violet sighed unhappily, hanging her head. "I can read. How did you know?"

Breaking into a grin, Sarah grabbed her by the shoulders. "One evening last week as I joined you on the porch, you suddenly blew out your candle. Later, I found a book under the cushion of the chair where you'd been sitting."

Violet's eyes widened. "You must be the one who put it back in the bookcase!" When Sarah nodded, Violet said, "I've wondered all week how it got there."

"So you'll teach me?" asked Sarah.

Fear covered Violet's face like a veil. "It's against the law for me to know how to read!"

"Against the law? Then how did you learn?"

"When I was a little girl, I was put with Master Lucas's crippled daughter, Becky. I helped her up if she fell down and held her hand when she climbed the stairs. Becky didn't want to go no place without me, and when she and her brothers learned their lessons from the tutor, I listened."

Violet's huge eyes filled with tears. "Becky died when she was about fifteen. That's when Master Lucas sold me. I guess I reminded him about his daughter."

"But you were a little girl. How could you know you weren't supposed to learn? Anyway, that's a silly law."

"The laws here got teeth, just like a bulldog, and I don't want to get bit," said Violet, her voice flat.

Undaunted, Sarah went on. "Mrs. Bowman's going to a meeting of the library auxiliary after breakfast. Then she's having lunch with some friends. We'll hurry through the chores, and we'll have—"

"But it ain't right," interrupted Violet.

"Is it against the law for me to learn to read?"

"I don't think so."

"And can you forget what you learned?"

"No, course not," Violet said, her face mirroring her confusion.

"Then how is it breaking the law for you to teach me to read?"

"Seems like it would be, that's all."

Taking a step closer, Sarah locked eyes with the younger girl. "Violet, I want to learn to read more than anything. Will you please, please teach me?"

Closing her eyes, Violet nodded.

෨

"I was beginning to worry about you." Mrs. Bowman added a teaspoon of sugar to her cup of coffee. "You must have slipped out of here pretty early. Where did you go?"

"The wharf by the farmer's market," said Sarah, pulling out a chair as Willie Mae set a cup of coffee on the table in front of her.

Mrs. Bowman's eyebrows shot up. "The wharf? Promise me you won't go there alone again. Some of the people lurking around seaports are not to be trusted."

"I won't. I'm sorry if I worried you."

"That's a good girl. Now, I've told you about my plans for today?"

"Yes, ma'am."

"Judge Rarick may be coming for supper again, so I'd like you to remind Violet to set the table with the Wedgwood dishes."

"I will," said Sarah, knowing that she'd be doing it herself once her employer left. Mrs. Bowman's Charleston home—many times smaller than Magnolia Bend—required such little upkeep that one servant could keep the general portion of the housework done. Willie Mae, a white woman hired every spring, took care of the cooking and kitchen, while laundry was picked up on Mondays and returned on Wednesdays by Mrs. Turner.

Sarah's duties were to shop for groceries and supplies, help Mrs. Bowman dress, and be on hand for a chat or game of chess whenever Mrs. Bowman had a blank place on her calendar. Over Violet's protests, Sarah insisted on helping with the housecleaning, but she did it discreetly, so as not to upset her employer.

Sarah didn't understand why Mrs. Bowman had said, "It isn't good for Negroes to have white people performing servant jobs in front of them." For someone who could be so kind, her employer had horribly wrong beliefs about black people.

Sarah's reflections were interrupted—and reinforced—when Mrs. Bowman sighed and said, "I'd love to have Jonathan here with us. I do worry so about him being all alone."

Almost two hundred slaves, yet she feels he's alone, Sarah thought.

❧

"And so Farmer Smith. . .plowed his corn fields. . .with . . .great care." Looking over the *Hartlet's Book of Elementary Prose* she'd bought in April, Sarah sought Violet's eyes. "Well?"

"That was good. You learn fast," said Violet, smiling.

"You're a good teacher. I think I'm ready now."

"Ready?"

"Someone I knew once gave me a notebook of things he'd written down. I've never been able to read it, but I'd like to try."

"Do you want me to help?"

Sarah gave Violet's hand a squeeze. "I haven't let anyone read it. Can you understand?"

Violet shrugged. "Course. We'd best be getting out of the kitchen anyway, before Miss Willie Mae gets up from her nap."

Hurrying quietly to her room, Sarah took the leather-bound notebook from her chest of drawers. Settling in a chair by her window so the June sun could light the pages, she opened the cover.

"Violet!" Sarah banged on Violet's cellar-room door.

The door opened immediately, and Violet, puzzlement showing on her face, let Sarah in.

"I can't read any of it!" Sarah cried, her cheeks splotched red. "Look!"

Taking the notebook that was thrust out at her, Violet opened it. Suddenly, she laughed.

"It's not funny!" exclaimed Sarah, bursting into a fresh torrent of tears.

"I'm sorry," Violet apologized. Turning the notebook so Sarah could see the pages, she explained, "This is script."

"Script? But that's not what you taught me."

"Not yet. It comes after you learn to print." Pointing to a letter, Violet said, "What letter does this look like?"

Sniffling, Sarah took the book from Violet. "Is it a b?"

Violet nodded, her face beaming. "Most of the script letters look like the printin' that you already know. It won't take long to—"

"I can't wait any longer!" said Sarah. "I want you to read it to me now."

The girls sat on Violet's quilt-covered bed and Violet turned to the first page of the notebook. "Gracious, Sarah. It's a book of Scripture!"

"Yes, that's what David said it was."

"David?"

"The friend who gave me the book."

Violet's dark eyes lit up. "I haven't seen a Bible since I came to Magnolia Bend. You don't know how I've prayed to be able to read Scripture again. Just listen, Sarah!" Clearing her voice, she read slowly and reverently:

My sheep hear my voice, and I know them, and they follow me: And I give unto them eternal life; and they shall never perish, neither shall any man pluck them out of my hand. My Father, which gave them me, is greater than all; and no man is able to pluck them out of my Father's hand.

"My Father's hand," repeated Sarah, eyeing Violet's face thoughtfully. "You're a Christian, aren't you?" she asked. "Why didn't you tell me?"

"I wanted to, and sometimes I could feel the Lord telling me to talk to you about Him, 'specially when we'd study your reading together, but I was scared."

"Why?"

Violet wiped a tear from the corner of her eye. "Right before you came, Miz Dora used to be in a real bad way. She even accused us of poisoning her food! One day I was cleaning in her room while she was in bed, and she started crying."

Wiping her other eye, Violet continued. "I felt the Lord telling me to tell Miz Dora all about Him so she could learn to have joy—just like He's been telling me to talk to you. Only, when I tried to, she got mad at me and slapped my face. She said that somebody who don't have a soul shouldn't be so uppity as to preach to her mistress."

"Oh, Violet. I'm so sorry. I wish I'd been hit instead of you." After a long silence, Sarah asked, "You really can feel God telling you things?"

"Yes," said Violet. "I know that don't make a lot of sense, but—"

"No, it makes sense!" Sarah interrupted, grabbing Violet's shoulder. "Because I've felt something calling me, and I wondered if it could be God."

"Glory be!" exclaimed the slave girl. "That's how I felt before I got the new birth!"

Sarah shook her head. "Now you're not making sense."

A smile spread across Violet's face. "I'd best start at the beginning." She pursed her lips. "You see, God lives in a place called Heaven, where there's no sin—not even a little speck."

"I know about Heaven," said Sarah. "Mrs. Carlton told me about it. People go there when they die."

"Good!" said Violet. "But, the problem is we're all sinners, because we can't help but sin once in a while. We got that from the first man and woman, Adam and Eve."

"I've heard about them, too. They lived in a garden until they ate some fruit that God told them not to eat."

"So we've got that sin inside us, and remember what I said about Heaven?"

"Not a speck of sin," answered Sarah, her face solemn.

"Don't look so sad. That ain't all there is!" said Violet. "See, there was a man named Nicodemus who was real important back in Jesus' time. You know who Jesus is, don't you?"

"Yes. He was the Son of God."

"Not was," said Violet. "He still is. He was living in Heaven with God, the Father, but He came down to earth in a body like ours a long time ago. Anyway, Nicodemus felt that callin' that you and I felt. He couldn't sleep one night, so he went to where Jesus was staying."

Sarah's eyes filled with longing. "I wish we could do that."

"Wouldn't that be nice!" Violet said. "But we can still talk to Him."

"Prayer?"

"Prayer. And He can talk to us—if we listen—by making us feel things in our hearts that He's trying to tell us. We can read the things He said, too."

"Scripture," said Sarah.

"That's why I was so glad to see some," breathed Violet, hugging the notebook to her chest.

"But what about Nicodemus?" asked Sarah.

"Well, he was a mighty good man. He didn't kill nobody, went to church, and told the truth the best he was able. But he still wasn't satisfied."

Sarah's voice fell. "He knew there was something he needed, but he didn't know what it was?"

"And you know what that feels like," said Violet. "Do you know what Jesus told him? He told Nicodemus he had to be born again."

"But how?"

"That's just what the man told Jesus! And you know what he was thinking—that Jesus was telling him to be a little baby all over again." Violet rolled her eyes. "As if! You know what Jesus told him after that?"

Sarah shook her head.

"He said, 'That which is born of the flesh is flesh; and that which is born of the Spirit is spirit.' We're all born of the flesh, 'cause we're human beings. But the only way to get into Heaven is to be born of the Spirit. That means asking Jesus to save us, and when we do, He cleans the sin out of our hearts and sends the Spirit to live inside us." Violet leaned forward, studying Sarah's face. "Do you understand?"

"Some of it," she answered. "Mrs. Carlton had a little silver cross with Jesus on it. When I asked her about it, she said he died for us and came alive again three days later, but I didn't understand why."

Violet was thoughtful for a minute. "Do you remember just a little while ago when you said you wished Miz Dora had slapped you 'stead of me?"

"Yes."

"Well, Jesus did the same thing. He looked down at us from Heaven, and He seen that we was going to be punished for our sins. That made Him so sad that He told his Father, 'I wish it could be me to be punished instead of them.' That's why He came down and died on the cross. He took our sins on His own self, and shed His blood to pay for them."

"So how do you get born again?" asked Sarah.

"By asking God to let Jesus' sacrifice on that cross be for your sins, too, and trusting Him to do that."

"That's all?"

Violet grinned. "I know it sounds too easy, but He wanted it simple enough for an ignorant slave like me to understand."

Sarah grinned back. "Or an ignorant Brit like me. I want to think about all this." Reaching out and touching the leather cover of the notebook again, she asked, "Would you read some more to me?"

"For as long as you want me to," answered Violet.

Watching her friend's brown face filled with joy, Sarah remembered back to that terrible dinner party at the Nortons'. *If God knows everything, He must know that I don't have a father*, she thought. *Does it matter to Him?*

Just then the sound of Violet's voice penetrated her thoughts. "A father of the fatherless. . .is God in his holy habitation."

☙

Sarah had just walked through the front door with a basket of grocery parcels when she heard a familiar voice in the parlor. *Jonathan Bowman*, she thought, retreating.

"Sarah, is that you?"

Not able to pretend that she didn't hear Mrs. Bowman's voice, Sarah stepped into the den.

"Yes, ma'am," she said, ignoring the man who stood as she entered the room.

"Haven't you noticed Jonathan, here? I was just telling him how much Judge Rarick reminds me of him, don't you agree?"

Smiling through clenched teeth, Sarah said, "Judge Rarick is a gentleman."

"See?" said Mrs. Bowman, beaming up at her son. "Sarah sees the resemblance, too."

The corners of Jonathan's mouth curled up. "It's good to see you, Sarah. I've been here in town on business for a couple days, and I wanted to see Mother before going back."

"I don't know why you didn't stay with us," pouted Mrs. Bowman.

"This house is so small. I didn't want to make anybody uncomfortable."

"Well, goodbye, then," said Sarah. "I'd better put these groceries away."

"Wait." Jonathan held a hand up. "May we talk on the porch for a few minutes?"

Startled, Sarah looked questioningly at Mrs. Bowman.

"Jonathan told me you might be taking another position and not returning to Magnolia Bend with me in October. I don't think I could go back there without you," Mrs. Bowman said. "I told him to talk you right out of that foolish notion! If it's more salary you need—"

"I'll handle it, Mother." To Sarah, Jonathan said, "Would you please talk with me now?"

The two walked out to the porch, and Jonathan leaned his tall frame against the rail. "I don't think you're concerned about salary," he said, "but I'll be happy to raise it if you'll stay with Mother."

"The salary I receive already is more than generous," said Sarah, shielding her eyes against the bright August sun. "I must confess that I haven't looked for another job yet. I've been so happy here."

"Really?" His eyebrows lifted.

"Yes, sir. Violet has been teaching me about God."

Jonathan laughed. "I hope Mother hasn't heard her teaching you religion." Turning his back to the sun, he asked, "You think you'll be coming back, then?"

"I don't know," said Sarah. "I'm wondering if you. . . ."

"If I plan to act like I did last time?"

Sarah lowered her eyes. "Yes."

"I'll tell you what," said Jonathan. "You tell me how to act around you, and I'll do it. I promise."

"You promise?"

"I just said I did."

"I want you to leave me alone," said Sarah. "If I go back, you mustn't buy me any gifts or touch me."

"And you'll come back if I do those things?"

She sighed. "I want to think about it. May I have a week to decide?"

"Yes," he said. "Tell Mother your answer. And Sarah?"

"Yes, sir?"

"I'll be a perfect gentleman—just like Judge Rarick."

❧

Pushing open the wrought-iron gate in front of the stuccoed house, Jonathan heard tapping overhead. Gazing down from a second-story window, Trudy was waving and smiling.

Has she been in that window all morning? wondered Jonathan, remembering how he'd waved goodbye at her from the street earlier. He'd evaded his mother's questions about where he was staying, knowing how appalled she would be if she discovered her son was staying with the notorious Widow Dalton.

Letting the gate swing behind him, Jonathan stopped. Squinting, he judged the distance the sun was from the horizon. *I could make it back to Magnolia Bend before dark if I started right now,* he thought.

The face behind the upstairs window looked confused. *What did I ever see in her?* Jonathan wondered. Her bawdy laugh irritated him, along with her insistence that she be with him every waking moment. It was a wonder she hadn't followed him to his mother's! *What would Mother have thought—or Sarah?* he mused, reminding himself that a servant's opinion didn't matter.

Touching the brim of his hat in farewell, Jonathan turned on his heel and went back through the gate to where Luther was tethered to a hitching post.

❧

It's no use. I can't sleep! thought Sarah, punching her pillow. *If I don't decide soon, Mrs. Bowman might hire somebody to take my place.* The thought of being separated from Violet was too terrible to consider, but Sarah didn't want to constantly keep her guard up around Jonathan Bowman. And what if his sincerity had been an act? Sarah was determined that what had happened to her mother was not going to happen to her.

Slipping out from under her sheet, Sarah walked to the window and pressed her forehead to the glass. The moon was a sliver over the darkened houses lining East Bay Street. *I'm the only person awake in Charleston,* she thought.

If only she could talk to someone. She couldn't discuss her struggle with Violet, who'd told her that she'd run away if Sarah didn't come back to Magnolia Bend. She didn't want Violet doing something that would endanger her life!

Suddenly, David's face came to mind. *I've got his office address in the notebook,* she thought. Hadn't he told her to come to him if she needed help? She remembered that day in Washington Park when she had seen him with the well-dressed lady. Perhaps he was married to her.

What difference does it make! Straightening, Sarah crossed her arms. *I'll just ask for advice as a friend.*

❧

"Five more months!" exclaimed Kathleen Harvey, white spots rising on her flushed cheeks. "You told me David would be gone for only six months. It's already been four!"

Sighing, Mr. Harvey held out his beefy hands helplessly. "This assignment he's working on—I'll need him over there a little longer."

"But you said—"

"I know, I know. But he's doing a good job investigating opportunities, and he needs to go to Liverpool to close out an agreement. Good business can't be rushed."

Kathleen leaned forward, her clenched fists on top of her father's desk. "You'll let your own daughter suffer so you can make more money, is that it?"

Mr. Harvey slammed down his palm on a stack of detail papers, sending the top sheet flying. "Listen to me, young lady," he growled. "Making money is what I do well, which is a good thing because you and your mother spend it as fast as I make it. Now go count your dresses or something, and let me get back to work!"

Kathleen hurried from the private office, glancing back to see her father concentrating on his work as if she'd never visited. *I'll be an old maid, and what does he care?* She strode past clerks with their heads bowed over their ledgers as if they hadn't heard her father yell at her. She would love to slap them all for pretending to work while, inside, they were laughing at her! Throwing the front door open with all her weight, she nearly ran over a young lady.

"Why don't you watch where you're lurking!" stormed Kathleen, finally able to vent her wrath on someone.

"I'm sorry," said the girl. "I didn't expect the door to open so quickly." Her face brightened. "Perhaps you can tell me. Does David Adams still work here?"

Kathleen's mouth dropped open. *So, this is why David broke our engagement!* She lifted her chin haughtily as she studied the intruder. The waiting girl could be called pretty, though she lacked sophistication.

"David is overseas on business now," Kathleen said icily. "When he returns, we'll be getting married. He'll be too busy to entertain visitors."

"Oh!" said the girl, her face turning crimson. "When you see him, please tell him that Sarah Brown came by."

"I'll do that," said Kathleen as she turned on her heel to leave.

Mrs. Bowman looked up from the book in her lap when Sarah walked into the parlor.

"If you still want me, I'll go back to Magnolia Bend with you," said Sarah.

Chapter Twelve

Never having seen Magnolia Bend in autumn, Sarah was unprepared for the burst of warm colors. "Is there any time that it isn't lovely here?" she asked Mrs. Bowman, who was seated opposite her in the carriage.

"I used to wonder that myself, but as I get older, I find it more and more difficult to leave Charleston," said the older woman, sighing. "I guess I'll always be a city girl at heart."

"Perhaps a certain judge has turned your head." Jonathan winked at his mother beside him.

"Oh, watch how you talk!" said Mrs. Bowman, gently slapping his hand and turning to address Violet. "And what did you think of Charleston?"

Violet's eyes shot open in surprise. "It was nice, Missus."

"Well, I'm certainly bringing you back next year. The house looked so nice. You practically did the work of two people!"

Had not Mrs. Bowman and Jonathan been seated across from them, Sarah would have burst into laughter. As it was, she averted her face and pretended to watch squirrels playing on a nearby limb. She knew that if she looked at Violet, they'd both have trouble keeping straight faces.

Later that evening, the girls unpacked Sarah's trunk. "How do you feel about being back?" Sarah asked.

"Maybe things'll be better around here—at least for the house servants. You sure have caused a change in the missus."

Sarah shook the folds out of her sea-green poplin dress. "I don't know what I did, except maybe have a good appetite."

"What?" Violet tilted her head to look at her.

"I'll tell you one day."

When the last dress and nightgown were put away, Sarah reached into the almost-empty trunk for her leather notebook. "I'll keep this in the top drawer of my chest. Whenever you want to read it, help yourself."

Violet flashed an easy smile. "You sure you don't need me to read it to you anymore?"

Shaking her head, Sarah smiled back. "I almost wish I hadn't learned to read script. Those days were special."

"It was the words that was special," said Violet. "You can't read the Lord's words without feeling a stirring in your soul." Her face grew serious. "Have you thought any more about asking for the new birth?"

"Many times, but I keep thinking I should wait until I feel worthier."

"Sarah, there most likely ain't anybody on this earth as good as you. You've helped me with my work, bought me those two dresses in Charleston, and you're just plain nice to everybody, colored or white.

"But," Violet continued, "compared to Jesus, none of us is worthy. We've all got some sin in our hearts. You've just got to repent—that means be truly sorry for your sins—and ask Jesus to cover them with the blood He shed on the cross. That way, when God looks at you, He don't see any unworthiness at all, just the purity of His own Son."

"All right," said Sarah. "I want to do that now."

"Glory be!" exclaimed Violet. "Do you want me to leave?"

"No, please stay. Do you think I could pray standing at the window? I'd feel closer to God if I was looking out at that sunset."

"I don't see why not."

Both girls stood at the window, feeling the nippy October air against their faces. "Should I pray out loud?" asked Sarah.

"Why don't you just be still for a minute and let God speak to your heart. Then you'll know how to do it."

Resting her hand on the windowsill, Sarah watched the orange rays of sunlight turn the clouds into hues as varied as the oak leaves in the lane. "Oh, Lord," she finally breathed. "I don't see why You would want me as Your child, but it says in David's notebook that You want to be my Father. Please forgive my sins and save me now."

When Violet didn't speak, Sarah turned to find her friend wiping tears from her eyes.

"Why don't I feel any different?"

"Feelings don't have nothing to do with it. It's what God promised in His Word that counts," said Violet. "But I think those feelings will come before too long. Wait and see."

Violet was right about the feelings, thought Sarah as she lay on her pillow later that night. *I feel like the part of me that was missing is here. At last I have a Father.*

৯

"Have you ever ridden a horse?" asked Jonathan, holding out an apple for Sarah to feed to Lady.

"Oh. Hello, sir." Sarah took the fruit from his hand. The mare's nostrils quivered at the smell of the treat, and lowering her head over the stable door, she pulled the apple into her mouth, dripping juice on Sarah's hand.

"Don't wipe it on your shawl. I keep a handkerchief around for such emergencies," Jonathan said, pulling a square of linen from his shirt pocket. "Don't worry. It hasn't got yellow birds sewn on it."

Sarah laughed. "I'll clean your handkerchief and return it to you," she said.

"Well," repeated Jonathan. "Have you ever ridden a horse?"

"Never." She eyed Lady wistfully.

"Would you like to learn?"

"Now?"

"Why not?"

Her eager expression was quickly replaced by wariness. "No, thank you," she said, reaching up to rub the horse's muzzle one last time.

"Let me guess why," said Jonathan. "You don't want to be alone with me."

"Are you surprised?"

Kicking a piece of hay stubble with his foot, Jonathan sighed. "I suppose not. I guess you're never going to forgive me for my rudeness that day."

"Forgiveness is something I've learned a lot about lately," Sarah answered. "I can forgive you, but I would be foolish to put myself in the same situation again."

"What if we stayed on the river road and Isaac rode with us?" he asked, nodding toward the slave who was soaping a saddle a few feet away.

"Well," Sarah smiled at the dark-skinned young man. "Would you mind?"

Isaac gave a vigorous nod. "I like to ride horses."

Sarah's face fell as she turned back to Jonathan. "I haven't got a riding skirt."

"Mother used to ride all the time, and she's almost as slender as you. I'm sure she'll be glad to lend you one." Pointing to the house, Jonathan added, "Why don't you take care of that, and I'll help Isaac saddle up the horses." He turned to Isaac as Sarah left. "Bring me two bridles."

"Yassir," said the slave, coming around the sawhorse where the saddle hung. He'd only taken a step or two when he stopped, letting out a groan as he bent over slightly.

Sarah wheeled around at the sound of Isaac's cry. "What happened? Is he hurt?"

"It ain't nothing. I'll be fine in a—ouch!" he cried, trying to take another step. "I'm sorry, Massa," he said to Jonathan, his face a mixture of pain and disappointment. "My back give out this mornin' when I was chasing that one-eyed colt back in its stall. I don't see how I can get up on a horse."

"I'll get a couple men to help you to your cabin," Jonathan said. Turning to Sarah, he shrugged his shoulders. "Some other time?"

"Is he going to be all right?"

"Oh, don't you worry none, missy," said Isaac. "This ain't the first time it's happened. I just got to lay me down for a day or two."

Sarah was about to leave again, when she saw the look of concern for Isaac on Jonathan's face. *He cares about them after all,* she thought. Hesitating, she took a step forward. "We can still ride, if you want to."

"Are you sure?" Jonathan asked. "We wouldn't have anyone to go with us. I don't trust any of the Negroes but Isaac to ride my horses in the saddle."

Sarah nodded. "I'll go ask Mrs. Bowman about a skirt."

When she was gone, Jonathan turned to Isaac. "Come help me saddle these horses. Then stay out of sight for a couple days. Have Anson do your work."

Straightening up, Isaac brought some bridles from the tack room. "Massa," he said meekly as he held out a bridle, "I didn't like fooling the missy, there."

"Did I hear you say something?" said Jonathan, stopping to glower at the young slave.

Isaac looked down at his shoes. "No, sir."

&

"By this time of year, work changes on a rice plantation," Jonathan explained to Sarah as their horses sauntered down the dirt road. Over to their right and stretching out to the river were the rice fields, left in stubble from the harvest.

"The rice was shipped last week, and most of the food crops have been gathered. Before winter hits, we'll have the Negroes repair the dikes and mend cabins and fences. Repair broken tools, too. A little later, they'll be butchering the livestock."

They rode on in silence. Finally, Sarah spoke. "I don't understand how one person can own another."

Lifting an eyebrow, Jonathan looked over at her. "You're not an abolition-ist, are you, Sarah?"

"I've been thinking about it a lot since I came to America, and yes, I believe I am."

"The Negroes here have it much better than the free ones in the cities up North," said Jonathan. "Their housing, food, medicine, and clothes are provided, and they get taken care of when they're old. How can you see anything wrong with that?"

Mindful that Jonathan was her employer, Sarah replied, "Sir, I worked for two different households in England. The first family didn't pay me anything, even though I worked hard helping my mother in the kitchen. The second family paid me a pittance, when that."

Taking a deep breath, she continued. "They provided all those things that you mentioned, but I was resentful when I got old enough to think about it. My life was not my own, but theirs—and to be had cheaply."

"But that was different. You could have quit."

Her eyes widened at his blindness. "Don't you see? That makes slavery much worse. Will you allow your workers to leave if they're not happy?"

"It doesn't work that way," he said crisply. "And besides, my people are happy."

There was another silence. *I've made her dislike me even more,* thought Jonathan. After all his planning to be on his best behavior and win her confidence, they were having an argument.

Surreptitiously, Jonathan drew back on the reins so that Luther would slow his pace. Sarah seemed not to notice that her horse was slightly ahead of his. Embarrassed by speaking so bluntly, she had turned her face toward the river.

Taking advantage of the opportunity, Jonathan studied Sarah unobserved. The steady November wind played with the hairs about her face, pulling out whispery tendrils from the thick braid which hung down her back. Her posture, surprisingly erect for one who'd been a servant all her life, showed off her tiny waist. Though he couldn't see them, he imagined her deep-set dark eyes, eyes which made him uncomfortable by their quiet assessment of him.

He'd seen more beautiful women, but none had captivated him like Sarah. *She's bewitched me,* he thought, a frown creasing his forehead. Why had he even brought her to Magnolia Bend? He'd been satisfied with life the way it was.

"We'd better turn around," Jonathan said, realizing how foolish it would be to "accidentally" get caught by the night. "It gets dark in a hurry this time of year," he added.

"Oh, yes," Sarah stammered, giving him an appreciative look. "I hadn't noticed."

When they'd turned the horses around and were headed back toward the plantation, Jonathan said, "I'm sorry if I was rude to you a little while ago."

"You weren't rude," Sarah replied. "I criticized the life you've had since you were born. Perhaps I had no right to speak. After all, slaves prepare my food and clean my clothes. But I will always think slavery is wrong."

"Then can we ever be friends?" he asked, his nerves growing taut when she hesitated.

"Yes, if you like." Sarah leaned forward to pat Lady on her neck. "I appreciate your teaching me how to ride."

"Then you'll come riding with me again?"

"I'd enjoy that very much."

સ્ર

Three weeks later, Violet came into Sarah's room with a bucket of glowing embers for the fire. "You awake?" she asked.

Sitting up in bed, Sarah kept the quilts up around her shoulders against the chill. "Yes. Thank you for the fire. Do you have time to read some of the notebook with me?"

Violet shook her head. "Maybe after supper's cleared up. Miz Bowman wants me to get with Trudy in a little while and let her teach me how to sew. One of the girls that helps Trudy make clothes for the servants, her eyes are going bad. I'm glad, 'cause I like to make things with my hands, 'stead of just cleaning all the time, but I might not be able to visit with you as much."

Having laid the ember and kindling, Violet sat on the edge of the bed and faced Sarah. "I need to talk to you about something."

"All right." Sarah studied her friend's face. "It's something serious, isn't it?"

"That depends. You been out riding horses a lot with Master Bowman lately, and that's got me worried."

"But he hasn't tried—you know—since we came back here."

"That's good," said Violet. "How do you feel about him?"

"Do you mean is there a romance between us?"

Violet nodded, her eyes grave. "It ain't none of my business, but—"

"We're just friends," said Sarah hastily. "I like him, but I'm not in love with him."

"You're sure?"

"Very. Now, what's this all about?"

Violet's shoulders relaxed. "I was worried that you were falling in love with him. Some 'round here say he's got an evil heart."

"Really? Why do they say that?"

"The field hands don't hardly talk to us house servants. They say we're uppity, and maybe some of us are when we shouldn't be. So we don't hear a lot of the talk that comes from the quarters. But I did hear that Master Bowman got in some trouble with one of the woman field hands a while back."

Violet put a couple logs over the blazing kindling in the fireplace. "I don't want to see you get hurt," she said, her back to Sarah. "I don't think a Christian should marry someone like Master Bowman."

"Marry!" Sarah laughed. "Violet, you were afraid I'd marry him?"

Turning, Violet's face was a picture of hurt. "Yes, I was afraid it might come to that."

"I'm sorry!" said Sarah, slipping out from under the covers to rush over and hug her friend. "I wasn't laughing at you! The idea of me wanting to marry Jonathan was so—"

"You called him Jonathan just then."

"Well, yes. He asked me to. But we're just friends. Besides, I talked to him yesterday about trusting Jesus, and he said he'd think about it."

"He did?" It was Violet's turn to look surprised. "Well, I guess if ol' Saul can be changed, then there's hope for Master Bowman! Just. . .I hope it's 'cause he's really interested, and not just to get on your good side." Suddenly, she looked down at Sarah's feet. "Better get you some slippers on before you catch some kinda sickness!"

Chapter Thirteen

"I want to spend a couple weeks in town," said Mrs. Bowman from the other side of the chess table. "The weather always turns nasty after the beginning of the year, so this is the last time I can go until spring. I'd like to do some Christmas shopping, too."

She's missing Judge Rarick already, thought Sarah as she moved a pawn diagonally. The quiet, gray-haired man had been by the house for Thanksgiving dinner. His bushy eyebrows looked comically out of place over a neat mustache, but Mrs. Bowman thought him the most handsome man in Charleston.

The transformation in Mrs. Bowman's appearance since she had met the judge that spring was remarkable. She fussed with her hair and dressed with great care. *Perhaps they'll get married,* thought Sarah, *and she can always live in Charleston, where her heart is.* Increasingly, Mrs. Bowman complained about the inconveniences of living in the country.

"I want you to come with me," she was saying. "We won't be taking any servants, as some good friends have invited me to stay with them."

≈

Glenda Wallis and Murial Hinton were widowed sisters quartered in a brownstone on Barkley Street. Why Mrs. Bowman had wanted Sarah to accompany her remained a mystery to the girl. When Mrs. Bowman wasn't shopping and gossiping with the sisters, she was being entertained by Judge Rarick. Fixing Mrs. Bowman's hair and helping her dress were Sarah's only responsibilities.

During her free time, Sarah explored the city. At a bookstore on Canton Street, she bought Violet a black Bible wrapped in brown paper. On the shopkeeper's recommendation, she purchased herself a copy of *The Pilgrim's Progress.* She had that book wrapped as well, for she still had to do her reading in secret. What would happen if anyone learned that Violet had taught her to read, Sarah didn't know, but she didn't want to risk her friend's life.

As she walked back from the bookstore, Sarah thought of the slave who'd been hanged for having an abolitionist pamphlet. Jonathan knew better! Would he send a young woman to the gallows as well? Why not? Any system that would force human beings to work in the stagnant water of the rice fields—without a share in the profits—would easily sacrifice the life of a slave who dared to take some control of her life.

Am I helping such a system by working for the Bowmans? Telling herself that the Bowmans would continue to own slaves whether or not she was in their employ wasn't working anymore. From reading the Scriptures in her well-worn notebook, Sarah had concluded that Christians had to take stands against evil, even if they stood alone or the effort appeared to be futile.

I should resign my position right now, she thought. Mrs. Bowman was much kinder to the servants, now that she realized they hadn't been plotting against her. *But what about Violet? I told her that I'd stay.*

That's when the idea hit her. She would buy Violet from the Bowmans! At first the thought was so repulsive that Sarah felt nauseated. But on further consideration, she realized it was the only way. *I'll pay for her, then set her free!*

"Free!"

The curious stare of the woman sweeping the sidewalk in front of the lace shop made Sarah realize that she'd spoken aloud. Giving the woman a wink, she hugged her packages and continued walking, resisting the urge to skip.

As she continued planning, Sarah realized she didn't know how much a slave would cost. Would the seventy-five dollars saved from her wages be enough? She bit her lip. Mrs. Bowman didn't run Magnolia Bend, so she probably had no idea.

I'll have to ask Jonathan when we get back, Sarah thought. *Please, Father,* she silently prayed, *show me a way to help Violet gain her freedom.*

ॐ

The clamor of wheels and hoofbeats brought Jonathan to his feet. Tossing his book back into the chair, he crossed the room and walked out the front door to the porch.

He paid no heed to the biting December chill that greeted him. Squinting, he struggled to glimpse down the oak-lined avenue. *They've come back early,* he thought. Had his mother tired of shopping—or of the judge? Had Sarah missed Magnolia Bend? It seemed like so much longer than a week since she'd gone.

Suddenly the farm wagon came through the shadows, and Jonathan could make out Jason's brown face and a couple wooden crates. Jonathan slammed his open palm against the top of the railing. Bolting down the stairs, he waved the wagon to a stop.

"Who sent you to town?" he demanded, glowering at the slave.

"Mista Gatewood sent me to see if these here tools he ordered last month was in."

"I'm supposed to know about supply trips. Why wasn't I told?"

Jason's face was a mixture of confusion and fear. "Mista Gatewood, he done already told you, Masta. This mornin' before I left, at the back door. Remember he asked if you be needin' anything else?"

One of the horses hitched to the wagon let out a snort, nodding his great head as if laughing at him. Narrowing his eyes, Jonathan studied the slave's face for any signs of mirth. Being embarrassed in front of a servant was a new experience for him, and he didn't like it. "Go on," he ordered.

"Wait a minute, Masta. I got some letters here, too," said Jason. "You wants me to bring them inside?"

"No. Give them here."

The wagon had only gone a few feet when Jonathan called out, "Jason!"

"Yassir?"

"Tell Isaac to have Luther fed and saddled first thing in the morning," he said, grinning at the envelope clasped in his hand.

ъ

David stood at the foredeck of the *Great Western*, watching the hull slice through the whitecaps. He'd be home in time for Christmas. Smiling to himself, he thought of the Christmas gifts he'd purchased in Europe for his parents and sister. He hoped he'd be allowed to take at least a week off from his job, to visit them in Jasper. *If I still have a job, after Mr. Harvey realizes I haven't changed my mind about marrying Kathleen.*

ъ

Sarah was well into the third chapter of *The Pilgrim's Progress* when a tapping sounded from her door. Closing the book, she pushed it under her pillow.

"Come in," she said, standing up and brushing the wrinkles from her blue calico dress.

"Miss Brown, you have a visitor," said Charlotte, a round-faced maid with rosy cheeks.

"Me?" There'd been visitors every day since Mrs. Bowman and she had arrived in Charleston, but none for her. Pausing at one of the dressers

crammed into the room, Sarah glanced into the mirror. *Should I hurry and pin up my hair?* she wondered, knowing that it would take at least fifteen minutes. Deciding that it would be rude to keep her guest waiting that long, she picked up a boar-bristle brush and ran it through her thick chestnut hair. Then she ran down to the parlor.

"Mr., I mean, Jonathan."

Sarah smiled and nodded at Charlotte's offer to bring tea, then turned back to the man who was standing in front of an overstuffed sofa. "I'm sorry, but your mother and some of her friends are having breakfast at the Russell house."

"It's you I came to see," said Jonathan, taking his seat only after Sarah found a place in an opposite chair.

For the first time in weeks, her face became wary. "Why?"

"You received a letter yesterday. I thought it might be important." From inside his gray frock coat, he pulled out the envelope. "Would you like me to read it to you?"

It's David! The thought leaped into Sarah's mind as she started to reach out her hand. *Wait. You're not supposed to be able to read,* she reminded herself. Putting her hand back in her lap, she asked, "Would you mind?"

Jonathan tore open the envelope and unfolded some sheets of paper. Glancing through the letter, he frowned. "This is from my cousin, Elizabeth Mobley. She says that a letter arrived for you late this summer at her parents' old address, and she's just getting around to sending it on, from a Julie Martin."

"Miss Martin!" Sarah sat up in her chair, her face lit up. "Please, read it to me!"

"You have the most beautiful smile," said Jonathan, oblivious to the letter in his hand. He blinked as if startled by his words. "I'm sorry. I know you don't like me to talk like that."

Sarah was grateful for the arrival of the tea tray just then, making it unnecessary for her to respond. Though Jonathan had professed to love her months before, she hadn't believed he meant it. But during the fall, she'd noticed him staring at her while pretending not to and making excuses to be near her.

Could he really be in love with me? She hoped not, for he'd been so kind lately, and she didn't relish the idea of hurting him.

Turning to the enclosed letter, Jonathan began to read:

Dear Sarah,

    Forgive me for not writing sooner, but things have been quite busy around here. I want to thank you and your employer, Mr. Carlton, for giving me back my home.

Sarah wondered what Miss Martin meant by that until she remembered a conversation she'd had with the Carltons. After she'd been with them for some months, she'd told them about how Miss Martin had suspected that her attorney had plotted with the Gertys to take away her home. Mr. Carlton had told Sarah that he'd write Miss Martin a letter, advising her to get another attorney and have the matter looked into. They'd not heard from Miss Martin since.

    As Mr. Carlton suggested, I contacted a solicitor with a reputation for being honest, and he was sympathetic with my case. It took a full year of tracking down so-called creditors to discover that I hadn't been as deeply in debt as my former attorney had stated and that it was unnecessary to sell my house. From there, we informed the constable.

    During the investigation, Mrs. Gerty dismissed me and I had to move into a boarding house, but it was worth it! Mr. Gerty and his attorney were brought to trial in June and are both serving prison sentences for fraud and theft. Mrs. Gerty, alas, was sent to the insane asylum near Crawford, as she caused quite a row when the eviction notices were given.

Miss Martin's letter went on to say that Agnes and Frances were doing well, having received substantial raises in their salaries. Ginny and her husband had come back to work. After more words of gratitude to Mr. Carlton and Sarah, the letter ended.

Jonathan grinned with amusement. "This Miss Martin thinks you're quite a heroine! How does it feel to have someone so deeply in your debt?"

"I owe her more than she could possibly owe me," said Sarah, earnestly. "If it hadn't been for her, I'd still be working for Mrs. Gerty back in Bristol."

"Oh yes, the one in the insane asylum. A rather interesting letter. You'll have to tell me about these people."

Smiling, Sarah repoured his tea. "It's so good to hear that they're doing well. I left them less than two years ago, yet my life is so different now."

"Does that mean you're happy?"

"Oh, yes!" Sarah said. "God has been so good to me."

Leaning forward, Jonathan's expression was hopeful. "Have I done anything to help bring about this happiness?"

"Of course. If you hadn't hired me, I wouldn't have met Violet." Immediately, Sarah realized she had not given the answer he had expected.

"You and your mother have been kind to me, too. I shall never forget you."

Jonathan frowned slightly. "You sound as if you're going somewhere."

"No, not me, but I'd like to talk to you about something."

Jonathan sat with an air of expectancy.

"Would you, uh, consider," she stammered, "selling Violet to me?"

"What?"

"Violet. I have seventy-five dollars, and I want to—"

"I heard you the first time," Jonathan said, crossing his arms. "Has our little abolitionist decided she needs a slave after all?"

"Certainly not! I want to give Violet her freedom."

Leaning back in his seat, Jonathan laughed. "Such high ideals in a woman of—how many years? Only eighteen? So, you want to pay me so you can set Violet free."

"What's wrong with that?" Sarah said, lifting her chin so that she could look him in the eyes.

"Nothing, my dear. You have a tender heart, and I admire you for it. But Violet's not for sale."

"Why not?"

"Well, for one thing, you don't have three hundred dollars."

"That much?" she whispered, her face falling.

"A bargain price these days, I assure you."

Sarah wiped her eyes with the back of her hand. "It would take two years to save three hundred dollars."

"Seems like I'm always around when you need a handkerchief," Jonathan observed, reaching out to hand his over. "Actually, you'd only have to save two hundred twenty-five, since you said you have some already. But that's not the only obstacle. It's against South Carolina law to let slaves go free."

"But there are free black people in Charleston. I've seen them!"

"Yes," he agreed. "They were set free either long ago by people without any foresight or recently by provisions in their owners' wills."

"Their wills?"

"And you know what has to happen to carry out the provisions of a will. I'm not prepared to die so that Violet can pretend to be white."

Sarah's face reddened. "Have you any sympathy for these people?"

"Yes, I have. Some. But you can't change the way things have been for the past century."

Blowing her nose into Jonathan's handkerchief, Sarah shook her head. "I was so excited, and now it's going to take so long." Abruptly standing, she made a motion toward the door. "I'm sorry. I'm not feeling well. Can you let yourself out?"

"Wait," said Jonathan. "Please sit down. I know a way you can help her."

Taking her seat again, Sarah waited. Jonathan was struggling to find the right words.

"You could become her mistress another way."

The wary expression returned. "How?"

"By marrying me."

The blood in Sarah's body felt like it had turned to molasses, and her heart pounded.

"Don't you have anything to say?" asked Jonathan, testily. "You look like I told you to sleep in a graveyard!"

"I can't," Sarah finally said.

"Because you don't love me." He shrugged his shoulders. "Do you think me a moon-faced young simpleton? I know you don't love me. I'd prefer that you did, but I want you for my wife regardless."

Sarah looked down at her hands. "How would my marrying you help Violet? Even if I were her mistress, she'd still be a slave."

"Not if we let her go."

Jerking her head up, Sarah narrowed her eyes. "You just said that was against the law."

"We could take her with us on our wedding trip up North and forget to bring her back, with no one the wiser."

"You mean, just leave her?"

"With some money to help her get started." Grinning, Jonathan said, "Your seventy-five dollars should be enough, don't you think?"

"I don't know. It doesn't seem like a lot to live on."

"It seemed like a lot of money to you a few minutes ago. You were trying to buy a slave with it." He winked. "All right. I'll give her a hundred dollars, too. I think that's pretty generous, considering I could sell her tomorrow for—"

"I'll do it," Sarah whispered, closing her eyes.

Jonathan tilted his head as if he hadn't heard her correctly. "Do what?"

"I'll marry you."

"Right now?"

Sarah's eyes shot open. "Now?"

"The sooner we get married, the sooner we can set Violet free." He studied her face. "You don't mind having a small wedding, do you? I find guests and all that tedious."

Shaking her head, Sarah murmured, "Where?"

"How about right here? I can find a minister who'd like to earn some extra money, and we can be married by this evening."

Sarah tried to think rationally. "Your mother. What would she think?"

"Of course," Jonathan said, slapping his forehead. "We need to make sure she's here. What will she think? She'll be delighted. She's been pestering me for years to give her some grandchildren. I suppose it'd be wise to wait until tomorrow morning. That way, you can pack for our honeymoon, and I can send for Violet. Would you like me to buy you a new dress for the wedding?"

It was all happening too fast. "No. I'll wear my green one."

"Be sure to wear your hair down around your shoulders," he said. "You said Mother is at the Russell house? I'll drop by and let her know our plans, so she can have the satisfaction of making a little fuss. She may insist on that new dress. Do you mind?"

"It doesn't matter," Sarah said flatly.

"Well, I'm off then." Jonathan rose to his feet. "Do you think you could spare a kiss for your fiancé?"

Obediently, Sarah stood, bracing herself. Taking a step closer, Jonathan put both hands on her shoulders, his blue eyes crinkling at the corners while a smile played about his lips. Bending slightly, he brushed her forehead with a kiss and was gone.

❧

Sarah was trying on the new ivory silk dress when Mrs. Bowman called to her from outside the door.

"Sarah, dear, may we come in?"

"I'll get it," said Gretchen, the maid who'd been fastening the row of covered buttons on the back of the dress. Opening the door, she stepped aside for Mrs. Bowman and the sisters, Glenda and Murial.

"Don't you look lovely!" exclaimed Mrs. Bowman. "And wait till you see what Priscilla is making for your hair—tiny satin roses with seed pearls."

Glenda pursed her lips. "The dress drags. We should have Priscilla take up an inch or so."

"Good idea," said Murial. Turning to the maid, she ordered, "Go tell

Priscilla to bring some pins right away."

"I'll finish buttoning you up," said Mrs. Bowman, motioning for Sarah to turn around.

Murial nudged her sister. "We'll let you two talk. We have a lot to get ready by tomorrow morning."

"I'm afraid this is turning into quite a lavish affair, contrary to Jonathan's wishes." The last button fastened, Mrs. Bowman turned Sarah around by the shoulders. "Glenda and Murial are so excited that it's hard to keep things simple."

Sarah smiled. "I don't mind. How do you feel about. . . me?"

"To be blunt, a few years ago I would've thrown a fit. Marrying a servant is frowned upon by my friends. Does that offend you?"

"When you've been a servant all your life, you understand how things are," answered Sarah honestly. "I'm not offended."

Mrs. Bowman gave a relieved smile. "When you came to Magnolia Bend, I was ready to lose my mind. I can't believe I had you switch trays with me!"

"It wasn't without some fear at first," laughed Sarah.

Wiping the corner of her eye, the older woman continued. "Remember the nights when I was afraid to go to sleep, and you came in my room and held my hand? You didn't treat me like a crazy woman, and your calmness helped me get over my silly fears."

Impulsively, Sarah stepped forward and gave Mrs. Bowman a hug. "Who will play chess with you while we're gone?"

Mrs. Bowman winked. "You've become quite skillful, but Judge Rarick is a master—or so he thinks. He's asked me to marry him several times, but I turned him down. I didn't want to leave my son for good until he had a wife."

"So, you'll reconsider the judge's proposal?" asked Sarah.

"Most definitely!"

❧

Changing back into her blue calico dress and wool cloak, Sarah slipped down the winding staircase and walked quietly through the massive living room. She closed the front door gently behind her, then sat in the nearest rocking chair. *They can handle the rest of the wedding preparations without me,* she thought. *I'm going to wait right here until Violet comes.*

Resting her head against the high back of the rocker, she closed her eyes, listening to the sounds of carriages in the street. Something didn't feel right, now that she had time to herself.

"You told me you weren't going to marry Master Bowman!" Someone was urgently shaking her shoulder.

Blinking her eyes, Sarah looked up into the face of her friend. "Violet!" she said, jumping up to give her a hug. "I couldn't wait to see you. I've got wonderful news for you!"

Violet's eyes widened. "Wonderful news! Don't you remember what I told you about him?"

"Let's go for a walk before it gets too dark," said Sarah, glancing back at the front door. When they were out of earshot of the house, she explained. "I'm marrying him for your sake."

"My sake? Oh, Sarah. I thought you was sensible, but something's—"

"Just listen." Sarah held up a hand. "Jonathan said he'd set you free up North if I married him."

"Set me free?"

"Yes, free! We're going to take a schooner to Boston tomorrow after the wedding, and you'll have enough money to take care of yourself until you find a job. A real job, Violet. You won't be somebody's slave!"

Violet didn't reply as they walked down the sidewalk lining Barkley Street. The shadows of the palmettos and magnolia trees were growing longer as the sun hugged the western horizon, bringing a noticeable drop in the temperature.

"Is your shawl warm enough?" Sarah finally asked, disappointed that her friend didn't seem excited.

Drawing the worn shawl tighter to her slim body, Violet looked at Sarah. "If it wasn't, would you give me your cloak?"

"Of course," she said, her fingers reaching up for the top button.

"And what would you wear to keep warm? My shawl?"

Confused, Sarah paused at the second button. "Yes, I suppose."

"Then I'd be warm and you'd be cold. But you'd be happy, 'cause you love me."

"What's wrong with that?" asked Sarah, coming to an abrupt halt on the sidewalk. "Why are you talking like this?"

Violet turned to face her friend. "You're giving me your cloak—your freedom—and taking my shawl—slavery. Did you think that I would be happy about that?"

"But I'm not going to be a slave!"

"Do you love Master Bowman?"

"Well, no," said Sarah. "But he promised to—"

"If you don't love him, then you're going to be his slave."

Sighing, Sarah reached for her friend's hand. "It won't be like that. He loves me, so he'll treat me well."

"And what about the things the field hands say about him?"

"Did you ever find out what he did?"

"No, but I don't trust him, and I don't want you to marry him!" Violet's tone softened. "Sarah, have you prayed about this?"

"There hasn't been time," she answered, her face solemn. "I was so happy when he promised to set you free that I felt it was a good thing to do. Don't you want to have your freedom?"

The slave girl sighed. "It's what I've prayed for many times. But this way ain't right."

"I said I'd marry Jonathan, and it's too late to change things," said Sarah, her voice suddenly firm. "Let's enjoy our time together while we still have it." They'd walked a few more yards when she asked, "Do you still love me?"

"Yes, my sister," whispered Violet.

"I have something for you in my room. I was going to give it to you for Christmas, but—"

"You're givin' me the chance to be a free person. That's enough, don't you think?"

"It's a Bible," said Sarah. "I bought it yesterday, and you won't have to hide to read it, either."

"A Bible." Shaking her head in wonder, Violet put a hand over her heart. "I can't hardly take the joy that's runnin' through me right now."

Sarah's eyes became moist. "Would you sing for me one last time?"

As they walked hand in hand down the brick sidewalk, Violet's clear, perfectly pitched voice sang out through the evening shadows:

> *Gone to take that boat, 'cross the River Jordan*
> *For to see my Lord, for to see my Lord.*
> *His shining face will be there to meet me*
> *He'll say "well done," He'll say "well done."*

Chapter Fourteen

"It's a good thing the weather held until we got back," said Jonathan, wincing at the clap of thunder that rattled the windowpanes. "I hope the dikes hold up in the fields."

"Yes." Sarah's answer was a distracted murmur. Leaving the window, Jonathan walked to the chair where she sat staring into the fire.

"What's wrong with my girl?" he asked, kneeling to take her hands. "Are you thinking about Violet?"

Giving him an unreadable look, she turned her eyes back to the fire. "I miss her."

"But this is what you wanted," he said gently.

Sarah nodded. "It is. But I didn't realize how much it would hurt. I haven't felt so lonely since my mother died."

Jonathan's heart sank. While he knew Sarah didn't love him, he'd figured that he could change that with time. They'd been married for almost a month, and though she was kind to him, he saw no flicker of love. *How long will it take,* he wondered, *before she loves me as much as I love her?*

Suddenly, he had an idea. "What if I took you to Boston to visit her?"

Sarah's eyes blazed with hope. "You would?"

"Yes, of course." Gratified by the success of his idea, he added, "We'll have to wait until fall, after the rice is harvested and shipped. Can you wait that long?"

"Oh, yes! I thought I'd never see Violet again," she said. "You're so good to me."

He pressed her hands to his lips, closing his eyes. "You've done more for me than I could ever do for you. I never realized how good it would feel to be this much in love.

"But Sarah, I want you to do something for me," he continued, his face serious. "If I can't go riding with you, don't go alone. The ground is frozen and slippery. If Lady slips and breaks a leg, you could be lost out in the cold. Take Isaac with you, but don't go alone."

"All right." Sarah ran her fingers through Jonathan's thick dark hair. "It's nice to have someone worry about me."

"It is?" His expression was hopeful. "You do care about me, don't you?"

She smiled. "I care about you."

❧

The bell over the door tinkled a welcome as Violet walked into the shop. The sharp smell of fabric dyes greeted her nose. Stacked bolts of cloth covered shelves on three walls.

"May I help you?" The white lady coming toward her was young and had copper hair pinned loosely into a bun.

"I saw the sign in your window," said Violet, "and I'd like to apply for the job."

"I'm Louise Johnson. I own this shop. Have you worked as a seamstress before?"

Resisting the urge to look down at the floor, Violet kept her head level. "I learned to sew shirts at the plantation where I lived. They weren't much fancy, but my stitches were straight and even."

"What about dresses?"

"No ma'am, I ain't had a chance to sew on a dress." She glanced around the shop at the fashions hanging from smooth wooden posts. "I could do it, though."

The owner looked doubtful. "I need to hire someone with more experience with ladies' dress clothes. Perhaps you should try one of the tailor shops?"

"Ma'am," said Violet, taking a deep breath. "Why don't you let me work for one month? I have money to live on for a while, so I won't take pay during that time."

"Oh, I couldn't let you do that," said the lady.

Violet pressed on. "I can get a job at a shirt factory, but I want to make dresses. I love the feel of good cloth and the way colors are put together to make a dress pretty. If you'll give me a chance to prove it, I'll learn fast, and you won't be sorry you hired me."

The lady studied Violet's face. "Where are you from?"

"Charleston, ma'am."

"What is your name?"

"Violet Bowman."

"Well," said Louise Johnson, smiling, "I'll give you one month. You'll get a salary, but if I'm not pleased at the end of that time—"

"Yes, ma'am!" Violet's dark eyes shone. "Thank you!"

❧

"But the way you see it, everyone is bad." Jonathan shook his head. "That's ridiculous, Sarah."

"I didn't say that. I said we're all sinners. Surely you'll admit that you've sinned at least once in your life."

"Well, of course I have—like everyone else," said Jonathan, moving his knight on the chessboard. "But that doesn't make me a sinner."

Sarah thought for a moment. "What if Lucy brought you some water and said that she let one of the dogs take a lap from the glass. Would you drink it?"

"Which dog, Luke?"

"I'm serious," Sarah said, crossing her arms.

"All right, let's see. No, I wouldn't drink the water."

"Why?"

He sighed. "Because it would be dirty."

"From just one little bit of dog saliva?"

"You're making some kind of point here. Would you care to fill me in?"

"Delighted to," she said with a smile. "If it takes just a drop of saliva to make a cup of water dirty, how many sins does it take to make someone a sinner?"

"Uh, fourteen?"

"One."

"And now you're going to tell me about Jesus dying for my sins again."

Pain washed across Sarah's face. "It's the most wonderful story I've ever heard, how someone so great could love us enough to do that. Don't you want to hear more about it?"

"Frankly, no," said Jonathan, reaching over the board to pat her on the arm. "If it makes you feel good to pray and do all that, I'm happy, really I am. But don't worry about me. I haven't been perfect, but I don't think I've done anything that would send me to hell."

Sarah sighed. Jonathan looked at her, wondering if he'd made her angry. After a long pause, he asked, "Did Mother tell you?"

"About Judge Rarick?"

Nodding, he added, "They plan to marry as soon as planting season starts, when she moves back to Charleston. Then she'll live there for good."

"He has a beautiful home, and she's happy in town. How do you feel about it?"

"I'm glad, of course," he said. "I just hope he doesn't expect me to call him Daddy."

"Daddy," she echoed, smiling.

Relieved that he'd brought a smile back to her face, he spoke again. "You'll need to leave with Mother in the spring. I'll come to Charleston as often as I can, but I won't want you around here then."

Her face solemn again, she gave a slight nod. "I'll pray that you don't get sick."

"Well, it can't hurt to have an angel pray for me," he said warmly. "But don't worry. I've never had so much as a cold."

❧

"It's a small family gathering," explained Mr. Harvey.

David Adams watched his employer's eyes. They were confident, even smug. *He's used to getting what he wants,* David thought. *He fully believes he can get me to change my mind.*

"Sir," he said aloud. "I've made plans for tonight. But thank you for the invitation. Please give my best wishes to Mrs. Harvey and Kathleen."

"I don't remember saying anything about tonight," said Mr. Harvey. "The invitation is for tomorrow night."

"But you said," David exhaled audibly, his shoulders falling. "I'm afraid I can't come tomorrow night, either."

"Let me guess. You've got other plans?"

"No sir, I haven't. It's just not a good idea for me to see Kathleen."

"But you've seen her already. I watched you, young man, when she walked through the office yesterday. You did a good job of pretending to work, but you couldn't keep your eyes off her."

David ran a hand through his sandy hair. He hadn't noticed Kathleen, but he needed to say something that wouldn't cause Mr. Harvey to lose face. "She's a beautiful young woman," he replied truthfully.

"But you're not interested." His employer's face hardened. "So you plan to keep hiding from her, like a coward?"

David squared his shoulders. "I don't plan to hide from Kathleen. Because I don't accept your invita—"

"Then why haven't you been to church since you came back from England?" Mr. Harvey interrupted.

"I have been—every Sunday."

"We haven't seen you. What do you do? Hide up in the balcony with the coloreds?"

"No, sir." David cleared his throat. "I've found another church."

"What!" Mr. Harvey's eyes grew twice their size. "So that's why you've decided to reject my daughter! Don't tell me you've become a papist. What have you done, taken some strange vow of celibacy?"

His cheeks coloring, David rose from his chair. "I've simply joined a congregation of believers a friend told me about. Perhaps you'd like to visit us. We meet in a house on Allyson Street."

"That'll be the day!" Mr. Harvey snorted. Picking up a pen, he waved his hand at the door. "Proceed with your work, Mr. Adams."

≈

"What did those men want, and why did they have those dogs?"

Jonathan turned away from the window. "What?"

"Those men—is anything wrong?"

Glancing back toward the window, Jonathan gave Sarah a distracted smile. "Albert Jordan lives about ten miles upriver. One of his slaves ran away, and Mr. Jordan wanted permission to look around."

"You think he might be hiding here?"

Jonathan shook his head, walking over to put his hands on his wife's shoulders. "They said he's been gone for a week. It'll be nigh impossible to track him in this snow."

A shiver ran through Sarah's body. Somewhere, a man was being chased by a dozen men with guns and dogs. "What will happen if they find him?" she asked faintly.

Jonathan's face was somber. "That's none of our business, and I don't want to talk about it."

Hesitating briefly, Sarah gave a nod, wondering why he wouldn't look her in the eyes. *He must realize I'm hoping the slave doesn't get caught.*

≈

David was surprised to find Elizabeth Mobley standing in the open doorway instead of a maid. "Um, Mrs. Mobley?"

She absentmindedly smoothed the sleeve of her worsted mauve dress, elegantly cut, though a bit worn. "Yes?"

"Do you remember me? I'm David Adams. I looked at—"

"I remember you, all right." Her eyes narrowed. "You and your prissy little fiancée tried to cheat me out of a fair price for my house last year." A look of triumph came to her face. "Well, I sold it anyway, and got much more than you two were willing to pay."

"That's good," David replied, genuinely relieved. "I felt badly about the way we changed our minds."

"Well, now you can rest easy," she said sarcastically. "Good day to you."

"Wait." David put out a hand before she could close the door. "I was wondering if you could help me. I'm looking for a maid that worked for your parents, a Sarah Brown. I thought you may have heard something about her."

"Elizabeth!" A man's voice boomed through the doorway. "Shut the door. You're letting in the cold!"

"Please?" asked David quickly. "Anything?"

Glancing back over her shoulder, the woman sighed. "Was she the little girl from England?"

His face lit up. "Yes!"

"She got married a couple months ago," she said, just before the door clicked shut with finality.

๛

"I'll only be out for a little while," said Sarah, kissing her husband on the forehead as he sat propped up by his pillow. "Isaac is going with me, so don't worry."

Jonathan's response was ambushed by a violent fit of sneezing. Wiping his reddened nose with a handkerchief, he said, "Be careful, and don't stay out too long."

"I'll stay with you if you'd rather."

"No," he said, waving a hand. "The horses could use the exercise. Anyway, I'm going back to sleep." He blew his nose again. "How long do these things last?"

"About a week," she said sympathetically.

"Wonderful."

"How about if I read to you this afternoon?" she asked. "I think you'd enjoy *The Pilgrim's Progress*."

"That might be nice." His brow wrinkled as he rubbed the stubble on his chin. "You know, it amazes me how quickly you learned to read."

"I had a good teacher," she answered truthfully.

"But all I did was explain the alphabet, and two months later, you're reading books!"

She gave him a smile. "I'll be back before lunch."

≈•

"And you stirs a little sugar in the milk before you pour it on the snow," Isaac was saying as the horses padded their way through the morning woods on a blanket of snow. "The children likes it that way." He looked over his shoulder suddenly, as if embarrassed to have anyone else know what he was going to say. "I still likes it, too."

"My mother used to make that for me," Sarah said, smiling at the memory. "Sometimes with cream. I thought she made up the recipe herself, but I guess not."

Isaac's hearty chuckle pealed through the snow-numbed stillness. "Likely, children all over the world knows about it if they live where it snows. Maybe they all be thinkin' their mamas thought up the idea."

Her laugh was cut short when Isaac shot an arm out, trying to grab Lady's reins. "Let's turn around now, miss!"

Startled, Lady reared back on her hind legs, pitching Sarah onto the ground.

"Oh, what I done!" Isaac cried, jumping from Luther's back. He ran over to where Sarah was struggling to sit up in the snow. "Miss Sarah, is you all right?"

Dazed, she wiped her face on the sleeve of her coat. "I think I'm all right. Will you help me stand up?"

Taking her by the arms, the slave pulled her to her feet. "You can walk?"

Sarah nodded, trying a couple steps to be sure. "Why did you do that?"

"I'm sorry, missy," he said, his face stricken as he stepped over to take Lady by the reins. "Let's go back now."

"Why?" Brushing snow from her eyelashes, Sarah tried to see what had startled Isaac on the trail.

"You ain't going to want to see it."

"See what?"

"Never you mind," said Isaac, his voice respectful but firm. "I'll come back by myself after we gets you home."

Fear and the cold set Sarah's teeth chattering. As she put her left foot in the stirrup and swung into the saddle, she concentrated on staring at Lady's mane. She was just about to turn the horse around, when she glanced up.

"No!" she cried, her face draining of color. "Isaac, it's—"

"It's dead," said Isaac, flatly. "Let's go."

Everything inside of Sarah wanted to leave, but she couldn't tear her eyes away from what lay on the trail ahead of them.

"Miss Sarah?"

She shuddered. "Please go see if he's really dead."

"Masta gone be mad at me if I let you 'round that body." Isaac's eyes were wet. "That ain't something a lady needs to see."

"I'll tell him I made you. Please, Isaac."

She watched as, reluctantly, Isaac climbed down from Luther's back. Lowering her eyes to Lady's mane again, she listened until his footsteps, muffled by the snow, ceased. "Is he?" she asked, her voice shaking.

"He done froze to death," sobbed Isaac.

Her eyes filled with tears. "Who is he?"

"I don't know. He's just a child."

"A child!"

Isaac was coming back, wiping his eyes with the back of his glove. "We can't help him, Missy Sarah. I'll come back with some of the others and get him." Catching Luther's reins, he looked over at her. "Let's go."

❧

It had been almost an hour since Isaac, Mr. Gatewood, and two other men had gone back into the woods with horses and a wagon. "They must have gotten back by now," said Sarah to Jonathan, who was pacing the floor of the library. As soon as Sarah had run upstairs to tell Jonathan about the child, he'd dressed quickly and come downstairs.

"You look pale." Dorothy Bowman eyed her son. "Why don't you go back to bed. You're too sick to be up. We'll let you know—"

Her words were interrupted by a knock at the door. "Come in!" said Jonathan.

Betty, one of the downstairs maids, came through the door and held it open for Mr. Gatewood, the overseer. "Mr. Bowman," he began, his face solemn. "May we speak alone?"

Glancing at Sarah before starting for the door, Jonathan nodded. "Come on. I'll get my coat and we'll go on the porch."

"You'll do no such thing!" exclaimed his mother. "Sarah and I will go upstairs so you can speak privately. You don't need to be out in this weather while you're sick!"

With a look of resignation, Jonathan shrugged his shoulders.

When he finally came up to their room, Jonathan looked numb. He walked over to the bed and lay down, not even removing his boots.

Rising from her chair by the fireplace, Sarah quickly stepped over to where her husband lay and put a hand on his forehead. His skin wasn't feverish. "Jonathan?"

He reached up with his right hand and took her hand, pressing it to his chest. "It was the runaway slave—Albert Jordan's."

Sarah gasped. "But that was a child we saw in the woods!"

"I didn't want to tell you that the runaway was a child. I was afraid it might upset you."

"A boy?"

"Yes."

"How old?"

"Ten."

"Ten," she repeated, sniffling. "Why did he come here?"

Jonathan looked at her. "I don't know."

Sarah was trying to coax Jonathan to eat some food from his lunch tray when the commotion began outside. "Listen!" she said, tilting her head. "Do you hear that?"

"What is it?"

"I don't know. At first I thought it was one of the dogs, but it sounds like a person."

Hitting the side of his head with the heel of his hand, Jonathan swallowed hard. "My ears feel stopped up. I can't hear anything."

"I'll go see," Sarah said, putting the dish of stewed peaches back on the tray.

"Wait," he called when she was near the door. "Maybe I should go too."

"I wish you'd stay in bed," she said, turning the knob. "I can ask Lucy what's going on." The sound grew louder as she pulled the door open.

"Who is that?" Sarah asked Mrs. Bowman, who was standing in her doorway.

"I don't know," she answered, her eyes wide. "Let's go down and see."

The sound—which could now be recognized as a woman shouting—grew still louder as they hurried down the stairs and through the living room. Several of the house servants were gathered at the large window near the front door.

"Who's out there?" asked Sarah, noticing that the noise had stopped.

They all turned to look at Sarah and Mrs. Bowman, their expressions uncertain. "Her name be Nettie," said a young girl. "She's havin' a bad spell."

The slaves moved aside from the window so that Sarah and Mrs. Bowman could see. Sarah could hear Jonathan's footsteps on the staircase as she stepped up to the glass.

Outside, a woman was struggling with Mr. Gatewood and Isaac, who were trying to prevent her from climbing the steps leading up to the front porch. The woman, though smaller than both men, was making some headway toward the steps. Suddenly, she started to scream again.

"You done killed him! Massa, you killed my baby!"

Sarah turned to look at Jonathan, who was right behind her, clad in his nightshirt and some britches he'd hurriedly pulled on.

"You killed him! You murderer!" screamed the woman outside.

In a flash, Jonathan was through the front door. "Take her away, Gatewood!" he barked.

Mr. Gatewood's face was red from effort as he struggled with the woman "We're trying, Mr. Bowman," he said breathlessly.

Sticking his head back through the doorway, Jonathan motioned to two male servants. "Ben! George! Help them!"

"I hates you, Massa! I hates you till I die!"

"Sarah, go back upstairs. You too, Mother," ordered Jonathan before disappearing through the doorway again.

About to obey, Sarah looked back through the window. The woman, overpowered by four men, had gone limp, her screams turning into deep, pitiful wails. The men half carried, half dragged her away.

Suddenly a huge black man came running up from the direction of the barns. He held out his arms as he got closer to the woman. "Nettie!" he cried, his voice thick with emotion. Nettie uttered one more cry of anguish, then fainted, her head dropping forward as the men held her upright.

"I'll take my wife, please," said the man.

Looking hesitantly at Jonathan, Mr. Gatewood ordered the slaves to release the woman. The large black man scooped her up into his muscular arms and with a glance at Jonathan, carried Nettie back to the slave cabins.

Sarah watched Jonathan step to the east end of the porch, his eyes glued to the black man and his wife. Cold air from the still-open front door gusted through the house past motionless figures.

The spell was cut by the sound of Jonathan's footsteps as he came back inside, closing the door behind him. Without a glance at the group assembled at the window he walked briskly through the room and up the stairs.

He sat slumped in a chair by one of the bedroom windows when Sarah clicked the door shut behind her. Though she didn't understand what was happening, she knew it was serious and that her husband had some guilt in the matter. *I have to know*, she thought, even as fear of what the answers might be made her blood run cold.

"Jonathan." He didn't move.

"Jonathan, what was she talking about?"

"Nothing," he barely whispered. "She's confused."

Anger stiffened her back. "Don't think me stupid. You tell me, or I'll go and find her."

Jonathan sat up, his blue eyes incredulous. "No, you won't. This has nothing to do with you!"

Suddenly, Sarah remembered Violet's warning about Jonathan having had some trouble with one of the woman field hands. The explanation came to Sarah in an instant, drying up any feelings of affection she'd had for her husband.

"The child was yours, wasn't he?" Sarah spoke in a flat, bloodless voice.

Jonathan's face registered guilt, but his expression quickly changed to one of misunderstood innocence. "My child?" His laugh was forced, hollow. "Do you hear what you're saying?"

Abruptly Sarah crossed to the peg where her cloak was hanging.

"Sarah, I forbid you to talk to that woman!" Jonathan said, rising to his feet.

"You do?" Her eyebrows raised. "Do you plan to lock me in this room for the rest of my life?" Holding her cloak in her arms Sarah stepped toward him. "Because that's what you'll have to do to stop me from finding out what happened!"

Jonathan's fists clenched at his sides. A great sob tore through him. "Sarah, don't hate me!" he cried, throwing himself into the chair.

Her jaw set, she took a step toward the door, then stopped. "Tell me the truth, then," she said softly over her shoulder. "The truth!"

"All right," he said, covering his face with his hands as he leaned forward. "Only, promise me that you won't leave me."

"I can't make that promise. Tell me now, Jonathan."

He nodded, sighing. "Please sit down."

When she'd sat in front of him, Jonathan looked at her, his face wretched. "The boy was mine. I sold him to Albert Jordan when he was seven, about three years ago."

Her face paled as her hand shot up to her heart. "Why?"

"Because he was beginning to look like me. It was embarrassing to see him running around with his blue eyes and light skin." After a pause, he said, "I wasn't proud of what happened, and the boy was a constant reminder."

"What did happen?" she asked icily.

"Oh, Sarah. Please don't look at me like that! I was only nineteen, and so drunk I couldn't see straight."

"Tell me."

"I came home late from a party at one of the plantations. Nettie—I didn't even know her name then—was outside near the stables. I don't know why she was walking around at night. I would have left her alone if she'd ignored me and kept on walking, but she looked at me with fear on her face and took to running."

Taking a deep breath, Jonathan continued. "I was young, remember. I chased her on horseback, cutting her off every time she went in a different direction. It was funny to me, to see how afraid she was." He shook his head. "She didn't scream. If only she'd screamed, I'd have left her alone."

"So you raped her."

His eyes met hers. "I did right by her. When I found out that she was. . ., I bought back Jim, her husband, from the man I'd sold him to."

"You'd sold her husband?" Sarah demanded.

"I didn't know it at the time. Gatewood handles all those details for me. When he told me, though, I bought him back. I even paid more than I'd sold him for. They had other children, later."

Sarah looked past Jonathan. The raw ache she'd felt when her mother had left her at Mrs. Gerty's came back, bringing tears to her eyes.

"He wanted to see his mother," she said, her voice dull.

"What?"

"That's why he ran away. He missed his mother and died in the woods from cold before he could get to her."

Jonathan's hands began trembling. "How could I know he was going to run away?" he pleaded.

Studying his face, Sarah's eyes turned cold. "I don't know who you are."

"Don't say that!" he roared, starting to rise from his chair. "I'm your husband. I love you!"

Sarah shot to her feet, holding out a hand in front of her. "Don't come near me. I'm leaving."

"No!" He stepped toward her. "Sarah, let me make it right."

"Don't touch me!" she commanded as she backed up. "Are you going to make that little boy come alive again? You're an evil man, Jonathan."

He stopped in the middle of the room, his shoulders sagging. "If you leave me—" His voice broke. "I'll kill myself!"

She locked eyes with him. "All right."

"All right? You'll stay?" His face was incredulous, hopeful.

"No. Go ahead and kill yourself!"

Chapter Fifteen

Isaac brought the trunk into her old bedroom in the Bowmans' summer home. "Set it right here, please," said Sarah, motioning toward a place on the floor near the chifforobe.

With a grunt, Isaac slid the trunk down from his shoulders. Straightening, he looked sympathetically at Sarah's red-rimmed eyes. "I'd best put the horses away 'fore it gets too dark," he said gently.

Sarah nodded. "That's a good idea. You shouldn't be traveling back this late."

"Miss Sarah?" Isaac took the brown felt hat from his head and clutched it in his hands. "I ain't goin' back in the morning."

"You're not?"

"No, ma'am. Masta Jonathan tole me to stay here so's I can look after you." Looking down at his hat, Isaac added, "I s'pose there's a room downstairs where I can stay?"

Sarah shrugged. "I don't need anyone to look after me, but I know you won't go back if he told you to stay." She walked toward the door. "I'll show you where the room is."

Isaac didn't move. "There's one more thing, missy," he said, still talking to his hat.

"Yes?" she said, pausing by the door.

"He tole me to give you this money," Isaac replied, reaching a hand into his back pocket, "so's you can—"

Her eyes flew open. "Money! He thinks I'm going to take his money!"

Isaac looked embarrassed. "Now, missy. How you gone to eat if you don't buy food?"

"I'll get a job and leave this house, too. His money's got blood on it, and I don't want it!"

"Yes'm," the young man said resignedly.

Later that night, Sarah tossed restlessly in her bed. She couldn't get the little boy out of her mind. What was it like to freeze to death? All alone in those cold, dark woods, did he cry for his mother?

If only she could sleep! She was exhausted, but her mind raced feverishly from one image to another. Why hadn't she listened to Violet? There could have been other ways to set her friend free. And why hadn't she prayed about it?

Wrapping a blanket around her shoulders, Sarah got up and tiptoed across the cold, oak-planked floor to the fireplace. She squinted at the mantel clock only inches away, but she couldn't make out the hands in the dark. Carefully, she picked it up and carried it to the window, drawing a curtain aside so the moon would illuminate the clock's face.

Four-thirty, she thought. *I may as well lay some fires.* She could have the house warm and be dressed by daylight. That would leave a full day to look for a position.

The house was used rarely in the winter, but Sarah knew a stack of wood was stored in a lean-to against the carriage house. Slipping on some woolen hose and leather slippers, she put her cloak over her nightgown and made her way to the kitchen door.

Shivering as the icy February wind stung her face, Sarah slowly advanced toward the lean-to, walking carefully on the slippery cobbled walk. The return trip was more difficult because the load of wood upset her balance.

Only a few feet from the kitchen door, she moved a little faster. She bent over slightly and raised her knee to support the load while she reached for the doorknob. The top log began to slide. She grabbed for it and lost her footing.

She screamed as her arm hit the frozen ground.

❧

"I think she's 'bout to wake up."

Sarah opened her eyes to find Isaac and a short, bald man at the side of her bed. "Who?"

"I'm Doctor Lemoine," said the man with a slight French accent. He nodded toward her arm. "Are you in much pain?"

Lifting her head from the pillow, Sarah looked down at her right arm. It was stretched out along her side and wound with a thick layer of white bandages.

"I've put splints on your arm so you can move it while the break heals, but you must be careful. Do you need some laudanum?"

"I don't think so, but thank you."

The doctor nodded, touching his mustache. "Nonetheless, I'll leave some here and check in on you next week."

Isaac returned to Sarah's room after seeing Doctor Lemoine to the front door. "Miss," he began, shaking his head. "You should'a let me tote that firewood."

"It's not your fault," said Sarah, managing a weak smile.

"Yes it is. I didn't think to bring in any wood last night." His eyes began to glisten. "I been bringin' you bad luck since yesterday."

He looked so miserable that her heart went out to him. "Isaac, it was good that we found the boy. He needed to be buried properly, not left out in the woods."

"But now you and Masta—"

"That's none of your doing. I found out what he's really like."

Isaac weighed his next words carefully. "I'm gone have to go out for a little while," he finally said. "There ain't hardly nothing in the kitchen, 'cept a little flour in the can and some molasses."

"You're not going to buy food with his money!" Sarah exclaimed, raising her head from the pillow.

"Now Miss Sarah, you got to think." Isaac held up both hands. "How we gone to eat if I don't get some food?"

Her head sank back into the pillow. Her rumbling stomach reminded her that she hadn't eaten since noon the day before.

"Go buy some food," she murmured listlessly, staring up at the ceiling.

❧

The empty bottle crashed against the fireplace bricks, throwing glass slivers over the hearth and rug. "Who needs her anyway!" Jonathan bellowed, wiping the spittle from his mouth.

The knocking at his locked bedroom door had ceased hours ago. Maybe his mother had gone to town, as well. *Let them all leave!* he thought. *I'll burn the place down!*

His bleary eyes found the lavender nightgown Sarah had neglected to pack in her haste to get away from him. He jerked it from its peg on the wall. Stumbling toward the fireplace, he brought the gown to his face. Tears gathered in his eyes as he recognized the faint scent of rose water.

"I'll burn you, too!" Jonathan mumbled, pitching the gown into the blazing fire. Sparks flew as the gown fell against the orange logs.

"No!" Jonathan cried, lurching forward. Falling on his hands and knees, he reached into the flames. Oblivious to the pain, he grabbed the gown and pulled it onto the hearth, jumping up quickly to stomp out the fire with his boots.

He scooped up the scorched garment, then looked down in puzzlement at the red stain on its bodice. He turned over his left hand. A jagged shard from the broken whiskey bottle was imbedded in his palm. Wincing, Jonathan grabbed the glass with his left hand and pulled it out.

Maybe I'll bleed to death, he thought, cradling the gown in his arms. "No!" he murmured, "I didn't mean that!" Furiously, he pressed the bleeding wound against his chest. "Don't let me die without seeing her again!"

⁊◣

"I don't understand what all this is about," sniffed Dorothy Bowman. She leaned her head against the back of the Queen Anne chair. "I know it must have been a great shock to find the little boy in the woods, but haven't you been away long enough?"

Sarah's heart filled with compassion. "I'm sorry, but there's more to it than that," she said gently. "I'll never be able to go back to Magnolia Bend."

Mrs. Bowman's face fell. "You're not thinking about a divorce, are you?"

"I don't know. It hurts to think too much."

"If you could only see him, Sarah. He's barely left his. . .your room. He hasn't shaved or taken a bath in two weeks!" Mrs. Bowman covered her face with her hands. "I think he might be losing his mind!"

Slipping out of her chair, Sarah knelt in front of her mother-in-law and took her hand. "I know you love your son," she whispered, "but there's nothing I can do for him right now."

⁊◣

"I wish you wouldn't go slippin' out of the house in the mornin' without telling me," scolded Isaac. "That's how you got your arm broke, remember? I'm s'pose to be looking after you."

"I'm sorry. I won't do it again," said Sarah. "I only walked a couple of blocks, though, so you needn't have worried." She rubbed the back of her neck. "Will you loosen my sling a little for me?"

Isaac lowered the knot in the wide strip of muslin. "I've just took some biscuits out of the oven," he said. "I was worried they'd be cold before you got home."

"You're turning into quite a cook," Sarah answered, smiling. "Do I smell bacon too?"

"I believes you do!"

When they'd settled at the breakfast table, Sarah told Isaac about a sign she'd spotted over the door to a house on Allyson Street. "It said 'Worship

Services every Sunday morning at ten o'clock,'" she said. "The house was a little larger than this one, so there can't be many people who attend. Would you still call it a church?"

"I reckon, missy. You plans to go there sometime?"

"This Sunday, perhaps. Why don't you come with me?"

Isaac looked uneasy. "I been wantin' to go to church, but maybe you should go by yourself the first time and make sure they don't mind me comin' too."

"If you like," Sarah said. "Isaac, are you a believer?"

"I'm 'shamed to tell you, but I am." He frowned, lowering his eyes.

"Why are you ashamed?"

" 'Cause I helped Masta play a mean trick on you a while back, and every time I look at you I remember how I lied."

Sarah thought. "Your back—it wasn't hurt, was it?"

"No, ma'am. It wasn't. And I knew about what Masta done to Nettie, but I let you go off alone with him."

There was an uneasy silence. "Well, he didn't try anything," Sarah finally said. "And I'm sure Jonathan made you do it."

"That don't make it right. You're s'pose to do right, even when you might get punished for it."

"Then I forgive you."

Slowly, Isaac raised his eyes. "Don't see how you can."

Sarah smiled. "We're supposed to forgive."

Isaac paused, as if weighing his words. "Does that mean you're gone to forgive Masta Jonathan?"

Sighing, Sarah answered, "I don't know."

ಶ

The Allyson Street church met in the living room of Pastor John Varner's white clapboard house. Sunday morning, some members came early to gather chairs from all over the house into the living room. One morning, people had begun filtering through the front door as David Adams was setting up the last chairs.

"David, is John upstairs?" asked Mrs. Oliphant, a kindly middle-aged woman who stood at the door to take coats and hats from people as they arrived. "We have a visitor this morning."

"I think so," said David glancing over his shoulder. "I'll go—" He froze. The young woman standing at the door had her back to him as Mrs. Oliphant helped her remove her shawl, but the long chestnut hair flowing from under a straw hat looked familiar. The woman turned around.

"Sarah!" David said.

"You know each other?" asked Mrs. Oliphant, looking from his glowing face to her startled one.

David took the young woman's left hand. "We met a long time ago." To Sarah, he asked, "Do you remember me?"

"Why, yes," she stammered. "David from the ship."

"What happened to your arm?"

She smiled, sheepishly. "I slipped on some ice last month."

"I'm sorry," he said, his brow furrowed with concern.

"It's almost healed."

"Wonderful! Would you like to sit down?"

When about thirty people were seated about the room, the worship service began. Sarah listened as David's clear baritone joined with the other voices and sang hymns. She was not familiar with them—the songs Violet had sung for her were the only ones she knew about the Lord—but she thought them beautiful.

I can't believe I'm sitting here next to David, Sarah thought. Her happiness at seeing him was suddenly marred by feelings of guilt. *I'm married. Perhaps he is, too. I shouldn't be this close to him.*

After the singing, Pastor Varner, a bearded man of about fifty, stood at the front of the room. His text was the story of the prodigal son from the book of Luke. Sarah listened to the story about the son who wasted his father's money on sinful living. Tears came when the pastor told of how the father forgave his son and welcomed him back into the family.

Lord, Sarah silently prayed. *Are You telling me to forgive Jonathan? How can I? What he did was so awful!*

When the sermon ended, David introduced Sarah to Pastor Varner and his wife, as well as to some other church members. She smiled when they asked her to come back the next Sunday, knowing that she could not. But when David offered to walk her home, she agreed.

They'd taken only a few steps down the sidewalk, careful not to walk too close to each other, when David asked about her husband.

"I was married in December," Sarah said.

"Why didn't he come with you?"

"He's not a Christian," Sarah answered truthfully, not wanting David to know the unhappy details of their separation.

"I'll pray that he will be one day," said David. "And what about you?"

"The Lord used your book of Scripture and a good friend to draw me to Him."

"I'm glad." They turned the corner onto Oakdale Street. "Perhaps you could persuade your husband to come with you next week."

Sarah didn't know how to respond. "David," she began, "I was happy to see you this morning, but I won't be coming back to your church."

"Why?"

"It's best that I go somewhere else to worship. I'll find another place."

He stopped on the sidewalk, under the bleak shade of an overhanging birch tree. "Will you tell me the truth if I ask you something?"

"Yes."

"Is it because of me?"

She nodded slowly. "It is."

Reaching a hand toward her cheek, David drew back suddenly. "I've wondered about you for so long. Tell me, have you thought about me at all?"

"Many times," Sarah said, tears forming in her eyes.

"Then, why didn't you contact me before you decided to get married?"

"I went to your office, but you were in England." Sarah swallowed hard. "I met a lady who said she was engaged to marry you."

"Kathleen." Pain covered David's face. "That's been over for a long time."

"It has?"

He took a deep breath. "We weren't right for each other, and I couldn't get you out of my mind."

"You couldn't? But you never tried to find me."

"Like an idiot I waited too long. When I did, Mrs. Mobley told me you were married."

They resumed their walk in silence, oblivious to the horses, carriages, and wagons that passed by. Too soon, they were at the wrought-iron gate in front of the house. David unfastened the latch and held the gate open. "You know, you could come back to my church," he said impulsively. "We could sit apart and not speak to each other."

Tears ran down Sarah's cheeks as she closed her eyes. "I don't think I could bear it!" With that, she turned and made her way through the gate to the house.

David watched her disappear through the front door, his fists clutched at his side.

☙

"Did you speak to her?" The question was out of Jonathan's mouth before his mother could get down from the carriage.

Dorothy Bowman's face was grave. "Yes."

"How is she?" he asked, reaching up to offer a hand to his mother.

"The splint is off." Dorothy stepped to the ground. "Her arm looks good, if a little pale, but she has a haunted look."

"Do you think it's because she misses me?" he asked, daring to hope.

Mrs. Bowman shook her head regretfully. "Let's go inside, son. I'm rather tired."

Arm in arm, they walked toward the front steps together. "I was able to persuade her to stay in the house," she said. "It took some doing, but she finally listened. I told her that it would embarrass me greatly if she took a job, especially as a servant."

"You gave her the money?" he asked as they entered the front door.

"I gave it to Isaac. She doesn't want to admit to herself that you're supporting her."

Mrs. Bowman took off her cape and gloves, hanging them on the hall tree. "She won't be coming to my wedding—not with you there." She sighed. "I wish one of you would tell me what happened to cause this unhappiness. I know it had something to do with the little boy who died, but, sad as that was, I don't understand how that could keep you apart for two months."

"I don't understand, either," he mumbled.

Jonathan was spending more time in bed, leaving control of the plantation to Preston Gatewood. It was unusual for Jonathan not to check the rice fields for the coming spring planting, but he felt uncomfortable around the field hands. Although they were respectful, he could see the accusation in their eyes, and when they lowered their voices to each other, he imagined they were talking about him.

He had started keeping himself clean, again, but only after becoming nauseated at his own stench. The simple acts of grooming and dressing himself required more effort each day, and his appetite was waning.

She said I was evil, he told himself repeatedly. *She doesn't understand. I never meant to hurt anybody.* He knew many planters who had relations with their Negro women. It wasn't talked about, but almost every plantation he'd visited had a handful of light-skinned children. Compared with most slave-owners, he'd been a model of restraint.

If I could only talk to her again, I could make her understand. Every time that thought came to Jonathan, he'd remember his mother's warning: "She said she'll leave Charleston for good if you try to see her."

ə▲

"I'm beginnin' to worry," said Isaac as he walked inside the kitchen with a basket of groceries.

A long string of potato peeling plunked into the bucket at Sarah's feet. "About what?"

"I keeps on seein' that same white man on the sidewalk 'cross the street. He was out there just now, but when he seen me comin' he walked away."

Setting the paring knife down, Sarah lifted a hand to her throat. "Do you think Jonathan has someone watching me?"

Isaac looked worried. "That did come to my thoughts, but why would Masta do that?"

"I don't know. What did he look like?"

"Nice suit of clothes, but not real tall." He motioned toward his head. "And he's got that light-colored hair."

Sarah clutched the edge of the table with both hands, fighting the consuming urge to run outside. "I know who it is," she murmured.

"Ma'am?"

"He's someone I used to know."

ə▲

"You pathetic dolt!" David said under his breath as he walked the four blocks to his office. "Spending your lunch hours hoping to get a glimpse of a married woman!" How had he let himself become so obsessed with someone he shouldn't be thinking about? He felt a pang in his heart. How long had it been since he'd prayed? What kind of Christian was he, really?

Slipping into a dark alley a few yards down from his office, David got down on his knees, ignoring the pebbles that pressed sharply against the cloth of his pants.

Father, forgive me for not keeping my heart in tune with Your will, he prayed silently. *I ask for the strength to stay away from Sarah's house. And please take care of her.*

Chapter Sixteen

Sarah was taking the carriage back from St. Michael's Church when she caught a glimpse of a woman who looked like Mrs. Bowman. Just as she was about to ask Isaac to stop the horses, she got a better look at the woman's profile. The unfamiliar face turned and looked at her, as if wondering why she was being stared at.

She's probably left for her honeymoon by now, anyway, Sarah thought, sitting back in her seat. *I hope her marriage is happier than mine.* Four months was a long time for a married couple to be apart, and Sarah knew things couldn't stay as they were for much longer. Yet she hated the thought of going back to Jonathan.

It would have been easier had he been cruel to her. *He made me feel special, cherished,* she thought. *I could have been content—even happy—with the man I thought he was.*

❧

Jonathan waved Lucy away when she approached him in the library with a tray. "Not hungry," he said, wiping his face with a handkerchief.

"Your mama tole us to make sure you eat your meals," she said timidly.

"What?"

"Leah done cooked fried chicken and dressing for you."

"Why do you care if I eat?" he growled. "You'd all be happier if I starved to death!"

When she made no response, he narrowed his eyes. "Wouldn't you?"

"No sir."

"Well, everybody else would! How long are they going to hold this grudge?"

"Don't know, Masta," said Lucy, placing the tray on the coffee table. "You gone to eat now?"

With a shrug, he moved to a chair near the food. "Wait a minute," he said as Lucy turned to leave.

"Yes, Masta?"

"Why aren't you mad at me, too?"

"Ain't my place to judge you. Fact is, Masta Jonathan, I feels sorry for you." Fear flashed across her face. "I better go now," she said, lowering her eyes as she took a step back.

"No," he ordered. "Sit down."

Obediently, Lucy perched her slight body on the edge of a straight-backed chair, her eyes fastened on the hands she'd clasped at her knees.

"Oh, relax, Lucy! You look like I'm going to hit you!" he said through clenched teeth. "You've lived here since I was a boy. Have I ever mistreated you?"

She shook her head. "No, sir." After a pause, she added, "You ain't never mistreated the dogs and horses, either."

"And what's that supposed to mean?"

Lifting her chin, Lucy asked, "How many children do I have, Masta Jonathan?"

"I don't know—three or four," he said impatiently.

"Five children, all grown. I had six, but my youngest died eight years ago."

"I remember that, Lucy. He drowned while swimming in the river."

"Charles. We didn't get to bury him," she said, her tired eyes watering. "But I carry this around with me all the time." She reached behind her head and untied a leather cord, pulling it out from under her dress. "This here has a button from his shirt inside," she said, holding up the cord so that a small cloth pouch dangled from it. "When I gets to missing him so much that I can't stand it, I takes out this button and holds it to my cheek."

Jonathan fidgeted in his chair. "You've carried that around your neck for eight years?"

"Sometimes I has to make another pouch, when this one gets worn. Don't know why, but it helps some." Tying the cord back around her neck, she looked at Jonathan again. "I'd give up the rest o' my life if I could have him with me for just a day, Masta. Just a day."

A big tear rolled down Lucy's cheek. "We colored folks loves our children, just as much as white people loves theirs. We ain't like the hen out in the coop. She forgets about her first batch of biddies when another hatchin' comes along."

When he didn't speak, she continued. "And the colored children—they loves their mammas and daddies. I was 'bout thirteen years old when I came here on a boat from New Orleans with some other slaves. I thought my heart would wear out from grieving for my folks."

"When my father died," Jonathan said softly, his eyes staring blankly at the wall, "I cried every night for weeks, where no one could hear me." He was quiet for a spell, lost in thought. Abruptly he sat up, startled that he'd spoken out loud. "Take the tray back, Lucy. I don't have an appetite in this heat."

She'd retreated to the door when Jonathan stopped her. "Wait."

"Yes, sir?"

"You said you felt sorry for me a while ago. Why?"

"Because you 'bout the loneliest man I ever seen."

༉❧

Jonathan hugged his arms together under the sheets. How could it be so cold? He'd roasted from the July heat all day, yet suddenly he was too cold to get a quilt from the chest just a few yards away.

A picture of worn fingers caressing a pouch flashed across his mind. Just as quickly, another image took its place: a boy, shivering. What had Lucy said? "Colored children—they love their mammas and daddies."

The little boy had set out, all alone, because he missed his mother. Did he know who his father was? Did he wonder about his blue eyes and straight dark hair? Jonathan clutched the top of the sheet as a dreadful thought hit him. *I didn't know his name!*

༉❧

"I believe I'd like to go fishin' in the mornin'—get us a big mess of perch to fry." The steady motion of Isaac's straw fan matched the thump of his rocking chair against the front porch floor.

"Perch would be nice," said Sarah. She pointed over the treetops. "The evening star is out rather early. See?"

Isaac's attention was on the horse-drawn wagon pulling to a stop in the street in front of the house. "Looks like we have company," he said, rising from his chair. "Why, it's Anson and Lucy from the house!"

Anson's face was grave as he jumped down from the wagon seat and came through the gate.

"What's wrong?" asked Sarah as she stood up.

"He's dreadful sick, ma'am. The doctor won't come out to the river durin' plantin' season, so Mista Gatewood said to bring him to you. Mista Gatewood says he can't leave right now, 'cause too much work in the fields."

Hurrying down the walk with the two men, Sarah went to the wagon and peered over the side. On a mattress under several quilts was her husband. His cracked lips were open and his eyes closed. His face nearly matched the white pillowcase on which his head rested.

"Is he dead?" Sarah asked.

Lucy shook her head. "Not yet. Can you send Isaac for a doctor while we bring him in the house?"

An hour later, Dr. Lemoine frowned, putting his hands in his pockets. "Malaria. Why has he waited so long to get help?"

"Lucy, one of the servants, said he wouldn't let them," Sarah explained. "He told them he didn't deserve to live. The overseer finally made them bring Jonathan here."

"Well, I think he's better off here than in the hospital," said the doctor. "Give him a dose of this medicine every three hours, and I'll check on him every day. Don't give him so many covers. It runs his fever up."

੨*

"I didn't dream it. You came to see me," Jonathan murmured, watching Sarah through half-opened eyes.

Sarah brought an enamel basin to the side of the bed. "Do you know where you are?" she asked as she squeezed water from a cloth and put it on his forehead.

His eyes flitted to the windows. "Charleston."

"You don't remember coming here yesterday?"

"No." A weak smile came to his lips. "You're here with me, Sarah."

She reached under the quilt for his hand. "Are you thirsty?"

"Thirsty," he echoed, but he wouldn't let her leave him to get a glass of water. With her free hand, Sarah managed to dip a clean cloth into the water in the basin. She brought it to his lips, squeezing out a few drops.

"We've sent a message to your mother," she whispered. "I don't know when it'll reach her, but—"

"New York," Jonathan mumbled. "Wedding trip."

Her eyebrows shot up. "You remember?"

"My mind isn't completely gone," he said slowly, and dropped off to sleep.

An hour later Jonathan woke again. "Please give me another quilt," he asked through chattering teeth.

Sarah turned away from the curtain she'd just opened. "You're awake?"

"Cold."

"I'm sorry, Jonathan, but Doctor Lemoine said only one quilt." She crossed the room to sit on the side of the bed. "You want to get better, don't you?"

"I'm not going to get better."

"Of course you are!"

He gave his head an almost imperceptible shake. "Will you forgive me?"

"Forgive you?"

"For what I did." Tears welled up in his eyes. "You're right. I'm an evil man."

"I forgive you," Sarah said, taking his hand.

"Not enough. Can't undo it."

"Sometimes you can't." Sarah wiped her cheek. "But I still forgive you."

The corners of Jonathan's mouth turned up slightly. "You forgive me? I love you, Sarah."

"I. . .I love you too," she said truthfully.

He closed his eyes for a minute, but when she thought he'd dropped off to sleep, he opened them again.

"I'm going to die."

"Don't say that!" exclaimed Sarah. "You're going to get well."

"Sarah," he whispered, turning his face toward her. "I'm scared. I've been having dreams."

"Bad dreams?"

"I don't know what's going to happen to me after. . ."

Sarah's heart lurched. "Jonathan, ask Jesus to forgive you. I know He will," she said urgently.

New tears came into his eyes. "Can't."

"You can't ask?"

"Can't ask. You don't know some of the things I've done."

"Jonathan, He'll forgive you if you ask Him."

"Why would He?"

"Because He loves you."

"No."

"Yes!"

Lord, Sarah prayed silently. *Help him understand.*

"Jesus let people kill Him so people like us could be saved," she explained. "And He's in Heaven now waiting for you to ask Him to save you. Please, Jonathan!"

He was silent. Finally, he nodded slightly. "Show me how."

Sliding closer to him, Sarah laid her head gently on his shoulder. "Lord Jesus," she prayed between quiet sobs. "Please forgive Jonathan of his sins and cover them with Your precious blood so he'll appear spotless before our Father in Heaven. Save him, Lord."

She felt Jonathan's hand in hers tremble. Lifting her head, Sarah moved closer to his lips so that she could hear him.

"Lord, I'm not worth it," he whispered. "But Sarah says You'll forgive me if I ask. Please, forgive me—and save my soul."

With her fingers, Sarah wiped the tears from Jonathan's cheeks and stroked his hair.

The next day, Doctor Lemoine drew Sarah aside. "Give him all the blankets he wants," he said gently.

"But you said—" Suddenly, Sarah understood. "Is there no hope?"

The doctor shook his head. "Perhaps if I'd seen him earlier. Just keep him comfortable."

&

"How do you feel?" asked Sarah, forcing lightness into her voice. She took the bowl of beef broth from Lucy and brought it to Jonathan's bedside.

"Clean," he rasped. "Feel clean." He managed a smile through trembling lips. "But still cold!"

"This warm soup will help." She turned to Lucy. "Please get more quilts."

Lucy gave a meaningful look before going over to the chest. "Plenty of warm quilts in here, Masta Jonathan," she said softly.

After he'd had most of the broth, Jonathan asked for Isaac. "Go tell Mr. Earl Powell. . .my attorney. . .on Beech Street."

"You wants him to come here, Masta?" said Isaac, his brown face a picture of sadness.

"Yes. Tell him, now."

When he'd left, Jonathan turned his head away from the broth that Sarah held near his mouth. "Don't want more. Want to talk to you alone."

Sarah nodded to Lucy, who took the dinner tray and left. "Why do you want to see your attorney, Jonathan?" Sarah wondered if he'd guessed how close he was to dying.

"Never made a will," he whispered. "Want to make sure Magnolia Bend goes to you."

She couldn't speak for a moment. "Please, don't," she said. "I don't want to own any slaves."

"Want to free them."

"What?"

"Let them go. When the rice comes in, divide money up so they can go North."

"Jonathan, you believed in slavery," Sarah said, still in shock. "Why are you doing this?"

"Want to make things right." He coughed, then, with some effort, gave her one of his old grins. "Okay?"

"Yes," she said, her voice trembling.

"You can live in this house. Lease plantation to company from town. They'll use hired workers. Tell them, let the old Negroes stay if they want to."

Nodding, Sarah put her hand on his cheek. "Don't worry about me," she said softly.

One blue eye winked at her. "You don't worry about me, either. Not afraid anymore."

❧

David had read about her husband's death in the *Chronicle* some six months earlier. In spite of the many times he'd wished Sarah hadn't gotten married, he felt for her pain.

He yearned to see her, but he recognized her need to mourn. So many times he'd been tempted to walk on her street and try to catch a glimpse of her.

With a sigh, David set the box of hymnals down. Church was about to begin. Their tiny congregation was growing, and there were plans to start work on a church building when weather got warmer. Most of the members were married. *What would it be like, he wondered, to have Sarah by my side every Sunday?*

"David?"

He wheeled around. She was standing in front of him, a smile lighting her beautiful face.

"I didn't think you'd come back," stammered David.

"Neither did I, at one time. Do you mind?"

"Not at all," David replied. "Will you sit with me? And may I walk you home?"

"Yes, I'd like that," she answered, and the two joined the other worshipers.

They didn't have another opportunity to speak privately until after the service was over.

"I had to leave my job," said David as they walked down the sidewalk, the January wind turning their noses and cheeks red. "But I found a better one right away. I work for someone you may know, a Matthew Wesley."

"Mr. Carlton's shipping company!"

He nodded. "I have to travel quite a bit up and down the coast, but I like seeing different cities."

She looked over at him. The same boyish grin that had charmed her two years earlier was on his face. *I hope I did the right thing,* she thought. *He must realize why I came to his church today.*

They reached an icy patch on the sidewalk, and David shyly offered Sarah his arm.

"You know," he explained, "Mr. Wesley said when he hired me that if I ever got married, I could take my wife on business trips."

"Your wife would probably enjoy traveling with you. Will you ever get to Boston?"

"At least twice a year. You like Boston?"

"Yes," she replied. "A good friend lives there."

"Boston, New York—all kinds of places. It'd be fun, wouldn't it?" He covered her hand and squeezed it. "I'm afraid I don't get to travel this time of year, though. Weather's too bad."

"Well, do you know how to play chess?" she asked.

"Yes. I like chess."

"Then, if you ever get married, your wife probably won't mind staying home with you in the winter."

The Sure Promise

JoAnn A. Grote

Chapter One
Minnesota 1877

"They're not going to chase me away!" Laurina Dalen stood alone on the edge of the bluff, silhouetted against the vast pearl gray sky of early morning, and flung her declaration into the air with bright determination. "For fourteen years I've waited to return to this beautiful wild prairie and I'm not going to let some grasshoppers chase me away now."

Her brown cotton skirt billowed out behind her in the wind that rose with the sun each day on the prairie. The deep brown of the wool shawl clutched about her to ward off the chill in the morning air was drab beneath the rich chestnut curls cascading about her slender shoulders.

But Laurina's mind wasn't on the cold nor on the wind that playfully tugged at her hair. Her thoughts followed the gaze of her large brown eyes to the covered wagons in the cottonwood grove of the village below.

Bellows of oxen, the voices of men shouting orders, and the creak of wagon wheels were carried up the bluff by the wind and sounded loud to Laurina compared to the usual silence of the plateau. Beneath the waving, empty branches of the cottonwoods, men scurried about loading last minute supplies and women hugged friends and neighbors farewell. The stripped branches, more typical of the branches in December than the last week in July, were a grim reminder of the grasshoppers that were forcing these people from the fertile lands of western Minnesota.

The voracious green creatures were gone now. They had left over a week ago in one large, dark cloud. But they were still chasing away her friends—the strong, vital people she had come to know this past year. The wagons were heading farther west, some to the gold fields of the Black Hills, some beyond to the Pacific. The people would find new lands, build new homes, dream new dreams.

But Laurina's dream was here in Chippewa City. In spite of the grasshoppers, the drought, and the hailstorm that had combined to wreak havoc with the crops, she had never been so gloriously happy. Just living with her father again after fourteen years was cause enough for joy.

And there was Matthew—Matthew Strong, the only doctor in Chippewa County.

"Thank You, Lord. Thank You that Matthew isn't leaving," she breathed softly. Her smile deepened as she pictured his hair that shimmered like soft gold when the sun shown on it, his wide face with its lively eyes the blue of

Minnesota's lakes on a sunny summer day, and his cheeks that were always ruddy from the sun and wind.

She hadn't seen him for five days, but it wasn't uncommon for Matthew Strong to spend days out on the prairie of southwestern Minnesota visiting patients. His office was here in Chippewa City, but he felt such a responsibility for the scattered settlers that he visited the more distant settlements at least once every few weeks.

Laurina knew that Matthew tried to see as many patients as possible on each trip so the hours he spent bouncing across the lonely prairie on a hard buggy seat would not be wasted. The prairie grapevine, still amazing to Laurina after her many years in the East, preceded him as he came near their homesteads. As she looked out over the valley, Laurina smiled to herself. What was it about Matthew that caught her heart when she had been immune to the young men who had courted her back east? Was it his sense of responsibility, his dedication to helping people, that kept him here on the prairies of western Minnesota where his patients often couldn't afford to pay for his services?

Or was it the way Matthew rejoiced in just living? Despite the heavy responsibilities he carried on his broad shoulders, he had the most joyous spirit of any man she knew. Perhaps, above all else, it was his love of life that drew her to him. When she was with him, she felt like a carefree schoolgirl rather than an aging spinster of twenty.

How she loved him! But Matthew, the only man who filled her waking and sleeping hours with dreams of a future together, had never spoken of love or marriage, had never kissed her. Instead of flirting with her, he normally spent any time they were together teasing her. Sometimes, when the teasing in his voice and eyes turned to tenderness, she let herself hope he might return her love. A thousand times she had imagined being swept into his muscular arms, his voice husky with emotion as he confessed his love for her, his eyes—

"Morning, Miss Boston."

Laurina jumped as the voice that had been playing in her mind spoke from behind her, and she whirled around to look up at the young giant. If he only knew what she, a minister's daughter, had been thinking, he wouldn't call her by that proper nickname! As usual, his flashing smile and sparkling blue eyes caused her heart to skip a beat. She tripped over her simple words of greeting.

"M. . .Matthew! I mean, Dr. Strong. I. . .I didn't hear you come up."

Matthew pushed the broad-brimmed black hat back on his head, exposing his blond hair to the morning's rays, and warmly smiled down at her. "Thought the 'hoppers stripped the prairie of flowers, but I can see now I was wrong."

Confused but pleased at his words, Laurina lowered her lashes over flushed cheeks. She hugged her shawl more closely about her shoulders in an effort to muffle the beat of her runaway heart. Unsuccessfully, she struggled to think of an appropriate answer.

"Not going down to say goodbye to anyone, Boston?"

She brushed back tendrils of coppery hair the wind was whipping into her face and shook her head. "No, I've said my goodbyes."

She turned back to the scene in the valley—it was easier to keep her thoughts together when she wasn't trying to meet those captivating eyes. *Such a thing to worry about when our friends are leaving their homes,* she reprimanded herself silently as she watched the bustling people below. "I feel sorry for them, Dr. Strong. It must be hard to leave. They all had so many dreams when they came here."

"They'll make new dreams, Boston. They're a tough lot, for the most part."

"Father is down there. Some of the people asked if he'd pray with them before they left. I thought...," she hesitated, then continued with a rush, "I thought I'd pray for them from up here. Somehow, it seemed appropriate, as though the blessing would float down and settle over the tops of the wagons." She glanced up at him. "I guess that seems silly."

The blue eyes she loved looked down at her. "Doesn't sound silly to me. Expect they can use those prayers. Mind if I join you?"

Laurina stared at him in surprise as he bowed his head. They had never prayed together before.

They stood next to each other, etched against the slowly bluing sky, as Matthew brought their request before God. "Lord, we lift our departing friends before Thee. We ask that Thou keep them safe as they journey and supply their daily needs. Guide each family to the place Thou hast reserved for them alone and refresh their spirits with hope. We leave them in Thy arms, Lord. Amen."

"Amen," Laurina repeated softly. *We haven't even touched, yet I've never felt so close to him.*

"The wagons look like loaf after loaf of frosted bread, don't they?" she said, breaking the comfortable silence.

"Might wish we had some bread here before the winter's up, frosted or not. Looks as though only one field in the county survived the 'hoppers. Won't be half enough flour to go around this winter." His tone was matter-of-fact, with no hint of bitterness.

As she contemplated his comment, Laurina's fingers played idly with the edge of her shawl. Last year the grasshoppers had turned their ravenous appetites on the waving fields of wheat in Chippewa County and approximately half the crops had been lost. This year was far worse—even the gardens of Chippewa City had been invaded. There were no vegetables to be had anywhere, at any cost.

The people who remained spoke of a brighter future. Laurina was fiercely proud of the way they held to their hope in the midst of poverty, in the face of the stagnation of the young community. She was glad to be one of them.

She lifted her pointed chin a trifle and determination glinted in her usually soft eyes. "Well, a few green pests aren't going to chase me away!"

Matthew's laugh rang out on the morning breeze. "A few green pests? You know, you make a pretty good prairie woman for a lady from Boston."

Laurina drew herself up to her full five feet, squared her shoulders, and looked up indignantly at him. "I was living on the Minnesota prairie long before you."

"Until you were six years old. Hardly counts as pioneering," he chided playfully.

"You can't look down your nose at me too much, Dr. Strong. After all, since no one lived here ten years ago, everyone in Chippewa City is a transplant. Some of them even come from Boston."

"Ah, yes," he agreed amiably, disciplining the smile on his lips though not succeeding with the laughter in his eyes. "But there's a mighty difference in the transplanting of a farmer or a blacksmith and the transplanting of a proper Boston maiden. Yet, I admit I'm *fairly* impressed with your progress." As he looked at her, he rocked back on the heels of his dusty boots, lifted his eyebrows, and tilted his head.

Was that a hint of admiration she saw lurking behind the laughter in his eyes? "I'm going to pretend you meant that as a compliment and change the subject." She turned her back on him primly and looked out over the valley again as he chuckled.

Below them, simple log and frame buildings straggled bravely alongside the dusty main street at the bottom of the bluff. Her eyes roamed past the river that bordered the town and the stripped cottonwood grove with its band of wagons, to the far bluff and beyond to where the prairie resumed its unending flat expanse.

"I'm glad Father's cabin is built up here where the view goes on forever, rather than down in the valley. It seems impossible that there will ever be more buildings up here on the bluff, what with so many people leaving."

"But the town fathers have plans for this village, Boston. It's not going to stay trapped down there forever." Matthew swung around, taking in the plateau behind them with the sweep of his arms. "They don't see just a one-room schoolhouse and a half-dozen log homes up here like there are now. They see rows and rows of tall, fine houses, with churches there, and there, and there." His broad index finger stabbed the air. "And maybe over there a university, a large brick university standing solid and majestic against the prairie winds. With a library beside it, filled with the knowledge and literature of the world. And trees, trees everywhere—elms and oaks and maples and cottonwoods—stretching their limbs out over wide streets, sheltering fine carriages pulled by matched mares." With a wink and a grin, he looked over his shoulder at her. "Carriages filled with beautiful women." He rested his hands on his slender hips, his eyes shining over the barren plateau. "It's going to be a fine town, Boston."

Laurina smiled at his enthusiasm. "I can almost see it growing before my eyes when you talk about it like that." *This is what I love most about him,* she thought, *the eager way he approaches life.*

"It's the most up-and-coming town on the prairie, Boston. Even the *St. Paul Press* says so."

"Those statements were made before the grasshoppers came, Dr. Strong."

He brushed her argument aside with a wave of his hand. "The 'hoppers are gone now, and the most reliable reports say they won't be back next year."

"The people are leaving, also," she reminded gently, nodding toward the crowd bustling about the wagons in the valley below, "and not only the farmers. The probate judge has already left, and one of the owners of the mill. And now the sheriff, the tinsmith, and the farm implement salesman are leaving."

"Merchants from the East and immigrant farmers poured into the area before the 'hoppers came, and they will again, you'll see."

Before she arrived last year, Laurina thought the destruction of the crops affected only the farmers. She hadn't realized that the entire economy of a new town on the edge of the frontier was dependent on the farmers for survival. Chippewa City was less than ten years old and hadn't the capital to withstand the economic blow dealt by the grasshoppers.

Wind-tangled curls brushed her shoulders as she shook her head. "You are an eternal optimist."

His beautiful smile flashed. "So are you, or weren't you just telling me a few minutes ago that the 'hoppers weren't going to chase *you* out?"

"Well. . . ." A grin tugged at the corners of her mouth, and she bent her head, studying the ground to hide the laughter in her eyes.

"So here we are, two optimists in the middle of a county entirely destroyed by 'hoppers. And what's wrong with that?" He shrugged his broad shoulders. "Remember the verse your father preached on last Sunday?"

Laurina stared at him in surprise. First he prayed with her and now he was talking about Scripture?

"You remember, Boston, the verses from Joel 2," he urged.

"I remember, it's just—" she swallowed her astonishment. "I remember. 'And I will restore to you the years that the locust hath eaten, the canker-worm, and the caterpillar, and the palmerworm, my great army which I sent among you. And ye shall eat in plenty, and be satisfied, and praise the name of the Lord your God, that hath dealt wondrously with you: and my people shall never be ashamed.' "

Matthew nodded emphatically. "That's the one. 'I will restore to you the years that the locust hath eaten.' I believe that. Besides, looking on the dark side of things never solved any problems. Sure never built any cities! And Chippewa City will be a fine city one day, Boston. You'll see."

I can see a lot of things I haven't seen before, Laurina thought, *and I like what I see.* "If everyone else *did* leave this town, I declare you'd build it yourself, Dr. Strong."

"Wouldn't have to build it *all* by myself, Boston, since you're determined to stay put." The look he gave her sent chills scurrying all the way down to her toes.

Laurina's gaze seemed glued to his. She tried to swallow the lump growing in her throat. Unsuccessful in the attempt, she forced her voice past the maddening obstruction. "S. . .sounds like building that town you described is more your vision than it is the town fathers'."

"That's only a piece of my vision." Matthew turned back to the broad, empty plateau, his hands on his hips, a distant look gentling his face. "I want a hospital here, Boston. A place where people can come when they're sick, instead of lying in dirty sod huts and cold log cabins scattered across the prairie where I can't reach them in the middle of a blizzard." The usually laughing voice was quiet, and Laurina could almost feel the aching need underlying his statement.

For a moment, Laurina thought that his shoulders were sagging as if under some unseen weight. But that couldn't be—his shoulders were as broad and strong as his wonderful, unfatigable spirit. Weren't they?

Yet even his voice sounded tired as he said, "Wish that hospital were a reality now, well-staffed with doctors whose wisdom far exceeds mine." The wind didn't cover his deep sigh as he nodded toward the wagons. "Wells wanted to leave with those wagons."

"Harlan Wells?"

He nodded. " 'Hoppers took his crop this year and last year, too. Had to sell his oxen to qualify for a seed loan last spring. Mortgaged his wagon and farm equipment. He doesn't have any way to carry his two kids away from here. Sure wish I could have saved his wife. Things are rough enough for him without losing her."

Laurina's heart twisted unbearably at the pain in his voice. She wished to reach out and comfort him. Instead, she said only, "I know you did everything you could for her, Matthew." His Christian name slipped from her lips without either of them noticing.

"Wasn't enough."

Laurina's mind filled with the picture of Harlan Wells beside his wife's grave the day before. How bleak and lonely the gravesite looked on the wide, treeless prairie! The young farmer with his chalky face and drooping shoulders was so filled with grief that she had felt afraid for him. Her father tried to talk with Mr. Wells and comfort him, but the widower said he just wanted to be alone.

The noises from the valley below changed and the creaking of the wagon wheels became a screeching sound.

"They're pulling out!" Matthew swung around, grabbing Laurina's elbow and pulling her with him.

Laurina slipped on a loose tuft of prairie grass that the grasshoppers had somehow missed and clutched at Matthew's coat to regain her balance. His strong arms steadied her, though they had the opposite effect on her nerves.

"Can't have you tumbling down the hill. Might land in one of those wagons and end up at the Pacific, and then who'd help me build this town?"

Laurina felt her heart tumbling down the hill after the tuft of grass she had loosened.

"Thank you, Doctor," she managed in an almost normal tone. Reluctantly, she moved to release herself from his hold, but his hands remained lightly at her waist.

"Don't you think it's about time you stopped calling me Doctor? My name's Matthew."

As if she didn't know. As if she hadn't repeated his name with words of love over and over again in her dreams since meeting him a year ago.

A tender glow slowly replaced the laughter in Matthew's eyes as he smoothed back a lock of her hair. Laurina knew she couldn't credit her recent slip for her breathlessness as the hand that had soothed so many fevered brows caressed her cheek with trembling gentleness. As Matthew bent to lay his lips on hers, she was only vaguely aware of the call of a robin soaring overhead and the brightness of the morning sun. It was a sweet, questioning kiss, and she rejoiced in its beauty.

"Laurina Dalen, I love you." The familiar voice was husky with the words that sang in her heart, and she didn't resist as his arms folded her tenderly against his chest.

She whispered her love for him, and was filled with wonder at the joy that lit his eyes at her words, the words she had hidden inside herself for so many months. Her stomach tied into knots as he kissed her again, not a questioning kiss this time, but a kiss of exultation and promise.

The screeching of wagon wheels, still rolling across the valley, slowly filtered through Laurina's senses and she pulled away from the beautiful world of Matthew's arms.

"We shouldn't be. . .not here!" she answered his questioning gaze. Before he could make one of his teasing comments, she blurted out, "Well, ministers' daughters don't kiss men on the bluff in full view of the entire town and. . .and the wagon train and. . .and everyone!"

His arms caught her again, drawing her back to him possessively, a twinkle in his eyes. "I think it's the perfect place for this minister's daughter to kiss this man. The entire county will hear about it by nightfall, and I won't need to worry about your other suitors any longer."

She turned her head just in time to escape his tempting lips. "The entire county *will* hear about it, including Father."

Reluctantly, he released her. "You win, Boston, this time." He reached for her hand. "Don't mind if your father sees me walking you home, do you?"

She shook her head shyly, and fell into step beside him. With her free hand, she drew her shawl closer about her shoulders. The sun was well up now, and she shouldn't feel so cool, but with the warmth of Matthew's arms removed. . . .

"House over there is mighty empty," his voice broke in on her thoughts, and he nodded toward the two-room house off to their left. "Sure would be nice to have a pretty wife to come home to after bouncing around the prairie looking after patients."

Laurina's face turned a soft rose color the prairie skies could never match.

Matthew stopped and reached for her free hand. "When we know the 'hoppers aren't coming back and my debts are paid off, I'm going to ask you to marry me, Boston."

To think he was promising a future together! How she yearned to plead, "Don't wait. Ask me now!" But of course, a lady couldn't say such a thing.

"Are your debts so large, then, Matthew?" she dared to venture. "Even after a year of practice?" Would he hear the plea in her words?

"My patients are like everyone else, Boston. After two years of 'hoppers, they've no money to pay their bills. And very little with which to barter, except for hope."

Laurina lifted her brave little chin and looked him in the eyes. "They may not be able to buy or barter with hope, but I can live on hope."

His lips brushed hers quickly, before she thought to pull away. "On hope and love, Boston," he promised.

At his words, her heart filled with a glorious joy, but she planted her hands on his chest and firmly pushed herself away from him, not willing to be caught again in a public embrace.

Matthew chuckled and drew her arm through his as they began walking toward her parents' cabin once more. "My proper, reserved Boston maiden."

She didn't feel proper and reserved! Not with the blood coursing through her veins with a wild abandon like the Chippewa River roaring through the peaceful valley below after the spring thaws.

She had always imagined she would be wearing her best frock when he said he loved her. And here she was in her everyday brown cotton, with her hair hanging down like a schoolgirl's. She should have taken time to put it up, as is proper for a woman. Fear that she would have missed the departure of the wagon train caused her to leave it as it was—the waves falling from her loosened braids.

But he loved her! And that made her feel beautiful in spite of the common dress and loose hair.

"Who's that in front of your cabin, Boston? Thought you and I were the only ones in the county not down saying goodbye to the wagons."

Laurina looked up at the log cabin still a hundred yards away, sitting quite by itself next to a leafless grove of slender elms planted the year before. Matthew was right, someone was in front of their cabin. No, it wasn't someone. There were two people—a man and a child. Laurina bit her bottom lip. Had they seen Matthew kiss her?

A moment later, they heard an unusual sound, almost a whispering, carried by the wind. "Oh, Matthew, the child is crying!"

Laurina rushed forward, pulling her voluminous skirt out of the path of her feet, the shawl sliding unnoticed to the ground. Matthew ran easily beside her.

As they neared the cabin, Laurina recognized the slender man with the dark beard as Reverend Adam Conrad, Matthew's closest friend. The curly haired child beside him was Johnny Wells, Harlan Wells's son, and he wasn't crying. The sobs were coming from a little girl in Reverend Conrad's arms.

"Johnny?" came the girl's tiny voice through her sobs.

"Johnny is right here, Pearl," the pastor reassured her in his deep voice. The sobs became sniffles. "Johnny? Pearl scared." Sniffle.

Johnny reached up as far as he could to awkwardly pat the girl. "Don't cry, Pearl. We made it. We're at Pastor Dalen's house." His words quivered.

"Why are the Wells' children with you, Adam? Has something happened to their father?" Matthew asked in a low voice.

"I don't know. When I saw them passing my house, I invited them in.

But Johnny insisted on going to Pastor Dalen's, so I came with them."

"Well, Johnny," Laurina tried to keep her voice cheerful, "it's certainly nice to have such fine company. But why are you visiting me?"

"We're not visitin' you, Miss Laurina. We're visitin' Pastor Dalen." The answer was given with the unembarrassed straightforwardness of a six-year-old.

"You want to visit my father?"

"Yes'm, Miss Laurina." The boy lifted his head topped with loose blond curls and looked up at Matthew with wide, sober blue eyes. "Hullo, Young Doc."

Laurina disciplined a smile. Even this child called Matthew the name by which he was known throughout the county. In spite of their respect for his medical knowledge and their requests for his opinion on every major decision in the county, the people of the area couldn't help thinking of Matthew, with his zest for life, as anything but a youth.

Matthew treated Johnny with the same respect he would show a man, reaching out to shake his hand soberly and matching the boy's serious tone. "Hello, Johnny. What are you doing in town so early? Where's your pa? Did he go down to see the wagons leave?"

The blond curls bounced as Johnny shook his head vigorously. "No, sir. Pa didn't come to town."

"Then why aren't you at home with him, Johnny?"

"He's not there, Young Doc. Yesterday he went to put Mama in her new bed, and he never came back. Pearl cried and cried. I told her somebody would come, but nobody did. When the sun came up, we were hungry, and there wasn't anythin' to eat, so I thought we better go to Pastor Dalen's house. Pa always said to go to the Pastor's house if there was anythin' we were needin'."

Laurina's glance flew instinctively to Matthew's face as they considered Johnny's news in the silence broken by Pearl's continuing sniffles. The fear Laurina felt at the graveside the afternoon before returned to sweep through her veins in a chilling flood. Why hadn't the children's father returned from his wife's funeral?

Chapter Two

Laurina set the heavy wooden water buckets down in the bluestem prairie grass, flexed her fingers, and breathed deeply of the August air. The steep climb from the spring at the bottom of the ravine always took her breath away. Shadowed by her blue calico sunbonnet, her eyes searched the horizon restlessly. Would the men never return?

After hearing Johnny's story, Matthew and Reverend Conrad had left to search for Mr. Wells. That evening, they stopped by her father's home. They had been to the graveyard, to Wells's soddie, and to the homes of Wells's few neighbors. There had been no sign of Mr. Wells. Mrs. Dalen made up sandwiches for the two men who then mounted fresh horses and continued their search.

Laurina picked up the buckets and started across the plateau toward the cabin. She had never understood how such a deep friendship had developed between Reverend Adam Conrad and Matthew. They were as different as the prairie from the timberland. It wasn't just their looks, although where Matthew was broad, blond, blue-eyed, and clean shaven, Reverend Conrad was slender, with black hair and a thick but trim beard. His brown eyes beneath straight brows were deep set and sober. That was the real difference. Matthew filled every day with laughter; Reverend Conrad seldom smiled. But he was a gentle, kind man, Laurina reminded herself. She had learned that during the many evenings he spent with her father, arguing theological questions over the checkerboard.

Laurina stopped to watch a group of small children playing at a cabin near her parents' place. Johnny was playing with the neighbor's two boys, tossing a ball back and forth, while Pearl sat nearby playing quietly with her corncob doll. As Laurina watched, one of the boys threw the ball to Johnny. Johnny didn't try to catch it. He didn't even see it. He was scanning the prairie toward his home.

Watching him, the now-familiar, chilling fear clutched at Laurina's heart. *Silly to feel so uneasy,* she admonished herself, *to feel so certain something is definitely, irrevocably wrong.* Yet she couldn't shake the conviction. It hung like a stone around her neck.

Laurina straightened her shoulders and gave herself a mental shake. Matthew and Reverend Conrad would find Mr. Wells. All she could do now was pray they would find him safe.

With a sigh, Laurina shoved the heavy door of her father's cabin closed behind her, shutting out the wind that was their constant daytime companion. The cabin was hot from the cast-iron cookstove where Hannah, her father's second wife, was preparing dinner.

Laurina wished the door could be left open, but she knew if it were, the cabin's two rooms and loft would soon be filled with dust. The dust crept in soon enough without the invitation of an open door. She crossed the room to set down the buckets before removing her sunbonnet and shaking the dust from her skirt.

Hannah was dropping dumplings from a wooden spoon into the prairie chicken stew simmering on the stove. Usually the smell of her cooking made Laurina ravenous, but she wasn't interested in food today—not with her mind filled with worry for the Wells family. Besides, everything tasted like grasshoppers these days.

The wiry, gray-haired woman wiped perspiration from her weathered brow and smiled over her shoulder at Laurina.

"Thanks for getting the water. Rough climb down the ravine. Maybe soon we'll have a well dug nearby. The men are talking about it. With six houses and the schoolhouse here on the plateau, we need a well."

"I don't mind getting the water." Laurina took a rag from the rough wooden counter, dipped it into the cool water in one of the buckets, and handed it to Hannah. "Wipe your face and rest a few minutes while I set the table. There's nothing more to be done at the stove until the stew is ready, anyway."

Gratefully, Hannah took the damp rag and sat down on the bench beside the rectangular table in the middle of the small room.

Laurina took heavy plates from the crude open shelves and set them on the table along with knives and forks. "I saw Johnny and Pearl playing with the Anderson children a few minutes ago. I don't think Johnny's heart was in it. He kept watching the prairie, as if willing his father to return."

"That's only natural, I suppose," Hannah responded matter-of-factly.

"Doctor Strong and Reverend Conrad have been gone two days. Surely they must have discovered something by this time."

"They'll be back as soon as they can, Laurina. Easy for a man who doesn't want to be found to hide in this country. You need to learn to wait patiently and trust in the Lord. He'll help them find Mr. Wells, if He wants him found."

"Wait patiently! I wish I were out there looking for Mr. Wells with them."

"You've been needed here to look after the children, Laurina."

"But—"

"Why don't you go round up Johnny and Pearl? The dumplings are almost ready. And tell Father to leave that woodpile out back and come in."

Laurina started toward the door. How could Hannah stay so calm? Pray and wait. Women always had to pray and wait while the men went out to meet difficulties head-on. She was tired of praying and waiting.

With a jerk, she opened the door and stopped in surprise. "Matthew!"

Matthew and Reverend Conrad, having tied their horses at the fence in front of the cabin, were almost at the door.

"Hello, Boston." Matthew smiled wearily down at her, his usually laughing eyes set in dark smudges of sleeplessness. Even in her relief at his return and her eagerness to know what he had discovered, her heart went out to him in his exhaustion.

Holding the door open wide, she invited, "Please, come in and sit down, both of you. Hello, Reverend." She flushed slightly as she realized how completely she had ignored the young pastor in her excitement at seeing Matthew.

As they entered, the men removed their dusty hats and greeted Hannah.

"Thank the Lord you're back," Mrs. Dalen welcomed them fervently. She motioned toward the recently set table. "Set yourselves down while I get you water."

She handed each man a thick cup, and they murmured their thanks before thirstily draining the cups.

Why didn't one of the men say whether they had found Mr. Wells? Laurina bit back the question as Matthew rested his forehead on his hand. Dust from the ride accentuated the lines of fatigue on his face.

Laurina jumped as the door flew open and her father rushed inside, his shirt sleeves rolled up above his tanned forearms, the ax still in his hand from chopping wood. "I saw you ride up. Did you find Wells?" The words tumbled out of his thick gray whiskers.

Mrs. Dalen perched her hands on her bony, apron-covered hips. "Let the men catch their breath before you pounce on them, Father. They're tired and likely hungry."

The older man stared blankly at his wife, then at the weary men seated at his table. "Oh. Of course. Won't you have something to eat?" he asked. "Smells as though Hannah has supper about ready."

Reverend Conrad shook his head. "We're too tired to eat. Thanks just the same. But we wanted to let you know what we found out before we go home to get some sleep." He paused a moment. "Are the children here?"

"They're at the Andersons'," Laurina said.

"Good." Reverend Conrad and Matthew exchanged relieved glances.

Suddenly, Laurina wasn't sure she wanted to know what they had discovered. Why did this situation keep reminding her of her own childhood, the years spent in the East with only letters connecting her with her father?

"How's Johnny doing?" Matthew asked, looking up at Laurina standing beside him.

"As well as can be expected. He asked about his father first thing this morning, but he hasn't asked since. Not in words, at least." Laurina remembered again the constant, unspoken question in the little boy's eyes, the intense gaze searching the road toward his home.

"Did you find Mr. Wells?" Pastor Dalen repeated impatiently.

"We found him," was Reverend Conrad's quiet reply. "He was at a half-way house west of Kragero Township."

The three Dalens waited expectantly for him to continue, but he averted his eyes and swallowed hard.

"But why hasn't he returned with you?" Laurina blurted out the question that had been on the tip of her tongue since their arrival.

Matthew took her hands. Looking into her anxious eyes, he spoke gently. "He isn't coming back, Boston."

The silence in the room beat against her ears. "Is he dead?"

"No, he's all right. Physically, that is. But he says that he's never returning. He isn't headed anyplace in particular, just away from here."

Reverend Conrad shook his head slowly. "The last few years seem to have crushed the life from him. We all know how hard the last two years have been for the farmers; seldom enough of a crop to feed their families, let alone to sell for profit. And now that Wells's wife has died, he says he hasn't any fight left."

Laurina could hear Hannah murmuring beside her, could hear her father's fervent, "God help him," even as she asked in a hollow whisper, "But the children? What about the children?"

Matthew squeezed her hands tighter. "Wells said he can't help them. He can't provide for them sufficiently."

"But—" she started.

"He's mortgaged all the personal property he can," Reverend Conrad explained, lifting his hands slightly in a gesture of defeat. "In order to get assistance for food for the winter and for spring seed, he had to sell his oxen. Without the oxen, he can't plant next spring. If he leaves the children here, he knows the local government will provide for them somehow. Probably send them to an orphanage. At least then the children will have food and clothing."

The utter helplessness in his deep-set eyes convinced Laurina of the truth more than his words did. How would they ever tell Johnny? How could he endure losing both parents within a week?

"There's always a chance he'll change his mind," Mrs. Dalen encouraged.

No one argued with her, but from the look on the young men's faces,

Laurina knew they were convinced there was no chance Harlan Wells would return. Sometimes, Laurina thought, waiting was better than knowing.

The door opened once more, and this time little Johnny Wells entered. "I saw the horses," he began eagerly, his glance sweeping the homely room. A puzzled frown creased his forehead. Johnny looked first at Matthew and then at Reverend Conrad. "Where's my pa?"

Laurina started toward him, but Matthew's hands restrained her as Reverend Conrad knelt beside the now wary boy. Laurina said a silent prayer, begging the Lord to give Reverend Conrad wisdom and to wrap Johnny in His protective cocoon of love.

The young pastor reached out to place his hands on Johnny's shoulders. "I saw your pa today, Johnny. He asked me to say goodbye to you for him. You see, he has to go on a long journey."

Johnny's eyes didn't waver from Reverend Conrad's. "When's he goin' to be back?"

"He may not be back, Johnny."

"He won't ever come back?" the boy's voice was steady.

"Not ever, Johnny."

"Did he go to heaven to be with Mama? He told me he was goin' to miss her somethin' awful. He cried. Mama isn't comin' home anymore, either. Pa told us."

"No, Johnny, he didn't go to be with your ma."

"Am I goin' to be the man of the house now, Rever'nd? When Pa had to go to Benson to buy supplies, Mama said I was the man of the house."

"No, Johnny, you won't be the man of the house."

"Then who will take care of Pearl?"

Laurina pulled away from Matthew's hold and knelt beside Johnny. "We will. We'll take care of both you and Pearl, Johnny."

Johnny gave a big sigh, and the load he had been carrying for the last few days slid from his too young shoulders. Then his pointed chin began to quiver, and tears welled up in the eyes that had looked into Reverend Conrad's so bravely only moments before. "I wish my pa would come back."

Reverend Conrad's arms wrapped tightly about the boy as Johnny's arms slid around his neck.

"I'll go find Pearl," Laurina murmured. As she left, she could feel Matthew's eyes on her back and she wondered fleetingly if he was thinking she was a poor candidate for a pioneer woman after all. But she couldn't add to Johnny's grief by allowing her tears to spill over in front of him. Johnny and Pearl needed the adults in their lives to be strong now.

A minute later she heard the door behind her open and close.

"Boston?"

She turned desperately toward Matthew's voice. "Oh, Matthew!"

His arms were around her, surrounding her with their strength, and he was murmuring words of comfort as his cheek rested against her hair. She burrowed her face against his coarse black coat, heedless of the dust and sweat that covered him. Safe in the refuge of Matthew's arms, she cried out her sorrow for the two whose loneliness and fear must be so enveloping. Cried out her knowledge that the love and protection she and her friends would offer could only begin to heal the wound of broken trust for Johnny and Pearl.

❧

An hour later, Laurina and Matthew sat on a rock near the edge of the bluff in the twilight. She was exhausted from crying. Only an occasional sob escaped her.

Matthew's arms slipped around her shoulders from behind. "Are you okay now, Boston?"

Laurina nodded. "I'm sorry. I haven't cried in years." She brushed away a late tear. "I should go back and help with Pearl and Johnny."

"Your folks and Adam can take care of them."

She didn't argue. She was too tired to move.

"It reminds you of your own childhood, doesn't it, Boston?" His voice was low.

"Yes," she murmured.

His hands slid along her arms. "I don't know the whole story, only that your parents sent you to live with relatives. Do you want to tell me about it?"

Laurina nodded, but it was a couple of minutes before she could speak.

"I was only six." Her voice was barely a whisper.

"The same age as Johnny."

She nodded again. "Chippewa City didn't exist then. Only Indians, fur traders, and a few missionaries, like my parents, lived around here, but we visited a Sioux village on the bluff on the other side of this valley. Father preached to them, and I remember playing with some of the children. But we were staying with some settlers about forty miles east of here when it happened."

"When what happened?"

"The Sioux uprising."

Matthew's hands gripped her arms. "You were in the middle of that?" His voice was husky with shock.

"Mother awakened me in the middle of the night and bundled me into a wagon while Father gathered our few worldly goods. There were other wagons in the yard, filled with women and children huddled together, sobbing.

The men held rifles as they drove, urging the frightened horses toward Fort Ridgley, away from the fires that lighted the sky. The fires were like pyramids of orange and yellow flames and the air was filled with smoke.

"But it's the eyes of the women I remember most. They were large with fear, not only for themselves, but for their husbands and children. When I think of those eyes, I can't blame my parents for sending me east to live with Aunt Miranda and Uncle William, Mother's sister and her husband."

"I'm so sorry that happened to you, Boston," he whispered into her hair.

His sympathy grabbed at her heart. She blinked quickly and bit into her lip to keep from crying again. "I wonder what happened to the Indian children I played with, how many of their fathers were killed in the uprising, or by the army as a result of the trials afterward." She took a deep, shaky breath. "I wonder how many of those children were never reconciled to their parents, like I've been to Father."

"Why didn't your parents send for you sooner?"

"Mother died a few months after they sent me to Boston. Father stayed to minister to the Indians after the uprising. Many of them were tried and hung, and the rest were sent farther west to reservations. Then he helped the settlers that remained to start again. 'Helping them grab hold of God's strength,' he called it." She was quiet a moment, remembering. At times in the East, her faith in God was the only thing that connected her to life as she had known it. She had learned then, as young as she was, to grab hold of God's strength herself—to grab hold and never let go.

"Father traveled a lot during those years," she continued. "It would have been difficult for him to have a small child along. And, of course, the Civil War was being fought at that time, making travel inconvenient. He and my aunt and uncle felt it was best to leave me in Boston."

"Were your aunt and uncle good to you?"

"Yes. They had no children of their own, and they lavished toys and beautiful clothes on me. But I missed my father. There wasn't a day I didn't wake up hoping that that would be the day Father would come to take me home."

"And now with Wells leaving Johnny and Pearl, it's like you're living through it all over again, isn't it?"

"Yes." She strangled back the sob that rose in her throat. "Why is it always the children that have to suffer?"

She felt his hands on her shoulders. "It's not only the children, Boston. And God's promised to be with us through the pain. Let's pray for Johnny and Pearl." He waited for her to begin.

But the words wouldn't come. "I. . .I can't find the right words. I just want so much for them not to hurt."

Matthew squeezed her shoulders. "It's all right, Boston. God knows your heart. He can hear you without the words."

Laurina hoped so. The ache inside her was so painful, and she knew it was nothing compared to the pain Johnny and Pearl were going to experience.

"Will you be all right?" Matthew asked as they neared the door of her father's cabin a few minutes later.

Laurina straightened her shoulders and forced a smile. "Of course. After all, I'm a pioneer prairie woman now. My courage just got a little soggy for a while."

"That's my girl, Boston."

When Matthew gave her a quick kiss on the cheek before leaving, Laurina clenched her hands into fists at her sides to keep from reaching out and clinging to him. She wasn't going to be a quitter. The children needed her to be strong and cheerful.

When she entered, the family was eating. Reverend Conrad had left. Johnny and Pearl were sitting together on the long bench beside the rectangular table in the middle of the room. Pearl's curls rested against Johnny's faded red flannel shirt and made it difficult for Johnny to eat the prairie chicken stew Hannah had set in front of him. With his left hand, he lifted a large spoonful of the stew shakily toward his mouth, watching it carefully. Only a little spilled down the front of his shirt. With a deep breath, he tried again. This time the entire spoonful made it into his mouth.

In spite of Reverend Conrad's assurance that Johnny wouldn't have to be the man of the house, Johnny obviously felt he was still in charge of Pearl. Laurina's face relaxed into a natural smile and she sat down beside Johnny. How wonderful for Pearl to have such a fine big brother. Laurina wished she had had one herself when she was sent across the country to live with an aunt and uncle who were strangers to her.

While they ate, the adults tried to speak of everyday things, united in their efforts to keep Johnny from dwelling on the news of his father.

At least she and her father and Hannah weren't complete strangers to the children, as Aunt Miranda and Uncle William had been to her. Maybe that would make it a bit easier for the children.

Before Johnny finished his stew, he was having difficulty keeping his eyes open. Laurina stooped to pick up Pearl. "Come on, Johnny. I'll tuck you in."

He climbed over the bench slowly, yawned, and rubbed his eyes with his fists. "Good night, Pastor Dalen. Good night, Mrs. Dalen," he mumbled.

"Good night, Johnny," they said almost together.

Pearl only opened her eyes once as Laurina undressed the girl and laid her in the narrow bed.

"Ready to climb in, Johnny?" she asked.

"Have to say prayers first, Miss Laurina." His mouth widened into a large yawn. "Mama said I must always say prayers before goin' to bed."

Laurina flushed slightly. "Of course you must, Johnny. I'm glad you reminded me."

She sat down on the bed as he kneeled on the bare floor, rested his folded hands against the bed, and squeezed his eyes shut. "Dear Jesus, please take care of Pearl and me while we sleep. And take care of Pa. Good night." He started to his feet, then dropped again to his knees. "I mean, Amen."

Laurina swallowed a giggle. "That was a very nice prayer, Johnny."

He crawled in beside his sister, and Laurina pulled the quilt up and tucked it under his chin. His big blue eyes stared up at her, asking nothing, asking everything. Impulsively, she bent forward and kissed his forehead. "Good night, Johnny. Just call out if you need me."

She climbed down the ladder from the loft and joined her father and Hannah. "Haven't the children cried at all?" she asked as she sat across from them at the table.

Her father nodded, his gray whiskers brushing the front of his shirt. "Johnny cried for a few minutes after you and Young Doc left, but he dried his tears when Hannah asked him to go find Pearl."

Laurina smiled a tired little smile. "He feels so responsible for her."

"I think you're the one feeling responsible, Laurina." Hannah looked her squarely in the eye.

Laurina's brows drew together in a puzzled frown. "Of course I feel responsible. The children have no one to care for them."

"But they aren't your family." Hannah didn't blink or smile.

"What are you trying to say?" Laurina asked slowly.

Her father coughed into his whiskers and moved toward the empty fireplace, his back to the table.

"I'm saying that we can't keep the children here indefinitely. And you mustn't let them think they have a home with us," Hannah said firmly. "It will only make it harder for them when they leave."

It was a moment before Laurina comprehended what Hannah was saying. Then she turned toward the fireplace where her father was laying an unnecessary fire. "Father?"

"I'm sorry, child, but Hannah's right." He didn't turn toward her.

"We don't wish to be hardhearted, but wise choices aren't always easy choices. We can't afford to raise the children," Hannah explained, rising to clear the table.

"But the Bible says we're to care for orphans."

"We'll try to find someone in the community to take them in," her father said from behind her.

"And if we can't?" Laurina challenged.

"Then the town fathers will likely send them to an orphanage, as Mr. Wells himself said," Hannah replied coolly.

Laurina stared at her, speechless. Over the last year, she had grown to love Hannah. She knew her father's wife was a tough woman, not given to sentiment. Still, she had seen Hannah act with compassion toward those enduring hardship this last year and believed her to have a kind heart beneath her rough exterior. She couldn't understand how the woman could be so cold toward Johnny and Pearl.

Her father patted her on the shoulder as he sat down beside her. "Everything will turn out all right, child. God looks out for the fatherless, you know."

"What if He wants to take care of them through us, and we don't listen to Him?" Laurina lashed out.

Blood rushed to her father's face, and the expression in his eyes made her feel as though she had betrayed him. Instantly, she regretted her harsh tone. "I'm sorry, Father. That was disrespectful. But—"

"It will all work out, child," he repeated. "Tomorrow I'll begin looking for a home for Johnny and Pearl."

And Laurina had to be content with that for the moment.

Chapter Three

Laurina slipped down the shallow bank to the large gray rock that had become her familiar haven since moving to the settlement. The Psalmist may have looked "unto the hills" for help, but she sought the whispering river when her heart was filled with pain and cried out to God for strength.

After two weeks of asking, even begging, people of the settlement and farmers in the area to give Johnny and Pearl a home, no one had opened their arms to the children. The economic hardships that had been the inevitable result of the depression that had spread across the country since 1873, coinciding with five years of grasshopper visitations in Minnesota, had spread their paralyzing tentacles through every aspect of the young community. Everyone seemed to have poverty knocking on their door. Worse than the lack of food and clothing, worse than unpaid debts, was the robbery of spirit. Barely able to meet the needs of their own families, people were unable to reach out to help others in need. Laurina had been aware of the hand-to-mouth existence of many in the area, but until now, she had heard the people speak mainly of hope in God and the future.

The last two weeks she had seen the poverty-broken spirits again and again as she, her father and Hannah, Matthew and Reverend Conrad sought a home for the children. The people would listen quietly and then there would be the shamed dropping of their gaze to the floor and the drooping of their shoulders already bent from life's struggles as they shook their heads and mumbled the too familiar story of their own desperate need. The few families that weren't destitute themselves felt it unfair to take in children who could be sent to an orphanage when there were so many others in the area that needed help.

A few families had offered to take Johnny, who would soon be old enough to help with farm chores, but Laurina refused to allow the children to be separated.

Today her father had spoken of allowing the court to take over the children's future.

Laurina had protested vigorously, pleading with her father and Hannah to allow her to raise the children in their home. But all of her protestations had been in vain.

Tears pooled in her eyes. "How could they?" she whispered to the unresponsive river. "How could they turn away those defenseless children?" The powerless feeling she had known as a child when her parents sent her east returned with shocking familiarity. She couldn't allow Johnny and Pearl to be sent away!

"Not going to catch any fish without a line, Boston. Thought even eastern ladies knew that."

She turned to find Matthew leaning casually against the trunk of a cottonwood behind her. The teasing twinkle in his eyes lifted her spirits for a moment. "Hello, Matthew. How did you know I was here?"

He settled down beside her, resting his arms on his knees. "Your father said you'd gone for a walk. I figured this was a likely place to find you. You've always said it's your favorite spot." His beautiful smile flashed.

It warmed her heart to realize he had tucked such trivial information away and knew immediately where to locate her. She lifted a quick prayer of thanksgiving to God for blessing her with the love of this man.

"Think the water has finally lost the smell of grasshoppers," Matthew said, pushing his hat toward the back of his head. "Fish are probably more thankful for that than we are. 'Hoppers aren't on their usual diet."

Though she laughed at his foolishness, she was glad herself that the smell was gone, and the fish and poultry they ate no longer tasted of the insects upon which the fish and fowl had feasted.

"I'm glad you're back, Matthew. You were out of town on your calls longer than I expected."

"I've been over in Kragero Township for two days. The doctor there is taking a trip south to find a new place to locate and he asked me to look in on some of his patients for a few weeks."

"Yes, the newspaper mentioned the doctor was away. It said Mr. Binkley, the attorney, was away looking for a new location, also. 'One goes one way, and one another. Anywhere to get away from the grasshoppers,' is the way the editor phrased it."

"Others will come to take their places eventually, you'll see. Or we'll grow our own. I would have been back in town yesterday, but a young Norwegian couple in the township had a new youngster that afternoon. The husband ran me down when I was returning from my calls yesterday." He smiled down at her. "Seeing a man's expression as he looks on his first child, well, it always makes me forget how many hours it's been since I've slept."

His tender gaze drove her lashes down in confusion. She knew somehow that he was thinking of the time he would look on his own firstborn, and the realization filled the innocent moment with intimacy.

Matthew is going to be a wonderful father someday, she thought. Maybe the idea that had been growing in her mind the last few days was actually possible.

"Children like you, Matthew. You can always make Johnny laugh, which isn't easy, I assure you. I think you're his hero."

Matthew shrugged, and tossed a twig into the water. "He's a good youngster."

Laurina smiled at him. "I think his admiration means more than you are willing to admit." She rested a hand lightly on one of his. "I've seen little of your carefree spirit since we came on the children with Reverend Conrad at Father's cabin."

His gaze penetrated her own, but he didn't answer.

After a minute of uncomfortable silence, Laurina removed her hand. "Did Father tell you of his decision?"

"That he thinks it's time to take Johnny and Pearl's situation before the widow and orphans' court? Yes, he told me."

"If only he and Hannah would let Johnny and Pearl live with them! I would watch over the children. I don't understand how they can just turn them away!"

"Your father's salary is paid by the same people who lived through the last two winters on beans and pork supplied by the government. Your folks have given away almost everything they have to help others weather these hard times. It's all your father can do to keep the three of you."

"Everyone is having hard times. Surely they can care for two little children."

"Your father's congregation is still meeting in members' homes because they can't afford to build a church, even though land was donated three years ago," he reminded her. "Maybe your father feels that other members of the congregation need the little he has left to give more than Johnny and Pearl, who can receive shelter and food at an orphanage."

Laurina didn't answer immediately. She recalled the barrel received a few weeks ago from a church back east that she had helped Hannah unpack. Every item that was removed brought a radiant smile from Hannah followed by, "The good Lord must have known how badly the neighbors need this." Soon, the contents of the barrel had been spread like manna from heaven among the needy settlers. It was only after a long argument that Hannah agreed to keep a piece of gray wool to make herself a badly needed dress.

Laurina sighed deeply. No, her father and Hannah couldn't afford to keep the children anymore than anyone else in the community.

"I can hardly believe I'm the same foolish woman who only two weeks ago prattled on about not letting the grasshoppers chase me away from here." Laurina shook her head. "I knew many of the people who stayed are poor because of the grasshoppers, but I had no idea how poor. Most have hidden the extent of their poverty behind words of hope. When we asked people to take Johnny and Pearl into their homes, the facades crumbled."

"Don't be too hard on them, Boston. Pride is about the only thing some of these people have left."

She brushed a twig from the rock, and watched as the river carried it away. "I can understand why no one else has been able to take the children in, Matthew, but I can't give up on Johnny and Pearl." Laurina pictured Johnny with his curly hair and enormous blue eyes as he questioned Reverend Conrad: "Who will take care of Pearl?" and recalled her own impassioned answer. "I promised the children we'd take care of them, remember Matthew?"

"I remember." His lips set in a firm line, and he looked away from her toward the far bank. "What about your aunt and uncle back east? Maybe they can help. I understand your uncle is a banker."

"Uncle William was a banker. The bank went under in the Panic of 1873. When he died three years later, he was bankrupt. He and Aunt Miranda lost everything. The creditors allowed Aunt Miranda to live in their home until her death, as they knew she was ill. She died last year, penniless. That's when I came out to join Father."

"I see. Then I think your father's plan is the best thing for Johnny and Pearl."

Her dark lashes flew upward as she turned to him in shock. "Matthew Strong, it is *not* the best thing for them. The judge will send them to an orphanage."

"That's the reason for orphanages, to care for orphans and abandoned children. You have to be reasonable, Boston. The youngsters will receive good care, and maybe they'll be adopted."

"I don't mean to say that orphanages are terrible places, Matthew. But if Johnny and Pearl are sent to an orphanage, they'll be at least one hundred miles from everything and everyone they know. And what if they aren't adopted by the same family and they lose each other in addition to their parents? We mustn't let it happen!" She was clutching both of his hands now, willing him to understand her burning desire to keep the children.

"At least they'll have food, Boston, and be warm in the winter. After all, their health is the most important thing here."

"It's *not* the most important thing!" she flared. "I mean, it's important, of course, but they're already so lost without their parents. It's terrifying to be placed among strangers when you're young. I *know*."

"I know you do, Boston." His voice was as gentle as the water lapping against the rock. "But it's for Johnny and Pearl's own good. Surely you can see that."

"I was sent away for my own good, too," she reminded him bitterly. She swallowed her anger and tried to speak calmly. "Matthew, think of all the children you see every day. Their clothing is inadequate and they haven't as much food as their parents would like them to have. But it's not the children who are unhappy. It's the adults that are fearful. The children only want to be loved."

"The children simply aren't old enough to know when to be afraid, Boston. And when their stomachs hurt from lack of food and they haven't enough clothes to keep them warm in the winter, they definitely *are* unhappy."

Laurina drew her hands back quickly. Never had Matthew spoken to her so sharply.

Matthew's lids closed over his angry eyes and he sighed deeply. He opened his eyes and his arms at the same time. "I'm sorry, Boston," he said quietly as his arms folded her to himself. "I wish you weren't hurting so deeply. Living out here, well, you learn quickly that life can be harsh. You know your parents can't keep the children. The county will pay to send them to an orphanage."

Matthew's white cotton shirt felt cool against Laurina's flushed cheek as she traced an imaginary design on his sleeve. She was glad he couldn't see her face as she suggested, "There is one other alternative, Matthew."

"What alternative is that?"

Was he really unaware of what she was thinking? Wouldn't he say the words she longed to hear? Her heart thumped loudly against her ribs. Surely he would feel the pounding and realize that she was waiting for him to speak, to open the door to the perfect solution. As she waited, the palms of her hands grew sweaty and her breath came more quickly.

She felt his hands playing with the hair that had slid from its proper bun, felt his cheek warm against the top of her head. "What alternative, Boston?" he murmured.

It felt so right with his arms about her. Surely it couldn't hurt. She dampened her dry lips with the tip of her tongue before venturing tremulously, "Are you really going to make me ask such an unladylike question, Matthew?"

The fingers that had been winding themselves in her hair stopped. "What do you mean?"

Was his voice wary? Did she dare continue? *Oh, God, please let him see the wisdom in this,* she pleaded silently. She grabbed her fleeing courage. "You did say you love me, Matthew."

The arms around her tightened. "I do love you."

Still the words she waited to hear did not come. But he loved her! She grasped his words to her heart, the blood pounding in her ears as she forced herself to ask casually, "Then why don't we take care of the children?"

Matthew remained very still and Laurina held her breath, and continued to trace the imaginary pattern on his sleeve, pretending she hadn't just committed the blunder of proposing marriage to a man. Why didn't he say something? She was dimly aware of the river playing merrily against the rocks, the birds singing cheerfully in the overhanging boughs of the cotton-woods.

"You know we can't get married now." His voice was harsh.

"Why not?" Laurina was glad her cheek still rested against his chest and he was unable to see the embarrassment in her eyes as she persisted with her impertinent questions.

"I told you weeks ago. I can't afford to get married now."

"But the children need someone, Matthew. Besides, almost everyone in this part of the country is poor when they start out. Look at the couple Father married last week. They're living in a dugout and will have only the crops they can raise to support themselves. But they didn't let their poverty stop them from marrying."

He grasped her shoulders firmly, pushing her from him, his blue eyes gazing steadily into her own as he explained his case patiently. "You know I have debts, Boston. All I have is a two-room house that doubles as my office. Where would I put a wife and two children?"

"We could find another place, Matthew."

"And pay for it with what? Don't you realize that most of the patients I've treated the last year haven't been able to pay? When they have paid, as often as not it's been in food that they couldn't afford to be giving away, or in help cleaning my office or mending my clothing. Not in the cash I need to pay my own debts."

"Surely we could get by, Matthew. Things can't go on this way indefinitely. There's a good chance the grasshoppers won't be as destructive next year and then everyone's business will improve. You said so yourself." The haunting thought of Johnny's eyes forced her to continue pleading.

Matthew ran his hands through his long blond hair distractedly, knocking his hat to the rock. His eyes pleaded with her to understand. "I'm not a farmer, with only myself and my family to consider. I'm a doctor—the only doctor in the county. So far, I've been able to keep the drugs and supplies I need in stock, and most of the little money I have goes to keep me out of debt with the companies that supply the drugs. With a wife and two children," he shrugged his large shoulders helplessly, "my family would have to come first, and what would happen to my patients?"

The spark of hope that had been burning inside Laurina flickered out.

"If there were no alternative, if there were no orphanage, you know I'd agree to take the children. I love you, Boston. I'd like nothing more than to make a home with you. You do know that, don't you?"

She couldn't raise her eyes to his. If there were no alternative. How often she had heard those words from the lips of others in the community the last two weeks. She had never expected to hear them from Matthew. She had believed his faith was too strong for such an attitude.

"I need to get back to the office, Boston. Will you walk back with me?"

She turned away from him and gazed into the water flowing by swiftly, wounded pride overwhelming her. "I think I'll stay a while."

His hands squeezed her shoulders. "I'll come by this evening."

"You needn't bother, Dr. Strong."

She felt him tense.

"What are you saying?"

She caught her bottom lip between her teeth.

"Boston, look at me." Matthew's voice was low.

She turned, and his hands cupped her rigid shoulders. "What are you saying?"

"I thought your values were the same as mine, Dr. Strong, but I was wrong. How could I ever have thought I loved you?"

His eyes widened in disbelief. "Boston, I—"

"Please, just go." She pulled away from his hands and sank down onto the cool, pitted surface of the rock, her back to him.

A minute later, she heard his boots on the soft dirt of the riverbank as he left. Wrapping her arms about her skirt-encased knees, her heart cried out, *How can You allow it, God? How can You sit up there and let little children be abandoned?* Throughout her own separation from her parents, she had been able to hold strongly to her faith in God's goodness and His promise in Romans 8 that "all things work together for good to them that love God." In her inability to help Johnny and Pearl, her faith wavered.

And Matthew. He had prayed for the children and helped her try to find them a home, but he hadn't the courage to help her care for them.

She sat up straight, brushing the tears from her face and setting her jaw defiantly. She had cried more the last two weeks than in the rest of her life, even more than when she was separated from her own parents. Well, she would not cry again. As Matthew said on the bluff the day he first said he loved her, looking on the dark side of things never solved any problems.

What did it matter that Matthew wouldn't marry her? Other women, widows, managed to raise children without men in their lives. She would raise the children herself and make a happy and good life for them. Surely there must be some way she could manage it. There must!

Chapter Four

The next morning, Laurina swayed with the motion of the wagon as she sat beside Reverend Conrad on the way to the Wells's homestead. Sleeping Pearl's curly topped head rolled against Laurina's calico-covered chest. Laurina's arms were growing weary from bracing the girl's limp body on her lap, but the girl's trust warmed her heart.

Johnny sat wedged tightly between her and Reverend Conrad, his eyes listlessly scanning the horizon.

Reverend Conrad kept his gaze straight ahead, the reins held loosely in his long fingers. He had said little on the drive. Laurina wondered whether they were imposing on his kindness, in spite of his offer to drive them to the homestead.

She wished her father were the one driving them. It was difficult for her to leave his home, even to move only a few miles away. He hadn't been as angry as she expected with her decision to move to Harlan Wells's farm, but she had seen the pain in his eyes as he tried to talk her out of it last night. Hannah had just tightened her mouth and left the arguments to Laurina's father. In the end, her father had shook his head and said that as her mind was evidently made up, he would have to leave her in God's hands.

He had planned to drive her and the children out this morning. Then when he had lifted Laurina's trunk to the wagon bed, he had hurt his back. She wouldn't hear of his riding over the rough road in such a condition. Secretly she had been relieved to have a reprieve from being on her own with the children for a few more days while her father's back strengthened. But when Reverend Conrad stopped by and volunteered to take them over, she felt that she couldn't refuse his offer to assist them.

A brown prairie dog poked his head up, eyeing the creaking wagon as it jolted along. Laurina pointed the curious creature out to Johnny and was rewarded with a soft laugh. A moment later, it darted underground.

"I always think of the prairie as flat, but it's really not, is it?" Laurina said to no one in particular. "Instead, it rolls, with slight rises here and there. Not much higher than the dirt around that prairie dog's home, but high enough to hide a homestead on the horizon."

Reverend Conrad looked out over the prairie and nodded solemnly.

Laurina wondered again how this somber man could be such a close friend to boisterous Matthew. How she would miss Matthew's joyful ways! If he were driving them today, he would have had them all laughing. A small sigh escaped her, and the reverend darted a questioning look toward her.

She managed a small smile. "It looks more like spring than the middle of August, with the primroses and prairie roses blooming amid the bluestem grass. I was afraid we might not see any more prairie flowers this year, after the grasshoppers destroyed so many."

His gaze drifted slowly over the landscape and he nodded again. "They're like hope. They cheer one's spirit."

She almost giggled. He was hardly the picture of a cheerful man. But when he turned his face back toward her, she saw the faint glimmer of a smile hidden deep in his eyes. *The woman who falls in love with this man will have her work cut out for her, always wondering what he is thinking and feeling,* she thought.

He was right, though. The small prairie flower blossoms covering the land were a cheerful sight. For weeks, wherever one looked, only brown, dead, and dying plant life had filled the prairie. Now, it was good to see life being renewed.

Since leaving Chippewa City, they had passed only a handful of homes. Most of them were barely specks on the horizon. The Homestead Act allowed people 160-acre tracts. In this fertile farming land, people had been eager for the acreage before the grasshoppers came. The few homesteads close enough to the rough road to be seen were humble places, all but one built of sod.

"Have you ever seen the Wells's home?" the reverend asked.

Laurina shook her head. "I realize it won't be elegant, but it will be a roof over our heads."

"It's a sod house, Miss Dalen. It's very. . .primitive."

A sinking feeling filled Laurina's stomach. A sod house! Could she live in a house of dirt? She had been inside a few in the area. They were dark, dreary, and always dirty. She tried to shut the picture out of her mind. Only two weeks ago she had bragged to Matthew that she was a pioneer prairie woman and now she was quaking at the thought of living in a sod house. What was that to fear when it meant she had a place to take the children?

She set her lips in a firm line. "Many people live in sod houses in this country. I can live in one, too, and be glad for it."

There was only the slightest change in the intensity of the reverend's brown eyes. It was impossible to tell what he was thinking. His face never showed his thoughts the way Matthew's open face did. "It will not be easy for you, but if you believe this is what God wants you to do, then of course you must do it."

The defenses Laurina had built up against her father and Hannah's rejection of her plan began to dissolve. Reverend Conrad's statement made her decision sound reasonable, even inevitable.

When they turned off the road onto a rutted path, Johnny bolted upright and pointed eagerly. "Look! There's my house!"

As they drove up to the soddie, the only signs of life were three hens and a rooster scratching in the yard. The house was rectangular, about twenty-feet long and fifteen feet wide, Laurina guessed. Two windows looked out on the yard, one on each side of the wooden door.

Facing the house was another, somewhat smaller, sod building. It had no windows, and Laurina decided it must be a barn. She was glad to see the well in the yard. At least there would be no long treks to a river or pond for water, assuming there was a river or pond nearby.

Reverend Conrad climbed out of the wagon and Johnny clambered down behind him. The boy raced across the yard toward the rooster, his hat blowing off unheeded. "Hullo, Pete! We're back!" He slid to his knees in the dirt beside the fowl. The rooster squawked and darted a few feet away, then jerkily walked back to the boy, clucking loudly.

Laurina cringed at the thought of the dirt being driven into the knees of Johnny's pants, then shook her head. Boys will be boys. It was good to see he was glad to be back home. She wouldn't begrudge him a few minutes of joy, even though it meant more scrubbing for her.

Reverend Conrad wrapped the reins about the brake and walked around the buggy to reach for Pearl. When they stopped, the child had awakened and was blinking and yawning as she looked about her.

As Laurina handed her to Reverend Conrad, Pearl twisted her head to keep the house in sight. "Home. Pearl home," she said as she pointed a pudgy finger at the soddie.

"Yes, Pearl, you're home," the reverend said as he stood her on the ground.

His hands rested lightly against Laurina's waist as he helped steady her while she climbed down. "It's your home, too, now, Miss Dalen," he said quietly from behind her.

The words were like blows to her chest. The sod house staring at her with those empty, lifeless windows was her home. She pushed away the terror that threatened to engulf her. "It's more than a home," she challenged. "It's my only opportunity to care for Johnny and Pearl."

She took Pearl's hand and began walking toward the house, head high and shoulders back. "Yes, it's my home, too. I think it needs a name, don't you, Reverend? Like the country estates back east, a name to grow up to. I'll call it," she hesitated, searching for something appropriate. The reverend's words about the new prairie flowers blazed in her mind. "I'll call it Hopeland. What do you think of that, Reverend?"

He looked at her with his always somber expression. "It's a valiant name, Miss Dalen."

Pearl pulled her hand from Laurina's and began running in her bouncy way toward the soddie, now only a few feet away. "Mama! Pearl home, Mama."

Laurina's feet rooted to the ground and one hand clutched the base of her throat. She hadn't anticipated this. She should have remembered that the children hadn't been here since the day after their mother's funeral, and of course a two-year-old child couldn't understand the finality of death.

The reverend's hand cupped her elbow, gently urging her forward. "You can handle this, Miss Dalen." His voice was firm and reassuring, but left no hope he would try to deal with the situation for her. That was best, of course. She was going to be the one in charge of the children.

Pearl was reaching for the latch, trying to push the heavy door open. "Mama!"

As she lifted Pearl into her arms, Laurina forced the dismay from her voice. "Your mama isn't here now, Pearl." Maybe she could put off the inevitable for a while longer.

"Mama's dead," Johnny stated flatly from beside her. He had heard his sister's calls and had come running. His eyes had lost the eager look they had held minutes earlier.

Reverend Conrad rested a hand on the boy's shoulder.

"I want Mama," Pearl demanded, twisting in Laurina's arms.

"I know, dear," Laurina said soothingly. "I know. But Mama isn't here now. Would you help Johnny show me your home?"

Pearl quit squirming and eyed Laurina warily for a moment. Then she nodded and struggled to be set down. Laurina breathed a sigh of relief at a crisis temporarily passed and opened the door.

Pearl waddled inside and Johnny followed slowly.

Laurina hesitated and looked up at the reverend. "Perhaps moving here wasn't wise."

"You're doing just fine."

Taking a deep breath, she stepped over the threshold.

Even with no trees to block the sun's morning rays, the house was dark. It smelled of damp earth. Laurina's heart dropped to her shoes. One glance showed her that most of the walls hadn't been whitewashed to brighten the interior and make it seem less rustic. Only mud plaster covered the walls, except by the beds.

"This bed is mine and Pearl's." Johnny's voice was filled with pride.

Laurina dragged her heart up from the floor and watched Johnny doing a somersault on a quilt-covered bed in one corner of the long room. Pearl was climbing onto the bed, too, her blue eyes large with laughter at Johnny's antics.

A laugh escaped Laurina as Pearl attempted unsuccessfully to copy her brother's trick. The laughter was as refreshing as wading in a cool pond. *Why, I haven't laughed in weeks,* she realized. She would have to search for things the three of them could laugh at together. Laughter was healing for children.

Suddenly, it seemed brighter inside the humble home.

Another bed joined the children's in an L-shape, allowing more living space in the tiny house than if they had been placed beside each other. The mattresses looked flat and uncomfortable, but Laurina had grown accustomed to the straw-filled mattress at her father's home during the last year, and seldom thought anymore of the soft feather mattress she had slept on in her uncle's Boston home.

Laurina puzzled over the dingy white canvas cloth covering the walls beside the beds. Then it dawned on her that it had once covered a prairie schooner, perhaps the one in which Harlan Wells and his wife had come west.

The ceiling was covered with dirty cheesecloth. Laurina knew it was not for decoration but to catch the mud and creatures that might tunnel through the roof. She glanced at it doubtfully. It hardly looked strong enough to do its duty.

Could she bear it here? Could she? Silly question. She must. "I can do all things through Christ, who strengthens me," she whispered.

"Amen."

She turned at Reverend Conrad's deep voice. She had forgotten for a moment that he was still here.

Assurance glowed in the eyes that watched her, the most emotion she had ever seen in his face. "You can do all things with Him, Miss Dalen."

Laurina took a deep breath and rubbed her hands down the sides of her skirt. "I hope so, Reverend. I feel so inadequate. But at least He's given us a h. . .home."

Through the years she had often quoted Scriptures to help her through difficult times. Now she was claiming strength from the God she was blaming for abandoning Johnny and Pearl. It made no sense. How could she reconcile her reliance on His promise to His inexplicable failure to take care of these children?

To hide the doubt her face might reveal, she looked down at the table beside her, trailing her fingers along its top. The table was simple and made of oak. The indentations and worn finish told that it was a work table in addition to being a dining table. Glancing about, she saw there was not another surface on which to prepare meals.

There were no chairs about the table. Instead, along one side there was a crude bench; a trunk did double duty on the other side.

On the wall opposite the door was a cast-iron stove with four lids and a pipe that went out the roof. Between it and the beds sat a plain oak rocking chair with a worn braided pad. A Bible rested on the sewing basket beside the chair. On the opposite side of the stove was a wooden crate filled with twisted hay; a cupboard stood tall beside the crate. A trail of flowers had been carved along the top of the cupboard, an unexpected attempt at beauty in the rustic home.

Curtains of faded yellow gingham trimmed the two windows. From where she stood in the room, Laurina could see small holes in the material. She recognized the signs of the voracious grasshoppers that hadn't been satisfied with destroying only crops.

Johnny tugged at her skirt. "I'm thirsty, Miss Laurina. Can I please have a drink of water?"

Pearl stood beside him and nodded her head emphatically. "D'ink."

Laurina smiled and ruffled Pearl's curls. "Of course you may." She glanced about the room. "Where is the bucket?"

Johnny was already pulling the door open. "There's a bucket at the well." He dashed across the yard with Pearl right behind him, her blond curls bouncing in time with her wobbly gait.

As Laurina and Reverend Conrad walked out of the soddie, a horse pulling a black sulky galloped into the yard in a cloud of dust. Chickens squawked and flapped out of harm's way as the driver pulled hard on the reins and the two-wheeled vehicle swayed dangerously.

Laurina gasped and one hand clasped the high collar of her dress. "Matthew!"

It was the first time she had seen him since. . .since she had asked him to marry her. The warmth of a blush flooded her face. She forced herself to stand tall with her head held high, though she quivered inside at the memory of her unladylike behavior.

Matthew leaped out of the sulky and strode across the yard, anger in every step, wind whipping his unbuttoned coat out behind him. Ignoring Reverend Conrad, he stopped a foot away from Laurina and settled his hands on his hips. His blue eyes flashed above beet red cheeks. "Just what are you trying to prove, Boston?"

Laurina's concerned glance sought the children. They were standing beside the well, an empty bucket in Johnny's hands, watching Matthew with large eyes. "I will thank you to lower your voice, Dr. Strong. You are frightening the children."

He shot a look at Johnny and Pearl. "Frightening the children? It's *you* who frightens me." His tone was fierce, but he had lowered his voice.

Laurina lifted her chin, her heart pounding wildly. "I can't imagine why anything I do should concern you, sir."

Matthew grabbed his hat from his head and smacked it against his leg, setting dust flying. "Stop acting like an eastern school marm and look around you. Do you really want to live in a soddie, Boston? You have no idea how rough life is for a woman alone in a place like this."

Laurina clutched her hands into fists at her sides. He refused to help her raise the children and now he presumed to tell her how the three of them should live. "It may surprise you to know that the prairie has no monopoly on poverty and hardship, Dr. Strong. Boston has its share of the unfortunate poor, I'm sorry to say. I am sure we shall do fine here."

"It's dangerous out here, Boston. This isn't the civilized Massachusetts countryside. The Jesse James gang was caught one hundred miles from here last summer, remember. There are claim jumpers in the area, too, keeping the homesteaders hopping."

She felt herself pale at the mention of the notorious James gang, and dug her nails into the palms of her hands to keep from weakening. "I can't see why any claim jumpers should want the grasshopper-destroyed claims around here."

A muscle jumped in his cheek and she knew a moment of satisfaction in his lack of an adequate response.

"How are you going to support the children? What are you going to use for money?"

"I intend to find a job."

His jaw dropped and for a moment he was speechless. Then, he spread his arms wide. "That should be easy. There are so many jobs available in this county now. Maybe you can take over for one of the men who left with the wagon train, like the farm implement salesman. Must be very knowledgeable about farming, having been raised in the city. Or maybe you'd like to be sheriff. That position hasn't been filled yet, and every frontier town needs a sheriff."

Laurina could feel the blood rushing to her face. How dare he speak so sarcastically to her?

"That's quite enough, Matthew." Laurina was surprised to hear the veiled threat in Reverend Conrad's voice. "Remember that you're speaking to a lady." He moved closer to her side, squeezing her elbow lightly. Would he feel the trembling that Matthew's words had set off within her?

"And you, Adam!" Matthew turned on him. "What were you thinking of, assisting her in this crazy scheme? You should have been trying to talk her out of it."

"What kind of minister would I be if I tried to talk someone out of doing what they believe God expects of them?" he replied evenly.

"Don't you think God wants her to act sensibly?"

"I think you owe Miss Dalen an apology, Matthew." Laurina could feel his fingers tighten on her elbow, and realized in amazement that the quiet pastor was having difficulty with his temper.

Matthew snorted. "An apology, my foot. She deserves a paddling."

Laurina gasped.

Reverend Conrad stepped forward, partially blocking Laurina as he rested a hand on Matthew's arm. "Calm down, friend, before you go too far."

Matthew yanked his arm free. "You're not doing those youngsters any favors, Boston." He emphasized his point by jabbing his hat toward her.

"Thank you so much for your faith in me, Dr. Strong." As soon as the words left her lips, she was ashamed of herself for her sarcasm. Aunt Miranda brought her up to believe a lady should be above such an uncouth reaction as sarcasm. But she wouldn't apologize. Matthew might think she was weakening.

Matthew ignored her cutting remark and turned to Reverend Conrad. "I thought you had more sense, Adam. It's not a kindness to encourage her in this." He wheeled around and stomped toward his sulky, ramming his hat on his head as he went.

"I'd best see to the children," Laurina murmured, looking over toward the well. Johnny and Pearl had turned their backs on the adults soon after Matthew arrived, and appeared to be struggling with the bucket. She hoped her shaking legs would carry her all the way over there.

"I'll go," Reverend Conrad said as he started toward them.

Laurina turned to watch Matthew's retreating back, her heart still beating frantically from his verbal attack. He reached for the horse's reins, then stopped, resting his hands and forehead on the horse's side. The animal snorted and shook his mane.

She swallowed her surprise as Matthew turned and walked back to her.

They stared at each other silently for a moment, then Matthew's gaze shifted above Laurina's head. She saw the muscles working in his cheeks as he searched for words.

When his eyes met hers again, she was shocked at the sorrow she saw in them. It crashed against the barriers she had thrown up and her belligerence crumbled. She longed to reach out and touch him, to kiss away the pain in his eyes, and clutched her arms tightly across her chest to keep from doing so.

He spread his arms in a gesture of helplessness. When he spoke, the anger was gone. "Boston, what are you going to do when Johnny and Pearl look at you with those big eyes and tell you they're hungry and you don't have anything to feed them?"

Laurina couldn't pull her gaze from the awful question that hung in his eyes. She had no answer to give him. Finally, he turned and walked swiftly to the sulky.

Laurina's throat ached with her loss and frustration while she watched the sulky carrying Matthew away grow smaller and smaller as it crossed the prairie.

Chapter Five

Throughout the day, her confrontation with Matthew haunted Laurina's thoughts. When she had decided to raise the children herself, she had known that it would not be easy. Why did he have to go out of his way to make it more difficult?

As she fed the children supper that evening, Matthew's words rang in her mind. "What are you going to do when they tell you they're hungry and you don't have anything to feed them?" Thank God for the basket of food Hannah had insisted on sending with them that morning. Laurina had been surprised when grim-faced Hannah handed it to her. Her disapproval of Laurina's intention to raise the children herself was plain. Laurina shook her head. This was just another sign of the compassion Hannah hid beneath her gruff exterior. Laurina thought she would never understand the complex woman her father had married.

For supper, she and the children ate cold biscuits from Hannah. The basket also held small amounts of flour, cornmeal, lard, and molasses. "Don't know what ya might be finding at the soddie," Hannah had said. Laurina knew she wouldn't be able to feed the children for long on Hannah's gift, but at least she would have meals for a few days, if she was careful.

Reverend Conrad left soon after Matthew. As he was leaving, Laurina's heart cried out in sudden terror at the thought of being left alone in the dreary house with the two children. But she smiled bravely and thanked him for his assistance. He promised to stop back later that day to be certain she wasn't needing anything. *I should have told him that wouldn't be necessary,* Laurina reprimanded herself, *but it's comforting knowing he'll be stopping.*

≈

They were just putting away the dishes when Reverend Conrad drove up in the mule-drawn wagon. Laurina and the children welcomed him warmly.

Johnny reached for his hand and tugged him inside the soddie. "It's storytime, Rever'nd."

"Father read to them from the Bible every night after supper." Laurina smiled fondly at Johnny. "I guess we're going to continue the practice here. Would you like to join us?"

When he agreed, Laurina picked up the worn Bible from the top of Mrs. Wells's sewing basket and handed it to him. Accepting it as though it were only natural that he be the one to read God's word, he sat down beside the table on the old battered trunk, drawing Johnny up on one knee.

Laurina sat in the rocking chair with Pearl cuddled on her lap. The hard wood of the chair was wonderfully relaxing after the long, emotionally draining day. As she and Pearl rocked, the child's peace and trust seemed to flow into Laurina, warming her heart and refreshing her spirit. Surely Matthew was wrong; surely she had made the right decision.

The reverend began reading from the Gospel of Luke. "And he said, 'A certain man had two sons.' "

So it will be the story of the prodigal son tonight, Laurina thought. The creak of the rocker was a rhythmic background to the reading.

What a homey scene we must make, Laurina thought. *Almost like a family, sitting together while Adam reads. If Matthew had agreed to marry me and raise the children, if he were sitting in Adam's place, even this horrid dirt house would seem wonderful.*

No! I'll not let myself think that way! Matthew Strong will never be a part of our lives. She forced her attention back to the reading.

In his slow, deep voice, Reverend Conrad read the familiar story of the son who had left his father's home, and returned, hungry and homeless, after he had spent all of his inheritance.

" 'And bring hither the fatted calf, and kill it; and let us eat, and be merry: For this my son was dead, and is alive again; he was lost, and is found.' " The reverend closed the book and looked down at Johnny. "And that is the story of the prodigal son."

Johnny wrinkled his young brow. "What's a prod. . .prod. . .?"

"Prodigal?" Reverend Conrad prompted.

Johnny nodded. "Uh-huh. What's a prod'gal son?"

"What do you think a prodigal son is, Johnny?" Reverend Conrad asked.

"Well," Johnny scrunched up his face and gave the matter serious thought. "I think it's a bad boy who runs away from home."

"That's a pretty good explanation, Johnny. The boy's father still loved him, though, didn't he?"

Johnny nodded. "He killed a fat calf for dinner."

Laurina smothered a giggle. She thought she detected the hint of a smile in Reverend Conrad's voice as he said, "That's right, Johnny. His family had a special dinner to celebrate because the son was back home where he belonged. Believing in Jesus is like coming home. It makes our Heavenly Father happy, too, when people come to believe in Jesus."

"Mmm." Johnny's attention was beginning to wander.

Reverend Conrad looked over Johnny's blond head at Laurina. "I guess theology is a bit too much for him tonight."

Laurina peeked at the face of the little girl whose cheek rested against her.

"For this one, too. I think she's asleep."

Reverend Conrad set Johnny off his knee and walking over to the rocker, lifted Pearl carefully. Her head rolled against his shoulder and a tiny sigh escaped her pink lips.

"She's always fallin' asleep before prayers," Johnny said disgustedly, brushing at the curls that fell over his forehead.

As she passed Johnny, Laurina lifted a finger to her lips. She folded the worn blanket back on the narrow bed Pearl and Johnny shared, and the reverend laid Pearl down gently.

"It's time for you to go to bed, too, young man," Laurina said in a low voice to Johnny. She pulled from her trunk the nightshirt he was quickly outgrowing, and he dutifully changed for bed.

Bless him, she thought, *he always does as he's asked without an argument.* Was it because he was by nature a gentle soul? Or was his normal boyish spirit crushed from the multiple tragedies of poverty and loss of his parents?

"Are you goin' to listen to my prayers, Rever'nd?" Johnny looked up at the slender man.

"If you like."

Johnny nodded solemnly. "I like."

He's so eager for a man in his life, Laurina thought as she watched Johnny kneel beside the bed. So as not to waken Pearl, Reverend Conrad carefully sat down next to Johnny on the bed and bowed his head.

Johnny looked over his shoulder to where Laurina stood beside the table. "Aren't you comin', Miss Laurina?"

Laurina sat down on the other bed and folded her hands.

As usual, Johnny's prayer included a petition for God to take care of his pa. But this time he added, "And please bring Pa home, like the prod'gal son, so we can be happy again."

His request drew a moan from her tender heart that Laurina bit back quickly. She had to keep herself from clutching him to her chest as she bent to touch her lips to his cheek. "Good night, Johnny."

"Good night, Miss Laurina. Good night, Rever'nd."

"Since we're friends, Johnny, you can call me Adam instead of reverend, if you like."

Johnny appeared to give this serious consideration. "I never had a real man friend before. Is Pearl your friend, too?"

"Yes."

"Can she call you Adam, too?"

"Do you think she can say 'Adam?' "

"I think so. It's not a very hard word."

"I guess you're right."

"Is Miss Laurina your friend?"

"Yes."

"Why doesn't she call you Adam?"

Laurina saw color flood the man's face above his beard, but his voice didn't betray his consternation. "I'd be pleased to have her call me Adam, if she so chooses."

Johnny seemed satisfied. Adam rose.

"Rever'nd. . .I mean, Adam, are there prod'gal pas, like the prod'gal son?"

Pain twisted Laurina's heart and she clutched her hands in front of her chest. So he had been thinking of his father while he was listening to the Bible story. Thank the Lord she had been able to understand that it was for her safety her parents had sent her to the East. What did Johnny's little mind think of his father's abandonment?

"Yes, Johnny," Adam was answering, "there are prodigal fathers, too."

"I guess Pa is a prod'gal." Johnny's fingers played with the edge of the blanket.

"Maybe."

"But God takes care of prod'gal's, doesn't He?"

Adam rested a hand on Johnny's head. "He sure does, Johnny."

With a sigh of relief, Johnny snuggled deeper under the blanket. "I thought so. Good night."

"We'll be right outside if you need us, Johnny." Laurina's voice was hoarse.

Adam closed the door behind the two of them and they moved together toward his wagon. His mule hee-hawed a greeting. "Almost early lamp-lighting time already," he said. "Days are getting shorter."

Laurina looked out over the prairie. She could no longer see the sun but the cloudless sky was still bright. The winds had died down, as they so often did in the evenings. "Thank you for stopping, Rever—Adam."

"Is there anything you need; anything I can bring you from town?"

Laurina shook her head, brushing a loose tendril of hair back from her face. "We seem to have enough for our immediate needs. Hannah sent a basket with us, as you know, and there's a little in the pantry and root cellar here."

"How much is a little, Miss Laurina?"

It was strange to hear him call her by that name. In the past, he had always addressed her by the more formal Miss Dalen.

"Very little, Mr. Adam." She didn't try to hide the twinkle in her eyes and voice. His face reddened at her teasing. She pretended not to notice and counted off on her fingers the few provisions she had found. "A half-dozen old potatoes, perhaps half a pound of coffee, a pound of shorts, some salt and baking soda, and one old onion. Oh, and almost a pound of butter in the crock in the well."

Adam's thick eyebrows met above his deep-set eyes. "Not much."

"No, but combined with Hannah's basket, we've enough to get by for a while. Except for milk, that is. I guess I'll need to walk to town tomorrow to buy some."

"There'll be no need. I spoke to Stina Lindstrom today. She and her husband, Olaf, have the next farm to the east." He pointed in the direction of the Lindstrom farm, but she couldn't see it. "It's about a mile-and-a-half from here. It's the Lindstroms that have been caring for the Wells's chickens, you remember."

Laurina nodded, watching the rooster strutting near their feet.

"I stopped there today and told them you'd be living here. I arranged for them to keep you supplied with milk."

Her head jerked up. "What do you mean, you arranged for it?"

He didn't answer immediately. Laurina was dimly aware of the mule moving restlessly in his harness and the chickens chuckling nearby as she waited impatiently for him to speak. Her gaze probed the shadow beneath the small rim of his round hat but it was impossible, as usual, to read anything in his eyes.

"I paid for a month's supply of milk and butter."

It was the first time she had heard uncertainty in his voice. Well, he should be uncertain of his actions. He should be ashamed!

"If you'll wait a moment, Reverend, I'll get my reticule and repay you." The words came through stiff lips. She whirled around and started toward the house.

"Miss Laurina!"

She kept walking, her chin high.

In a few strides, he caught up to her and grabbed her arm with just enough pressure to stop her. She set her chin in silent defiance, chest heaving with anger.

"You don't need to repay me. That wasn't my intention."

"It was my decision to take on Johnny and Pearl. They are my responsibility now. I won't be taking charity." Her words were frosty in the warm August air. She slapped angrily at a mosquito on her hand and brushed ineffectually at another buzzing around her ear.

"Do you have any money, Miss Laurina?"

"Yes!"

"How much?"

She stared at him stonily. His calm did nothing to alleviate her temper.

"How much, Miss Laurina?" His firm tone demanded an answer.

"Six dollars and twenty-three cents." She snapped the words. The money was all that remained of the little she had brought from the East last year. She knew from his quickly indrawn breath that he was shocked by her meager savings.

"Miss Laurina, please, accept the milk and butter. Not for yourself, or even for Johnny and Pearl, but for me. So I can do something to help those two fine youngsters." His voice was humble.

Did he think she was so gullible? She opened her mouth to refuse when a picture of another man flashed through her mind. Mr. Jensen, with a shamed look on his kind face when he had told her he and his wife couldn't afford to take Johnny and Pearl into their home.

Laurina had seen by Adam Conrad's actions of the last couple of weeks that he did care for Johnny and Pearl. He had stopped almost daily at her parents' home to check on them and worked tirelessly searching for a family that would take the children. She realized his plea to be allowed to give to them came from his heart. Still, it was hard to swallow her pride and accept his gift.

She locked her fingers in front of her skirt, looked down at them, swallowed hard, and nodded. "All right."

"Thank you." She could hear the relief in his simple words. If she were ever again in a place to help another, Laurina knew she would not forget how awful it felt to accept charity.

"I'll stop again often, if you don't mind. I'd like to keep up with Johnny and Pearl—see how they're getting on."

She hoped her smile didn't look as cold and tight as it felt. "You'll always be welcome, Adam. I apologize for my anger, but I need to learn to supply the children's needs myself. Yet I'm grateful for your support, truly I am."

He touched his hat. "My pleasure, Miss Laurina." As he swung himself up to the high wagon seat, Laurina noticed that the evening insects had begun their chorus.

"Adam?" She hesitated.

He waited.

"Adam, I hope your assistance to us won't harm your friendship with Dr. Strong."

"If you're thinking of what happened here this morning, don't let it worry you. It would take more than that to destroy our friendship." He picked up the worn leather reins. "Don't be too hard on Matthew, Miss Laurina. He's angry only because he loves you, and he's frightened for you."

He spoke to his mule and left before she could reply.

The rumble of his wagon crossing the yard and starting across the prairie toward town was lost in her thoughts. What would she have said if he had expected an answer? That she didn't want a love that wasn't strong enough to include Johnny and Pearl? "Why can't Matthew care for the children like Adam cares for them?" she whispered.

But the broad, darkening heavens covering the prairie gave back no answer.

Chapter Six

Laurina sank wearily onto the bench beside the table, opened her black nankeen reticule, and poured out what little money she had left. As she counted each piece, her spirits sank lower and lower. Eighty-one cents. After five weeks at the soddie, she was fortunate to have that much left.

Even at the "rock bottom, grasshopper prices" advertised by the general store and mercantile, she could barely afford to purchase necessities. The owner of the general store offered to allow her a small amount of credit, as she knew he offered many others in these hard times, but having no foreseeable means of repaying him, she was reluctant to accept his generosity.

Laurina leaned her aching head on her hand. It was more difficult than she had suspected—raising the children by herself. She had known it would be hard, but she hadn't anticipated the emotional and physical exhaustion that resulted from having the constant and sole responsibility for two other lives. Not that she regretted her decision.

Yet, how it tore at her when Johnny or Pearl asked for another helping at a meal and she had to refuse. Each time she recalled Matthew's words from the first day at the soddie, the fear would invade her heart that one day she would have nothing at all to feed the children.

Laurina did have some assistance about the place. Adam Conrad and her father had helped her plow the garden and a few acres of broken farm land, turning the plants the grasshoppers had stripped beneath the prairie sod for the winter.

She flinched as she brushed her hair back from her forehead—even that small act tore at her cut and blistered hands. Her hands had lost their soft white skin soon after she had joined her parents in Chippewa City, but then, living with her parents, she had helped only with normal woman's work. Using a scythe to cut the wild bluestem grass for hay to be used to cover the floor, and twisting and tying it into small bundles to burn in the stove, were not tasks to which her skin was accustomed.

To try to soothe her hands last night, she had used the last of the rose-scented lotion her friend, Caroline, had sent from Boston last Christmas. There was no money to spend on more.

Digging the leathery oval roots of the teepsenee hadn't helped her hands, either. Her father had taught her to recognize the hairy, grayish plant and to use her coffee mill to grind the dried roots into flour to supplement the precious flour she had purchased at the general store. Pastor Dalen had learned to use the teepsenee plant during the years he had spent working as a missionary with the Sioux. When her father said the roots were tasty raw, Laurina had been skeptical but she found that they were rather starchy and mealy but that their white interiors did have an agreeable flavor. She didn't dare turn down anything that would add to her store of food.

How did men ever learn to trust God for daily bread for their families, she wondered? It was much harder to trust Him to meet the children's needs than she had ever found it to trust Him to meet her own. She had tried to keep her faith, but she was finding it more and more difficult to trust God's promises. It frightened her more than anything she had ever experienced to feel her faith slipping away. In its wake was an emptiness deeper than that of a childhood spent without her parents, and a future without the hope of Matthew's love.

At least Pearl had finally stopped asking for her parents. Her constant pleas for her mama and pa had lacerated Laurina's heart. She found it was impossible to explain the word "forever" to a child.

Johnny never asked about his parents, not since the story of the prodigal son. Often, she would find him standing in the yard, staring down the rutted path toward town, and knew he was hoping to see his father return. In spite of her attempts to add fun to their lives whenever possible, Johnny seldom smiled. Whenever they left the homestead, both children refused to let her out of their sight.

She brushed her hair back again from her sweaty face. She had been baking bread and the heat from the stove, along with the smell of burning hay and the yeasty odor of the fresh bread, filled the room. Golden loaves were lined up across the small table, their buttered tops glistening in the morning light that shone through the two windows. The sleeves of her brown calico dress were rolled up to her elbows, and she unbuttoned the top button at her collar to cool her throat.

The milk and butter that Adam Conrad supplied had been a blessing, but the month for which he had paid had been over for a week. Thorburn, Stina's strapping sixteen-year-old son, had continued to bring the milk each day, saying nothing of her lack of payment. Laurina had grown accustomed to his daily visit and had forgotten until this morning that she was overdue in paying. She wondered how much it cost. She hadn't asked Adam, but it was most likely more than the eighty-one cents she had left.

Thorburn's milk stops were a blessing in more ways than one. There was always a smile on his wide, Norwegian face; his straight blond hair reminded her of Matthew's; and the boy's visits were the highlights of Johnny's days. No matter how busy he was, Thorburn took time to talk or play with Johnny for a few minutes before he left. Occasionally, he brought his seven-year-old brother, Nils, to play—a treat for Nils and Johnny both. Thor even helped

Johnny build a fort from tumbleweeds, something of which Laurina would never have thought, and a plaything that gave the children hours of pleasure.

As she looked at the money on the table, a sigh slipped out. Maybe, if she used the churn in the pantry to make the butter herself, she could save a little money. One more thing to add to her already filled days.

The rumble of a wagon and Johnny's joyful shout of welcome startled her from her bleak thoughts. Thorburn, or Thor as Johnny called him, must have arrived.

Laurina could see through the window set deep into the three-foot-thick wall that Thorburn wasn't alone today. Beside him sat a plump, middle-aged woman with a round face. Thick blond braids wrapped across the top of her head. Could this be Stina? She hadn't yet met Thorburn's mother.

Laurina's hand flew to the back of her neck to grasp the braid she had left hanging down her back during the busy morning. Too late to pin it up now.

She rubbed the palms of her sore hands down her flour-covered apron and darted a nervous look around the simple room. She would have to invite the woman inside. Her gaze dropped to the tabletop. The money! She swept the coins into her reticule. It wouldn't do to let the woman see the small size of her funds.

Hurriedly, she pulled down her sleeves and struggled with the button at her throat, securing it just as she heard Johnny's call to her.

"Miss Laurina?" Johnny was pushing the door open. "Mrs. Lindstrom and Thor are here. Come on, Thor, let's play outside."

Thor set the bucket of milk down beside the door. As usual, a twine-tied piece of cloth covered it for protection against dirt on the trip over. The boys went out together, leaving Laurina and Mrs. Lindstrom alone in the one-room house.

Mrs. Lindstrom's face was filled with her smile and her blue eyes twinkled. A brown plaid dress covered her ample frame. "Welcome to our home, Mrs. Lindstrom. I'm Laurina Dalen."

Round, reddened hands reached out to her in greeting, and Laurina found herself grasping them with her own. "Ya, Reverend Conrad, he told us about you. Is such a good thing you do, being mama to the little vuns."

Laurina's discomfort melted away in the sunshine of her neighbor's friendliness.

"Won't you sit down and have a cup of coffee, Mrs. Lindstrom?" Laurina gestured toward the rocking chair. "I'll just get it from the pantry."

There was very little coffee, if the truth be told, but it was considered inhospitable not to offer a visitor coffee. Laurina had saved the few cups of coffee beans Mr. Wells had left behind so she would have some to offer company, but the only company she had had so far were her parents and

Adam Conrad. Laurina served them a hot drink her father had taught her to make from the root of the wild licorice plant that grew on the unbroken land on the homestead.

It's fortunate I'm baking bread, Laurina thought as she filled the heavy coffeepot with fresh water and set it on the stove to heat. She wouldn't need to waste precious twisted hay to heat the stove just to make a couple of cups of coffee.

"Soon vinter vill be here. The cold, it makes it hard to do the chores. But the snow I like. It reminds me of home," Mrs. Lindstrom chattered amiably.

Laurina sat down on the trunk beside the kitchen table. "And home is Norway, Mrs. Lindstrom?"

"Ya. Telemarken, Norvay. The land, is not so good for farming, but the mountains are beautiful."

"How long have you been in America, Mrs. Lindstrom?"

"Four years we live here. Ve came to Minnesota first thing."

Laurina liked Mrs. Lindstrom's singsong accent.

"My husband, Olaf, he vill be going to the north voods to look for a yob in the lumberyards now harvest is over." Her plump shoulders moved up and down as she chuckled. "Is silly the government says men must be on their own farms during harvest or lose their homesteads, ven the 'hoppers hev left nothing to be harvested, ya?"

Laurina smiled slightly. "Yes, very silly, indeed." Would she ever be able to laugh at life's problems again? The perking of the coffee added a cheerful song to the room and the wonderful aromas of coffee and freshly baked bread surrounded the women with warmth as they continued to visit.

Before the coffee finished perking, the women were on a first name basis, and Laurina had learned that Stina had five children besides Thorburn, who was the eldest. The youngest was Johnny's friend, Nils. Laurina thought they were fortunate to have such a kind, good-natured mother.

When the coffee stopped perking, Laurina took two of Mrs. Wells's china cups and saucers from the hand-hewn cupboard. "I couldn't believe my eyes when I saw these lovely dishes," she told Stina as she set the delicate blue-and-white pieces on the old table, "though I admit I've enjoyed using them. They add a bit of beauty to this dark room."

"Ya, Emily, she said they vere vedding gifts."

Laurina handed a filled cup on a saucer to Stina. *I'll have to find a way to buy some cheap dishes,* she thought. Emily's wedding presents should be saved for Pearl. It would be a shame if they were broken.

"Tell me more about Emily, Stina." She would write down everything Stina told her. Someday, the children would want to know more about their parents.

Stina took a sip of coffee and leaned her braid-topped head against the back of the rocker. "Vell, she vas a sveet young thing, alvays smiling and cheerful. She vould sing hymns vile she vorked around the house. She loved the Lord Jesus very much." Stina nodded, a smile on her lips as she remembered her friend.

"And Harlan, vell, he joost live for Emily." She pointed to the top of the cupboard. "He carved the flowers there ven the 'hoppers eat her flowers by the front door. Emily vas already very poorly then, and he said to me, 'I could 'most forgive the 'hoppers for eating my crops, if they yust vould hev left Emily's flowers.'" Stina blinked tears away with her blond lashes and smiled. "Ya, he love her much."

Laurina said nothing. She couldn't understand how such a man as Stina described could abandon his children.

"You speak English good. Vould...vould you read the newspaper to me?"

The question caught Laurina by surprise. "Why, of course. You speak English well yourself."

Stina looked down at her lap. "*Mange takk.* I mean, thank you. We try to speak your language in our new land. But I cannot read your language." She chewed her bottom lip. "No vun in my family reads English."

"Well, no one in my family speaks *or* reads Norwegian."

Stina smiled broadly at her. "I'll get the newspaper from the vagon."

The woman pushed herself out of the rocker, her wide hips scraping the arms of the chair.

A couple of minutes later, she was back with the newspaper. "Olaf, he brought it from town ven he bought supplies yesterday. Sometimes Reverend Conrad or Young Doc stop ven they go by und they read to us. But ven ve come here today, I think maybe you vould read."

Laurina poured another cup of coffee for Stina before she reached for the *Valley Ventilator*. The Chippewa City newspaper had been in operation for only a few months.

"The first article says that the *Lac Qui Parle Press* has discontinued operations due to a lack of funds. That's the second newspaper in this area to be discontinued in the last month. The *Valley Ventilator's* editor says 'Times are tough, but there's none so poor they can't afford the price of a subscription. Just twenty-five cents for a year.'"

Laurina swallowed. Twenty-five cents. What she could buy with twenty-five cents! None so poor they can't subscribe, indeed.

There was an article about the distributions made from the local poor fund and her heart went out to the people whose names were listed. How it must hurt their pride to need charity, and have that fact spread throughout the community! She tried hard to keep her voice normal as she read of the distributions made to Dr. Matthew Strong in payment for his services to destitute citizens.

In spite of the ads of local retailers selling "everything at grasshopper prices" and lists of mortgage sales, the editor insisted things weren't as bad as people from the outside reported them.

When Laurina brought up the subject of the milk money, she was surprised to see Stina's wide face redden. "I vas vondering. . .vould you be agreeable to teaching Thor to read and vrite English language? Ve could gif you milk and butter for pay."

Laurina couldn't believe she had heard correctly. "You mean, in return for giving Thor lessons, you'd give me milk and butter free of charge?"

"Ya." Stina nodded vigorously.

A frown creased Laurina's forehead. "I'm not sure I can teach. I don't know how to speak Norwegian and that will make it difficult for Thor and me both."

"I know you can do it." Stina's voice held no doubt.

Laurina took a deep breath. "Then I'll try."

A broad smile burst across Stina's face. It was agreed that lessons would begin the next morning when Thor delivered the day's milk.

It would be hard to find time to work with Thor. As it was, there were never enough hours in the day. But she would make the time somehow.

All too soon, Stina and Thorburn left to return to their home. With a smile on her face, Laurina turned back to the room. It seemed brighter in the dark soddie now. A pleasant glow from their visit seemed to linger in the air. She liked Stina—she laughed so easily. The comforting smells of coffee and baking bread added a homeyness to the place. *And why not?* she thought. After all, it was her home now, hers and the children's.

She was humming as she picked up her reticule from the table and went to put it in her trunk, happy that it was no lighter than when Stina arrived.

As Laurina started to fold the newspaper, her glance fell on the story of the local cheese factory. The factory had opened for the first time in June and was run completely by women. She had been so sure she could find a position there. But Mrs. Anderson, the head supervisor, had explained gently that, even before Laurina began looking for work, all the positions had been filled by other women who were forced by the 'hoppers to seek employment. Laurina hated to accept the pound of cheese Mrs. Anderson offered her but knew she couldn't turn down food for the children.

Everywhere she went it was the same. As Matthew had warned, there were no jobs to be had in the valley. She couldn't even make her living as a seamstress, since she couldn't compete with those who had a sewing machine. Besides, few were paying others to sew for them now. Everyone was wearing patched clothing, "making do" and "making over."

She was going to have to swallow her pride and ask for help from the local poor fund. Her cheeks burned at the thought of her name spread across the county through the newspaper. Still, she couldn't let her pride keep her from providing for the children. Winter would be here soon and Johnny needed a new coat. The sleeves of his old coat reached barely past his elbows and it wouldn't even button across his chest any longer. At least Pearl could wear Johnny's old coat, even though it would be large on her. They both needed shoes. It was up to her and the poor fund to supply for them now.

Laurina reached up and ran her fingers over the flowers Harlan Wells had carved for his wife in the cupboard. She would never understand what men call love. Why couldn't Harlan see that the most wonderful thing he could do for his wife would be to take care of their children? And Matthew claimed to love her, but he refused to care for the children, too.

She stamped her foot in exasperation, the sound unsatisfyingly dull against the packed earth floor. Why did her mind insist on going back to that man? She didn't love him anymore, not now that she knew what he was really like. She didn't!

Chapter Seven

Laurina brushed straw from her face as she joined Johnny, Pearl, Adam, and the Lindstroms in the final verse of *Yankee Doodle*. The group had been singing for the better part of an hour and Laurina was growing accustomed to hearing the Scandinavian accents blending with the American ones. As they rode along in the back of the Lindstroms' straw-filled wagon, their voices drifted out over the prairie. Thor drove and Stina sat beside him on the high seat. Laurina was grateful for the straw that protected her from bumps and bruises as they lurched across the uneven prairie land. Blue gentians and white asters dotted the prairie, brightening the expanse of browning prairie grass.

She had been surprised when Adam stopped after church and insisted that she and the children join him and the Lindstroms for a day of fishing and picnicking at the river. As she watched Johnny and Pearl's eyes shining in the midst of their dirty faces, she was glad Adam had persisted until she agreed. It had been an unusually warm day for October, and it was a joy to relax beside the river. She hadn't been to the river since moving to the soddie, and she had missed the waters that were so restful to her spirit.

Soon, they pulled into the yard of the soddie but the group hung onto the last notes of *Yankee Doodle* longer than normal as though loathe to let the afternoon end. The children stood up as the wagon came to a stop, laughing at each other as they wobbled on their "sea legs" after the rocky ride.

"Won't you stay for a while, Stina?" Laurina asked as she got up on her knees.

She barely heard Stina's "Ya." Matthew's small, two-wheel sulky was sitting beside the sod barn and his horse was staked beside Adam's mule. Her heart started racing faster than the rabbit that had dashed from the path of the wagon wheels minutes earlier. She hadn't seen Matthew since the day they moved to the soddie. Why had he come?

"Who's here?" Johnny asked, noticing the sulky.

"Doctor Strong." Adam's gaze didn't leave Laurina's as he answered Johnny and helped Laurina from the back of the wagon.

Johnny gave a whoop and raced toward the house. "Young Doc! Young Doc! See the fish I caught!"

As usual, Pearl followed after him. "Fishes, fishes!"

Laurina hurried behind them on unsteady legs.

Matthew was standing beside the pantry door, the sleeves on his cream-colored shirt rolled above his elbows, a thick brush in one hand, a bucket in the other, and a wide grin on his face. Goosebumps chased each other from the tips of Laurina's toes to the top of her head at the sight of him standing in the house that had become her home.

Johnny was tugging at one of Matthew's legs. "C'mon, Young Doc. Come see my fish."

"Hi, Boston," Matthew greeted her with a wave of his brush.

"What are you doing here?" She hoped her voice didn't sound as breathless to him as it did to her.

"Sorry, got to go see some fish." He handed her the brush as he and Johnny passed her on their way out the door.

"Doctor Strong!" she said.

But he was following Johnny to the group of Lindstroms beside the wagon.

She stamped her foot impatiently. "Oh, that man!" She looked down at the brush in her hand, and held it away from her straw-covered blue calico dress. Whatever had he been doing?

She turned back to the room and caught her breath. The dirt walls were covered with white lime. Compared to their previous state, they seemed to fairly shout with light. Tears came unbidden to her eyes. "Oh, Matthew," she whispered. She walked slowly to the middle of the room, looking about her in wonder.

"How beautiful! Laurina, is this not vonderful?" Stina's hands were clasped prayerlike in front of her chest. Her wide frame filled the doorway.

Laurina started to dash the tears away with her hand, and realized she was still holding the brush. "Yes, wonderful," she mumbled.

Matthew was back a few minutes later. She handed him his brush. He took it with his usual grin but there was no answering smile on Laurina's face.

Stina seemed to sense the tension between them for she hurried her children outside. "Please don't leave, Stina," Laurina urged. "I was hoping you and the children would stay for dinner. We can fry the fish."

"Ve need to go home and tend to chores. I vill come in the morning with Thor to show you how to pickle the fish." She closed the door behind her, leaving Matthew and Laurina alone.

Now that they had privacy, Laurina didn't know what to say. The brightness in the room this late in the day amazed her. It would be marvelous having white walls, but how could she thank him? She didn't want him to think he could parade back into her life without so much as a "by your leave."

For the first time she noticed the white lime splattered in his hair and on his nose. Even that didn't distract from his good looks.

It was Matthew who broke the silence. He leaned toward her slightly and asked in a conspiratorial whisper, "Did I hear her say you're going to pickle fish? Are you sure it's edible?"

His choice of subjects was completely unexpected and Laurina laughed in spite of herself, for she had asked herself that very question. The thought of pickled fish didn't particularly appeal to her. But it was food and she might be glad to have it before winter ended. Stina, however, thought it a delicacy.

Her laughter seemed to give Matthew courage. "I didn't mean to offend you, Boston, whitewashing the walls. But I kept thinking how depressing this place was when I stopped to check on Mrs. Wells when she was sick." Lines seemed to grow in his face, and his next words were so quiet Laurina strained to hear them. "I couldn't bear thinking of you living in such a dreary place."

Her heart leaped at his words. He still cared for her! She immediately reined in her betraying thoughts, reminding herself that she no longer cared. She had to fight to keep her voice steady. "You've no right to come into my home unannounced, Doctor."

His lips tightened into a thin line. "No, don't suppose I have." He threw the brush into the empty lime bucket on the floor. "If it makes any difference, I intended to be gone before you got back."

"It makes no difference. I cannot afford to pay you for the lime."

"I'm not asking you to pay for it. A patient over on the Lac Qui Parle River offered it to me in payment of a bill. I had no use for it at my own place."

Laurina folded her arms over her chest, trying to protect herself from the feelings that flowed through her at his nearness.

He ran a hand impatiently through his blond hair. "Boston, you can be plain impossible sometimes."

She lifted her chin a trifle, but before she could snap back a reply, Adam walked in with Pearl in his arms.

Adam's gaze shifted from Laurina to Matthew and back again. "Think this little one needs a nap, Miss Laurina."

Pearl rubbed her forehead back and forth against his shoulder, her round arms hugging his neck. "Fishes want a nap, too."

Laurina caught back an exasperated sigh. Why were these children so enthralled with the fish?

"Fish don't take naps, Pearl. I tried taking one to bed with me when I was a tyke about your age. Want to hear about it?" Matthew held out his arms to Pearl. She nodded and leaned toward him. "Well, it happened like this." He sat down on the bed with her in his lap and launched into his story.

Adam's expression didn't change a bit. He just turned on his heel and walked out the door.

Was he hurt at the quick way Pearl turned to Matthew? Laurina wondered. She looked at Matthew, deep into his tall tale with Pearl. He shouldn't be here, acting as though he had every right to whitewash the walls without asking her, as though he were an everyday part of the children's lives. Still, she could hardly pull him away in the midst of his story to Pearl.

Laurina pulled the door shut behind her as hard as she could.

Adam was in front of the barn cleaning the fish on the top of an old barrel. Her skirt flapped in the wind and when she brushed at the stray hairs that blew across her eyes, pieces of straw poked at her. *I must look a sight,* she thought, dismayed that Matthew had seen her in such a state, then instantly angry at herself for caring.

She smiled at Adam, trying to ease any rejection he might feel. "Pearl was just tired, Adam. You know you're her favorite 'real man friend,' as Johnny says."

He didn't look up from the fish he was filleting. "It doesn't matter. Miss Laurina, it's my fault he's here. When I told him I hoped we'd be going on the picnic, I didn't know he was planning to whitewash your walls. If I'd known, I would have warned you."

"I know that, Adam. It's not like you to be a party to deception."

After a few minutes, Matthew joined them. Laurina hated the longing for him that pulled at her.

"Pearl's asleep. Guess I'll be leaving." Matthew started toward his horse, then turned back, almost tripping over Pete and receiving a sound scolding from the rooster. He pulled an envelope from the pocket of his shirt and handed it to Laurina. "Almost forgot to give this to you. The postmaster asked me to deliver it."

She glanced at the familiar handwriting on the thick envelope. "It's from Caroline!"

Laurina tore open the letter from her Boston friend as Matthew went to hitch his horse to the sulky. Johnny abandoned Adam and the smelly fish cleaning to chase after Matthew. "Can I ride your horse, Young Doc?"

"Johnny, mind your manners!" Laurina admonished.

Johnny stuck his hands in his pockets and kicked at a granite pebble. Then his face brightened as Matthew said, "Sure, pardner. Jump on up here." He lifted the boy easily to the horse's bare back then untied the large chestnut animal and led him around the yard.

Johnny's shining face as he rocked back and forth on the back of the doctor's horse kept Laurina from urging Matthew to hurry his leave-taking.

She turned her attention back to the envelope. A newspaper clipping was folded in with the letter, but she ignored it, eager to read what her friend had to say. The hooves of Matthew's horse padded softly against the ground through the knee-high grass. "Oh, my goodness!"

The knife in Adam's hand stilled as he looked up from the fish. "Is it good news, Miss Laurina?"

She looked up at him with a grin that felt foolishly large. "It seems I'm now a newspaper woman."

He looked at her steadily, waiting with his usual unexcited patience for an explanation.

"Just before the wagon train left this summer, I wrote to Caroline, telling her about the devastation caused by the grasshoppers. She read the letter to her husband, David, who is a reporter for a Boston newspaper. He showed my letter to his editor. And Adam," she could hardly say the words, they sounded too good to be true. "Adam, the editor printed what I wrote about the grasshoppers. Caroline sent me money for the article! The best part is, the editor wants me to write more articles about life on the frontier."

His face flooded with a joy that humbled her. It started, of course, in his deep-set eyes, moved to his mouth into an honest-to-goodness smile, and then filled his entire face. "Thank you, Lord Jesus."

His fervent words stilled her breath for a moment. It hadn't even crossed her mind to thank God. "It doesn't pay very much," she rushed to explain, knowing she was trying to excuse herself for not acknowledging this as God's gift. As soon as she had realized her oversight, she knew she wasn't ready to thank Him. Why *should* she thank Him when there were still so many things wrong with the world, and with her life and the children's lives in particular?

"But it's something, Miss Laurina. Every bit helps."

She nodded. "Yes, every bit certainly does help."

"Congratulations, Boston."

She turned in surprise to find Matthew standing behind her, staring at Adam with a strange look on his face. He lifted Johnny down from his horse and went to hitch up his sulky without the usual bounce in his step.

Why did he have to come here today, Laurina raged inwardly as she watched him. The last few months, she had worked so hard to stop dwelling on the pain of knowing he would never again be a part of her life. Now she would have to learn all over to live without him. The white walls would be a constant reminder of him. There would be memories of him inside her home, laughing, teasing her, and worst of all, pretending to befriend Johnny and Pearl. *Oh, God, how could You do this to me? Wasn't life difficult enough, Lord?*

Before she knew it, he was climbing up on the seat of the one-man buggy and leaving without saying goodbye to anyone. "Doctor Strong!" she said.

He reined in so quickly that his sulky rocked precariously. When he had it and the horse in hand, he turned to her, waiting.

"Let's take the fish inside, Johnny," she heard Adam say behind her, and was grateful for his thoughtfulness.

She shouldn't have called Matthew back, but when he started to drive away, she couldn't bear the thought of his leaving, not knowing when she would see him again.

"I. . .I do appreciate the whitewashed walls, Doctor."

"Are you ever going to call me Matthew again, Boston?" he asked quietly.

His gaze held hers and her chest ached with longing for the freedom to let herself love him once again. She had been a fool to call him back. She was only making things harder for herself. The breeze rattled the papers in her hand, breaking the spell between the man and woman. "Goodbye, Doctor."

He snorted and drove off with dust rolling up behind his wheels.

ঽঌ

There was no Bible story time that night. The children were exhausted from their holiday. Laurina wiped Johnny's face and hands and Adam listened with her to Johnny's prayers.

"I'll walk out with you," she offered after they tucked Johnny and Pearl into bed and as she was reaching for the brown-fringed shawl on the back of the rocker.

He paused beside the door and looked back at the room, brighter than normal now in the lamplight. "It is nicer with the walls whitewashed."

"Yes."

He didn't speak as he hooked his mule to the wagon but his silence didn't bother her. She was growing accustomed to his quiet ways.

She leaned back against his wagon and looked up at the twilight sky. "Thank you for today, Adam. The memory of it will refresh me for weeks. It was wonderful for the children. Johnny hasn't been this happy since his father left." She dropped her eyes from the sky to his face. "Your approval has made it much easier for me to care for the children, Adam. Everyone else seems to think I was a fool for taking them."

He rested one hand on the front wagon wheel. She couldn't see his eyes beneath the rim of his hat in the darkness. "You're not a fool, Laurina." He cleared the huskiness from his throat. "Psalm 68 tells us that 'God setteth the solitary in families.' God's been good to Johnny and Pearl, setting them with you." He pulled himself up into the wagon. "Good night, Miss Laurina."

She stood in the yard long after his wagon was lost in the darkness. The creak of its wheels, which could be heard for many minutes after she could no longer see him, sounded foreign among the night sounds. Soon the weather would be too cool for the songs of the evening insects. The fall had been mild so far.

She pulled the shawl closer about her shoulders against the slight breeze.

"God setteth the solitary in families," she repeated, facing the thought she had been trying to push away since Adam left. Was she, by herself, a family? Didn't a family include a husband and father? Wouldn't it have been better for Johnny and Pearl if Matthew had married her and provided a true family for them?

She was tired of trying to believe the promises of God when she could see no evidence of their being fulfilled. It took so much of her strength to try to believe and there was so little strength left after the long days spent caring for the children.

Laurina looked about her at the plain soddie homestead. Hopeland. How foolishly optimistic she had been when she named this place. "False hope, that's all God's promises are," she whispered fiercely. "Just false hope."

Chapter Eight

On November twenty-ninth, Laurina settled herself and the children on a bench near the front of the schoolroom for the Thanksgiving Day service. Laurina didn't feel thankful. In fact, every Sabbath she felt more bitter as she and the children sat in the midst of the people that hadn't helped Johnny and Pearl and listened to sermons on the God who supposedly loved them all.

In the last few months, she had considered more than once leaving the church, but she wasn't quite brave enough to face her father with her doubts about his God. More importantly, she remembered how vital her faith was to her when she had been separated from her parents as a little girl. Johnny and Pearl needed to believe in God's goodness now and she couldn't make herself take that away from them. So she continued to take them to church whenever the weather permitted, to have Bible story time nightly, and prayer at meals and bedtime.

Sometimes a prayer for the children or the things they needed would slip out before she could catch herself. It made her angry to find herself praying for them when she no longer believed God answered prayers.

Today, she and the children sat quietly with the other women and children on the crude school benches. The men and older boys stood against the wall, since there weren't nearly enough seats for everyone. The special service brought a much larger crowd than the Sabbath services. The schoolhouse was the best building in town, the only one with shingles. It stood on the plateau halfway between her father's home and Matthew's house.

Laurina looked down at Pearl who was wearing the black wool coat that once belonged to Johnny. Beneath it was a dress Laurina had made by hand from an old one that had belonged to Pearl's mother. Laurina had found three dresses in the trunk that stood at the bottom of the bed Mr. and Mrs. Wells had shared. Two of the dresses were barely more than rags and all were years out of fashion. But then, fashion wasn't nearly as important here on the frontier as back in Boston, although most women liked to stay as fashionable as their circumstances allowed. At the least, they attempted to have one "good Sabbath dress."

Laurina knew the third dress she had found was more than a typical good Sabbath dress. It was the dress Mrs. Wells wore in the wedding picture Laurina had discovered in the Wells's Bible. Though its color was faded somewhat, the dress was in very good shape. Laurina would like to save it for Pearl to have when she was grown but perhaps Mrs. Wells would prefer that her daughter have some decent dresses now.

As people visited while waiting for the service to start, voices and laughter filled the room. How could they be so happy? Maybe it was all a façade, the kind she had seen crumble when looking for a home for the children.

Suddenly, one voice penetrated the rest and she turned her head sharply to see Matthew talking with some of the old settlers, as the earliest inhabitants of Chippewa City were called. He was gesturing grandly with his hands and his face was as animated as usual as he told a story. Pain twisted her heart at the sight of him. She didn't love him, she assured herself, but she did miss the laughter his lighthearted ways brought to her life.

The murmurs quieted as Reverend Conrad moved to the front of the room and announced the opening hymn, *O For a Thousand Tongues to Sing Our Great Redeemer's Praise.* Before the people could begin singing, Pearl pointed a pudgy finger at him. "Adam!" she squealed. Adam refused to look in their direction, trying to retain his usual composure as the congregation twittered at Pearl's outburst. Laurina leaned down to gently hush the child. When Laurina sat up, she caught Hannah staring at her with a tight mouth and hard eyes. What was wrong? True, children were to be seen and not heard in public, but Pearl wasn't yet three, and her actions hadn't been that abhorrent. Puzzled, she joined the hymn in the midst of the first verse.

In his sermon, her father reminded the congregation of Joel 2:25 and 26, which he had preached on in the midst of the grasshopper invasion last summer: "And I will restore to you the years that the locust hath eaten."

As she listened to her father read the verse, she remembered Matthew standing tall against the early morning prairie winds with the sun's rays gleaming off his blond hair as he proclaimed, "I believe that, Boston." She had believed it, too, then. That had been the day he had said he loved her.

"We've much to be thankful for this day," her father was saying. "It's an exciting time, as we see God fulfilling this promise. The railroad has set up offices in Granite Falls, only fifteen miles away, and the railroad is expected to reach Chippewa City this summer. Some of you may find jobs with the railroad. Report is that the 'hoppers didn't leave behind enough eggs to threaten next year's crop. Land sales and business are picking up. Mr. Moyer opened a bank last week, the town's first." As he talked, his gray beard moved up and down on the front of his long black coat.

"Many of you sought God's forgiveness during the day of fasting and prayer for deliverance from the 'hoppers in April. God has seen the repentance in your hearts, and has started to heal the land. If you continue to seek Him with all your hearts, He will bring about complete healing, and make this land and your lives fruitful."

Several in the congregation responded with "Amen" or "Bless Thee, Lord" but Laurina didn't join in them.

Following the service, the congregation milled about inside the school-house, loathe to leave the company or the warmth of the potbellied stove. Three weeks ago, the first snow of the season had covered the prairie and the river froze over. If her father hadn't picked Laurina and the children up in the wagon last evening, they wouldn't have been able to walk in the cold to the service today. Her father and Hannah had invited Laurina, Johnny, and Pearl to stay the night with them and join them for the Thanksgiving meal following the service. The congregation had given her father and Hannah a turkey to celebrate the day. If there was one thing for which Laurina thought she might possibly thank God, it was for that turkey.

Johnny begged to go outside and play with the other boys, and Laurina reluctantly agreed after tying his wool muffler securely over his head and wrapping it around his neck and chin. It was the first time he had willing-ly left her presence when away from the soddie and she beat back tears with her lashes as she watched him run out the door. She and Pearl remained inside where Laurina visited with the women. Hollers and laughter drifted through the walls from the children playing outdoors and became a muffled background to the adults' voices inside.

Gradually, Laurina became aware that the shouts from outside had changed and were no longer cheerful sounds of play. She followed some of the others outside. The horses in the yard were tugging at the ropes that secured them, neighing nervously. Then she saw two boys fighting in the midst of a ring of children. Was Johnny one of the boys fighting?

She breathed a sigh of relief as she saw Johnny standing in the ring of spec-tators, but her heart continued to pound rapidly. Johnny's face was screwed up in anger and his mittened hands were curled into fists as he watched the fight. Moments after she caught sight of him, he darted into the circle and started pummeling one of the fighting boys for all he was worth.

"Johnny, no!" Laurina cried. She tried to hurry to him to pull him away from the danger, but Pearl was in her arms and the snow and her long skirt tripped her up. "Johnny!" He was so small! What if he were hurt?

Then Matthew was in the middle of the circle, lifting Johnny by the back of his coat and easily setting him aside before separating the other boys. One of the boys darted back to continue the fray, but Johnny and the other boy, recognizing Young Doc, stood with their chests heaving beneath their winter coats, small clouds of air forming in front of their faces.

Matthew grabbed the insistent fighter by his shoulders. "Whoa, there! What's the problem?"

The boy pushed unsuccessfully against Matthew's hands. "He called me a sissy!"

"He wears girls' clothes," the other boy defended himself belligerently.

Laurina heard a soft sigh come from beside her as she realized that the target of the taunts was indeed wearing slacks made of faded blue-flowered calico.

The woman next to her was dressed in a shabby gown covered by a worn wool shawl, a tattered brown scarf tied over her head. She hurried to the boy in calico as Laurina and Pearl went to check on Johnny.

As she knelt beside Johnny, Laurina was dimly aware of Matthew dispersing the crowd of boys and girls that had gathered to watch the fight. "Are you hurt, Johnny?" She set Pearl down and moved Johnny's muffler gently to search for bumps and bruises. There was only a small bump below one eye, growing more colorful by the moment.

Johnny wasn't aware of any physical pain yet. "That boy was bein' mean to Willie, Miss Boston! Just 'cause Willie doesn't have good clothes like us. That's mean, isn't it? Why are people mean like that?"

"I don't know, Johnny." Her heart fought over whether to feel sorry for his pain or be glad for his tender heart.

Willie's mother stopped beside her with Willie's hand in hers. "Thank you for wanting to help my boy," she said to Johnny. But Willie pulled his hand from hers and bellowed, "I didn't need his help. I can fight by myself!" and tore across the schoolyard to the row of wagons on the other side of the building.

His mother turned to Laurina. Her face was lined and leathery from the prairie winds and sun, but her eyes were a soft, gentle brown. "I'm Rose Beck. You have a fine son." Her voice was as soft as her eyes.

Laurina stood up and slipped her hands over Johnny's shoulders. "Johnny's not my son, though I'd be proud if he were. I'm Laurina Dalen, and this is Johnny Wells."

Mrs. Beck smiled. "I'm so glad to meet you, Miss Dalen. I've heard how you took on the care of Harlan and Emily's young ones. It's a fine thing."

The wind was cold, rushing across the snow, unhindered for miles. Laurina shifted her scarf to better protect her chin. As they started back toward the warmth of the schoolhouse, Laurina said, "I'm surprised we haven't met before, Mrs. Beck. I thought I knew everyone in Father's congregation. Or maybe you attend Reverend Conrad's church?"

"I'm ashamed to say we haven't been to any church service for a long time. We live a good piece from town and haven't any horses or oxen to pull a wagon. We had to sell them, you see, to qualify for a seed loan."

Laurina nodded. Harlan Wells had to sell his, also, she recalled.

"My husband is dead," Mrs. Beck continued. "We have five children, four of them girls. Willie is our youngest. Keeping the girls clothed has been hard, but not so hard as finding clothes for Willie. The girls can share things and pass them down, but Willie needs things new, being a boy. He's shot up like a weed this year, and there wasn't anything to be making pants out of but an old calico dress." Her smile didn't hide the tears in her eyes as she added, "It's hard to make a boy understand that you can't buy material for pants when there's no money for food."

"Yes," Laurina murmured. "It is hard." Here it was again—more evidence that God didn't care about people. Her chest burned in anger at the God she had once trusted and loved.

"I've been ashamed to bring the family to church or send Willie to school, since we're so poorly dressed. I try to teach him at home and we read the Scriptures and sing hymns on the Sabbath, but it's not the same. Lately, I've been seeing the Lord God cares more for our hearts than the clothes we wear to church. So when my neighbor asked if we'd like to ride to the service today in their wagon, I said 'Thank you, kindly,' and here we are."

Laurina forced a smile. "I'm glad you've come. You're right, the clothes don't matter." But they do matter for your little boy, she thought. She wished she could afford to give Mrs. Beck money for material and thread. She hated the stingy, dirt-poor way it made her feel to be unable to give. Was that how the people had felt when she had asked them to give Johnny and Pearl homes, and they couldn't?

"Some people think Mr. Wells is shiftless and no good for leaving, I've heard talk," Mrs. Beck was continuing, "but I can understand why he left the children. He wanted them to have a better life than he could give them." She looked toward her daughters, standing together in a quiet circle a few feet away, and smiled sweetly. "I'm not as strong as he is; I can't separate myself from my children."

The wife of the owner of the local general store stopped to talk with Mrs. Beck, and Laurina excused herself. Other women stopped her to chat, and Laurina made an effort to seem attentive, but her mind remained with Mrs. Beck. Laurina felt chastised by her words. As Mrs. Beck said, Mr. Wells had left the children in order to provide them a chance for a better life. She had taken them back to the sod house, and with no income, expected to care for them. The small amount she had received from the poor fund, and the few dollars her newspaper articles brought, were not enough to support them. If it weren't for Adam and her father and Hannah, they probably would have spent many days before this with empty stomachs. Had she tried to save Johnny and Pearl, only to bring them to the extreme poverty Mrs. Beck and her family knew? Would the day come when she could no longer suitably clothe the children? She shivered from a chill not caused by the cold drafts.

Laurina heard Matthew's voice behind her and turned to see him introducing himself to Mrs. Beck, who was now standing in a corner of the room with her daughters. Mrs. Beck thanked him warmly for breaking up the fight. Laurina could barely hear his next words—his voice was much quieter than usual and there was still a large number of people visiting in the one-room building.

"Mrs. Beck," he was saying, "my barn needs cleaning, and I need some kindling cut. I was wondering if your boy would be available to help me one day soon. I expect it would be worth the price of a pair of pants to me."

Laurina couldn't see Mrs. Beck's face on the other side of Matthew's broad back, but her voice sounded radiant. "Bless you, Doctor. I'm sure Willie'd be glad to help out."

How kind of Matthew to think of a way to save Mrs. Beck's pride and offer her the much needed pants at the same time! Laurina's heart swelled with love for him, and the realization shook her to the core. Why did he always slip back into her heart unexpectedly, when she tried so hard to keep him out?

"I'm going to be leaving now to get that turkey started for supper," Hannah said from beside her. "Are you and the children ready?"

Laurina nodded, suddenly aware that she had been eavesdropping on the conversation between Matthew and Mrs. Beck. As they moved toward the door, she heard snatches of conversation. Everyone was talking about the exciting things that were happening in Chippewa City and the way God was fulfilling His promise.

Things hadn't happened soon enough for Mrs. Beck and her children, Laurina thought. *And many of the settlers are still without food for the winter and seed for spring planting. Why hast Thou waited so long to restore the years of the locust?* she thought as her heart challenged God.

Walking back to the log cabin, Johnny tugged at the sleeve of her gray wool wrapper. "Miss Boston, Willie doesn't have a pa, either."

She enclosed his hand in her own black-mittened one. "I know."

A thoughtful frown creased his forehead. "If I were God, I wouldn't let kids' pas go away."

She squeezed his hand and felt as though he had squeezed her heart. *I wouldn't either,* she thought. Maybe God could restore the businesses of Chippewa City and the land of the settlers, but could He ever restore the lost dreams and broken hearts?

Chapter Nine

In the weeks following Thanksgiving, the temperatures moderated. Soon, the early winter snows melted. Laurina was glad for the reprieve from winter weather. It meant she could use less of the precious fuel to heat the sod house, and that meant she didn't need to twist as much hay.

The unseasonably mild temperatures brought rain instead of snow, and the last week had been damp and misty when the heavens weren't pouring down rain. Laurina had discovered that sod houses keep out the cold well in winter and the heat in summer, but sod was not meant to keep out rain.

Two weeks after Thanksgiving, a rainstorm lasting two days struck the area. At first, Laurina and the children were snug and dry in their sod home, but by the second evening, muddy water was dripping through the roof, through the cheesecloth, and onto everything in the house.

Amidst many grunts and groans, Laurina managed to remove the canvas from the wall beside her bed. Dragging the children's straw-filled mattress over, she tugged it on top of her own and covered both with the canvas. She tucked the rocking chair beneath the edge of the canvas, not wanting the rain to ruin their only decent piece of furniture.

To help dry the building, a fire had to be kept going in the stove, around the clock. Laurina's hands were more scratched and sore than usual from trying to keep up with the demands for twisted hay. After two days of storms, what hay she had left was damp if not soggy, and didn't burn well. It didn't help that she had a wood stove rather than a sheet metal, hay-burning stove, but she had grown accustomed to making do with what was available.

Even with the constant fire and unseasonably warm temperatures, the dampness seeping into her bones made it more difficult than usual to keep up her cheerful front with the children.

The morning of one day dawned clear and bright outside, but it continued to rain indoors. Laurina carried what items she could outside to dry. She sent the children out to play, setting the tableside bench next to their tumbleweed fort so they would have someplace to sit that wasn't muddy.

She wasn't so fortunate inside the house. She pulled the table next to the stove to where the roof and floor were a trifle drier than the rest of the room, and started to mix some flapjacks for lunch. The faded brown cotton housedress that fit her perfectly when she had moved to the soddie hung loosely about her now. In an attempt to keep her hem out of the mud as she worked, she hitched up the skirt, exposing her legs halfway to the knees, and tied her apron strings around it.

Caroline would never believe it if she could see me now, Laurina thought, as she glanced about at the drizzle. She grimaced. *I guess I've found the topic for my next article.*

She was so engrossed with her attempts to dodge the muddy water while mixing the batter it took her a while to realize that Adam had arrived.

He surveyed the situation with his usual calm. Laurina watched as his gaze took in the muddy drizzle, the canvas over the bedding, and the floor that was beginning to look like Chippewa City's main street after a storm. Without changing expression, his dark eyes swept quickly over her unusual dress.

He held up a dead goose. "I shot this on the drive out here, Miss Laurina. Perhaps I'd best leave it in the wagon for now."

"You might set it in the pantry. And thank you, Adam. It's been a while since we've had fresh meat.

Since prairie chicken season had ended, Laurina's father and Adam had brought them duck and pheasant whenever they had had some to spare. Laurina salted and dried as much meat as she could. The birds had been numerous during the fall months, before it snowed and Laurina had enjoyed the honking of the geese that had flown over by the thousands. Now, only a few were left since the cold spell at Thanksgiving. In hopes of bringing home meat, both Pastor Dalen and Adam carried their rifles with them when they made calls on parishioners. Sunday was the the normal hunting day for the local men, but both pastors felt it wasn't proper to enjoy the sport on the Sabbath.

Adam moved past her through the small door beside the cupboard into the minute room that served as a pantry. A moment later, he was back. "Miss Laurina, you haven't much on the pantry shelves."

Did he think she didn't realize how meager their supplies were? "I know, but—"

"I was thinking," he interrupted, "perhaps I could use some of those shelves to cover the worst of the places on the floor. The shelves are short and narrow, but they'd provide some protection. Of course, I'd leave enough shelving for your supplies."

"Bless you, Adam!" Her heart felt as though it had grown wings. "That's a wonderful idea."

Adam left for the barn in search of tools and Laurina turned back to the flapjack batter.

Splat!

Laurina almost dropped the heavy bowl as batter spattered across the top of her apron. "What in the world?" she muttered as she looked into the bowl. Was the batter wiggling? "Oh, my goodness!"

She rushed to the door and flung the remaining batter out as one would a bowl of dirty dishwater.

"What was that for!"

Laurina saw in dismay that the batter had landed on Matthew and was covering his white shirt and vest. Johnny and Pearl broke into peals of laughter.

His arms spread wide, Matthew looked down at himself in shock. "New way of greeting company, Boston? I don't think it's going to catch on."

Mutely, she pointed to the batter-covered snake wiggling away in the mud at his feet. Matthew burst into a belly laugh.

"It's not amusing!" Laurina slammed the door in his face and stalked back to the table through the muddy drizzle. She set the bowl down smartly on the table. An entire bowl of ingredients wasted by that stupid garden snake! Didn't it know it was supposed to be hibernating? "Is it too much to ask for some winter weather during a Minnesota December, Lord?" She stamped her foot in exasperation and was instantly sorry as mud spattered over her partially exposed stockings. Something else that would need washing.

"It'll wash out." He shrugged his broad shoulders good-naturedly. "I brought you a load of wood. One of my patients has a timber claim by the river and he gave me a cord in return for helping deliver his wife's baby yesterday. I have enough to keep me for a while and thought maybe you could use it."

Laurina struggled with her pride. She didn't want to accept anything from him, but the thought of having wood to burn instead of twisted, soggy hay was too great a temptation. "Thank you."

Hands on his hips, he surveyed her makeshift tent over the mattresses. "Boston, for an eastern lady, you're downright amazing, thinking of protecting those mattresses that way."

"You're just in time to help me put down some floor, Matthew," Adam greeted his friend as he returned from the barn. Quickly, he explained his plan to Matthew.

"Good idea," Matthew congratulated. Just then, a piece of mud found its way through the cheesecloth; with a grimace, he wiped it from his face. "Maybe we can stop this deluge first. Boston was pretty smart, using this canvas, but there's another piece left on that wall." He pointed above the mattressless bed and explained his idea to Adam and Laurina.

Soon, the two men had removed the second canvas piece from the wall and were nailing it up to the single row of timbers that sat along the top of the sod walls to support the roof. When they had finished, it covered a good portion of the main area of the room. Then, they attached the piece of canvas Laurina had settled over the narrow mattresses to the area above the beds. Soon, the small room was virtually free of rain, if one ignored the small areas beyond the canvas coverings. "You'll have to drain the canvas when the water and mud get too heavy, but for the time being, this will keep you a might drier," Matthew said as the three surveyed the results. "Of course, it will take longer for the stove to dry out the sod this way."

While the men went to work on the floor, Laurina took a brush and towel outside. At the well she freshened up as Pearl jabbered about her cornhusk doll and Johnny rode circles around her on the plain stick he had adopted as his fiery steed. She knew there was no hope of removing all the mud from her clothing. *Matthew must think there's not a trace left of the proper girl he once courted,* Laurina thought, as she removed her batter-soaked apron and let her dress drop back down around her ankles.

Retrieving the goose Adam had put in the pantry, Laurina carried it outside, where she cleaned it and set it to soak in cold, salted water. They would have some for supper this evening and she would have to find the time to dry the rest.

Soon, the men were done with the floor. The shelving didn't begin to cover all the floor, but the planks made it possible to walk around the worst of the puddles.

The raining sod was a symphony of soft plunking notes against the canvas, but Laurina observed from the doorway that she could look across the room without raindrops blurring the opposite wall. The changes renewed her courage.

"Thank you. Thank you, both. Would you," she hesitated, "would you like to have some flapjacks with us?" Laurina directed the question to both men. She hated to ask Matthew, but he did deserve something in return for the wood and his help with the house.

"I'd be much obliged, Boston, long as they don't have any snakes in them. Guess I'll just unload that wood." When he left, the room seemed empty.

A smile tugged at her lips. The snake wriggling away in the batter had been rather amusing after all.

"Do you have enough food to share with us?" Adam asked.

Laurina smiled, grateful for his consideration. "We'll make do. Please join us."

He nodded his acceptance. "I brought a trunk out for you. It's from Boston," he added as he left to get Matthew to help him carry it inside.

Even with the boards on the floor, there was nowhere to put the trunk out of the mud except on one of the remaining shelves of the pantry, and it barely fit there.

"Aren't you going to open it, Miss Boston?" Johnny pleaded, hopping around the room.

Her cheeks burned at she met the laughing eyes beneath Matthew's raised brows. Did he think she had asked them to call her by his pet name for her? "I'll open it later, Johnny."

"But don't you want to know what's in it?" he persisted.

"I do know what's in it. Caroline sent it. Watch out for the puddle!" She grabbed for his arm as he slipped off the edge of one of the boards, but he righted himself fine after stepping in the mud.

"What's in the trunk?" he demanded with shining eyes.

"None of your business, young man."

"Is it something for Christmas, Miss Boston?"

Laurina settled her hands on her hips and said in mock disapproval, "Now, is that anything for a boy to be asking two weeks before Christmas?"

His voice and eyes filled with laughter. "Yes!"

Pearl started giggling just because Johnny was. Soon, Johnny was clutching his stomach as he laughed. In a moment, Matthew and Laurina were laughing, too, and an indulgent smile even slid onto Adam's lean face.

When the hilarity died down somewhat, Laurina sent Matthew, Adam, and the children outside to clean as much mud off themselves as possible, while she went back to the flapjacks. The batter sizzled as she dropped a large spoonful into the cast-iron skillet.

The table was crowded with three adults and two children. Johnny entertained Adam with the tale of the battered snake. There wasn't much conversation among the adults. Laurina spent most of the meal trying to avoid Matthew's eyes. She wondered at the unusual quiet between him and Adam. They had been congenial enough when working on the house.

"Do you have patients to visit out this way, Matthew?" Adam asked suggestively when the meal was over and the children had gone back outside to play.

Matthew smiled at him easily and folded his arms on the table. "None that need me right away. Thought I'd stay and visit with Boston a bit."

Laurina's heart skipped a beat at his words.

Adam gave her a long look, and Laurina knew she only had to ask and he would stay also. He seemed to realize her discomfiture around Matthew. But her curiosity had to know what Matthew wanted to say.

Laurina brought Adam his hat from its shelter beside Matthew's on the canvas-covered bed and walked with him to the door. The sun blazed down from a cloudless sky.

"Thank God He stopped the rains." Adam settled his round hat on his dark hair.

"Yes." Laurina looked down at the fingers she laced together in front of her, hoping he hadn't noticed her bitterness. She would have been more thankful if God would have prevented the storm in the first place. The rest of today and likely all of tomorrow would be filled with cleaning up after the storm and drying things out, as if she had the time to spare. The thought of the laundry alone was enough to exhaust the hardiest woman.

Before reentering the soddie, she took a deep breath and wished that Matthew had left, yet part of her was traitorously glad he had stayed. The determined look in his eyes made her quiver inside and she began unsteadily to clear the table as he urged the children outside. The china cups tinkled cheerfully against their saucers and Laurina set them down quickly, afraid her shaking hands would break them.

"Boston, will you sit down so we can talk?"

"I'm sure I can hear you just as well while I work."

When he didn't say anything, she glanced at him. His chin was set in unyielding determination. She stood where she was on the opposite side of the table, folding her hands together in front of her demurely, hoping he wouldn't notice their trembling.

"Are you and Adam. . .are you. . .?" He stumbled over the words in a manner most unlike his usual confident self.

She stared at him in shock. "I don't think I like what you are not quite suggesting, Doctor."

"Boston, I'm not suggesting anything improper. I'm just wondering if . . .if you're promised to him." He looked like someone had just pulled one of his teeth.

"I hardly think that's any of your affair."

"Quit freezing me out like that. He's here every time I come out here. How do you think it looks? People are bound to start talking."

Ladies do not yell, she reminded herself firmly. Taking a deep breath, she forced herself to speak in a civil tone. "This is hardly the conversation of a gentleman, Doctor Strong."

"I suppose it's more gentlemanly to let a woman turn herself into a spectacle in front of the entire community, and ruin her reputation!" he blazed, rising from the bench and leaning heavily on the table.

"I've done nothing to ruin my reputation!" She stamped her foot, surprised by the satisfying "plunk" it made against the pantry boards. She swung around, dragging in ragged breaths. The man was infuriating! There, she had gone and raised her voice after all. "I think you'd best leave."

"If he's not courting you, why didn't you ask *him* to leave?"

She turned on him, throwing out her arms to take in all of the soddie. "I don't ask him to leave because I don't have a husband to help me care for my home or the children, and he's often helped us." Her fists perched on her calico-covered hips. "What do you think it did for my reputation to have my neighbors find you whitewashing my walls as big as you please without an invitation?"

A muscle jumped in his cheek. "I was here one time, Boston, not every-day like Adam."

"Adam is not here everyday." She turned and stared unseeing out the deep-set window.

Suddenly, he was behind her, and her knees wobbled dangerously at the things his nearness did to her heart. His hands burned her shoulders and she felt his groan deep within her. "I can't bear seeing you live like this, Boston. Move into my place with the youngsters."

Joy and an overwhelming feeling of escape filled her chest and made her heady with happiness. He wanted to marry her and raise the children with her after all! She turned into his arms, all of her instinctively saying yes to life with him. Love tingled through her in waves of thanksgiving.

"Move into my place," he repeated. "I'll move out here to the soddie."

Her heart felt as though it had crashed into a wall and broken into a thou-sand splinters. Roughly, she pushed herself from the arms she would have welcomed so completely only seconds before. "That should do wonders for my reputation." She could barely get the words out for her anger and humiliation.

"Boston. . . ."

Quickly, she stepped away from the hands that reached for her and she clutched the cast-iron door handle for dear life as she held the door open for him. "Goodbye, Doctor."

He stopped in the doorway and cupped her cheek in his hand. Fire raced through her at his touch. "You don't belong here, Boston."

The husky voice almost undid her resolve. She was tired of being strong for the children. She was worn out from comforting the children and hav-ing no arms to comfort her in return. Just a moment, one moment to rest in his arms.

How could her body and mind betray her like this? She knew if she gave in she would have to pay a big price for that moment. Not wanting him to know how his touch unnerved her, she made herself speak. "I do belong here, Doctor. I'll always belong with Johnny and Pearl."

Chapter Ten

A few days later, as he passed on his way to the home of an ailing parishioner, Pastor Dalen dropped Hannah off for a surprise visit. Laurina was glad that most of the mess from the rains had been cleaned up now. Fresh straw had been spread on the floor, the planks were swept clean of dried mud and re-layed, the mattresses had been refilled with fresh hay that she had taken from its storage in the barn and dried in the sun for a day. The mattresses had been aired and their clothing washed. When Adam came again, she would ask him to help her remove the canvas pieces so she could clean them. The weather was growing colder and she doubted she would need to worry about an indoor rain again before spring.

As Hannah settled herself in the rocker, Laurina set the cool iron she had been using back on the stove and replaced it with the one she had been heating. She wanted to have the ironing done before Thor arrived for his daily lesson.

While Laurina worked, Hannah shared news of the area. Laurina heard little of what was said; her mind kept returning to Matthew's insulting insinuations about herself and Adam Conrad.

When she was almost finished ironing her brown cotton dress, she sent Johnny for a bucket of fresh water to heat so she could offer Hannah a cup of hot licorice drink. She was pleased when Hannah set a cup of ground coffee beans on the table. Hannah set about making the coffee while Laurina finished ironing and put the folded clothes in her trunk.

As Laurina took down the coffee cups from the cupboard, the smell of wood burning in the stove blended with the aroma of perking coffee and the smell of hot cotton. Laurina liked sitting at her table, visiting with another woman while the children's shouts and laughter came dimly through the walls as they played in the yard. *What I told Matthew yesterday is true,* she thought, *the children are my home now.* And she was pleasantly surprised at the realization.

The thought of Matthew reminded her again of his accusations and before long she told Hannah about his suspicions of her relationship with Adam. She expected Hannah to be as outraged as she had been herself.

Instead, Hannah set her cup down, put her worn hands in her lap, and lifted her wrinkled, skinny face. "That's the reason I came today, Laurina. Fact is, Matthew's not the only one to wonder about you and Reverend Conrad. Gossip is getting pretty thick about the two of you."

Dismay flooded her. "But no one could think Adam would do anything that was. . .improper."

"Funny how quick people can be to judge another and how happy to point out another's sin. I know there's nothing wrong happening between the two of you, Laurina, but you must think of your reputation."

Laurina opened her mouth to protest, but Hannah lifted a hand and hurried on. "It takes mighty little gossip to wreck a woman's reputation for good."

Laurina bit her lip, knowing what Hannah said was true, but wanting to fight against it with all of her being.

"Adam Conrad is a preacher of the Gospel," Hannah continued in her matter-of-fact voice. "Not the same church as your father, but a preacher of the Gospel just the same. Satan would love to have sin—real or imagined—linked to his name to stop him from saving souls for the Lord God."

Emily's blue-and-white china cup felt almost too fragile between her fingers and Laurina wondered whether the hands she had wrapped around the delicate cup would shatter it.

Dry, bony hands surrounded Laurina's younger ones. "I'm expecting if you and Reverend Conrad were planning to marry, you'd of told your father. But if you are, you'd best announce it soon. If not," Hannah's voice was gentler than Laurina had ever heard it, "then you must think of your own good name, and Reverend Conrad's, too."

Hannah slapped her hands down on her knees and straightened her back. "Well, I've said my piece. Did Reverend Conrad ever get that trunk that Caroline sent out to you?"

Laurina blinked at her sudden change of topic. *How like Hannah to state the facts and leave the decision to me,* she thought.

She had just opened the trunk to show Hannah the contents when Thor drove up with Stina and Nils. Stina was on her way to town to pick up some supplies and would pick up Thor and Nils when she returned home. Laurina convinced her to stay a few minutes to see what Caroline had sent.

Thor pulled out a bench from beneath one of the windows and settled down with the Bible to practice his reading while Johnny and Nils played in the tumbleweed fort. Pearl tagged after them as usual.

Laurina explained briefly to Stina how Caroline stored her trunk when she came west, then opened it to reveal the treasures of her former life. There was a beautiful doll with a porcelain head, dressed in lace-edged, faded blue silk. "I'm going to clean her up and give her to Pearl for Christmas." She handed it to Stina, who handled it as though it were an irreplaceable piece of art.

Then, Laurina showed Stina and Hannah the old dresses, bonnets, and petticoats she had worn, and the bed linens, tablecloths, napkins, and dresser scarves she had embroidered or crocheted for her hope chest.

Upon opening the chest the night before, Laurina had wondered whether she would ever bring her hope chest to a marriage. Would any man want to marry her, a woman with two small children to raise? If so, could she ever love anyone as much as she loved Matthew? Hope seemed a useless word in her world now, where daily living was hard, and God's promises seemed unbelievable. The time to use the items in the hope chest was now.

Laurina pushed away the unhappy thoughts, refusing to let them crowd in and remove the joy she was having in sharing the contents of the trunk with the other women. She told them how she planned to use as many items as possible to remake into clothes for the children. Holding up a rose dress trimmed in velvet and lace that had been new five years earlier, she said, "I wanted to make a Christmas dress out of this for Pearl, but with such a short time left before Christmas and no sewing machine, I'll not have it ready in time."

"Vy not use my sewing machine?"

Laurina looked at Stina in grateful amazement. "Stina, that is a very generous offer. But I couldn't possibly take you up on it. I'm sure you have much to sew for your own large family."

"My Christmas sewing, it is already done. The greatest gift is vat you gif to Thorburn—a future. A man must know how to read the language of our new land."

So Laurina humbly accepted Stina's offer.

That afternoon as the children napped, Laurina hummed softly while mending a pair of Johnny's worn pants. Her heart warmed at Stina's friendship and a small smile played on her lips as she sewed.

The sound of excited chickens in the yard and the rattle of a wagon brought Laurina to her feet. She could see through the window that the two men in the wagon were strangers. One horse pulled the empty wagon and another was tied behind.

Their mission dampened her spirits. They were there for the wagon and farm equipment Harlan Wells had mortgaged to obtain the right to a seed loan. No, they didn't know anything about the land.

It just went to prove that she had been right and God wasn't looking out for them at all, Laurina thought as she watched the men drive away with the second horse drawing the Wells's wagon filled with the Wells's farm equipment.

That night, Laurina paced the soddie restlessly in the gentle light from the oil lamp on the table, her flannel gown tickling her toes. For a while that day she had been happy about the trunk and Stina's sewing machine. Then she had been cast into despair when the men took away the wagon and farm equipment. But in the quiet evening hours, she remembered Matthew and Hannah's comments about Adam, and her heart smarted.

She wasn't in love with Adam. The way her body betrayed her every time Matthew was near and the impossibility of putting the young doctor out of her mind was proof enough she still loved Matthew, though she rebelled at the thought of loving a man whose ideals were so far removed from her own. And Adam had never indicated he felt anything but friendship for her, in spite of Matthew's suspicions.

She stopped at one of the windows beside the door, leaned against the wide sod ledge, and stared out at the stars spread like a million candles lighting the inky blue sky. She had been so happy when she came back to the prairie. Life had been good, overflowing with the possibilities this new land offered. Where was the person that she had been? Would she ever know that happiness again?

"It's so unfair, God." Her broken whisper was breathed against the cool pane of the glass. Adam was only a friend, like the brother she had never had, but she and the children could not have made it all these months without him. After all that God had taken from her and the children, would He take Adam's friendship away, too?

There was a time in her life when she would have immediately said, "Whatever is right, Lord; whatever Thou askest, I will gladly do." But tonight she looked at the incredible sky that God had created and wondered why One who was so powerful would demand so much from one who was weak. As she turned from the window to turn out the light, she said firmly, "I *won't* ask him to stop coming. You can't make me, God. We need someone here to help us."

In the darkness, she stumbled to her bed.

ॐ

Laurina's days grew longer as she made time to use Stina's wonderful machine. While at the Lindstroms', she would hold English lessons with Thor and as many of the Lindstrom children as could steal away from their chores would surround them the entire time. Their eagerness to learn was exciting to Laurina.

But her own chores had to be done after the hours she stole to sit at Stina's machine. There were items she was making for Christmas that didn't require a fancy machine and she had to make time for them, also.

One evening the week before Christmas, Laurina settled in the rocker beside the warm stove. Opening Emily's sewing basket, she took out the piece of lace she had retrieved from one of her old dresses. Earlier in the week she had bleached and starched it and it was as lovely as if it were new. Picking up needle and thread, she began attaching it to a small square of linen with tiny, even stitches. The handkerchief would be the children's Christmas gift to Hannah.

The blanket separating the beds from the rest of the room moved and Johnny stood quietly in his flannel nightgown watching her. "I'm thirsty, Miss Boston," he said when she looked up.

After he had had a drink of water from the dipper in the bucket next to the door, he stood staring at her.

"Is something wrong, Johnny?"

"I'm not tired."

"Maybe you'd like to sit with me by the nice warm stove."

He nodded, and climbed into her lap.

Laurina tried not to show how surprised she was that he willingly sat on her lap. Pearl wanted to be hugged and loved as often as Laurina would make the time, but Johnny acted like a reserved little man and held back from anything more demonstrative than a good night kiss on the cheek. Laurina respected his boyish feelings and tried to show him in other ways that she cared.

She rocked slowly, her sewing set aside. "Would you like me to tell you a story, Johnny?"

He nodded, the back of his head resting against her chest and his thumb in his mouth.

Gently, she removed his thumb as she began the story. "Once upon a time, near Chippewa City, lived a little girl named Laurina."

"That's your name." Johnny twisted his head around to look at her.

"That's right. She and I had the same name." He twisted back around and she continued, telling about the Indian uprising, her mother's death, and how she had been sent to Boston to live with her aunt and uncle. She told how she had missed her parents and longed to be back with her father.

"Is this a real story, Miss Boston, or a pretend story?"

"It's a real story, Johnny. I was the little girl in the story and I was just your age when my mother died and I had to leave my father. Sometimes I cried, because I missed them so much, but I tried to be strong."

"Boys aren't s'posed to cry," Johnny mumbled around his thumb, looking down at his lap.

"Oh. Is Jesus a boy?"

"He's a man."

"I see. Well, do men get to cry?"

Johnny shook his head, his blond curls catching the light from the lamp on the table. "Pa cried when Mama died, but mostly men aren't s'posed to cry."

She leaned her cheek against the top of his head for a moment. "Do you remember the Bible story we read about Lazarus tonight?"

"Yes."

"What did Jesus do when He heard Lazarus was dead?"

The little flannel-covered shoulders shrugged all the way up to meet Johnny's ears.

"Well, let's read it again and find out." She turned to Luke and read through the story until she came to where Jesus was told of His friend Lazarus's death. " 'Jesus wept.' Wept means he cried, Johnny."

Johnny looked down at the pages. "Jesus cried?"

"That's what it says."

Johnny leaned back against her, sucking hard on his thumb while he considered this. "Sometimes I miss my pa and mama, Miss Boston."

She let her arms tighten slightly around his waist. "I'm sure your father misses you, too. You and I and Pearl will always remember your father and mother, won't we?"

"Miss Boston, do you think if I ask Jesus, He would tell my mama I miss her?"

She tried to swallow the lump in her throat. "I'm sure He would, dear."

"Do you think He would let her come back to me and Pearl?"

Laurina gave up trying to be reserved and hugged him close. "I'm afraid not, Johnny," she whispered through a tight throat. "But one day you'll see her in heaven. Until then, Jesus will help you when you miss her especially much."

"Did Jesus help you when you were little?"

"Yes, Johnny, He did." A tiny bit of Christ's peace slipped into her frozen heart as she remembered the way she had clung to Him as a child in a strange land.

They sat together a long time, with the winter winds noisily blowing past and the fire dying in the stove beside them as the two of them remembered the mothers they had loved so much, yet had known for such a short time.

Chapter Eleven

By December twenty-fifth, winter had returned to the prairie with crisp temperatures and bone-chilling winds. That evening, Laurina and the children hurried across the bluff with her father and Hannah to the schoolhouse for the community Christmas party. Yellow squares of light fell from the windows, beckoning them across the prairie.

It seemed the entire community was there when they arrived at six-thirty. The wire that had been strung to keep stray cattle from damaging the building now corralled scores of buggies, sulkies, and wagons. Laurina's gaze searched the assorted vehicles and horses. Was Matthew's among them? *Don't think about him!* she exhorted herself.

Once inside, Laurina could barely get the children to remove the rabbit-fur mittens her father had made for them. They were too busy craning their necks to see the decorations.

Paper garlands hung across the ceiling from each corner and in the very middle of the room, a large paper star painted yellow hung where the garlands met. Fragrant pine boughs filled the window ledges. Ginger cookies shaped like animals hung in the windows, fastened with red and brown tea twine.

The room was filled with chattering, laughing people dressed in their Sabbath best. Her father and Hannah were immediately stopped by parishioners. Laurina and the children pushed through the crowd toward the front of the room, stopping often to greet friends on the way. Adam was able to only say hello before an elder's wife demanded his attention.

The woman darted a contemptuous look at Laurina and she moved away in shock. Did the woman believe the gossip about her and Adam? Laurina recalled that when looking for a home for the children, this woman had said if Johnny were old enough to earn his keep, she and her husband would consider allowing him to live with them. How dare she judge Laurina and Adam on the basis of gossip? Was she even now warning Adam to watch out for Laurina?

Johnny tugged at her hand, eager to get to the front of the room to see the display of presents. Pearl followed docilely, her hand in Laurina's, her head thrown back, her large blue eyes staring in wonder at the star and garlands above her head. More branches topped the picture of George Washington that hung in stately honor on the wall above the teacher's desk. The spicy odor of pine mixed with the scent of burning candles and the heavier wood smoke from the stove.

A few of Chippewa City's wealthier women bustled about, contented smiles on their faces as they tempted guests with platters of cookies and sliced cake. Laurina blanched at the thought of the costly ingredients that went into the desserts.

Finally, they reached the front of the room. On the teacher's desk was a manger carved of cottonwood and cornhusk dolls of Mary, Joseph, and the Baby Jesus that had been made by Stina's daughters. Laurina and Pearl were fascinated by the miniature scene and examined it in wonder until Johnny pulled them away to investigate further.

Instead of a Christmas tree, there was a huge arch of evergreen boughs that had been taken from trees along the river east of Chippewa City. The arch was on the front wall, covered with small gifts and tapers. Below the arch were baskets overflowing with more gifts. Laurina wondered bitterly how the community could justify this extravagance when there were people in the area who were destitute.

The children had no such misgivings. Johnny walked slowly to the arch, reaching out to tentatively touch the fragrant branches. Pearl just stood with her hand in Laurina's and stared wide-eyed at the wonders before her. *Her eyes outshine the stars,* Laurina thought.

"Youngsters are amazing, aren't they, Boston?" Laurina jumped as Matthew spoke from behind her. "In spite of everything they still believe in the magic of Christmas."

As she turned toward him, she heard him gasp. The admiration in his eyes as they swept over her drove her lashes down over her cheeks.

"In that blue dress, you're prettier than any Christmas tree, Boston. Women should always wear their hair in soft curls like yours." His gaze lingered on her hair as though he longed to touch the chestnut locks she had caught up in combs at the sides and let tumble down below the small hat that matched her dress.

Laurina wanted to give him a scathing reply that would prove to them both she was unaffected by his bold statements, but her mind refused to come to her aid. His eyes made her wonderfully glad that the trunk from Boston had arrived before Christmas. She glanced down at the seven dark blue velvet bows primly running down the middle of her princess robe from her neck to the hem. A deep ruffle ran around the hem and the train made the skirt difficult to walk in after her simple house dresses.

"See Pearl dwess," Pearl insisted excitedly, holding her skirt out as far as possible with one hand in order to give Matthew a better look. "Pwetty." She was wearing the dress Laurina had made with the help of Stina's machine. It was soft rose and trimmed with bits of lace at the collar and cuffs, with a black velvet bow at the throat and a larger one catching a ruffle at the waist in back.

Matthew's eyes sparkled with suppressed laughter as he bowed from the waist. "It's a beautiful dress, Miss Pearl."

Pearl smiled widely in satisfaction, bringing the hand still holding the skirt of her dress to her mouth as she rocked back and forth.

Pastor Dalen announced it was time for the Christmas program to begin and Laurina was uncomfortably aware of Matthew standing beside her as the people raised their voices in the Christmas celebration hymn, *Joy to the World*. Following a prayer by Pastor Dalen, more Christmas carols were sung without accompaniment and recitations and skits were presented by children of the village. Pearl craned her neck to see Johnny play the part of a shepherd boy in the Christmas story. Tears stung Laurina's eyes as she watched him kneel beside the basket with the babbling six-month-old baby who was unknowingly playing the prize role.

The new banker and his wife, Mr. and Mrs. Moyer, lit the tapers on the arch and children and adults alike oohed and aahed at the illumination. Pastor Dalen led the people in singing *Silent Night* while they enjoyed the wonder of the brilliantly lit arch.

Laurina stole a glance at Matthew to see his reaction to the beauty and found his eyes, filled with warmth and longing, on her face. It was a long minute before she could pull her gaze from his and join again in the hymn.

Forcing her attention from Matthew, Laurina hoped she could remember the way everything from tonight looked and smelled. Christmas on the prairie might prove an interesting article to her Boston editor.

Before the flames could set fire to the dry branches, the tapers were extinguished, accompanied by the groans of many children. Cheers soon replaced the moans as Mrs. Moyer began removing the presents from the arch and distributing them.

As the presents were opened, Laurina was ashamed of her earlier accusatory thoughts and she realized how humble they were compared to the gifts of the year before. Last year each child had received a toy, a bag of candy, and an orange. The adults had fared well, also, with the school teacher receiving a book of poetry, the woman who led the Ladies' Aide receiving a mirror and brush for her vanity table, and Pastor and Mrs. Dalen receiving a barrel of apples.

But the 'hoppers hadn't caused nearly as much damage in the summer of 1876 as they did this year and the difference was reflected in the gifts. The children each received a tiny bag of popcorn and peanuts, Pastor and Mrs. Dalen were given a purse with a few coins from their parishioners, and Adam received a small basket of cheese, beans, and dried apples from his congregation. Other adults were not singled out. The people were even asked not to remove the apples on the arch, as they had been loaned for decoration only. Laurina's mouth watered at the sight of the forbidden fresh fruit.

The children didn't seem to mind that the gifts were less extravagant this year. It was Christmas, and even the most modest gift was considered a miracle.

The crowd was reluctant to leave after the program. A man in a tall hat and mutton chop whiskers claimed Matthew's attention and Laurina tried to ignore the emptiness she felt at the lack of his presence as she made her way across the room to speak with Mrs. Beck. Willie was dressed proudly in woolen trousers—were they the ones earned by helping Matthew clean his stable? Willie seemed to have shed his belligerence along with his calico pants. Soon, he and Johnny were seated on a bench, counting their goodies to be sure they had each received exactly the same amount.

Two days ago, her father had killed two good-sized bucks near the river and the deer would supply a good amount of meat. He had already offered some to Laurina. Thanks to the cooler weather, they had no need to worry whether the meat would spoil. Hesitantly and aware from her own experiences in accepting charity, Laurina offered a venison roast to Mrs. Beck. She wished she could think of a diplomatic way to offer it, as Matthew had done with the pants for Willie.

She needn't have worried. Mrs. Beck accepted her offer with a sweet smile. Laurina wondered whether it was because Mrs. Beck knew herself the joy of being able to share with another when you are poor. They agreed Mrs. Beck would pick up the roast after the party.

Finally, the crowd began to disperse. Mr. Moyer was having a Christmas ball at his home and the time had almost arrived for it to begin. Laurina would have to trust the reports of others if she added the ball to her newspaper article—as the minister's daughter, she would not be attending. They would be spending the night at her father's home.

Adam offered the Dalens and the children a ride home in his wagon and they gratefully accepted, as the winds had gained strength since they had walked to the party. Laurina hated to leave without wishing Matthew a joyous Christmas, but her pride would not allow her to cross the room to him.

As they rode to the cabin, the sky overhead was cloudy and not a star could be seen. The children though, searched diligently for the sight that had led the three wise men.

Johnny and Pearl showed Adam their new rabbit-fur mittens and begged him to come inside so they could show him the gifts they had received that morning. When the Dalens and Laurina extended their welcome also, he agreed.

After Mrs. Beck had picked up her roast and gone, Adam gave his gifts to the children. Johnny was thrilled with the hand-carved horse with reins of twine, and promptly named him Dan. The doll cradle that Adam had made for Pearl was lovely with roses carved along the sides; the doll Laurina had given her fit in it perfectly. When Adam asked Pearl her new doll's name, she said with a decided nod, "Bos'n," and Laurina blinked away sudden tears.

Johnny gave a demonstration of how to ride a bucking bronco on the stick horse Laurina had given him. She had made the horse a face from a scrap of gray wool and stuffed it with hay, using buttons for eyes and cornhusks for the mane and tail. Compared to the plain stick he had been riding about the soddie yard for months, this was almost as good as a real horse.

Laurina handed a small package to Pearl and whispered in her ear. Pearl ran across the small room to lay the package in Adam's lap, leaning against his knees as he sat on the bench beside the table. "Pwesent fo' you, Adam."

Laurina was learning to recognize the smile that sometimes occurred deep in Adam's dark brown eyes, and she could see that he was pleased they had thought of him. The glimmer grew into a warm smile when he saw the cross bookmark she had crocheted. "Thank you. I'll treasure it."

Pearl smiled wide at his pleasure and went back to playing with her doll and cradle. But Adam's eyes seemed to linger longer than usual on Laurina's, and the breath of a warning whispered across her mind as she returned his smile. Was there a hint of something more than friendship in his gaze tonight? Just then, he turned to speak with Pastor Dalen. *No*, Laurina chided herself. Surely it was only the magic of Christmas that gave a romantic quality to his smile.

When Pearl had said her prayers and climbed into bed, Johnny began to climb in beside her.

"You haven't said your prayers yet, Johnny," Laurina reminded him.

He pulled the quilt up to his chin and mumbled, "I don't want to."

He had never forgotten nor refused to say his prayers in the past and Laurina wasn't certain how to handle his stubbornness. "Why not, Johnny?" she ventured in a nonthreatening tone.

Johnny pulled at the edge of the quilt with his fingers and didn't answer.

Laurina stood up. "Well, you can pray tomorrow night when you're not so tired."

"I wanted a fat calf," Johnny blurted out.

"A what?" She thought he had forgotten that story.

"I asked God for a fat calf for Christmas and now Christmas is over and He didn't give me one."

Pearl lay beside him, clutching her dolls and watching him with wide eyes.

Laurina sank to the bed, swallowing the painful lump that filled her throat.

Did he think his father would return home like the prodigal son if he had a fat calf to offer? "Sometimes, God doesn't give us what we ask for, because He knows it wouldn't be the best thing for us, or because He knows it would be better if He gave it to us at another time."

"Do you think He might give me a fat calf later, Miss Boston?"

She couldn't bear to quell the hope in his voice. "Maybe, Johnny. But even if He never gives you a fat calf, He will always love you."

Johnny didn't answer, but as she began to stand up, he scurried out of bed to drop to his knees. "Thank You for all the Christmas presents, God, especially for Baby Jesus. Please take care of my pa. Amen."

Laurina leaned down to kiss them both after he had climbed back into bed. His prayer seemed incredibly brave to Laurina. *I haven't handled my own doubts nearly so well,* she thought.

Before leaving the loft, she turned back for a last look at them, lifting the lamp high to cast its mellow glow on their beds. Pearl was snuggl -ing the new cornhusk doll, Betty, to her chest. Laurina watched as Pearl kissed both dolls on their foreheads in imitation of Laurina's good night kisses. "Thank You, Jesus," Pearl's little whisper floated to the top of the ladder.

When she walked him to the door a few minutes later, Adam slipped a small package into her hands. "I hope this isn't too personal," he said in a voice for her ears alone. His slender fingers rested on her hands.

She pulled them back self-consciously. "They're so rough."

"God didn't mean hands to be useless, Miss Laurina. Only giving hands are beautiful, and your hands are the most beautiful on the prairie." His dark eyes held her gaze for a long moment, but he said nothing more personal. Laurina gave a soft sigh of relief when he nodded and tossed his muffler around his neck. "Merry Christmas, Miss Laurina."

She was embarrassed he had noticed how unladylike her hands had become, but she welcomed his gift of rose-scented lotion. She caught her bottom lip lightly between her teeth. Had Matthew noticed her weathered hands, also?

Laurina leaned her forehead against the cool glass of the window beside the door and stared across the bluff. The schoolhouse windows were dark now, but lights shown from a handful of houses built on the opposite side of the bluff from her father's. One of those houses was Matthew's. Was he there now, alone as Christmas came to a close? Or was he at the Christmas ball, perhaps dancing with another woman? *It doesn't matter,* she reminded herself fiercely. *He isn't part of your life anymore.*

"Young Doc gave this to me at the party tonight and asked that I pass it along to you." As she turned in surprise from the window, her father handed her a small package in simple brown wrap tied with a red ribbon. He kissed her on the cheek, his gray whiskers tickling her skin. "Good night, child. Blessed Christmas." He left the gift in her hand as he turned to join Hannah in their bedroom.

Laurina lowered herself slowly into the rocker beside the dying fire, holding Matthew's gift in her hands. She stared at it for many minutes before opening the package.

It was a book of poetry by her favorite poet, Longfellow, and was bound in soft blue leather with lettering in gold. Matthew knew how she missed the books with which she had grown up. Her uncle's library had been sold with the rest of his belongings to satisfy his creditors and Laurina was always hungry for literature.

She gazed into the fireplace where embers glowed, a small flame occasionally shooting upward as a stray piece of kindling ignited momentarily. The crackle of the embers played a background song to her uneasy thoughts.

Christmas had been wonderful for the children and she couldn't help but be grateful for that. If it hadn't been for the arrival of the trunk from Caroline and the use of Stina's sewing machine, she would not have been able to give such satisfying gifts. But the children would still have had the mittens made by her father, the toy horse and cradle carved by Adam, and the party at the schoolhouse.

In spite of the gifts, something was missing from Christmas this year. Laurina relived memories of former Christmases until she discovered the missing piece. It was the comfort of hope. In the past, the Christmas promise of God's love and providence through the gift of His Son, Jesus, had warmed her heart with belief in the goodness of God and the triumph of goodness in life. Now, in spite of the richness that filled her life and the children's today, there was a part of her that was raw from living without hope.

She sighed slightly. Well, it did no good to dwell on it. At least they weren't yet reduced to the poverty of Mrs. Beck and her family. She ran her hand lightly over the leather of Matthew's gift, and opened it to a page marked with an attached ribbon. Her gaze fell on the words of The Native Land, translated by Longfellow.

> *Beloved country! banished from thy shore,*
> *A stranger in this prison-house of clay,*
> *The exiled spirit weeps and sighs for thee!*
> *Heavenward the bright perfections I adore*
> *Direct, and the sure promise cheers my way,*
> *That, whither love aspires, there*
> *   shall my dwelling be.*

Had Matthew placed the ribbon in hopes that she would read that particular verse? Did he somehow know she had lost her faith? "The sure promise," she whispered, her fingers tracing the words. She looked across the room at the cornhusk nativity scene from the party that now rested on the table. Smaller than the flickering light of a distant star, a glimmer of hope settled in her heart.

Chapter Twelve

Excitement bubbled up inside Laurina as she scurried around the soddie, packing the items she and the children needed. She could hardly believe that her father had asked them to move into the log house with him and Hannah! When Hannah added her approval to the request, Laurina accepted gladly.

The blizzard that hit Chippewa City the day after Christmas and left three feet of snow had been responsible for his change of heart. "I can't have you living out there any longer with no man to take care of you and the youngsters," he had said, shaking his head, his beard sweeping the front of his shirt. "Wouldn't be any kind of a father if I did that." She had hugged him exultantly and he had added in a voice that was suddenly gruff, "Besides, I'd spend too much time worrying about you instead of concentrating on my flock."

"The sure promise," she whispered as she folded a blanket and placed it in the round-topped trunk that had carried so many treasures from Boston. Was this God's way of showing her that He was finally keeping His promises? But she shied away from continuing with the thought. She wasn't ready to trust Him unreservedly yet.

She was ready for her father when he returned from his calls to pick her up. Together they loaded the trunks, the rocking chair, a bed ticking, the chickens, and the children into a wagon equipped with runners and started off across the snowy plain behind Old Bill. Blankets covered their laps and hot rocks sat at their feet—Laurina never noticed the cold.

"Has it ever looked so beautiful?" she asked her father, looking out across the snow, sparkling as though covered by diamonds because of the the sun shining brightly from the cloudless blue sky. The horizon was unhindered by trees, buildings, or fences and this added to Laurina's intoxicating sense of freedom. To think she would no longer have the sole responsibility for the children! Surely, with three adults looking after them, Laurina would not have to worry whether they would ever run out of food or clothing. Maybe she would even find that they had enough left over to help out Mrs. Beck a little. And Laurina would no longer have reason to worry about the people of Chippewa City gossiping about Adam's unchaperoned visits.

Her father had stopped by the Lindstroms' while making his calls and had explained Laurina's move to Chippewa City. Stina and Olaf agreed that Thor should make a trip to town two or three evenings a week to continue his lessons and deliver milk and butter.

Oh, yes, life was wonderful!

That afternoon, a barrel arrived addressed to the parsonage from Caroline and David's church in Boston. It was filled with old clothing, a bolt of material, a new quilt, cakes of raisins, and vegetable and flower seeds. The Dalens said a special prayer of thanksgiving and spent the rest of the day discussing which members of the congregation were most in need of the items. They all agreed some must be shared with Mrs. Beck.

That night, as she looked up at the moon spreading moonbeams through the window beside her mattress, she thought, *perhaps, just perhaps, God is watching out for me and the children after all.*

Laurina and the children quickly settled into their new life in town. Working alongside her parents seemed easy after the hard, solitary days at the soddie. She had never thought there would be a day when she would enjoy cleaning wooden floors or beating rugs.

While the snow lasted, the children enjoyed sledding with neighbor children fortunate enough to have sleds. On Friday night, Adam took her ice skating on the river and Mrs. Moyer kindly lent her blades. The moon gleaming on the snow from a cloudless sky made the night bright and she thrilled to the beauty of the blue shadows the tree trunks made against the ice. She was surprised to see a good portion of the townspeople enjoying the sport. But Matthew wasn't there.

In less than a week, her bitterness toward God began to weaken and she began to recall His many kindnesses toward them over the last months. As distasteful as she had found the soddie, it had been a roof over their heads. True, there had been no vegetables or fresh fruits, but no one here had those this winter, either. And Johnny hadn't been reduced to wearing flowered calico.

One evening, as Laurina and Hannah were beginning to clean up after supper, Reverend Conrad stopped with a letter for Pastor Dalen. "I picked up your mail along with my own," he explained.

"It's from the bishop." Pastor Dalen wiped a knife blade on a worn napkin and sliced the envelope open.

Laurina and Hannah continued clearing the table and heating water as he read. She rubbed the dishpan with soap and filled it before Laurina realized her father hadn't spoken again.

"What does the bishop say, Father?" Laurina turned around, her hands still in the dishwater, to find her father's tired eyes on her face. A wave of fear washed over her. She straightened slowly, drying her hands on her apron. "What is it, Father?"

He wiped a hand slowly over his beard. "The bishop says I've been transferred to a new congregation in the Dakotas, near the Black Hills."

"But that area is dangerous," she protested. "Why wouldn't they send a younger man?" And then she realized the importance of what he was saying and she barely heard him reply that it wasn't his place to question the directives of the church.

She and the children wouldn't be able to stay in the log cabin after her father and Hannah were gone. The new minister would move into the parsonage. Her father would no longer be there to help out with extra food or money. Worst of all, after being close to her father again for less than two years, he was being taken away once more. For a moment she considered the possibility of asking whether she and the children could join them in their move, but realized immediately that the idea was foolish. If the area was dangerous for her father, surely it was too dangerous for the children. Besides, they needed to stay in Chippewa City, in case Harlan Wells ever returned for Johnny and Pearl.

"When do we leave, Father?" Hannah asked. Laurina had to admire the way Hannah quickly accepted the inevitable.

"We're expected to be there the middle of February."

Laurina did some quick figuring. It would take at least two weeks to travel to the Black Hills. That meant he and Hannah would have to leave the end of January, at the latest.

She turned back to the wash basin and finished the dishes. To think she had almost begun to believe in God's promises again! It just went to show what a fool she was.

When she said it was time to go to bed, the children protested. They were having a wonderful time talking with Adam and playing with their Christmas toys on the colorful braided rug in front of the fireplace.

After she had the children in their bedclothes, her father read the Bible story, and she listened to their bedtime prayers. When she came down from the loft, her father stretched and said it was about time for him and Hannah to "hit the sack," too. As her father gave her a peck on the cheek, Laurina's eyes questioned him, but he avoided her gaze. They had never before left her alone like this with a man in their home.

Laurina sat down in one of the rocking chairs, glad for the warmth from the fireplace. She was chilled to the bone, and it was not caused by the winter winds that howled around the cabin.

Adam dropped down on the braided rug before the fireplace, only inches from her chair. "I'm sorry your parents are leaving, Miss Laurina."

Laurina swallowed the fear and sorrow that rose like a physical obstruction in her throat. "It will be hard without them, but the change will be difficult for them, also. The Black Hills is a dangerous place."

"I'm sure the bishop has chosen your father because of his experience in dangerous places. God will go with him, Laurina."

Would He? She smiled a brighter-than-normal smile and changed the subject. "Have you noticed the touching way Johnny watches out for Pearl? His solicitous ways remind me of you, Adam. Sometimes I feel you're the older brother I never had, watching out for us at the soddie." She hoped he hadn't noticed the catch in her voice.

Adam's face was bent above the toy horse he was turning over and over in his hands, and she couldn't see his expression. "Johnny and Pearl need a father."

"Yes," she admitted, "but we don't always receive what we need." Did her bitterness sound through her words? What would Adam think if he knew she was no longer certain she believed God cared what happened to individuals?

"I'd like to be their father, if you'll let me."

Laurina stopped breathing at the deep-voiced words and stared over his shoulder at the yellow and blue flames dancing merrily in the fireplace.

"I'm asking you to marry me, Miss Laurina."

Marriage to Adam? The idea had never crossed her mind. She looked into his lean, strong face, wondering what she could possibly answer.

"With your parents leaving, it will be impossible for me to continue to spend time at the soddie without. . .forgive me for being indelicate, Miss Laurina, but without soiling your reputation."

Laurina looked down at her hands, clutched together tightly in her lap. "Have. . .have people been questioning the. . .the propriety of your visits, Adam?" Her cheeks burned as she asked the question.

When he didn't answer immediately, she braved another glance at him. Surely her face couldn't be any redder than his was above his trim beard, but she doubted her eyes were as black with anger. "I'd hoped you hadn't heard the gossip, Miss Laurina."

Her chest ached at the unjust treatment he was receiving from the townspeople. "Is that why you're asking me to marry you?" Why didn't she just say no, she wouldn't marry him? But she couldn't force the words past her throat.

He dropped the horse on the rug and propped one elbow on a raised knee. "No, I've been wanting to ask you for a long while, but I didn't think you would agree to it. I thought. . .I thought you and Matthew would work out whatever had come between you, but that hasn't happened, and with Pastor Dalen leaving, the children need a father more than ever."

Now is the time to tell him that I don't care for him the way a woman should care for a husband, she thought. But she let the moment pass.

When she didn't respond, Adam continued, his eyes burning with an intensity hotter than the flames from the fire that warmed them. "I've grown fond of Johnny and Pearl. If I weren't single, I'd have taken the children into my own home as soon as their father left them, but I had no one to care for them when I had to be away." His hands surrounded her own. "I'd do my best to be a good husband and father."

"Of course you would," she said softly. *But marriage to you would mean removing Matthew from my life forever.* As the thought flashed in her mind, Laurina caught her lip between her teeth so she wouldn't cry out. Had the hope of spending life with Matthew been living in her heart all this time?

"Remember, Miss Laurina, 'God setteth the solitary in families.' We could make a real family for Johnny and Pearl."

Was it God's will that she marry Adam and together they provide a family for the children? Had she the courage to say "yes" to God's promise for Johnny and Pearl and close off all possibility of a future with Matthew? How could she do any less? "The sure promise," she whispered.

"What?" A puzzled frown creased Adam's forehead at her whisper.

"I said yes, Adam. Yes, I'll marry you."

Chapter Thirteen

The following weeks were filled with wedding plans. Laurina and Adam agreed to be married the last Sunday in January, the day before her father and Hannah would leave for the Black Hills. Her father would perform the service.

When she had told her father about their wedding plans, he had set his worn hands on her shoulders, looked deep into her eyes, and asked, "Are you certain this is what you want?"

Laurina flushed, but managed to keep her gaze steady as she answered. "Yes. It's exactly what I want, Father." She didn't tell him that "exactly what she wanted" was a father for the children.

Her father didn't look convinced, but patted her shoulders and said, "Then I hope you'll be happy, child."

Hannah was more forthright. She sharply nodded her thin face with its pointed nose sharply. "You've made the right choice. He'll make a good husband and father."

"Yes, yes he will," Laurina agreed. But would she ever learn to love him as she had loved Matthew?

❧

Two weeks before the wedding, Laurina sat before the fireplace while the children napped upstairs in the loft. With tiny stitches, she worked at the hem of the new petticoat Hannah insisted she needed before she was married. Laurina admitted that her tattered petticoat, stained from the mud floor at the soddie, was almost beyond hope. Her thoughts scurried away from the idea of Adam seeing her in such intimate apparel. She was thankful he had not kissed her yet, though she couldn't help wondering why he hadn't. The thought of being in any man's arms but Matthew's made her shudder.

Stina had offered her sewing machine to make a wedding dress, but Laurina politely refused. It seemed wasteful after the months of living on poverty's edge. Although Adam had a small frame house and his salary of two-hundred-seventy dollars a year sounded like a fortune after her experiences, she knew they would have to live thriftily.

Was she doing the right thing, marrying Adam? Of course she was, she answered her own question. She couldn't afford to continue raising the children herself. She would have to put away the longing for a marriage that included the kind of passionate love she had had for Matthew.

Perhaps real love was made up of respect and shared values, with no place for the overwhelming delight she had felt in Matthew's presence. *Maybe believing in the emotional side of love is as silly as believing in God's promises the way I once did,* she thought.

Since the day she had admitted that God had been with them through the months at the soddie, she had not been able to disclaim God's faithfulness as she once had, but neither did she trust Him completely. She tried not to hope anymore, so she wouldn't be disappointed by broken trust.

"Ouch!" The sharp needle jabbed her fingertip as a rap at the door interrupted her thoughts.

Her heart almost stopped when she discovered Matthew at the door. His usually laughing face with its wind-roughened skin was gray and deep circles dug hollows beneath his blue eyes.

Without stopping to think, she laid a hand on his arm. "Are you all right, Mat—Doctor?"

He reached to remove his hat, and her hand slid away. Embarrassed, she clutched at the door handle as he asked for her father.

"He and Hannah have gone to the general store for supplies," she said tersely.

He swallowed hard. "Lost a youngster today to typhoid, Boston. Three more in the family are ill. Doesn't look good for them."

A desire to hold him in her arms and still the desperation in his voice swept through her and she clung the harder to the door handle. "I'm sorry, Doctor. Do I know the family?"

He blinked and looked down at the hat he was turning in his hands. "It's the Becks. The youngest girl died this morning. Willie and his mother are the only ones without the typhoid."

Laurina covered a small gasp with her hand.

"Mrs. Beck would like your father to conduct the funeral."

"I'll tell him," she said hoarsely. "Are you going back out there?"

"Yes. Don't know if I can do any good, but the girls are in bad shape."

"Please, tell Mrs. Beck I. . .I'll be praying for them." Would God hear her prayers when she distrusted Him so?

"I'll tell her." He rubbed his red-rimmed eyes with weary fingers. *He looked tired unto death himself,* Laurina thought, every fiber of her being longing to help him. "I could use your prayers, too, Boston."

She tried twice before she could speak. "Then you shall have them, Doctor."

Matthew looked down at the large hands worrying the brim of his hat. Pain filled his eyes when he lifted them again. "I hear you're to marry Adam the end of the month."

Laurina caught her breath at his unexpected question. If she admitted the betrothal, would he ask her to marry him instead? With a pang of terror, she realized she had been hoping he would do just that ever since she had said yes to Adam.

"Is it true, Boston?"

"Yes," she managed, just above a whisper.

His mouth tightened into a thin line. When he spoke, his voice was as taut as his lips. "He's a fine man, Boston. You couldn't do better."

Couldn't I? her heart cried, but she only nodded.

He drew a ragged breath and settled his hat over the blond hair she loved so well. "Be happy with him, Boston."

Be happy with Adam? How is it possible when you are in the world? Unshed tears blurred her view as she watched him leave.

As soon as Matthew left, Laurina began boiling venison for broth, reasoning that with one child dead and three seriously ill, Mrs. Beck would not have time to prepare food. She placed the Dutch oven with the meat and broth into her father's wagon bed when he returned, along with a crock of milk and a loaf of bread wrapped in a towel. Hannah added a blanket the Dalens could ill afford to spare.

Within minutes of returning from the general store, Pastor Dalen called to Old Bill and started out across the prairie as fast as he dared go. By the time he returned to the log cabin the next day, two more of the Beck girls had died.

Laurina's heart went out to Mrs. Beck, and she immediately requested the use of her father's wagon and Old Bill to go to her friend, but Pastor Dalen shook his head. "Young Doc says he doesn't know what's causing the fever and he doesn't want folks coming around until he does."

"But everyone knows typhoid isn't contagious!" Laurina sputtered, outraged at being ordered to stay away from the hurting woman.

His wrinkled hand rested heavily on her shoulder. "The Doc doesn't have time to deal with those of us who are well coming around, child. He says there's four other families have the typhoid. It's best we listen to him."

Laurina checked the sharp retort on the tip of her tongue. Weariness sat on her father's aging shoulders like a cloud heavy with rain. Four other families wrestling with the fever! She didn't know the families, but her heart went out to them just the same.

Within a week, they received the news that Mrs. Beck's remaining daughter would live, and Laurina rejoiced at the news. But the typhoid was spreading. Now it was in eight families and fear filled the community like a living thing. Both her father and Adam were weary from visiting the ill.

Pastor Dalen wrote to the bishop asking that he be allowed to stay in

Chippewa City until the epidemic passed and the bishop agreed readily.

Adam and Laurina postponed their wedding date until the epidemic was over. The last Sunday in January passed with another funeral instead of their wedding. This time the victim was a young mother from Adam's congregation.

At Matthew's suggestion to Adam, Laurina reluctantly returned to the soddie with Johnny and Pearl. They would be more isolated there and less apt to come into contact with whatever was causing The Fever, as it was being called in hushed conversations throughout the county.

By the middle of February, The Fever had spread as far as Benson, and Matthew was traveling over forty miles each time on his rounds. Laurina expected daily to hear that he had contracted the dread disease himself. At least there was no longer any snow to hinder him and the temperature had moderated.

The next week when Thor brought their milk, he announced shakily that Stina and two of the children were ill. Laurina was determined she wouldn't let Matthew's former orders keep her away from Stina. When Hannah drove out to see her, Laurina ignored her protests and took her father's wagon to the Lindstroms', leaving Hannah with the children.

Laurina wasn't prepared for the sight that greeted her. Stina and the two youngest children were delirious, their lips covered with a brown crust, and their stomachs distended. The oldest daughters and Matthew were sponging the fevered bodies with cold water. After the first shock, she grabbed her courage in both hands and marched to Stina's bedside. "What can I do to help?"

When Matthew turned to see her standing beside him, unbuttoning her sleeves, he muttered something unintelligible under his breath.

The sight of him sent a wave of dismay through her. He was so thin! Hollows that replaced the healthy, ruddy cheeks of his wide face were only partially concealed by the beard he had grown. Handing the wet cloth to Thor, Matthew took her arm in an iron grip and led her outside where he ordered her in no uncertain terms to leave.

"I'll not leave. Stina has been like a sister to me since I moved to the soddie. She needs me now." She tried unsuccessfully to pull her arm from his grip.

"Typhoid is dangerous, Boston."

She tossed her head and raised her chin belligerently. "I've read that it's not contagious, Doctor."

"Maybe it's not, but I don't know why so many are coming down with it. If we don't know what's causing it, we can't stop people from getting it."

"But—"

He dropped her arm with a suddenness that made her stumble. Leaning wearily against the wagon, he dropped his head into his hands and dragged his fingers through his hair. "Boston, I don't want you to contract The Fever. If you do, what will happen to Johnny and Pearl?"

His humble tone disarmed her temper. What an awful choice to have to make! *Do I stay with my dear friend, or leave so I don't get the disease myself and cause more sorrow for Johnny and Pearl?* Everything inside her rebelled at leaving her friend in pain. Yet she knew Stina would understand the choice she must make and how much it would hurt her to make it. Stina would make the same choice for her own children.

Silently, she turned to get into the wagon and Matthew's strong arms assisted her. "Watch for the symptoms, Boston." The relief at her decision was evident in his voice. "If you have a fever, with a headache or backache, and maybe a stomachache to boot, send for me right away."

She lifted the reins and his hand closed over hers. "*Promise* you'll send for me if you have any symptoms!"

She nodded dumbly, and his hand slipped away.

As the week wore on, other members of Stina's family became ill and Laurina found herself begging God for their recovery, not daring to rage at Him as she had been doing for so many months. She had to satisfy her desire to help her friend by sending what food she could with Adam and her father when they passed the Lindstrom homestead.

And then, the last Saturday of February, Johnny complained of a headache and refused to eat.

Chapter Fourteen

Twenty-four hours later, Pearl was acting uncharacteristically grumpy, rubbing her head and refusing food. Laurina had no way to tell anyone of the children's illness unless she left them alone, and that she refused to do. Since so many of the Lindstroms were ill, Thor had made no milk visits for three days. Adam, her father, Hannah, and Matthew were all attending to the sick, and stopped by the soddie only when their rounds led them close by, and time permitted.

Laurina tried to keep her panic down by busying herself with the children. She made broth and urged the children to eat, depressed that she could convince them to try only a few teaspoonfuls. She read Bible stories to them and told them children's stories she remembered from her own childhood, but they tossed restlessly on their beds and slept fitfully.

Finally, at dusk the next evening, as she walked to the well, she spotted someone riding past about a quarter-mile out on the prairie. Dropping the heavy wooden bucket, she lifted her skirts and ran for all she was worth, tripping over clumps of dead prairie grass and calling at the top of her lungs. It was a stranger on horseback, but he stopped and listened to her breathless story, and assured her he would make certain the doctor or one of the pastors at Chippewa City received her message.

Laurina didn't sleep well that night. She didn't bother to change to her bedclothes, but sat up in the rocker with a blanket over her knees. She was afraid she would sleep too soundly and not hear the children if they called for her, but she needn't have worried. The slightest stir from their beds drove sleep from her. Once during the night Pearl started whimpering and Laurina brought her to the rocker, whispering soothing words as she held the child close.

Just after daybreak a wagon rumbled into the yard and she hurried to the door to see Adam racing toward the house. He grabbed her hands, his eyes questioning her anxiously. "It's the typhoid, I'm sure of it," she said, choking back a sob. She had tried to be strong and cheerful for the children, but the relief of having another adult to share the fears with tore at her defenses.

He squeezed her hands, whispering "Help us, Father God," and hurried to the bed. The children were both asleep, though Johnny was moaning slightly. Adam breathed a deep sigh of relief and came back to where she leaned against the door.

"It's not reached the critical stages yet."

"No," she agreed shakily.

"Matthew's at the Lindstroms'. Their youngest son, Nils, is at a dangerous stage and Matthew can't leave him. I promised to return right away to let him know how bad it is with Johnny and Pearl."

Relief flooded Laurina, leaving her limbs weak. She was glad for the door she leaned against, as she was certain her legs would not have held her up. Just to know Matthew with his knowledge was so close!

Shame washed over her. Her first thought was her own loved ones when her dear friend's son may be dying. *Forgive me, Lord,* she begged silently.

"I must go for the Lindstroms' pastor, also, Laurina." He hesitated, looking back at the children, his hands clenching repeatedly into fists at his sides. "I wish I could stay, but there's no one else to send."

She nodded, and prodded herself out of her own concerns. "You must be exhausted and hungry."

"I can eat later. Matthew will be waiting for my return."

Together they prayed for Johnny and Pearl and the Lindstrom children before he left.

Laurina got fresh water from the well and splashed it over her face. She folded the blanket she had used during the night and laid it over the end of one of the beds, noticing in surprise her rumpled skirt as she did so. *Why, I haven't been out of these clothes in two days,* she realized.

She changed quickly and brushed the hair that streamed down her back before braiding it and wrapping the braid around her head in Stina's Scandinavian manner. She had found it stayed up better that way than in the bun in which she normally wore it, and she didn't want to be bothered with such unimportant things as hair now.

Since the children hadn't awakened yet, she mixed some biscuits and heated a pot of coffee, thankful for the coffee beans Hannah had sent along when she moved back to the soddie. Talking with Adam had made her aware that she was hungry. She couldn't recall when she had last eaten. It wouldn't help for her to deplete her strength through hunger, and it was good to have something to keep her hands busy.

How she wished she could do more for the children! If only she had been trained for nursing. She had once entertained the possibility of training at the New England Hospital for Women and Children, but then her uncle had lost his money, and she had been needed by her aunt. And of course, then she had come west to be with her father. Until now, she had never regretted not training to be a nurse.

What had she read in Florence Nightingale's book, *Notes on Nursing: What Is, and What Is Not?* Oh, yes. The sick need fresh air, dainty food, the effect of drab surroundings, and cheerful, kind company. *Well, they certainly had the drab surroundings,* she thought, looking about her; though not so drab as before Matthew whitewashed the walls. There wasn't much hope for fresh air in the musty earthen building, or of dainty food, but she could try to be cheerful company. She pushed from her mind the memory of Stina and her children in their delirium. They hadn't known whether Matthew's company was cheerful.

"Stop it!" Laurina whispered to herself fiercely. She wouldn't allow herself to imagine Johnny and Pearl in that dreadful state. She wouldn't!

Pete's crows reminded her there was work to be done. She pushed the perked coffee to the back of the stove and checked on the biscuits. Only a couple of minutes more and they would be ready. Just the smell of the coffee and baking biscuits made her feel stronger and more able to cope.

Pulling her shawl over her shoulders, she tiptoed over to the children's beds and listened to their labored breathing. Then, she went out to feed the chickens.

They chattered at her urgently until she spread their seed, and she stood in the midst of them, the cool morning breezes refreshing as they caressed her face. She looked about her at the homestead: the sod house, the sod barn, the well, the tumbleweed fort where Johnny had spent so many happy hours making the world safe from evil. Hopeland.

❧

It was almost dark before Matthew arrived. She had the door open before he could knock. "Thank you for coming. How is Nils Lindstrom?"

His eyes sank deeper in their sockets and his shoulders sagged beneath the now too large coat. "He didn't make it."

Tears leaped to her eyes. Poor Stina! She wished she could go to her. "And the rest of the family?"

"I think they've all passed the critical point." He set his long, narrow medicine bag on the bench beside the table and dropped his hat on top of it. Laurina could see his hair had not been trimmed in a great while; it curved around his ears and hung over the collar at the back of his coat.

He wasted no more time in conversation, but lifted the lamp from the table and went directly to the children. When Matthew lifted Johnny's wrist to feel his pulse, Johnny awoke and stared listlessly at him. "Hullo, Young Doc."

Laurina blinked back tears that rushed to her eyes at the hoarse voice that came from between cracked lips. She wouldn't let the children see her cry. "Cheerful, kind company" Miss Nightingale recommended, and that's what the children would have.

Matthew gave Johnny a tired smile. He talked quietly as he examined him, telling about a puppy he had found on his rounds. Johnny's face actually showed a hint of interest when he heard of the black puppy. "A real puppy, Young Doc?"

"Yup, a real puppy."

"Could I see it?"

Matthew waited until the coughing his questions had started had ceased. Then he said, "Don't see why not, once you're feeling better."

"When Mama was sick, she died. Are Pearl and I goin' to die, Young Doc?"

Laurina turned quickly to the stove, clutching her hands together and forcing them to her mouth to prevent crying out. Had Johnny been worrying about dying all these days? She took deep breaths to steady herself, wishing she could believe Matthew without reservation as he said, "You won't die for a long time, Johnny."

Laurina walked quickly back to the bed, wiping the palms of her hands down over the sides of her striped skirt. "Does that puppy you found have a name yet, Doctor?"

Matthew smiled up at her and she thought she recognized gratitude for her diversion. "Not yet. Haven't been able to come up with just the right one."

"Johnny is good at names."

"How about it, pardner? Will you give it some thought and come up with a name for the puppy?"

Johnny nodded slowly.

"Would you like some broth, Johnny? Or some warm milk and bread?" Laurina asked.

Johnny shook his head and rubbed his eyes with his fists.

"You know, Johnny, you need to eat if you're going to get strong enough to play with that puppy," Matthew urged.

Johnny stared at him for a minute. "Okay."

Laurina turned to get the food and Johnny said, "Miss Boston's pa is leavin', Young Doc. He's goin' far away."

Laurina blinked back hot tears. Imagine him thinking of her at a time like this!

"Yes, Johnny, I know." Matthew held a cup of cold water to the boy's lips.

"Do you think she'll go away with her pa?"

"And leave you and Pearl? Not a chance. Don't you know you're everything in life to her?" His voice rang with conviction.

"We need to help her not be lonesome when her pa leaves, huh, Young Doc?" Another coughing spasm tore at his throat.

"Yes, we will," he assured the boy quietly.

Laurina dug a handkerchief from her apron pocket and blew her nose before going back to Johnny's bedside. Matthew was right. The children had become everything to her. What would she do if she lost them, as Stina had lost Nils? *Please, God!*

While Laurina fed a little broth to Johnny, Matthew checked on Pearl, who was awake now and whimpering. Pearl refused any broth, pushing away the spoon and rolling her head back and forth on the pillow. Soon, the children had dropped back into a restless sleep.

"They can't keep much food down," Laurina informed Matthew.

"It's important to keep trying. Don't let them get dehydrated, either."

"Will you have something to eat before you leave, Doctor? You look as though a strong wind could blow you away."

His grin was almost normal. "A few of these prairie winds have tried, but they'll have to blow stronger than usual to get rid of me." But he did sit down to the table for a simple meal of cold biscuits that he dunked in a bowl of broth, accompanied by a cup of coffee.

Laurina sat across from him, her hands wrapped about a warm cup of coffee. "They have the typhoid, don't they?" She finally asked the dreadful question.

Matthew lowered his cup to the table, a muscle working in his cheek. "Yes."

"I knew it must be, but I kept hoping. . . ."

"What about you, Boston? Do you have any symptoms?"

She shook her head, staring at her coffee cup.

He waited for her to look back up, then captured her gaze with his own. "Is that the truth?" he asked sternly.

"Yes." She took a deep breath and added, "But what about you, Doctor? You. . .you don't look well."

"I've not taken The Fever, Boston." He shrugged his shoulders and her heart ached anew at their surprising slenderness. His weary grin teased at her fears. "I've just been rode hard and put away wet."

She couldn't help but laugh at his use of the phrase that usually applied to a poorly treated horse, but she admonished, "You must take better care of yourself."

His grin died away and his sunken eyes stared at her sadly. "I'll be all right, Boston."

Her fears weren't lessened by his assurance.

A few minutes later, Adam returned and Matthew went on his way with a few cold biscuits wrapped in one of Harlan Wells's clean old handkerchiefs. Matthew assured her he would return at least every couple of days to check on the children, but that if the disease progressed normally, it would be a few days before the fever came to a life-threatening point.

ે

As she cared for the children, Laurina did her best to remain cheerful and kind in her best Florence Nightingale manner. She drew the rocking chair up in the corner of the *L* formed by the beds, where she could be near both Johnny and Pearl. When the children tired of Bible stories and the adventures she could remember from her own youth, she made up tales for them centered around Pearl's dolls and Johnny's horses. These stories seemed to keep their attention longer and diverted them from their pains for at least a short time. When they could no longer bear to hear stories or converse, but still wanted attention, she sang them every song and hymn she knew in her sweet Boston accent.

When the children slept and she hadn't the distraction of being cheerful for them, she sometimes allowed her fears to slip into her mind and wondered whether God was using the children's illness to punish her for doubting Him. She tried hard not to rail against Him and to ignore the question of why a good God would allow such an awful thing to strike innocent youngsters. Terror at the thought of losing them burned like an unquenchable fire in her stomach.

"Please," she pleaded with God, "don't take the children's lives in payment for my unbelief."

Chapter Fifteen

Two weeks after Matthew's first sick call, Johnny's headache became severe, his fever climbed rapidly, and his stomach became distended. Since the children had taken ill, Adam had been stopping by the soddie twice a day whenever possible. When he saw Johnny's worsened state, he rushed to find Matthew.

Laurina placed cool cloths on Johnny's head, but he constantly brushed the cloths away. She attempted to give him the powders Matthew had left to help with the pain, but Johnny couldn't force them past his brown crusty lips and tongue. When Johnny began muttering in delirium, it was all Laurina could do to keep at bay the fears that threatened to overwhelm her. While she bathed him with cold sponge baths, she shakily sang hymns to keep whimpering Pearl quiet. *Please, God!* The cry of her heart was too great to put into words.

By the time Matthew and Adam arrived, Pearl's fever was climbing, also. Still, relief swept over Laurina at the sight of the knowledgeable young doctor. On her own, she had felt as though she were drowning in ignorance.

As soon as they walked in the door, Matthew sent Adam for more cold water. The color drained from Matthew's face when he looked down on Johnny. "Help me, God."

His cracked whisper and the desperation on his face frightened Laurina all the more. To avoid thinking what it might mean, she concentrated on Pearl. The doctor began to bathe Johnny.

Adam spelled Laurina for a while. He and Matthew urged her to rest but she couldn't sit still. Instead, she made coffee, checked on the chickens, and went to the well for another bucket of water.

Soon, Adam announced he had to leave to see the family of a parishioner who had died the night before. Taking her hands, he looked over to where the children lay, both in a delirious state now. "I want to stay, Laurina." His voice broke.

"I know," she whispered. "I know." *He cares for the children as his own. It must tear him apart to have to leave,* she thought.

He pulled her closer; her arms slipped tentatively around him, wanting to comfort the man who had helped her care for the children all these months. She met Matthew's unreadable eyes over Adam's shoulder. "Thank God that Matthew is here," Adam said. "He'll do all that is humanly possible for them, Laurina."

She nodded, unable to speak.

"I'll be back as soon as I can. Until then, I'll carry you all in my prayers." He took her face between his hands, kissed her on the forehead, and left without looking back.

Why had he done that? she wondered as she went back to sponging Pearl. Not even when she agreed to marry him had he kissed her. Was it. . .was it because Matthew was here, to remind the doctor that she was betrothed to Adam now? But the thought seemed unworthy of the young pastor. Soon, she forgot the kiss entirely as she worked over Pearl.

Laurina and Matthew worked in a silence ripped by the children's labored breathing and senseless mutterings. *Please, God!*

In another hour, Johnny's voice stilled. Laurina turned in surprise and fear. Had he. . .had he died? But Matthew was tucking the worn brown blanket under Johnny's chin. "He should sleep peacefully for a few hours, now."

She collapsed into the rocker still sitting between the beds and clasped her cold, damp hands to her cheeks. "Thank God!" She raised happy eyes to his, tears streaming unheeded down her face. "He's out of danger now, isn't he?"

Matthew busied himself with Pearl. "Only for the moment. The fever could return. It usually doesn't, but. . . ."

"And if it does?" she asked slowly, not certain she wanted to hear the answer.

"We'll hope it doesn't," was the terse reply.

Laurina stood up. "I'll bathe Pearl. It was just the shock of Johnny's improvement that caused me to stop."

"Rest, Boston," he encouraged softly.

As she couldn't convince him to let her help, she made another pot of coffee. *Whatever did women do in such situations without coffee to make?* she wondered. She worried at the return of her sense of humor while Pearl was still delirious, then knew it was due to the relief of Johnny's improvement, however temporary. She brought more cold water from the well and only then did she insist again that she bathe Pearl.

She handed Matthew a cup of coffee. "I've been caring for the children for two weeks. You've been caring for the ill for two months. Please, sit down."

He took the cup and sank into the rocker beside her and she again began sponging Pearl's tiny body. It comforted her to be doing something direct-ly to help Pearl and she wondered if it was that feeling that kept Matthew going when he was obviously so spent. She would give her own life to stop the disease in the little girl she had grown to love! The golden curls were dark with sweat and drenched the pillow under her head. "Please, God, please spare her," she whispered as hot tears blurred her sight of the dear face.

It seemed forever before Pearl's fever dropped low enough to stop the delirium. With a shaky hand, Laurina brushed the girl's hair back from her forehead. "She still feels so hot." She darted a scared look at Matthew.

"Her fever is still high, and so is Johnny's, but that's normal at this stage. The danger is past for the moment."

Laurina moved to the kitchen area. "You must be famished, Matthew. Perhaps I could make some flapjacks, even if it is the middle of the night."

He didn't answer and she turned to find him staring at her strangely. "You haven't called me Matthew in a long while."

She felt color stain her cheeks, but did not respond. Instead, she handed him the large cast-iron kettle. "Would you fill this with water, please?" A tremor ran through her as his hand met hers when he grabbed the handle. "And would you bring some eggs?" she added breathlessly as he went out the door, taking a lantern from the wall to help light his way in the dark.

Together they ate the flapjacks in silence. When they were done, she filled the wash basin with warm water from the teakettle and set it in front of him. "Your hands must be frigid after all that cold sponging." Her own joints ached from the hours spent in the cold water, though she hadn't noticed that until she sat down to eat.

Matthew looked at her in surprise, then smiled as he stuck his hands in the water. "A number of women have fed me on sick calls, but none has given me warm baths for my hands. It feels good."

She went to sit by the children. She liked being close to the them, even if it was only a few feet closer than the table. It was safer to be a little farther from Matthew, too. Why, why couldn't she love dear, sweet Adam instead of Matthew? Any other woman would be ecstatic to be marrying such a fine man as Adam.

When Matthew finally dried his hands on the towel that she had laid beside him and had come to check on the children, she went back to wash the dishes. Her feet froze to the ground when she turned to find him on his knees beside Johnny's bed. Grasping her skirt, she rushed across the short distance between them, scattering the straw that covered the floor and clutching Matthew's shoulders. There were tears in the eyes he turned to her.

"Is he. . .is he. . .?"

Matthew jumped up and grabbed her shoulders. "Johnny's fine, Boston. He's fine. I was only praying for them."

She slumped against him, and his arms surrounded her. For a moment she was too weak with relief to move, then she put her hands against his chest and reluctantly pushed herself away. His heart hammered against the palms of her hands. She wanted to stay there, her head against his shoulder. It felt so safe with his arms about her. But it was a false safety, she reminded herself. His arms couldn't protect her from anything. He wasn't there to stay. So she stepped back and bit her lip at the regret that flowed through her as his hands slipped from her back.

She dashed the tears of relief away with the back of her hand. "If Johnny is fine, why are you praying, Doctor?"

"Because I've done all I can for Johnny and Pearl. Their lives are in God's hands now."

Laurina whirled around and strode back to the kitchen area, brushing angrily at the wisps of hair that curled about her face. She didn't want the children in God's hands! It was too risky. She much preferred them in Matthew's hands. At least Matthew would do everything he could to save them, while God—well, one never knew what to expect from God.

She dropped down on the bench beside the table and clutched her arms across her chest. "Forgive me, God," she whispered as she watched Matthew checking Pearl's pulse, and instantly felt like a hypocrite. She wasn't sorry for her thoughts. She just didn't want God to hurt Johnny and Pearl because of her anger.

Matthew touches them so gently, she thought as the doctor laid a hand on Johnny's forehead, then drew a thumb along the boy's hairline. What would she have done without him during the last couple of weeks? What would the entire county have done without his knowledge? How many mothers were thanking God that Matthew was here to help their families through the epidemic? The thought of his tears as he had prayed for Johnny and Pearl both tore and comforted her heart. She had thought Matthew didn't care for the children.

She caught her breath sharply, and he turned to her immediately to see what was wrong. She only shook her head. How could she tell him that she had suddenly understood what he had tried to tell her months ago beside the river—that helping her to raise Johnny and Pearl would have threatened his ability to help others? She realized now that Matthew did care for Johnny and Pearl, but was unable to place their needs above the needs of the rest of the community, above all the other children in the county.

He had had to make a choice, as she had had to choose between letting Johnny and Pearl be sent away, or trying to support them herself; and between staying with Stina or caring for Johnny and Pearl.

Adam knew the pain of making hard choices, too. His haggard face as he had to leave the children last night to go to the side of a grieving parishioner, flashed across her mind. Was that the way Matthew had looked when he was with Stina's dying son and heard that Johnny's fever had worsened?

"I don't understand your hope, Matthew," she said when he left the children to sit across the table from her. "How can you leave a child who has just died, and come here to two other children who are fighting death, and believe you can win? Where do you get that kind of faith?" Her eyes searched his, her heart truly longing for an answer, hungry for hope and peace.

He looked puzzled at her question, but answered immediately. "But that's why we're here, Boston, isn't it? To be, as much as is possible, God's answers to people's needs, to people's prayers." He looked over at the children sleeping peacefully, and something that looked strangely like regret flashed across his face. "As you've been God's answer to Johnny and Pearl's needs. We do as much as we can. The rest is in God's hands."

She stared at him. Did he really believe that she had been God's answer to Johnny and Pearl's needs, in spite of his protests to her actions?

Creaking wheels and the sound of a horse's hooves in the yard broke in on her thoughts. Glancing at the windows, she realized that the sun was rising. A minute later, Adam rushed inside.

While his hand was still on the doorknob, his eyes flew to Laurina, his face one large, anxious question.

She nodded, and smiled at him. "They're all right."

"Thank God!" He slumped against the door. Then, taking a deep breath, he crossed the room with his hand held out to Matthew. "And, thank you."

Matthew allowed him to shake his hand, but warned, "They aren't out of the woods yet, but it does look promising. Their fevers have continued to drop throughout the night, and they've been resting peacefully for a few hours now." He rose from the bench and reached for the jacket he had thrown across the other end of the bench hours before. "I'd better be going. There are other patients to check on."

"But you've not slept all night!" Laurina could cheerfully have bitten off her tongue as Adam darted a sharp look in her direction. She caught her hands together behind her back. "I'm sorry, Doctor. Of course, you must go to them."

Adam looked longingly at the children. "If you're sure they'll be all right for a few hours, I could drive you to the next patient's, Matthew. At least you could catch a couple of winks on the trip—if you can sleep sitting up, that is." He gave a weak grin.

Matthew clapped a hand on Adam's shoulder. "Thank you, friend. I'll take you up on that offer, though I probably shouldn't as you've not slept all night yourself."

Adam slid a hand down Laurina's arm. "You'll be all right while I'm gone?"

"Yes, Adam."

"We'll take my wagon and tie Matthew's horse behind it." He walked over to the beds, needlessly adjusting the blankets and resting his hands on the children's foreheads.

He just wants to touch them, she thought, *to assure himself they are really still alive.*

She turned to Matthew, who was slipping into his coat while he also watched Adam. "Thank you. Thank you for everything," she said softly.

"I'll be back to check on Johnny and Pearl as soon as possible, but if anything about their condition frightens you before then, send for me."

"I will." *I wish you could stay,* she wanted to cry out to him. *I wish you would stay with us always.*

"Ready, Matthew?" Adam said from beside her, and she dragged her gaze from Matthew's to say goodbye to the man with whom she had promised to spend the rest of her life.

Chapter Sixteen

To Laurina's relief, Johnny and Pearl continued to improve. A few days after their fevers peaked, Matthew turned from examining the children to slap Adam on the shoulder and say, "They'll be back to their mischievous selves in time for your wedding."

His casual reference to her coming marriage pricked at her heart even as joy flooded her at the assurance of the children's health.

As soon as possible, Laurina visited Stina and Mrs. Beck, bringing with her some of the precious flower seeds that had been included in the barrel sent by the Boston church. Some thoughtful woman back east had included them to brighten prairie women's homesteads, but they would grace the graves of their children instead, a reminder of the heavenly hope.

Laurina returned from the visits to clutch Johnny and Pearl in a close embrace, and felt wonder that God had spared their lives.

True to his promise to Johnny, Matthew brought his black puppy to visit as soon as he felt the children were well enough for the excitement of the lively fellow. Johnny and Pearl dissolved into giggles at the sight of the puppy rolling around on the bed trying to chew Johnny's toes. Johnny instantly and importantly named him Mr. Wiggly.

Matthew pushed his hat to the back of his head, scratched Mr. Wiggly behind the ears, and said in a practiced tone of concern, "You know, it's pretty hard on Mr. Wiggly when I'm off making my rounds, what with no one at my house to look after him. Think you two youngsters might be willing to take care of him for me?"

"Matthew Strong!" Laurina declared in an accusing voice, propping her hands on her apron-clad hips. "You're no better than a slippery-tongued salesman."

He grinned at her sheepishly as Johnny said, "Could we, Miss Laurina? Could we really?" and Pearl chimed in with, "Oh, yes!" and clapped her hands in glee.

Laurina shook her head. Here she was barely able to keep food on the table for three people, and Matthew handed her another mouth to feed. The bill for Matthew's services had yet to be paid, too.

She smiled at him innocently. "I assume that in return for giving the creature a house and home, you'll mark our bill paid in full."

He grinned back at her, his eyes twinkling, and she wondered if he was surprised at her unusual attempt at a jest. "Your bill was always marked paid in full." And she knew in spite of the grin, he meant it.

They didn't see much of him after the children began improving.

&

Laurina dropped the last of the cabbage seeds in the furrow and covered them with the rich black dirt. The ground smelled wonderful—the fertile odor of the promise of life. Earlier in the week, Thor had dug the garden for her with a hand plow. She straightened, brushing the moist dirt from her hands. Putting her fingers against her aching back, she stretched and turned to check on the children. They were still playing about their tumbleweed fort in the March afternoon sunshine.

The prairie grass was greening. It was time to think of planting the fields. She wasn't sure yet what she was going to do about farming the homestead, though she had claimed the seeds for a field of peas that Harlan Wells's sacrifices had earned from the state seed loan plan.

Soon, she and Adam would be married and perhaps there would be no need to worry about the farm. Still, the homestead acres might provide welcome income and food. She would have to remember to ask Adam what he thought they should do. The homestead was the children's; that is, it was the children's if the taxes were kept up and if the lien that Harlan Wells had taken out was paid off. Laurina wanted to do everything in her power to keep the land for which the Well's had worked so long in the children's hands.

She smiled as the children's laughter was carried to her on the prairie winds. How beautiful life was! Since the children's lives had virtually been given back to her after The Fever, contentment had filled her days. It was hard to believe she had lived with such anger for so many months.

Everything seemed to change with Matthew's words the night the children's fevers broke. "But that's why we're here, isn't it, Boston? To be, as much as is possible, God's answers to people's needs, to people's prayers." She still didn't understand why terrible things happened to people, but it comforted her to think she could help others when hard times came.

Maybe God had brought her back to Chippewa City two years ago just so she would be there to take care of Johnny and Pearl when they lost their parents. She recalled how angry she had been when Adam first suggested she was the family in which God had set Johnny and Pearl. She had been too bitter then to be grateful she could be used by God to help the children.

Laurina carried her gardening tools over to the small barn. How could she have thought God wasn't providing for them all those months? He gave them Hopeland, and the dairy products from the Lindstroms, and the newspaper job, and constantly provided meat through Adam and Matthew and her father. What did it matter that she hadn't known from one day to the next from where the meat would come? It did come, even if in the form of wild birds and venison she had to ask Stina and Hannah how to prepare.

She stepped over a chicken standing obstinately in the doorway of the barn and moved into the sunshine of the yard covered with the bright green stubble of new prairie grass. She had been so foolish. God had been true to His word and provided their daily bread. All the while she had raged at Him for not showing her from where next month's bread would come, and the bread for the month after that.

And He had given them Adam. Soon they would be the family God promised. Her heart still betrayed her sometimes in yearning for Matthew, but she was praying for God to remove her longing for him and replace it with love for Adam. She wanted to be a good wife to the man who had stood by her and the children all these months.

She had blinded herself to all the good things God had done for them, but she wasn't going to live that way any longer.

Her skirt flapped in the wind as she laughingly watched Pearl running toward her with her childish gait, her arms spread wide and a smile covering her face. She threw her little arms around Laurina's legs, bent her head back, and grinned up at her. "Pearl love Bos'n."

Laurina hugged her back. "And Boston loves Pearl." *Thank You, God, for giving them back to me.*

As she straightened up, she could see someone approaching across the greening prairie. They were too far away to tell yet whether they were coming to Hopeland. Well, perhaps she should put on a pot of coffee, just in case. She put a hand to her braid, and decided there was time to fix her hair properly, also.

It was Adam. Laurina watched smiling from the doorway as he stopped to examine the minute cut Johnny was showing him, the one he had received on the palm of his hand from one of the tumbleweeds. Then Pearl insisted on telling him a make-believe story about the imaginary bump on her knee. After all, if Johnny had a hurt, she must have one, also.

"I see they caught you up on all their bumps and bruises. They're going to love having you around all the time," Laurina said as he reached the door and the children hurried back to their makeshift fort. "I've made coffee. Would you like some?"

She didn't wait for an answer, but went to remove one of Emily Wells's fragile cups from the cupboard.

"Laurina—"

"Yes?" she asked as she reached for the heavy coffeepot.

"We need to talk."

"I agree. Now that the typhoid epidemic is over, Father will be leaving for the Black Hills. We must set the wedding date right away. I doubt there will be time to arrange a large reception like we planned before, however." She set the filled cups on the table and looked up at him in surprise. "Why, Adam, aren't you going to sit down?"

"Laurina, will you please be still and listen to me?"

She sat down on the edge of the bench, facing away from the table, her hands folded demurely in her lap, and gave him her full attention. Never had she seen him so agitated. "What is it, Adam?"

He paced the small room nervously while Laurina prayed silently for him. Finally, he stopped pacing, his hands resting against the cupboard, his back to her. "We mustn't marry, Laurina."

It seemed forever before Laurina comprehended and asked dazedly, "What did you say?"

He turned around abruptly, his face set in determined lines. "I said we mustn't marry."

"I don't understand, Adam. Have you fallen in love with someone?"

"No!" He wiped a hand over his face.

Laurina stood up and closed the few feet that separated them. "Adam, I am thoroughly confused."

"When the children were so ill, I saw the way you looked at Matthew."

"I was grateful to him for helping the children."

"And I saw the way he looked at you."

She opened her mouth to protest, but he laid gentle fingers on her lips and shook his head. "Matthew loves you, Laurina. He told me last summer of his hope to marry you, but something happened between you after that. He never told me what. As the months passed and the two of you didn't work things out, I began to hope you could love me."

She laid a hand on the sleeve of his black coat. "But Adam, I want to love you that way. I care for you very much. Surely as we live together, the love will grow."

He shook his head slowly. "It can't grow in a heart filled with love for another."

She looked away, unable to refute him, yet hating to hurt him. "But what about the children, Adam?"

"Matthew will be a good father to them."

"That is what he said about you!" She turned and walked angrily to the window, then returned to sink down on the bench once more and drop her head into her hands. She was doing it again, trying to argue a man into marrying her. Whatever would Aunt Miranda think of her now, after all her training in the mores and manners of proper young ladies?

Laurina sat up straight and took a deep breath. "I'll not beg you to marry me, Adam. But I don't understand how you can leave the children. I've seen the love you have for them."

"God knows walking away from them and you is the hardest thing I've ever done!" Anguish filled his dark eyes. "But I believe Matthew also loves all of you, and that it's God's will that you be together."

Laurina jumped up and stomped her foot ineffectually on the dirt floor. "Matthew Strong has no intention of spending his life with us!"

Adam took her hands and swallowed hard. "I selfishly hope that is true. If it proves to be the case, I promise you I will be back, begging you on bended knee to become my wife."

"But—"

"But, if I'm correct, God has someone else for me, and you are to marry Matthew gladly, with no remorse because of me." He squeezed her hands tightly. "Goodbye, Miss Laurina."

Without a backward glance, he hurried out the door as she stared after him, wide-eyed. She watched him stop to smile at something the children said. He stooped to pick up Pearl and kiss her on the cheek, squeezed Johnny's shoulder, climbed quickly into his wagon, and departed.

Guilt swept over her. Because she hadn't hidden her love for Matthew from him, Adam was separating himself from the children he had grown to love and the children were losing a second father. And it was all for naught. The idea of Matthew marrying her was laughable. Since the day he turned down her proposal, he had not once indicated he had any interest in marrying her.

She dropped into the rocking chair. "What now, God? Where is the family You've promised going to come from now?"

Had God decided that her faith wasn't strong enough for the wife of Reverend Adam Conrad? Adam did deserve the best woman on this earth. "Please God, bring a great love into his life," she prayed.

Well, God had shown her that He would supply everything she and the children needed. He would take care of them, whatever came. But she did feel somewhat lonely with both Matthew and Adam out of her life.

She walked resolutely over to the pantry. Enough of this self-pity. Look at the mess she had made of her life when she allowed herself to wallow in self-pity before. She would get lunch together for the children and let God take care of the tomorrows.

❧

Laurina was finishing the luncheon dishes when the racket of a racing horse filled the soddie. Matthew was inside before she could reach the door. "Are you all right?"

"Yes," she replied, bewildered. "Are you?" His hat was gone, and his string tie had blown over his shoulder. His blond hair faced every direction possible. She was glad to see he had begun to put on some weight again.

He grabbed her by the shoulders. "Sometimes I could shake you, Boston! Don't fool with me. What's wrong?"

Laurina pulled away from his hands. "The only thing that is wrong is that you're yelling at me, and I have no idea why." *And if my heart doesn't stop beating so wildly, I'll need medication for certain.*

His hands dropped to his sides. "You don't?"

She almost laughed at the bewildered look on his face as she shook her head and felt the bun start to slip down the nape of her neck.

He frowned and dragged a hand through his hair. "But Adam said you needed me. I was afraid Johnny or Pearl might have had a relapse, or maybe that you had contracted The Fever." He came a couple of steps closer and peered into her face. "Are you sure you're feeling all right?"

Laurina stepped back to avoid the hand he was trying to lay on her forehead. "Yes, Matthew, I'm fine. I think you must have misunderstood Adam." She continued to move away from him. She didn't want him to think that she was proposing to him again. "You see, Adam broke off our engagement today."

Matthew's jaw dropped. Why, she hadn't noticed until now he was clean-shaven again. She liked his face better without the beard.

His lips formed the familiar tight line. "I'm sorry, Boston. Sorry I stormed in here like a fool, and sorry about your wedding. I never took Adam for the kind of cad who'd walk out on his promise to marry a woman."

"Adam is not a cad." *Honestly, men could be so dense.*

The little she could still see of his lips turned white, but his cheeks reddened angrily. "You don't have to defend the man, Boston. You might still love him, but surely you can see he isn't acting like a gentleman."

Laurina opened her mouth to refute him, then snapped it shut. What could she say? That Adam cancelled their wedding plans so she could marry Matthew instead? The Minnesota prairie would turn into a desert first!

"Sorry." Matthew cleared his throat. "Seems like I'm apologizing a lot today."

Johnny's giggles and Mr. Wiggly's yips came softly through the thick sod walls. Matthew walked to a window and watched the children silently.

Laurina wished he would leave. True, she was learning to trust the Lord for her future once more, but the day had been quite trying enough with Adam breaking their engagement. And now Matthew was here, and the flames of longing for him that she had been trying to quench these many months were flaring up again. There was a limit to how much a person could endure.

"I read an article in the *St. Paul Pioneer Press* the other day, Boston." He continued to look out the window as he spoke. "It told how a home in St. Paul for destitute and neglected children was overflowing—three to a bed and even the hallways filled. They can't find enough homes for the youngsters. If it weren't for you, Johnny and Pearl could have been among them."

Then maybe it was true that God brought her here to care for Johnny and Pearl. *Surely, I can trust Him with our future,* she rejoiced.

Matthew moved to the oak table and sat down heavily on the bench, his head dropping into his hand.

"Seeing you take those young tykes under your wing with nothing but a hope and a prayer, it made me realize my faith hadn't any substance to it. It seemed I fought God all winter, trying to learn to trust Him like you do."

Laurina lowered herself slowly to the trunk opposite him. "But Matthew, my faith wasn't strong." She raised her hands slightly as she shrugged her calico-covered shoulders. "I discarded my faith for months."

He shook his head. "Faith isn't something you feel, it's something you act on. You took those kids out here and started living like anyone else would do with their own kids. At first I thought you were, well, not as bright as you might be," he flashed her a sheepish smile, "but then I saw God was taking care of you, just as you said He would."

"Matthew, I was angry at God. It was you who helped me understand that there will always be suffering and injustices in the world, but as long as we're willing to be God's instruments, there will also always be hope."

He smiled, and his smile sent trickles of joy and anticipation running along her spine. "Guess you must have learned it from me after I learned it from you."

She smiled tremulously. "Watching you with the children while they were ill, I finally understood why you. . .why you had to choose your profession over Johnny and Pearl. I hope you can forgive me for misjudging you so."

His gaze searched her face inch by inch, as if he had never seen her before. He shook his head slowly. "I don't understand Adam at all, walking away from a woman like you. I figured for sure God took you away from me and gave you to Adam because you deserved a man with a faith as strong as your own."

He paused, looking around the soddie. "You know, Boston, you were never so beautiful to me as that day I saw you standing in the rain inside this soddie, making lunch while ankle-deep in mud, all for those two youngsters.

Thought I'd burst, loving you so much. And it shamed me that my faith was so small."

Matthew propped both elbows on the uneven tabletop and rubbed his face with his hands. "I about prayed myself out this winter, asking God to forgive me, make me worthy of you, and. . .and let you love me again."

Laurina clutched her hands together beneath the table and tried to make her breath come evenly again. *Proper ladies do not fling themselves across tables at gentlemen,* she reminded herself sternly. *But they might find a way to make the right gentleman fling himself across the table at them,* a little voice seemed to say. Did she dare?

She leaned her own elbows on the table, and rested her chin femininely on her fingertips, forgetting how rough they had grown in the months at the soddie. "You know," she drawled, "a very wise man once told me that faith isn't something you feel, it's something you act on."

Aunt Miranda might have cringed at the misuse of the English language, but she would have approved the result.

Matthew's face was a picture of hope, and Laurina encouraged him with her most radiant smile. He reached across the table to engulf her hands in his own. "Laurina Dalen, Young Doc has come a-courtin'."

"It's about time."

Before she could draw another breath, he was beside her, drawing her into his arms with a joy that humbled her. *This is right,* she thought as his cheek met hers. Who would have thought joy and peace could coexist so perfectly? Matthew pulled back slightly to look into her eyes. "Is it too early to ask you again to marry me, Boston?"

She melted against him and looked up through thick lashes in an attempt at coquettish flirtation. "Is it shameful of me to accept so quickly?"

He smothered his laugh against her neck as his arms tightened exultantly. "Thank you, Lord," he whispered against her skin and her heart repeated his words. A moment later, she was lost in his kisses, kisses that promised he would never let her go again.

Eventually, he pulled his lips from hers, although he kept his arms about her. She rested her head against his shoulder in blessed contentment.

"God's really keeping His promise, isn't He, Boston? The town's bustling with new life now that the railroad's coming and the 'hoppers aren't a threat this year. Land office is doing a bumper crop business. Even The Fever is gone." He squeezed her closer. "But the most amazing thing of all, is the way He restored your love to me," he admitted in a husky whisper that sent delightful shivers dancing through her. "We're going to build that town together after all, Boston."

They bolted erect at Johnny's voice. "Pa always said kissin' Mama was like talkin' to the angels. Are you talkin' to the angels, Young Doc?"

Laurina was appalled at the thought of Johnny's father kissing his wife in front of the children. She had never seen her father kiss Hannah or Uncle William kiss Aunt Miranda.

But Matthew broke into a hearty laugh, his eyes showing his delight with Harlan Wells's picturesque description. "I reckon I am, Johnny."

"I thought so. Brother!" The disgust of thousands of six-year-old boys filled the word. "Let's go back outside and play with Mr. Wiggly, Pearl."

As the door closed behind the children, Laurina relaxed against Matthew's chest again. She ran a fingertip down his arm, feeling the muscle jump at her touch. "Do you think God can ever really heal Johnny and Pearl's lives, Matthew?"

His cheek slid across her hair. "He's already used you to begin to heal them. You were the perfect person to help them, considering what you went through when you were a youngster."

"But is that enough?"

"If we fill their lives with love, Boston, maybe God will use their lives the way He's used yours, to restore and heal other lives. In fact, I think He's already started. Remember the way Johnny jumped to Willie Beck's defense? And his concern that you'll miss your father when he moves?"

A sweet ache filled her chest at the memory of Johnny's determination to keep her from feeling lonely for her father. *Maybe God could heal Johnny and Pearl,* she thought, slipping her arms about Matthew's neck as Young Doc started talking to the angels once more. *After all, God's promises are sure promises.*

Dream Spinner

Sally Laity

To Don. . .a knight, if ever there was one.

Many thanks to Gertrude Cragle for the invaluable historical information she passed on to me; thanks also to Barb, Dianna, Sue, Wendy, and Rich for all their help and support while I was writing this story.

Chapter One

I never used to believe in dreams. . .
Not even the kind most little girls fancy,
Of knights and dragons
and princesses in need of rescue.
They seemed so far beyond my realm. . .
Until I met you.
Now I dream all the time.
Day and night,
Waking, sleeping. . .
And all my dreams are of you.
Strange, but now in my life
There really is a knight,
And a dragon,
And someone in desperate
need of rescuing.
I have no way of knowing
Whether or not daydreams come true,
But just this once
I hope with all my heart
They do.
Come dream with me for a while, my love. . . .

Noxen, Pennsylvania
1892

The first time she saw him, Starlight Wells knew he had to be the storybook knight Ma had told her about so many years ago. *Tall and straight, noble of bearing with wide-girthed shoulders, and riding upon a great, swift steed.* Hadn't those been Ma's own words? Starlight had heard the tale hundreds of times. . .by the fire at the end of a long winter's day, or on a summer evening when fireflies speckled the velvety darkness with tiny bursts of light. Once in a while she and Ma would sit out on the porch watching shooting stars or brilliant fingers of lightning tickling the night sky. *As Ma wove her wonderful fantasies,* Starlight mused, *it seemed the whole world became a magical place.*

Now, gripping the maple branch in front of her, Starlight steadied herself on her perch and peered through the summer-green leaves for a better look at the stranger. Her pulse quickening, she brushed a stray lock of wheat-colored hair aside.

Astride a splendid silver stallion, the gallant rider tugged at the wide brim of his hat, then rested a mighty hand on his thigh as he casually rode under the bottommost limbs of her tree, unaware of her presence.

Starlight felt a smile tug at her lips as she admired the resplendent figure in store-bought clothes and fine shiny boots, astride a saddle as grand as any she'd seen at the mercantile. She could almost smell the smooth leather as she drew in a breath and closed her eyes for a second in sheer pleasure. He probably had a good deep voice, too, she decided, one people would sit up and notice. The jacket of his black suit rippled across his back with each stride of the gray steed as he continued beyond the next tree, the rhythmic clopping of the horse's hooves growing ever fainter.

Dipping her head, Starlight sought unsuccessfully to find a better view, then climbed a few branches lower and swung down to the ground. Her bare feet landed silently, stirring tiny bursts of dust beside her. She brushed her hands on her faded brown calico dress and ducked unobtrusively behind the broad tree trunk. The knight must not see her. He was far too elegant for the likes of her, and he might make sport of her anyway, the way Pa always did. Pa thought nineteen was too old for tree climbing, but Starlight didn't hold to his opinion. High up in the boughs was her dreaming place where she could imagine herself on blustery days sailing the high sea, or on still days as princess, gazing down at her kingdom from the castle tower. She was absolutely certain she would want to climb trees until her dying day.

The horse and rider veered off in the direction of the lumber camp in Stull and soon were hidden from view by myriad trees top-heavy with summer crowns.

Starlight waited a few seconds before moving into the open. Then, confident she would not be seen, she ran across the space between her tree and the weathered story-and-a-half clapboard home she shared with her father, Abel Wells. With practiced ease she skipped over the broken bottom step on her way up to the rickety porch. She dashed inside the four-room house, allowing her eyes a moment to adjust to the dimness. When Pa came back from playing cards with that shiftless farmer, Dewey Blackburn, she knew he'd be hungry for dinner.

Out of habit she seized Ma's old apron to protect the front of her dress from the wear of rubbing against the sink and tied it around her. Its two sides, much too wide, met at her spine when she made a bow of the sash, and the long ends trailed down her backside. Scooping a handful of potatoes from the basket beside the sink, she set them on the sideboard, then reached for the peeling knife and set to work.

Starlight smothered a tiny smile as she thought of the strong and noble knight who had passed through her kingdom. Pushing aside a faded pink gingham curtain panel, she leaned to peer out the open window on the odd chance that he might come back. But the breeze-tossed birches and elms in the distance gave not the slightest indication he'd even ridden by. She settled back onto her heels again and resumed her task. Most likely he was on his way to aid a town of downtrodden peasants who lived in hopeless despair, she decided, or perhaps some fair damsel being threatened by a ruthless lord.

Her smile widened and her heartbeat quickened. *What must it be like to know someone like him, to be the one he was venturing through vast forests to see?* Whoever he was, she decided, he was no concern of hers, nor she of his. She would most likely never see him again.

A pile of nearly transparent parings brought Starlight back to reality. She pumped water to rinse the potatoes and added them to a steaming pot of venison stew on the stove, then wiped her hands on the apron. Foolish or not, it had been pleasant to pretend for a little while.

Her gaze flew fleetingly to the wall shelf in the next room where a worn picture book sat between the few volumes Ma had possessed. Later, when dinner was over and the kitchen cleaned up, she'd look once more at the pen drawings. Sometimes, if she tried hard, she could still hear Ma's voice making up stories to go with each beloved picture.

All of the pretty fantasies and stories her mother had lavished upon Starlight, her late-born only child, had come to an end with her death. In their place a hollow emptiness had invaded the girl, a feeling that dreams were absurd and impossible, and for months the storybook gathered dust. Finally, unable even to bear the sight of it, Starlight put the book away. She had come across the worn volume only recently while sorting through some old things in the cellar. All her treasured, bittersweet memories had come bursting to life again. Forcing herself to concentrate on the dinner preparations, Starlight peeled and chopped carrots and an onion and added them to the simmering broth with a pinch of herbs from the tin atop the stove.

As the delicious aroma filtered through the tidy, drab kitchen, she took two of the last four remaining bowls in Ma's blue hyacinth pattern out of the corner hutch and set two places at the dark pine table. Careful as she'd tried to be, many pieces from the set had been chipped or broken in the eight years since typhoid fever had taken Ma, leaving beside the bowls only three plates and a few cups and saucers. Starlight now guarded those with her life. Ma had loved pretty things, but now that she was gone Pa didn't have much use for them. Or anything else, to be truthful.

After a quick glance around to be sure she hadn't forgotten anything, Starlight ran out to the grove behind her house and gathered a bunch of violets to put in water on the table.

࿏

June's bright midmorning sunshine warmed Kirby Mitchell as he and his horse took the shortcut through the gently rolling wooded area on the outskirts of Noxen to connect with the country road to Stull. Tall trees made a canopy overhead and he nudged back the brim of his black felt hat in the mottled light. If anyone had told him a few short months ago that he'd be on his way to conduct a preaching service—his first—at the lumber camp at Stull, he would have laughed. He had yet to go to seminary. Nonetheless, here he was, thanks to his dumb horseplay of two nights ago. That little tumble over the porch banister at his sister Jessica's house shouldn't have hurt her husband, but Cook had broken his collarbone. Now it was up to Kirby to fill in the Sunday services his brother-in-law normally handled until his injury mended. Kirby prayed they'd go well.

Taking his small, worn Bible from the inside pocket of his jacket, Kirby patted the sheaf of notes still there. He leafed through the book to the opening chapter of First Corinthians and let the glorious passage about the wisdom and power of God fill him with awe. Over the past few days he'd studied hard to commit many of the verses to memory. But what if he stumbled over his own tongue, or worse, forgot a thought right in the middle? He hoped the listeners would be patient with him and make allowances for his first effort.

He quickly sent another prayer that the Holy Spirit would guide his words and speak through him. He'd always been grateful for opportunities to share his faith. Sometimes he even wondered if he might have a calling for the ministry. Within himself lay an insatiable desire for reading and studying the Word, and he had devoured most of his brother-in-law's theological books over the past several months. Cook, a circuit preacher, often invited Kirby to ride along with him to services. *Perhaps in time,* Kirby mused, *I'll have enough saved from my woodworking to go to theological college also and secure a few charges of my own.*

He took a deep breath, enjoying the freshness of a countryside washed clean by recent heavy storms. The leaves had taken on their glossy summer green and in the ditch alongside the road, collected water mirrored the same azure hue as Estelle's eyes. At once Kirby tightened his mouth and reined in his thoughts. Estelle Marsden—no, Barnett now—was no longer of any consequence to him. To mention her name in conversation was an effort, but a small part of him couldn't help wondering if she were happy, at least.

Surprisingly, he realized he had weathered his sadness since the initial humiliation six months ago, when he had been tossed aside for some spine-less "drummer" who peddled jewelry. How Estelle could have been taken in by that fast-talking swindler remained a mystery to him. As a result of that episode, Kirby had decided to commit his life to serving God. Never again would he allow some woman to distract him from this new, and exhilarat-ing, higher calling.

Up ahead the settlement came within sight. Kirby nudged Jericho's flanks.

The town lay two miles from Noxen at the base of North Mountain, clus-tered along the flatlands lining Bowman's Creek. Although most townspeo-ple were taken up with timbering the surrounding woods, the village also boasted a clothespin factory and other smaller enterprises. The normally bustling Albert Lewis Lumbering and Manufacturing Company became a sleeping giant on Sunday. No line of gray smoke trailed from the chimneys above the massive roof; the giant band and circular saws, whose shrill whines echoed against the surrounding hills beginning at seven every morning, were strangely silent. Even the smooth, mile-long wooden log slides that coursed downward from the mountainside were vacant. No steady stream of cut tim-ber plunged swiftly to the creek or to the rail site for processing, and no clap-ping of axes competed with the buzz from the lath mill as logs lay glistening and motionless in the mill pond.

The slanting sunlight illuminated the weather vane atop Hattie Thomas's boardinghouse, where workers and travelers alike could secure lodging and decent meals at reasonable rates. Kirby saw the proprietress come out onto the wide front porch of the two-story wooden structure and shake a rag rug over the banister before going back inside. He had taken an immediate liking to the sturdy woman on his previous visits. Not given to excessive levity, she nevertheless had a bit of a twinkle in her clear blue eyes and, despite her short stature, she didn't take much guff from the locals. As she and her waitresses bustled about tending to the needs of the regulars, Hattie always had time to lend a sympathetic ear.

Kirby's mouth watered at the thought of Hattie's substantial meals and strong coffee, but he knew that he would most certainly be invited to some church member's home for the noon meal.

A cluck of Kirby's tongue started Jericho past rows of simple houses and businesses toward the plain white schoolhouse with its multipaned win-dows, where Sunday services were conducted.

❧

The muffled thump of Abel Wells's crutch came haltingly up the steps and into the house and the torn screen flapped as the door swung shut after him.

He hung his black slouch hat on a hook and hobbled across the room. Propping the crutch upright against the table, he sank heavily into a chair and rested his lean arms in front of him on the bare tabletop.

Starlight brought heaping bowls of stew one at a time and set them down, followed by a platter of biscuits. "Did you win this time, Pa?" Pulling out her spindle-back chair, she took a seat.

Hollow, glittering black eyes flicked a disgusted glance her way as Abel's bony fingers combed through the thinning brown hair he wore slicked back on his head. "Almost did. But that Dewey has the oddest string o' luck, I swear. Jes' when I think I got him fer sure this time, the cards turn sour on me. Cain't figger it." A scowl darkened the long crevices of his unshaven face as he broke two biscuits apart and slathered butter on them. He dipped one into the broth, then put it into his mouth and chewed slowly. "Might go back after while an' give it another try." He wiped his fingers on his threadbare trousers before taking a gulp of coffee.

Starlight blew on a spoonful of stew, knowing better than to bring up the subject of her worn-out shoes. Or some of the chores that Pa had been neglecting since the loss of his foot last winter. She'd just have to make do with the hole in the sole for a while, until he hit a lucky streak and won back some money from that lazy Dewey Blackburn. Common knowledge had it that Dewey spent more time at card playing than he surely did tending his farm.

She inhaled the fragile perfume of the blue violets that brightened the stark room. Perhaps if she finished Mrs. Browning's dress and got another order from her, maybe there'd soon be enough extra money for some slippers. Fancy ones like the town girls wore, she decided, with buckles and everything. For now she'd just have to cut a thick piece of old blanket for the inside of her sensible brown shoes to keep out the stones and dirt. She didn't wear them much anyway. No princess anywhere had ever donned such plain or clunky ones as those.

"I'll have more," Abel said, shoving his bowl her way. Starlight rose and refilled it, wondering as she brought it back to the table whether the stew tasted good enough. Pa never had been one to praise or compliment anything, though he didn't have much of a problem finding fault when something didn't suit him. She was almost afraid to mention that was the last of the meat they had in store. Hopefully there'd be enough stew left over for supper. She didn't want to think about tomorrow. Right now they needed all the chickens for the egg money they brought in.

She took her dishes to the sink and filled the washpan with hot water from the stove. But her gaze kept wandering unbidden to the grove of trees where her knight had ridden. *Will I ever set eyes upon him again?*

Chapter Two

"That was a delicious meal, Mrs. Harding," Kirby remarked across the white linen tablecloth as he eased himself another scant inch away from her sixteen-year-old daughter in the next seat. A younger version of her mother, brown-haired Gladys Harding wore a blouson-style, flower-patterned dress that only added more bulk to her too-plump figure. And she never stopped smiling. At him. Avoiding her enraptured gaze, Kirby tugged at his collar and stared straight ahead.

"Thanks. Clem an' me, we's real glad ya enjoyed it." Mrs. Harding beamed as she set a generous slice of huckleberry pie in front of Kirby, then one before the girl. "We was pleasured to have ya preachin' this mornin'. Sorry to hear 'bout Reverend Singleton's fall, though." She placed another portion before her lumberjack husband, Clem, then one at her spot, before resuming her seat.

"Came as a real surprise," Clem said, the spindly fork he held all but swallowed up in his massive hand. He bent his grizzled salt-and-pepper head. "How'd it happen?"

Kirby could feel the heat that started to rise up his neck. He shifted in his chair and cleared his throat, while Gladys turned her braid-wrapped head his way, ready to hang on every word. "He, uh, sort of toppled over the banister of his porch." Noticing that his hostess had started eating her dessert, he forked a piece into his mouth.

A frown scrunched up Clem's sunburned face. "Don't that beat all. Well, we'll be prayin' fer him. You 'spect to do the preachin' till he mends?"

"Sure do." He would try to make the sermons last a little longer, too, he resolved, as new embarrassment rekindled the glow and flashed it upward. All those pages and pages of notes, covered in only ten minutes. How had he done it? How in the world did Cook fill the right amount of time when he preached? "We's lookin' forward to it," Mrs. Harding said graciously.

"Sure are," Gladys breathed.

"With folks 'round here workin' so hard all the time," her mother went on, "it's a pure treat bein' reminded of the Lord's goodness. Sorta helps keep things balanced."

Kirby nodded. He gulped the last mouthful of pie, then drained his coffee cup. His chair legs scraped the smooth plank floor of the company house as he got up. "Well, if you don't mind, I'd best be on my way to Mountain Springs for my second service. I sure appreciate the hospitality. It was a fine meal, Mrs. Harding. Clem. Miss Harding."

Gladys's blushing cheeks dimpled effusively.

Her mother brushed crumbs from the skirt of her mauve cotton dress. "We was glad it was our turn." Getting up, the heavy-set woman crossed the plain, simply furnished room to the door, which stood open in the summer heat. She tucked a few stray hairs into the severe bun at the nape of her neck. "We'll see ya next week at church. Maybe whoever feeds ya will give ya a chance to take a little walk down by the crick with our Gladys."

"Well, that may not be possible, I'm afraid," Kirby said, being careful to keep his attention centered on the older woman and not on the daughter who'd come to stand beside her. "My time in Stull is quite limited because of the other service. But I do thank you kindly."

Plucking his hat from a hook by the door, he went out into the heat of the Pennsylvania summer. He turned and waved upon reaching the street, then mounted Jericho, knowing better than to acknowledge the slightly flushed face of Gladys Harding eagerly watching him from the doorway. If there were one thing he didn't need right now, it was some young woman thinking he'd be coming around for any other purpose than to preach the Word.

Aware of darkening clouds overhead, Kirby decided to ride the train up the mountain rather than navigate the rough terrain beside the tracks as he and Cook often had. He nudged the horse forward and headed for the livery. He couldn't help but notice that even in Stull womenfolk saw to it that a rainbow of pansies, roses, and other summer flowers bordered the stark but homey dwellings, lending a cheery riot of color to the landscape. Lace curtains billowed from some of the open windows and here and there a brightly painted windowbox fairly overflowed with vivid blossoms. With threatening clouds amassing for a summer storm, the multicolored hues made a person feel good.

As he rode, Kirby didn't dare to cast a backward look toward the house where he'd shared the dinner meal. He had no doubt that he'd find Gladys Harding, in her bright ruffled dress, still staring after him.

❧

Mountain Springs, the small settlement at the top of North Mountain, was among Pennsylvania's colder spots in the winter, thus providing two important industries. The thick ice harvested from its bountiful supply in winter provided commercial ice dealers in Wyoming Valley with steady revenue as they shipped it to numerous markets throughout the state and beyond. The enterprise opened up an alternative method for preserving meat other than smoking and pickling and made it possible to ship fresh meat and perishables longer distances by rail.

But once the cold season was over, attention returned exclusively to harvesting the mountain's rich supply of pine, hemlock, and other timber. Included among the town's company homes and boardinghouses, a forty-acre log pond had been constructed for felled trees. Water from two splash dams propelled logs down a steep log chute to the mill pond over seven miles below in Stull.

Watching out the open passenger car window, Kirby mulled over his message once again as the train chugged upward past timbered-out areas and others yet to be harvested. Here and there along the mountain route he spotted low clumps of ginseng with its greenish-yellow flowers. He and Cook often brought some of the medicinal herbs back to Jessica. Farther on, around an outcropping of rocks, the train passed within yards of a congregation of the area's most prevalent denizen, the eastern diamondback rattlesnake.

Kirby's preaching engagement at Mountain Springs, though it went smoothly enough, was memorable for two reasons. Penelope and Priscilla Norton, his hostess's skinny and fidgety fifteen-year-old twins, had giggled and gawked at him all through church. He had never noticed them before on any of his trips with Cook. As he walked with the family toward their house after church, the girls all but pulled one another's blond curls out in an argument over who would claim the seat beside him at the supper table.

Looking over his shoulder at the family's younger son, Kirby saw an escape. He put an arm around the boy as they walked into the parlor and took seats on the worn couch to await the meal. "So, Wesley, do any fishing hereabouts?"

The lad's dark eyes lit up. "Do I ever. Me an' my buddy have a spot we ain't never told nobody about. We ketch enough for supper lots of times."

"I'll bet you do."

"Come on out back," Wesley said, springing up, "an' lookit my pole."

Breathing a prayer of thanks, Kirby gave an indulgent smile to the lad's father and excused himself. Hopefully there would be many interesting things to see out there.

When Mrs. Norton finally rang the dinner bell to summon them inside, Wesley wasn't about to let either of his sisters elbow her way next to the company. Straightening to his full height, he glared at one and smirked at the other as he deftly grabbed the chair beside Kirby. The meal was consumed in near silence as the twins pouted across the table.

Short, muscular Grady Norton peered through gold-wire spectacles astride a nose as solid as the rest of him. "How long d'ya expect Reverend Singleton to be laid up?" he asked as Mrs. Norton cleared away the roast.

His rail-thin wife arched her brows in curiosity beneath her chestnut waves as she returned with generous slices of chocolate cake the same shade as her dress.

"Several weeks, from what the doctor says," Kirby answered.

"Prob'ly won't get much fishin' done," Wesley piped in, "seein' as how he can't cast a line."

Kirby grinned. "No, I don't suppose he will."

"I think fishin's a waste of time," Penelope whined. She scrunched her mouth into a pout.

"And besides, they're smelly," her sister said with a toss of shoulder-length curls.

"Yeah, well what do girls know?" Wesley demanded. "I'm gonna take Preacher Mitchell to see my fort right after we're done eatin'. And there's no girls allowed."

The twins turned up their noses and ignored the lot of them all through dessert.

Making good on the lad's word, Kirby accompanied him to the secret haven built from scrap lumber several yards from the house. Kirby had to admire Wesley's handiwork, a similar version of one he'd constructed years ago as a youngster in Plymouth. He hadn't allowed girls in his either. *Too bad I let my guard down some years later with Estelle,* he thought with a wry smile.

"Well, what d'ya think of it?" Wesley asked, his eyes shining with pride.

Kirby clapped a hand on the lad's bony shoulder. "I think it's real fine."

"I only ever brought one other friend up here," the boy said quietly.

"Then that makes me feel real special. Thanks for showing it to me."

Thunder rumbled in the distance. Glancing through the overhead tree branches, Kirby shrugged. "Looks like we're in for some rain."

"Yeah, we'd best git back home," Wesley replied. He shoved the flap closed over the doorway and put his hands into his pockets, then he fell into step, measuring his strides to Kirby's. "I kinda liked what you said when you was preachin' before, about how we're like logs, and if we're in God's chute, we can git safe to heaven."

Kirby mussed the lad's unruly hair. "Just remember that God's chute is named Jesus. He made the way for us to come to Him, by sacrificing Himself on the cross to pay for all the wrongs we've done."

"Sounds simple, put like that."

"It was meant to be simple. God loved us all so much He wanted to make a way for us to reach Him. Man is the one who makes it all complicated by trying to earn his own way. That never works."

When they'd reached the house, Kirby followed Wesley inside where the lad's mother was drying her hands on a dish towel. "I'd sure like to thank you, ma'am, for that fine meal. It was truly delicious."

"Oh. Why, thank ya. When ya get tired, ya can stay the night in Wes's room. He'll sleep on the couch."

Kirby scratched his head. "Sure I wouldn't be putting him out?"

"You kiddin'?" Wesley piped in. "I'll show you where it is. I got more stuff to show you in there."

With a chuckle, Kirby winked at him.

As the train puffed its downward journey the following morning, Kirby reflected on the previous day and his first preaching experiences. Despite his initial nervousness and sweaty palms as he first met the sea of curious eyes, both services had gone smoothly. He couldn't have been more thankful. His late afternoon message had lasted almost twenty minutes, which wasn't too bad. Besides, something he'd said had actually stuck in Wesley Norton's mind. Most kids squirmed and whispered their way through church services.

He stretched a kink out of his back and yawned. The bed in Wesley's room sagged a bit in the middle, but Kirby would still have slept through the night if it hadn't been for a pair of cats that conducted a yowling match on the roof between thunderstorms. Not only had they awakened him, but all the neighborhood dogs as well and they joined into the chorus. Dozing after that had been impossible. It would be good to get back home to Alderson.

After disembarking at Stull, Kirby picked up Jericho and headed homeward. As they broke through the trees along the shortcut through the outskirts of Noxen, Kirby saw someone moving among some maples and elms ahead. He'd noticed the old house with its steep pitched roof yesterday, but he hadn't had time to stop and be neighborly. The least he could do was say hello and introduce himself since he'd be passing there a few more times before Cook recovered. He'd start by saying hello to the elusive tree dweller.

No one was in sight, however, when he arrived, and there was no response when he called out. With a shrug, he guided the horse back onto the road. Cook's preaching circuit had taken him through the area for several years now, and he pretty well knew everybody. Kirby would ask him about the place.

❧

Starlight peered down at the man from her roost. When he finally gave up the search, she released a breath she hadn't realized she'd been holding. A wisp of sun-gold blond hair brushed her knuckles as she gripped the sodden limb beside her.

A slow smile played over her lips as she watched him ride off. Today he was in a long-sleeved shirt with blue and black checks spanning his strong back, his black suit jacket folded and draped neatly behind the saddle. *He must have completed his daring mission,* she decided. The peasants were saved, the damsel avenged, and he looked even stronger and more daring in everyday clothes.

"Star," her father called as he came around the far side of the house. "Where are you, you fool girl?"

"Comin', Pa." Quickly she climbed down from her perch.

Abel shook his head as she hurried across the open space between them. "When're ya gonna quit that senseless tree scalin' an' git yer chores done?" he asked, shoving his hands into his pockets.

"Sorry," she whispered, brushing past him on her way inside. "I'll get right to them." Taking the broom from its corner by the door, Starlight went into the parlor where she pulled up the tattered rag rugs and took them outside to shake, then returned and started sweeping the floor.

Abel stuck his head in the open door. "I'm goin' huntin'. Back in a while."

"Yes, Pa." Resuming her task, Starlight continued on through the kitchen, then rounded up the dust and swept it into a pan which she dumped over the edge of the porch. Taking the egg basket from its hook, she looped the handle over her arm and went out to the chicken coop, peering into the distance for one last glimpse of the handsome knight.

❧

Kirby fastened Jericho's stall closed after brushing him down and walked to his own recently built house. Kneading the muscles of his neck, he mounted the back steps and went in.

The smooth wooden floor of the kitchen smelled damp and was still wet around the edges, evidence that Jessica had come over and whipped through with her mop. He'd have to thank her later. Unbuttoning his shirt, he headed for the stairs.

"Oh. You're home," his sister said, coming down somewhat clumsily. A big work apron covered her obviously swollen stomach and a checked kerchief tied back her wavy chestnut hair, which fell short of her shoulders in a side part. "How'd it go?"

"Not too bad for a first effort."

She gave an understanding smile. "You'll have to tell Cook and me all about it later. By the way, I made some coffee a while ago. Want some?"

He tweaked her chin with his finger. "Now that sounds great." Putting an arm about her, he gave her a hug and led the way, refastening shirt buttons as he went.

She nudged him gently to the table and crossed to the sideboard.

Kirby sank wearily onto one of the chairs and stretched out his legs while he watched his sister. Jessica's face had a refreshing beauty to it, with clear, expressive blue-gray eyes her most arresting feature. An easy smile appeared as she brought him a steaming mug. "Thanks, Jess. You shouldn't be working so hard, you know."

Jessica tossed off the comment with a shrug. "When are you ever going to finish this place?" she asked pointedly, but the sparkle in her eyes kept her tone light.

His all-encompassing glance roamed the open area around them. "Why? What's wrong with it?"

"What's wrong with it?" she echoed. "It's nothing but a shell. A bare, unfinished shell. That's what's wrong with it! No doors on your cupboards, no sills on the windows, no curtains, no mantel, no—"

"Hey, I get the picture," Kirby said tiredly. "But it's good enough for me. I can't see much point in making it fancy."

"You had some grand plans for it once," she said quietly.

"Well, that was then. This is now. I like it fine just the way it is."

She pulled off her kerchief and shook her hair loose, running a hand through the one side in a habitual gesture. "Whatever you say. I just don't know how you can be contented with it. It's not like you." She regarded him for a minute and her expression softened. "Coming over for dinner? The kids want you to. Cook could use some help with a couple things. You could stay to supper later too."

"Sure. Be there in a little while."

"Good. I'll go on home, then. Everything's done here."

Kirby met his sister's gaze with a sheepish grin as he drank the remainder of his coffee and took his cup to the sink. "Put it on my bill, as usual, huh?"

"I'm letting it accumulate till it adds up to a vast fortune," she said lightly. "For when I need new furniture or something. See you later." With the turn of her heel, she lumbered out toward the house directly across the road.

Watching Jessica out the kitchen window, Kirby fought against unwelcome memories. He'd had some rather grandiose plans when he'd started building this house, back when Estelle was in the scheme of things. But that was a lifetime ago. Or did it just seem that way?

≈≈

Starlight buttered a slice of warm bread and bit off a chunk to have with a glass of water. When Pa wasn't around she didn't fuss with meals. But while she ate she wondered what sort of fare a prince might have. She let her mind make a slow circle around the thought and imagined a great long table fairly sagging under the weight of fat roast pheasant and pig and broad platters of apples and grapes, the same as in the book. But princes, she knew, had all sorts of fair maidens to eat with. Despondently, Starlight cast her eyes downward over her almost colorless gray dress. It was hardly fit for eating in at home, let alone at a beautiful castle.

She sighed and brushed off her hands, then snatched up the elegant plum taffeta dress she needed to finish for Mrs. Browning and put the last stitches in the hem and the sleeve edges. The fine texture, so smooth against her skin, would be perfect on a princess.

"I declare," she muttered. "What good are dreams?"

But inwardly she smiled. Even now, leftover scraps from all the pretty dresses she ever sewed were being turned into a colorful coverlet for her bed. One fit for royalty.

❧

"I get him!" Betsy whined.

"No, me!" James said, elbowing his little sister aside as the two of them scrambled for a spot on Kirby's lap.

"Hey, you two," he said. With a hand on each small head, he ruffled their silky, copper-lit hair. "There's room for both of you, remember?"

"Oh, yeah," his three-year-old niece spurted. She hugged her ever-present rag doll close and straightened, enabling Kirby to pick her up and settle her on his left knee. Four-year-old James climbed onto the right one by himself.

Jessica smiled at them as she set places on the big oak table in the adjoining kitchen. The atmosphere of the six-room house reflected her good taste. Colorful touches throughout the dwelling blended together in a bouquet of comfort, from bright floral pillows accenting the dove-gray upholstery of the parlor to rainbow-hued quilts on the beds upstairs.

"So, you made out fair enough, Kirby?" Cook asked, coming in from the barn. Hunkering slightly, the result of his injury, the wiry redhead dried his hands a bit gingerly, then gave the towel a light toss on his way to the parlor. Jessica caught it by a corner, not quite managing to look stern. His deep-set blue eyes winked at her as he lowered himself cautiously into one of the overstuffed rose chairs.

Kirby watched the tender exchange with a twinge of longing and momentarily forgot the question. Then he took a deep breath and answered. "The people at the camps were pretty gracious, considering it was my first time and all." An uncomfortable grin broadened his face. "How *do* you make your sermons last long enough, anyway?"

With a chuckle, Cook rubbed a work-roughened hand across the bridge of his nose. Kirby noticed the way his brother-in-law's fair, sun-freckled complexion complemented Jessica's winsome beauty. His rugged face had an outdoor look that spoke of steadiness and trust. "It comes with practice. I had to learn, too, as I recall. Now my difficulty lies in knowing when to shut up!" He sobered a little. "Actually, when I quit trying so hard and let the Lord take over, that's when things started working the right way."

Kirby considered the comment as Betsy ran a chubby finger along his jaw-line. He smiled down at her and caught it gently in his teeth with a growl.

"I love you, Uncle Kirby," she said, her round, innocent blue eyes shining.

"Me, too," James piped in. "When can we go fishin' again?"

"James," Jessica said in her no-nonsense mother tone, "I told you not to ask your uncle for things."

He sank back against Kirby's chest as tears sprang to his eyes.

"I'll try to work it in next week, how's that, Freckles?" Kirby whispered with a hug.

The boy looked up with a secret smile.

"I think everything's ready," Jessica announced, and the family gathered around the table, Betsy in a high-seated chair and James on a pillow in a regular one.

Cook took his wife's hand, and she reached for one of Betsy's while Kirby took the other. James completed the circle as they bowed their heads.

"Dear Lord," Cook prayed, "we do thank Thee for the food Thou hast provided, the loving home, and all Thy other blessings. We're thankful for Kirby's safe return and ask that You'll continue to give him wisdom and safe passage in the coming weeks. In Jesus' name. Amen."

"Amen," the children echoed.

"What did the doc say about your shoulder?" Kirby asked, spooning browned potatoes onto his plate and passing the bowl to him.

"Just to take it easy," his brother-in-law answered with a wince. "It's not serious, or anything. But jouncing along on horseback isn't such a good idea, he says. Sure hope you don't mind filling in for me."

"Not at all. Figured I'd have to."

&

Starlight blinked to clear her vision in the lamplight, then set her sewing aside with a yawn. She wasn't going to stay awake all night waiting for Pa to decide to come home from Dewey Blackburn's, where he'd been since sup-per. Unfolding her cramped legs from beneath her on the sofa, she hobbled across the room and took down the treasured picture book, then hugged it to her all the way upstairs.

In her small bedroom with its sloped ceilings, Starlight opened the window and leaned out for a breath of mild night air. Honeysuckle and roses sent fragrant greetings as crickets and tree toads sang their appreciation. Starlight unbuttoned her dress and shrugged out of it. Her muslin night shift felt cool against the heat of her skin as she lifted her arms high above her head. Starlight touched a match to the oil lamp, then replaced the chimney.

Flickering light illuminated the plain unpainted walls, casting playful shadows around the pine bedstead and mismatched wardrobe along the opposite wall. Taking a seat on the bench at her dressing table, Starlight brushed the tangles from her hair the way Ma used to. Then she turned down the bedclothes and climbed into bed with the book, letting her gaze linger on the enchanting pictures once again.

Chapter Three

Kirby rode leisurely toward Stull early the following Sunday morning. Hopeful that this week his sermon would fill a decent interval of time, he ran over the outline in his mind. Idly he wondered who'd be feeding him today, since the townsfolk took it upon themselves to pass him around. He hoped the meal would be as good as the one he'd shared with the Hardings.

As he neared the dilapidated house he had passed last weekend, Kirby regretted he had forgotten to ask Cook about it. The place had many of the earmarks of an abandoned homestead, with its loose shutters and lopsided porch roof. But there was a lively brood of chickens in back. Looking closer, he noticed someone scrubbing laundry in a washtub in the side yard. He guided Jericho over that way.

A waif of a girl looked up as he approached, her doe eyes, too big for her face, wide with fear. He watched her glance around as if looking for a place to run and hide, and finding none. Her gaze returned to him for the most fleeting of seconds before she bent her head and worked at her task with renewed vigor.

Kirby smiled, taking note that not only was she young and slight of frame, but in her shapeless nondescript dress and bare feet, she looked in need of a few decent meals. Nevertheless, her loose, sun-streaked hair glistened and she looked clean, particularly up to her elbows, submerged as they were in lye soap. He nudged back the brim of his hat. "Morning, miss. The name's Mitchell. Kirby Mitchell. Might I have the honor of knowing your name?"

She raised her face and locked eyes with him momentarily, then appraised him curiously from head to toe. She opened her mouth to speak but was interrupted by an older, bony man hobbling out of the house on a rude crutch.

"Thought I heard somebody out here," he stated in a gravelly voice.

Removing his hat, Kirby gave a nod to the man glowering from the porch landing. "How do you do, sir. Name's Kirby Mitchell. I'm passing through on my way to conduct Sunday services at Stull and Mountain Springs. Thought I'd stop by and say hello."

"A pulpit-thumper," he spat with a disparaging shake of his head. "Mighta figgered. If ya was from around here, ya'd know I'm Abel Wells, an' this here's my daughter. An' ya'd know we ain't got much use fer religion. So's ya'd best be on yer way."

Kirby raised his brows good-naturedly. "Ah, well, I'm from the Alderson end of Harvey's Lake and will be passing this way for the next few Sundays. I just wanted to be neighborly, is all." He glanced pointedly at the logs strewn haphazardly near the dwelling. "Would it put you out if I were to come by and chop your wood sometime? You'll need it put up for winter."

Wells didn't alter his expression. "Suit yerself. Don't have no money to pay ya." He turned and started ambling away.

"No matter," Kirby said, keeping his tone even. "As I said, I like to be neighborly. Good day to you, sir. Miss." Nodding to them in turn, he slapped his hat back on, turned his horse, and cantered toward Stull.

ও

Starlight swallowed a lump of wonder as she watched the gallant horseman ride away beneath the dazzling splendor of the sun. *Kirby Mitchell,* her mind sang. *Sir Kirby.* He was better than she'd imagined. Strong of tooth and limb, eyes blue as the summer sky, a voice pleasant and low and ringing with authority. His shiny brown hair looked as though the wind liked to play hide-and-seek among its tousled strands. And his face! Open and honest, one that would never lie or be mean. Even though he hadn't smiled much, he hadn't appeared to look down on her either. He seemed different from some of the townspeople, especially the ones her age. They treated her as though she carried some death plague around in her pockets, intent on scattering it over unsuspecting folks like so much chicken feed.

With a sigh, she leaned over and rested her elbows on the rim of the tub for a last long glimpse of the black-suited knight. He did look like a preacher, she decided. Or at least the way she pictured someone who would take up the mission of telling people about God, like those who had been friends of the man named Jesus. Ma had talked about them when she told her stories from the Bible but Starlight could barely remember them now. Something about a flood, a white-haired man smashing stone tablets, a younger one who wasn't afraid of lions, and a real sad tale about a cross.

Unconsciously she glanced toward the house. Ma's Bible was on the shelf in the parlor, next to where the storybook had been. Sir Kirby would appreciate knowing she and Pa had God's Book right inside, if he ever came back, as he said.

Putting her hands again into the washtub, Starlight pulled out one of Abel's shirts and wrung it before flopping it into the basket beside her. Flinging her arms wide in a spontaneous gesture, she spun joyously around, splaying drops of soapy water about her, and ran to hug her maple tree.

ও

From a bend in the road, Kirby watched the touching childlike display in puzzlement. For some unknown reason, he had stopped and looked back toward the forlorn house as he breathed a prayer for its occupants. Now as he watched the girl grasp the bottom branch of the tree and swing easily onto it before disappearing into the thick leafy boughs, he smiled to himself. No wonder there had been no one around the last time he'd come by. The little wood nymph had been hiding! "What do you make of that, Jericho? Quite the disappearing act."

The horse flicked its ears and tossed its head with a shake of its dark mane.

Kirby chuckled and patted the animal's neck. "It does explain a few things. But we'd best be getting on," he said, lingering for another long stare at the lush maple by the house. Then, drawing a deep breath, he turned the horse and continued toward Stull. For the remainder of the ride he tried to force his mind to concentrate on his upcoming sermon. But despite his good intentions, thoughts of an elusive golden-haired girl got in the way.

She sure was different, he conceded. Not at all like Estelle, whose fine porcelain features and pleasingly rounded form had once seemed to him the utmost in womanly perfection. Now that a fair amount of time had gone by, he recalled a certain coldness in Estelle's blue-green eyes that he'd refused to acknowledge before, an aloofness in her smile and manner. Odd that he hadn't seen them from the beginning. She hadn't deceived Jessica, but then not much got past his older sister.

The little wood nymph wasn't what one might consider pretty by some standards, that was for sure. Her huge sleepy-looking sable eyes seemed to take in everything at once, when they weren't searching for someplace to escape, and she had an overgenerous mouth. She looked as if a strong gust of wind could whisk her away to Ohio. Yet there was something about her that teased a man's mind. Delicate cheekbones, a neat straight nose, silky shoulder-length hair, a supreme innocence he'd rarely encountered. . .and a vulnerability he could almost taste. Not that he truly cared. But she could probably use a few prayers.

Shaking off his musings as the town came into view, Kirby eased Jericho toward the schoolhouse.

そ▲

Starlight wiggled her toes to make space for them over the piece of heavy blanket she'd cut for inside her shoe. Didn't feel too awful bad, but she'd be glad when she got done at Mrs. Browning's and could kick them off again. Moving to her dressing table, she ran the brush through her hair and tied it back with a strip of colored material she'd cut from some goods a while back. She then stepped away to assess her reflection in the cracked mirror. Her spruce gingham skirt and white shirtwaist had seen better days, but it was the best she had. *Oh, pshaw!* What did she care what the townspeople thought anyway? She was hardly ever there unless she had to deliver a dress or run for supplies when Pa forgot.

The half-hour walk to town took Starlight through pleasant rolling forest land, past rambling stonewalls she delighted in navigating, and beside a gurgling brook where she performed a stone-hopping jig. All around her, robins and meadowlarks sang their glorious songs. Leaning over to catch sight of herself in the water, she stared for a moment, then with a toss of her head, sighed and continued on, a basket of eggs dangling from one forearm, the widow's new dress draped over a shoulder.

Mrs. Browning's house was the second building on the way into town, gabled and two-storied, an immaculate white structure with forest green shutters. The turret on one side of the front, like a castle tower, fascinated Starlight. Paying no mind to people coming and going from houses and business establishments farther on, Starlight mounted the painted gray steps and crossed the wide porch. She knocked at the glass-paned door, never ceasing to wonder that such a huge place housed but one person.

"Oh, Starlight," Mrs. Browning said warmly as she opened the door. Her smiling face had few lines for someone "nearer fifty than forty," as she'd once confessed. "You've finished my dress so quickly?"

"Yes, ma'am." Starlight set down her basket and held the edge of the garment out a bit as proof.

"Well, do come in, child." Deep red stones in the woman's rings glittered as she gestured with a tapered hand toward the entry hall just inside. "You truly are a marvel. I was certain you wouldn't be done for at least another week. Let me have a look."

Starlight let her gaze wander over the fancy house dress the elegant, slender woman wore with grace. Navy with tiny white dots, the soft material draped casually over her handsome figure and complemented nicely her creamy skin and coiled, silver-streaked brown hair.

The widow raised light green eyes and smiled. "Why, you've done a lovely job on it, Starlight. Every bit as nice as anything I've gotten from the catalog, I must say."

"Thank you, ma'am."

"Yes," she continued, a mischievous glint in her eye, "Hazel will be so envious when I wear this to the social on Saturday. I'm certain she'll run right out for a nice piece of goods herself so you can make one for her. Wait and see if she doesn't."

"Maybe," Starlight answered. Between Hazel Camp and Violet Browning, she had a steady stream of sewing jobs. Rivalry between the two widows had been legendary for some time as they tried to outdo one another in catching the eye of distinguished Mr. Malcolm, the new lawyer who came up from Wyoming Valley twice a week. The women seemed to have no qualms about talking to Starlight about him, since she had no one to whom to carry on the tales.

"Well, come along, child," Mrs. Browning said, turning and walking through the apricot-hued hallway toward the parlor. "I must get you some money."

Following her, Starlight admired as always the woman's lovely possessions. Charming figurines of birds and old-fashioned damsels adorned assorted wall shelves and the hall lowboy, and a gold-edged looking glass between candled wall sconces tossed back the daylight. Starlight wouldn't have dreamed of touching such fine objects and walked especially softly even as she passed them, lest the breeze created by her movements send them toppling to the floor.

In the parlor with its silver and blue flocked wallpaper, polished mahogany furniture gleamed beneath blue glass lamps that dripped glass prisms from their shades. But Starlight's eyes were drawn as if by a magnet to, in her mind, the grandest piece of all, a dark upright piano. She crossed to the instrument and trailed her finger lightly along the keys, making not a sound.

"Would you like me to play a song for you, my dear?" Mrs. Browning asked gently.

"Oh, would you? I'd truly love that."

The widow gave Starlight's hand a squeeze as she moved to the stool and sat, her fingers poised above the "ivories." She played an intricate arpeggio and continued on into a hymn, her clear voice singing along:

"Rock of Ages, cleft for me, let me hide myself in Thee. . . . "

Starlight closed her eyes and let the glorious melody flow over her, through her, and around her, filling her world with music. A piano must surely be the most wonderful thing a person might possess, she was sure. At the sound of it she wanted to laugh and cry at the same time, though she did not understand the strange words the widow was singing. As the song came to an end, she opened her eyes.

"Thank you, ma'am. That was truly beautiful."

With a friendly smile, Mrs. Browning rose. She picked up a velvet drawstring purse that lay atop the instrument and dug through it for some coins, then took Starlight's hand and pressed them inside, curling the girl's fingers over them. "And thank you, my girl, for your lovely work. Now, I have some elderberry scones out in the kitchen for you and your father." She hesitated. "And if you have the time, I did pick up another bit of fabric, but I hate to impose on you. I know young people have other things to do at times."

"Oh, don't worry," Starlight said eagerly, slipping the money into her skirt pocket. "I'll be glad to sew anything you need." She scrunched her toes inside her worn shoe and smiled.

On her way out of W. F. Brown's General Store a quarter of an hour later, Starlight came within a hair's breadth of slamming right into Dewey Blackburn, who was on his way in.

"Sorry," she said, sidestepping the short, wiry man as she took a firmer hold of the sack that held her supplies.

"Well, now. Little Starry Wells," he rasped. In a seemingly mocking gesture, he whipped off his old hat, revealing his balding head. His hazel eyes flared as he slid them over her. "Ain't ya a purty sight. Glad to give ya a ride home in a couple minutes." He smiled insinuatingly, displaying discolored teeth.

The man always made her feel uncomfortable. "Thanks, no." She forced a smile. "I have another errand to run." Hardly regretting the lie, she flew down the steps to the street hoping he'd go inside so she could find a big rock to hide behind, like the one in Mrs. Browning's song, until he was gone. But the hotel across the street offered quicker refuge. She ran over and flattened herself against the side of it, occasionally peeking around the corner of the building.

After he'd come out of the store and driven away, Starlight started up the wide street for home.

A few buildings beyond the store and hotel, she passed the big yellow Honeywell house, the grandest in town. Starlight cringed as she saw spoiled and haughty Emily Honeywell. She knew the wealthy girl from the brief period she'd attended school. Emily and two of her fashionable friends lounged in the dotted shade of a big elm sharing glasses of lemonade. The flower-trimmed brims of their summer hats shielded their skin from the scourge of freckles.

As she passed the white picket fence along the front edge of the yard, Emily whispered something behind her hand that made the others giggle. Starlight ducked her head and hurried on. To her dying day she would dislike them all. She preferred having no friends at all than being with people who looked down on her.

A bitter memory surfaced unchecked of a school Christmas program held at the schoolhouse one year. All the girls had voted to wear white dresses, all except Starlight who had no such outfit. The classmates had all contributed to a special fund to provide a new white dress for her, and Starlight had worn it proudly while she and the others quoted their memorized pieces and sang carols to the parents. In truth the frock was much finer than any she'd ever had. Before the program she had caressed the soft taffeta with reverence while Pa had done up the buttons in back. Afterward, seeing Emily's sneer and overhearing her snide remarks, Starlight had gone out to the privy and slipped the white dress off. After tearing it to shreds, she shoved it down into the hole and ran all the way home. Pa hadn't even cared that she had never gone back. He didn't think there was any need for girls to learn such useless things as reading or writing anyhow.

With a decidedly hateful glance over her shoulder, Starlight lifted her chin and took the shortcut through the woods.

At least at home she was comfortable. Without the world at her heels she was even, dare she think it, a princess.

Chapter Four

Humming a nonsensical tune as she emerged from the woods, Starlight stopped dead.

Dewey Blackburn's wagon was in front of the house.

With a sinking feeling, she pictured the man's leering eyes and uncouth manner. Not altogether sure she wanted to go home yet, she tightened her lips. Pa would be mad if she stayed out too long, but perhaps Dewey would be leaving soon. Skirting the edge of the property, she stole quietly into the fragrant shelter of a cluster of honeysuckle bushes and set down her sacks and the empty egg basket. Then, lowering herself to the spongy ground, she straightened her skirt and lay back with her head resting on her hands.

Billowy clouds inched slowly across the sky. Through a break in the higher branches Starlight traced the ever-changing outlines of puffy castles and dragons as she wondered where today's noble ventures had taken the knight of her dreams. Last Sunday seemed ages ago. Without closing her eyes she could still picture him tall and straight atop his silver charger. The memory of his low voice played a lullaby across the strings of her heart as her eyelids grew heavy.

He said he would return sometime to perform neighborly kindnesses, and he had to have spoken truly. Knights took vows about that. A delicious warmth flushed her cheeks as her lips spread into a secret smile.

"Starlight!" Her father called from the porch, his grating voice interrupting her musings. "Starlight, girl. Where are ya?"

Grimly she sprang to her feet and grabbed her things. "Comin', Pa," she answered, purposely making her voice sound farther away. Then she dashed back several yards to the knoll within sight of the house and angled over to the path. She emerged from behind the rise, swinging her sack nonchalantly in case he were still watching. To her relief, he was not. She expelled a sigh and trudged the rest of the way.

She could hear her father and his friend guffawing as she mounted the steps and swung the door open.

" 'Bout time, girl," Abel said flatly as she entered.

The door clacked shut behind her.

"Told ya b'fore not to dawdle. Dewey here says he offered ya a ride. Shoulda took it. We been waitin' fer some coffee."

"I needed to stop by Mrs. Browning's," Starlight said self-consciously, lowering her gaze as she reversed the order of events. "She gave me some more goods to work on." Refusing to meet Blackburn's appraising dark eyes, she crossed to the sideboard and measured some fresh grounds into the coffee pot, then added water and set it atop one of the hot plates on the stove.

"Shore is a comely little thing," Blackburn remarked. "Gettin' purtier ever'-day, I swear."

Starlight ignored the man's comment, though a chill skittered up her spine. Even with her back turned she could feel his eyes boring through her. More distasteful to her than Dewey Blackburn, however, were his two ill-mannered boys, Calvin and Marvin. Thankfully, he had left them behind.

While the coffee brewed, she picked up the clothes basket and hurried out the back door to take down the sheets. Despite trying to stretch out the chore, she finished within moments and carried the folded linens inside.

"If it wasn't that things was pressin' on me right now," Dewey Blackburn was saying to her father, "I'd be more'n glad to give more time. But the way things are. . . ." He let his words trail off.

Abel rubbed a hand up and down over one cheek in thought. A scowl drew his shaggy brows together. He looked Starlight up and down, then met her eye and looked pointedly at the stove.

She removed two blue tin mugs from the cupboard and filled them with hot coffee. She'd heard little of their conversation, but the air seemed thick with something that made her uncomfortable. As she set the cups before each of them, she only barely escaped Dewey Blackburn's swarthy hand as he reached for her arm. "I—I have some sewing to do, Pa," she said. Hurrying over to her sack with the new fabric, she snatched it up and ran upstairs to the haven of her room.

Starlight flung herself onto her bed. Had it been all that many years ago, when as a little girl she used to sit on that lecher's lap? Ma had been alive then, and Mrs. Blackburn. The two families had shared meals and good times together. Starlight and the boys, one a year older than she, the other a year younger, had fun fishing and wading in the creek. But when Ma took sick and passed on, Pa withdrew, spending entire days out by himself, not caring about the house or the little motherless girl who mourned the loss too. Mrs. Blackburn's almost daily visits became less and less frequent and then stopped altogether when she took a fever and died two years later. The sons no longer seemed to have a guiding hand; they turned into pranksters and bullies and Starlight hated even to be near them.

Starlight shuddered. They weren't her main concern now. Their father was. Dewey Blackburn, with eyes that undressed her, a smirk that unnerved her, and a touch that repulsed her, made her wish she were a hundred miles away. She wished he'd stay home on that farm he'd let go to ruin. If he didn't, she'd have to find someplace else to be whenever he came around, pure and simple.

When finally she heard him go out to his old wagon and pull away, she breathed a sigh of relief. It was time to start dinner. She'd best hurry downstairs before Pa got upset.

The sickening stench of liquor hovered in the kitchen when Starlight descended the stairs. She glanced at the table where Abel glowered in silence, his eyes glazed as he stared at nothing. An almost empty bottle of whiskey sat beside the coffee mugs. Giving her father a wide berth, she went to the counter board and chose some potatoes to fry from the basket below and began peeling them. While she worked, she looked up at her father from time to time.

After a while, Abel's gaze shifted to her, and he frowned.

Starlight attempted a smile. "Want some dinner?"

He shrugged a shoulder, staring wordlessly at her, a distressed expression crimping his features. "I want ya to start being nicer to Dewey when he comes here," he said. "It's important. I owe him."

❧

Riding back toward Noxen after Sunday services the following week, Kirby guided Jericho toward the Wells home. There was still enough daylight to chop a bit of wood and stack it, and he could rehash his messages as he worked. The services at Stull and Mountain Springs had gone well and Kirby wondered whether there were towns farther on in need of regular preachers. Once Cook had mended, Kirby would be without a pulpit.

There was no one about as he drew near to the tumbledown house belonging to Abel Wells and his daughter. Recalling the young lass and her escape route into the thick branches of the big maple, he smiled to himself. She might be there even now, looking down at the world from her shaded aerie. He dismounted and looped Jericho's reins around a slat in the banister rail along the porch and then went up and knocked at the door.

Silence followed.

After waiting a reasonable time, he bounded down the steps and took his ax from the saddlebag. Around in the sideyard pieces of wood were still strewn about in no particular order. It was a place to start, anyway, he decided. He rolled up the sleeves of his gray striped shirt and began to whistle the opening notes of "Jesus Paid It All." He picked up the first log, placed it onto the chopping block, and halved and quartered it. But the physical effort called for more than a mere whistle. Reaching the chorus, he claimed his mighty tenor voice as the words resounded from the rocky, hilly terrain.

"Jesus paid it all; all to Him I owe; sin had left a crimson stain, he washed it white as snow."

From the corner of his eye, Kirby caught a flicker of light blue from the direction of the climbing tree, but he kept his attention fixed on the job at hand, singing and working steadily until the last log chunk had been cut and stacked. His repertoire of memorized hymns exhausted, he brushed his hands and strode to Jericho.

୨ଈ

Breathless, Starlight watched Sir Kirby replace the ax in the saddlebag and swing easily into the saddle. She convinced herself that if she'd been inside the house when he arrived, or even tending the chickens instead of high amid the branches of the maple, she might have taken him a glass of cool water or at least said hello. After all, it would have been mannerly to greet him. He didn't seem at all frightening. She imagined herself gliding gracefully from behind the house, a fold of wondrous flowing silk held lightly in her fingers, a welcoming smile upon her lips. *Hello, sir knight. How noble of you to come by. I'm Lady Starlight Wells, mistress of this manor. May I offer you some cool spring water? Nectar, perhaps? You have labored long and hard and must be in need of refreshment.* But alas, she couldn't be caught on her childlike perch.

Nonetheless, she hadn't even tried to keep her eyes from following his every movement, the strong muscles that flexed in his arms as he positioned logs and swung the ax. Why would a stranger take it upon himself to be so neighborly? Most of the townspeople barely acknowledged her father's or her existence.

Starlight didn't allow herself to breathe as the knight and his steed rode directly beneath her. How mortifying it would be to have him discover her!

"Ah, Jericho," he said, in low soothing tones touched with deep disappointment. "Too bad Miss Wells wasn't at home today. I'd have liked to say hello to her and her father. Well, maybe next weekend when we pass through again."

Warmth flowed over Starlight and filled her being. He had wanted to see her. Talk to her. She nibbled the inside corner of her lip and watched until he was completely out of sight. Slowly, she sank back against the tree trunk and closed her eyes with a smile.

The lilting melodies of his songs still echoed all around, as if from this moment on she could listen at will and hear them whenever she wanted. Strange melodies, to be sure, like the one Mrs. Browning had played on her piano, with words and phrases she could not comprehend. Maybe they went with some of the things he talked about when he went preachering. They sounded ever so interesting. One of them had a vague familiarity about it. Ma had sung that one to her long ago. Maybe sometime, someday, her knight would teach it to her.

&

Kirby had fought a strong impulse to look right up at Starlight when he and Jericho passed beneath her hiding place. Curious, how someone could be so shy that she'd keep her very presence a secret. She must not have many friends or she'd surely be used to people dropping by.

He wondered how many more visits it would take before she'd come down from her maple tree and pass the time of day with him while he worked. The more wood he chopped, the more things he had noticed that needed to be done around the place. The bottom two porch steps needed to be bolstered, or even replaced, the rail had some slats missing, and even the roof above it sagged toward the far end. And that was just the outside. The girl couldn't be expected to see to things like those, and her father wasn't in any condition. Maybe both of them could use a friend.

In any event, they needed to know about the Lord and the truth of His goodness. Even though Abel Wells flatly denied that fact, his daughter was far too young to harbor such bitter feelings toward God. The empty sadness in her eyes had haunted Kirby's sleep ever since they met. She needed to learn to trust.

Chapter Five

"My goodness, something has you in a state," Jessica said knowingly as she poured Kirby a cup of tea and set it before him at her kitchen table.

"Hmm?" As if only suddenly aware of his sister's voice, Kirby looked up. He ran his fingers through his glossy hair.

"I said, something has you in a state," she repeated.

He expelled a lungful of air. "Oh. Sorry. Were you talking about something in particular?"

"No, you just seem to be a few continents away, that's all. Need a listening ear?"

The corners of his mouth turned upward into a hint of a smile, but he shook his head. Picking up his cup, he sipped the tea.

Jessica felt her growing baby stir and she positioned her hand over the bulge in her abdomen. She continued observing her younger brother as he bit into a biscuit spread with butter and jam. Although it had taken him months to crawl out of the bitter pit he had plunged into since Estelle's insensitive action, he'd made considerable progress recently getting on with his life. At least until a week or two ago. Since then it seemed as though something were eating at him, something he was reluctant to discuss. *Could he and his former fiancée have crossed paths?* Jessica wondered anxiously.

With a sigh, Jessica drained her own cup. She'd been no great admirer of that uppity Estelle Marsden from the first time Kirby had brought her home. The young woman was far too caught up in herself. For her brother's sake she had made an effort to put aside her reservations and include her in family activities. But Estelle never really entered in. She couldn't be bothered answering the children's endless questions, and she was reluctant to enjoy an outing for fear she'd soil her stylish dress or muss her perfect hair. She was forever opening her little drawstring bag and checking her appearance in a tiny, silver-framed mirror. Any enthusiasm on Estelle's part regarding family togetherness was only halfhearted at best. She wanted Kirby all to herself, and, in fact, had all but admitted it to Jessica once in an unguarded moment.

After the initial shock of Estelle's elopement, Jessica had felt profound relief. Kirby deserved a woman more like himself, with a heart for God, a desire to help others. But still, Estelle Marsden's thoughtless treatment of Kirby had offended Jessica, and because of that, she had been fighting a battle of her own ever since, one of forgiveness. Though her brother seemed to have made allowances for the despicable act, and even accepted it, he nursed deep wounds. Some of them were still visible. His once laughing face now bore a strange, somber expression.

Reaching for the teapot, Jessica met Kirby's eyes. "Well, Cook's out in the barn studying. I'm sure he'd welcome a break, if you need to talk." She lifted the pot questioningly and, at the negative shake of his head, refilled only her own cup. A new thought occurred to her. *Could it be possible that Kirby had found someone else?*

≈

Hands in his pockets, Kirby strode out onto Jessica's back porch. Normally he looked forward to being here in his sister's cheery, comfortable house with its feminine touches, but today there was too much on his mind. By rights he should be studying, too, for tomorrow's sermon. He still hadn't decided on a passage. Rattling around his big empty house all day, he had been unable to concentrate. Glad for the standing supper invitation, he'd come early, *hours* early, while the kids still napped. It would have been better if they'd been awake, to keep him occupied and too busy to think. Now the quiet seemed unnatural.

The willow off to the right moved lightly in the summer breeze, its crown of long fronds graceful and thick and almost touching the grass beneath it in an undulating circle. In the distance, robins and meadowlarks tried to outdo one another with cheery songs as the tall meadow grasses dipped and swayed in unison. Maybe Cook would appreciate an interruption, Kirby decided in frustration.

Kirby found his brother-in-law in the small office cubicle in the corner of the barn. Cook had finished off this room for the sole purpose of acquiring some peace and quiet for his devotions and sermon studies. He rapped lightly on the door.

"Come in."

Kirby turned the knob and went in. "Mind a diversion?"

"Not at all, not at all. What's up?" Cook closed the book he'd been reading and turned his round, ruddy face Kirby's way in earnest.

"Just thought I'd come say hello. What are you studying?"

Cook tilted his head in the direction of the volume. "An exposition on Romans. Fascinating."

Kirby nodded. "How's the shoulder?"

"Coming along. Ready to preach again tomorrow?"

"Sort of." He raised his gaze to the heavily laden bookshelves that occupied the wall on the other side of Cook. "Know anything about the people of Noxen?" he asked suddenly.

"In general, or in particular?"

Propping an ankle on his opposite knee, Kirby met Cook's puzzled expression. "I was wondering if you'd come across Abel Wells, on the shortcut we take to hit Stull."

Cook rubbed his chin in thought. "Kind of a scruffy character, right? Walks with a crutch, lives with his daughter in a house that's seen better days."

"That's the one."

"What about him?"

Realizing with chagrin that what he really wanted was some information about the elusive young woman with wide doe eyes who scurried up a tree whenever he came by, Kirby hesitated. He didn't want to give Cook the wrong impression. He tried to formulate a reasonable query, discarding questions one by one as they came to mind.

"Well," Cook said, breaking into the silence, "I do know he's got absolutely no interest in anything that concerns the Lord." He laced his fingers together over his belt and leaned the chair back on its two hind legs. The buttons on his red plaid shirt strained slightly against the buttonholes.

"I gathered that already," Kirby stated flatly. He flicked a minuscule speck of paper off the corner of the plain wood desk as Cook continued.

"Tell you the truth, I never had much contact with the man. Saw his daughter once or twice, though."

Kirby's attention rose a notch but he managed with some difficulty to maintain his casual expression.

"Strange little thing, I must say," Cook went on. "Has some odd, magical name or other. Can't think what it is. Anyhow, she seemed mildly interested in going to the town church when I mentioned it. Don't know as she ever did, though. Her pa probably squelched the idea soon as it was mentioned."

"I can believe that," Kirby admitted. "He as much as told me to keep my religion to myself." He paused. "But I couldn't help noticing there were a few chores crying out to be done out there. I offered a hand."

Cook gave a silent huff. "How'd he take that?"

"He said it was up to me. Can you believe it? He didn't care one way or the other."

"Well, sometimes that's the only way to reach a person, through helping them out. I don't see much harm in it, myself, if you have the time to do things that far away."

"I have nothing but time," Kirby admitted. "I haven't had any new orders for cabinets or furniture for a while."

❧

Abel Wells hobbled up the overgrown yard to Dewey Blackburn's squat, rundown house by the creek, an unlit corn cob pipe clenched in his teeth. His gaze took in the dead, strawlike geraniums from years gone by in the window box off the kitchen as he went in the open door.

"Heard ya comin'," Dewey said, getting up from a lumpy upholstered chair by the empty fireplace. He brushed off his baggy serge trousers with one hand. "I'll just run to the outhouse fer a second. Make yerself to home."

Abel sank wearily onto a wood slatback chair at the kitchen table and propped his crutch against it. He slipped off his brown jacket and looped the worn collar over the spindle of the next chair. The sounds of Dewey's two sons carried from the bend in the creek where they were either wading or fishing. How a man could abide having two able-bodied, almost grown boys around who did nothing but eat and squabble was a mystery to Abel. Even a skinny daughter with her head in the clouds was better than that.

"So. Come fer some more card playin'?" Dewey asked on his return. He crossed the plank floor of the dismal room to the pine sideboard and grabbed a jug and two spotty glasses. He plunked them on the table by the ever-present deck. The breeze stirred the threadbare calico curtains on the open window at their side.

"Why not?"

With a smirk, Dewey took a seat and brushed away some bread crumbs at his place. "Bring any of the money ya owe?"

Abel scowled. "You know I ain't got nothin' but what the gal puts in the jelly jar. Told you that."

"An' I told you I'm needin' some cash money. Bad. I got people after me, too, an' I need a new roof before winter," Dewey said evenly. "What you owe would put a roof over my head an' git them off my back."

"An' I said I'd pay ya when I can, so shut up an' deal." Abel was feeling lucky today. He'd pay off his pal one way or another. He watched Dewey pour two full glasses of corn liquor from a jug and shove one his way. It went down slick and fiery, adding a measure of confidence to his optimism.

Dewey shuffled the cards and dealt them five each, then set down the remainder.

Abel tried not to let his pleasure show when his three sevens took the first hand. Meeting with success several more times, he glanced at the little stack of chips beside him. Fifty dollars already. He was on his way. Lady luck had finally begun to smile on him. If he kept this up, soon he'd be the one with money owed him.

In rapid succession, Dewey fired another hand of cards around.

The breath in Abel's lungs almost didn't emerge as his eyes absorbed the threesome of jacks, a four, and a deuce. "I'll draw one," he said, returning the deuce. He picked up a four of hearts. His hopes soared. Dewey sure couldn't beat a full house!

Dewey took three to replace his own discards.

"Why not double or nothin' this time?"

"Fine with me," Dewey said, a gleam in his ferret eyes as he shuffled and dealt them each a hand. He sat back and scanned his cards, then in satisfaction smacked down four aces and a six of diamonds.

Abel's mouth dropped open. "That finishes me," he said emptily.

"Well, guess we should tally up then," Dewey said in a measure of triumph.

Chapter Six

On Saturday Kirby rolled his good suit inside his blanket roll and set out for Noxen. He could put in a fair day's work at the Wells place and then go on to Stull, where he'd get a room for the night at Hattie's. By the looks of the clouds gathering off to the northwest, he would be prudent not to have to travel far tomorrow morning anyway. As he rode he thought of another point for the sermon he'd prepared. Taking out his little Bible, he read over the passage he'd chosen, the ninety-first Psalm. His eyes traced the familiarwords:

> *He that dwelleth in the secret place of the most High shall abide under the shadow of the Almighty.*

The verse reminded Kirby of the welcome coolness he felt when riding out of direct sunlight into the fragrant shade of the wooded hills. It was like that to know the Lord, to be able to leave the sweltering confinement of life's pressures and spend time in His restful presence. *How did anyone even find contentment without Him, without His blessings?* he pondered as myriad thoughts assailed him. Where did unbelievers turn in times of trouble? Why did they waste their lives acquiring wealth and possessions when those things could vanish in an instant? How could they be satisfied to exist under a haze of alcohol, disregarding their family's needs and destroying their own health? Liquor offered no solutions to the problems of life.

A rabbit hopped across the road ahead, drawing Kirby's thoughts back to the present as he came within sight of his destination. He could make out Abel Wells dozing in a porch chair that faced the opposite direction, his legs propped on the banister.

Kirby's anxious eyes roved the rest of the property. Tossing feed to the chickens, Starlight's minikin figure looked graceful in a white shirtwaist and faded blue calico skirt, and she'd tied her tawny hair back at the nape of her neck. Purposely, he nudged Jericho off the road and into the seclusion of some bushes and trees. She wouldn't be able to see him coming. With an inward smile, he stopped and watched her momentarily as she shooed the chicks out of the way and slipped out the gate with a basket of eggs.

After she'd taken them inside, Kirby emerged from his cover. He stopped between the house and the maple tree. "Morning, Mr. Wells," he called lightly.

Abel Wells gave a little snort in his sleep and straightened with a start. He swung his legs down, propping the maimed one on a wooden stool. "What're you wantin'?"

"Nothing much," Kirby answered evenly. "Just thought I'd bring by some things from my sister's garden." He indicated two sacks tied behind the saddle. "And I brought a piece of chicken wire. Thought I'd mend the pen."

"Suit yerself," Abel muttered.

Well, what did I expect? Kirby wondered. *His undying gratitude for chopping a little wood?* He dismounted and took down the burlap sacks containing the vegetables, setting them by the front door. Then he unfastened the roll of wire and removed some tools and nails from the saddlebag. As he strode over to the pen, a dozen fat white hens fluttered to the far corner and clucked in a nervous huddle. Ignoring them, Kirby set to work.

He kept watch in the direction of the front porch while he pounded the flimsy posts more securely into place and attached the new section of fencing. Even if the girl did come out, he knew she couldn't exactly run and climb her tree with him at such close proximity. Perhaps she had another hiding place he didn't know about.

A respectful, olive-skinned young man who Kirby had met last week in Stull came to mind. Nelson was about the same age as this lass, and he had the same quiet way about him. If he knew of her existence. . . .

But when the door squeaked open, and Abel Wells's daughter moved partly into Kirby's range of vision and shook out a ragged mat over the banister, he changed his mind. *No, not Nelson. Polite as the lad was, he was far too clumsy and gawky for someone like her.*

"Might as well set another place," Kirby heard Abel grouse. "Likely the gospel monger'll be workin' up an appetite."

The girl didn't answer and slipped back inside.

After the pen had been mended, Kirby gathered his tools and canvassed the area in search of a scrap of lumber that could be used to repair the porch step. He found one that would do behind the small shed in back, beside a pile of rotted shingles that looked as though they'd been there forever. A quick brush with a rag rid the board of spiders, then Kirby tucked it under an arm and went for more nails. Already the aroma of rabbit stew was flavoring the immediate area around the house. His stomach growled in earnest.

"Dinner," Abel announced grudgingly a short while later. "We don't have no money to be payin' ya, but we kin see that ya eat."

"Thanks." Kirby moved to the rain barrel alongside the house and scooped out a dipperful to wash his hands. Upon entering the cheerless dwelling, he found Abel and his daughter already seated at the pine table. He took one of the empty chairs.

The stew heaped in each of their bowls smelled delicious, and while Abel reached for the plate of biscuits, Kirby bowed his head and offered a swift, silent prayer. When he looked up, he met the daughter's eyes for a second before she quickly averted her gaze.

"Mighty fine stew, Mr. Wells. Miss," he said to each of them after he'd sampled it. "I appreciate the hospitality." Then he turned his attention to the father. "Have you and your daughter been living in Noxen long?"

Abel swallowed grumpily. "All my life. My wife come from up New York way, though." He mopped some broth with another biscuit and stuffed it into his mouth.

Kirby nodded, unable to keep from noticing the sad shape of the interior of the hovel, the saggy shelves, the threadbare rugs. A rusty spring was in full view on one side of the sofa seat in the room just off to the side. But there was a glass of violets on the tabletop and another one with two pink roses on the windowsill above the sink. The curtains appeared to have once been that same delicate pink, and a subtle hue just as fragile tinged the girl's cheekbones beneath the long lashes she lowered over her eyes.

"How did she like this area?" Kirby inquired in an effort to keep the topic general.

"Liked it fine, I expect. Been gone, now, for nigh onto eight years."

"Sorry to hear that. I'm sure you must miss her."

"Yep. Well, nothin's to be done about that." He dunked another biscuit. "Ya still spreadin' fables at the Stull camp?"

Kirby nodded, not taking offense. "And Mountain Springs. I'm just filling in temporarily for my brother-in-law."

"My wife used to believe in such truck. Me, now, I got no use fer it. Cain't see how no lovin' God would let a little gal go through most her life without her ma."

A quick glance toward the girl revealed a moist sadness gathering in her wide brown eyes. She blinked it away and continued eating.

"Some things are often hard to understand," Kirby admitted, but he did not elaborate. He felt as though Abel Wells were baiting him, waiting for him to start sermonizing so he could banish him for good. That was the last thing Kirby wanted.

Abel drained his glass of water and wiped his hands on his trousers, then got up.

Kirby hadn't quite emptied his bowl. He wondered fleetingly if he were being dismissed until the man spoke again.

"Need to go out back fer a second. You finish up."

Watching Abel Wells hobble outside, Kirby felt the girl fill with an almost tangible panic. He smiled at her as he raised his spoon to his mouth. "This is some of the best rabbit stew I've ever eaten."

She appeared to relax a measure. "Thank you," she whispered, not quite meeting his eyes.

He wondered if he'd ever heard such an airy voice as hers.

Starlight felt her lungs pressing in on themselves, squeezing out all the breath inside. She reached for her glass, almost knocking it over with suddenly shaky fingers. It took great effort to control her hand. *How mortifying it would be to spill water all over company,* she thought fearfully, sure that if she did such an inexcusable thing she'd drown herself in the castle moat, if there was one. She wished for all the world that Sir Kirby would go. . .yet at the same time she hoped he never would.

"I don't think I know your name," he said softly.

She swallowed. "S—Starlight," she stammered. "It's Starlight."

Kirby tilted his head and studied her.

She half expected him to laugh and make light of it, the way the town kids always had, but he gave only the hint of a smile. She wondered what a real smile would look like on his handsome face, one wide enough to glow in his sky blue eyes. Embarrassed at her bold thoughts, she reached for a violet and drew it to her nose, inhaling the sweet perfume.

"Starlight," he repeated thoughtfully.

"Ma said I was born at night," she said, surprised to hear the words come tumbling out of her thoughts. "She was sittin' and watchin' a star shower when the pains first started. She said she wanted to name me somethin' that would always bring back the remembrance of that magical night."

"Must be why it suits you."

Starlight tried to quiet her racing heart, to stay the blush that crept slowly upward. But she lost the battle on both counts. Could he see how quivery it made her to have him right here in her own house? Did he know how she'd hung onto his every word, or that even without looking right at him she could see him in her heart? She sighed unconsciously. Probably the other maidens in the kingdom knew how to be elegant around royalty. They would never blurt out the first thing that came to mind. There was no reason for him to give someone so poor and out of fashion the time of day. Feeling at peace, Starlight made a silent resolution. *Ever after, even if he never sets foot in my home again, he will still fill my dreams.*

The muffled thump of Abel's crutch sounded from the path outside, then from the porch. "Storm's comin' on," he said to Kirby. "Ye're welcome to spend the night in the shed out back. Ain't got no other place."

"Thanks, but no," Kirby said politely. "I'll head for Stull when I get my things together."

"Suit yerself."

Starlight felt the gloom from the sky wrap itself around her.

Chapter Seven

The following morning Kirby enjoyed a splendid breakfast of eggs, bacon, and biscuits with gravy at a window table at Hattie's boardinghouse. Outside, leftover raindrops dripped from the sloped roof, forming rings in the ditch below the eaves. Most of the cloudbank had passed, but the sky showed no indication of clearing soon. Thunder still rumbled occasionally in the distance. As he idly watched rivulets of water funneling down the mountainside and into Bowman's Creek, Kirby found his thoughts drifting back to Noxen. Had Starlight Wells and her father kept warm and dry during the storm, or was the roof on that sorry house as worthless as the rest of it?

"How 'bout some more coffee?" Hattie asked at his elbow.

Kirby smiled into the older woman's pleasant face and twinkling eyes. Despite her petite build, something about her good-hearted nature made people snap to attention. "Thanks. Nobody makes it like you, you know."

"Pshaw! There's plenty of good coffee to be had in this world, but I thank you for the compliment. That brother-in-law of yours on the mend, is he?" Resting a knuckle on the curve of her hip, she lingered with the coffee pot in hand.

"Seems to be. I imagine he'll be back on the job pretty soon."

"That's good news. Glad it wasn't somethin' more serious." Nodding, the chestnut brown bun set high on her head bobbed and she moved to the next red and white checked table and the one after, pouring refills and speaking with patrons along the way.

Kirby took out his watch and checked the hour, then gulped the last of his strong coffee. Time to get over to the schoolhouse. He knew he should have used his free time this morning studying his notes but his mind kept wandering. Finally he gave up and forced himself instead to concentrate on the names and faces of the worshipers with whom he'd become acquainted over the last couple of weeks. He was enjoying getting to know the people of the area who, for the most part, seemed hard-working and decent folk. Removing some change from his pocket, he left it on the table to pay for the meal, then rose and returned to his room to gather his things.

After church—an hour and a half later—Kirby felt elated. For the first time, he'd actually managed to stretch the sermon out to a full half hour. But what was even more gratifying, yet humbling, a newcomer at church had accepted the Lord when Kirby had given the invitation. His heart sent a prayer of thanksgiving heavenward.

The Mountain Springs service also went well later that afternoon, though the following supper hour came up far too quickly to suit Kirby. He had overindulged at noon on pasties, a favorite meat and potato pie, and was not in the least hungry. Nevertheless, not wanting to hurt the feelings of the generous Roberts family, he feigned a show of appetite as he accompanied them home to eat. He gave serious thought to fasting the next day.

Jethro and Ida Mae Roberts, the parents of three lively daughters between the ages of eleven and fourteen, seemed delighted to have a turn to feed the preacher.

Their oldest, a rather shy, plain-looking brunette named Nancy, blushed in rosy profusion whenever Kirby so much as looked her way. He tried not to add to her discomfort, concentrating instead on getting acquainted with Nancy's fidgety younger sisters, Martha and Selina, who giggled and chattered ceaselessly. All the while Kirby sat waiting for supper, the Roberts's fat gray-striped cat, Muffin, climbed all over him shedding its light hair, while its sharp claws pricked him through the layers of his shirt and suit jacket. Time and again he found himself plucking the animal gingerly off his shoulder and nudging him gently away, but none of the girls seemed to notice. When everyone gathered around the table, Kirby somehow managed to stuff down what he'd been served, while the cat rubbed against first one leg, then the other.

"With the sodden trail, an' all," Jethro Roberts said after dessert, as he scratched his balding head, "we'd be right happy to put you up for the night out in the barn."

"Thanks for the kind offer," Kirby answered as he shoved his empty plate away. "But I need to start for home." Politely as he could, he took his leave a few minutes later.

A few tentative raindrops speckled his slicker as Kirby guided Jericho carefully along the road. Memory of the day's giggly echoes and girlish blushes faded into thoughts of timid brown eyes and tawny hair, and an ethereal maiden with a magical name that could belong to no one else.

When Kirby finally reached the clearing that bordered the Wells place, he paused to see if he might catch a glimpse of Starlight. He couldn't explain why, but even with cool rain trickling from the wide brim of his hat, he had to try. He veered over closer to the house.

A light glowed in one of the two upstairs rooms, and when a graceful form in white moved past the window he presumed that bedroom was Starlight's. Wearing an ivory nightdress, her silky hair draping her slim shoulders, she stood poised with an open book extended out in one hand. As Kirby watched in wonderment, she tilted her head slightly, then dipped and twirled, dancing without music. Her dreamy movements enthralled him, until he felt a twinge of guilt for intruding on her private moment. His heart beating faster, he turned the horse toward home.

ða

"That smells mighty good," Dewey Blackburn said, leaning back in the kitchen chair and peering Starlight's way as he rounded up the cards and shuffled them for still another game. He and her father had been playing for what seemed like endless hours, and with each hand Abel seemed to grow more morose.

Starlight ignored the remark and added another pinch of dried basil to the vegetable soup, then gave it a stir with a wooden spoon.

"Yeah, what is it?" Calvin Blackburn asked, thumping into the kitchen. He nosed over toward the stove and with a smirk on his pudgy, mottled face, leaned around Starlight to see into the pot, absently snapping his suspenders with his thumbs. "I'm hungry."

Starlight replaced the lid without comment, then eased herself a comfortable distance from Dewey's older son. Calvin always made a nuisance of himself and she disliked having him underfoot. He was always staring at her and following her every move in a way she found most distasteful. Anyway, wasn't it time for the three of them to be going home?

To her relief, Calvin finally meandered into the next room, snooping into everything he passed along the way until he sank down onto the couch and dangled one leg over the arm with a yawn. His raggy denim jeans were nearly as grimy as his bare feet jutting out of them.

"Might as well stay to supper," Abel said, squelching Starlight's only shred of hope. He turned to her. "We kin add another potato to the pot, cain't we, girl?"

Returning her attention to the soup, Starlight closed her eyes for a second. What a waste of the beautiful vegetables from Sir Kirby's royal garden. After all, he hadn't bestowed his generous offering upon all the peasants in the kingdom. They'd been given to her and her pa, and she'd been trying to make them last as long as possible. *Of course,* she rationalized, *if the Blackburns happened to be chained up in a dungeon somewhere, I might possibly deign to take them a crust of bread and a sip of water once in a while.* But this! She gritted her teeth, stooped to remove the last few carrots and potatoes, then began peeling them. None too gently, she hacked random-sized chunks into the simmering broth, fighting the impulse to bump the entire salt box into it while she was at it.

"Hey, Cal!" Marvin Blackburn's taunting voice carried from outside. "C'mere."

"Aww, what d'ya want?" his brother moaned. "I jest set down."

Not to be ignored, Marv stuck his head around the doorjamb, his protruding ears outlined by the daylight behind him. He grinned, displaying a mouthful of yellowish, overcrowded teeth. "Got somethin' to show ya." He shoved his fingers through his oily, unkempt hair, leaving indentations among the blondish strands.

Calvin gave a deep sigh, then got up with reluctance and tromped out. In moments, rakish laughter sounded from behind the shed.

Starlight could only imagine what they were doing. Probably plucking feathers from some poor, squawking chicken or annoying another unsuspecting woodland creature. Many a kitten or stray dog had mysteriously disappeared, thanks to the Blackburn boys. Moving to the cupboard, she took down some soup bowls, making sure only she and Pa would use Ma's pretty ones. With a glance toward the table she caught Dewey's fixed stare. Starlight looked away and busied herself gathering silverware.

When at last it was time to eat, Starlight stared in disbelief at the ensuing free-for-all, with Cal and Marvin grabbing the plate of biscuits and slapping butter on them. It was impossible to talk above their slurping. She couldn't help but wonder how their mother would have felt. There wasn't a single shred of politeness between the two of them.

Marvin sidled up to Starlight afterward while she washed the dishes and brushed against her. "Why don't you an' me go out behind the shed?" he whispered in her ear.

Sure of his intentions, Starlight straightened and narrowed her eyes. "Leave me alone," she hissed under her breath.

"You botherin' the gal, son?" Dewey asked.

"Naw."

"Well, git away, then, an' leave her be. Go round up that brother of yers. It's time we was headin' on home anyways." He gave Starlight a suggestive smile as Marvin went to do as he was told. "Thanks fer the invite." Then with a clap on her pa's back, he plunked on his worn floppy hat. "Remember what we talked about, hear?"

To Starlight, the remark sounded less than casual. And so did the look he and her pa exchanged. Uneasiness pulsed through her.

Pa's only response was a grunt, then Dewey left.

After the sounds of their old wagon faded into the distance, Starlight finished wiping the dishes and putting them away. She crossed to the far side of the couch where Pa had put the partially finished dress for Mrs. Browning. Starlight had been working on it at the table before the Blackburns arrived and she hoped to set in the sleeves before retiring for the night.

As she picked up her sewing, her gaze fell upon the length of lace trim atop the pile. Her eyes widened in dismay. A coffee-colored stain marred most of it and the moisture had spotted the raspberry bodice as well. The stain was fresh and Starlight was fairly sure she'd be able to sponge it out of the dress fabric with cold water. But the trim was another story. "Pa! How did this get dirty?"

He shrugged. "Cal must've spilled his coffee, I guess. That's about where he was settin'."

"It's ruined," Starlight said ruefully. "Ruined. Now I'll have to get some new lace before I can finish it." Her lips in a tight line, she went back to the kitchen and took down the jelly jar. It felt surprisingly light. She peered inside, then turned and leaned her spine against the cupboard as she met her father's eyes.

"Had to pay Dewey some o' what I owe. An' that wasn't hardly enough to start."

"*What?*" Starlight stared incredulously at him. "You took it all?"

Abel slammed a hand down on the table. "Shut up, girl. I don't want no lip from ya. I keep clothes on yer back, don't I?"

Starlight's mouth gaped at his unnatural outburst and tears sprang to her eyes. She felt herself tremble and mustered as much control as she could. "But how are we supposed to buy food, Pa?" she asked in a small voice.

He let out a huff. "I dunno. With the egg money, I s'pose."

"Eggs. They don't bring in but a few cents each, did you know that?" Starlight put a hand to her forehead. "Oh, this is awful. Awful! Without more lace, I can't even finish my sewing. I can't go to Mrs. Browning and tell her I've ruined her new dress!" Despite the struggle to maintain her composure, her brimming tears spilled over. "I can't take care of everything by myself, Pa. I need help." Starlight hated the way her voice shook, but she felt like everything had been dumped on her shoulders a long time ago. She was weary of the hopelessness that faced her day after day. Pa needed to stop his card playing and find a job. He wasn't completely helpless.

Abel had the grace to look guilty as he rubbed his unshaven jaw. "I know, girl, I know. But I'm in a pickle. It was all I could think of."

Her misery did not waver as she kept her gaze fixed on him.

He shifted in his seat and took a deep breath. "Dewey's come up with a sort of suggestion I'm considerin'."

Starlight blinked slowly. Nothing that man could come up with would ever benefit anyone but himself, of that she was certain. Whatever it was, she would have no part of it. She didn't even want to hear it.

"From now on," Abel stated, "you treat him good."

A feeling of dread clutched at her throat and she did not respond. Determinedly, Starlight hiked her chin and dried her cheeks, then went to the sink and pumped some cold water into a bowl. She plunged the lace into it to soak. With a moist, clean rag, she sponged away the spots marring the raspberry frock. When her efforts showed success, she carried the materials wordlessly upstairs to her room and closed the door.

Chapter Eight

Near the end of the following week, Kirby drove Cook's wagon toward Noxen, its bed containing lumber and supplies for a good day's work. Last time he'd been at the Wells house he had measured the slats in the banister so he could cut proper replacements for the missing ones. So far Abel hadn't put up an argument about having someone fixing things, and, in fact, he seemed moderately thankful he didn't have to expend his own energy on it. Kirby made up his mind he'd keep doing whatever was needed until the man put a stop to it, or until the house was a fit place for habitation, whichever came first. Until now he'd been limited to bringing along only what would fit inside his saddlebags or be tied behind them, so progress had been slow. Hopefully after today the improvements would be more noticeable.

Only some nearly transparent mare's tail clouds feathered the blue Pennsylvania sky. Kirby had been looking forward to this jaunt since the rainy spell. He kept assuring himself that it was gratifying to be helping out, that he'd be doing the same for anyone in such desperate need. To keep a damper on his enthusiasm, which seemed to be increasing with each passing mile, he picked up the Bible from the seat beside him and read a few Psalms.

❧

Starlight, momentarily lost in a daydream that she was feeding the royal pheasants instead of common laying hens, curtsied a greeting to an imaginary silver knight. The crimson plume in his helmet swayed gently as he emerged with a smile from behind the lilac bush, leading his magnificent velvet-draped horse. "Good day, milord," she said breathlessly, pausing to allow his response. What she heard instead was the sound of approaching wagon wheels crunching over the gravel. Jerking her head around, dried corn still clutched in her hand, she looked into the distance and recognized Kirby Mitchell. Her heart skipped a beat.

A chicken brushed past her just then and its tail feathers tickled her leg.

Starlight suddenly remembered herself. She dipped into the sack she held and scattered a handful of corn, watching the clucking birds flock to it and gobble it up. Her own pulse fluttered as if she were one of the skittish hens.

"Morning, Starlight," Kirby called out as he drew up and stopped the rig. He jumped down easily. "Your pa around?"

She shook her head, afraid to trust herself to speak at first. She cleared her throat. "He went out checkin' traps for a spell."

"Ah." Kirby nodded.

He didn't look in the least put off by her announcement, she noticed. She might have sworn he nearly smiled. Frowning in puzzlement, she quickly tossed the rest of the chicken feed and stepped outside the enclosure, fastening the newly mended gate behind her. She saw that Kirby was already unloading things from the back of his wagon. For a few golden seconds she allowed her eyes to wander over him, drinking in his maroon plaid shirt, slightly worn jeans, and shiny boots. She cast a disparaging glance over her old brown and gray striped skirt and off-white shirtwaist. How she wished she had put on her green calico this morning.

Kirby turned and smiled. He held something out to her.

Starlight took the slightly worn braided rug and shyly met his eyes.

"Hope you don't mind a castoff. My sister just made herself some new ones and was getting rid of this."

"It's real purty," she whispered, unfolding it so she could see its size. It would go nice in front of the sink and would be soft to stand on when she was doing dishes, even warm in the winter. Unconsciously, she hugged it to herself.

"She doesn't need these curtains, either," Kirby said, "if you'd like to have them, of course."

Starlight stared in disbelief at the barely used dimity panels, two pairs of them. Crisp and white, they had tiny embroidered lavender violets along the sides and bottom edges. She'd never seen such lovely things, and for someone to be discarding them. . . . She had to fight back her tears.

"Jessica's always sewing things," Kirby explained. "Especially when she's in the family way. She whips through the whole house with new colors everywhere. Kind of a quirk of hers. Think they'll fit your windows?"

Not knowing whether to laugh or cry, she only nodded. "I'll go see." As she turned and floated inside, she heard Kirby unloading lumber and stacking it by the porch.

The rooster will crow any minute and awaken me from this wondrous dream, Starlight assured herself, but until that happened she would enjoy every minute. She pushed one of the kitchen chairs over to the window by the sink and climbed up onto the seat. Her fingers shook as she slid the almost colorless gingham panels off the rod and replaced them with the loveliest curtains she'd ever laid eyes on. They were even prettier than Mrs. Browning's yellow ruffled ones which Starlight had secretly coveted. There were even embroidered lavender strips to tie them back in the middle. She'd go find some nails later.

The second pair fit perfectly on the other kitchen window by the back door. Once the floor had been swept in front of the sink, she would lay the new rug in place. Smiling, Starlight stepped back and memorized the glorious sight.

"Hey, they look just right," Kirby said from the doorway. "I'll get some tacks and fix the sides for you."

Before Starlight could tell him he didn't have to bother, he was gone and back. With a few taps, he put nails in the right places and she slipped the ties onto each panel.

"Perfect," he said, smiling broadly.

She had never seen him smile so completely, and she wasn't at all surprised that his incredible blue eyes now held the leaping flames of an inferno. She smiled back. "It's gettin' near noon and you must be hungry. I'd best be startin' on dinner."

"I brought more vegetables from Jessie's garden," he said. "She grows way too many, another of her quirks. And there's some canned fruit she's put up that needs to be used. I'll go bring the stuff in."

Suddenly Starlight remembered there would have been nothing to feed him except eggs. Not even a crust of bread. But when he strode back inside with a bounty of vegetables, canned fruit, jams, fresh bread, a smoked ham, and even a sweet butter cake, the entire situation was reversed. For the first time ever, she couldn't decide what to fix. She nearly laughed aloud.

Pa wasn't one to accept what he called charity, Starlight knew, but when Sir Kirby explained he had more than he needed, she felt it was the neighborly thing to do to accept it. But all the same, she planned on hiding some of it before Pa got home, in case he'd be mad.

As Starlight busied herself preparing the noon meal, she was conscious of Kirby's presence just outside while he replaced all three of the porch steps with the new boards he'd brought with him, then tackled the banister. The midday sun intensified the July temperature and cicadas droned periodically in the background. Taking two of Ma's pretty plates out of the cupboard, she put a lettuce leaf on each one, then sliced hard-boiled egg rounds and arranged them in vertical rows with edges slightly overlapped, the way Mrs. Browning once had fixed for her when she'd spent a day in town mending for the widow. Some thick slices of ham and buttered bread, carrot and celery sticks, and bowls of canned plums completed the fare, with generous portions of the butter cake on the side. She filled two tall glasses with water and hoped Sir Kirby would find her efforts acceptable.

After assessing the table from a few steps away, Starlight brushed her hands on her apron and took a deep breath. What if he preferred to eat outdoors instead of having to stop completely and come inside? Momentary panic filled her. Hesitantly she went to the open door and cleared her throat. "Dinner's ready."

Kirby hadn't needed the announcement. He'd been listening to her fussing about inside for some time and felt her presence at the doorway before she'd spoken. He was glad for the welcome break and also famished. "I'll wash up and be right in."

Entering the house moments later, he couldn't help noticing how cheery the place looked with the new additions. Starlight had gathered some wildflowers and glasses of them graced the table and the windowsills. Her cheeks glowed as he took the chair opposite her. She lowered her lashes.

Kirby debated for an instant. "Would you mind if I said grace? It looks so good I'd like to thank the Lord for it."

At the shake of her head, he bowed his and clasped his hands. "Dear Heavenly Father, we thank You for Your kindness to us and for this beautiful day. We ask Your blessing upon this home and the bountiful food You've so graciously provided. May You keep Your hand upon Starlight and her father in the days to come. In Jesus' name."

When Kirby looked up, he saw a strange expression clouding Starlight's face. He cut a piece of ham and smiled. "Something wrong?"

"Does God really hear your prayers?" she asked. She lifted her fork, but merely played with her food.

"Absolutely."

"And God knows about us? Me and Pa?"

"Sure does. I talk to Him about you every day."

"Why would you do that?"

Her simple sincerity touched him deeply, and so did the questions in her eyes. "Because I pray for everyone who's important to me, and that includes you and your pa."

Starlight smiled. "Ma used to talk about God and about Jesus when I was little. Even sang songs to me from church." She raised an egg slice to her mouth and bit it in half.

"Ever go to church with her?" he asked.

She nodded and swallowed. "But Pa won't let me now. He was different after her passin'."

"That's one reason I pray for him," Kirby said gently. "God can heal the things that hurt and make people bitter. He wants everyone to know and love Him."

"What do you tell God about me?" she asked softly, her brown eyes wide and shining.

Kirby thought to himself. He prayed all kinds of things about Starlight Wells. That God would send someone into her life who would take her away from all the drudgery. That He'd make things easier for her, surround her with beauty, take away whatever made her seek a haven high in a maple tree.

Most of all he prayed that she'd come to know Jesus as her Savior, be clothed in His righteousness, and know His peace, His joy. "That you need a friend," he finally answered.

Starlight felt warmth surge through her. She couldn't imagine anything more wonderful than the handsome man who this minute sat at her table. Until a few weeks ago she hadn't been aware that he even existed in this world; now she no longer felt afraid when she saw him coming. He filled her dreams day and night, but it was not fear that made her hands tremble. All she knew was that having a friend couldn't be better than what she felt right now.

But as she watched him eat, she knew that a glorious and daring knight like Sir Kirby Mitchell probably had a legion of beautiful maidens awaiting his rounds. Once he finished performing his good deeds here, he'd probably not give another thought to a poor dull-witted girl like herself. Accepting the reality of her situation, she had to force herself to enjoy the lovely butter cake that tasted as light as a cloud.

Chapter Nine

The house seemed strangely empty after Kirby drove off. With her hands cushioning the base of her spine, Starlight leaned against the doorjamb and watched after him until the wagon disappeared over the rise. Never had he spent so much time with her. Never had they been together when Pa wasn't around.

Pa! She needed to hide some of the food Sir Kirby had bestowed upon them. Hurrying to the sideboard, she put half of the fresh vegetables into another burlap sack and set them behind the woodbox where the broom stood against the wall, all but shielding them from view. Three quart jars of canned fruit slipped easily behind the bowls on a bottom shelf in the cupboard; another pair she took upstairs and hid in her closet. That left just two she'd have to explain. The ham wouldn't be difficult. After all, it was a small one, and since he'd come for the whole day he'd brought it for his dinner, obviously expecting to share it. Noticing the two jars of preserves still in sight, she tucked the peach ones among her lye soap and rags under the sink, leaving just the strawberry out for use. Satisfied that the remainder looked more like neighborly offerings than charity, she brushed her hands on her apron and set the table for supper.

&

Kirby whistled absently as Cook's horse, Dusty, clopped over the rutted road toward Alderson. The day had passed swiftly. Thinking of what he'd accomplished at the Wells place made the ache in his weary muscles lessen. He shifted on the hard seat. A few more such workdays and he wouldn't have to go back there anymore.

That thought brought a jolt. He couldn't remember a time in his life when he'd felt so useful, so satisfied. Though his woodworking business drew regular contracts as new people moved into the area and built homes, he knew that if he hadn't had a shop, folks would have found somewhere else to buy furniture and cabinets, possibly even build their own. Most of his savings had gone into his own house, fixing it the way Estelle had wanted it. Now, considering tuition, lodging, and all, it could take several years before he'd acquire money enough to go away to theological school.

He wondered if the Lord had other plans for him. As much as he'd enjoyed filling in for Cook, he'd heard talk in the settlements of organizing real churches and obtaining ordained pastors to live there and be part of things, men with degrees from colleges. The need for circuit-riding preachers was diminishing. But a person could be a witness for the Lord no matter where he was or what he did. Maybe carpentry was his calling, and being around for Jessica and Cook, being an uncle to James and Betsy. Maybe even someday provide them with some cousins.

He chuckled to himself. He'd pretty much given up on the idea of being a family man now, since Estelle. Kirby took off his hat and raked his fingers through his hair. Surprisingly, when he'd thought of her this time there had been no ache, no longing, not even that familiar deep hurt that once twisted him all up inside. Only a peaceful kind of emptiness, one somehow transitory. He'd found other things to fill his life besides thoughts of marriage to her. He was beginning to feel needed again. A warm satisfaction flowed through him.

Sweet pictures of Starlight Wells replaced the void of unfulfilled yesterdays. How those huge eyes of hers had glowed at the sight of used curtains and a discarded rug. Kirby had to admit the new furnishings had alleviated some of the bleak cheerlessness of what she and her father called a home. But it needed more. So much more.

Then an uneasy feeling made itself known. Would Abel Wells rebel at the sight of so many improvements all at once? Would he take offense at the offerings of food and a few belongings another had no need for anymore? Kirby hoped he hadn't brought trouble on Starlight with all his good intentions. After all, he wasn't trying to make her life worse. Perhaps he should have hung around in Noxen until her pa had come home. He could have offered a proper explanation, one Abel would understand and even welcome.

The sound of a logging train drew near as a steam engine chugged around the curve, hauling pine and hemlock from the camps down to Wilkes-Barre and other parts of Wyoming Valley. Halting the wagon, Kirby waved to the engineer while it passed, then continued on in the fading light.

When silence settled around him again, he remembered Starlight sitting across the table from him, her expressive face aglow with a sort of shy delight over her new possessions. She was such a strange, innocent creature. She probably hadn't had a gift of any kind from anyone in a long time.

Kirby wished he knew a young man around her age who could befriend her. He went over the entire list of lads he'd become acquainted with at the camps, but not one seemed right. They were either too young or already wed with families of their own. Of course, if she weren't so young herself, perhaps even *he* might give serious thought to being that friend. But twenty-six was too old for her. Starlight didn't appear to be more than fifteen or sixteen. Seventeen, maybe. Her pa would certainly object to having a grown man coming to call on his daughter. No, that was out of the question entirely.

But he still had some things to rectify before he'd ride off and never go back. No one—especially someone who was able to find beauty in even the most drab situations, the way Starlight did—should have to live under the conditions she endured so matter-of-factly. Kirby wouldn't be completely satisfied until he did more to make her life better. And he definitely wouldn't make an exit without telling her about Jesus. That was his main priority anyway. Starlight appeared to be showing interest along that line, and his working around the place merely supplied opportunities for him to talk to her about spiritual matters.

Yes, that was it, he surmised with satisfaction. He would be her friend as long as he could. But after that. . . .Somehow Kirby didn't want to think about after that.

⁊⦿

Starlight trudged up Mrs. Browning's gray painted porch steps and hesitated at the front door. Today the gables and turrets resembled the face of a prison. She imagined herself shut up for a long time, all alone, with no company but the rats that came to nibble on whatever crumbs might fall from the dried crust of her bread rations. She'd never hear another human voice until she was old and gray and feeble.

She cast a forlorn glance down at the ruined lace clutched in one hand. Her insides had felt quivery all the way into town and a dull ache began in her head. How was she going to explain? Her mind went over one story after another, then rejected the lot. She couldn't imagine Sir Kirby lying to anyone. She'd tell the truth and get it over with. Taking a deep breath of resignation, she rapped on the frame of the screen door.

All too soon the widow appeared. "Why, Starlight, dear." A look of surprise wrinkled her forehead as she stood there in a pretty butternut house dress with chocolate piping on the bodice. "I wasn't expecting you so soon. Surely you couldn't have finished that new gown so quickly."

"No, ma'am. Almost did, but. . . ." Starlight swallowed a lump and extended her hand, displaying the spoiled trim. "I'm dreadful sorry. But coffee got spilled on this, and it won't come out. I soaked it in cold water for a couple days, but it didn't help." She felt the heat of a blush stain her face all the way up to her hairline.

Mrs. Browning took the lace and perused the damage. "Well," she said with a shake of her head and a patient smile, "accidents happen. We'll just have to get another length of it."

Starlight couldn't believe her eyes and ears. Regarding the widow's expression thoroughly, she felt herself relax. "I'm dreadful sorry," she repeated. "You can take the cost of it out of my earnin's."

"Nonsense. Why, I won't hear of any such thing. It isn't as if you dumped something on purpose to ruin it, now, was it?"

"No, ma'am," Starlight said most sincerely. "It wasn't even me."

"Well, then," the woman said, her kind green eyes smiling, "all the more reason just to replace it. I'm quite certain I have a little more of this same pattern right inside. Go sit and enjoy the nice breeze, dear. I'll be right back." Swiveling around on her gray leather heels, she closed the door.

Starlight heard her soft footsteps fade away. Aware of the lighter feeling in her chest, she stepped over to the white wicker chairs and admired the rich floral needlepoint cushions adorning them. In minutes she heard Mrs. Browning returning.

"Yes, how fortunate," the woman said, coming outside and taking the other chair. She held out a new piece of lace trim. "I had this upstairs with some other things. It should be enough, don't you think?"

Starlight unraveled it and nodded. "Just fine. I sure do thank you, ma'am, that you weren't mad at me."

With an indulgent smile, the widow's countenance softened even more. "After all the wonderful work you've done for me since I first heard of your skills, how could I hold one little accident against you? Especially one that wasn't your fault. That wouldn't be very Christian."

"No, ma'am, I s'pose not." She studied the older woman. "Christian has somethin' to do with God, doesn't it?"

"Yes, dear," Mrs. Browning said, patting one of Starlight's hands where it rested on the arm of the chair. "It has everything to do with God. Being a Christian means I believe in His Son, Jesus, who died to take away my sins."

Starlight nibbled her lip. "But someone like you wouldn't be needin' help from sinnin'. You're good already."

A smile broadened the widow's face. "Believe me, my dear, no one who ever lived on this earth was ever good enough not to need God's forgiveness. It isn't the bad a person does that makes him a sinner. We sin because we have the sin nature passed on to us from Adam, way back in the beginning, in the Garden of Eden. But God sent His only Son, Jesus, to die for us, and the blood He shed for us washes away the stain of our sins."

Trying to fathom the strange words, Starlight stared absently. "Guess I need to think about that for a spell. I do thank you, though, for tellin' it to me. I wonder about thin's sometimes."

"Most people think about God sooner or later, dear. I've been praying for you for some time."

Starlight smiled in wonder. "Somebody else said that to me too. God must be gettin' tired of hearin' my name."

"Oh, no. He never tires of us. He loves us all." The soft wind stirred loose silver and brunette hairs along her neckline and ears.

The thought, though comforting in some ways, seemed hard to take in all at one time. Starlight looked at the widow in puzzlement for several minutes, then rose. "Well, I have to be gettin' on home before Pa starts to worryin' over me. I do thank you for the new trim. I'll have your dress quick as a wink. That's a promise."

"I believe you will, my dear. I'm looking forward to it."

With a smile, Starlight turned and began walking toward the steps.

"Wait, child," Mrs. Browning said quietly from right behind her. "Before you go, I wanted to give you something."

She paused and looked back over her shoulder.

Opening the screen door, the widow reached inside and picked up two folded pieces of yardage, one a medium blue floral cotton, the other an off-white dimity. "I've had these forever but I haven't been able to decide what to do with them. There's not nearly enough fabric for a dress for me but I thought perhaps you might be able to make something for yourself. A skirt and shirtwaist, perhaps, or something else you might prefer. They're going to waste not being sewn into something useful." She held them out hopefully.

Starlight assessed the goods incredulously. New material? For her? Aware that her mouth was gaping, she took the proffered gift as her eyes swam with tears. "I—I don't know what to s—say. I never—" With a sob, she grabbed the widow's elegant form in a hug. "Oh, thank you. Thank you."

Mrs. Browning blinked quickly and cleared her throat. "You're most welcome, child. One of these times when you come to town, I expect to see you wearing something real pretty of your own. Do you hear?"

"Oh, yes, ma'am. I will. I truly will. I promise." Starlight skipped down the steps toward the homeward path, her steps made lighter by a carefree heart.

Chapter Ten

It was all Starlight could do the next two days to put the finishing touches to Mrs. Browning's new dress. All the while she worked her eyes returned time and again to the fabric the widow had given her for herself. Starlight couldn't remember the last time she'd had something new of her own. Occasionally someone would pass on a hand-me-down or discard an item no longer in fashion, and even those seemed new—but this! She couldn't wait to sew the blue floral goods into a beautiful skirt. Already she knew which pattern she'd use to make the soft ivory dimity shirtwaist, one that would be fit to be worn anywhere. She'd never known such happiness.

She paused in her stitching and stared out her bedroom window at the distant cloud puffs. Mrs. Browning's words had hung in Starlight's mind as well. Pa's bad feelings about Christians didn't make sense to her. Both Mrs. Browning and Sir Kirby spoke easily about knowing God, and they were the kindest people Starlight had ever met. Both were thoughtful and generous and gave of what they had to help someone else, without expecting anything in return. Both of them assured her that God loved her and Pa and wanted them to know Him. A warm feeling flowed through her just knowing that two such wonderful people were praying for her. Surely God had meant for people to be decent and good and joyful, not all scowly and vexed like Pa. But the idea of Jesus dying on a cross was hard to understand, and so was the part about sins and forgiveness.

Coming finally to the last stitch, Starlight knotted the thread and bit it off with her teeth. She held the dress at arm's length and scrutinized her handiwork, then went to her dressing table mirror and held the garment up to herself. The silky raspberry taffeta would look so pretty with Mrs. Browning's shiny brown hair and green eyes. The pattern was the latest style, and the widow's hand-crocheted lace made it extra special. Satisfied with the finished product, Starlight ran downstairs to put the iron on the stove to heat. Tonight she could cut out her new skirt! What a lovely week this had been!

ॐ

Abel swallowed a mouthful of moonshine slowly, letting the whiskey burn its way down his throat. He couldn't have lost the last dozen hands of poker, not when he'd been doing so well. How could his luck have turned on him all of a sudden? He was so close to getting on top of things and now he wouldn't so much as break even. He knew that by rights he should have quit an hour ago, before things soured on him. But feeling cocky and overconfident, he decided to make up to Starlight for taking the money she'd worked so hard for. Only Dewey had that uncanny knack for turning up one more ace all the time. Now Abel was in the hole and had to keep on playing until he hit another winning streak. There was no other way.

Dewey shuffled back inside from the outhouse, a shifty expression on his face. One side of his mouth curled upward as though the recent run of good luck was his due. "How 'bout a couple more hands?" he asked, grabbing another bottle from the cupboard and plunking it down on the table.

Abel kneaded his jowls, the stubble on his chin pricking his hand. "Don't see that there's much point, but might as well. Things gotta turn my way again sooner or later."

"I 'spect." Dewey shuffled the cards again and dealt, then set down the remainder of the deck. With his thumb he fanned out the ones he held and perused them. "Y'know, that gal of yers could help out."

Turning his eyes slowly upward, Abel kept his expression even. "I know. Ya told me b'fore."

"Well, like I said," Dewey continued, "I haveta hire a laundry woman in town to wash our clothes, an' that widow lady from down by the tannery comes by once't a month to sweep out the place. Way I figger it, Starry could do them things easy. It'd start payin' on that debt ya owe."

"The girl's got enough to do with her sewin' and lookin' after our place. An' I don't want her walkin' by herself in the woods to git here."

"She wouldn't haveta *come* here if she *lived* here." His shrewd gaze leveled at Abel. "I'd do it all proper, a'course. I'd be willin' to marry up with her."

Abel slapped his cards down. "Now where would ya git a fool idea like that? Ya got a son older'n her!" Shaking his head, he gave his pal a look of disbelief and stood. "I had enough card playin' fer one day. I'm gittin' home."

With a shrug, Dewey grimaced. "I think ya need to consider it. I got heavy bills of my own, y'know. An' I need the new roofin' bought an put on. Place leaks like a sieve ever'time it rains."

Abel gritted his teeth so hard they hurt. He grabbed his crutch and stomped out the door without looking back. He might be bad off, but just thinking about what Dewey was saying made him sick. He'd have to come up with some other idea. Star was the only thing he had that was worth anything, and Dewey Blackburn knew it.

But an even more nauseating thought gnawed at his brain. Starlight might be the only way out of this mess.

❧

The sound of hammering echoed from the upstairs of Kirby's house as

Jessica let herself in the kitchen door. No longer able to navigate the steps with ease or grace, she ambled clumsily toward the source, pausing at the top to catch her breath. "Kirby?" she called out.

"In here," he answered from the front bedroom.

She found her brother on his knees surrounded by stacks of assorted sizes of lumber as he measured along one of the boards and drew a cutting line.

He looked up as she entered. "You should have hollered, Jess. I'd have come down. You don't need to be going up the steps these days."

She smiled patronizingly. "I'm fine. This isn't my first experience with budding motherhood, you know."

"All the more reason to use caution," he said with exaggerated sincerity. "You're no spring chicken."

"Oh, thanks!" she gasped in mock horror. "I needed a reminder." Her smile dismissed her harsh tone. Looking around the large, plain room, she noted that the once open closet now had a serviceable door, a new sill graced the side by side windows, and a good-sized dresser was taking shape. "What's all this?"

Kirby smiled sheepishly as he stood and brushed off his knees. "I had some time on my hands. You were right, the place was looking pathetic. Thought it was about time I did something besides feel sorry for myself." He set down his pencil and measuring tape. "Where are the kids?"

"Outside tagging after Cook while he tends the cow and chickens." She moved to one of the windows and stared at her own home across the wagon road, noticing that the red and white roses entwining her arbor were especially lovely this year. "He feels quite fit today, actually."

"That's good to hear."

"Yes. He's anxious to get back to his preaching. I wouldn't be surprised if he were to start in again this Sunday and relieve you of the burden of filling in. He's really appreciated your help, though, I'm sure he's told you enough times."

Kirby nodded, shrugging off a sinking feeling. He knew that his brother-in-law had improved over the past week or two. Most of the soreness in Cook's shoulder had dissipated and he had almost his normal mobility. Truthfully, it would be a relief for Kirby not to have to go back to the lumber camps again. As much as he'd enjoyed meeting and getting to know the church families there, and reveling in the lofty position of temporary pastor, he'd felt inadequate without formal training. He harbored serious doubts that the ministry was truly his calling after all. It seemed that he'd used the opportunity for selfish reasons instead, as a way to hide from his own life. But with the realization that he wouldn't be going back again, a profound emptiness invaded his heart. One for which he had no explanation.

Jessica turned from the window and met his gaze. The sunlight behind her made a bright halo of her hair as she stood silhouetted in her yellow linen dress. "Will half past five be all right for supper?"

"Hmm? Oh, yeah. Whatever you say."

When the supper hour drew near, Kirby followed the delicious aroma of roast beef wafting his way from Jessica's house. Betsy and James burst out the open door at the sound of his footsteps coming up their walk.

"Uncle Kirby!" Betsy latched onto one leg, hugging so hard there was no circulation in it for several seconds.

"I wish you'd come before," James announced, "when Daddy and I took out the kite."

"Sorry, squirt," Kirby said, giving the reddish waves atop the boy's head a teasing ruffle. "I was busy over at the house."

Betsy let go and looked up at him, her guileless face alight with love. "Are you busy now, Uncle Kirby? Would you read us a story?"

With a chuckle, Kirby bent and hugged his blue-eyed niece. "I'm never too busy for you, princess. Even if I were doing something real important, I'd stop and read to you."

"Oh, goody," she said. Slipping her tiny hand inside his huge one, she tugged him toward the door and inside, then eagerly shoved him toward the couch in the parlor.

"Mama," James said, racing past them and into the kitchen. "Uncle Kirby's going to read to us. Where's the Jesus storybook?"

"By the bottom step, remember?" she answered. "We were going to take it upstairs for your bedtime."

"Oh, yeah. I forgot."

"Tell your uncle only one story now. Supper's almost ready."

"I will." Making a beeline for the stairwell, James grabbed the worn volume and then raced to occupy the vacant spot on Kirby's other side, holding out the book.

"Which one would you like?" Kirby asked, taking it from James. He looked from one to the other.

"Jesus waking up the dead girl," Betsy said.

"No, not that one, Bets," James said authoritatively. "The one about Naaman, the leper."

Kirby chuckled. "Tell you what. We'll read Betsy's now, and then after supper we'll read yours. How about that?"

"She's always first," James grumbled.

"That's because she's a girl, and girls are special to us men. Someday you'll find that out for yourself. Now, let's see. . .we'll see if we can find hers." Flipping through the pages until he came to it, Kirby settled back against the sofa and began reading as the children sat enthralled.

An hour later, after stuffing himself with Jessica's tender roast and a generous slice of apple pie, Kirby noticed an odd expression on his sister's rounded face across the table. He frowned slightly in question.

She tossed her head. "Do you suppose one of you two handsome men might consider going for the doctor?" she said breathlessly. "I thought it was my imagination a while ago, but now I'm pretty sure the baby's about to make his or her appearance tonight."

Cook went ashen and gulped down a mouthful. "*What?*" Springing to his feet, he shoved his chair out with the backs of his legs. "I'll go right now."

"Oh, no you won't, Papa," Kirby said teasingly. Only a step behind his brother-in-law, he clamped a hand on Cook's shoulder, halting his flight. "You stay with the little mother, here. I'll go and get the doc."

"Thanks," Jessica breathed. "And when you get back, would you mind taking James and Betsy with you overnight?"

"Glad to." He smiled at the children. "While I'm gone, you two go get your night clothes and some clean ones for tomorrow, so you'll be ready when I get back."

"And the storybook," James hinted.

Kirby shook his head in amazement. "And the storybook."

The children were so excited at the opportunity of spending the night over at "Uncle Kirby's," he doubted they'd ever unwind when he took them to his house. Ignoring his own concern over Jessica in labor, he'd ridden them horseback on his hands and knees, read nearly half the book to them, and even played hide and seek for a little while. Finally after plying them with some of Jessica's ginger snaps and a glass of milk, some huge yawns overcame their determination to stay awake as sleepy eyes fought to blink open again.

Asleep at last on cots in his extra bedroom, they looked angelic and peaceful. *What a pair,* Kirby thought as he gazed at them. He now had more respect than before for his sister and brother-in-law. To think they did this every day! Closing the bedroom door softly, Kirby stretched the kinks out of his back and realized he hadn't been this tired in a long time.

Or this happy.

Chapter Eleven

Starlight's shaking fingers fumbled as she buttoned her pretty ivory shirt-waist, then tugged her new gathered skirt over her head. As it settled around her, she adjusted it so the button on the waistband would fasten at one side. Smoothing the folds, she stepped over to her dressing table. Even with the crack in the mirror the reflection that met her eyes looked like a stranger. She'd soaped her hair twice that morning and rinsed it with rainwater, the way Mrs. Browning had once told her when Starlight had commented on the woman's shiny hair. Now it lay smooth as gold over her shoulders. Giving it one last stroke with Ma's old hairbrush, she picked up the ribbon she'd made from the selvage of the blue fabric and tied her hair back at her neck. Then, sure that she'd never looked finer in her whole life, Starlight flew down the stairs.

"Where do you think you're goin'?" Abel asked, his narrowed eyes taking in everything at once.

"Nowhere, Pa. Just outside is all." She smiled nervously, then twirled, her full skirt flaring around her. "Isn't it just the purtiest thing you ever saw?"

His scowl looked forced as he nodded. "Should save it fer special."

Starlight couldn't imagine anything more special than being dressed like all the other young maidens in the kingdom. *And it was Sunday!* Sir Kirby was sure to notice when he passed by on his way to his preachering. "I will, Pa. But I want to wear it for a little while first." With another smile, she raced outside.

Abel filled his lungs and watched her go. He'd never seen it before, taken up with all his sorrows, but there was a lot of Josie in her. The way her hair shone, the way her eyes lit on pretty things, the way she smiled. *She was all growed up already,* he realized soberly. One of these days he'd be chasing boys off the place with a stick. The thought gnawed at his gut. He'd done wrong by his daughter. She deserved better than this miserable life, a hundred times better than Dewey Blackburn and his sons put together! He should have seen to her schooling, like Josie wanted. He should have been a better pa.

The steady ache in his head persisted, tightened, then took to throbbing. He needed a drink. Last night he'd been in such a rage over Dewey's outrageous proposition that he'd poured what little whiskey he had all over the dirt outside. It had been years since he'd thought with a clear head, and now it hurt to do so. Hobbling over to the stove, Abel filled a blue metal mug with strong coffee and drained half of it in one gulp. Then he maneuvered back to the table and slumped down onto a chair.

Starlight, pausing as she gathered daisies and black-eyed susans, strained to listen. Yes, there it was, the sound of hoofbeats. She tried to calm the incessant throbbing of her heart. What would Kirby think when he saw her? She tapped the toe of one shoe nervously against the grass. He should find her in some elegant but natural pose when he passed, not as if she'd been waiting for him for hours. Brushing a tendril of hair away from her eyes, she reclined ever so gracefully against the nearest tree and raised the bouquet to her nose to inhale its sweet perfume.

"Good morning, Miss Wells," a strange voice called as the rider drew near.

Her heart stopped. She peered around the tree trunk. There was a man dressed like a preacher; she'd seen him often over the past months from high in her tree. But it wasn't Kirby.

"Just passing through on my way to the church meeting at Stull. Tell your father Reverend Singleton sends his best." Nudging back his black hat with the edge of one finger, he nodded and continued on his way.

Starlight swallowed hard. Fighting hot tears, she cast a disparaging look down at her fashionable attire and raised her chin. She drew a shaky breath and walked woodenly inside. Passing by her pa on her way up to her room, she knew he was right. Pretty clothes should be saved for special occasions. She would look back on this Sunday as one of the blackest days of her life.

All those hours I'd spent sewing something pretty so I could look special for one brief moment were wasted, she reflected bitterly. Someone as grand as Kirby Mitchell could never be happy with one as lowly as she. With grim determination, Starlight slipped out of her new things and hung them carefully on two nails in her open closet, then pulled on her faded yellow gingham dress. She didn't need the ribbon either, so she tugged it off and shook out her hair before returning downstairs.

Bravely, Starlight cleaned up the breakfast dishes in silence and swept out the kitchen. Then she tended the chickens. When Abel ambled off on his crutch to check the traps, she climbed up into her castle in the old maple tree and sobbed her heart out.

Sir Kirby was dead, that was it. He had to be. After all, knights faced the peril of battle every day, from evil soldiers to lurking dragons. She imagined him stretched out on a velvet-draped slab in his shining armor, hands crossed over his chest, his magnificent stallion pawing the ground at his side, bewildered and nervous. All the while hordes of other knights and nobles and beautiful damsels from the surrounding kingdom filed past his lifeless form in solemn silence. He'd died bravely, of course, defending some downtrodden peasant. A town would be named in his honor, an eternal memorial, and forevermore children would hear of the glorious tales of his adventurous life. Never again would a more daring knight than Sir Kirby walk the land.

A sob caught in Starlight's throat and she lay her forehead in her hands and wept. She was too old to daydream about knights, and too old to climb trees. Besides, there weren't any knights, not anymore. Knights only existed to delight children at bedtime. She'd best climb down and do the rest of her work, like everyone else in this sorry world. Kirby Mitchell had better things to do than come here, that was for sure. She and Pa had gotten along without him before. They would again.

Determinedly, she wiped her eyes then swung down to the ground and hurried to the house. But the sight of the new porch steps made the tears start all over.

☙

Kirby lugged the new kitchen cabinet over against the wall, then moved back to check its position. Needed to go a few inches to the right. After making that adjustment, he brushed off his hands and slid them into his back pockets. Some white enamel would finish them perfectly. Jessica was sure to be impressed.

At the thought of his older sister, he smiled. Her healthy, nine-pound son, Benjamin David, with dark hair and big blue eyes, the exact replicas of his mama's, was a week old already. Cook hadn't stopped strutting. James already had made plans to show his baby brother the best trees to climb, the best spots for fishing. And Betsy! Her own doll in hand, Betsy was a little mommy herself, copying everything Jessica did as she cared for Benjamin. Kirby chuckled inwardly. He'd never seen such a happy home as theirs, the kind he'd always dreamed of having.

No sense letting the day go to waste, he decided. He went down to the cellar for the paint he'd bought ages ago and brought it to the kitchen. But as he stroked it onto the cabinets, thoughts of a rundown place a few miles away ate at his conscience. He'd started a job there. He couldn't quit until he was finished. What kind of testimony would that be? Abel Wells was probably smug in his satisfaction that the "gospel-monger" had finally left them in peace. Yet Kirby knew all too well that was the least of his reasons for returning. In all good conscience he *should* stay away. But Starlight . . . what about her?

Again, as he'd done for days, Kirby tried to squelch memories of hair that shone like gold in the sun and a smile that stirred the deepest longings of his soul. His efforts met with a measure of success, in the daytime.

But nights were another matter. When he lay awake in his bed and the moon traced its silver path across the dark sky, visions of Starlight Wells taunted him. He'd close his eyes and see her darting among the trees with a smile. He'd open them and see her almost crying with joy over castoff curtains. Her voice was a whispery song in the night that stirred his heart with haunting melodies.

Suddenly aware that he'd stopped in the middle of a stroke, Kirby saw white splotches of paint on the floor. He groaned and put down the brush, then rubbed the spots away vigorously with a turpentine-dampened rag.

You know you have to go back. The thought was almost audible, it came at him so clearly.

"I can't!" he railed aloud vehemently. "Don't you understand?" His voice echoed off the bare surfaces in the room. "I can't go back," he repeated with less force. "I want to, but I can't."

❧

"Why, Starlight, dear," Mrs. Browning said when she answered her door. "How very pretty you look."

Starlight smiled and turned once around. "Thank you, ma'am. I hurried to finish my new things so you could see them when I brought your dress." She handed the woman the neatly folded garment.

Tucking it under an arm, the widow gestured for her to come inside. "I just made some fresh lemonade. Would you care for some?"

"I surely would, thank you," she hastened to add. She followed Mrs. Browning into her almost blinding white kitchen with its black and white linoleum floor. Through the parted yellow curtains the afternoon sun intensified the glossy shine of the cupboards. Starlight could only imagine what it would be like to live in such a beautiful place and cook at the huge black coal stove with two warming ovens and fancy claw feet.

The older woman pulled out a maple chair for her. "Have a seat, child. July is always so hot, and you've had such a long walk." Crossing to the sideboard, she filled a tall glass with the pale liquid and set it before Starlight, then she shook out the newly made garment and looked it over. "Why, this is your finest work ever. I'll feel grand at the ice cream social this Saturday night."

"I'm glad." She forced a smile.

Mrs. Browning got another glass of lemonade and joined Starlight at the table, moving a doily with a vase of flowers aside slightly. "Is something the matter, my dear? You don't look quite yourself today."

With dismay, Starlight's eyes brimmed and the woman blurred before her. She blinked. "Nothin's wrong. I'm fine. Honest." Her cheeks burned as tears slid down them.

"Well," the widow said with a comforting pat on the arm, "if you ever have a problem, I hope you know you can come to me. I can't solve everything that comes up, but I can talk to the Lord about things and ask for His help and wisdom."

Starlight nodded, then gave a little huff. "I s'pose you can. But some things aren't important enough to bother God."

"Oh, you're wrong, child. He cares about everything that concerns His children."

The thought, though said kindly enough and with Mrs. Browning's sincerity, only made Starlight more despondent than before. God probably did take care of those who were His. But what about those who weren't? She drank the rest of her lemonade and set down the glass. "Thanks for the drink. I'd best be gettin' home now."

"Well, let me get the money I owe you. I'll be right back."

Waiting for the widow's return, Starlight pondered her own feelings. If she knew the Lord the way Mrs. Browning did, would her way be easier? Would her heart be lighter? Would Sir Kirby return to claim her?

Chatper Twelve

After dropping off her sewing project, Starlight ran down to W. F. Brown's General Store, lowering her gaze whenever anyone passed her on the street. *How shameful that Pa had gambled away all the money in the jelly jar,* she thought, when they needed so many things. Her earnings would barely cover white flour and coffee. She'd hidden some of the bounty Kirby Mitchell had brought with him that last time, but his supplies were all but used up now.

Trying to distract herself from the tender memories that always flooded her consciousness at the mere thought of her former knight, she browsed through the myriad goods. How did other folks manage to get money for luxuries like washing machines, ice boxes, or fancy clothes when she and Pa had to scrape the bottom of the barrel to stay alive?

Against the far wall, on floor to ceiling shelves, bolts of all kinds of fabric stood proudly side by side, each displaying a different pattern or unusual sheen. Starlight moved toward them and gazed longingly at the lot, running her fingers lightly over an especially fine chocolate colored wool. In her mind she could envision a grand winter coat trimmed with soft rabbit, with a muff to match. She sighed and turned her attention to the rest, recognizing some she'd made into dresses for the Widow Browning. It came as no small satisfaction that not a single one of the printed cottons was as pretty as her own blue flowered skirt.

Starlight raised her gaze to the selection of trims nearby and her eyes caught a spool of ribbon the exact shade of her skirt. Dare she even ask the price of a small piece of it? Her heart began to pound as she opened her fingers and stared at the coins in her palm. Then she made up her mind. Instead of saving the change for the jelly jar after she'd purchased the items she'd come for, she'd use some for herself. Fighting the feelings of guilt over her decision, she made her way to the counter and requested flour and coffee.

The bell above the door clanged as a threesome of laughing town girls entered. Starlight felt their presence at the same time they spotted her; their giggles stopped and the whispering took over. She cringed as they sashayed across the room toward her.

"Well, if it isn't Starshine," Emily Honeywell said patronizingly. "Oh, excuse me, I mean Starling. That's right, isn't it?" She tilted her face questioningly in overstated innocence, her blond ringlets dangling from behind a wide yellow ribbon that matched her organdy frock.

Her two snickering friends smothered their mirth behind lace-trimmed handkerchiefs.

"Coming to the social this Saturday?" Emily went on. "We could chip in for a new dress."

Starlight felt spots of color heat her cheeks but she clenched her teeth and ignored the insult. Grabbing the packages the clerk had wrapped for her, she fled without waiting for the change.

&

Kirby had been surprised and puzzled to find no one home at the Wells house when he arrived. It wasn't unusual for Abel to be otherwise occupied, but where was Starlight? He checked the shed, the maple tree, and even knocked tentatively on the outhouse door, but to no avail. With a shrug he took the sacks of food he'd brought to the porch and set them down, then parked the wagon in back where it would be handy for unloading the wood he'd chopped at home. He stacked the wood against the side of the house, figuring the goodly supply would likely keep Starlight and her pa warm through the winter.

When he was done, he dusted off the new hinges he'd gotten for the shutters. Kirby finished the front ones first, then those on the one side. He'd progressed around to the rear windows when the faint sound of someone crying interrupted his task. He set down the screwdriver and peered cautiously around the corner.

Starlight was huddled miserably against the maple, sobbing.

The sight wrenched his heart. What could have happened? Torn between going to her and leaving her be, he hesitated. He'd never been much good comforting crying women, having endured Jessica's emotional displays as they'd grown up, and whenever she was expecting a baby. But someone needed to do something here and now, and he was the only person around. Inhaling a deep breath, he walked soundlessly over to the tree and knelt down. "Starlight?"

She jerked up her head and a look of shock crossed her features. She buried her face in her hands with a moan.

"What's wrong?" he asked gently. "Are you hurt?" He placed a hand on her shoulder.

She jumped with a start and he lowered his arm.

"Sorry. I didn't mean to offend you." He watched her struggling for control, and for a few moments, wished he hadn't intruded on her private pain. A motherless girl as she probably never had anyone to whom she could confide. What made him think she would open up to him, a marginal acquaintance at best? "Sometimes it helps to tell another person what's troubling you," he began.

Starlight sniffed and shook her head.

Kirby reached into his back pocket and took out his kerchief. He pressed it into her hand and got up. "Then I guess I might as well get back to work. If

you feel up to talking later, I'll be here for a while before I have to go home."
He was amazed when she nodded. So there it was, a dismissal. Some pastor
he'd make. Obviously he had no talent whatsoever in counseling someone
with a problem. With resignation, he stood and returned to his chore.

Her swollen eyes and tear-stained face ate away at him and he found it
difficult to concentrate. She was dressed in new clothes, he'd noticed, and
somehow they made her appear especially vulnerable. If Abel were responsible for this, if he had done something to hurt his daughter, Kirby would
flatten him, crutch or no crutch.

In a few minutes he heard Starlight at the rain barrel, washing up. When
she finished, there wasn't another sound until she came shyly around to
where he was fastening the last hinge in place.

Kirby looked at her and knew the effort it took for her to raise her head
and slowly meet his gaze. He'd seen that look from Betsy now and again and
fought the impulse to sit down and draw Starlight onto his lap. Instead he
gave a slight nod to acknowledge her presence.

Starlight didn't know why she'd come to him. She didn't know what to say,
how to explain that she'd been feeling sorry for herself. She should have been
over being hurt by what Emily Honeywell said or did. But the rich girl's jabs
always went so deep, and the humiliations were always public. Starlight had
felt so special in her new things. It wasn't fair for Emily to ruin it in an
instant. But even if the Honeywells had ten daughters as cruel as her, it did-
n't matter anymore. *Sir Kirby was alive!*

He cleared his throat. "Say, I don't suppose you might have a glass of water
you could offer a thirsty worker," he said hopefully.

Thankful that he'd put her at ease, Starlight smiled. "I surely do. I'll go
and get you some." She turned and took a step away, then peered over her
shoulder. "It's almost suppertime. Are you hungry too?"

"Now that you mention it, I guess I am."

"Then after I bring you a drink, I'll fix somethin' to eat."

"Thanks." Kirby watched her go, noting with some gratification that her
step was lighter again. He breathed a prayer that the Lord would take care
of whatever had troubled her. Her life was hard enough without something
adding to her burden.

When Starlight called him to the table a short while later, Kirby washed
quickly and took his empty glass inside. He set it on the sideboard, then
took the seat across from her where she had set his place. At once he saw
her clasp her hands and bow her head.

He did the same. "Dear Lord," he prayed, "we thank You for the kindness
of this home and the lovely feast before us. Bless our food and the hands
that prepared it. In Jesus' name, Amen."

Starlight didn't quite meet his eyes as they both raised their heads. She reached for her glass and took a sip of water.

"Looks good," Kirby remarked, assessing the assortment of fresh cooked vegetables from the new supply he'd left on the porch. Thick slices of Jessica's braided sweet bread were toasted and spread with butter and chunks of cheese rested on lettuce leaves. A plate of cinnamon cookies occupied the middle of the table alongside a glass of daisies and clover, and she'd dished out two small bowls of canned plums.

"It's. . .kind of you," she said, "bringin' all this food when you come. Pa, I mean, we—"

Kirby smiled. "My sister Jessica has way more than she needs, so often she'll make something for the sole purpose of giving it away. It makes her happy."

"Does she live with you, your sister?" Starlight nibbled her toast.

"No, but her house is right across the street from mine."

"Where is that?"

"Pretty near the lumber mill at Alderson, on Harvey's Lake. Jessie had a new baby about a week ago, made me an uncle for the third time. Been keeping us all hopping." He bit into his cheese and set down the remainder.

Feeling better all the time, Starlight tried to imagine a knight like Sir Kirby as some child's uncle, but it didn't seem to fit with the rest of her fantasies. Knights weren't supposed to be like other mere mortals. They lived grand lives; they were champions.

"By the way," he said, "you look real nice today. I meant to tell you that before when I first noticed."

A flush crept over her cheeks and she went all fluttery inside. Though she tried especially hard to be casual around him, Kirby Mitchell always caused the most peculiar feelings, and now was no exception. "Thanks. A lady I sew for in town, Mrs. Browning, she gave me some extra material to use for myself." At once she wished she had kept quiet. He wouldn't be interested in something that trivial.

"Oh? Well, you do really nice work. And the color looks good on you. Real good."

Unable to prevent herself from glancing down at her clothes, Starlight felt the warmth of another blush. He must think she was a complete ninny by now, especially after finding her bawling her eyes out earlier. "I—I'm sorry," she stammered. "About before. The cryin' and all."

"You don't have to be. It's part of being human, you know. It says in the Bible that even God's Son wept when He lived on earth."

"Truly?" Surprise widened her eyes. "I never heard that before."

Kirby nodded. "He was sitting where He could look out over Jerusalem, a city that He loved. And knowing that its people not only refused the message the prophets had brought to them about His Father but murdered them as well, His heart was broken thinking of the judgment that would befall the city."

It was a strange, sad story, she thought, one she'd put with the things Mrs. Browning had told her and think about later, when she was alone. "We have a Bible here, me and Pa," she said, motioning vaguely toward the parlor with her head. "It was Ma's. She used to tell me the stories when I was little. But I didn't get much of a chance for schoolin', and, well, there's a lot of hard words, and all." Suddenly embarrassed by her confession, she looked down at her fidgeting hands in her lap.

"Reading's something a person can learn anytime," Kirby said evenly. "There's no hurry."

He always knows the right thing to say, Starlight thought as she felt herself relax. She lifted her gaze to his. "Mrs. Browning talks about God sometimes, like you. She's a Christian too."

"That right?" Kirby found the news encouraging. Maybe the woman was praying for her, too, as he was. Starlight seemed open to hearing spiritual things, yet Kirby was afraid that if he pressed her, she'd tell her father, and Abel would order him never to darken their threshold again. Or worse, she could revert to hiding from him again. He'd worked too long and hard to get her to be herself around him.

Kirby felt his lungs deflate. Again he was forced to face the truth of the matter. He was concerned about her spiritual condition, but all this coming around, the helping out, it wasn't a bunch of good deeds meant just to win her father over or show God's love to an unbeliever. *I'd done it for her. All for her.* He wanted Starlight Wells to accept Jesus, true enough. But just as much, Kirby wanted her to trust him. He wanted that more than anything he'd ever wanted in his entire life. Since the first moment he had looked into her haunted brown eyes, his soul had been touched by her in a way too deep for words.

Suddenly realizing that he was staring at her as if in a trance, Kirby blinked and reached for his glass. In his haste, his hand knocked it over instead. "Sorry," he muttered, his palm mopping helplessly at the spilled water that even now was dripping onto her pretty new skirt.

Brushing herself off, Starlight sprang up. "No harm done. I'll get a rag."

Kirby felt himself go red up to his hairline as, open mouthed, he watched Starlight's lissome flight, and her graceful return. Her capable hands belied the little girl before his eyes. This was no helpless waif, no mere wood nymph. As if someone had removed the blinders from his eyes, he saw before him an enchanting and desirable young woman.

He was in big trouble.

"I, uh, had better start home. . .before it gets dark."

Chapter Thirteen

Kirby lectured himself for being a fool as he drove Cook's empty wagon away from Starlight's house and headed toward Alderson. Had he truly considered that silky-haired backwoods princess a child? Had he actually believed that since Estelle had crushed his spirit and broken his heart he'd never again be capable of falling in love? Because he might as well admit it. The feelings he once saw as the mere concern of a good Christian neighbor had grown far beyond that. They had grown into a deep and abiding love.

The wooded countryside passed in a blur as Kirby relaxed the reins and gave Dusty his head. All his visions of Starlight merged into one as he recalled her surprise when he suddenly announced his departure. The questions in her eyes, the way her brows had dipped in bewilderment, and the delicate flush on her high cheekbones were noted duly as she caught the screen door before it slammed and stood peering through it. All Kirby wanted was to turn and leap back up the steps and take her into his arms, to kiss her unsmiling and tremulous lips.

He shook his head. The way she'd jumped when he'd so much as touched her shoulder when she was crying, he could imagine how terrified she'd be if he tried something more familiar. What her pa would do if he saw it! Kirby let out an unsteady breath. Abel would be able to spot right off the change in the way he felt. It was sure to show. But what if Starlight felt the same way?

Starlight Wells was far too innocent in women's wiles to put on airs or concoct schemes to entice a man. Kirby couldn't for one second believe she'd ever been anything but natural whenever he'd been there. There had been the odd time when he'd caught a dreamy, faraway expression in her eyes, but then she'd blink and it would vanish, and she'd be back to herself. She wasn't like other young women, batting eyelashes at him and trying to make him notice her.

But still, even if by some odd turn of events everything else should be in his favor, there was the reality that Star had not accepted Christ and His teachings. She did appear open to hearing about the Lord, but that didn't make her a believer. It would be an act of disobedience to God to be yoked to someone who didn't share the desire to travel the same heaven-directed path he would always seek.

He'd have to make this a matter of serious prayer.

❧

Starlight absently cleared away the dishes as the sound of the wagon faded away. It seemed so quiet in the house now. So empty. Even with the meadowlarks trilling their pretty songs and the soft breezes stirring through the woods, the stillness around her made her feel she should walk on tiptoe.

Her mind replayed the day's events, from the time she'd felt shattered and hopeless on through the discovery that Sir Kirby still existed, and beyond. She'd never known anyone like him. How she wished fate could have made her a town girl, one who'd had proper schooling and nice clothes, one who went to ice cream socials, church, and Sunday school picnics. She hadn't missed those things before. But since Kirby Mitchell had befriended her and Pa, she realized how lonely and colorless her existence had been all the years since Ma's death, and how much she looked forward to Kirby's visits. He had ridden into her heart, that first day, with his sky blue eyes, his almost-smiles, and his kindnesses. . .and now nothing would ever be the same.

He said his kingdom was at Alderson. Starlight had seen it in her mind dozens of times: a huge white castle with gold spires that crowned a hilltop, its brilliance reflected in the shining mirror of Harvey's Lake. Young pages in red and black velvet who called him Uncle Kirby attended his every need, and a lovely woman named Jessica, in flowing blue gowns, brought him trays heaped with the most sumptuous food.

But the look he'd given her when he'd said goodbye seemed different somehow. Final. He would have no more use for a simple peasant girl now that he had finished repairing her humble cottage.

Starlight cast a despairing look down the empty road. How would she live without her knight, if he never crossed her path again?

❧

Jessica heard the wagon drive up while she nursed Benjamin. Kirby had been gone much longer than he said he'd be and it was not like him. But then, he hadn't exactly been himself for the last couple of weeks. He'd been distracted and moody, and sometimes when she was in the middle of talking to him, she'd see that she'd lost him somewhere along the line. Even when Betsy and James were making pests of themselves, it was as if Kirby were only aware of them on the surface. It was time for a talk. If there were something wrong, she wanted to find out what it was.

When he didn't pop in to say hello and see if she had anything left over from supper, she worried all the more. She buttoned the front of her dress and propped the baby on her shoulder while she patted his back. When a soft burp came from his sleeping rosebud mouth, she smiled and took him upstairs to the cradle beside the big four-poster bed she and Cook shared, then went out to the barn.

"Honey?" she said, finding her husband in his study reading.

Cook raised his head, and as always, smiled at her with his eyes.

"Isn't Kirby here?"

"No. He unhitched Dusty and put the wagon away, then said he had to go. Why?"

Jessica frowned. "I'm just a little concerned about him, that's all. He hasn't been himself lately, have you noticed? It's almost like those first days after Estelle ran off."

Rubbing his jowls, Cook thought for a moment. "Well, I noticed he hasn't been very talkative. But if something serious were bothering him, I'm sure he'd have confided in us, asked us to pray with him about it."

"I used to think so," she said shaking her head, "but now I'm not so sure. Would you mind reading up at the house for a bit while I take some cake over to him?"

"All right, big sister." Getting up, he moved close and slid his arms around her. He moaned softly and nibbled her earlobe. "But I'll miss you."

"You'd better." She laughed silently and hugged him. "I won't be long, sweetheart."

Only one light glowed inside her brother's house as she went around back and up the kitchen steps. She tapped lightly and let herself in. "Kirby?"

Hearing no response, she set the cake plate on the table and tiptoed to the parlor. The room was in darkness, but she could make out a figure sprawled in the one upholstered chair. His head lay back on the top edge as he stared at nothing. "Kirby?"

He lifted his head and looked in her general direction.

Jessica let out a breath. "Mind if I light a lamp?"

"No. Make yourself at home."

Crossing to the carved mantel her brother had recently finished, she slid the matchbox open and took one out, then lit the wick of a kerosene lamp. Crazy shadow patterns danced about as she replaced the chimney. She stared at her brother. "What on earth is wrong? You have me worried out of my mind. Is there something I can help you with, pray with you about?"

He didn't answer.

"Does this have anything to do with. . .Estelle?"

Kirby finally met her eyes with a cockeyed, disbelieving half-smile. "No, it has nothing to do with her. And no, there's nothing you can help me with."

"But something *is* wrong," she prodded. "Please don't shut me out, Kirby. I love you."

"Jess." Leaning forward, he rested his elbows on his thighs and let his hands dangle. "I do have a problem, but it's between the Lord and me, something I have to work out on my own. Don't worry about it. I'll be all right."

Only slightly mollified, she paused, then changed the subject. "I brought you some cake, chocolate cake."

"Hey, now that does sound a bit helpful," he said teasingly. "And too good to pass up."

She smiled. "It's on the table. I'll put on some coffee too."

Kirby followed her out to the kitchen and pulled out a chair for her, then one for himself. Sitting down, he stretched out his legs and rested an arm on the tabletop, watching his sister fuss for him. *Did Cook truly appreciate her?* he wondered, then chided himself for the silly question. He'd seen the way they looked at each other. He knew that neither felt complete without the other.

The knowledge made him feel all the worse. He ached to know that same kind of relationship, the wholeness that came from being with the one person God had made for him.

Once he thought it was Estelle, and he'd been dead wrong. Now, with Starlight, it felt right, but in a different way. A better way. *Was she the one?* Or was he merely trying to convince himself and the Lord of that?

If only he'd told her more about God, how to accept Jesus as her Savior. But he hadn't. He had been afraid to turn her off completely. And now that he'd repaired everything he could think of at her place. . . . He tapped his finger against his pant leg.

There was always that woman in town, Mrs. Browning, was it? Starlight said she talked to her about the Lord. Perhaps something she said would open Starlight's eyes to her need for salvation. There was that hope, at least.

"Here you go," Jessica said, pouring a cup of hot coffee and putting it before him. The rich aroma smelled soothing and welcome.

"Thanks, sis. I appreciate it."

"That's always nice to know," she said lightly. She filled another cup for herself, then put a slice of cake on a dish and pushed it toward him with her fingertips as she sat down. "You were late getting back this evening."

"I know. I didn't come straight home. I had some thinking to do."

"Oh. How'd the work go at the Wells homestead? Cook said it's beginning to look like a different place, with all the improvements you've made."

"It's coming along. I'm nearly finished." His casual tone surprised even him. "Might only need to go back one more time." *If she only knew the truth of that statement,* he thought with a jolt. Before he poured out the complicated mess to Jessica, he sliced a chunk of cake with his fork and stuffed his mouth.

But it only slowed him down. Suddenly he heard his own voice blurt into the silence, "I. . .think I'm in love."

Chapter Fourteen

"*What?*" Shiny waves spilled over Jessica's shoulder as she turned from rinsing out her cup at the sink. Her eyes flared wide in surprise.

"You heard me," Kirby replied miserably, wishing he'd kept quiet. He hadn't meant to tell her yet. He wanted time to think things over, pray about them, and then come to a decision. Then, and only then, would he have informed his family about the situation.

"Kirby," his sister said, coming over and sitting across from him, the expression on her face somewhere between a smile and a puzzled frown. "When did this happen? Who is she? Someone you met at the lumber camps?"

He shook his head. "On the way." At her look of complete confusion, he decided he might as well tell her the rest. There was no point in trying to keep anything back now. "It's Starlight Wells."

"From Noxen? Where you've been working?"

Resting his chin in his cupped hand, Kirby nodded. "I don't know when it happened. It was a gradual thing." He paused, and a chuckle shook his shoulders. "It's funny, actually."

"What do you mean?"

"Well, all the while I was filling in for Cook at the lumber camp services, it seemed like mothers at both places were trying to encourage me to show some interest in their daughters. Heaven only knows why. It's not as if I'm a qualified preacher or even someone who could offer any real prospects, know what I mean?"

Jessica gave a hint of a smile but she did not interrupt.

"And with Starlight, it was the complete opposite. After Estelle's actions, I'd closed myself off from the possibility of ever loving anyone again in the same way I'd loved her. It never entered my mind that I'd even be vulnerable to the idea!" He reflected silently for a moment. "Starlight wasn't like other girls from the very first. To say she had no scheming ways or secret plans to entice the substitute preacher is an understatement. The first few times I even passed their place, she ran and hid, if you could imagine that! I thought if I displayed God's love to her and her father and started being a friend, she'd come out of her shell of fear and be—I don't know. Like other people, I guess. Able to relate to someone else who might happen by sometime. Maybe, in time, somebody would be able to get through to her and her pa and tell them about Jesus. I was only trying to lay the foundation, plant the seed. I never for a minute harbored selfish reasons of my own, I swear."

Tilting her head slightly to one side, his sister looked right into his eyes. "Hey, I know you, remember? You don't have to try to defend yourself to me.

And I know without a doubt that you haven't a dishonorable bone in your body."

Kirby flashed a sheepish grin. "Thanks for the vote of confidence. I don't know why it does, but it helps."

She squeezed his forearm on the table between them. "When exactly did you realize things had changed?"

"Earlier today, while I was there. It hit me, like the old bolt out of the blue people have talked about. Just in case you ever had any doubts, let me tell you. . .it really happens like that."

Jessica pondered the information for several minutes. Then she met his gaze. "Does she share your feelings?"

"I wouldn't know. I didn't hang around to find that out." He paused. "Thing is, she and her father claim to have no use for religion, or at least he is opposed to it. She's a little more open when I bring up spiritual matters. But all the same, it's not enough merely to show interest. I keep thinking about how light can't have fellowship with darkness, the unequal yoke and all that. It doesn't seem right to try to develop a closer relationship with her when we're instructed as Christians not to tie ourselves to unbelievers."

"I see what you mean," Jessica said quietly. "That does explain why you haven't been yourself lately, with all this on your mind. I wish I could help you." She patted his hand comfortingly. "Well, I can do one thing, at least. Why don't we pray together about it?"

His fingers curled around hers and gripped them firmly. "I'd appreciate that, Jess. I was afraid you'd rail at me about how I should know better. But I swear, I never expected this to happen, not for one minute."

She smiled. "I guess that's how life is, isn't it? Ever so predictable until we find ourselves a little too comfortable. . .then comes a surprise to make us sit up and take notice. And who's to say that even something like this can't 'work together for good,' just like all the rest of our lives as Christians?"

"You know," Kirby said, suddenly feeling a new surge of hope, "I'm glad I told you. I forgot what a blessing it is at times to have an older sister to turn to."

With a smirk more playful than angry, Jessica shook her head. "That's what I love about you. You never let me forget I'm three whole years older than you."

Chuckling, they both stood. Kirby held out his hand and Jessica took it, and together they walked into the parlor and knelt side by side by the overstuffed chair.

"Our dear Heavenly Father," Jessica began. "How we thank You that we can come to You at any time, knowing You care about us and about what is happening in our lives. Often we don't understand the whys of some of the trials that face us. But nothing takes You by surprise, for You know our lives from the beginning to the end. So we ask for Your guidance and wisdom for

Kirby as he seeks Your will concerning these new feelings for Starlight Wells. Thank You for her openness to the Gospel. May her desire to know more about Jesus bring about a deep longing to know Him as her Savior. And keep Your hand upon us as a family. May we be faithful always, for we pray these things in the name of Your Son."

"Dear Lord," Kirby said. "Thank You for the blessings of home and family and people who care. I commit all the desires of my heart to You and ask that You show me what to do regarding Starlight. Help me to be a testimony to her and her father, and if there's a way for You to open their eyes to the glorious light of the Gospel, I pray it will be done. Help me not to do anything that would hinder Your work in their lives. May both of them come to an acceptance of the truth. I thank You for hearing our prayers. In Jesus' name, Amen."

As Kirby raised his head he met his sister's eyes. Without a word he embraced her.

&

Abel breathed out long and slow as Dewey rounded up the cards and patted them into a neat deck once more. How was it possible that things had gone from good to bad in so few hands? He could not understand it. For weeks now, even months, he'd have hope within sight, only to be snatched from his grasp before he had a good fingerhold. Yet he'd been dumb enough to think that sooner or later, time and chance would turn and be on his side.

What would Josie think of the mess he'd made of things? Because she'd never held to card playing, he'd resisted Dewey's invitations, and the two men had stuck to fishing and hunting whenever their two wives wanted to get together. From the beginning Abel hadn't much cared for Blackburn's rough ways, but Josie had known Minnie Blackburn from years back when as young girls they both moved into the area around the same time. She hadn't wanted to part with one of her oldest friends. Gradually Abel accepted Dewey's self-indulgent manner and laziness, for Josie's sake. But after her funeral, when Abel submerged himself in misery and didn't care any longer what he did to get through a day, he'd drifted into gambling whenever Dewey had the time. Though at first it was merely a distraction—and an enjoyable one in some ways—lately they went at it far too much. Now instead of being on top of things for a change, as he'd hoped, Abel was in over his head again. He cast a scathing look at the worn deck that had cost him his peace of mind and resisted the impulse to strike a match to it.

"So is that it fer the night?" Dewey asked, his countenance not unlike that of a cat in a henhouse.

Meeting Dewey's eyes, one of which sported the yellow-green of a bruise that was healing, Abel shrugged one shoulder and stood. He positioned his crutch under his arm. "Yeah. Better git on home."

"Ya can borrow the lantern," Dewey suggested.

Abel nearly didn't answer. "I know the way," he finally said as he thumped across the room dejectedly.

"Look, Abel," Dewey began placatingly. "I'm sorry about that string o' bad luck that's been hangin' on yer back. But remember, Clem an' Billy Jake Houser are after me too. So far they only gave me this black eye. Who knows what they'll do next time if I don't come up with some o' what I owe 'em. That's why I keep houndin' ya to pay up. I'd hate to have to sic the law on ya, bein' my friend, an' all. I jes' don't see no other way."

Abel glared back from the doorway in shock. That someone who was supposed to be his friend could consider such a step was unthinkable. Maybe he'd been too blind or drunk to realize that Dewey Blackburn considered him more of an easy mark than a friend. "The law?" he managed to ask. "Gamblin's not legal here, ya know. There's nothin' the law could do but get us both in trouble."

"Mebbe. But a debt is still a debt. I got yer signed paper, all right an' proper like. Don't see as how the law could ignore that, since they don't hafta know why ya owe me. An' as yer friend, I wouldn't be askin' if I wasn't bad off myself. Ya know that, Abel. But I gotta have that money. I gotta have it now."

"I ain't got no money, and well ya know it!" Abel said through gritted teeth. "I ain't got nothin' to sell, and I ain't got nothin' in the world that's worth anythin' to anybody."

Dewey raised his scruffy chin a notch. "Ya got one thing. Abel Wells. I tole ya I'd marry up an' make it all proper. If I had Star to hire out an' bring in some cash money, it'd be a real help."

Abel felt as if the wind had been snatched out of him. There had to be some other way. "Why don't ya hire out them two lazy critters ya call sons?" Abel spat, seeing nothing the least friendly in Dewey Blackburn's black eyes. "They'd bring in twice as much."

"Them two ain't fit fer much but sleepin' an' eatin', an' never been. Ain't nobody who'd give 'em a hog's chance. But tell ya what. I'll let ya have two or three days to pay up before I haveta call in the law." He drummed his stubby fingers against the tabletop, pressing his advantage. "If ya end up gettin' locked in a cell someplace, ya know, the gal'll need someone to look after her anyhow. I'm tryin' to help clear up yer troubles. It's up to you. Think on it, ya hear? Mull it over real good. Three days."

❧

Starlight lay awake in her bed for the longest time trying to sort out all her new feelings. Sir Kirby had only been gone for a few hours, yet it seemed like forever. She could still feel the wild joy that had coursed through her when she'd realized he was still alive after all. He hadn't shown anything but kindness even when he had caught her blubbering all over her new clothes. Anyone else might have made things worse by wanting to know what she was crying about, or made her feel like a baby for shedding tears at all. But not Sir Kirby. He'd acted like it was the most normal thing in the world for a body to cry, and even told her about God's sadness. Such a wonder he was. Even now, the scent of new lumber he'd used to repair the porch and its roof sweetened the night air. The quiet warmth of his smile and encouraging words caused a tingling glow inside her.

When Abel finally came home from Dewey Blackburn's, he was in one of the foulest moods Starlight had ever encountered. Though she could tell that Sir Kirby's latest repairs had not escaped his notice, he stomped wordlessly to his room and slammed the door. Now his snores punctuated the quiet night.

Rising, Starlight rested her arms on the windowsill and leaned slightly out of the open window. The silvery glory of the three-quarter moon crowned distant treetops and spread over the meadow, making the world glow in a warm and magical way. She smiled and breathed deeply of summer's fragrant perfume. Mrs. Browning had told her that God sent His only Son into the world to die for sin. Sir Kirby had told her that Jesus had wept over the sins of Jerusalem.

Did He still know what people thought and did? she wondered. Ma had sung her songs about God and told her Bible stories, and even Pa used to go with them to church. But now Pa was angry with God, and his pal, Dewey Blackburn, used the Lord's name in a foul way. If God still loved the world, then things like that must still make Him sad. She hoped there was nothing inside of her that would cause God to grieve. But there was no way to be sure. Perhaps after her chores were done tomorrow, she'd call on Mrs. Browning and ask her how a person could come to know God.

The warm breeze feathered Starlight's hair and she smiled at the moon, then beyond. Truly having the Lord for a friend, like Mrs. Browning and Sir Kirby, must be the most gladsome thing a person could ever experience, she decided.

Far across the meadow, a deer strolled in the moonlight, making not a sound. Starlight's mind returned to a grand silver horse with a brave knight astride. Tall and straight and noble of bearing, his blue eyes squinted from sunshine and his hair was tossed by the wind. A gallant champion who had driven out of the kingdom hours ago, he wore a look of supreme sadness as though he might never return.

The moonlit meadow blurred behind a veil of tears.

Chapter Fifteen

The next morning dawned heavily overcast with a promise of imminent showers. Starlight gazed moodily at the dreary sky as she hastened through her chores. It appeared unlikely that she'd be able to venture into town to see Mrs. Browning as she'd hoped, but she decided that one more day wouldn't hurt anything. Returning inside, she saw that Abel had come down to breakfast.

"Mornin', Pa. Want some eggs?"

"Just coffee. Stomach's a mite uneasy."

Starlight studied him at the table. She couldn't remember when he'd looked worse. "The Widow Browning says sometimes chamomile tea helps a sick stomach. Should I make you some?"

"Huh-uh. It'll pass. Have somethin' to take care of. That oughta take my mind off the queasiness."

"I suppose." Moving to the stove, she reached for the coffee pot and filled a mug with the steaming liquid, then put it before her father. The odd way he peered up at her made her feel funny. "Somethin' wrong, Pa?"

He looked her up and down in one quick motion and let out a breath. "Cain't say just now. We haveta talk later." He raised his cup and blew on the steamy brew, then took a sip, watching her all the while.

Starlight felt that something wasn't right but she couldn't put a finger on anything in particular. Rather than dwell on it, she sat down with the old kitchen throw rug and began darning one of the thin spots. It wasn't nearly as grand as the maroon and gray braided one Sir Kirby's sister had discarded, but even threadbare and colorless it would be nice to step out of bed upon it when the weather started getting colder. She'd tried it out already, anticipating the needful purpose it would serve.

Laying the hole over the wooden spool, she ran long parallel stitches across the opening, then began weaving vertical stitches over and under the strands. *Probably not even the dungeon at Sir Kirby's castle had such ragged mats on the floor,* she thought, amused by the idea. But then last night's sadness filled her mind and her smile wilted at the edges. Kirby Mitchell wouldn't likely brighten another day out here. She'd best start forgetting her silly dreams and face the real world. Morose but determined, Starlight tightened her lips and worked harder.

Abel regarded his willow-thin daughter as she bent to her task, her nimble fingers making short work of the patching. Even from the earliest days, Josie had taught the child well. She could mend and sew with stitches so fine Abel's eyes could hardly see them. It was shameful that all her sewing went to townsfolk. If it weren't for him wasting the pittance she earned all the time, she could have had some decent stylish clothes of her own.

She was nearly a woman now, comely and graceful as Josie. Even after eight years the hurt of not having Josie still burned inside. She was the one good thing that had happened in his life. God shouldn't have taken her. He looked again at Star. The summer sun had sown wheat-gold strands among her silky hair and put roses in her cheeks. When she smiled it was with the innocent delight of a child, and it tore at Abel's heart. By rights, she should have had a string of young bucks stammering and tripping over their own feet long ago in their eagerness to take a wife. To keep such a tight rein on her hadn't been smart; he'd shut her off from other young folk. *Why haven't I thought clearly before?* he wondered.

What Dewey Blackburn needed was a chunk of air between his ears. Letting out a deep breath, Abel shot a look at the hunting rifle that hung above the mantel. No one would even miss the scoundrel, that was the truth of it. But though such a remedy would be instant and simple, it would only murk up things all the more. The law was sure to find the culprit, and then Star would be left alone and at the mercy of those kids of his, or maybe someone even worse. There had to be another way.

He rubbed at the stubble on his jaw. Maybe Joe Rawlins, his old boss at the tannery, would have an opening for a laborer. No matter what job it was, from unloading hemlock bark from the railroad cars to pickling hides or putting them into vats of tannin, even pressing the dried leather to remove wrinkles, he'd do anything, foot or no foot. He'd start earning the three hundred dollars to pay off Dewey Blackburn.

Maybe somebody new in town needs a house, his thoughts went on. He and Star could go stay with his Uncle Ray, down in Luzerne, and he could find a job in the mines sorting coal. All he needed was time. But Dewey said three days, and one of them was passing by even while he sat. First he'd go outside and sharpen his razor and take a bath in the crick. Then he'd decide what to do.

An hour and a half later, he turned away from the tannery, downcast. Joe Rawlins's voice still rang in his ears. *Sorry, Abel. You know I'd hire you in a minute, but we just signed three new guys. We're full up. Why don't you try the mill?* And it was the same story there. No work. Abel's good foot throbbed and burned by the time he hobbled back home in defeat. His armpit was rubbed raw from the pressure of the crutch as he sank down onto the porch step in despair and dropped his forehead into his hands.

Starlight's cheerful laugh carried from the henhouse. Abel raised his head and watched as she sprinkled dried corn liberally from her splayed fingers.

As she finished scattering the last of it, she let herself out and fastened the gate closed. Then she did a barefoot jig to the back door.

Abel felt a heavy load of guilt press hard on his insides.

⁂

Starlight watched the huge cloud puffs glide across the fresh blue afternoon sky. Stepping around a puddle in the path, she felt damp ferns graze her leg. She giggled and swiped away the water drops with her hand, then continued on. When she finally reached Mrs. Browning's house, she ran up the steps and crossed the porch to the door.

The widow answered her knock within seconds. "Oh, Starlight. How nice to see you. I didn't have you working on something I forgot about, did I?"

"Oh, no, ma'am." Suddenly losing her boldness, she studied her old brown shoes and fidgeted with one of her buttons, trying to gather courage to look up. "I—I just wanted to ask you about somethin'."

A patient smile widened the woman's well-shaped lips. "Well, in that case, come inside. I just made a pitcher of iced tea in the kitchen." Her ivory house dress made a soft swishing sound as she turned and led the way.

Starlight pulled out the kitchen chair she normally occupied and settled gratefully onto it. While the glasses were being filled, she admired the red geraniums in the windowbox outside. Their bright bonnets seemed to be glorying in the warm sunshine and they looked especially bright against the crisp curtains.

"Here you are, my dear."

"Thank you, ma'am." She took a sip to fortify herself, then noticed Mrs. Browning was staring at her curiously.

"You said there was something you wanted to ask?"

Starlight cleared her throat. "Um, yes. Somethin' I was wonderin' about."

"What is it, dear?"

She took a deep breath. "About God. And how we can know Him like a friend. I. . .wanted to ask about that. If you have time, and all."

"There's always time to talk about important things, child."

"Then you don't think I'm stupid for not knowin' already?"

Mrs. Browning patted her hand lovingly. "Not at all. The Lord wants all people to come to Him, you know. The Bible says that whenever someone accepts the Lord as his Savior, even the angels in heaven rejoice."

"Truly?"

"Oh, yes, child." The older woman thought for a moment, idly tapping a fingertip on the rim of the glass she held. "Since before the world even began, there's been a great battle going on between the forces of good and the forces of evil. It started in heaven when Satan, the most important angel of all, grew proud and decided he wanted to take over the kingdom. But God, being all powerful, cast Satan out of His presence."

Starlight had no difficulty picturing the event. She listened enraptured as the widow continued.

"Satan hated God then. And when God created this world, Satan wanted control of the earth, and of God's new creation, man. He tempted man to be proud the way he was, and his plan succeeded. Man disobeyed God and sinned. So now, the Bible says, we are like wandering sheep without a shepherd, and the devil, Satan, is like a roaring lion, walking about, seeking whom he may devour."

"How scary," Starlight said breathlessly.

"But," Mrs. Browning said with a smile. "God knew we couldn't help ourselves, so He sent His only Son, the Prince of heaven, as a sacrifice for our sin. His blood washed away the stain of sin. When Jesus died on the cross and rose again, Satan was defeated forever. It says in the Gospel of John, the third chapter, sixteenth verse, 'For God so loved the world, that he gave his only begotten Son, that whosoever believeth in him should not perish, but have everlasting life.' "

Shades of unbelief fell from Starlight's eyes. She could see it all. . .the vision of a great silver knight conquering an evil black lord who had domineered a kingdom of helpless peasants. The Son of God dying for the sins of the world. . .for her sin. Angels cheering whenever someone finds God. She felt tears coursing down her cheeks. Wordlessly she reached across the table and grasped Mrs. Browning's hands in hers. "I should thank Jesus for dying for me," she whispered.

"Yes, Starlight," the widow said, her own eyes brimming with tears of joy. "I'll kneel right by you while you do."

❧

The world took on a breathtaking brilliance as Starlight walked homeward. The sky had never looked bluer, nor the clouds more magnificent; birds had never sang in sweeter melody. She felt an incredible peace inside unlike anything she had known. She was a child of God. Angels had re-joiced as a new soul was born into the eternal family. *God so loved the world.* As though her steps weren't light enough to suit her, she started skipping over the path.

Halfway home, she heard voices near the creek. Recognizing Cal and Marvin Blackburn's cocky tones, she slipped behind a tree trunk and listened.

"Shore will be somethin' havin' a ma the same age as us," Marvin said. "Whooee!" He whacked Cal exuberantly on the back.

"Hey!" Suddenly off balance, Calvin grabbed his younger brother's suspenders and the two of them landed on their backsides in the shallow water, sputtering and guffawing. Then Cal sobered and tossed his head. "Well, I have me some plans fer after next week. Don't see why Pa should be the only one benefitin' from the sitiation."

Marvin studied him for a second with a crafty smile, then picked a pebble from the water and tossed it. "Y'know, that ain't a half bad idea!" He led another round of boisterous laughter.

Starlight's heart plummeted with a thunk. She wasn't sure who the Blackburns were talking about, but recalling Pa's peculiar mood this morning, a dreadful sense of foreboding oozed through her veins.

Skulking backward away from the tree, she turned and broke into a run.

Chapter Sixteen

Tears stung Starlight's eyes as she ran blindly through the woods. *Cal and Marvin had to be talking about me.* That explained the odd way that Pa had been looking at her, watching her. He was going to marry her off to Dewey Blackburn! Dewey Blackburn! *How could Pa even think such a thing?* she thought helplessly.

A sob caught in her throat. Stopping abruptly, Starlight's eyes darted about in a frenzied search of the surrounding area. She couldn't go home. She had to find someplace to hide. Somewhere no one would ever find her. But where? She'd never been far from home. She rested her spine against a huge elm then slowly sank to the ground. There was no place to go. Even if Mrs. Browning were kind enough to offer shelter, Starlight knew they'd find her there.

Thought of the kindly older woman brought back her recent experience in Mrs. Browning's kitchen. Starlight could still see herself kneeling with the widow's comforting arm around her own shoulders. She could still hear herself asking Jesus to come into her life, still feel the sweet peace that had flooded her being. It had taken place such a short time ago and already her heart felt all shriveled up like a dried leaf. *Oh, God,* she prayed. *What Pa's thinkin' isn't right, or even decent. I don't know what brought him to considerin' such a thing. I thought he loved me.*

Too fearful and miserable to cry, Starlight hugged herself, surprised to feel gooseflesh on her upper arms on such a warm day. It spread over her entire form when the wind stirred through the leaves. She drew up her knees and wrapped her arms around them, then closed her eyes. *Jesus, God, I'm new at this, seein' as I just learned how to know You. But Kirby Mitchell—he's a preacher friend of mine—says You know all about us. If that's true, then You know I got nowhere to turn. Please help me.*

No more words would come, so she pressed her lips together and waited for a sign or a miracle, some way to know her prayer had been heard. When even that small hope faded, she got up and brushed herself off and trudged homeward, the long way. Thoughts of being by herself in some strange place after dark were scary to think about. Even if she didn't go in the house ever again, she needed to be close enough to see it at least. But she'd be careful to keep out of Pa's sight.

❧

Sitting in the upholstered chair in his parlor, Kirby stopped reading his Bible and looked up, perplexed. Something wasn't right, he could feel it. Since noon he'd had an uneasiness nagging at him. He wanted to see Starlight again, of that he was certain. But the reason to ride over there needed to be better than his own selfish desire to feast his eyes on her or hear her sweet voice. Somehow he needed to find out where things stood between them. If by some miracle she seemed agreeable to having him come to call, somehow they needed to work through her spiritual problems as well. He gave a sigh and rubbed the bridge of his nose. What if none of this was the Lord's will for him? What if he were just trying to force things to happen his way?

He slapped his knees and rose. He needed some coffee. Halfway to the kitchen to warm the dregs from breakfast, a knock sounded on his back door.

Cook stuck his head inside. "Anybody home?"

"Sure. Come on in." Indicating a seat at the table, Kirby took the enamel coffee pot and dumped the vile contents down the sink so he could put on a fresh pot.

His brother-in-law tossed a good-natured grin Kirby's way as he watched him run water and add grounds. "Hear you've come to a ripple in the stream of life," he said without his usual subtlety.

With a withering glare at him, Kirby set the container on the stove. "Well, I can see I have your sympathy," he quipped.

Cook winked. "Actually you do, pal. Thought I'd come by and offer you my advice is all."

"And what might that be?" Kirby grabbed the spindle of another chair, spun it toward himself and straddled it, resting his arms on the chairback as he faced his sister's husband.

Cook had the grace to look concerned, Kirby decided, watching him rake his fingers through his rust-colored hair.

"Well, the way I see it," Cook began, "you have a right to some happiness, like anybody else. If you think you've found some, and feel it's of the Lord, then I can't see you have much to worry about."

Letting out an unsteady breath, Kirby met his gaze. "That's just it. I don't."

"Don't what?"

"Don't know for sure if this is God's will. Starlight and her father don't seem too inclined toward religion, you might say."

"Hmm. I never got that feeling around her. Seemed to me it was more her pa's opinion holding her back. If you ask me, he's the only one who's closed off God."

"Maybe you're right. She shows some real interest in anything I say about the Lord. In fact, she told me that one of the town ladies she does sewing for talks to her about God. A Mrs. Browning, or something."

Cook brightened. "Say, I've met her. Fine Christian woman. If Starlight Wells is around her very much. I'd say it's only a matter of time till she comes to the Lord."

"That's encouraging. I only pray you're right." Kirby shifted in his seat.

"But that still leaves her father."

"Oh, I don't know. I've been praying for that pair since the first time I crossed by their property. So has Jess. Counting you, now, and Mrs. Browning, that's four of us already. Considering the power of prayer, the man hasn't got a chance, right?" He sputtered into a laugh.

Kirby only grinned and nodded.

When his mirth subsided, Cook grew serious. "The real reason I came over was to see if you wanted to ride to Stull with me."

"When?"

"Soon as I pack up. I've been asked to perform a wedding this evening, and since there's a service tomorrow anyway, I thought you might like to tag along. We can get rooms at Hattie's for the night."

"Sounds all right. I'd enjoy that." Checking over at the stove, Kirby saw a column of steam rising upward from the spout of the coffee pot. "How about some coffee first?"

⁂

Abel maneuvered himself out onto the porch and peered toward town. Star should have returned hours ago, but there'd been no sign of her. He stepped to the banister. "Star!" he called. Cupping his hands around his mouth he tried again. "Starlight! Where are you, girl?" Watching for a few more minutes, he finally gave up and went back in. It wasn't like her to go off and cause him worry. Not like her at all. Young girl like her, alone in the woods, no telling what harm could come to her. If she didn't come in the next half hour, he'd have to go looking for her. A sick guilt slithered through him. Star needed to know about his decision. Much as it had galled him to agree to Dewey's demand, he hadn't been able to find another way to pay him the money.

Within twenty minutes he plunked on his hat and headed out the door. Daylight was already starting to fade. There wasn't much more time to waste sitting and waiting for the girl to come home. Could be she was in trouble somewhere. "Star!" he yelled into the stillness. But there was no response. He'd check the path she usually took to town first.

Dampness from the rain earlier in the week made Abel's progress along the wooded path slower than usual as his crutch made deep impressions in the spongy ground. By the time he'd covered half the distance to Mrs. Browning's he was hoarse from yelling.

With a deep sigh, Abel stopped and stared ahead in the waning light. She couldn't be around here or she'd have answered. He'd have to try another direction. Leaving the worn path, he cut across in the direction of Stull. Could be the Widow Browning had bragged about Star's sewing to some woman at the camp and sent the girl over to her. It was worth a try anyhow.

"Star!" he croaked, grabbing his scratchy throat with his free hand. He navigated clumsily around a cluster of white birch.

The sudden ominous rattle caught Abel off guard. Startled, he lost his grip on the crutch and pitched forward with a yell. Sharp fangs sliced through his trousers and into his good leg. *Fool,* he thought grimly. *Ya knew better than to move when there's a rattler starin' at ya.* Sitting up, he whipped out his kerchief and tied it around his leg above the wound.

❧

"What was that?" Kirby said, drawing up on Jericho's reins. "Did you hear someone cry out? Sounded like it came from over there."

Cook nodded. "I think you're right."

Kirby gave Jericho a sharp nudge with his knees and the gray stallion bolted in the direction of the sound. Although Cook was following a few paces behind, he scanned the darkening woods desperately. Finally, in the distance, he focused on a man sprawled on the ground. Coming up on him, Kirby skidded his mount to a stop and jumped down. He knelt and turned the man over. "Abel!"

Dark eyes opened barely a crack. "I. . .I been. . .snakebit."

Instantly Kirby saw the kerchief tied around Abel's calf. He reached for his pocket knife as the other horse approached. "Cook! It's Abel Wells. Ride for Doc Tibbins and tell him to go to the Wells place. I'll probably have him home by the time he gets there."

"Will do."

While Cook rode off in a flurry, Kirby ripped Abel's pant leg open to his knee. Even in the dimness of the forest, two angry red dots were noticeable on the whiteness of the man's leg. Kirby retied the kerchief. He opened his knife and cut across the wound twice, then bent and sucked out the acrid venom, spitting it forcefully before repeating the action several times.

"S-s-sorry. . ." Abel barely managed to say. "Didn't mean. . .to hurt her."

The faintness of the man's voice alarmed Kirby. He breathed a silent prayer as he poured water from his canteen over the cut, then bandaged the already swelling leg with his own handkerchief. He tried to ignore Abel's words. What had he meant, *hurt her?* Obviously he was out of his mind from the snake poison. He'd have to get him home so he'd be there when the doctor arrived.

In one swift movement, Kirby hefted the man's dead weight and tossed him face down onto Jericho's back. Fairly certain he was secure, he then led the horse quickly toward the tumbledown house a few thousand yards away.

Soon he would see Starlight. Perhaps together they would pray for Abel.

Chapter Seventeen

High in the branches of an elm tree still within range of her house, Starlight saw Sir Kirby leading his silver stallion. She drank in the sight of her dashing knight for several seconds until the wind's breath ruffled a handful of leaves aside, clearing her view. Suddenly she caught her breath and gulped aloud. Pa was dangling facedown across the saddle! Forgetting her own peril, she sprang to her feet on the limb directly beneath her and, with more haste than caution, climbed downward until she reached the lowest branch. As her feet touched the ground, she saw Kirby carrying Abel inside. Heart pounding, she ran across the meadow and up the porch steps.

No one was in sight. Starlight flew up the staircase to Abel's room and met Kirby's dire expression as she went to the bed and knelt beside her father's unconscious form. His forehead felt clammy to her touch. "What happened to Pa?" she whispered, not able to tear her eyes from the pallor of his face.

"A diamondback." Kirby put a comforting hand on her shoulder.

"No," she said almost inaudibly as her tears muddled his form. He'd gone downhill so much already since Ma passed on that she dared ask herself the inevitable. What if he never got better and needed to be taken care of? What if he died? Desperately, she stood and buried her face in Kirby's chest. "Please don't let my pa die."

Starlight's heart-wrenching plea was Kirby's undoing. He wrapped his arms around her and crushed her to himself. She melted against him, trembling with the force of suppressed sobs. He'd never felt so utterly helpless in his life. Cupping the back of her head, he rocked her gently, clenching his teeth at the irony of the situation. He'd have given anything to have Starlight Wells willingly in his arms, clutching him tightly the way she was. She probably didn't even know she was doing it. He breathed in deeply and slowly. "My brother-in-law rode for Doc Tibbins," he said quietly. "I've done what I could."

He felt her swallow and stiffen a little, as if suddenly realizing where she was. But instead of drawing away, she sniffed and raised her chin as she searched his eyes with a shake of her head. "No, you're a preacher. You have to pray for him."

Kirby hadn't stopped praying since he'd seen Abel lying on the ground, but as Starlight eased out of his hold, he knew that an audible prayer would do much to comfort and strengthen her. She sank to her knees and clasped her hands and watched as he followed suit. Then she bowed her head and closed her eyes.

Kirby's shirtfront was damp from Starlight's tears, and his arms felt so empty he struggled against an almost overwhelming need to put one of them around her again and hold her while he prayed. Instead he reached for her hand and held it tight, hoping to impart some of his strength to her. "Father, we bring Abel Wells before You in prayer. You know the needs of his heart and his body, and we ask that in Your mercy You will meet them. We humbly ask You, as the Great Physician, to lay Your healing hand upon this man and restore him to health. And if it is Your will, give him another opportunity to reach out in faith and find Your hand there, open and filled with all that he has ever needed. We pray that You'll give the doctor wisdom in treating Abel, and that You'll give Starlight and me hope and strength as we wait for Your will to be done. In Jesus' name we pray these things, thanking You that You hear and answer the prayers of Your children. Amen."

"Oh, God," Starlight began, her soft petition falling like rose petals on Kirby's surprised ears. He opened his eyes in wonder and saw a childlike faith glowing over her lowered face. He quickly bowed his head again. "You know I'm kinda new at this prayin', and all. But I thank You for sendin' Sir Kir—I mean, Kirby—along when Pa needed him. Please help the doc to come fast, and please make my pa better. He needs Jesus. Amen."

The door downstairs banged open then and two pairs of feet charged upstairs.

Kirby and Starlight stood and moved aside as kindly and efficient Doc Tibbins, in his usual black suit and tie, came into the room with his worn medical bag. He moved to the bedside and set the bag on the night table. Taking out a few shiny instruments, he looked up soberly. "If you don't mind, I need to examine the patient."

"Of course." Kirby put an arm around Starlight's shoulder and drew her out of the room. Cook had already exited. "Maybe you could make some coffee for us all," he suggested, hopefully. "It may be a long night."

With a nod, she went dejectedly down the steps.

Following her, Kirby looked at Cook. "Think you can get along without me tonight?" he asked.

"Sure. I think you're needed here more than at somebody else's wedding. I'll check in on my way back tomorrow, in case things...." He gave a meaningful shrug, then he reached over and gave Kirby's shoulder a squeeze.

"Thanks. And keep praying."

❧

For most of the next three days, during which Abel lay unconscious and near death, Kirby and Starlight took turns staying by the bed while the doctor kept a close watch for any change in his patient. The ravaged leg swelled alarmingly and turned incredible shades of red and purple. Abel's pulse raced erratically and his temperature fluctuated. Starlight assisted in applying cool cloths whenever they were needed.

Sitting in the faded upholstered chair in the parlor where he'd been praying almost constantly night and day whenever he was alone, Kirby heard soft footsteps on the stairs and looked up.

Starlight gave him a small smile from the landing, her hand resting on the knob of the banister.

"Any change?"

"Not yet. But I have this feelin' inside that everythin's gonna be all right. Ever have that?"

"Every now and then." He was afraid to voice the fears that he'd had at the beginning, when his main thoughts had been of her should Abel die. But for the last two days, the simple realization that Starlight had given her heart to the Lord had brought Kirby an incredible peace. He knew that no matter what happened, she'd have the strength to get through it. He'd make sure she did.

"Are you gettin' hungry? The doctor's wantin' some dinner."

"Guess I could force something down," he said with a grin. In total agreement, his stomach growled.

With a nod, she went into the kitchen where Cook had delivered a supply of Jessica's baked and canned goods early that morning.

Kirby took the steps two at a time and went to chat with Doc Tibbins. "Any improvement?"

The doctor looked over the tops of his spectacles and cocked his head back and forth slightly. "Holding his own. Wakes up once in a while, but still talks out of his head. After I have a bite to eat, I think I'd better go see a few of my other patients. I've a mother-to-be who's ready to deliver any day. You and the girl can watch Abel. It's all in God's hands anyhow."

Taking the comments as a sign of hope, Kirby nodded. "I'll sit with him while you go have some coffee."

"Thanks. I appreciate it."

As the doctor left the room, Kirby took his chair. He put his hand on Abel's chest and said a prayer for him.

"Th—that. . .you. . .pulpit. . .th—thumper?" came Abel's whisper.

Kirby looked into Abel's glazed eyes. "Yes. Don't try to talk."

"Have to." A long silence passed. "Star. . . . Didn't mean. . .to give her. . . away."

"What?" Kirby tried to absorb the statement. Maybe the doctor had been right about Abel being delirious.

"Owed. . .money," Abel rasped urgently, as if he feared he might die. "Th—three. . .hundred dollars. . .to Dewey." Slowly he breathed in and out, as if gathering strength. "Said he'd. . .take. . .Star. No. . .other way." In exhaustion, Abel's eyes drifted closed and he dozed off again.

As Abel's earnest expression penetrated Kirby's mind, a disbelieving haze gave way to mounting rage. Abel thought he could pay off a debt—with his daughter? Kirby's fingers curled into fists. It was all he could do to keep from strangling the man, half dead or not. He rose with a contemptuous glare at Abel's limp form and strode downstairs.

Starlight was about to start up. "Dinner's ready. I'm gonna look in on Pa, then I'll be back."

Kirby fought to control his anger as he watched her go. "Thanks." Though he'd suddenly lost his ravenous appetite, he forced himself to take a chair at the table and eat what Starlight had fixed.

Doc Tibbins drained the last of his coffee and set down his cup.

"You're right," Kirby said. "Abel seems to be waking up now and then."

The physician nodded. "The man's lucky. I'd say the worst is past. Might be a spell before he gets his strength back, but he'll survive."

"*Good.* *Because as soon as he's up and around, I want to kill him myself,*" Kirby's mind added facetiously. "Say, Doc. Know anybody by the name of Dewey?"

A smirk creased the man's features. "That'd be Dewey Blackburn. A no-account crony of Abel's about three-quarters of a mile east of here. Spends most of his time gambling and has amazing luck whenever he needs it. . .if you catch my drift."

"Yes, I do."

"Well, I'll check in on Abel and be on my way." He rose and turned for the stairs.

Kirby stayed him with a hand on his arm, holding out a few folded bills in his other palm. "Is this enough to cover your trouble?"

"Plenty. Thank you." The physician deposited the money into a trouser pocket, then gave a nod and left.

Sinking again onto one of the chairs, Kirby released a deep breath. *Dewey Blackburn. Three-quarters of a mile east.*

"The doc thinks Pa's gonna be all right," Starlight said, her airy voice breaking into Kirby's musings as she took the seat to his right. He'd never even heard her coming down and had no idea how long she'd been there.

"I know."

"I told the Lord thank you the minute Doc Tibbins told me, seein' as this is His doin'. He says he has to go now."

The dazzling hope that lit Starlight's brown eyes tugged at Kirby's heart, and her tremulous smile made him all the more resolved to carry out his plan. "Listen. I have something I need to take care of at home. It's urgent. Will you be all right for a little while? I'll come back as soon as I can."

She looked downcast but recovered quickly. "God'll still be here with us. No need to worry about Pa, knowin' that, is there?"

Kirby smiled gently and rose to his feet. "No, none at all." He tried to leave it at that and go, but his boots seemed nailed to the floorboards while he filled his eyes with her. There was something he had to do here, now, before he left. He held out a hand. When Starlight placed her smaller one in his, he almost forgot how to breathe as he drew her, unresisting, into his arms.

His heart thrummed against hers as he crushed her to his chest, breathing in the fragrance of her hair, astounded at the awareness that her pulse was keeping pace with his. She had been through so much, and if it took him forever, he'd see to it that nothing ever hurt her again.

Now was not the proper time to kiss her, he knew, but he could not predict the way she smiled at him just then with her eyes. "Oh, Star. . . ." With a little moan, Kirby lowered his mouth to hers.

Chapter Eighteen

Even with several shortcuts the trip home to Alderson and back to Noxen to Kirby seemed never ending. His jaw muscles ached from clenching his teeth and he had to remind himself more than once to relax. Abel Wells's admission had both stunned and enraged him once he could absorb its significance. If Abel hadn't been so intent in that moment, fearing death, the utterance might have been disregarded. Kirby pressed on with grim determination, finally arriving at what he figured was Dewey Blackburn's place, a small cabin tucked against a wooded hillside.

Once the dwelling had probably been a charming homestead, Kirby surmised, but now, in complete disrepair, it made Abel's house, even without the recent improvements, seem like a mansion. The entire front porch sagged listlessly onto the weed patch surrounding the dwelling, the empty frame of a screen door hung haphazardly from only the bottom hinge, and two of the windows in sight had rotting boards nailed over the broken panes. The smaller side porch had been bolstered on the outer edge with an upended log but looked useable at least. After dismounting, Kirby draped Jericho's reins over the protruding branch of a wild bush, then strode determinedly up the five creaky steps to the open side door. A swarthy face looked up from within the dismal interior.

"Dewey Blackburn?" Kirby asked, trying not to inhale the sour stench that emanated from the kitchen.

"Who wants to know?" Dark eyes narrowed in suspicion.

"A friend of Abel and Starlight Wells. Name's Mitchell."

Looking unconvinced, the man rose from where he'd been sitting and came to the door. "What d'ya want?"

Kirby stared straight on. "I'm here to pay a debt. Three hundred dollars, I believe." Reaching into his pocket, he withdrew a roll of bills and held them in his open palm.

Blackburn eyed the offering greedily, then with a smirk, but shook his head. "Well, ya see, it's too late. Abel an' me, we made other arrangements. I don't want yer money."

"Well, now," Kirby began, anger and impatience rising to the fore, "that's too bad 'cause this is all you're going to get."

"Says who?"

In no mood to play games, Kirby grabbed the scrawny man's dingy shirt-front and stood him on his toes, nose to nose with himself. "Look, Blackburn, I want Abel's note," he said in distinct, measured words, "and I want it now."

The farmer's eyes bulged in renewed purpose. He swallowed. "I—it's over in the cupboard," he squeaked through his compressed vocal chords.

Releasing his grip, Kirby curved one side of his mouth but maintained his glare. "Thought you'd see it my way, eventually."

The man raised his scruffy chin a notch and, drawing in some air, brushed off his shirt. Then without a word he crossed the room and opened the door of a cabinet. He returned, a wrinkled scrap of paper clutched in his hand. He peered down at the money Kirby still held, then breathed out as he reluctantly surrendered the note.

Kirby slapped the bulk of his savings into Blackburn's palm. Forcibly restraining himself from expressing his thoughts, he turned in mute silence and went back to his mount.

❧

Starlight had hardly moved since the timeless moment some hours ago when Sir Kirby had kissed her. Time and again the remembrance of the warm shelter of his arms and unspoken longing in his eyes drew her back to the tender embrace they had shared.

Thinking back, she knew that when he opened his arms to her, she could do nothing but step into them. Nothing in her life had ever felt so right as when his quiet strength had surrounded her, pressing her close to his heart. Starlight realized there had neither been any false play nor coyness in their relationship. She'd once overheard some girls giggling about ways to entice a boy. Kirby had merely come into her heart one day and stayed there, and now it was hard to remember what her life had been like before. She touched her lips with her fingertips and closed her eyes, reliving that most treasured moment.

When the sound of an approaching horse finally carried from outside, she felt her heart skip a beat. To still the trembling of her hands, she clasped them together in front of her and went to the door to wait.

Sir Kirby smiled when he came in. He raised a hand to her hair, and brushed lightly through the strands in a caress. "Hello, Star."

Starlight couldn't find her voice, her eyes were so filled with him that her throat closed up.

His smile widened slowly in an endearing way as he placed his other hand on her shoulder and drew her close. "How's your pa?" he whispered against her hair.

"Doin' better. He took a few spoons of broth a while ago."

"I'm glad." Kirby rocked her for a few minutes. Then, easing her away slightly, he brushed the backs of his fingers along her cheekbone. "Think he's up to some company yet? If he's awake, I mean."

"Don't see why not." Reluctantly stepping out of his embrace, she smiled and offered a hand. When he closed his around it, she turned to lead the way.

Kirby tightened his hold and didn't move.

Starlight paused on the first step. She looked back over her shoulder.

"Not yet," he pleaded softly. "I wanted to say something to you first, before we go up."

Drowning in his gaze, Starlight looked questioningly at him. "W-what is it?" Butterflies fluttered through her.

"I love you, Starlight Wells."

Her breath caught at the awaited words and for a heartbeat she couldn't think straight. "Truly?" she heard herself ask.

A smile played over his face, crinkling clear blue eyes that were almost even with hers as she stood on the first step. "Truly. More than life."

Starlight let out a shaky breath. With a little half-laugh, she leaned toward Kirby and slid her arms around his neck. "I love you, too. Sir K—" She pressed her lips together and her entire face blazed pink as a quizzical frown drew his dark brows closer together. "I. . .love you, too," she managed. "Kirby."

Kirby regarded the tawny-haired beauty before him with a steady gaze. Twice he'd caught that slip of her tongue, or almost caught it, anyway. Could it be possible that she knew someone with a name somewhat similar to his and got the two tangled together? But the momentary question vanished as he looked into her dreamy eyes. Whatever it was, he didn't care. She was here now, and she loved him. Nothing else mattered. He kissed the tip of her nose. "I think we should talk to your pa, if he seems up to it."

Abel, in a fresh but worn nightshirt, looked pale and listless as Kirby accompanied Starlight into the subdued glow of the stark bedroom. Kirby expected the man's sleepy gaze to fasten on them, and it did. But the feeble hint of a smile was a bonus. "Abel," he said, coming to the bedside.

"Preacher." He blinked heavily. "Ya saved my life."

"Anyone who happened by would have tried," Kirby replied.

"Mebbe." A weary sigh raised and lowered his chest and when he spoke it was with labored phrases. "Only I ain't worth it." He breathed slowly in and out. "Not after what I done. I'm ashamed o' myself." The effort of speaking made him look all the more tired.

"There's probably no one in the world who didn't make a decision he'd regret later," Kirby admitted.

The older man gave a weak nod.

"But," Kirby went on, "things are all right now. Thought you might rest better knowing you don't have to worry over it."

Abel blinked twice, as if to clear his vision. "Ya mean what I told ya?" He lifted his eyes toward Starlight and back.

Kirby nodded.

"How can that be?"

"It's been paid off."

In the heavy silence that ensued, Starlight rinsed out a folded cloth and lay it on her father's head. Her expression conveyed her apprehension, but she appeared relieved.

"Who paid?" Abel finally managed.

"I did." Kirby's gaze didn't waver.

Pondering the revelation, Abel looked mildly stunned. "Why would ya do somethin' like that?" he asked, his voice faint and raspy. "I didn't ask ya to. It was somethin' I owed."

Kirby smiled. "Someone once did the same thing for me, paid a debt I couldn't pay. It was a debt of sin."

A strange emotion clouded Abel's heavy-lidded eyes. He had been rendered speechless. His leathery hand came up from under the sheet and scratched his jaw.

"I was the one in the wrong," Kirby continued. "But it was Jesus who paid the penalty. He did the same for all of us. The whole world."

Abel's forehead wrinkled in thought. "Never saw it like that b'fore."

Starlight turned a sweet smile Kirby's way and caught her bottom lip in her teeth.

Kirby bent and gave Abel's shoulder a squeeze. "I know. But it's as simple as that. Think about it while you get back your strength. Sometimes when a man is forced to lie on his back, he finally starts looking up."

A sheepish smile widened the older man's mouth. "See what ya mean. An' somethin' else. . . ." He took a few steady breaths. "Ya live what ya preach. I saw that. I'll do some thinkin'."

"Good. I'll pray that you do." He paused to bolster his own courage. Abel looked washed out but his fiery spirit seemed to be in evidence. Shifting his weight to his other foot, Kirby cleared his throat. "I know you're tired, but there's one more thing you need to think about while you're resting up." He held a hand out to Starlight and she placed her trembling one in his. Kirby gave a comforting squeeze and returned his attention to her father. "I'm in love with your daughter. I hope you don't mind if I come calling on her from now on."

Abel looked from one to the other, then gave a resigned nod. "Cain't say I didn't see it comin'." He aimed a meaningful grin at Kirby. "She coulda done worse."

Her heart bursting, Starlight strolled hand in hand with Kirby through the meadow. If she lived to be a hundred she was sure she'd never know greater happiness than she did right now, knowing she had won the heart of the noblest knight in the land. She couldn't stop smiling, and yet at the same time, she could feel tears of joy forming behind her lashes. *If I can't hold them back, what will Kirby think?* she wondered.

Kirby stepped in front of Starlight, blocking her path as he wrapped his arms around her. The rhythm of his heart was strong and rapid against hers. "I don't know how I kept from doing this for so long," he murmured as he stroked her hair. "I guess I thought you were afraid of me."

She raised her head from where she'd rested it against his chest and let her eyes wander freely over all the facets of his face. "No one could fear a knight like you," she began, and then added, "Sir Kirby." Her heart waited breathlessly for his reaction, wondering if he'd think her silly.

His brows met above his nose in query, but he smiled. "You know, I thought I heard you say that once or twice before. But then I was sure I'd imagined it."

She returned the smile. "But you didn't. You've always been Sir Kirby, my brave and noble champion, from that first time you came ridin' by our place."

"Under your tree, you mean?" he asked teasingly.

Starlight's eyes widened. "You knew I was up there?" Feeling a blush flame over her face, she buried her nose against him.

He hugged her close. "Why did you suppose I sang all those songs that day? To entertain my horse?"

Despite her embarrassment, Starlight giggled. "Yes, I did. Truly. But. . . he's not just a horse, you know."

"Is that right?"

She nodded up at him. "He's your silver stallion. Your great, swift steed."

"I had no idea." He traced her jawline with the edge of his fingers, entering her dream. "I should have treated him with the respect due a noble charger and given him more time to roam the pasture with the mares of the kingdom."

Starlight couldn't hold back a delighted laugh and Kirby joined in. When their mirth finally subsided, he brushed a lock of hair from her eyes and tipped up her chin. For a sweet moment, her breath mingled with his. "I'll always protect you, my little dream spinner," he vowed. "I'll never let anything hurt you." Then, ever so slowly, his lips claimed hers in a tender kiss of promise.

As they drew apart, a shooting star streaked across the darkening sky.

"Oh, look," Starlight cried, and Kirby followed her line of vision. "Ma used to say that when a star fell it wrote a secret in the sky that only the angels could read."

Kirby inhaled deeply and held her tight. Having the love of Starlight Wells was more than he could ever have hoped for. He wanted to spend forever being enthralled by her fanciful tales. She had a way about her that made him feel he could be a knight, if that's what she wanted him to be. For the briefest moment, as he looked into her eyes, a glint akin to silver armor flashed back at him. He brushed her mouth with his. Then, taking one of her hands, he lowered himself to one knee and placed his other hand over his heart as he bowed his head. "Would the fair damsel, perchance, deign to marry this humble servant?" He raised his head and looked up.

A tear fell from the corner of Starlight's eye as her lips spread into a brilliant smile. Taking a corner of her skirt in her fingers, she dipped into a curtsy. "She would deem it the greatest honor, my lord. As soon as my pa says I can."

ঽৱ

Late afternoon sunshine lent warm brilliance to the August sky as Starlight smiled at Abel. He looks young again, she decided, all dressed up and with that peaceful look on his face that came from knowing God. She placed her hand lightly on his black-suited arm and stepped from Jessica's bottom porch step onto the grass. When she trembled, he patted her hand.

Mrs. Browning started working the foot pedals of the pump organ, then began the opening notes of the wedding march. Ahead, Jessica started slowly up the path toward the rose-covered arbor.

Through the filmy veil, Starlight saw Kirby waiting for her in a silver pinstripe suit, smiling her way. She took the first step forward, rustling the taffeta bridal gown she'd sewn lovingly and breathing in the fragrance of her bouquet of roses and daisies. With hand-crocheted lace and pearls adorning the bodice, the short train caressing the ground after her, no princess had ever looked more enchanting.

When at last she and Abel reached the trellis and Abel placed her hand in Kirby's, she met his eyes. The love that filled his face stole her breath away.

"Hello, my princess," he whispered, for her ears only. He tightened his fingers on hers as they stood on the brink of a lifetime and heard the traditional ceremony begin.

After the brief words of encouragement and the haze of vows, Cook finally smiled at Kirby. "You may kiss your bride."

Kirby raised Starlight's veil and closed his arms around her as she tipped up her lips to meet his for a breathtaking moment. From far away there came the sound of soft clapping.

Starlight wished she could thank Ma for telling her those stories so long ago. When this shining knight had come along, *tall and straight, noble of bearing with wide-girthed shoulders, and riding upon a great, swift steed*, her heart had recognized him at once. "I love you, Sir Kirby," she whispered.

As a smile spread slowly across his face, he whispered back, "My kingdom is yours forevermore, fair bride of my heart." He then claimed her lips once more.